D0382941

ALSO BY CALEB CARR

The Italian Secretary
The Lessons of Terror
Killing Time
The Angel of Darkness
The Alienist
The Devil Soldier
America Invulnerable (with James Chace)
Casing the Promised Land

THE·LEGEND
OF·BROKEN

CALEB·CARR

THE·LEGEND·OF
BROKEN

RANDOM HOUSE · New York

Published in the United States by Random House, an imprint of The Random House Publishing Group, a division of Random House, Inc., New York.

RANDOM HOUSE and colophon are registered trademarks of Random House, Inc.

ISBN 978-1-4000-6283-6
eISBN 978-0-8129-9408-7

Printed in the United States of America on acid-free paper

www.atrandom.com

2 4 6 8 9 7 5 3 1

FIRST EDITION

Book design and panel artwork by Simon M. Sullivan

This book is dedicated with the greatest gratitude and affection to

DR. HEATHER CANNING

DR. BRUCE YAFFE

THOMAS F. PIVINSKI, M.S.

who have made my life physically and emotionally possible;
and to

EZEQUIEL VIÑAO,

a steadfast friend who always encouraged this project;
and, finally, to

PRUDENCE K. MUNKITTRICK,

who did so much to see it through before she even
knew what it actually was

INTRODUCTORY NOTE

Some years ago, while doing research at one of our major universities on the personal papers of Edward Gibbon—author of the multivolume classic *The Decline and Fall of the Roman Empire,* published from 1776 to 1789—I came across a large manuscript in the collection, contained in an unmarked box. On further investigation, I discovered that the work was not entered in either the university's card catalogue or its computerized list of holdings. Intrigued, I began to read the document, and soon realized that it was a narrative concerning the fate of a legendary kingdom said to have ruled over a portion of northern Germany from the fifth to the eighth centuries. The tale had never been published, during Gibbon's lifetime or since; I only knew of the thing because I'd run across references to it in several unpublished letters that Gibbon had written to his countryman and colleague, the great Edmund Burke. Burke's own masterpiece, *Reflections on the Revolution in France,* had appeared just as did the last volume of Gibbon's *Decline and Fall;* and, as a token of his esteem for what he had immediately recognized to be a seminal achievement on his friend's part, Gibbon had attempted to present Burke with a copy of his latest discovery.

But Burke had subsequently returned the gift, and sent Gibbon a cordial yet sternly phrased warning against any attempt to publicize it.

At the time, I didn't quite know what to make of the manuscript: although detailed in its descriptions, its provenance could not be immediately proved, and any tale that made such remarkable claims about a largely unknown and unknowable chapter of history (for northern Germany during most of the Dark Ages remains one of the notable blank spots in the record of European civilization) required at least that much. I knew from Gibbon's letters that the original document had been translated into English by a linguistic and historical scholar of impressive talents; but I also knew that this character had nonetheless chosen to remain as assiduously anonymous as had the manuscript's original first-person narrator. Exploring his personal history would therefore be of no further aid in terms of verification. Certainly, the English vocabulary and idioms that he employed throughout the translation were consistent with the late eighteenth century, containing no anachronisms of the kind that would have quickly betrayed a fabrication or hoax produced during a subsequent era; yet something more was required.

Recently, that something more has begun to surface, in the form of documents dating back to the last days of Hitler's Germany. These documents (which are only now in the process of fully emerging) apparently reveal that not only Hitler himself, but some of his most trusted advisors, as well, were aware of both the Broken Manuscript and the historical evidence that supported it: so aware, in fact, that they became determined to eradicate all trace of any written or archaeological evidence of the kingdom of Broken's existence from the record of German history.

Taken together with Gibbon's statements, these facts are sound enough to demonstrate that the manuscript is quite probably factual; and I have therefore decided to present this, the tale of the kingdom of Broken, embellished with Gibbon's and Burke's original correspondence on the subject, as well the former's footnotes to the text, to which I have added my own explanatory notes. (*Throughout the text, the accompanying back-matter notes are indicated by a series of symbols.* These notes are offered simply for clarification; the reader *should not* think that reading them is necessary to understanding or, hopefully, enjoying the book itself; they can be read as one proceeds, reviewed after each chapter or when one has finished, or ignored altogether.)

As to the elements central to the manuscript's actual story, I can only say this: there developed, particularly after first the Elizabethan and then the Victorian eras, a feeling that tales set in the Dark or Middle Ages must necessarily have a certain formality and fussiness, not only of style, but of subject. Yet, especially in the case of early medieval Germany, nothing could be further from the truth. The legends that emerged from that time and place were driven by both language and plots that we would today recognize as very similar to works of more recent eras: indeed, examples such as the Broken Manuscript could be considered almost modern. Certainly, by relying on such themes as obsessive kings, diminutive peoples of the forest, buried scrolls, and, ultimately, a vanished civilization (elements that would, obviously, become staples of certain schools of literature in our own time), as well as by relating these elements in the informal manner that it does, the manuscript contributes to a trend that Bernd Lutz, in his masterful essay on early medieval German literature, called "a monument to vernacular dialect."†

—Caleb Carr
Cherry Plain, N.Y.

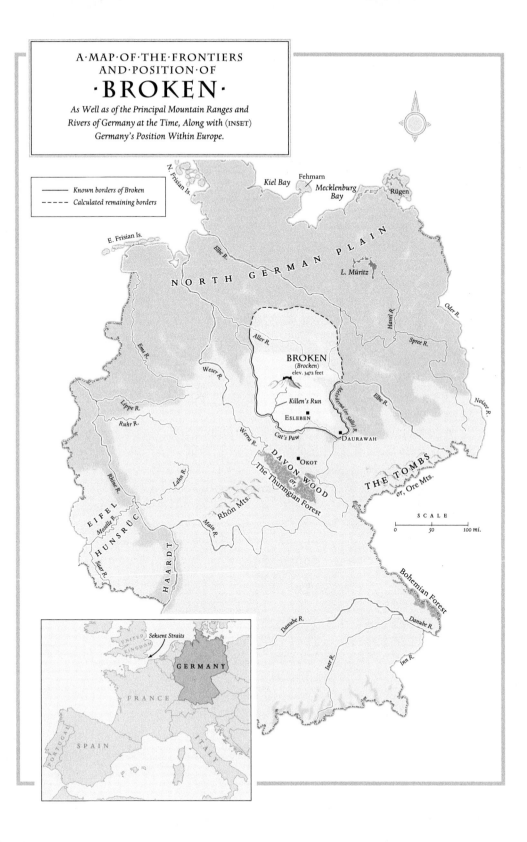

A·MAP·OF·THE·FRONTIERS
AND·POSITION·OF
·BROKEN·

*As Well as of the Principal Mountain Ranges and
Rivers of Germany at the Time, Along with (INSET)
Germany's Position Within Europe.*

———— *Known borders of Broken*
- - - - *Calculated remaining borders*

N. Frisian Is.

Kiel Bay   Fehmarn
Mecklenburg
Bay   Rügen

E. Frisian Is.

Elbe R.

NORTH GERMAN PLAIN

L. Müritz

Ems R.

Aller R.

Havel R.

Oder R.

Spree R.

Weser R.

BROKEN
(Brocken)
elev. 3472 feet

Lippe R.

Killen's Run

Weidorna (or Salle) R.

Elbe R.

Notsee R.

Ruhr R.

ESLEBEN

Werra R.

Cat's Paw

DAURAWAH

Rhine R.

Lahn R.

OKOT

DAVON WOOD
or,
The Thuringian Forest

THE TOMBS
or, Ore Mts.

EIFEL

Moselle R.

Rhön Mts.

HUNSRÜC

Main R.

SCALE

0   50   100 mi.

HAARDT

Saar R.

Bohemian Forest

Danube R.

Danube R.

Seksent Straits

UNITED
KINGDOM

GERMANY

FRANCE

Isar R.

Inn R.

PORTUGAL

SPAIN

ITALY

PART·ONE

THE·MOON·SPEAKS
OF·DEATH

NOVEMBER 3, 1790
Lausanne

Are there reasons to count the central elements of the tale credible?

There are. First, the location of the small but evidently powerful realm of Broken can easily be calculated: The narrator's mention of it as lying outside the northeastern borders of the western Roman empire place it somewhere in Germania, while his descriptions of the dramatic countryside call to mind not only the fertile fields of the Saale and Elbe River valleys, but, even more pointedly, the dense, timeless forests of Thuringia and Saxony, in particular the Harz mountain range—the highest point of which is a summit called *Brocken* (the "c" was evidently dropped in the Broken dialect, with the result that the word was pronounced much as it would have been, and is, in Old and Modern English). This mountain has ever been infamous as the supposed seat of unholy forces and unnatural rites,[†] and its physical attributes conform closely to the mountain atop which the city of Broken is said to have stood (particularly its summit of stone, which bears some resemblance to the Gallic stronghold of Alesia, although it was far superior from a military perspective).

As to the customs and culture of the people of Broken, they were certainly more developed than anything that can be found in central Europe between the fifth and eighth centuries A.D., the period during which the greater part of the kingdom's history seems to have transpired. But this difference can, I believe, be accounted for by the unidentified narrator's assertion that the kingdom's founding ruler, one *Oxmontrot,* and several of his tribesmen once fought as barbarian auxiliaries for both the Western and Eastern regions of the Roman empire. Evidently this chieftain possessed not only a brutal sword arm, but a potent intellect, as well, which absorbed and made use of many of the most beautiful, noble, and administratively effective Roman traditions.

Unfortunately, he also legitimized the beliefs of his less perspicacious companions, who had been drawn into several of the most extreme Roman cults of sensuality and materialism that had been organized around such deities as Elagabalus [var. Heliogabalus] and Astarte, and who wished to form a similar new faith of their own. This longing took the form of a similarly secret and degenerate cult, one that was permitted by Oxmontrot to become the new faith of the kingdom of Broken, for reasons that will become clear. The faith was organized around what had, until then, been a minor deity in Rome's eastern provinces, one called *Kafra;* and his dominance would lead to the second most important development in the early years of Broken, the creation of the race of exiles known as the *Bane.*[†]

—Edward Gibbon to Edmund Burke

My pitted skull sees once more, and my bleached
jaws crack to tell the secrets of Broken . . .

AND SO THESE WORDS have at last risen from the ground in which I will inter them, defying Fate as my homeland of Broken never can. The city's great granite walls will remain shattered, until they again become the shapeless raw stone from which they were fashioned. Do not pretend, scholars unborn, that you know of my kingdom; it is as windblown and forgotten as my own bones. My purpose now is to tell how this tragedy came to pass.

Do you wonder at my saying "tragedy"? How can I say anything else, when I know full well that historians of your day will be unable to state with conviction whether Broken ever existed at all, despite its magnificent accomplishments? When I know that its enemies, as well as some of its most loyal citizens—to say nothing of Nature itself—shall work as hard as they evidently have done to dismantle the great city's magnificent form? And that I, from whose mind that magnificence sprang, still deem the destruction just . . .[†]

Above all, consider this, before going on: You are embarked on a journey in which every cruelty, every unnatural urge, and every savagery known to men plays a part; yet there is compassion here, too, and also courage, although it is one of the peculiarities of the tale that each of these qualities appears when it is least expected. And so: let strength of heart guide you through each period of confusion to the next point of hope, keeping despair from your soul and allowing you to learn from this history in a manner that my descendants—that *I*—never could.

Yes, I became utterly lost . . . Do I remain so? My own family whispers that I am mad, just as they did when I first spoke of recording these events with the sole purpose of burying the finished text deep in the Earth. Yet if I am mad, it is because of these visions of Broken's fate: visions that began unbidden long ago and have never departed, regardless of how desperately I have begged more than one Deity for peace, and no matter what intoxicating potions I have consumed. They weight me down, body and spirit, like a stone-filled sack about the neck, dragging me under the surface of my Moonlit lake, down to those depths that teem with so many other bodies . . .

I see all of them, even those that I never truthfully saw in life. They ought to have faded: it has been more than the span of most men's lives since I returned from the wars to the south[†] and the apparitions began, and it has been half again as long since I came back from my voyage to the monks across the Seksent Straits,[‡] who revealed to me the meaning of my visions, that I might record all that I know to be true, against the day when someone, when *you,* would stumble upon my work, and determine if the mind that had created it yet deserves to be called mad.

But there will be time enough for all such deliberations, while there is precious little, now, to explain what you must know about my kingdom before our journey can begin. Yet the monks under whom I studied warned against plain recitation; and so—imagine this:

We tumble together out of the eternal heavens, where all ages are as one and we may meet as fellow travelers, toward the more constrainèd Earth, which is, at the moment of our approach, in an era earlier than your own, yet later than mine. Passing through the mists that envelop a range of mountains more impressive than lofty, more deadly than majestic, we soon come to the highest branches of a perilous expanse of forest. The variety of trees seems nearly impossible, and the whole forms a thick green roof over the wilderness below; a roof that we, in our magical flight, shall penetrate with dreamlike ease, eventually settling on a thick lower limb of one obliging oak. From our perch we are afforded an excellent view of the woodland floor, lush and seemingly gentle; but its wide carpets of moss frequently conceal deadly bogs, and its stands of enormous ferns and thick brambles are capable of cutting and poisoning the toughest human flesh. Even beauty, here, is deadly: for many of the delicate flowers that emerge from the mosses or cling to the trees and rocks offer fragrant elixirs fatal to the greedy. Yet those same extracts, in the hands of the less rapacious, can be made to cure sickness, and ease pain.

Yet what of man, in this place? It was once believed that humans could not survive, here; for we have entered Davon Wood,[††] the great forest that the people of Old Broken said was made by all the gods to imprison the worst of demons, in order that they might know the loneliness and suffering that they inflicted upon those creatures that they tormented. The Wood has always provided an impenetrable southern and western frontier for Broken, one whose dangers have been plain even to the wild marauders[†] that first appeared out of the morning sun generations ago, and that yet ravage neighboring domains. Only a few of these invaders have even attempted to traverse the Wood's unmeasured expanse, and of that small number even fewer have reemerged, scarred and crazed, to declare the undertaking not only impossible but damned. The citizens of Broken were once content to view the Wood from the safety of the banks of the thundering river called the Cat's Paw, which provides a perilous break between the wilderness and the richness of Broken's best farming dales to the north and the east. Yes, once my people were content, with this limitation as with so many;[‡] but that was before—

Lo! They arrive ere I can speak their name—look quickly. There— and there! The blur of fur and hide, the glint of furtive eyes, the whole fluid: between, under, and over tree trunks and limbs, around and through nettle bushes and vine tangles. What are they? Look again; try to determine for yourself. Swift? Impossibly swift—they find pathways through the Wood that other animals cannot see, still less negotiate, and they navigate those courses with an agility that makes even the tree rodents stare in envy—

They begin to slow; and perhaps you note that the "hides" of these quick beings are in reality animal skins stitched into garments. Yet not even in Davon Wood do beasts go clothed. Could they perhaps be those cursed demons about which the people of Old Broken told such fearful tales? Certainly, these small ones are damned, in their own way, but as to their being demons—examine their faces more closely. Beneath the soil and sweat, do you not take note of human skin? And so . . .

Men.

Neither forest beasts, nor dwarves, nor elves. And not human children, either. Watch a moment more: you must realize that, while these travelers are unusually small for fully grown humans, they are not *too* small.[††] It is something else that disturbs you. Certainly, it is not their agile, even entertaining, movements, for these are as marvelous as any troop of tumblers; no, it is something more obscure that leads to the conviction that they are somehow—*wrong* . . .

Forgive me if I say that your judgment is not complete. They are not "wrong" of themselves, these little humans. The wrong you sense is the result of the grievous manner in which they have *been* wronged.

But wronged by whom? In one sense, by myself, in that I gave life to my descendants; but far more by the new "god" of my people, Kafra,[†] and more still by those people themselves, who despise this small race more than any vermin. Do I confuse you? Good! In this mood, you will raise your eyes up to the heavens and appeal for relief; but you will encounter, instead, only more marvelous sights. First, the sacred Moon,[‡] deity of Old Broken, although discarded within my lifetime for that newer and more obliging god; then, lit by the Moon's sacred radiance, a great range of mountains miles to the south of the peaks that we passed on our journey here, a range known in Broken simply as the Tombs. Further north and east, the shimmering band that you see cutting across the enviable farmlands that are shielded by the mountains (lands that are the kingdom's chief source of wealth) is the Meloderna River, the teat at which those rich fields suckle, and the kinder sister of the rocky Cat's Paw.[††]

And in the center of this noble landscape, protected as some royal child by Nature's powerful guards, stands the lone mountain that is the kingdom's heart. As torturously forested on its lower slopes as is Davon Wood, yet as barren and deadly as the Tombs above (if more temperate), this is Broken, a summit so frightening that, legend has it, the single great river that burst out of the surrounding mountains at the beginning of time split into many at the mere sight of it. Great and imposing as the mountain is, the greatest sight we shall witness is atop it: the walled wonder—bejeweled, from this distance, by flickering torches—that is both the proverbial heart and the sinful loins of the kingdom. Miraculously carved out of the solid, nearly seamless stone that is the stuff of the mountain's summit, the city was once the favorite of the Moon, but incurred that Sacred Body's wrath when it embraced the false god Kafra:

Broken . . .

Yes, we shall go there. But we have not finished with the Wood, yet. For this tale begins with those scurrying little humans below us. Never forget that word: for it is the one supreme fact of this entire history. Those soil-crusted, furtive beings that spark such curiosity in you are *human*. The people of Broken allowed themselves to forget as much, for centuries; and on tempestuous Moonlit nights below the windswept peak of the terrible mountain, you may yet hear the wail of their condemnèd souls, as they bemoan their most grievous error . . .

$$1:\{ii:\}$$

Of the Bane: their plight, their exploits, and their
outrages; and of the first of several remarkable events witnessed
this night by three of them . . .

T HE SCENT GIVEN OFF by the three hurrying forms is odd—
less human even than their stature. But of their many peculiarities, this one is their own doing: for to be identified as human in
Davon Wood is to be marked as easy meat, and so they work hard to
disguise their odor. This means, first, the use of dead leaves, plants, and
rich soil from the forest floor, as well as water, when they have it to spare,
to scour their bodies free of sweat, grease and food, and the remnants of
their own waste. They then apply fluids drained from the scent bags of
animals both clawed and cloven-hoofed, and the result of this careful
preparation is that even the cleverest predators, along with the most ob-
servant prey, become confused upon the approach of the three travelers,
an effect heightened by the incongruous aromas that arise from the burgeoning deerskin sacks they carry on their shoulders. The tantalizing
fragrances of the Wood's rarest herbs, roots, and flowers; the crisp smell
of medicinal rocks and bones; and the hint of fear from a few small cages
and traps that contain captured songbirds and rare, gregarious tree
shrews; these and more besides blend to increase the threesome's chances
of never being precisely identified. Thus do these small, cunning souls
complete their near-mastery of Davon Wood.

The three are of the Bane, a tribe made up of exiles from the city on
the mountain, as well as the descendants of those who suffered similar
punishment; a tribe whose survival in the Wood is ensured by foraging
parties like this one, which are dispatched to seek out rare goods prized
in Broken for their curative or pleasuring qualities. In return for undertaking risks that even the desperately avaricious merchants of Broken
will not dare, the Bane receive in trade from those same merchants certain cultivated foodstuffs that cannot be grown in the forest, as well as
such rudimentary bronze and iron implements as the rulers of the great
city feel it safe for the exiles to possess. Woodland foraging, even for the
Bane, is dangerous work, and the governing council of the tribe—called

the Groba[†]—will send only the cleverest and most daring of their men and women to do it. This sometimes includes (as in the case of our three foragers) those who have broken the tribe's laws: a productive term of foraging can absolve such ungovernable souls of all but the worst of sins, and cure almost any tendency toward their repetition, so great are the hazards encountered during the span of these missions. As for those who undertake foraging willingly, out of concern for the tribe, they can expect to receive high honors from the Groba—should they return with both their bodies and their minds intact.

Thus the Bane have survived in the Wood: and over the course of two centuries they have developed a society, laws—in fact, a civilization, bestial though it looks to their uneasy neighbors. They even speak the language of Broken, though so inventive a race has modified the tongue:

"*Ficksel!*"[‡]

The forager who travels to the rear of the quick-moving pack has spat the insult (an urgent if impractical suggestion that its object withdraw and fornicate with himself) at the tribesman in front of him; yet no sooner has he done so than his face—a blur of scars interrupted only by two hard grey eyes and an enormous black gap amid his teeth, the remaining number of which are ground to sharp points—turns about, to search for any danger approaching from behind. His lips, split so many times by blows that they might be those of an agèd man, curl into an ugly frown of disgust as his whispered insults go on; but the clear, cutting eyes never cease to scan the forest expertly. "You always were a lying sack of bitch's turd, Veloc,[††] but *this* . . ."

"The Moon's truth, Heldo-Bah!" the one called Veloc answers indignantly (for the Bane still worship the patron of Old Broken). Veloc's round, dark eyes spark and his well-formed jaw sets firmly, an attitude of defiance that ripples through his shoulders as he makes certain that first his deerskin foraging sack and then his finely worked short bow and arrows are in place. Save for his size, he would be considered handsome, even in Broken (indeed, at least a few women of the city do secretly think him so, when he breaks Bane law and steals within the mighty walls), but he is no less alert for his looks: despite the heat of argument, he watches the thick tangle to either side of the speeding column as carefully as his comrade studies the rear. "It seems I must remind you that I was nominated for the post of Historian of the Bane Tribe—and that the Groba Fathers almost approved the post!"

Heldo-Bah bounds a fallen ash, scarcely jostling his sack of goods and grumbling, "Great collection of granite-brained eunuchs . . ." At the sound of twigs cracking in the distance, he suddenly produces his favored weapons: a set of three throwing knives originally taken from an eastern marauder by a soldier of Broken, one who was later unlucky enough to encounter Heldo-Bah across a tavern table in Broken's trading center on the Meloderna River, the walled town of Daurawah.[†] "There's no need to remind me of anything, Veloc! Lies breed like groin rot, and 'historians' are only the whores who spread it—"

"Enough!" The command, though issued by a woman of even smaller stature than the men, is instantly obeyed; for this is Keera, round-faced, dusty-haired, and the most skilled tracker in the whole of the Bane tribe. At three feet eleven inches tall, Keera is shorter than Heldo-Bah by two inches, while her brother Veloc stands taller than her by a full three; but no advantage of height can outweigh her knowledge of life in the Wood, and her quarrelsome companions are accustomed to doing as she says without question, resentment, or hesitation.

Keera deftly leaps onto the rotting stump of a collapsed oak, her knowing blue eyes seeing in the forest ahead what no other human can discern. Heldo-Bah's expression has changed aspect from angry annoyance to concern with a speed that is almost clownish, and characteristic of his tempestuous moods. "What is it, Keera?" he whispers urgently. "Wolves? I thought I heard one."

Wolves in Davon Wood grow to extraordinary sizes, and are more than a match for any three Bane—even these three. Keera, however, shakes her head slowly, and answers: "A panther." Veloc's face, too, fills with apprehension, while Heldo-Bah's shows childlike panic. The solitary, silent Davon panthers—which can reach lengths of twelve feet, and weights of many hundreds of pounds—are the largest and most efficient killers known, each as lethal as a pack of wolves and, like all cats, nearly impossible to detect before they strike. They are particularly fond of the caves and rocks near the Cat's Paw.

Keera listens intently to the Wood, leaning forward on a worked maple staff with which she has humbled more men than would ever admit to the experience. "I sensed him some time ago," she murmurs. "But I do not believe he stalks us. His movements are—strange . . ." She cocks her head. "Hafften Falls[‡]—near the river. The rocks are high and hidden, hereabouts—good ground for panthers. *We,* however"—she reaches into her bag for a stick with well-oiled, charred rags wrapped in tight layers around one end—"will need torches. At this speed, in this darkness, we may go over the bank and break our necks, before ever we realize it. Veloc: flint." As her brother goes into his own sack, Keera frowns at Heldo-Bah, so that her small nose points in accusation. "And by the Moon, Heldo-Bah, stop complaining! This poaching was your idea; it's your stomach that can't bear any more wood boar—"

"They're made of nothing but fat and gristle!" whispers Heldo-Bah.

"We're going, are we not?" Keera answers sternly. "But stop drawing attention to us with your eternal grumbling!"

"It's not my fault, Keera," Heldo-Bah says, tossing his own torch on the ground before Veloc. "Tell your fool brother. These lies of his—"

"They're not lies, Heldo-Bah—it's history!" Veloc's face and voice grow improbably pompous, as he produces sparks for the three torches that he has sunk into the moist Earth in front of him: "If you choose to ignore facts, then you're the fool—and the simple fact is, long before Broken, all men were of roughly the same height. The Bane did not exist, nor did the Tall—the names meant nothing. It has been recorded, Heldo-Bah!"

Heldo-Bah grunts: "Yes—by you, no doubt. Written on the rump of some other man's wife!" Glancing about for something on which to inflict his bitterness, Heldo-Bah sees only a creeping orange tree grub on a moss-covered log. In a startling flurry, he slices the creature into four pieces with his deadly knives. "It's bad enough that you make these insane tales up to charm women into your bed—but to then try to pass them off as 'history,' as though no one would ever question you . . ." Heldo-Bah picks up the four oozing[†] segments of wood grub—and drops them, one after another, into his mouth, chewing ferociously and seeming satisfied by a taste that would cause most humans to erupt from both ends.

Keera watches in revulsion. "Do you never consider, Heldo-Bah, that wood boar may be the least likely cause of your ailments?"

"Oh, no," Heldo-Bah says simply. "It is boar—I have studied the matter. And tonight, I will have beef! What do you see, Keera?"

"We've angled our run well—we should reach the Fallen Bridge in a few minutes, and then should cross straight onto Lord Baster-kin's Plain."

Heldo-Bah moans delightedly, seeming to forget the panther. "Ah, shag cattle . . . Good beef, and beef belonging to that pig Baster-kin, too."

"And the Merchant Lord's private guard?" Veloc asks his sister.

Keera shakes her head. "We will have to get closer before I can answer that. But—" She lifts her staff, hooks it onto a leafy birch, and pulls the fluttering green curtain aside to reveal the distant summit of Broken, perfectly framed by the trees. "All seems quiet in the city, tonight . . ."

At the sight of the torch-lit metropolis, fountainhead of power in the kingdom of Broken and wellspring of misery for those who dwell in Davon Wood, a passionate silence falls over the party, and, soon thereafter, over many of the forest creatures that share this sudden glimpse of the northern horizon. The eerie calm is not broken until Heldo-Bah spits out the last bit of his vile meal. "So—the Groba has *not* dispatched any Outragers," he grumbles; and it seems he finds this last word infinitely more sickening than what he has just eaten.

Veloc glances dubiously at his friend. "Did they consider it?"

"There was talk of as much, among that last group of foragers we met," answers Heldo-Bah. "They claimed to have witnessed one of the Tall's death rituals at the Wood's edge, and sent a man back to Okot with the news. When he returned, he said that the Outragers had argued that the act required a response—for the Tall did their killing on our side of the river."

Keera presses: "But are they certain it was the Tall who were responsible? The Groba are forbidden to dispatch Outragers unless they are sure, and the river spirits are very active, following spring thaw—they may have coaxed a forest beast to attack one of Baster-kin's men—"

"And I might have stones the size of a shag bull's," Heldo-Bah answers, spitting again. "Save that I don't. Rock goblins and river trolls . . ." The forager's cynicism is answered by even louder crackling on the forest floor nearby. His face reverting to childlike fear, Heldo-Bah snatches a lit torch from the ground and glances in all directions. "The existence of which," he declares in a clear voice, "I accept as an article of faith!"

Keera is over to him in a few bounding steps, and claps a hand over his mouth. Her eyes and head always moving, she whispers, "The panther . . ." Keera creeps to the very limits of the flickering glow created by the three torches, holding her maple staff at the ready. "I may have been wrong—he may be stalking us. Yet it did not seem so . . ."

Veloc comes to her side. "What can we do?"

"Run?" Heldo-Bah whispers, joining them in a bound.

"Yes," Keera says, "but we will not manage fifty yards, even holding torches, unless we give the panther something else to think about. An offering—where is the boar joint from yesterday?" Veloc produces a piece of bone and meat, wrapped in a bit of hide. "Leave it here," Keera commands. "It will draw him, and the fire of the torches should remove any lingering interest he might have in us."

"And catch the interest of Lord Baster-kin's Guard," Veloc replies, even as he follows his sister's orders.

"We will extinguish them at the Fallen Bridge," declares Keera, her mind, as ever, solving problems before Veloc and Heldo-Bah even contemplate them. "Come now, quickly—away!"

Having resumed their characteristic pace through the Wood, the three Bane need only moments to reach the craggy, deafening banks of the churning Cat's Paw river, where they find themselves near the thick, hundred-foot trunk of an enormous red fir, whose roots have recently given up the desperate struggle to grip the scant Earth of the high riverbank. The ancient sentinel's mighty body now points directly north across Hafften Falls, one of the most daunting of the Cat's Paw's many cascades: it has sacrificed itself to provide the most reliable of several natural bridges between Davon Wood and Broken—bridges that many of Broken's military commanders would like to see destroyed, and with them the threat posed by the mischievous and sometimes murderous Bane. But the merchants of Broken, although they despise the exiles, make enormous profits from the goods that the tribe's foragers bring out of the wilderness: a child in Broken, for example, who does not number among his possessions a little Davon tree shrew like those that now huddle in cages in the sacks carried by Keera's party can depend upon the disdain of his play fellows, while any woman who cannot drape herself with sufficient jewelry made of the silver, gold, and precious gems found in the wilderness will leave her house only at night, or elaborately veiled. Worse yet, a husband or father who cannot afford to buy such things is seen as faltering in his devotion to Kafra—

Kafra: the strange god whose image was first brought up the Meloderna valley centuries ago, and who, with his love of beauty and riches, quickly stole the souls of citizens of Broken away from the pragmatic tenets of the old Moon faith—and so changed the very basis of their lives. But we must speak more of Kafra soon; and it will sicken me enough then . . .

Nimble as ever, the three foragers prepare to cross the bridge, not so much alarmed as amused by the crashing waters below it. Their escape from the panther, the thought of enjoying a meal suitable for the wealthiest of the Tall (and above all stirring trouble in the otherwise peaceful night), combine to make them increasingly boisterous. As soon as they have mounted the bridge, they boast of how they will knock one another from it, and play at doing so, the two men finally able to shout all they want: for between the rocky banks, the roar of the river overwhelms the sound of their voices.

It would require something dire to put an end to their games; but such sinister signs are precisely what Keera has a gift for detecting. As she puts her nose to the light breeze, her body goes taut; and then, with a quick wave of her maple staff, she once more silences her companions.

"What now?" Heldo-Bah whispers. "Not that cat—"

"Silence!" Keera hisses. Then, at a run, she leaps back off the bridge, and begins to search the rocky ground on the southern bank of the river, following an unmistakable scent:

"Someone has died," Veloc announces, following his sister.

"Aye," Heldo-Bah noises. "And been left to rot . . ."

Within moments, the three are upon the remains of a young man of Broken. Once he had been as tall and well formed as any; now, he is a rotting carcass, from whose ribs protrude several beautifully crafted arrows: shafts of wood overlain with gold leaf, flights made of Davon eagle feathers, and heads of fearsome silver.

"This must be the fellow." Veloc's voice betrays some small measure of sympathy, although the rotting man would likely have spat on the Bane forager, had the two ever crossed paths. "The one who was slain in the ritual you spoke of, Heldo-Bah. He's scarcely more than a boy . . ."

Heldo-Bah grunts, repelled: "Look at the arrows—Moon strike me dead if they did not come from the Sacristy of the city's High Temple."

Keera nods agreement; yet her face betrays more complex suspicions. "But there has been no mutilation—his head, arms, and legs are all intact. And they killed him on *our* side of the river—why?" She moves a few steps closer, still puzzling with the sight. "And what of scavengers? The body has not been disturbed; yet wolves and bears should have strewn it over this part of the Wood. What could—"

She stops suddenly, her face wrinkling up with some newly detected aroma that makes her immediately retrace her steps. "Keep back!" she orders, holding her torch higher. "His flesh is not merely rotting—it is diseased. Even scavengers would sense as much—it's why they have not touched it."

"Well, then," Veloc muses, moving away from the remains. "They killed him because he was sickly. They've done it many times before."

"But it makes no sense," Keera insists, strangely alarmed. "Look at him—there is nothing to suggest that he was anything but a perfect young man of Broken. Tall, well formed, no lameness in the bones of his limbs, a good skull . . . And they slew him on this very spot, whereas the sickly have always been simply abandoned to the Wood—it is the ritual they call the *mang-bana*."[†]

"A criminal, perhaps?" Heldo-Bah wonders. "No—no, you're right, Keera, there's no mutilation. A criminal would have suffered some such."

"We must find out the meaning in this death," Keera announces.

"And who may we ask?" Veloc betrays nervousness at his sister's determination. "We are foragers, Keera, raiding for decent meat—shall we inquire of Lord Baster-kin's Guard what took place here?"

Keera's purposeful manner never weakens: "If we must, Veloc."

Heldo-Bah smiles wide, revealing the black gap in his teeth. "So—this night promises amusement! Not only poaching, but capturing one of the Merchant Lord's soldiers, too . . ."

Keera looks at the dead man once more. "There is nothing amusing in this, Heldo-Bah. This is the worst evil: that made by men, be it sorcery or mere murder."

"Then it calls for evil in return, does it not?" Loosening the straps that hold his deerskin sack on his shoulders, Heldo-Bah moves back toward the Fallen Bridge. "We leave our goods here—take only weapons." Planting his torch in the ground, Heldo-Bah nimbly clambers to a high maple branch, and ties his sack to it. "Keep everything above the ground—I don't want scavengers destroying three weeks[‡] of work."

Veloc cannot conceal satisfaction of his own at the party's new mission—but he is vexed about his sister, as well. Alone of the party, Keera has a family awaiting her return to the Bane village of Okot, which is a full day's run to the southeast, even for these three. The handsome Bane approaches her confidentially, while Heldo-Bah is busy.

"Keera," Veloc murmurs, placing his hands on her shoulders, "I believe you are right about what we must do—but why not let Heldo-Bah and me attend to it, while you wait here? After all, if we meet with misfortune, no one will weep for us—but Tayo[†] and the children need you to return to them. And I pledged that you would."

. Keera, though touched by her brother's words, frowns a bit at this news. "And what right had you to pledge my return, Veloc?"

"True," Veloc says, his manner growing contrite. "But I bear the responsibility for your being here—your own children know it."

"Don't be foolish, brother—what was I to do? Allow those Outragers to beat you both senseless, simply because they enjoy the favor of the new Moon priestess? No, Veloc. Tayo and the children know the injustice of this term of foraging—and the best thing that I can do for them is to learn if what has taken place here endangers our tribe."

Veloc shrugs, knowing that the guilt he already feels for Keera's punishment by the Groba will become unbearable, should some mishap befall her now. Having long ago learned not to argue important matters with his wise and gifted sister, however, he begins to climb into an oak that stands near Heldo-Bah's maple. "Very well—hand me your bag. Heldo-Bah is right, we must travel light, if we are to do as you wish."

"I do not wish it," Keera says, loosening the straps of her sack. "I could wish we had not discovered this nightmare. For you are wrong, Heldo-Bah."

"Undoubtedly," the sharp-toothed Bane replies as a matter of course from above. "But what, pray, am I wrong about on *this* occasion, Keera?"

"You said that evil calls for evil."

"You think it does not?"

"I know it does not," Keera says, handing her sack up. "Evil *breeds* evil—spreads it like fire. It parches men's souls, just as the Sun burns the skin. Had you paid attention to the basic tenets of our faith, you'd know that this was how the first Moon priests determined that all devils spring from that same Sun, while the Moon, by night, reminds each human heart of its solitary, humble place in the world, and so fills it with compassion. But we will find no compassion across the river—no, we are walking into evil, I fear. So both of you, please—try not to fall into the trap that evil has set for us." The Bane men stare at her in confusion. "No killing," Keera clarifies. "Unless absolutely necessary."

"Of course," Heldo-Bah replies, dropping to the ground, his thick legs absorbing the impact easily. And then he adds under his breath, "But somehow, I suspect it will be . . ."

$$1:\{iii:\}$$

On to the city atop the mountain, now!, and learn
of its virtues, its vices—and the vexations of a soldier . . .

WE TAKE TO THE SKY once more, you and I, across the fields and dales that seemed so serene on our arrival, but which, perhaps, you now find less idyllic; up the slopes of the lonely mountain, first through thick trees and undergrowth on the lower reaches, and then into a still more treacherous maze of rock and harsh scrub; and finally, to the heights, where scattered stands of defiant fir trees give way at last to stone formations, bare of any life and rising, as if of their own accord, to the ultimate and ordered demeanor of mighty walls . . .

"Sentek?"†

Sixt Arnem‡ sits in a shadow beneath the parapet, staring at a small brass oil lamp atop a folding camp table that he has had brought up from the barracks of the Talons.

"Sentek Arnem!" the sentry repeats, more urgently.

Arnem leans forward and folds his arms on the table, his features becoming distinct in the lamp's glow: light brown eyes, a strong nose, and a wry mouth that is never entirely concealed by a rough-trimmed beard. "I'm not deaf, Pallin," he says wearily. "There's no need to shout."

The young pallin slaps his spear against his side in salute. "I am sorry, Sentek." He has forgotten, in his excitement, that he addresses no ordinary officer. "But—there are torches. On the edge of Davon Wood."

Arnem stares into the smoky lamp once more. "Are there?" he says quietly, poking his finger into the yellow flame and watching black soot collect on his skin. "And what is so interesting about that?" he muses.

"Well, Sentek—" The pallin takes a deep breath. "They are moving toward the river and Lord Baster-kin's Plain."

Arnem's eyebrow arches a bit higher. "The Plain?"

"Yes, Sentek!"

Rising with a groan, Arnem sweeps his wine-red cloak behind him, revealing well-made, well-worn leather armor. A pair of silver clusters worked into the shape of outstretched eagle's feet and claws attach the cloak to his powerful shoulders. "All right, Pallin," he says, approaching the eager youth. "Let's see what makes your heart race so."

"There, Sentek; just by the Wood!" the pallin says triumphantly; for to rouse the interest of Broken's greatest soldier is indeed an accomplishment.

Arnem eyes the distance with the calm, all-encompassing gaze of a seasoned campaigner. Even in the light of the rising Moon, the dark mass on the horizon that is the northern frontier of Davon Wood reveals no details about these dancing pinpricks of light. Arnem sighs ambiguously. "Well, Pallin—there are, as you say, a series of torches. Moving just inside Davon Wood, toward the river and the Plain."

Then, as the two men watch, the lights in the distance suddenly disappear. Arnem's features sag mildly. "And now they're gone . . ."

The pallin watches incredulously as Arnem returns to his small stool by the camp table. "Sentek—should we not report this?"

"Oh, Kafra's stones . . ." The blasphemy—common among the poor, but no less extreme for its popularity—has escaped Arnem's lips before he can stop it. He studies his pallin's youthful, clean-shaven features, so resolute beneath the unadorned steel plate helmet[†] that is standard equipment among the Talons; and when he sees how deeply the boy is shocked by his vulgar reference, he cannot help but smile. "What's your name, Pallin?"

"Ban-chindo," the young man replies, again snapping his spear to his side so that its point rises above his six-foot-three-inch body.

"From what district?"

The pallin looks surprised. "Sentek? Why, the Third."

Arnem nods. "A merchant's son. I suppose your father bought your way into the Talons, because the regular army wasn't good enough for you."

The pallin looks straight over Arnem's head, injured but not wishing to show it. He knows about Sixt Arnem's past, as does every soldier in the Talons: born in the Fifth District—home to those who have displeased Kafra with their poverty or unsightliness—Arnem was the first man to rise from pallin in the regular army to the rank of sentek, master of the fates of five hundred men. When he was placed in charge of the Talons, the most elite *khotor*[†] in the army, many of the officers of that larger force sneered; but when he repelled a months-long attempt at invasion by an army of Torganian[‡] raiders, so hardened that they were willing to brave the few passes through the Tombs that remained open at the height of winter, the people of Broken took him wholly to their hearts. Though his family still lives in the Fifth District, Sentek Arnem is acknowledged to be a favorite of both Kafra and the God-King—

None of which, the pallin finally decides, is an excuse for bad manners. "Kafra favors those who succeed in the marketplace, Sentek," he says, keeping his gaze steady but away from Arnem's eyes. "I don't see why their sons should shrink from defending his city, in return."

"Ah, but many do, these days," Arnem replies. "Too many, Pallin Ban-chindo—and those that do serve are forever asking for a place in the Talons. We soon shall be without a regular army altogether."

The pallin is in deep water, and he knows it: "Well—if those who *will* serve can afford a place in the finest legion in the army, is it not Kafra's will? And why should they shy from the glory—*or* from the danger?"

Arnem chuckles in an unmistakably friendly manner. "No need to be so nervous, Pallin Ban-chindo—that's a fine sentiment, bravely stated. I am well rebuked." Arnem rises, and grips the young man's shoulder for an instant. "All right. We have seen several torches, making their way from the Wood to Lord Baster-kin's Plain. What shall we do?"

"That—that is not for me to say, Sentek—"

Arnem quickly holds up an open hand. "Now, now—between one future sentek and one former pallin. What would *you* do?"

"Well—I would—" The pallin stumbles ever more clumsily over his words, angering himself: how can he deserve higher rank if he cannot seize this opportunity? "I would—report it. I think."

"Report it. Ah. To whom?"

"Well, to—to Yantek Korsar, perhaps, or—"

"Yantek Korsar?" Arnem feigns amazement gently. "Are you sure, Pallin? Yantek Korsar has the worries of the entire army of Broken to occupy him. In addition to which, he is on in years—and a widower." The sentek grows pensive, for an instant, thinking not only of his commander and old friend, Yantek Herwald Korsar,[††] but of Korsar's dead wife, Amalberta.[†] Known as "the Mother of the Army," Amalberta was one of the few people Arnem had ever encountered in whom he recognized true kindness, and her death two years earlier had shaken the sentek almost as much as it did Korsar—

But Arnem must not dwell on sadness; for such sentiments are precisely what he came up on the walls to avoid. "All of which," he says, recapturing his authoritative tone, "makes our commander doubly fond of what little sleep he can manage. No, I don't think we want to risk a burst of his infamous temper, Ban-chindo. Isn't there someone else?"

"I don't—perhaps—" Ban-chindo brightens. "Perhaps Lord Baster-kin? The torches are moving toward his land, after all."

"True enough. Baster-kin, eh? And this time you are certain?"

"Yes, Sentek. I should report the matter to Lord Baster-kin."

"Ban-chindo . . ." Arnem strides deliberately up and down the thick stone wall. "It is now past the Moonrise: the middle of the night. Do you know the master of the Merchants' Council, by chance?"

"He is a legendary patriot!" Ban-chindo snaps his spear again.

"You'll bruise yourself, boy," Arnem says, "if you can't bridle your enthusiasm. Yes, Lord Baster-kin is indeed a patriot." The sentek has an unusual respect for Broken's Merchant Lord, despite the tensions and rivalries that have ever existed between the Merchants' Council and the leaders of Broken's army. Yet he knows, as well, that Baster-kin is a short-tempered man, and he shares this fact with Pallin Ban-chindo: "But his lordship is also given to working all hours of the night, and he does not suffer trivial concerns lightly. Now, shall I barge into his residence, where he is doubtless poring over ledgers and accounts, and start slapping my own spear about like some dog-bitten lunatic,[‡] saying, 'Excuse me, my lord, but Pallin Ban-chindo has seen several torches moving toward your plain, and believes that something must be done right away—even though your Personal Guard *do* patrol the area'?"

The pallin lets the spear drift, staring at the stone walkway. "No . . ."

"How's that?"

Ban-chindo straightens. "No, Sentek," he replies. "It's only—"

"It's only the boredom, Ban-chindo. Nothing more."

The young soldier looks Arnem in the eye. "You know . . . ?"

Arnem nods slowly, looking first to his left and the nearest turreted guard tower, then to his right, at a similar squat stone structure some fifty feet away. Near each of these, a young man much like Pallin Ban-chindo stands vigilant. Arnem lets out a leaden sigh. "We've been a long time at peace, Ban-chindo. Eight years since the end of the Torganian war. And now . . ." The sentek leans against the rough parapet. "Now our best hope of action is to fight a tribe of scavengers half our size, in a cursed forest that only a dwarf could master and a fool would attack." He hammers a fist gently on the surface of the parapet. "Yes, Ban-chindo. I understand your boredom . . ."

And only wish I truly shared it, Arnem muses silently. He reminds him-self again that there is no reason for the commander of the Talons to be standing guard duty, and concentrates his attention on the area in the distance where those terribly small lights danced so briefly, hoping they will reappear, and that some warlike crisis will arise to keep his mind from the troubling personal thoughts that have gnawed at him for days. But the lights are gone, and the sentek turns in disappointment to look out over the city that stretches away before him.

Broken lies largely asleep, waiting for the day of feverish trading that will begin with the dawn. From this vantage, Arnem has an unob-structed view of the marketplaces and merchants' houses of the Second and Third Districts, the largest sections of the city, at this hour all dim and serene. Farther to the north, in the wealthy First District, such re-spite is unknown: six-foot-high oil and coal braziers burn perpetually outside the High Temple of Kafra, fed day and night by diligent acolytes. Arnem's soul is thrown into deeper turmoil at the sight of it, and he seeks solace in the Fourth District, to his right, where the main force of the army of Broken is quartered, and then in his own Fifth District, to his left, its nighttime peace riven by those who have failed in the fierce com-petition of the marketplaces and can find solace only in drink.

The distant roar of a crowd erupts, and Arnem looks northward again, to the city Stadium, which stands just beyond the Temple and, for more years than the sentek can remember, has been ordered open and active day and night. Arnem has often been assured that the development of physical prowess and beauty so essential to the worship of Kafra is facili-tated by sporting competitions; while the money that trades hands among the gamblers in attendance creates new fortunes, revealing newly favored souls, and punishing those who have lost their zeal. The sentek has tried hard to accept this reasoning; at the very least, he has kept himself from openly stating that the youths who spend their hours in sport or gambling would be better off serving their kingdom and their god in the army. But recently this self-control, this keeping his questions to himself, has become a difficult chore. For of late, the priests of Kafra—whom Arnem has ever obeyed faithfully—have asked of him something that he cannot give:

They have asked for one of his children.

Arnem's eyes are drawn farther north, once more, to the smooth granite walls of the Inner City and the rooftops of the royal palace beyond. Home to the God-King,[†] his family, the Grand Layzin (highest of the priests of Kafra and the God-King's right hand) as well as the beautiful high priestesses known as the Wives of Kafra, the Inner City has not been visited by any common citizen in the more than two centuries of Broken's history, and remains the city's supreme mystery—which is precisely why Arnem is reluctant to send the second-born of his sons to serve there, although such an act is expected of all families of even moderate stature in Broken society. Children who enter the service of the God-King are never permitted to see their families again; and a childhood spent in the alleys of the Fifth District long ago planted a powerful distrust of such secrecy in Arnem. Perhaps the service these children undertake is pious, and worthier than any life spent in Broken's outer world; but it is Arnem's experience that virtue, while it may sometimes need a veil, never requires utter obscurity.

But was it not Oxmontrot who wanted it all this way? Oxmontrot,[‡] Broken's founder, first king, and greatest warrior, and a hero to lowborn soldiers like Arnem. More than two centuries ago, Oxmontrot (himself lowborn, and able to lead his people only after long years as a mercenary in the service of that vast empire that the citizens of Broken call *Lumun-jan,*[††] although scholars know it as *Roma*) had been labeled "Mad,"[§] because of his ferocious determination, following his return home, to force the farmers and fishermen west of the Meloderna River valley and north of Davon Wood to carve a granite city out of the summit of Broken. Previously, the great masses of stone atop the mountain had been used by tribes dwelling below only as settings for human and animal sacrifices to their various gods. Yet the Mad King had also been shrewd, Arnem muses, on this night as so many: Broken had truly been the finest point from which to build a great state. From its summit, the people of the valleys and dales below could withstand onslaughts from the southeast, the east, and the north, while the remaining approaches to the kingdom were sealed by Davon Wood. No warrior of the Mad King's time could find fault with the ambitious plan, nor has any since: for the sole enemies to have pierced the city's defenses have been the Bane, and Arnem knows that not even Oxmontrot could have been expected to foresee what an unending problem that race of exiles would become . . .

The fact that the Mad King had been a heathen, a Moon worshipper like the Bane, could not have helped his foresight in this regard, Arnem knows; yet despite his personal beliefs, Oxmontrot had presided over the building of the Inner City as a sanctum for his royal family, in his later years, and he had not opposed the introduction of the faith of Kafra and all its secret rituals into his city. Indeed, Broken's founder had seen that the Kafran religion (brought home by several of his mercenary comrades in the service of the *Lumun-jani*) could be made to work to his kingdom's advantage, precisely because it emphasized so strongly the perfection of the human form and the amassing of wealth. His new kingdom, like any other, needed strong warriors and great riches, as much as it needed masons to build its structures and farmers to supply their food; and if a religion could urge Broken's subjects to strive for ever-greater strength and wealth, while casting out those who would not contribute, what matter the private beliefs of the king (the *God-King,* increasing numbers of Broken's citizens began to say, although Oxmontrot consistently refused the title)? Let the new faith flourish, he had declared.

Yet there had been a harsh side to this utility: soon not only those who *would* not work toward the kingdom's safety and wealth, but those who *could* not—the feeble, the weak-minded, the stunted, all who did not embody the goals of physical strength and perfection—found themselves exiled by Kafra's priests to Davon Wood. The wilderness's dangers would provide an ultimate solution to the problem of their imperfect existence, or so it was thought, among both the Kafran clergy and the rising merchant class that built the great houses lining the broad avenues that met near the High Temple to their smiling, golden god. So plain and pervasive had become the priests' severity that even before Oxmontrot fell victim to a murderous plot led by his wife and eldest son, Thedric,[†] there were rumors that he had realized the error of taking advantage of the new faith, rather than forbidding it. Indeed, it had been his doubts on this point, many said, that had sealed the Mad King's fate. Officially, the Kafran priests' version of history had said that the blasphemous perpetuation of Moon worship had caused his death; and while Arnem's discomfort with the recent demands of the Kafran priests has not led him so far as taking up the ancient faith, there have been moments, of late, when he wishes that it would—for absolute belief in *something* must be better than his silent uncertainties.

This recent silence has become especially difficult because the son whom Arnem wishes so earnestly to keep out of the reach of Kafra's priests is anxious to undertake his service to the God-King in the shrouded Inner City; whereas his mother—Arnem's wife, the remarkable Isadora,[†] renowned for her work as a healer within the Fifth District—is equally adamant that her husband's long and loyal service to the kingdom ought to free any and all of their five children from religious obligations that will break the family into pieces. Arnem himself is torn between the merits of the two arguments: and religious doubt, while perhaps troubling for those whose daily lives involve no regular confrontations with violent Death, is an entirely different breed of crisis for a soldier. To feel that one is losing faith in the same god to whom one has prayed fervently for luck amid the horrors of battle is no mere philosophical vexation; yet Arnem knows he must resolve this crisis alone, for neither his wife nor his son will give any ground. His household has been in exhausting turmoil ever since several priests of Kafra arrived to inform Sixt and Isadora that the time had come for young Dalin, a boy of but twelve, to join their elevated society; and that turmoil is what has driven the sentek up onto the walls every evening for a fortnight, to spend long hours beseeching Kafra—or whatever deity does guide the fates of men—for the strength to make a decision.

Arnem takes a small piece of loose stone from the parapet and tosses it lightly in one hand, gazing down at the mighty outer walls of Broken. When originally carved from the natural stone formations that made up the summit of the mountain, the walls followed the basic shape of that peak, a roughly octagonal pattern, with massive oak and iron gates cut into each face. Staring at the portal beneath him, Arnem catches sight of two soldiers of Broken's regular army. Though on sentry duty, the pair are trying to steal a few minutes' sleep: they struggle to obscure themselves beneath a bridge that spans Killen's Run, a stream that emerges from the mountain just outside the city wall, although its subterranean course begins within the Inner City's eternally clear, unfathomably deep Lake of a Dying Moon.

From the point of its emergence under the southern wall, Killen's Run rushes down the mountain to join the Cat's Paw; and once, many years ago, these guards who now seek to hide on its banks would have been Arnem's comrades. The sentek remembers vividly the weariness that drives regular soldiers to steal what rest they can. But the sympathy he feels for their plight cannot now stay his commander's hand, and he drops his bit of stone downward, where it strikes one of the soldiers on the leg. The sentries leap from the cover of the bridge and look up angrily.

"Ah!" the sentek calls to them. "You wouldn't feel such anger had that been a poisoned arrow from a Bane bow, would you? No—you'd feel nothing at all, for the wood snake venom would already have killed you. And the South Gate would now be unmanned. Keep vigilant!"

The two soldiers go back to their posts on either side of the twenty-foot gate, and Arnem can hear them grumbling about the easy life of the "blasted Talons." The sentek could have both men flogged for their insolence; but he smiles, knowing that, exhausted as they may be, they will now perform their assigned task, if only to spite him.

Footsteps echo: an eager yet entirely professional step that Arnem recognizes as that of Linnet Reyne Niksar,[†] his aide.

"Sentek Arnem!"

Arnem turns to face the linnet, without standing. A golden-haired ideal of Broken virtue, Niksar is the scion of a great merchant house, who five years ago gave up command of his own *khotor* (or legion, each *khotor* being composed of some ten *fausten*[‡]), it was said for the honor of serving so closely with Sentek Arnem. In fact, Niksar was suggested for the post by the Grand Layzin because he came from one of the oldest houses in the city: the ruling elite of Broken, unlike the rest of its citizens, do not fully trust the sentek from the Fifth District. Arnem himself suspects that Niksar is an unwilling spy; but he admires his aide's dedication, and the arrangement has not yet produced either friction or any question of divided loyalties.

As the linnet approaches, Arnem smiles. "Good evening, Niksar. Have you seen the torches on the edge of the Plain, as well?"

"Torches?" Niksar answers in worried confusion. "No, Sentek. Were there many?"

"A few." Arnem studies the deep lines of concern above Niksar's light brows. "But a few are very often enough." The commander pauses. "You bring a message, I see."

"Yes, Sentek. From Yantek Korsar."

"Korsar? What's he doing up at this hour?" Arnem laughs affectionately: for it was Yantek Korsar who first recognized Arnem's extraordinary potential, and sponsored him for high rank.

"He says it is most urgent. You are to bring your aide—"

"Yourself."

"Yes, Sentek." Niksar is fighting hard to maintain his discipline. "Bring your aide to his quarters. There is to be a council at the Sacristy of the High Temple. The Grand Layzin is to attend, and also Lord Basterkin."

Arnem stands up straight and glances at Pallin Ban-chindo, who, although he keeps his gaze fixed on the horizon, cannot help but smile at this news. Arnem urges Niksar a few paces further down the wall.

"Who told you this?" Arnem's tone is earnest.

"Yantek Korsar himself," Niksar replies, no longer concerned with shielding his uneasiness from watchful sentries. "Sentek, his manner was strange, I've never seen him . . ." Niksar holds up his hands. "I can't describe it. Like a man who senses Death hovering nearby, yet makes no move to avoid it."

Arnem pauses, nodding slowly and scratching at his short beard. He does not truly believe that this summons can be related to the heated debate over his son's entry into the royal and sacred service—if it is, why involve such high officials of religion, commerce, and the army, to say nothing of young Niksar? But the possibility is unsettling, nonetheless. At length, however, the sentek shrugs once, affecting merely mild consternation. "Well—if called, we must attend."

"But, Sentek, I—I have never been summoned to the Sacristy."

Arnem understands Niksar's apprehension: for the Grand Layzin can order anything from a man's banishment to Davon Wood to his ennoblement, without any explanation that base mortals might comprehend. To be summoned to the Sacristy, seat of the Layzin's power, is therefore cause for great celebration or for deep dread; and even Niksar—a man who could not display any more obvious signs of Kafra's favor—cannot greet the call with confidence.

How much more, then, should an older, less handsome man—one lacking great wealth and certainty of faith—feel cause for alarm?

But Arnem has confronted greater terrors. "Pull yourself together, Niksar," he says. "What interest can the Layzin have in you?" Hastening Niksar toward the nearby guard tower, the sentek adds with a laugh, "Why, you make even *me* look like a Bane forager . . ."

Just before he descends the spiral stairs, Arnem claps his previous companion on the shoulder. "Stay alert, Ban-chindo—you may get your action yet!"

The pallin draws in a proud breath and smiles. "Yes, Sentek!"

Inside the guard tower, where torchlight dances on stone surfaces, Arnem and Niksar prepare to start down the winding steps; but before they can, they, along with every other soldier on the southern wall, are frozen by an unmistakable sound:

Echoing up from the far side of Lord Baster-kin's Plain comes a horrific shriek of terror and pain, one clearly made by a man.

Rushing back out, Arnem and Niksar see that Ban-chindo's spear now drifts from his side uncertainly. "Sentek?" he murmurs. "It comes from the direction of the torches . . ."

"It does, Pallin." Arnem listens for further cries; but none come.

"I—have never heard such a sound," the pallin admits softly.

"Likely some Bane has fallen prey to wolves," Niksar muses, his own face knotted with puzzlement. "Although we heard no howling . . ."

"Outragers?" Ban-chindo's voice is scarcely more than a whisper, revealing the extent to which the Bane raiders are not only disdained but feared in Broken. "Attacking one of Lord Baster-kin's Guard? Surely the others heard him cry out, if we were able to."

"Perhaps," Arnem murmurs, as the three soldiers move to the parapets. "But sound plays evil tricks on a man, near the rocks of the Cat's Paw. We once campaigned for a month down there, and lost many men to wolves—you could hear them attacking from a mile's distance, yet they could take a picket off without his nearest comrades detecting a thing. And yet, as Niksar says, we have heard no howling . . ."

"A panther?" Niksar suggests. "They are silent during attack."

"So is their prey," Arnem replies. "Difficult to scream with a set of panther's teeth embedded in your throat."

Pallin Ban-chindo's dread rises, as his superiors discuss these grim possibilities, further freeing his young tongue: "Sentek—I know that those who live in the Wood are unworthy, but—I pity the creature who made that sound. Even if it was a Bane. What can have caused it, if neither wolves nor a panther?"

"Whatever the full explanation, Ban-chindo," Arnem pronounces, "understand that what you have just heard is the unmistakable voice of human agony. Understand it, respect it—and get used to it. For such are the sounds of the glory you seek so desperately." Arnem softens his tone. "Keep careful watch. Like as not the torches and this scream were not connected—but if a party of Bane Outragers *has* got past Baster-kin's men, it means that they intend to enter the city. And I want them stopped—*here*. Send word along the walls—and alert those two shirkers below, as well." Ban-chindo nods, his mouth too dry to speak. "I can count on you, Pallin?"

Straining hard, Ban-chindo finds his voice. "You can, Sentek."

"Good man." Arnem smiles, and moves Ban-chindo's spear so that it is tight against the young man's shoulder once more. "At attention,† lad. There's worse to come, if I'm any judge—and we must *all* be ready . . ."

1:{*iv:*}

The Bane foragers secure a fine meal for
themselves—and for the wolves on the Plain, as well . . .

HAVING HEARD THE SCREAM, though not quite so distinctly as the men atop Broken's walls, Keera and Veloc have leapt from their hiding place on the northern, or Broken side of the Fallen Bridge. They rush through the rich spring grass that rises above their knees to join Heldo-Bah, who has gone to scout for any members of Lord Baster-kin's Guard who may be patrolling this portion of the boundary of the great merchant's plain. Keera seethes with anger, as she keeps her nose in the air to locate their troublesome friend.

"I told him!" she hisses. "You heard me, Veloc, I said no killing!"

"No killing *unless* it was necessary," her brother answers evenly, lifting his short bow over his head, reaching for an arrow from the small quiver at his waist, and nocking it. "That is, in fact, what you said, Keera—and perhaps it *was* necessary."

"'Perhaps it was necessary,'" Keera mocks. "You know just as well as I do that—"

But they have reached a small circle in the grass, flattened violently as if by a struggle. At the edge of the circle, hidden in standing grass, they find not only Heldo-Bah, but a soldier of Broken. The latter is young, muscular, and would stand at well over six feet—if his legs were not bent at the knees and bound so tightly with strong gut-line to his arms that his feet are crushed painfully to his thighs. Heldo-Bah, cackling quietly, stuffs moist sod into his captive's mouth. The soldier bleeds near one knee; but his well-bred face shows more terror than pain.

"It seems they've just changed the watch," Heldo-Bah tells Keera, getting up. "We should be safe enough while we finish our business."

"You suppose so?" Keera demands angrily, letting her fists fly at Heldo-Bah's arm. He stifles a small bark of pain. "With that cry that he gave? How could even *you* be so stupid, Heldo-Bah?"

"Can I help it if the man's a coward?" Heldo-Bah replies, sullenly rubbing the spot on his arm that Keera struck. "I hadn't touched him, and then he suddenly saw my face, and screamed like some frightened girl! Besides, I made sure that he was patrolling alone." Looking at the soldier's face, Heldo-Bah's own features fill with delight once more: his grin displays the filed teeth with their black gap, and he pokes the young man's red-brown leather armor with one of his marauder knives. "Not your night, Tall," he says, removing a wide brass band encircling the muscles of the soldier's upper right arm. The center of the band has been beaten into a bearded, smiling face with empty almond eyes, a thin, flaring nose, and full lips—the image of Kafra. It marks the captive soldier as what the three Bane expected to encounter: a member of the Personal Guard of the Lord of the Merchants' Council.[†] It is a fact with which Heldo-Bah toys even more delightedly than he does with the shining trinket.

"Baster-kin will probably sentence you to be mutilated for this failure," he laughs. "Provided *we* don't kill you first, of course."

The soldier begins to sweat profusely at these words, and Veloc examines him disdainfully. "A fine specimen of Broken virtue," the handsome Bane decides. "Keep him alive, Heldo-Bah—the Groba will have our stones, if we come away from this with no useful information."

"You won't have to wait for the Groba," Keera says, eyes ever on the landscape about her. "Kill him and I'll geld you myself, Heldo-Bah. I've told you, we are not Outragers—" She stops, nose to the breeze once more. "The cattle," she says, leading the way further east.

A dozen yards further on, and the tall field grass gives way to close-chewed pasture. The three Bane go onto their bellies at its edge, and from there they can make out the silhouettes of well-fed shag cattle against the deep blue of the horizon. "The Moon has cleared the trees," Keera says, pointing to a half-circle of light that shines bright in the sky east of their position.

"A good omen," Heldo-Bah declares. "You see, Keera—"

"Be silent, blasphemer!" Keera orders impatiently. "A good omen for the Bane—when they're neither defying the Groba nor *stealing*. We must be quick—the light increases the risk." She turns to her brother. "All right, Veloc, let's get the grumbler his dinner. Heldo-Bah, question that soldier, but *do not* harm him."

Veloc eyes the cattle. "We'll take a steer. I know women who will do anything for ground shag horn, they say it heightens the pleasure—"

Keera smacks an open hand to her brother's head. "Do not finish that statement, pig. By all that's holy, the pair of you will drive me mad . . . Be sure it *is* a steer, Veloc, and not a bull—bad enough to kill any horned animal when the Moon is high, let alone a sacred bull—"[†]

"Sister," Veloc chides, "unlike Heldo-Bah, I know the articles of our faith. I'm not likely to commit such serious sacrilege."

"Well, stones or horns, bring me beef," Heldo-Bah declares. "I'll need a decent meal by the time I've done with our friend . . ."

Veloc is on his feet with his short bow drawn, advancing into the pastureland. He and his sister are among the finest archers in the Bane tribe, and Veloc scarcely bothers to take aim before loosing a shaft. Immediately, a strangled moan comes from a shag steer, and the Bane can see that Veloc's arrow is protruding from the beast's neck at what appears an ideal spot: even at half the distance, it would be a remarkable shot.

Heldo-Bah pounds Veloc's back with a congratulatory hand. "A fine shot, Veloc—we'll eat well tonight! Quick, now—you two fetch the haunches and the back straps, while I talk with our prisoner!" Veloc and Keera trot away, Veloc grinning at his friend's praise. "That's right," Heldo-Bah adds, under his breath. "Go and get me my dinner, you vain ass . . ."

Turning to stride delightedly toward the struggling soldier, Heldo-Bah pauses when he hears Veloc cry in stifled alarm. Glancing back into the pasture, the gap-toothed forager sees that the shag steer has risen unexpectedly from the ground and come close to goring its would-be executioner: The arrow has not pierced the animal's flesh as deeply as they had thought. Comprehending her brother's predicament, Keera races faster to aid him; Heldo-Bah, however, only shakes his head with a small laugh. "I'll mate with one of Keera's river spirits before I'll chase a wounded shag steer about in the dark . . ."

The captive soldier lets out a low moan; and when Heldo-Bah turns to him again, the forager's aspect has changed to something more unsettling than anything we have yet witnessed. Anger, foolishness, despair, jocularity: Heldo-Bah has already exhibited all of these—

But now, for the first time, when he is alone with the soldier, it becomes clear that his casual comments about murder have some root in experience.

The soldier senses this, and his moans become more pitiable. "Oh, don't carry on so, Tall," Heldo-Bah says quietly. "Think of this as a small taste of Bane life." He gives the collar of the young Guardsman's tunic a painful tug, pulling the captive up onto his knees. In this position, the two can just look each other in the eye: Heldo-Bah puts his head close to the Guardsman's, then turns both his own and his captive's faces to watch the shining Moon. "Things look different from this point of view, eh?"

The youth's widening eyes indicate clearly that he thinks Heldo-Bah mad, and his panic makes him take too large a breath, shaking dirt loose from the sod in his mouth. He begins to choke as the dirt catches in his throat: if Heldo-Bah does not help him, he will soon die, and both of them know it. Yet the Bane forager goes on studying him calmly.

"Bad feeling to be treated no better than a useless animal, eh, Tall? I've an idea—I'll save your life, that should finish your Broken pride for good and all!" Heldo-Bah then works the sod out of the Guardsman's mouth, after which the captive spits, and retches yellow slime. He catches his breath, heaving noisily—and quickly finds one of Heldo-Bah's knives at his throat. "Now, now—no noise or crying out, Tall. You'll be dead before anyone hears you."

The soldier can only gasp: "Are you going to kill me?"

"That—is a distinct possibility." Heldo-Bah keeps his knife leveled at the soldier's neck. "How willing are you to educate me?"

"To—*what?*" stammers the Guardsman.

"Educate me!" Heldo-Bah answers plainly. "I am only a Bane forager, Tall, I know nothing about the truly important things in life: your great society, for instance, and the laws that keep it great . . ." Heldo-Bah lets the knife at the soldier's throat draw a little blood, then shows the sticky blade to the young man, who can see the precious liquid clearly in the Moonlight. "For instance—why would the priests of Kafra deliberately kill a sickly comrade of yours on our side of the River?"

"What are you talking about?" the captive moans.

The question brings the forager's knife back to his throat. "I can cut deeper, Tall, if you play at ignorance with me. You're a member of Lord Baster-kin's Guard—you know all that has gone on in this part of the frontier."

"But—" Heldo-Bah's mounting pressure on the knife is moving the young man to tears of despair. "But this is my first patrol, Bane! I know nothing save what has happened tonight!"

Heldo-Bah's air of delighted menace collapses. "You're joking."

"Joking? *Now?*"

"Then you're lying. You must be! Your *first* patrol? Not even *my* luck is that bad!"

The Guardsman shakes his head as emphatically as the Bane's knife will permit. "I tell you, I know nothing—" And then, a faint light of recognition fills the man's eyes. "Wait."

Heldo-Bah looks quickly out at the pasture. Veloc and Keera are stalking the mortally wounded steer, whose death throes make it ever more dangerous. "Oh, I'll wait, Tall—that much is certain. I'm certainly not joining *those* two . . ."

"I did hear something—in the mess. Earlier. About an execution."

"Good! Your chances of surviving the night have improved enormously. Now—*who* was executed? And why in that manner?"

"What manner?"

"In the manner he was killed, damn you! Why force him across the bridge, shoot him down with ritual arrows, then leave the body untouched, with the arrows still in it? You Tall haven't suddenly lost your taste for religion or wealth, have you? Those arrows were from the Sacristy of your High Temple, we know this, and a lot of gold and silver went into the making of them—what does it all signify?"

"I—I don't know any more than I've told you, I swear it! I heard two soldiers talking about an execution that took place some days ago—one asked the other if he thought it had succeeded."

"Succeeded?" Heldo-Bah does not hide his skepticism. "With nearly half a dozen arrows in him? Of course it succeeded! What's your game, Tall?"

Again the knife presses hard, and the Guardsman must strain not to cry out. "I don't think—that is, it seemed they were speaking of something else! Not as if they had succeeded in killing the man, but—something else."

"Such as?" Heldo-Bah draws another bead of blood from the youth, close to the vital pathways throbbing on the powerful neck.

"I don't know!" the captive sobs. "In the name of Kafra, Bane, I would tell you, if I did—why would I *not*?"

Heldo-Bah rises up, as if making ready to cut the youth's throat; but at the sight of the tears streaming unchecked down his cheeks, he relents, and shoves the knife angrily into the sheath that holds all three of the blades. "Yes, I suppose you're telling the truth, Tall—and I suppose my luck simply *is* that bad. Tonight as always . . ." Looking out into the pasture once more, the forager hisses. "Blast it.[†] And those two still haven't got my meal!"

Out amid the cattle, Veloc is being chased in a tightening circle by the wounded steer, as his sister moves to grab hold of the long, bloodied hair that dangles from the animal's neck and shoulders. Keera is close to success—until the steer flings her a dozen yards away with a toss of its head. She sits up, dazed but uninjured. "This evening looks to be a thorough disappointment," Heldo-Bah moans.

"You won't kill me?" the captive dares, some nerve returning.

"Oh, I'd *like* to, make no mistake. Save that the woman you see out there would render me worse than dead, were I to do it . . ."

"Truly? I—I did not know that the Bane understood mercy."

Heldo-Bah gives an angry laugh. "*Us?* It's you lofty demons that inflict suffering without a bit of remorse! Besides, what of Kafra, and his little brother the God-King? Won't they save you from our terrible wrath?"

The Guardsman's voice suddenly boils with indignant rage: "Do not soil those names by speaking them, you unholy little—"

Heldo-Bah laughs more heartily. "Good, Tall—good! Let's keep things simple—you hate me, and I hate you. Each on principle. I don't like confusion." He snatches a gutting blade from his belt, and points into the pasture once more. "You take my friend there—do you know, he has spent this evening savaging my ears with those old lies about all men having once been of an average height? I ask you, what half-witted—"

A stifled cry of alarm comes from Veloc, who is waving frantically at Heldo-Bah; but Heldo-Bah only smiles and returns the wave.

"Listen, Bane," the captive says, feeling ever bolder, now that he realizes these three do not intend murder. "You know my comrades will return soon. You should release me now—"

Heldo-Bah considers the matter as he watches events on the Plain. "And *you* had best hope my friends avoid that steer's horns," he answers, in a blithe manner that renews much of the young man's fear. "Because if it's up to me, boy, you *will* die. But let's return to this puzzling question of height for the moment. I'll tell you what—help me solve it. And then, perhaps, I'll let you go."

"What is it you want to know?"

"It's troubling," Heldo-Bah answers, squinting at the soldier, his voice still a blend of threat and congeniality. "If it's true, this business of all men having been of one size before your accursed city was built,[†] that would mean that the creation of the Bane wasn't the act of any god, yours *or* ours—wouldn't it? That would mean that the Tall somehow brought it about themselves—wouldn't it?" Heldo-Bah again puts his face very close to the youth's. "That would mean that you have a lot to answer for—*wouldn't it?*"

The forager is interrupted by a louder cry from the shag steer, followed by a very unsettling sound that Veloc makes as he runs with his buttocks just inches from the dying animal's thrusting horns, while Keera dashes alongside the animal once more.

Heldo-Bah frowns. "Well . . . I suppose I shouldn't have expected anything else. This is the price of being a martyr to one's digestion, Tall . . ."

He grips the gutting blade (which is almost as long as his forearm) tight enough to whiten his knuckles. "Stay at your post," he mocks, as he bends down to cut a fresh piece of grassy sod and stuff it into the Guardsman's mouth. "I'm just going to finish that steer." Heldo-Bah drops the captive's brass armlet on the ground. "Here," he says. "Let your god keep you company. And pray, boy . . ."

Only when Heldo-Bah is out in the open plain does he realize that he and his friends have wasted too much time with their various amusements: other members of Lord Baster-kin's Guard will arrive before long, to find out what has so upset the cattle. Heldo-Bah takes the ball of hatred that has been fixed all his life on Broken, and momentarily redirects it to the wounded animal: he locks eyes with it, in a manner that transfixes the steer just long enough to allow Heldo-Bah to leap onto the beast's thick neck and gain an unshakable purchase with his strong legs. Then, in one expert motion, he reaches around with his gutting blade and slits the animal's throat, sending a spray of hot blood across the winded Veloc's legs. In seconds the steer has collapsed, and Heldo-Bah leaps back to the ground, rubbing dirt into the blood on his tunic.

"Trust you to bungle it, Veloc," he says, as Keera prostrates herself before the head of the dead steer.

"An excellent maneuver, Heldo-Bah," Veloc answers angrily. "A pity you couldn't have managed it earlier!"

"Be still!" Keera orders; and then she turns to the steer again, murmuring several phrases indistinctly, yet earnestly.

"She fears its wrath," Veloc whispers. "It did not die quickly."

"No—and we've tarried too long here, as a result," Heldo-Bah replies—although not loud enough for Keera to hear.

Within seconds, Keera is on her feet, having begged the steer, as Veloc said, for mercy. "Hurry, both of you," she says, as she cuts away one of the steer's haunches. "Heldo-Bah, if you want your precious back straps, you can cut them out yourself."

Heldo-Bah quickly gets the carcass of the steer open and its guts out onto the Plain in a steaming mass. Working deeper, he neatly harvests the long pieces of muscle that run astride the spine, delicacies he has dreamed of for many days; and he does all of this in less time than it takes the other two foragers to remove the second haunch. The three make ready to run back to the river and their waiting bags—but they go only a few steps before Keera stands alarmingly still, ordering the other two to wait. Heldo-Bah and Veloc see fear suddenly widen her eyes.

"The panther?" Heldo-Bah whispers.

Keera shakes her head once quickly. "No—wolves. *Many . . .*"

Veloc looks back at the remains of the steer. "Come for the carcass?"

Keera shakes her head, disturbed. "They may have smelled the blood, but—they're in *that* direction. The place where we—"

The noises that erupt from the spot where the three Bane left the bound Broken Guardsman make further explanation unnecessary: none of the foragers needs to see what is happening to know that the pack of wolves has decided to move in swiftly on the easiest meal. The agonized screams of the helpless soldier indicate the pack is working fast: in half a minute the screaming is stifled, and the howls are replaced by the growls of feeding.

Keera knows that any wolves that do not get an immediate place at the Guardsman's body will come looking for other meat, and the smell of the steer's blood will so embolden them that they will take long chances against humans. "We must move in a wide circle and back over the river," she says. "Quickly—the other soldiers must have heard that." She starts to move, and Veloc keeps pace behind her; but Heldo-Bah hesitates.

"You two go ahead," he declares. "I want that brass armlet."

"Don't be an idiot," Veloc snaps. "You heard what Keera said."

"Take the back straps," Heldo-Bah answers, tossing the bloody pieces of beef to Veloc. "I'll meet you at the bridge!" Before waiting for further argument, Heldo-Bah vanishes quickly.

Intending to give the wolves a chance to move on to the steer carcass, Heldo-Bah works a wide circle through the field to the spot where he left the Guardsman. As he runs, the forager's thoughts turn to the young man, but with little remorse: to a greater extent he is curious—about how much of the body the wolves will consume before going to the steer, and how it must have felt for a youth who had known comfort for most of his short life to have faced, on his first night of patrol, all the horrors of the wilderness, without weapons, comrades, or even freedom. This last thought brings a smile to Heldo-Bah's face, as he reaches a spot from which he can hear those few wolves who have not already been drawn to the richer meat of the steer snarling over the soldier's remains. When these sounds cease, Heldo-Bah creeps closer once more. But even he cannot maintain his smile when he finds the remains:

The wolves have torn away the young man's limbs, along with the gut-line that bound them, and slick white bone sockets shine out from the bloody groin and shoulders. The armor has frustrated attempts to get inside the body, but the head lies to one side, almost fully severed, the wide eyes slowly ceasing to reflect the Moon. Heldo-Bah studies the remains, then retrieves the shining armlet from the ground and sets out for the river. He pauses after just a few steps, however, and turns to stare once more into the dead, terrified eyes of his young captive.

"Well, boy," Heldo-Bah murmurs. "It's a Bane's education you've had tonight." His cracked lips curl a final time, displaying something more complex than cruelty. "A shame you'll never have a chance to use it . . ."

Turning back to fetch the soldier's short-sword from about his ravaged right shoulder, Heldo-Bah is soon running fast enough to catch his companions before they reach the Fallen Bridge.

$$1:\{v:\}$$

Arnem's long march into the heart of Broken, and the
mystery he encounters along the way . . .

"SO IT WAS WOLVES," Linnet Niksar pronounces, having heard the terrible sounds that have reverberated up from the Plain below Broken; and though his words are conclusive, his tone lacks the certainty to match.

"Yes, Linnet," agrees young Pallin Ban-chindo, who tries to hide his relief at this Earthly explanation for the agonized cries. "Shall I stand the watch down, Sentek?"

Like his aide, however, Sixt Arnem does not share the young pallin's certainty. "I wouldn't, Ban-chindo," he murmurs, eyes narrowing and deepening the scar-like creases at their corners: the product of a lifetime spent studying what ordinary eyes are slow to detect. "No, I would not . . ."

"Sentek?" Ban-chindo asks in surprise.

Arnem slowly lifts a finger to trace the black horizon of the forest. "Why the lengthy pause? Between the initial scream and the final attack?"

"That's not hard to explain," Ban-chindo answers, again letting his mouth move faster than respect dictates. "Sir!" he adds quickly.

"I'm delighted you think so," Arnem chuckles, once more resting his forearms on the parapet. "Please share this easy explanation that eludes both Linnet Niksar and myself."

Ban-chindo's face twists with discomfort, as he realizes that his next statement had better be considered, deferential—and above all, accurate. "Well, Sentek—the first cry was one of alarm. A reaction, upon spying the pack, and a warning to the other members of his patrol."

Arnem nods slowly, settling the pallin's spirits considerably. "That may have been the intent behind it—yet what would such tell us about the man who cried out?"

Ban-chindo's mouth falls open. "Sentek?"

"Come now, Ban-chindo, think," Arnem says, firmly but without anger. "You, too, Niksar. What have we said about the tricks that sound can play on a man near the Cat's Paw?"

Linnet Niksar's features fill with comprehension. "If he is part of Baster-kin's Guard, he would know the others are unlikely to hear him."

"True. Unless . . ." This has always been Arnem's way: to draw ideas from his men, rather than to bellow indictments of their blindness.

Ban-chindo snaps upright once again: he has used the moment well. "Unless—he was a new recruit. He may have been unaware of local conditions, and patrolled too far from the rest of the watch."

Arnem smiles and nods. "Yes, Ban-chindo," he says, offering the young man a look that any soldier of Broken would endure great hardship to receive. "Yours is the best explanation." As quickly as it brightened, however, Arnem's face grows dark. "But it is not particularly reassuring . . ."

Ban-chindo is too confused to speak, leaving Niksar to ask: "Why not, Sentek? It's no joy to lose a man, but better to wolves than—"

"My dear Niksar," Arnem interrupts a bit impatiently. "You don't find it strange that wolves should know to pick an ignorant new recruit, at an ideal distance from the river, when there are so many easier targets? The cattle, for example—what pack of wolves risks a struggle against men, when grazing livestock are to be had? No . . ." Arnem gazes out at the faraway edge of Lord Baster-kin's Plain a final time, as if he will tease more clues from it with his eyes alone. "There is more to this business than we yet know. Something, and even more likely someone, was certainly lying in wait for just such a target as our unfortunate new recruit . . ."[†]

A few quiet moments pass, as Niksar and Pallin Ban-chindo watch their chief further puzzle with the problem. Eventually, Niksar must step forward. "Sentek? The council in the Sacristy—"

"*Hak!*"[‡] Arnem noises, rousing himself. "Curse me for a buggered Bane . . ." It is another of the popular oaths, the use of which mark the sentek as an outsider among the ruling classes of Broken, but which have helped forge his close bond to his men. "Yes, Niksar, we must be away. Ban-chindo—eyes and ears open, eh? If anything of further interest happens, you'll bring the news to me yourself—understood?"

"I—am to report to the High Temple?" the young man replies, once more the very image of Broken pride. "Yes, Sentek!"

"Good. Come, Niksar, before Korsar's impatience turns to rage."

And the two officers of the Talons finally vanish into the chisel-scored walls of the guard tower, and down its worn stone steps.

The carving of Broken's outer walls took more than twenty years to complete, even under Oxmontrot's ferocious direction. It meant death for thousands of laborers, and misery for many more. But the impenetrable barrier that finally surrounded the Mad King's fortress-city was, on its completion, a source of awe even for those who had suffered cruelly during its construction. And there were many ways to suffer: for in the early years of Oxmontrot's reign, the first of the banishments took place, as a pragmatic means of ensuring that those citizens of the infant kingdom who were too feeble—in body *or* mind—to contribute to the great undertaking would not occupy its members' energies with pointless care-giving, consume any of the initially thin streams of foodstuffs that came up the mountain, or waste space in the crude shelters that were built for the healthy.[††] Cruel reasoning; yet effective.

Arnem and Niksar make their way swiftly to the foot of the guard tower steps, and, once outside, proceed along a pathway that runs at the base of the city's outer walls, and is kept clear at all times for the passage of troops. Taking a left turn, Arnem decides to cut the distance to Yantek Korsar's quarters by taking Broken's main avenue, the Celestial Way,[§]

which bisects the city by originating near the southern wall, running north between the Fourth and Fifth Districts, then continuing on, through the market stalls of the Third District and then the more formal shops and sturdy residences of the Second, before finally terminating in the public square before the steps of the High Temple. Weary of his family worries, the sentek turns his mind to his duties, and to the possibilities that may be unfolding: *Must it be the Bane?* he wonders, in silent frustration. *Will no more worthy enemy present themselves?* He thinks of his months fighting Torganian raiders amid the frozen passes of the Tombs, and of the ferocity of those southern tribes: surely, he has not survived many years of faithful service only to discover that the soldiers of Broken are to be given the humiliating task of chasing a race of wretched exiles through an impenetrable wilderness. And why chase them? Simply because of the occasional crimes of the Bane Outragers? Whatever god does rule the affairs of men, Arnem decides, he or she would not permit so noble an instrument as the Talons to be bent to so petty a purpose. Perhaps it will be an eastern campaign: an attempt to finally confront the horsed marauders who press Broken's borders with a regularity that nearly matches that of the rising Sun, out of whose blinding brightness they prefer to attack; or perhaps the fearsomely organized soldiers of *Lumun-jan* have returned once more—

Neither these ambitious ruminations nor his underlying anxieties about the possible connection between the dilemma facing his family and this unexpected council can dull the physical instincts first sharpened during Arnem's childhood: as he and Niksar pass the mouth of an offal-strewn alleyway that feeds the Celestial Way from the west, the sentek ducks to keep his head from being struck by a hurtling object. A clay wine jug smashes into the mortared base of a house just a few feet from him, with force enough to kill. As he looks up he sees Niksar searching the area, his short-sword drawn; and then they glimpse a thickly made, unkempt man standing in the alleyway. The man grins and lets out an idiot's laugh.

"Off to lick royal arse, are you, Tall?" the drunkard cries. "May you choke on it!" The man vanishes back through the alleyway in the direction of the Fifth District, Niksar moving to pursue him; but Arnem grasps the younger man's arm.

"We've far more important business, Reyne," the sentek says; yet he pauses long enough to consider the drunkard's words. "Tall?" he says in wonderment, as Niksar sheathes his sword. "That man was too big to be a Bane—I thought only they used that term for our people."

Arnem is answered by yet another voice, this one disembodied, disturbingly serene and floating out of the shadowy rear doorway of the nearby house:

"The Bane aren't the only people who resent your kind, Sentek . . ."

Arnem and Niksar watch in some confusion as the shadows produce an ancient, bearded man. His hair is no more than a mist surrounding his head, while his robe, once an elegant design in black and silver, is now a faded testament to years of hard luck. The man steadies himself on a staff as he limps painfully forward. "Have you visited the Fifth District of late?" the old man asks.

For the second time tonight, Arnem must prevent apprehension from manifesting in his demeanor. "Indeed," he says, approaching the man calmly. "It's where I was born, as were my family. We live there still."

"*You?* Then you are . . . ?" The old man stares at Arnem with recognition that makes the sentek ever more uneasy. "You *are* Sixt Arnem . . ." Milky eyes turn first to the stars and the ascendant Moon, and then squint at the beacons outside the High Temple in the northern distance, until at last the old man murmurs, "But am I ready . . . ?"

"'Ready'?" Arnem echoes. "Ready for what?"

"For what is likely beginning," the man says calmly. "You go to the Sacristy, Sentek—I suspect . . ."

Unlike Arnem, Niksar is unable to master his wariness of the agèd specter, and approaches his commander. "Come, Sentek. He is mad—"

Arnem holds a hand up to silence his aide, then says, "So, we're bound for the Sacristy?"

The old man smiles. "You will hear lies there, Sentek—though not all who speak them will be liars."

Arnem frowns, growing less patient and more relaxed. "Ah. Riddles. For a moment, I thought we might actually avoid them."

"Mad or taunting, his words are treasonous," Niksar says; then he scolds, "Be careful what you say, old fool, or we must arrest you."

"The Bane are the cause of your summons." The old man raises his staff from the ground. "This, I believe, can be stated with certainty."

"There's no prescience in that," Arnem says, affecting carefree laughter. "You've likely heard the screaming on the Plain." The sentek resumes his march. "Why Kafra should have chosen to number those wretched little beings among his creations, I'll never—"

Arnem and Niksar have not gone a dozen paces before the old man declares, "It was not any god who created the Bane, Sixt Arnem—we of Broken bear that responsibility!"

The two officers quickly retrace several of their steps. "Stop it," Arnem tells the old man urgently. "*Now*. Whatever your madness, we are soldiers of the Talons, and there are things that we cannot hear—"

Arnem suddenly ceases to speak, as his eyes go wider. The old man's face is still nothing but a strange mask of misfortune—but his robe . . . Something about the faded silver and black, and the fine cut—something about the robe looks disturbingly yet inexplicably familiar.

"You do not remember me—do you, Sentek?" the old man asks.

"Should I?" Arnem asks.

His mouth curling, the old man replies, "No longer. And not yet . . ."

Arnem tries to smile. "More riddles? Well, if that's all you offer—"

"I have given you what I have to offer, Sentek," the old man says, raising his staff a few inches higher. "If you go to the Sacristy tonight, you shall hear lies; but not all who speak them will be liars. And it will be your task to determine who disgraces that allegedly exalted chamber with deceit!"

Rage flushing his cheeks, Niksar can no longer contain himself: "We should kill you here," he declares, a hand to his sword. "You speak one heresy after another!"

The old man only smiles again, looking at Niksar. "That has been said," he replies, raising the hem of his robe with his free arm. "*Before* . . ."

In the dimness of the avenue, with Moonlight playing off water that flows quietly in the gutter, Arnem and Niksar can see that the old man's left leg is far darker than his right; but it is only when the agèd arm taps the staff against that left limb, producing a hollow knock, that the two men guess the truth. The old man smiles at their horror, and continues to tap the wood strapped to the stump of his thigh.

"The *Denep-stahla!*"[†] Niksar whispers.

"The young linnet knows his rituals," the old man answers, dropping the hem of his robe. He continues to tap his staff against the makeshift lower leg, producing a sound that is more muted, but no less dreadful, than that which preceded it.

Arnem's gaze does not leave that leg: for the sight has brought with it understanding of his earlier uneasiness, as well as memories of his own days as a linnet, when he was part of more than a few escort parties that accompanied the priests of Broken to the Cat's Paw river, where they performed, where they still perform, their sacred, bloody rites of punishment and exile. Although a post of honor, it was not a commission to which Arnem was suited, and he did not hold it long—long enough, however, to plant the seeds of his doubts about the faith of Kafra.

At length, he looks the old man in the eye again. "Have we met before?"

"You will remember my name at the appropriate time, Sentek," the cripple answers.

"And how did you escape the Wood?"

Again the agèd lips curl grimly. "The unholy are often cunning. But should you not be concerned about something else?" The old man pauses, but Arnem says nothing. "I am *here,* Sentek—is it not against the laws of Broken for exiles to return to the city without permission? Have I been granted such?"

With the old man's words making ever less sense, and his infernal tapping growing ever more relentless, Arnem approaches him one last time. "If you have endured the *Denep-stahla,* friend, then you have been given trouble enough for one lifetime—and ample reason for your madness. Leave the city—we will forget this encounter."

But the old man only shakes his head slowly. "You will try, Sentek. But do not trust my word alone. Wait for another voice to sound, this night— to sound more times than it ever has before . . ."

Arnem tries to dismiss this latest riddle by lifting a stern finger; the movement is awkward and ineffective, however, and becomes instead a simple signal to Niksar. The two men move speedily down the Celestial Way once more. In the distance, however, they can still hear the steady tap of the old man's staff against his wooden leg, prompting Niksar to say, a bit nervously, "Well—an attempt at murder and an insane heretic. Not the best of omens for this council, Sentek."

"Have any officers been attacked in this area?" Arnem asks, wanting to forget the old man and, above all, hoping Niksar will not ask why the peculiar character believed Arnem might remember him.

"There have been a few incidents, but most have occurred within the Fifth District itself. It's the newcomers—young people from the villages along the Meloderna, for the most part—who continue to pose the problem. They're coming in increasing numbers, and when they arrive . . ."

"And when they arrive, they find no priests of Kafra handing out gold on the streets. They find they have to work, just as they did at home."

"But most know nothing of the kinds of work to be found here," Niksar says, nodding. "And so they pass their days begging, and their nights in taverns. Or at the Stadium."

"They ought to pass them in the barracks," Arnem declares. "A few years of campaigning would take the idiocy out of them . . ."

Turning off of the Celestial Way, Arnem and Niksar enter a street that leads directly to the main gate to the Fourth District, home to Broken's army—and also Arnem's only true sanctuary, of late, being as his own house is relentlessly filled with such turmoil as only a petulant youth doing hourly battle with his mother can generate. As soon as the two officers see the district's massive pine palisade ahead, they quicken their march; and they grow visibly relaxed as they near the enormous gate flanked by square sentry towers, which, like the palisade, are constructed of mighty pine logs, neatly hewn, notched, and joined, which, where upright, are narrowed to sharp points.[†] Together, these elements form an awe-inspiring main entryway to a world unlike all other parts of Broken, one that, no matter how often Arnem passes through it, has an exhilarating effect on his spirit. The groan of the iron-banded gate as it opens, the steady rhythm of booted feet on the upper walkway, the smell of horse dung and hay from the stables, and the eternal pall of dust raised by the ceaseless drilling of the city's soldiers: these are finally enough to take Sixt Arnem's mind from matters of family and faith, and to fix it on the calling that is his terrible passion:

"Kafra's stones, Niksar," Arnem says, as he puts a fist over his heart in salute to a sentry. "A war would do this kingdom good!"

The Fourth District of Broken is a series of open drilling and training quadrangles, each bounded on all sides by low wooden barracks. The quarters of the Talons are hard by the eastern gate of the city, traditionally the first point of an enemy's attack, as the eastern face of the mountain is easiest to ascend (although even that approach presents a devilish set of problems). Yantek Korsar, as commander not merely of the Talons but of the entire army, keeps his headquarters and personal residence near this same gate, so that his gruff manner and eternal vigilance can be sensed by any soldier, no matter how humble. After passing through drilling courts where linnets bark orders at night patrols, keeping them moving and ready to respond to any sudden threat, Arnem and Niksar enter a wide, empty parade ground, at the end of which rises a log structure higher than the barracks around it. Making quickly for this building, the two officers bound onto its wooden stairs, Arnem's doubts and concerns having transformed into the anticipation that he always feels with a new commission. The city *must* be in real danger, he allows himself to think; it is the only explanation that makes the list of worthies called to the Sacristy this night comprehensible. He shall get the "true" war he craves, a war that a professional soldier can be proud of, and one that will begin to finally purge the city of that mischievous idleness, the effects of which he himself witnessed only moments ago.

At the top of the stairs, a sentry must move with great agility to bring his right fist to his chest while using his left hand to get a nearby door open in time for the rushing Arnem and Niksar to pass through it without incident. Both officers return the salute without breaking stride; and once inside, they find Korsar's enormous frame seated at a broad table, his weathered face and full white beard suspended over a parchment map of the kingdom: an encouraging sign, Arnem thinks—

But when Korsar looks up, the sentek needs only a brief glance to realize that Niksar's earlier assessment was disturbingly accurate: although the oldest and most experienced commander in Broken, Korsar's deep blue eyes—the right bent by an ancient scar across his brow—bear an unmistakable sense of doom, augmented by resignation.

"You've precious little to be excited about, Arnem," the yantek says, standing and rolling his map. "It looks as if it's the Bane, after all."

As he lifts his fist to his chest in salute, Arnem notices that Yantek Korsar has donned his finest armor, meticulously worked leather embellished with elaborate silver embroidery. "But why all the secrecy, Yantek?" Arnem asks. "And at this hour? We saw torches in the Wood not long ago, and heard screaming—have Outragers gotten into the city?"

"So it seems," Korsar replies, as a pair of aides fix to his shoulders a deep blue cloak edged with the fur of a Davon wolf, one that the yantek himself killed during a foray into the Wood many years ago. "And they're growing extraordinarily audacious—to say nothing of powerful!"

"Yantek? What are you saying?"

"Only that they've tried to murder the God-King, Arnem. Or so say the Layzin and Baster-kin."

Korsar's flippancy is as unsettling as what he relates, and Arnem feels his own confidence draining still more. "The God-King? But how?"

"How *does* one murder a god?" Yantek Korsar picks up the foot-long wood and brass baton—topped by a small, sculpted image of Kafra with the body of a panther and the wings of an eagle—that is the emblem of his rank and office,[†] and taps Arnem's shoulder with it. "Sorcery, my boy," Korsar goes on, smiling for the first time; but the smile quickly transforms into a frown of skeptical distaste. *"Sorcery . . ."*

With a startling flood of nerves such as he has rarely experienced in battle, Arnem suddenly recalls the identity of the mad old man in the street. *But it can't be,* he thinks; *I myself saw him die . . .*

"What in the name of all that's unholy is wrong with you?" Korsar has paused to study Arnem; and what he finds is not much to his liking.

Arnem quickly attempts to recover his wits. "Only the activity we observed in the Wood, Yantek," he says swiftly. "Just before your orders arrived: should we not suspect some connection to all of this?"

"I doubt it," Korsar says, still unsatisfied with the sentek's explanation of his peculiar mood.

The two men have known each other since Arnem's earliest days in the army of Broken, and Korsar is aware that since those days he has played something of the role of father to Arnem, who began his life in the Fifth District as an impoverished orphan; or rather, he has always said that he is an orphan. Korsar suspects that Arnem's mother and father simply abandoned him, or sold him into some menial servitude that young Sixt cleverly escaped—for he had been a boy with a gift for planning all manner of troublesome behavior, and an even greater talent for organizing other rootless children to participate in the same. Whatever the truth of his origins, it was this life of mischief, and not any youthful sense of patriotism, that led to Arnem's enlistment in the army, as a means of escaping arrest for a long list of petty crimes. But Arnem found that military life suited him, and he soon brought himself to Korsar's attention when, during a battle that took place in a river valley beyond the Meloderna,[‡] he was the only man in his *khotor* to stand fast against a charge of eastern marauders. Arnem's brave action inspired fleeing soldiers to emulate him, and prevented the collapse of the center of Korsar's legion: Arnem had revealed himself to be both brave and a gifted leader, although it was only in subsequent years, when he demonstrated new-found loyalty to the kingdom, that the path to his present high rank opened. But Yantek Korsar has never forgotten the troublesome youth he once knew, and he is always quick to detect evasiveness on the younger man's part.

Tonight, the yantek has no time to draw Arnem out, and instead leads the way back through the door and then to the stairs as fast as he can manage. Arnem follows, and then Niksar, along with one of Korsar's aides. The latter pair stay a few steps behind, so that they cannot over-hear the older men's conversation; but they are still close enough to be of use. "It seems," Korsar continues, as they descend to the parade ground, "that the attempt was initiated some few days ago, although I'm not cer-tain how. I'm not certain about many things, if the truth be known, Arnem."

"But you consider what little explanation you have been given far-fetched?" the sentek asks quietly; and he is disturbed when his com-mander makes no similar effort at discretion.

"My opinion doesn't much matter." An additional pair of guards—regular army pallins—fall in as they reach the far side of the parade ground. "Lord Baster-kin accepts it, and the Grand Layzin has embraced it zealously—"

Arnem smiles. "Which does not tell me what you believe, Yantek. With respect."

"Demons take your respect, Sixt," replies Korsar, affection bleeding through his gruffness. "All right—do I believe that the Bane attempted to kill the God-King, His Radiance, Saylal the Compassionate?" Korsar shrugs carelessly. "They *want* him dead, certainly. But this . . ."

"You find it unlikely," Arnem says. In reply, Korsar tilts his head and lifts a skeptical brow, causing Arnem to venture: "And I agree, Yantek. The Bane have shown great audacity, at times, but never—"

"Be careful, Arnem." Yantek Korsar takes Arnem's forearm, clutching it hard as he gazes at the district's main gate. "Mind how quickly you fol-low my example, tonight. It may not be wise . . ."

It is an inexplicable comment, one to which Arnem can form no re-sponse during the few moments that it takes the group of men to reach the gate; then, just as he recovers his wits enough to ask Yantek Korsar to explain his true meaning, half a dozen soldiers emerge from the darkness outside the Fourth District, and quickly intercept Korsar's party. The newcomers' armor is like that worn by troops of the regular army; but each, on his upper arm, wears a wide, finely worked brass band, its surface beaten into the semblance of a smiling, bearded face . . .

Arnem is surprised to find that Yantek Korsar is neither shocked nor irritated by this intrusion on the part of Lord Baster-kin's Guard. There has long been bad blood between Broken's army (especially the Talons) and the Merchant Lord's troops, an animosity fueled by the fact that, although they wear the same armor as any *khotor* in the kingdom, the Guard train and are quartered in the First District, under the personal supervision of the Merchant Lord. This apparent slight—the implication that the regular army and the Talons are inadequate for the protection of the Merchants' Council—is not one that any soldier, much less the proud Korsar and his subordinates, could suffer without resentment, and there have been occasional brawls between the two forces. Arnem has always been inclined to view these as meaningless mischief, for he believes Lord Baster-kin to be above such trivial rivalries; yet there have been times when even Arnem has found the Guard insufferable, and he quickly realizes that this is going to be one such.

A young linnet of the Guard—typically tall and well-proportioned, with curling, carefully arranged black hair, paint accenting his eyes, and an arrogant manner—steps in front of the detachment.[†]

"Yantek," this man says, with a tone to match his manner; an impression that is deepened when he offers Arnem, his superior in both rank and experience, nothing more than a quick nod. "Sentek. His Eminence and His Grace have ordered us to escort you to the Temple."

"Did they also order you to ignore deference to rank, Linnet?" Arnem barks harshly. "I very much doubt it." The linnet smiles, at this, and half-heartedly covers his heart with his right fist. The rest of his men do the same, with a similar impertinence; and Arnem is about to strike the linnet a resounding blow, when Yantek Korsar stays his hand.

"Calm yourself, Arnem," Korsar says, with plainly false cordiality. "No doubt this is only for our own safety."

"No doubt, sir," the linnet of the Guard replies, with equal duplicity.

Korsar turns to Arnem: an expression of warning is in the old warrior's blue eyes, despite the smile beneath them. "Apparently, things have reached so desperate a state that you and I need nursemaids. And pretty nursemaids they might be, were they actually the women in whose manner they paint themselves." The Guardsmen bristle as one at this; but Korsar only smiles and holds up his hands. "A poor attempt at humor, Linnet, I apologize—we see so little true fashion in the Fourth District that we become awkward in its presence. Please, take no offense. Rather"—the yantek points to the Celestial Way, keeping his eyes on the leader of the Guardsmen—"escort us, if you will. Yes, by all means, escort us . . ." With a wave of his hand and a nod, Korsar dismisses his own men, so that only Niksar—now looking as troubled as he did when he first appeared on the southern wall to fetch Arnem—remains. The Guardsmen encircle their charges, and the party marches on in the direction of its hallowed destination: the High Temple of Kafra.

For what seems a long interval, Yantek Korsar is silent; and when he begins to speak again, his words are cause for further concern in both Arnem and Niksar. The yantek offers more mocking comments on the possibility of the Bane having attempted the life of the God-King, sentiments that Sixt Arnem shares and might have echoed, mere minutes ago; but now his mind and heart are in turmoil. The identity of the old lunatic in the street (a realization so fraught with evil possibilities that Arnem dares not speak the man's name aloud, even to Korsar), as well as this detachment of Lord Baster-kin's Guard, combine to make the yantek's air of caustic dismissal seem ill timed. *No*, Arnem suddenly realizes; *it is more than that—it is careless.* Carelessness: a trait that even Korsar's enemies among the younger leaders of the city—who have never known the perils of war, and who see little in Yantek Korsar save an old man of sacrilegiously ascetic habits—have never accused him of exhibiting. Yet the yantek seems consumed by it, even though the Guardsmen are plainly committing every deprecating word to memory. Whatever the case, Korsar's mood quickens his pace along the Celestial Way, so that the younger men must rush to match his speed.

When the group passes into the First District, the yantek's behavior changes yet again: his stream of cynicism seems to be exhausted, and Arnem, trying hard to focus on duty rather than doubt, hopes that his commander has finally realized that he should do the same. But a mere glance at Korsar's face offers no such assurance. As the yantek silently casts his scarred, seasoned gaze at the splendid stone residences of Broken's wealthiest nobles and merchants—structures known as *Kastel-gerde*,[†] which rise to two and even three stories in height, and are built from the blocks of granite cut from the mountain to create the seamless expanse of Broken's outer walls—unmistakable disgust emerges through the grey beard and under the long, tangled eyebrows.

"Observe, Arnem," Yantek Korsar says, and Arnem studies anew structures that he, like his commander, disdains. Disdains, not merely for their size, but for the statues of their illustrious forefathers with which the various merchant clans have filled their gardens: all are rendered with legs of exaggerated power and idealized features that Arnem finds absurd. "You didn't see much of this as a boy, did you, Sixt? Not really the style, in the Fifth District."

"The people of the Fifth find their own ways to obey Kafra, Yantek," Arnem replies. "And I can assure you that, though humble, they are equally—*enthusiastic.*"

Korsar's broad chest heaves with a lone laugh that betrays no true merriment. "Yes. I suppose that everyone in this city, even the miserable souls of your district, must find some way to perpetuate the dream of a god that loves them for both their avarice and their cruelty."

"Yantek?" Arnem whispers urgently; but Korsar ignores the younger commander's concern, forcing Arnem to try to draw the yantek into a safer discussion. "The society that venerates achievement and perfection also venerates hope and strength, Yantek—your own life demonstrates it. Only consider your actions in my case. In what other kingdom would a commander elevate a man with my past to the command of a noble legion?"

Korsar laughs: once again, without humor. "Dutifully recited, Arnem." Then, to the linnet of Baster-kin's Guard, the yantek adds, "I trust you take note of the sentek's piety, Linnet! As for me—" Yantek Korsar coughs up a smattering of phlegm, and spits it hard onto the cobbled avenue; and with it seems to go, finally, the last of his defiance, and his voice is transformed from a deliberate bellow into a resigned murmur: "I can see neither hope nor true strength in any of it. Not anymore . . ."

"I don't take your meaning, Yantek," Arnem says. He has known Korsar to be irascible and moody since the death of his wife; and he has known him to take great chances as a commander, as well; but he has never seen him court personal disaster in so fatalistic, so defeated, a manner.

"You *will* understand, Sixt, my friend," Korsar replies, in an ever more melancholy tone. "All too soon, I fear."

Arnem says nothing, but is deeply alarmed, for all his silence: Korsar's words are uncomfortably close to those the sentek heard from the apparitional old man he met on his way to the Fourth District . . .

The detachment, keeping a brisk pace, is now approaching the High Temple, which stands atop the mountain's highest formation of granite; and as they do, the sounds of the Stadium beyond that sacred structure grow louder. Some of the hundreds of voices are frantic with enthusiasm, while others cry out in desperation; and occasionally the crowd, which can number in the thousands when the Stadium is full, breaks into wine-slurred song. But these chants always fall back, after only a few repetitions, into the deep, disorganized moaning that attends so many disappointed hopes. Yantek Korsar seems to grow sadder, on hearing these sounds: even his sarcasm can find no voice strong enough to rise above the roars of the three-tiered stone oval.

Trying to explain Korsar's melancholia to himself, Arnem returns to thoughts of the yantek's wife, the foreign-born Amalberta, and especially to memories of her death. The couple had endured a childless marriage for many years; for so long, in fact, that the yantek had resigned himself to Amalberta's being barren—until, at the remarkable age of thirty-seven, she conceived, safely carried to term, and delivered herself of a son. Amalberta's joy was great, although perhaps not so great as that of her husband, whose pride took a particularly martial form, inspiring his planning and successful execution of that same campaign against the eastern marauders during which the conduct of young Sixt Arnem first came to his attention. Arnem has always felt that the yantek's championing of his own interests was due in no small part to Korsar's new paternal instincts, which the sentek believes had so welled up over the years that, once loosed, they could not be confined to one object of affection. Whatever the truth, the first ten years of the child Haldar's life were the most important of Sixt Arnem's, as well: for it was largely through the example of the yantek's family that the talented soldier from the Fifth District came to know a side of Broken that had been remote to him, as it was to most who hailed from that part of the city—a side that prized faithful service, and valued perfect affection as much as perfect appearance. Thus, for Arnem as for many soldiers, Haldar Korsar became a symbol: as much a breathing talisman as a boy. It seemed natural and good when, at the age of twelve, Haldar announced his desire to enter military service as a *skutaar*†, which would require him to serve a linnet selected by his father, and to live within the Fourth District. After this term of service, which would conclude with his own elevation to linnet, Haldar would naturally assume a position of importance somewhere in the army, and carry on his father's work—

But such had not been the will of Kafra. At the coronation of the God-King Saylal (a ceremony during which the new monarch was never actually seen by anyone save his priests, though he had full view of the large audience inside the High Temple), Haldar, along with two or three other youths and young ladies, was noticed by the Divine Personage amid a children's chorus composed of the offspring of Broken's most successful families; and priests soon arrived at the Korsar's door, to announce that the boy had been selected for service to the God-King. Honor though such selection was, the thought of losing forever a child whose arrival had been so long delayed was a mortal blow for the yantek and his wife; and there were those who said that Amalberta's heart began to wither the day she saw her son disappear forever through the gates of the Inner City. By this time, Arnem had married, and fathered the first of his own children, also a son: he could scarcely imagine having such a scion as Haldar snatched away so young, no matter the spiritual rewards that a life of service in the Inner City might bring. Yantek Korsar was a creature of duty, and eventually learned to exist, if not truly live, with the loss; not so Amalberta, who, after several years of trying to make a life without the boy who had become her life's purpose, as well as her solace when Korsar was campaigning, seemed to simply surrender her will to live. Korsar, frantic over his wife's steady decline, begged the Grand Layzin to release Haldar from divine service; but his requests were consistently refused, the last disappointment proving too much for Amalberta, whose heart quietly ceased to beat when the yantek brought her word that there was no hope of their ever being a family again.

Having been at the yantek's side during this ordeal, Arnem developed a deep fear of the day when he would be asked by the priests of Kafra for one of his own children; and now, with that request finally made, the sentek finds that it has brought a distressingly deeper understanding of the twin burdens that Korsar has carried for so many years. The loss of Amalberta, his one truly intimate companion, following hard on the loss of the boy who had embodied his hopes for a meaningful legacy, seemed to shrink Korsar's world: it was then that the yantek abandoned his own house (one of the more modest dwellings in the First District) and went to live in his headquarters, plainly intending to do nothing more than continue attending to the work of keeping Broken safe, until his worries as a commander would exhaust and destroy him.

But now Arnem must wonder, given the yantek's strange behavior, if the business of Broken's safety is all that Korsar has been pondering, during his long nights pacing those quarters that were never meant to be a home.

The small detachment of soldiers at last reaches the wide granite steps of the High Temple. At the foot as well as the top of these steps burn enormous bronze braziers, throwing their golden light onto the massive granite façade and the twenty-foot columns of the Temple. Given this setting, made all the more awe-inspiring by the time of night, the sentek feels that he is following Korsar into something more complicated than a council of war—a feeling confirmed when the yantek throws a heavy arm around Arnem's neck, and urgently whispers:

"I meant what I said, Sixt. Whatever happens inside, you're to stay out of it. The army will need you now, as never before."

"You sound as though you expect to be relieved, Yantek."

"That is certainly *among* the things that I expect," Korsar replies, grunting. "But it will hardly be the most important. No . . ." Korsar takes his arm from the sentek's neck, looking out over the city, and smiles: not in the false manner that has marked him thus far tonight, but in the manner of . . . Arnem gropes for words, and remembers Niksar's earlier statement: *Like a man who senses Death hovering nearby, yet makes no move to elude it.*

"Unless I'm very much mistaken, Sixt," Korsar continues, with something that is strangely like anticipation in his voice, "I will never see the sun set over the western walls of this city again . . ."

$$1:\{vi:\}$$

The Bane foragers witness a disordering of Nature,
before the Moon summons them home . . .

"LIES! LIES, LIES, AND STILL MORE LIES!"

"You dare question my honor *again?*"

Keera splays her small, slender fingers over her face, as Heldo-Bah and Veloc rail at each other. *It is remarkable,* the tracker thinks: *the shag steer stew has been in their stomachs for less time than it took to remove the pot from the fire, yet they are ready for more senseless bickering . . .*

"There is no end to it," is all that Keera has the patience to murmur aloud, as she stares through the dark, dense tangle of vegetation that surrounds their camp, alert for any sign of movement. Having led her party south of the Fallen Bridge at a good pace, Keera has decided that it is safer to allow Heldo-Bah to enjoy some of his precious beef now than it would be to attempt the journey back to Okot with him complaining every step of the way. She has found a fortunate site for their meal: a small clearing surrounded by thick ferns and briars, and sheltered by fir trees which obscure the light of their fire, if not its smell. As her companions continue to argue, she begins to wish that she had been less thorough: if they were not so well-concealed, she would have good reason to tell both men to keep their mouths shut. As it is . . .

"Listen to me, Veloc," Heldo-Bah says, as he leans into the fire, unconscious of its heat, and holds his back strap beef over a high flame with one of his knives. "That foul city has never meant anything save suffering for the Bane tribe—all your other 'historical' discussions only confuse that one supreme truth!" With his free hand, Heldo-Bah snatches up a stick of firewood and pokes at the bright coals mere inches from his deerskin boots, sending sparks flying at Veloc.

"Here!" Veloc cries, swatting at the glowing embers. "Unprovoked immolation is a crime, Heldo-Bah, even under Bane law!"

"Oh, I've been provoked!" Heldo-Bah counters, the beef having revived his strength. "By falsehoods from a festering philanderer!"

Veloc returns to the calm condescension that is ever his course of last resort when he is losing ground to his friend's bullying: "Perhaps your own luck with women would be better, Heldo-Bah, had your father not eyed a sow with lust and produced a son with the face of a pig."

"Better the son of a sow than a patron of Broken whores!"

"Whores?" Veloc's false demeanor is shattered. "Why, you ape, I have never paid any Tall for her favors—each has offered herself to me!"

"And I suppose that you have never been indicted by the Groba for the trouble your failure to pay these 'willing' women has created?"

"Dog!"

The two men face each other across the fire, seemingly ready to fight to the death; yet Keera exhibits no great concern, for she knows how the exchange will end. Both Veloc's and Heldo-Bah's jaws tremble with anger for a silent moment; and then, with a suddenness that might bewilder anyone unfamiliar with their friendship, each bursts into laughter, throwing dirt harmlessly and rolling on the forest floor.

"It seems folly to bicker so," Keera remarks, to herself as much as to her companions, "when, on every occasion, you only end by—"

Suddenly, the Bane tracker gets silently up on her legs, keeping them bent so that she can spring in any direction. Her remarkable nose is in the air, while her hands cup her ears. Heldo-Bah and Veloc stifle their laughter and creep noiselessly to Keera's side: in much the same manner, she notices, as her three small children do when frightened. The men listen to the Wood, but are unable to catch the noises or scents that have alarmed her so.

"Again he moves," Keera whispers in frustration. "But I cannot *understand* his movements—he neither hunts nor makes his den . . ."

"Not the same panther . . ." Veloc murmurs in disbelief.

Keera nods slowly. "I was worried that the smell of the stew might draw him, if we crossed paths again. But such an encounter seemed unlikely—I deliberately chose a different route. And yet there is no mistaking that step. It is so . . . *odd*. Hesitant, anxious, searching—he could be wounded, I suppose. Or I may be wrong, he may stalk us. Whatever the case, we must seek refuge. Heldo-Bah—"

But when Keera turns, Heldo-Bah has already disappeared. She worries for an unreasoning instant that her noisy friend has been taken silently by the panther, for the great cats are more than capable of thus picking apart a group of humans without ever being heard or seen.

Soon, however, Keera hears grunting from above and sees Heldo-Bah, his deerskin sack slung over his shoulder, scaling the straight trunk of an ash, one of many trees that, due to the thickness of the forest canopy, have no lower limbs to offer a panther an avenue of pursuit. "By the Moon!" Keera murmurs. "Up the tree before I've given the word!"

"Waste your explanations on your fool brother," the squirming Heldo-Bah hisses, by now some twenty feet up. "I'll be no cat's dinner!"

Veloc and Keera quickly follow Heldo-Bah, using their powerful feet and legs to climb two neighboring trees. Once lodged in the closely clustered aeries provided by the extended branches of their protectors, the three Bane watch expectantly—but the dreaded panther fails to appear.

"You're certain it comes, Keera?" Veloc whispers to his sister.

Keera lifts her shoulders in confusion. "Ordinarily, I would say that the fire might be keeping him away—but this cat was close enough to both smell and see the flames, yet he continued to venture nearer . . ."

"Likely it's deciding what order to eat us in," Heldo-Bah hisses, clutching his sheathed throwing knives with moist hands. "But I'll—"

Keera raises her hand; and then a resonant growl can be heard outside the hemisphere of light created by the fire below. "At last," Keera whispers, allowing a small smile. "You almost made me look a fool, cat . . ."

The panther rumbles; but it is a confused sound, neither aggression, nor pain, nor any other noise that so experienced a tracker as Keera can understand. Her smile quickly reverts to an aspect of consternation.

And then he appears: his great paws of the darkest gold padding against the Earth of the clearing, the panther enters[†] the light of the camp. He is young, but large (well over five hundred pounds) with short tufts of hair about the neck and shoulders.[‡] The dark spots and stripes on his nine-foot body are pronounced, giving the animal a distinctly masculine coat. This is significant: the Moon faith teaches that uniformity and richness of color in a panther's coat are signs of divine favor, and certainly of mature (and usually feminine) wisdom. Though lacking such, this animal yet displays evident power in his long, thick muscles—which makes his interest in the diminutive foragers more mysterious, for he could easily take down a stag or wild horse, or even one of Lord Baster-kin's shag cattle, any one of which would be a better meal than a human.

As the newcomer circles the camp, he shies, yet does not run, from the fire, which would ordinarily keep the majestic beast at a safe distance:

but this male has an apparent purpose that emboldens him. With each step, his thick muscles cause the rich, iridescent fur to ripple ever more splendidly in the firelight, as though he is attempting to intimidate a rival or display his power for a mate. Yet Keera is right about the complexity of the panther's behavior: for the amber eyes are glazed with passion, and, along with the quick panting of the tongue and mouth, they create an impression of consternation that belies the purposeful body.

"What is it, cat?" Keera says softly. "What agitates you so?"

As if in reply, another form slowly enters the light of the fire: two feet taller than even Veloc, it is a young woman, her seemingly flawless body moving easily inside a black silk robe edged in red velvet.† Visible through slits up the sides of the garment are long, beautifully formed thighs and calves, the movements of which mirror those of the panther's four legs, as he paces on the opposite side of the fire. Sheets of black hair fall to the woman's waist, and her eyes—which glitter an alluring green in the torchlight, a green the color of the best emeralds the Bane have been known to bring out of Davon Wood—are fixed on the amber orbs of the panther, which already betray some sort of enthrallment.

"A woman of the Tall," Keera whispers. "In Davon Wood!"

"And one of rare form," Veloc adds with approval, his gaze lustful. "She's no farmer or fisherman's wife, and no whore, either." But then Veloc's attention turns from the woman's flesh to her raiment; and his stare becomes quizzical. "But—her robe. Heldo-Bah, am I mistaken, or—"

Heldo-Bah shows the black gap in his vicious teeth. "You are not."

Keera looks at the gown. "What is it that he is so correct about?"

Heldo-Bah's whisper takes on a killing tone, without either increasing in volume or losing its air of delight. "She is one of the Wives of Kafra."

"A Wife of Kafra!" Keera nearly slips from her branch with the news, although she, too, keeps her voice from rising. "It can't be. They never leave the First District of Broken—"

"Apparently, they do." Heldo-Bah holds a knife by the blade between the thumb and first two fingers of his right hand, judging carefully the distance to the ground. "And by the Moon, this is one that won't get back again—not tonight, at any rate."

Veloc looks uneasily at his friend: the dim light and the shifting shadows of the leaves are transforming Heldo-Bah's face into an exaggerated mask of delighted bloodlust. "You would murder a woman, Heldo-Bah?" Veloc whispers.

"I would murder a panther," comes Heldo-Bah's answer. "There are better uses for the women of the Tall—and not the kind you're thinking of, Veloc. Or not *merely* that kind. She could also bring a ransom such as we have never demanded: weapons that the Tall have always refused us—"

"Stay your blade," Keera whispers urgently, putting her staff before Heldo-Bah's arm as he lifts the knife. "You'll murder neither woman *nor* panther—not unless the cat attacks us. They are possessed of powerful souls, and I want no such enemies—" Her lecture stops short. "Hold . . . ," she says, more perturbed than ever. "What sorcery is *this*?"

The Wife of Kafra keeps her eyes on the panther's as she squats before the animal, her long legs angling out through the slits in her gown. The great beast begins to growl again, and to shift from side to side nervously—but just then, as if seeing the fire and the stew pot for the first time, the woman glances about quickly, beginning to hurry her apparent ritual.

"Has she seen us?" Veloc asks, withdrawing deeper into the leaves of his tree with no more sound than that of a flitting thrush.

"Steady." Heldo-Bah, too, nestles further into his perch, looking even more pleased. "She's seen nothing—but we, apparently, are going to see a great deal . . ."

The Wife of Kafra quickly unties a golden cord that gathers her robe at the waist. With impressive confidence, she strides directly to the panther, as ever staring into his eyes intently; then she kneels, and puts her nose to the throat of the beast.

"She invites death!" Keera says. "Unless she *is* a sorceress . . ."

The foragers grow silent once more. The woman's long hair falls in front of her breasts as she moves her cheeks against the cat's face in long strokes. The panther growls, but the noise soon fades into a loud purr: the beast, still confounded, is now completely enthralled.

"Oh, Moon," Keera whispers. "This is sorcery, indeed."

"If she persists," Heldo-Bah cackles, leaning forward eagerly, "what that cat will do to her will be anything but sorcery . . ."

As the panther continues to purr and only occasionally growl, the woman begins to run her long fingers through the thick golden fur as she might a human male's hair, coaxing the animal to fold his forelegs; and then, with a swiftness that startles the Bane foragers but not the cat, she slides onto the animal's back, looping the golden cord that girdled her waist about its thick neck. When the woman pulls back on the cord with authority, the panther stands; and when she tightens her knees on the cat's shoulders, he starts forward slowly.

Heldo-Bah clearly fears that his prized quarry will escape, however unbelievable the method; and he produces the same knife once more, ready to do what he must. But then he, his two companions, the Wife of Kafra, and even the panther snap their heads toward the southeast, expressions of alarm on all their faces:

Through the forest comes the low call of a powerful horn, its sonorous, steady drone slow to reach its peak but full of urgency. Called the Voice of the Moon, the massive instrument rests against a high hill in the Bane village of Okot, and is as old as the tribe itself. It was fashioned from clay taken out of the bed of the Cat's Paw, after the first of the banishments resulted in the exile community's establishment two centuries ago; and it has been used ever since to order tribesmen home, throughout as much of Davon Wood as its twenty-foot tube and ten-foot flaring bell—so enormous that the Horn requires huge bellows to produce its single, mournful note—can penetrate.

The foragers silently wait out the sounding of the Horn, hoping that they will not have to descend while the Wife of Kafra and the panther are still present. But after a few seconds of silence, the enormous instrument calls out again, and with greater insistence; or so it seems to Keera, who is keenly aware that danger in Okot means danger to her family. "Come!" she murmurs. "Two blasts, we must—" But Heldo-Bah points to the ground without comment:

The Wife of Kafra, on hearing the Bane Horn, seems to have disappeared atop the panther. Likely she is moving through the northernmost portions of Davon Wood toward home as swiftly as she can urge her unusual mount to go, the fiery Bane thinks; but his face says that they cannot yet be certain.

The great Bane Horn grows silent again; and only when Keera can detect neither scent nor sound of the woman as well as the panther does she nod, at which Heldo-Bah throws his knife angrily toward and into the Earth. *"Ficksel!"* he declares, shaking a fist in the direction of Okot, the Voice of the Moon, and the Bane Elders who ordered the sounding of the mighty alarm. "Bloody Groba," he grumbles, making his way back down his ash. "No sense of timing!"

The three are soon on the ground, Keera deftly leaping from ten feet. "Two blasts of the Horn," she says. "What can have happened?"

"Try not to fret, Keera," Veloc says, pulling Heldo-Bah's knife from the ground, tossing it to his comrade, then quickly starting out for the southeast. "Why, I've heard the damned thing sound for no more reason than—" He stops with an awkward rattle of his sack, however, when he hears the Horn sound yet again; and then he turns, not wishing to appear as concerned for Keera's husband and her children as he feels. "*Three* blasts . . . ," he says evenly, looking to Heldo-Bah; but all he finds playing across his friend's scarred features is worry to match his own.

"Can either of you remember so many?" Keera asks, her composure deteriorating.

Heldo-Bah forces a smile onto his face. "Certainly!" he says, with an affected lack of concern: for he knows well that something undeniably important, and likely sinister, is happening. "I recall it well—so do you, Veloc. When that detachment of Broken soldiers chased an Outrager party into the Wood—the Groba ordered at least three blasts, and I'm fairly certain there were more. Isn't that so, historian?"

Veloc understands Heldo-Bah's intent, and quickly replies, "Yes—yes, it is." He can dissemble in no greater detail, and the three foragers stand motionless as the third blast wanes; but when the Great Horn immediately issues another, Keera moves quickly to her brother's side.

"It doesn't stop!" she cries. "Why would they issue so many? It will bring the Tall to the village!"

Veloc puts an arm tight around her, trying to make his voice as gentle as his words are hard: "They may already *be* attacking Okot, Keera—that may be what is happening . . ."

"*More* bitch's turd!" Heldo-Bah declares. "Pay him no mind, Keera— the Tall can't *find* Okot, much less attack it. Besides, do you not find it even a little odd that we should hear so many Horn blasts on the same night that a Wife of Kafra entrances and then makes away with a Davon panther?" He tousles Keera's hair. "What is happening has naught to do with any attack on Okot—something of a different nature is going on, I'd stake my sack's earnings on it. But we won't know anything until we get there—so let's be off."

"If you're saying that you *do* suspect sorcery here, Heldo-Bah," Veloc says, as the group strap their sacks tight and Keera buries their fire, "then I must tell you that Bane historians have determined that, since the expulsion of the sorcerer Caliphestros following the reign of Izairn, the Tall have forsworn—"

"Ah, the scholar speaks again," Heldo-Bah declares, as he leads the party away. "What's *your* explanation, then, cuckolder? Has all of Nature been stood on its ear during the Moon we've been away? Do women now seduce and ride upon great cats, and will *you* rule in Broken, come sunrise?"

Veloc, at the rear of the little column, rolls his eyes toward eternity and sighs heavily. "I did not say that, Heldo-Bah. But it is a fact that—"

"Oh, fact, fact, fact!" Heldo-Bah spits, as he increases the party's pace to a steady run. "I've no use for your facts!"

Keera has no strength to stop her companions from arguing, nor to take her usual place at the head of the group. Heldo-Bah knows the way back to Okot, and it is all Keera can do to keep herself from growing frantic as she travels. *My family is in danger*—the phrase repeats itself silently in Keera's mind, along with all its terrible implications: *My family is in danger . . .*

1:{vii:}

Who speaks truth, and who insults Kafra with lies, in the Sacristy of his High Temple?

THE FIRST BLAST of the mighty woodland clarion had reached the ears of Arnem, Niksar, and Yantek Korsar, along with those of their escort from Lord Baster-kin's Guard, just as the group reached the marble-paved forecourt atop the steps outside the entrance to the High Temple in Broken.

"It's the Bane Horn—in Okot!" Niksar had pronounced, with more alarm than he would have liked. But if Arnem's young aide had been startled by the Horn, the detachment of preening soldiers from the

Guard, who had done nothing save laugh among themselves during the walk to the Temple, had been struck dumb with fear by it. Arnem and Korsar, for their part, had halted, at first showing little concern at the dour intonations; but as the number of blasts had continued to rise, both grew silent and speculative, wondering what could prompt such blaring from an instrument that seldom saw use.

Now, a fifth sounding of the Horn is echoing up the mountain and over the walls of Broken, bringing momentary stillness to even the crowded Stadium. Yantek Korsar gazes back over the slate-tiled rooftops and the southern wall beyond: from the group's vantage point atop the highest spot on the mountain, the old commander can discern the Moon-lit Cat's Paw's, and the edge of Davon Wood beyond it.

"That it is, Niksar," Korsar answers at length, softly and respectfully. "The Bane Horn. A powerful yet lovely sound, to be made by so blasphe-mous a people, wouldn't you say? It has a name, I seem to recall. What is it, now . . . ?" His question goes unanswered: the heightening effect of the Horn is such that the soldiers atop the steps scarcely even hear the yantek's words.

The few cartographers and soldiers from Broken who have been de-termined enough, in ages past, to press through Davon Wood and locate the Bane village of Okot have received harsh reward for their courage: either a gutting blade across the throat, a poisoned arrow sunk deep in the flesh, or the rougher hospitality of the Wood's other predators. Not a soul in the kingdom has ever seen the Great Horn that the Bane elders use in times of crisis to summon their people home. Yet, like the men under his command, Yantek Korsar has heard many outlandish rumors concerning the fabled instrument: of how its great, flaring bell was fashioned from mortar mixed with blood; of how that same bell is large enough to hold half a dozen men; and, above all, of the demons of the air that the Bane have enslaved to produce the powerful bursts neces-sary for its sounding. He finds such tales as the last absurd, of course; *and yet . . .*

Yet the yantek cannot disguise the admiration he has always felt for the Bane's having created such an ethereal, and powerful, means of link-ing their tribe. "It's been many years since last I heard it," he continues wistfully. "Do you remember, Arnem? We lost—what was it—two dozen men that night? And caught not one glimpse of the Bane . . ." The

Horn's mighty cry tapers off, and the men make tentative moves to cross the forecourt and continue on their way to the Sacristy—

But a mere instant later, the Horn roars to life again.

"Six calls?" Korsar says, attempting to toy with the already terrified men of Lord Baster-kin's Guard. "Rare to hear it sound even half so many times," he muses. "The Bane have always feared that it will aid us in finding their stronghold. Damn me, what do they call the thing, Arnem? Your memory hasn't been muddled by age, I very much hope."

Korsar turns to find that Arnem's eyes have opened much wider than is their habit, and that he has not heard his commander's question. The yantek moves closer to his trusted subordinate. "Sixt?" Korsar says, with genuine concern. "Blast it, man, what ails you tonight?"

Arnem shakes his head. "It's nothing, Yantek," he replies. "And I remember the name. They call it 'the Voice of the Moon.' Unless I am much mistaken . . ." Arnem glances at Niksar, who, to judge by his aspect, is coming to much the same realization as his commander, concerning events earlier in the evening. Seeing this, Arnem shakes his head just perceptibly, indicating silence, and Niksar nods quickly.

As he notes the peculiar looks that pass between his officers, Korsar scrutinizes Arnem yet again, and steps over to Niksar. "*Something* is eating at the pair of you," he determines, as the latest blast of the Horn fades. But before the yantek can press his inquiry—

A seventh droning of the Horn rises from the Wood, this one the loudest and most desperate of all. Yantek Korsar returns to the edge of the Temple forecourt. *"Seven?"* he says, with genuine incredulity. "What in the name of all that's holy . . . I don't know that *anyone* has ever heard the Bane Horn speak seven times."

"No one has, Yantek," Arnem says, glad that his commander's attention has been drawn away. "We heard four calls on the night of which you've spoken—when you dispatched my full *khotor* to pursue a party of Outragers into the Wood. That is the largest number of blasts recorded."

"So," Korsar muses. "Something affects the Bane so mightily that they risk seven soundings of their Horn—even as they are trying to kill our God-King. A remarkable collection of outcasts—eh?"

But Arnem's thoughts are fixed, not on what may be behind the calls of the Horn, nor even on the council inside the Sacristy, nor on any other immediate affairs. Rather, the sentek is thinking—and so, plainly, is

Niksar—of the earlier warning issued by that agèd, seeming madman in the street:

"Wait for another voice to sound, this same night—to sound more times than it ever has before . . ."

As the Bane Horn's seventh and final call begins to grow faint, Korsar approaches Arnem, seizes his shoulder, and shakes the younger man. "Arnem!" he murmurs. "Forget the bloody blaring, and listen to me— we've far more important matters to attend to, right now."

Arnem rouses himself, and tries to give his commander's words the attention their urgency warrants. "Yantek—I'm not sure I understand."

Indicating silence and lowering his voice to a whisper, Korsar leads Arnem aside, and puts his head close to the younger man's. "All this activity deepens my suspicions. And so, remember what I told you earlier: whatever happens, whatever you may hear or see, you must not take my part—in *anything*." Before Arnem can question this command, which is even stranger than those the yantek issued in the Fourth Quarter, Korsar goes on: "I would prepare you, if I thought it would do any good. Simply understand and obey—and by the Moon, get rid of young Niksar. The Horn helps us there—we can dispatch him to learn if the soldiers of the watch have seen any signs of Bane activity, or been able to approximate its location." Korsar raises his head, his voice regaining its usual gruff power. "Niksar! With us, son—quickly!"

A few long strides, and the conspiratorial council numbers three. "Back to the wall, Linnet. See what they've determined, if anything."

Niksar's face betrays both relief and doubt. "With all respect, Yantek— the orders were specific. I must report to the Sacristy with you."

"The responsibility is mine," Korsar says. "The sounding of the Horn changes the matter; the Layzin and Baster-kin will understand."

Niksar looks to Arnem and receives confirmation: "He's right, Reyne. Get back there and take charge. I'll join you when the council is adjourned."

A few final moments of silent uncertainty, and Niksar puts his fist to his chest. "Sentek. Yantek." He starts down the Temple steps, finally bringing the members of Lord Baster-kin's Guard out of their fearful daze. "Linnet!" calls the man who is equal in rank to Niksar, but far different in appearance—to say nothing of experience. "Stop! We were charged—"

"Your charge has changed, boy," Yantek Korsar declares. "And, speaking of that, you'd best resume it. Your master has no patience for men who dally gossiping."

The men of the Guard mumble among themselves for a moment, before they take up their positions around the commanders once more; and their momentary distraction provides Korsar with enough opportunity to give Arnem a meaningful glare, one that again underlines his last order. The sentek has no time to reply before the Guard have surrounded them, and then set a quick pace into the well-ordered forest of columns that support the portico of the Temple. The linnet of the Guard draws his short-sword and hammers its pommel against one of the massive brass doors. A system of locks are undone from within, and then the door begins to open, pulled back by a pair of straining priests whose heads are shaved smooth.

Both of the priests wear simple, elegant robes of black silk edged in silver and red, and in unison they beckon the soldiers to follow them down the nave toward the enormous altar that stands in the northern apse of the cavernous Temple.† The forty-foot-high interior of the structure is lit only by torches at the entrance, oil lamps along the innermost columns, and, in the apse, dozens of beeswax candles. Dominating this serene yet imposing scene is the distant sound of chanting: over a large chorus of bass and tenor men are layered smaller numbers of children and but a few women, singing, unaccompanied, in the classic Oxian style, which is named for its innovator. In his later years, the Mad King turned to music—among other pursuits—to pass the ever more idle hours of his life; and not a few members of his household were surprised to find that he had a sophisticated understanding of the art, gained how, when, or where, Oxmontrot never said. But the mode of composition he devised was one of his proudest legacies.

Arnem falls in next to Korsar, the better to hear any further explanation of his commander's extraordinary instructions; but the yantek evidently intends no such clarification. Instead, as the men walk northward between the long inner colonnades, Korsar silently enjoys the chanting, which grows in volume, and begins to pull at his beard, puzzling with something playfully.

"Seven blasts of the Horn," he suddenly murmurs, as much to himself as to Arnem. "A pity, really. I would have enjoyed being the one to discover their meaning . . ." He walks further behind the priests, and then pauses as they reach the Temple's apse. "But the golden god has other plans for me," the yantek adds, maintaining his strangely detached tone.

The most ornate feature among many such in the Temple, the altar is the most obvious statement of Kafra's love of wealth, of indulgence—and of those among his followers who worship him in a corresponding manner. A finely carved platform of various exotic woods supports an octagonal slab of granite, the eight sides of which are carved into reliefs depicting key episodes from the history of Broken. Each of these scenes is laminated in gold. The surface of the altar, by way of contrast, is composed of an almost faultless slab of black marble, quarried in a distant region of Davon Wood by the Bane.[†] To obtain it, the God-King Izairn (father of Saylal, the present ruler) and the Merchants' Council of his time were forced to offer the Bane not only goods, but something even more precious: knowledge. In particular, the Bane demanded—and Izairn's increasingly powerful Second Minister, Caliphestros, recommended giving them—building secrets that at least a few of Broken's merchant leaders and military commanders did not believe the exiles should possess: techniques of leverage and buttressing, of counterweighting and joining.

But those who sponsored the creation of the altar had not believed the trade dangerous: the Bane would never, they argued, be able to make use of such sophisticated techniques—a prediction that has thus far proved true, so far as anyone in Broken can determine. And few citizens of the kingdom, upon viewing the magnificent new locus of the most important rites of Kafra, would assert that the exchange was not worth the risk. Above the altar, seeming to confirm that the bargain was indeed an appropriate one, has been suspended a most arresting representation of Kafra: a statue, also laminated in gold and suspended in such a manner as to make its supports (a web of delicately wrought iron, painted darkest black) effectively invisible in the candlelight. This apparently miraculous figure depicts the generous god as a victorious young athlete; and on his face, as always, is the smile, that gentle, seductive curl of the full lips, which has ever sparked in his followers sensations that Arnem knows he and Yantek Korsar are intended to feel tonight: benevolence, love, and the delight in life available to the righteous.

On this occasion, the statue's serene expression prompts another of the yantek's grunting, humorless laughs, this one particularly strange: for it is Korsar's usual custom, at such moments in the Temple, to drink deeply of the beautiful chanting that drifts up from below the altar. So much is this the case that, for an instant, Arnem believes that he *must* have mistaken the yantek as the author of the caustic sound; but when it is repeated, and when Arnem places it in the context of Korsar's earlier and more peculiar words and behavior, the sentek is left to wonder anew if his mentor, comrade, and friend—the man Arnem admires more than any in the world—is in fact the simple, honest, and above all pious old soldier for which his protégé has always taken him.

The pair of silent priests touch Korsar's and Arnem's shoulders gently, urging them down the left side of a transept that crosses the nave before the altar and leads to a black marble archway that is the entrance to the Sacristy of the High Temple. The beechwood door below the archway— guarded by still more priests—opens; and in an instant, Arnem and Korsar find themselves within the Sacristy, the penultimate seat of power in the kingdom of Broken.

The sumptuous main room, off of which are located more intimate chambers, is a repository for those holy instruments—chalices, bowls, plates, and icons—as well as the various knives, axes, halberds, arrows, and spears, that came into use when Oxmontrot's pragmatic goal of banishing unfit and infirm citizens of Broken to Davon Wood was legitimized by the liturgy of the Kafran faith. The practical then became the sacred, and the tenets that resulted quickly became the unquestioned social and spiritual laws of Broken. Since then the Sacristy has provided at least a nominally accessible location from which religious and civic wisdom can be dispensed to various representatives of the populace. In addition, appeals to Broken's ever-remote royalty may be made through the Sacristy, provided there is no expectation of gratification or even reply.

The Sacristy's trappings reflect this portentous unity of spiritual and secular purpose. The stone walls are finely finished with glittering, durable mortar[†] that has been sand-ground to an alluringly smooth finish, one that, like so many aspects of the Temple and the Sacristy, is nearly irresistible to human touch. Over these walls, between large panels of exquisite tapestries woven by unrivaled artisans, hang the richest fabrics ever brought up the Meloderna by Broken's intrepid river traders: deep vermilion silks, crisp white and gold cottons, and rich burgundy wools. These drapes conceal no apertures in the building's walls, for no such openings exist: the concern for secrecy that is the very essence of the Broken's ruling tradition is too great to allow any such. Instead, the sumptuous draperies frame an astounding series of creations, whose effect is best appreciated during the daylight hours, as well as on nights like this one, when the Moon shines bright: the glowing results of another of the proudest achievements of Broken's artisans, their preservation of the ancient process of manufacturing glass—glass of almost any color, and, in the case of structures such as the Sacristy, any thickness. Into secure settings of translucent alabaster are mortared thick, rounded blocks of tinted glass, created in the expansive, well-guarded studios of such craftsmen as have disappeared from almost every society that surrounds Broken.[†] The Sacristy is thereby bathed in wondrous light that vividly supports the priests' claim to the near-divinity of the chamber. Most importantly, this effect is achieved with no reduction of the privacy of the chamber's business.

First among the ministers who conduct that business, and second in power only to the God-King and his immediate family, is the Grand Layzin, the human vessel and instrument through whom the will of Kafra and the God-King are made not only known, but comprehensible, to the mortal citizens of Broken. The furnishings within the Sacristy clearly emphasize this: at the northern end of the chamber rises the Layzin's dais, which runs the width of the Sacristy and is supported by granite arches which lead down into a wide entryway to the catacombs, out of which emerge the ethereal sounds of the Oxian chanters. The almost equally well-appointed furnishings before the dais (provided not only for superior citizens such as the members of the Merchants' Council, but for anyone who has business with the Layzin) are all oriented toward that superior level, coming to an end in a deep reflecting pool cut into the floor of the Temple: a serene spot which is both protective and intended to heighten the sense of separation between the Layzin and ordinary supplicants.

Upon the dais itself (the rear wall of which is covered by an enormous curtain), an expansive sofa occupies the left side, its cushions echoing the richness of the room's draperies and tinted glass. In the center of the space is the elaborately carved gilded chair from which the Layzin casts his serene reflection into the pool below. Two less ostentatious seats are positioned to either side of this near-throne, and are reserved for the First and Second Wives of Kafra, the highest ranking and most beautiful of the priestesses. One of the two is present now, and she sits utterly motionless in her chair, her long legs visible through slits in her black gown and her abundant golden hair falling freely onto her well-formed body. Occupying the remaining space on the right-hand side of the dais are a chair and gilded table covered with books, scrolls, and writing: communications from royal officials throughout the kingdom. Behind this, at a scribe's desk, sits a shaved priest, who records all words spoken in the Sacristy.

As Arnem and Korsar enter, they notice quickly (for both men are very familiar with this chamber) that the collection of messages from outside the city on the Layzin's table is unusually large. They acknowledge this fact to each other silently, in the manner of soldiers who have often had to communicate without words in the presence of authority, quickly determining that each has drawn the same conclusion from what they see: *Something dire troubles this city—indeed, the entire kingdom of Broken—tonight* . . .

For Arnem, such is far more encouraging a sign than it is, evidently, for Yantek Korsar, whose features have lost even their sardonic skepticism, and now reveal only hard determination to face the matter at hand. *But what matter is it?* Arnem asks himself; for if the threat to the kingdom is not the Bane, surely the supreme commander of the army will not be disappointed. His mockery of Arnem's desire for a glorious campaign aside, the yantek would actually relish, Arnem believes, facing an adversary other than the exiles. *Why, then, does the yantek's face grow so ashen . . . ?*

Atop the dais, two men stand at the table on the right, making their way through the reports at a hurried pace, but in hushed tones. The first looms large over the table, and is possessed of considerable strength, to judge by his broad back and shoulders. These last are covered by a cloak of rich brown fur, edged in pure white flecked with black: the seasonal pelt of the hermit stoat, known across the Seksent Straits as "ermine."[†] The second, seated man is, for the most part, obscured by the first; but Korsar and Arnem can see that his hands are moving papers about on the table with a speed seldom displayed in the contemplative stillness of the Sacristy.

The two priests leading Arnem and Korsar walk to the edge of the reflecting pool, while the detachment of Baster-kin's Guard take up positions by the doorway—a fact that Arnem finds ominous. But he nonetheless follows the priests, as does Korsar; and when the commanders have also reached the edge of the reflecting pool, one priest delicately calls to the men above:

"I beg your pardon, Eminence, but—"

The broad-shouldered man turns quickly, and steps to the side of the gilded table. Although graced with angular, handsome features, he scowls out harshly from beneath a bristling shock of auburn hair, the set of his jaws revealing little patience with distraction. Only the light, hazel-grey eyes hint at any gentleness, and even that is overwhelmed by condescension that could easily be mistaken for contempt. A tunic of loose-fitting scarlet wool does little to hide his physical strength, and the overall impression is one of enormous pride that can be supported physically or intellectually, depending on the opponent.

This is Rendulic Baster-kin, Lord of the Merchants' Council of Broken, scion of the oldest trading family in the kingdom, the embodiment of Broken's heritage and worldly status, and, although past forty, an impressive testament to those physical ideals that all of Kafra's followers strive to attain, but only the most devout achieve.

Behind him, standing in marked but not unpleasant contrast, is the Grand Layzin.[†] He is a man who possessed a name, once, just as he likely possessed a family; but when his service to Kafra, as well as to the God-King, progressed from simply devoted to so shrewdly capable as to be deserving of authority, both the name and the past life it signified (which the Layzin, like all such children, had forsaken on entering the royal and sacred service) were excised even from official records. Any citizen who now speaks of either can rely on arrest for sedition, a charge punishable by ritual death. The near-divinity of the Layzin's person is among Broken's eternal mysteries, and although it must remain—like his image in the reflecting pool—ineffable and intangible, it must also be (again like that reflection) undeniable. After all, a man who, alone in a kingdom of many tens of thousands, can move freely between the sacred world of the Inner City and the vividly material realm of Broken's government and commercial affairs, asserting authority in both realities, must have *some* spark of the divine in him. And yet the Layzin himself never claims as much; indeed, he forgoes personal arrogance, embodying instead an earnest holiness, as well as a compassion that not only stands in consider-able contrast to his near-absolute power, but has also been the source, during his fifteen years of executing the God-King Saylal's will, both of his enormous popularity and of the conviction held by the God-King's subjects that, while the Layzin may not be entirely divine, neither is he wholly mortal.

As Arnem and Korsar approach the reflecting pool before the dais, both Baster-kin and the Layzin offer further evidence of their comple-mentary natures: Baster-kin puts his hands to his hips in impatient irrita-tion, while the Layzin stands from his chair and smiles generously, honestly pleased to see these two men who have so often risked their lives for Broken and its God-King. Still young (somewhere between twenty-five and thirty years of age, Arnem would guess), the Layzin lacks the overbearing physical power of Baster-kin. His features are far more delicate, and he clothes his slender body not in animal hides, but in layers of white cotton covered by a brocade mantle[†] of gold thread woven into pale blue and soft green silk, a fabric at once heavy enough to mask his stature and delicate enough to accentuate his gentle manner. His hair is golden and straight, and it is his custom to gather it at the base of his skull with a golden clasp, letting it fall freely to his shoulders and beyond. His blue eyes and clean-shaven face radiate warmth, and the smile he of-fers Arnem and Korsar is sincerity itself.

"Our deepest thanks," says the Layzin, "for answering what must ap-pear a peculiar summons, Yantek Korsar. And you, Sentek Arnem."

At this slight indication that the gathering of luminaries in the Sac-risty has begun its work, the chanting in the catacombs suddenly stops.

"You are both well?" the Layzin asks.

As the two soldiers assure the Layzin that they are indeed so, the seated wife of Kafra, obeying some unspoken command, kneels before the Layzin briefly, and then departs through a doorway on the left side of the curtain behind the dais. The shaven-skulled priests disappear mo-mentarily into another chamber, and then return carrying a sloped wooden walkway that they position over the reflecting pool, to allow the Layzin to descend to the floor of the Sacristy: an unexpected and mag-nanimous gesture, and one of which, to judge by the sour look on his face, Lord Baster-kin does not approve. But the Layzin moves with deft grace to face Arnem and Korsar without the advantage of physical remove, apparently most earnest in his desire to ingratiate himself with them. He holds out his slender, soft right hand, the third finger of which is encircled by a ring with a large, pale blue stone that nearly matches his eyes. Korsar and Arnem bow and kiss this ring, detecting the sweet aroma of lilac on the Layzin's clothing.

"You're late," Baster-kin grunts, not to the two commanders, but to his own men, who continue to cower by the doorway. Then he looks at Korsar and Arnem. "I trust that they did not inconvenience you."

"Not at all," Korsar replies. "I fear it is we who have delayed them— some signs of activity in the Wood, beyond my lord's own Plain."

Baster-kin exhibits no alarm at the statement; indeed, he scarcely reacts at all. "But I presume it was nothing?"

"We do not yet know, but we live in hope, my lord," replies Korsar, in a blatantly disingenuous and uncharacteristic tone that surprises Arnem.

Baster-kin's face grows somehow gloomy as his eyes study Korsar; but before more words can be exchanged, the Layzin steps in. "You will, I hope, forgive the presumptuousness of our dispatching these men of Lord Baster-kin's Guard, Yantek. But the dangers that face our city and kingdom seem to be multiplying every hour, and we frankly feared for the lives of Broken's two greatest soldiers. Did we not, Baster-kin?"

"Yes, Eminence," Baster-kin replies. "We did." The man is still brusque, still very sure of himself. Yet he is genuine, too, or at least he seems so to Arnem. Unlike his commander, the sentek has never felt resentment or incomprehension in Baster-kin's presence: the Merchant Lord's frequent bouts of blatant rudeness strike Arnem as no more than plain honesty fired by an undeniably superior mind, one that labors tirelessly in the cause of patriotism; and this opinion is the source of the muted but genuine admiration that Arnem feels toward the most powerful secular official in the kingdom. "We have too great a need for both your talents now," Baster-kin continues, speaking directly to Arnem and Korsar, "to see you fall prey to drunken cutthroats. Or madmen."

Arnem's brow arches: is Baster-kin, who has lackeys in every part of Broken, aware of what the sentek and Niksar have seen and heard tonight?

Korsar bows deeply—to the Layzin. "You honor us both, Eminence." Rising, the yantek offers Baster-kin a small inclination of his head. "As do you, my lord. I have brought Sentek Arnem, as you wished. But I fear that I have dispatched his aide, Linnet Niksar, back to the southern wall. Should the activity in the Wood develop, we thought that it would be best to have an officer that we *all* trust in charge."

Surprise piles on surprise, for Arnem, and he again glances at his old friend: it is as close to an acknowledgment that Korsar is aware of Niksar's role as a spy, working for the men in this room, as the old soldier has ever come; and it is a very risky thing to say. Yet Korsar seems unmindful of danger: "Not that I think it will come to anything, Eminence. A few torch lights, the Bane Horn sounding, some vague shouting—nothing more."

Shouting? thinks Arnem. *It was screaming, and well he knows it—unless he did not believe my report. What's he playing at?*

"Beyond that," Korsar concludes, "I confess that I have seen little, inside the walls or out, that would indicate a desperate state of affairs."

"The Bane have learned new ways," Baster-kin says, eyeing Korsar more critically. "They behave more like the deadly vermin that they are with each day's passing—we chase them into one hole, and they strike from any of a dozen others."

Korsar makes no reply, but cannot keep a glint of dismissal from his agèd eyes; *and if I can catch that look,* Arnem realizes, *then how much more quickly can Baster-kin?*

And, to be sure, Baster-kin reacts with an expression of distaste—or is it regret?—and a disappointed shake of his head. Striding down the wooden walkway that spans the pool, the Merchant Lord descends to the soldiers, but with none of the grace that marked the Layzin's approach.

"May I ask what these 'new ways' are, Eminence?" Korsar says, his voice carrying a hint of continued skepticism. "There was mention of sorcery, in your summons . . ."

"A necessary ruse," the Layzin replies, "to mask the true nature of the danger from those who have witnessed its effects." The Layzin sighs heavily, deep distress revealing itself ever more in his face and voice. "It was, in fact, poison, Yantek. We do not yet know from which woodland creature they extracted the substance, but its effects are"—the sacred head bows, and the gentle shoulders slacken—"fever—painful sores throughout the body—all . . . brutish . . . savage."

Korsar's eyes go wide with what Arnem hopes the others will not recognize as disbelief. "Poison?" the yantek repeats. "In the Inner City?"

"Yantek Korsar forgets," Baster-kin declares, "that my own Guard patrol the entrances to the Inner City." Seemingly incensed by Korsar's skepticism, Baster-kin steps but inches from the yantek. "And it was they who were struck down by those misshapen little heretics."

"The poison," interrupts the Layzin, placing a hand gently on Baster-kin's chest and guiding him a few steps away, "was introduced into a well outside the Inner City gates. Near a military post. We must suppose that the Bane hoped that some of the tainted water would find its way inside, or that, once loose, the illness would spread like plague—for its effects are similar to that worst of all afflictions . . ." The Layzin's voice grows soft, and his delicate eyes fill with dread. "Broken is nothing without the God-King, Yantek. I need not remind you that Saylal has not yet been blessed with an heir, and should the line that began with the great Thedric—"

"With Oxmontrot," interjects Korsar, causing no little surprise throughout the room: the Layzin is not a man to be interrupted like any other, and he is even less one to be corrected on questions of royal history and faith. But Yantek Korsar persists: "Surely Your Eminence remembers?"

"*Oxmontrot?*" Baster-kin repeats. The Merchant Lord is indignant, at both the suggestion and at Korsar's interruption; but he controls his resentment, and calmly presses: "Oxmontrot was a lowborn heathen, Yantek. And, although we owe him gratitude for the founding of this city, he had, by all accounts, lost his mind, by his life's end."

But Korsar holds his ground calmly: "And yet he is still respected as the father of this kingdom. Or does my lord deny as much?"

The Layzin casts a glance of mild admonishment at Baster-kin, and turns back to Korsar, placing another pale, smooth hand on the yantek's wrist. He smiles gently, at which Baster-kin's tone seems to genuinely soften: "I do not deny it, Yantek. But Oxmontrot was unfortunate enough to have died without ever accepting Kafra as the one true god; thus, great leader though he was, he cannot be considered of the divine lineage."

Korsar shrugs carelessly. "As you say, my lord. But he was a devout man, in his way."

"He was a *Moon worshipper,* just as the Bane are!" Baster-kin exclaims, losing his momentary self-control. "Are you truly attempting to say—"

"*My lord . . . !*"

The Grand Layzin of Broken has been forced to raise his voice, if only slightly; but it is enough to make the shaven priests suddenly remember urgent tasks to be performed in adjoining chambers, while the men of the Guard shrink into the Sacristy's furthest shadowy corners. Arnem would join them if given the chance; but he must stand his ground and support Korsar—provided it does not lead to further inexplicable flirtations with blasphemies that, quite aside from being provocative, are unnecessary.

The Layzin's ordinarily cool eyes become quite heated, as he glowers at Baster-kin. "We are not here to discuss ancient history or Yantek Korsar's views thereof," says the Layzin, more sternly. "The attempted assassination is the subject at hand."

Baster-kin swallows any remaining bile when he looks into the Layzin's eyes; then he turns his own gaze to the floor and goes down on one knee. "Yes, Eminence," he says quietly. "I beg forgiveness."

The Layzin passes a generous hand over Baster-kin's head. "Oh, no need, no need, my lord. Rise, I beg you. We are all near distraction, at the thought of the Bane reaching into the very heart of this city. I am sure Yantek Korsar will forgive us."

Korsar, too, appears humbled by the Layzin's words, for all his defiance. "Eminence, I would not wish to appear—"

"Of course not," the Layzin replies, again full of sympathy. "But there is more news, Yantek. The God-King has reached a momentous decision—one terrible in its nature, but righteous in its purpose."

Korsar begins to nod, almost seeming to smile ever so slightly beneath the agèd grey whiskers, before he very carefully says, "He wishes the army of Broken, led by the Talons, to undertake the final destruction of the Bane tribe . . ."

The Layzin's gentle, pronounced lips part, and his face fills with surprise and approval as he brings his hands swiftly together. "There, now, Baster-kin! Yantek Korsar's loyalty makes the solution clear to him before ever I voice it. Yes, Yantek, such is the wish of our sacred ruler, and he directs me to charge you with its execution—although the involvement of the entire army hardly seems necessary. Sentek Arnem's Talons should be more than adequate to the task."

The Layzin clearly expects an enthusiastic response from the two soldiers—and is disturbed when neither displays one. Korsar stares down at his boots, shifting from one foot to the other uneasily, then tugs at his beard with his right hand in a similar fashion.

"Yantek . . . ?" the Layzin asks, mystified.

But Korsar does not answer; instead, he lifts his head, apparently growing settled in his mind, and looks into Arnem's bewildered eyes, his message so clear that, once again, no more than a silent reminder need accompany his speedy glance: *Remember what I told you—do not support me . . .*

And then Korsar turns to the Layzin, putting his arms to his sides and inclining his head in deference once more. "I—" The words do not come easily, to one whose life has been obedience: "I fear that I must— *disappoint* Your Eminence."

The proud smile that has lit the Layzin's face disappears with disturbing abruptness. "I do not understand, Yantek."

"With respect, Eminence," Korsar says, steadying one trembling hand by gripping the pommel of his raiding sword[†] and grinding the tip of its long, straight sheath into the marble floor. "I suspect that you do. I suspect that Lord Baster-kin has already warned you of what my reaction to such a charge was likely to be."

"*I* have?" the Merchant Lord asks, genuinely confused.

The Layzin glances quickly at Baster-kin, not at all pleased. "Yantek," the Layzin says, in a hushed, deliberate manner, "you cannot refuse a commission from the God-King. You know this."

"But I do refuse it, Eminence." Sorrow and deep regret grip the yantek's voice, just as his words tighten Arnem's own chest. "Although it makes me sick at heart to say so . . ."

A hushed awe falls over the Sacristy, as all wait for the Layzin's next words: "But this cannot be!" he finally cries, staggering back into a nearby chair. "*Why,* Yantek? Why should you refuse to fight the Bane, whom Kafra has made the very image of all that is unholy?"

Korsar grips the pommel of his sword hard enough to go white at the knuckles. Arnem, himself in the grip of emotions too profound to express, can see that his friend's next statement will be his most crucial:

"It was not the golden god who created the Bane, Eminence." Having made the break, Korsar can finally look up, strength returning to his voice: "It is we of Broken who must accept that responsibility."

A sudden chill runs through Arnem, in part because of the words that he is hearing, and in part because of how closely they resemble words that he has already heard, this night:

"*Visimar . . .*"[†] the sentek whispers, not yet willing to admit that he has so recently encountered the man; nay, not the *man:* he was a blasphemous criminal, Arnem silently declares, a mage in his own right, one who, worse yet, was the primary acolyte of Caliphestros, Broken's most infamous sorcerer. Visimar, who pilfered corpses for his master's rites, and who allowed his very form to be oftentimes transformed by his master, that he might enter Davon Wood unnoticed and fetch out strange animals and herbs and crystalline rocks, all to be used in the creation of evil charms. No, Arnem will not admit to the chance meeting—or *was* it chance? And if the dead do walk the streets of Broken, what reason can Arnem have to doubt the most chilling of Visimar's prophecies:

"*You shall hear lies in the Sacristy tonight, but not all the men who speak them will be liars. And it will be your task to determine who disgraces that holy chamber with falsehoods.*"

Arnem turns away from the other men for a moment, clapping a hand to his forehead. "You cursed old fool, Visimar," he murmurs inaudibly, as his blood races ever more rapidly. "How am *I* to determine such a thing?"

One separate conclusion the sentek has already reached, with terrible certainty: as punishment for what he has just said, Yantek Korsar will almost surely be exiled to Davon Wood, the effective death that is meted out to those who spread sedition. Precisely as Korsar himself predicted earlier in the evening, the old commander—the man who has ever been a father, not merely to Arnem, but to the army generally—will not see another sun set over Broken's western walls. "Kafra's stones," Arnem curses in a helpless whisper, despite his surroundings. "Kafra's bloody stones . . ." the sentek repeats, with the same soft desperation. "What is happening, this night . . . ?"

The Layzin stands and, without deigning to look at either Korsar or Arnem again, quickly recrosses the walkway and ascends to his dais. Moving to its most distant point and throwing himself upon the sofa, he calls, "Baster-kin!" in a tone authoritative enough to make the strong-willed Merchant Lord turn about like a household servant. Then the Layzin orders the scribe who sits opposite him to stop recording what is said: an ominous act, and one Arnem has never before observed.

Starting toward the walkway, Baster-kin pauses to glare at the two commanders, whispering only, "I assured him, earlier, that this was *not* a possibility. You two had better prepare some explanation!" And then he spins again, so quickly that both commanders are brushed by the swirling hem of his cloak, just before he marches up the walkway to face his much-displeased master.

Turning to Yantek Korsar, Arnem finds, for the first time, uncertainty in his old friend's face; but it is an uncertainty that gives way to private amusement (remarkably ill-timed, Arnem thinks), and Korsar sighs an almost hateful laugh as he quietly pronounces:

"Clever. Yes, clever—*my lord* . . ."

Arnem would have an explanation, and will press Korsar for one, if he must; but just then there is a commotion to the rear of the chamber. The men of Baster-kin's Guard are assuring someone that entry is forbidden— but whoever is on the other side is having none of this explanation.

"Linnet!" Baster-kin calls out from the dais, where he has gone into close conference with the Layzin. "What's that unholy noise?"

The linnet of the Guard strides quickly to the center of the chamber. "A soldier, sir—a mere pallin, from Sentek Arnem's command. He claims that he has an urgent report, which the sentek himself ordered him to bring."

"Did you so command?" Baster-kin calls to Arnem.

"Ban-chindo," the sentek mumbles; then, as calmly as he can manage, he replies, "Yes, my lord, I did. The pallin has been watching the area of the Wood in which we earlier observed activity."

"Well—see what he wants," Baster-kin says, and resumes his hushed conversation with the Layzin, a heated exchange that is evidently doing nothing for the Merchant Lord's infamous disposition.

In truth, Arnem would rather stay where he is, and use the moment to privately demand that Yantek Korsar explain his extraordinary behavior and statements; but all Korsar seems willing to offer is an additional order:

"You heard him, Sixt—go see what troubles your pallin."

Left without alternatives, Arnem tries to make his concern plain on his face, and puts his fist to his chest in salute to his commander; but Korsar only smiles again, that infuriating expression that is almost wholly hidden by his beard, and so Arnem must stride to the arched doorway in as bad a humor as he can remember experiencing. He moves roughly past the men of the Guard, and drags the winded Pallin Ban-chindo out into the transept of the Temple.

"I trust this is urgent indeed, Ban-chindo," he says. "What have you seen—more movement?"

"No, Sentek Arnem," the young man replies: "Yet another fire!"

The word drives all other worries from Arnem's mind, for an instant. "Fire? What do you mean, Pallin? Be specific, damn it all!"

"I am trying, Sentek," Ban-chindo says, only now getting the heaving of his broad chest under control. "But it has been a long run!"

"You wait until you have four or five Bane fighters anxious to take your head," Arnem scolds. "You'll remember running the Celestial Way as an amusing bit of exercise—now, *explain.*"

"We thought it the light of more torches, at first," replies Ban-chindo, doing his best to be soldierly and detached. "But it is much deeper in the Wood, and far larger. Flames as high as any tree! Linnet Niksar ordered me to tell you that he thinks it a signal beacon, or evidence of a large encampment."

Arnem takes a few moments with this news, pacing the transept. "And Linnet Niksar's opinion can be trusted . . ." he murmurs. "But that's all you bring?"

"Well, Sentek, you did say that if we observed anything else—"

"Yes, yes. Fine. Well done, Pallin. Now, back you go. Tell Linnet Niksar that I want the *khotor* of the Talons ready to march by dawn. The full *khotor,* mind you, with cavalry ready to ride—both *profilic* and *freilic*† units. Understood?"

Once again, Ban-chindo slaps his spear to his side as he stands to attention and smiles. "Yes, Sentek! And may I—"

"You may do nothing else," Arnem replies, knowing that the young man simply wants to express gratitude for the trust his commander has placed in him, but also knowing that there is no time. "Go, go! And keep your mind on those Bane gutting blades!"

Setting off at a run once more, and lowering his spear in the manner instilled by countless hours of drill—so that it hangs level to the ground at his side, ready either to form part of a bristling front line or to be thrown from farther back in the *khotor's* formation—Pallin Ban-chindo is soon out the brass doors of the Temple. Arnem, however, is no longer in a similar hurry: he has realized that all he will hear inside the Sacristy are more bizarre statements and angry recriminations, and, for a moment, he indulges the childish belief that if he does not enter, none of it will happen . . .

But the moment is fleeting; and he soon hears the linnet of the Guard calling out, to say that the Layzin and Baster-kin await his return.

$$1:\{viii:\}$$

The Bane foragers, journeying homeward,
encounter horror compounded by Outrage . . .

KEERA CANNOT SAY how long she has been running; but when she realizes that her brother and Heldo-Bah have finally sated their appetite for argument, she supposes that it must have been a considerable time. Heldo-Bah still leads, having chosen the most direct, if not the safest, route home to Okot: along the Cat's Paw. They turn into the deeper Wood only when the river does, and then will move south by east, atop the more shielded (and thus more dangerous) stretch of the river. Finally, they will say farewell to the waterway, and prepare to follow an ancient trail due south. Like a handful of similar routes in other parts of the Wood, this trail was marked by the earliest exiles with ancient Moon worshipper symbols,[†] carved glyphs upon rocks that no longer hold meaning for anyone outside the Bane, and for precious few members of that tribe. But the symbols' loss of significance has not diminished their quality of encouragement: for Bane returning from missions, the markings remain welcome indications that they will soon be among the smaller settlements that surround Okot, and, not long thereafter, amid the bustle of the central Bane community itself.

The final, writhing turn of the Cat's Paw to the east has long been infamous for its series of especially violent waterfalls, the noisiest cascades in an already loquacious and often lethal river. Generations ago, Bane foragers, in a moment of typically grim humor, named these falls the *Ayerzess-werten,*[‡] in acknowledgment of all those in their tribe who, dashing too carelessly through the Wood, had slipped and plummeted to their deaths in the narrow, well-hidden gorge. Keera's party are too expert to be tricked by any of the *Ayerzess-werten's* ploys, although they pay them healthy respect: when Heldo-Bah reaches the deceptively beautiful spot where flat granite and gneiss formations[†] jut out over the tiers of falling water, he carefully creeps to the slippery, moss-covered edge of the most dangerous precipice, then returns to mark the limit of safe ground for his companions with a rag of rough white wool that he ties to the lowest limb of a nearby silver birch. This important task completed, Heldo-Bah begins to look for the faded marks of the trail that will make up the final stage of the foragers' race to discover what vexes their people so severely that they have sounded the Voice of the Moon no less than seven times.

When Keera reaches the *Ayerzess-werten,* she looks up through the break in the Wood's leafy ceiling above the falls, at the position of the Moon and stars.[‡] She realizes that Heldo-Bah has set a far better pace than she had supposed: the tribulations of the heart, like those of the body, can make a lowly fool of that seeming master we call Time. Keera speculates that she and her companions should reach Okot by dawn— and yet, for the tracker who is above all a wife and mother, there is only additional dread in this seemingly reassuring consideration: for if Heldo-Bah were as certain as he claims to be that no great evil has befallen Okot, he would hardly have been likely to set and sustain such a rigorous pace over the most dangerous stretches of the Cat's Paw—particularly after having stuffed his belly with beef.

Despite her mounting anxiety, Keera herself soon halts the party's progress: for, carried on a gust of wind from the southeast is the scent of humans—filthy humans, to judge by what is more stench than scent. No foragers would travel so carelessly, nor would any other Bane familiar with Davon Wood; and so, without a word, Keera reluctantly stops just short of the area marked by Heldo-Bah's warning rag, and signals to Veloc. Veloc, recognizing in his sister's expression that strangers are approaching, calls as quietly as he can after Heldo-Bah, who has wandered some fifty paces from the river in search of the southern trail. But in the region of the *Ayerzess-werten,* fifty paces might as well be five hundred: Veloc's voice, even were he to bellow, would scarce rise above the sound of the waters. And so, with expert movements, he produces a leather sling from inside his tunic and reaches down, picking up the first acorn-sized stone he can locate. He flings the stone in Heldo-Bah's direction, intending, he tells his sister, to strike a tree in front of his friend. But Veloc misses his mark (or does he?) and the stone catches Heldo-Bah on the rump, drawing from him a single sharp cry of pain, and then, to judge by the contortions of his face, more variations on his formidable store of angry oaths. Heldo-Bah is yet close enough to the *Ayerzess-werten* for his voice, like Veloc's, to be swallowed up by the din of the river; and so his tirade poses scant danger of revealing the foragers' presence. He returns to his comrades, still mumbling curses as he prepares for a new battle of name-calling.

But rage becomes consternation when he finds his friends busily concealing their sacks and then their bodies within a series of crevices and caves that cut through a massive crag a short way upriver from the most treacherous ledges surmounting the *Ayerzess-werten:* ever cautious, Keera has so arranged matters that whoever is approaching from the southeast will have to cross those same dangerous spots before reaching the foragers. Heldo-Bah slackens the straps of his bag, which he sets on the crag.

"What in the name of Kafra's golden anus has got into you two?" he seethes.

Keera claps one of her strong hands over Heldo-Bah's mouth, and relates with a mere look the urgency of silence—an order that might seem superfluous, near the *Ayerzess-werten,* save that Keera is so deeply fretful. Veloc, for his part, tries to convey that men are approaching, with admittedly peculiar movements of his hands: the sole result is that Heldo-Bah's brow dances in bewilderment. Only when Keera puts her mouth tight to one of her blockheaded friend's malodorous ears and whispers, "Men come this way—from the south—*not* Bane," does Heldo-Bah grow silent and begin, with the alacrity he reserves for moments of unidentified danger, to search the crag for an especially deep crevice of his own, which he finds some twenty feet above the spot chosen by Veloc and Keera. He scouts the maw-like opening for obvious signs of animal habitation, and, finding none, stuffs his sack into the moist dankness below, and then wedges his body in tight above his goods, ever cautious to crush nothing of value. Finally, he produces all of his marauder knives, as well as his gutting blade,† and steadies himself for the fight that they all sense may be coming.

Soon, Keera can make out more than mere scents: voices are distinct, even against the noise of the *Ayerzess-werten*. But they are not martial voices, or at least Keera does not believe they can be—no soldiers, not even the sometimes arrogant young legionaries of Broken, would be so foolish as to allow the cacophonous blare of their calls and acknowledgments to resonate among the stands of especially giant and agèd trees that mark the line where the rich soil of the Wood gives way to the rock formations of the *Ayerzess-werten*. There is always the possibility that those who approach are trolls, goblins, or even giants, and that they speak without care because they fear neither humans *nor* panthers; but why would such beings give off so human a stench?

Keera takes some little comfort when she turns to see that Veloc has laid a series of arrows along the ridge of the crevice in which they have hidden, that he may snatch and loose them all the faster in the event of an attack, and that he already has his bow in hand: for every echoing voice out among the trees makes this prospect of a desperate struggle against some unknown group seem steadily more inevitable. Yet, in the midst of the foragers' preparations, another puzzle emerges: the mix of sounds takes on a different quality, losing its loudest male voices altogether. In the wake of this change, a new sound makes its way to the crag, one that is wholly unexpected by any of the foragers:

"Weeping," Keera whispers, and Veloc, emboldened, moves higher up to join Heldo-Bah in trying to steal a glimpse of what comes.

Seeing nothing, Veloc hisses down to his sister, "Who weeps?"

"A child," Keera answers, tilting her head to the southeast and cupping a hand around one ear. "A woman, as well."

"Ho!" Heldo-Bah noises, pointing. "Look to those beeches!"

And, indeed, from a stand of beech trees, the bush-like branches of which swarm with bright spring leaves, the careless newcomers emerge; but they are neither of the Tall, nor any race of woodland creatures. They are, in fact, Bane, but Bane who observe none of the tribe's ordinary precautions for forest roving; Bane who seem to care no more for the threats that may lurk in the Wood or the rocky riverbank than they do for the dangers of the Cat's Paw itself.

More surprising still, given their noisiness, is that they number but four—and one of these is a bawling infant, while two of the remaining three are women. The younger woman wears a well-shaped gown that, to Keera's eye, hangs as though it has silk in its weave; while the second woman, although agèd, is covered from head to ankle in an outer gown that also hangs softly; and the blanket in which the younger woman has wrapped the infant is no mean sheet, either. These are all signs that the wanderers are not destitute Bane, by any means; yet agonies of the body and spirit care nothing for rank, and the younger woman is so beside herself with torment that Keera worries she may somehow harm the child. The gestures the four employ when speaking and noising to each other allow Keera to conclude that the women and babe are of the same family, of which the man (perhaps a successful craftsman) is almost certainly head: but the pallor of their drawn faces and the stiff movements of their bodies speak of shared troubles having naught to do with mere age. Instead, all three of the adults display signs of severe illness, and from time to time each joins the infant in openly crying out in pain and despair.

Indeed, it would not surprise any of the foragers to see blood on the wanderers' clothing, for they behave as if they might be wounded. Perhaps, thinks Keera, they were set upon by those men whose voices are no longer part of the moaning chorus. Yet there is no evidence of any such misfortune. Worst of all, they are making directly for the sharpest precipice overlooking the *Ayerzess-werten,* and seem to take no interest at all in Heldo-Bah's plainly visible warning rag.

Keera, her own vexed mother's heart straining, can no longer contain herself: "Stop!" she shouts, believing that the newcomers must be blind, lost, or simple, and are therefore unaware that they are stumbling directly toward dangers that every healthy Bane knows are among the worst in the Wood. Her warning has no effect, however, either because her voice is consumed by the roar of the falls, or because the family chooses to take no note of it. But Keera will not be deterred; and, before Heldo-Bah or Veloc can scramble down to stop her, the tracker is out of the lower crevice as if hurtled, standing in plain view and again shouting, "No! The river!"

The members of the family on the rocky ledge still do not hear her, causing Keera to begin running toward them. She has only managed some ten paces before being stopped by the strangest of the family's behaviors: the man, his movements awkward and painful, approaches the young woman and the infant, and places his hands on the child, as if to take it. The hysterical woman[†] then releases the most shrill of all her cries of pain and lets go of the child, after which she collapses onto the slippery moss. Keera continues forward, but more slowly, now that the man has removed the babe from any harm that its mother might have inflicted in her madness. The older woman attempts to comfort the writhing tangle of hair and silken broadcloth on the ground; yet she cannot even kneel, so painful are her own movements. Despite their distress, the man ignores them both, staring down at the infant in his arms with what seems an expression of deep, fatherly love. But there is something else in the expression: some part of what Keera has taken for love soon reveals itself to be an obsession that drives the man, slowly yet relentlessly, toward the farthest point on the ledge above the *Ayerzess-werten.*

Two realizations rob Keera of breath: first, she sees that she has been wrong, terribly wrong, to think the mother the greatest danger to the infant; and second, she comprehends that the father's apparent love for the child has been perverted into something else; something not directed toward *saving* the babe, at all . . .

"No!" Keera cries with every bit of her exhausted heart; but, protest as she may, the man, now amid the cloudy spray sent up by the *Ayerzess-werten,* never halts his slow advance to the fatal precipice. And as he goes, he begins to raise the child up gently, holding it as far out as the excruciating pain afflicting his body will permit.

Keera realizes that, quick as she may be, she cannot move quickly enough to subdue the man—particularly as she must approach him over wet, mossy rocks that only become more difficult and dangerous, the faster one tries to cross them. And so, perceiving no other choice, she spins about and signals to her brother in wild-eyed dismay.

"Veloc!" she cries, so strongly that he can hear her over the falling waters. "Your bow—bring him down! *Kill him!*"

But Veloc, on the crag's higher perch with Heldo-Bah, has left both his arrows and his short bow below. He begins climbing down to retrieve them, but manages only a short part of the descent before he hears Keera call out in protest again. Veloc looks up to see that the man holding the babe is sobbing, clearly on the verge of surrendering to every form of torment a human can feel. The man offers a final entreaty to the Moon, raising the child up toward it—

And then lets the infant slip from his hands. Still screaming in uncom-

prehending agony and terror, the child plummets into the sharply protruding rocks and mercilessly churning waters below. The sight is so
terrible—but worse, it is so very much against Nature—that Keera's
knees buckle beneath her, like those of the shag steer she earlier helped
to kill. She drops to the ground to watch as the young mother—now, it
seems, so fully in the grip of her frantic grief and physical agony that she
can no longer muster the will or the power to even weep—crawls resignedly to another spot on the same precipice, and looks up at the defeated,
broken countenance of the weeping man.

Veloc senses further tragedy, and gets quickly to the ground to start
toward his sister, without retrieving his bow. And surely enough, before
he reaches Keera, the nightmare spins on: the woman who lies on the
ledge uses the last of her strength to simply roll off of it, silently disappearing into the falls, perhaps desiring, in her distraction, to be reunited
with the infant in the realm that lies beyond death, the realm that, the
Bane believe, is governed by the benevolence of the Moon.

By the time Veloc does reach Keera, he finds his sister so aghast that
she cannot move from the spot where she kneels. The old woman ahead
of them staggers unsurely but steadily toward the man on the ledge, in
precisely the manner that the younger woman did moments ago: slowly,
tormentedly, without hope or even desire for salvation.

"Stop them," Keera says to Veloc, getting to her feet in a display of
desperate purpose, as if her desire to know that her own family survives
has become bound up with the fates of the wretches on the rocks. "We
must stop them, Veloc—we must know why they are doing this . . ."

Keera and Veloc begin a cautious progress toward the two remaining
Bane, who now stand together, as steadily as their conditions will allow,
on the shelf above the *Ayerzess-werten,* their hands clasped, their eyes
looking up at the Moon. Their shared determination causes both brother
and sister forager to begin to move faster; and because of this, they issue
small noises of alarm when an entirely new man appears before them, so
suddenly that it almost seems that the mists of the *Ayerzess-werten* have
coalesced to form a *skehsel,*[†] the breed of malevolent spirit that all Bane
dread most—for the evil Natures of the *skehsel* would surely attract them
to such terribly stricken people as these, to work the unnatural idea of
self-destruction into their confused minds. In reality, the man has simply
been secluded behind the trunk of a gnarled oak that stands rooted to the

last patch of rich forest floor that borders the rock formation onto which the pain-racked Bane have made their way. This vantage point, and the fact that the man has kept himself hidden, suggest that his purpose is to ensure that events on the ledge unfold in the manner that the foragers have witnessed—and to prevent any passersby from interfering. In a dutiful, routine manner, the man blocks Keera and Veloc's path, silently telling the foragers to stop with one upturned hand.

So bewildered that they are momentarily robbed of their self-possession, Keera and Veloc obey the silent order: for the man before them, while not so imposing as the average citizen of Broken, is taller than both of the foragers—or, indeed, than almost any other Bane—by a good measure. But it is only when brother and sister notice the new-comer's garb that the matter is clarified. A shirt of expertly crafted chain mail—not iron or scale mail, but shimmering steel chain—that covers his body from elbows to thighs is layered by a leather tunic, as well as a wool cape and cowl, all black, the last with oxblood crimson wool lining. Crimson breeches lead down to knee-high black leather boots of a quality to indicate importance, an impression that is deepened by a long, be-jeweled dagger in a dark sheath that hangs from the first pass of a double belt, while from the second winding dangles a short-sword, a weapon that, to judge by its brass-banded sheath, is the exceptional work of one of Broken's bladesmiths. Finally, a well-crafted bow is slung over his right shoulder, completing an effect that is so sinister and imposing as to seem calculated. But the expression on the man's face is sincere; and as he tosses the left side of his cloak over his shoulder, he reveals a crimson crescent Moon stitched to the upper left-hand portion of his tunic—the emblem of a long tradition of terrible violence.

Keera and Veloc say nothing, less out of fear than stupefaction. On the crest of the crag, Heldo-Bah experiences no such befuddlement:

"Great Moon," he whispers, once the man has revealed the emblem on his chest. "Or whatever woodland demon has arranged this—" He begins to scramble quickly down the crag. "I thank you for it . . ." He takes the last ten feet to the ground in one strong jump, landing almost silently and looking up with sincere and gleeful hatred:

"An Outrager . . ."

With these words, Heldo-Bah glances about, making sure his various knives are still at the ready—

And disappears, apparently abandoning his friends to their fate.

In the clear ground between the oak tree and the rocks surrounding the *Ayerzess-werten,* the black-clad man immediately takes a commanding tone with Keera and Veloc: "Stay back, foragers," he calls. "You know who and what I am?"

"*What* is apparent," Veloc answers. "As for who—does it signify?"

"Not at all, little man—not at all," answers the Outrager; for such he is. "It's only that, should we come to blows, it may help you to meet Death with less shame if you know that you have been bested by Welferek,[†] Lord of the Woodland Knights."

Veloc's fear is apparently not strong enough to prevent him from scoffing: "*Lord of the Woodland Knights* . . . 'Outrager' isn't comical enough for you, eh?" He turns to Keera, his continued laughter indicating that he has abandoned all caution: for this Welferek could easily kill them both, and Veloc knows it. Keera stares at her brother in disbelief. "Tell me, sister," he inquires, with mock sincerity—and then Keera sees his true purpose: Veloc's insulting impertinence is distracting the Outrager from the unfortunates on the rocky ledge, who have taken one or two steps away from the precipice, and are watching what transpires near the oak tree intently. "Have we not spent as much time in the Wood," Veloc continues, "as any Bane alive?"

"Truly, brother," Keera replies, trying to disguise her emotions and play his game; but it is difficult. "And more than most Bane now dead."

"Which makes it odd—indeed, passing strange!—that we rarely if ever see any of these 'woodland knights.' And yet, here now is a *lord* of that noble brotherhood, in all his peacock finery!"

Welferek has been steadily losing the tolerance that had first marked his treatment of the foragers; and now, his hand slowly closes on the hilt of his short-sword. Yet he has also taken the bait: for his thoughts have wandered momentarily from the surviving Bane behind him. Veloc has been wise to gamble on the pride of the Outragers.

Chosen for their exceptional height and strength, qualities that allow them to pass into Broken without being immediately (or in some cases ever) identified as Bane, the "Sacred Order of the Woodland Knights of Justice"—or, in common parlance, the Outragers—are the divinely sanctioned instrument of Bane vengeance, the creatures of the Priestess of the Moon in Okot, who alone chooses and commands them. The violence that they perpetrate, within Broken's walls or among the villages of that kingdom, is infamous for its suddenness, its cruelty, and the often indirect way in which it is connected to individual injuries committed by the Tall against the Bane. A Bane forager run to death by the dogs of a Broken merchant's hunting party, for example, or a young Bane woman who is abducted and obscenely used by a detachment of soldiers from Broken's army, will nearly always result, not in retaliation against the particular Tall guilty of the crime, but in the torment and murder of Broken families in entirely different parts of the kingdom. This is not deemed cowardly, among the Bane—or rather, the High Priestess often declares that it should not be so deemed. Instead, it is reaffirmed on all Lunar holy days that the Woodland Knights of Justice have a divine right to strike wherever they will be least expected. Since the beginning of recorded Bane history, it has been the central secular tenet of the Lunar Sisterhood, from whom the High Priestesses are selected, that only by remorselessly engendering horror and shock throughout Broken can the Bane command sufficient respect among the Tall (even if it must be hateful respect) to ensure the flow of trade between the two peoples, and to keep the Tall from far more serious depredations against the tribe.

The knight now facing Keera and Veloc is a typical example of this philosophy. He is handsome enough, with well-proportioned features and a neatly trimmed beard atop a powerful frame more than five feet tall. But in his eyes is the same chilling aspect that Keera and Veloc have seen in the gaze of every Outrager they have ever encountered. It is the dark scowl of one who has known too much lonely bloodshed in his life; bloodshed, the weight of which is neither eased by the comradeship of warriors in battle nor made somehow comprehensible by the gratitude of one's own people; bloodshed undertaken at the obscure behest of priestesses; bloodshed that makes of a man something apart, something deadly, and of his soul, something already dead . . .

"You can have no interest in what takes place here," Welferek says evenly, keeping his sword sheathed, and attempting to hold his anger at bay. "Continue about your business, and quickly."

Keera's resentment at being thus dismissed is great, but she tries to sustain Veloc's ploy: "And what if we do have an interest? The deep Wood is the realm of the foragers, Outrager—it is *we* who say what is our business, here. Do you suppose we will submit meekly?"

In reply, Welferek finally draws the short-sword—slowly, to achieve the greatest effect. "I don't suppose it," he answers calmly. "I am certain of it. These deaths have been sanctioned by the High Priestess, by Her Lunar Sisters, and by the Groba. Those among the condemned who wish to die immediately may choose their own method of ending their lives. This family chose the *Ayerzess-werten,* as have others. They were escorted here at spear point by several of my knights" (*The careless male voices in the Wood,* Keera concludes silently) "and I am charged with making certain they fulfill their pledge. And if they do not, or if anyone attempts to interfere . . ." He shrugs.

"But—*why* is it happening?" Veloc asks. "What do you mean, 'those among the condemned who wish to die immediately'?"

Welferek scrutinizes Veloc with great suspicion. "If you truly do not know, forager, then it's not my place to tell you. For those sorts of answers, you need to see the Groba when you return to Okot. I've told you what my task is, and I advise you again to move along."

The ugly glare of lethal sincerity in Welferek's eyes intensifies, and is only slightly mitigated when the Outrager at last remembers his charges on the rocks: cursing both his inattention and the foragers' interference, he turns away to make sure the man and the old woman are proceeding on the path that the young mother and her child have already taken. Discovering that they are not, Welferek murmurs still more irritated oaths, while Veloc, realizing that his game has run its course, puts a gentle but persuasive arm around his sister's shoulders, urging her back. But Keera will have none of it, and Veloc, not knowing what recourse is left to him, begins to search first the crag and then the line of the Wood, in the hope that Heldo-Bah will soon offer support.

But he can find no trace of his friend among the Moonlit rocks and tree trunks, a fact that does little to encourage further defiance.

Welferek sends a sharp blast of air whistling through his teeth, fixing his own harsh gaze on the tormented eyes of the two Bane who are, apparently, the last business he has to attend to, at least for the moment. Taking a few long strides toward the *Ayerzess-werten,* Welferek holds his short-sword aloft, waving it through the air slowly, but with purpose, as his entire body assumes a posture of menace. His message could be no plainer: *There are but two choices available to you . . .*

The distraught pair on the ledge reluctantly select their fate: the man throws his arms around the now-weeping woman, tenderly yet very firmly (in the manner of a dutiful son, Keera cannot help but think), and whispers something into her ear that has at least a partially soothing effect. Then, with the last of his strength as well as another plaintive gaze up at the Moon, he guides the woman back to the very edge of the precipice and, with no more ceremony than would be required to drift into slumber, he falls with her from the ledge and into the spray of the cascade, from whence the two—ever locked in that same gentle embrace—hurtle down into the killing maelstrom, which cannot acknowledge these latest of its victims by allowing even a splash to escape its monotonous thundering.

Welferek sighs wearily. "Great Moon, they were a long time about it," he declares, trudging back to the oak behind which he had earlier concealed himself. He plunges his sword half a foot into the ground, produces a small wineskin from inside his tunic, and sprays a hefty amount of its contents into his mouth and down his gullet. Hiding the skin away again, he relaxes against the oak, wiping his mouth. "Ill as they were, you'd think they'd have been happy to go," he continues, still with nothing more than slight annoyance in his voice. Leaning more heavily against the tree, the Outrager reaches for his sword, pulls it back out of the Earth, and levels it at Keera and Veloc. "And I'm warning you two," he says, the wine working on his restraint. "Any more arguments and we will finish speaking. You"—he points the sword at Veloc—"I will kill quickly. Although *you*"—the tip of the sword moves to Keera—"I may take a little time with. You're not at all bad to look at, little forager. Yes, the two of us might find all manner of sport—provided you cooperate. If you won't, I won't hesitate to—"

Something flashes through the air just in front of the Outrager, whose arm is still leveled at Keera and Veloc; and, although his eyes go wide and his mouth opens to scream in apparent pain, the arm stays up, as if of its own choosing. Then a second hurtling flash cuts the Moonlit night, and Welferek's left arm slaps back onto the trunk of the oak, again without his seeming to will or wish it to do so. He screams again, and his shortsword falls; but his sword arm remains upraised, unable to reach across and offer any assistance to his left. Indeed, Welferek seems to have lost all ability to control his movements.

And then, from atop the same mossy rocks where the Bane family leapt to their ends, bitter laughter cuts through the noise of the falling water, taunting the Outrager:

"You've *already* hesitated, you puffed-up fool . . . !"

1:{*ix:*}

Faith, treachery, and treason in the Sacristy
of the High Temple . . .

UPON REENTERING THE SACRISTY, Sixt Arnem finds all the participants in the tragic finish of Yantek Korsar's career, and quite probably his life, positioned almost exactly where he left them long moments ago. Arnem is faced with a dilemma: as he walks down the center aisle of the great chamber—where the gentle Moonlight that drifted through the blocks of colored glass in the walls on his arrival has given way to the jagged illumination provided by torches, oil lamps, and a pair of braziers on the Grand Layzin's dais—he feels his body pulling toward what would be its ordinary place, beside and half a step behind Korsar. But as Arnem moves toward this position, he catches sight of Lord Baster-kin, standing behind the Layzin's gilded seat and staring directly at him; the Merchant Lord is plainly trying to tell the sentek this is no time for sentimental loyalty, but rather the moment to separate himself from his commander. Arnem is ashamed that he considers this directive, even momentarily, and tries to walk deliberately toward his original goal; but as he folds his hands behind his back, a peculiar thing happens:

Korsar, without looking at the sentek, takes half a dozen long strides away from him. The old commander has also caught Baster-kin's meaningful glance, and is trying to protect Arnem in his own way; but it is, nevertheless, a jarring moment, the first time that the younger man has ever felt that standing by Korsar—whether inside Broken's halls of power or on the field of battle—might be the incorrect thing to do. He will not insult the yantek by following him; but the loneliness that Arnem feels is a burden perhaps impossible for any who have not known combat—who are strangers to the manner in which true warriors must place their fates within each other's hands—to comprehend.

On the dais before them, in the meantime, the Layzin sits with his head in his hands; and when he looks up, Arnem can see that he has maintained that position for as long as the sentek has been outside the Sacristy, judging by the marks his fingers have left on his face. That face has lost its gentle aspect; and his jaws now stiffen as his words go cold:

"Yantek Korsar. You have spoken treason, and within the Sacristy. As I am sure you know."

"Eminence, I have spoken . . ." Korsar endures one last flush of self-doubt: doubt that seems to vanish only when he looks to Arnem, and finds his staunch friend standing quite rigidly, yet clearly on the verge of weeping. Korsar half-smiles at the sentek, then lifts his head proudly to face the Layzin again.

"I have spoken the truth!" he declares defiantly. At the words, the two shaved priests, who have been half-hidden in the shadows in the rear corner of the dais behind the scribe's desk, move to protect the Layzin, while the soldiers of Baster-kin's Guard advance toward Korsar. The Layzin holds up a hand, quickly and silently halting all activity; Korsar, by contrast, continues to rail: "Yes, it was we of Broken who made the Bane—not Kafra! For what *god* would condemn the misshapen, the sickly, and the idiotic to such vicious, wretched ends as lurk in every corner of Davon Wood?"

It is Baster-kin who answers; but the Merchant Lord's tone has changed, now. Gone are the attempts to challenge Korsar, to almost bully the yantek into more obedient and more pious behavior. In place of these efforts is resignation: confident resignation, to be sure, yet irritated confidence, as well, as if Fate has made its decision, and both men must carry out the irksome business of accepting it. And in this, Baster-kin and Korsar are not so different; yet each is a man of importance, and their words must be spoken, if only that they may be recorded by the scribe.

"A god of unsurpassed wisdom, Yantek," Baster-kin replies to Korsar's last demand. "A god whose design was long ago revealed so clearly that even the heathen Oxmontrot could not deny it, choosing instead to allow Kafran law to become supreme, even as he himself kept the old faith. Or do you not remember that the Mad King began the banishments?"

Korsar's gaze becomes hateful. "Yes, that's how you bend all facts to your purpose, isn't it, my lord? You know as well as I do that Oxmontrot used the banishments as a practical tool to strengthen his kingdom. But he gave his life, as you have said, to the old faith—"

"He did not *give* his life to anything, Yantek," says Baster-kin. "His life was *taken,* because it was of no more use—he could not see divinity when it was before his face, because his mind was so broken by heathen idiocies. The banishments were never meant simply to make this kingdom strong—they were a sacred gift, granted in the hope that Broken would *remain* powerful. They were an instrument, not of survival, but of purification, a sacred method to root out imperfections in the people, to keep them strong, in body, in mind—"

"And in purse—I know the litany, my lord," Korsar says, with rising anger. But his disdainful demeanor is interrupted when he sees the Layzin's head fall back into his hands, as if it has once again attained insupportable weight. "But it was a sin, Eminence," the yantek continues, with more urgency than pride. "I know this. Whatever else the God-King Thedric called the continuation of the banishments, it was a sin against Kafra, against humanity! To go on dooming creatures like ourselves, simply because of imperfections of the body and mind—to destroy families—when the city and kingdom were already secure . . ." Korsar takes several steps toward the walkway up to the dais, at which the priests rush quickly to guard the thing, ready to withdraw it instantly if they must. The soldiers of the Guard start again in Korsar's direction; but this time, Baster-kin himself stops them, realizing, it seems (as does Arnem himself), that every word the old soldier says only ensures his doom more certainly. "But they survived the sin," Korsar says eagerly, still speaking to the Layzin, who will not look up. "Those forsaken devils, dwarfish, sickly, mad, many of them still children—out there where death was all around and never merciful—enough of them survived to form a tribe and make a life, wretched as it was. As it is. And now, because of insatiable greed and ungovernable pride, Eminence, you would allow the Merchants' Council to take even that away from them?" Korsar turns on Baster-kin. "Well, I will have none of it—no, my lord, I say I will have none of your fanciful, murderous plots!"

At these words, the Layzin looks up and speaks, his voice so empty of emotion as to seem ghostly: "Do you say the poisoning attempt is a *fabrication?*"

"I do!" At the words, the Layzin clutches the arms of his golden seat tightly, anger casting a pall over his features. But the yantek will not be dissuaded by scowling, now that he has traveled so far down the path of blasphemy. "I've spent my life defending this kingdom, Eminence—I've killed more Bane than my noble Lord Baster-kin has ever *seen*. And I say that they are not a people capable of such audacity—though, Kafra knows, they should be. I say it before you all—this is merely a contrivance to establish our control over the Wood, and by doing so to allow our merchants to bring even more precious goods out of the wilderness than the Bane can carry on their small backs!"

For a moment, no one in the Sacristy is capable of speech. Arnem himself is concerned with somehow coaxing his chest to take in air, and with finding something upon which to steady himself. He is aware of what has happened, of the grievousness of Korsar's statements; but he cannot make sense of the scene, cannot grasp the reality of this moment that will shortly demand from him greater participation.

In the silence, the Grand Layzin's face slowly softens, the rage becoming, once again, an acknowledgment of tragedy. Nor is there anything in his expression that might admit satisfaction at the exposure of a traitor; there is only regret clearly embodied in his next words:

"Yantek Korsar, I do not know if madness or treachery has driven you to this outburst—your life and your service speak against either quality, yet what else are we to think? In the name of that life and that service, however, I offer you a final opportunity to recant your outrageous statements, and mitigate the punishment that must befall you."

But Korsar's clear blue eyes are illuminated by defiance. "Thank you, Eminence," he says, genuinely but unrepentantly. "I will stand by my words. Baster-kin and the Merchants' Council have sent enough warriors to die in the cause of filling their coffers. There must be an end. Make peace with the Bane, let them keep the Wood. Let us continue to trade with them, but on terms, if not of friendship, then at least of respect. It is little enough to offer, considering what we have done to them. But I know you will refuse any such idea. And so," placing his hands behind his back, Korsar plants his feet, "I am ready, Eminence, to face exile. No doubt Lord Baster-kin would like to escort me to the Wood himself."

Baster-kin, the Layzin, and Arnem react to these words in unison, each displaying a different kind of shock: but all are genuine. In Arnem, the stunning blow is deepened by sorrow; in the Layzin, it is accented by bewilderment; and in Baster-kin, the effect of the yantek's words is mitigated by something like pity.

"*Exile?*" the latter says. "Do you imagine exile could be considered an appropriate punishment for challenging the basis of our society?"

For the first time, Korsar exhibits surprise: "My lord? Banishment is the ordained punishment for sedition, it has always been—"

"For the weak-minded, or mere drunkards, yes," Baster-kin continues, still astonished. "Or for any other hapless fools in the Fifth District. But a man of your standing cannot be granted a punishment equal to that of a child with a withered leg—your position demands that an example be made of you, an example that will serve as a warning to any who might be swayed by your calumnies, and tempted to repeat them. Did you not at least consider that before you indulged in this insanity?" The Merchant Lord waits for an answer; but, receiving none, he holds his arms high and then drops them in resignation, shaking his head. "For you, Yantek Korsar, there can only be the *Halap-stahla* . . ."†

A low commotion runs through the soldiers and the priests in the Sacristy, while Korsar falls as if struck into a nearby chair. For the first time, Arnem starts toward him—but years of discipline and the yantek's own orders pull the commander of the Talons back again. Whatever his bewilderment and horror, Arnem knows that his friend has spoken nearly unprecedented treason against Broken, against the God-King and Kafra, against all that he once valued and that they both have spent their lives defending. *But why?* the sentek demands of himself. *Why now? What has driven him to do it?* And, most terrible thought of all: *Is Korsar the liar of whom Visimar spoke?*

"The *Halap-stahla*," Korsar breathes at length, the flame gone from his eyes and real fear in his voice. "But—not since Caliphestros—"

"Not since Caliphestros has there been such treachery," Baster-kin declares, still astounded at the yantek's failure to foresee the consequences of his own actions.

"The higher the position, the greater the betrayal," the Layzin adds mournfully. "And the God-King has entrusted few in this kingdom with as much power as it has been your privilege to exercise."

Arnem's heart is near to bursting, as he watches Korsar's body begin to tremble. The motion is slight, at first, but becomes ever more violent as he plainly imagines the fate that he has brought down upon himself.

Yet then he calms, suddenly and strangely, and turns to Arnem, managing a half-smile of trust and affection, as if to tell the younger man that he has done well to control himself, and must continue to do so, for the sake of both Sixt's life and Korsar's own composure; then, just as quickly, the smile vanishes, although the yantek does grunt another of the humorless laughs that have punctuated his conversation throughout the evening.

"Well, Baster-kin," he says, remaining seated. "I suppose you think this puts an end to it. But you are wrong, great lord . . ." Slowly, Korsar drags his heavy, agèd frame from the chair, to stand once more in defiance. "Oh, you may mutilate me all you wish, and call it religion—but what I have said will remain true. You are leading this great kingdom to disaster, you are exposing its guts to the blades of all the tribes that surround us; and if Kafra does not punish you, there will be another god to attend to it."

"Yantek Korsar!" The Grand Layzin stands suddenly, holding an arm out, no longer in outrage, but in warning; and in his voice, a corresponding plea is plain: "Your crime is sufficient—I beg you not to endanger your life in the next world through further sacrilege in this one." The Layzin then looks down the dark length of the Sacristy. "Linnet!" the Layzin calls. At this, all the soldiers of Baster-kin's Guard move forward behind the commander of their detachment. "I almost dread to say it—however, you must take Yantek Korsar away. With dispatch."

"It must be in chains," Lord Baster-kin declares, with neither venom nor satisfaction, but a perfunctory air of duty. His instruction has been anticipated, for one of the shaven priests now produces a heavy set of manacles from under his robe, and lofts them over the reflecting pool to the linnet of the Guard, who, as they crash to the floor before him, appears a different man than the insubordinate mass of conceit who escorted Korsar and Arnem to the Temple. With a nod, Baster-kin directs the hesitant linnet to put the manacles on Korsar's wrists and ankles, and make a mere prisoner of the most distinguished soldier in Broken: small wonder that the linnet—a man unfamiliar with momentous events—finds that his own hands tremble as he complies.

"Wake the commander of my Guard," the Merchant Lord tells the linnet. "Herwald Korsar is no longer to be addressed by the rank of yantek. He will be held in irons until dawn, when he will be taken to the edge of the Wood for the ritual of the *Halap-stahla*."

"No." The Layzin's voice is painfully dry. "In Kafra's name, my lord, let us not wait for dawn. My own priests will follow behind your men, when they have collected the sacred instruments. Let all be in place for the ceremony at the edge of the Wood, when the sun rises—we must not risk trouble inside the city, once word spreads."

Lord Baster-kin bows in response. "Wise, Eminence, as always." He turns to his soldiers. "Very well—you have your orders, Linnet. Rouse your commander, and have him assemble a ritual detachment. Take the prisoner to the southeastern gate, to await the sacred party."

With a suddenness that strikes horror into Arnem, the soldiers begin ushering the yantek—nay, no longer yantek, now, only the agèd prisoner Herwald Korsar!—toward the Sacristy's arched doorway. One Guardsman thoughtlessly takes Korsar's arm as they go, but at a look from the still-powerful warrior the young soldier relents, and forms, along with his fellows, a close but respectful ring around the prisoner.

Arnem's self-control is no longer sustainable: the emotions that have been battling within him have caused a glistening band to form on his brow, and his vision grows blurred. He is aware that this is the last time he will see Korsar; and he feels a violent urge to bid his oldest comrade farewell, if only to assure the condemned man that they will meet again. Of this Arnem is certain, for the one article of faith that every warrior of every army that he has ever encountered has shared—no matter their specific gods—is the notion of a great hall in the next world where this reality's bravest warriors will meet once more.[†] Yet Arnem is still of this world, an Earthly soldier not yet fallen; and so, to his own amazement, the habits of duty keep his feet immobile, and his mouth closed. He finds himself beseeching Kafra to allow Korsar, who is now past redemption, to give some sign—

And his prayer does not go unanswered. Halfway to the arched doorway, Yantek Korsar halts, and his guards do likewise. The old soldier turns around, facing Baster-kin and the Layzin once more, and the head he has held so proudly throughout this ordeal drops forward in respect.

"Eminence—my lord—will you allow me to take leave of Sentek Arnem, who must take my place at the head of Broken's army?"

Baster-kin strides to the table on the dais, and affects to busy himself with papers. "You can have no further interest in the business of Broken's army, Herwald Korsar. Nor may you—"

"My lord." It is the Layzin, his weary voice still compassionate. "How many scars of Bane attacks do you bear? Or do I? In the name of the man he was—we shall grant the prisoner this small request." And with a simple gesture of the supple hand that wears the blue-stoned ring, the Layzin tells the Guard to allow Korsar to approach Arnem.

"But you must take his sword," Baster-kin orders, "and do not allow close contact." As the linnet of the Guard draws Korsar's raiding sword, Arnem goes toward the prisoner, stopping when he hears:

"Close enough, Sentek." It is Baster-kin again. "Eminence, there must be no confidences exchanged." The Layzin nods, acknowledging the remark with as much muted irritation as agreement.

From some ten feet away, then, Arnem and Korsar must end a friendship that has been rooted in far more than friendship, a bond in which far more has been shared than mere blood. Arnem finds that words elude him, but Korsar is not so impaired:

"I beseech you—heed me, Sixt, it is vital." Arnem takes two steps closer to the prisoner, and inclines his head to listen to Korsar more carefully: "This is your war, now, Sixt—and it may be a calamitous one. You will have to fight it within the Wood, for the Bane will not come out to meet you on the Plain. Do not oblige them too soon—do not fight upon their ground until you are sure our men know what such a fight requires. Do you understand? Do not be bullied into it—you have *been* there, you know what the Wood can do to men. Beware it, Sixt . . ."

"Enough!" Baster-kin calls out, starting back down the walkway over the reflecting pool. "Sentek—this man is no longer your superior, you must not discuss military operations with him."

The Layzin can only lift his hands and declare: "Take him away, all of you—this is too much to bear . . ."

As the shaven priests attend the distraught Layzin, Baster-kin gives his men a decisive wave of his arm, ordering them to remove their prisoner with haste. Now fully appreciative of the changed world in which they find themselves, two of the Guardsmen take rough hold of Korsar's arms, while their linnet prods him toward the door.

But Korsar will not be silenced: "Remember that, if you remember nothing else, Sixt: beware the Wood—*beware the Wood . . . !*"

And then he is gone. Arnem, finally unable to contain the multitude of passions that burn up through his throat, takes one step to the doorway, unable to stop himself from weakly calling out *"Yantek!"* as burning tears cloud his vision. Aware of this last fact, suddenly, and hearing, in the new silence of the chamber, the rushing sounds of his surging blood and his own labored breathing, he turns away and works hard to regain his self-control. Daring only one glance up, his still-cloudy vision settles on the face of the Grand Layzin, who, through his own deep sorrow, manages the beginnings of a comforting smile, and inclines his gracious head as if to tell Arnem that he appreciates the terribleness of the moment, and does not fault the sentek for his reaction; and, finally, in those near-sacred eyes, there is an extraordinary reassurance that life in the kingdom will continue, and that all will, somehow, be well.

The sentek starts when he feels a hand on his shoulder; and he starts again when he turns to find Baster-kin, who is a good inch taller than Arnem, grasping the sentek's shoulder so tightly that Arnem can feel his fingers through the thick shoulder panels of his leather armor.

"Sentek Arnem," Baster-kin says, in a tone that Arnem has never heard this man use before; a tone he would, if speaking of anyone else, call sympathetic. "Come with me, eh? We have much to prepare, and little time. I know how deeply this business has cut into you. But you are a soldier of Broken, and the safety of the God-King and his realm rest with you now: for reasons, the complexity of which you cannot suspect."

It is a bewildering statement; and hoping for guidance, Arnem looks past the Merchant Lord to the Layzin. But His Eminence—overwhelmed, at last, by the emotion of the occasion—is being guided by the two priests, along with the Wife of Kafra (who has reappeared without announcement), toward and through one of the doorways that lead to adjoining chambers.

Baster-kin's eyes, too, follow the Layzin out of the Sacristy; and when he and Arnem are left alone, the Merchant Lord confides, "He has been working himself to exhaustion over this business—nobly so, more than nobly, but he must take care, and rely on the rest of us to do more than he is accustomed to allowing." Turning once more to the sentek, Baster-kin declares, "To do so, however, he must be presented with evidence that we are fulfilling the momentous duties with which we have been tasked—and for you to understand your portion of those labors, Sentek Arnem, I would have you come with me to the Merchants' Hall. We must be sure of your orders, and of what forces you will require; but above all, I must be sure that you understand why this war must be fought."

"My lord," Arnem manages to reply, "I can assure you, this duty comes as no surprise. We—I—have long expected it."

"Yes, but you cannot have understood the reasons that now compel us to act. *All* the reasons. I intend to be candid with you, Arnem—for you share many of Korsar's opinions, I know, but not all. And you must know why you should share none. You go to war to achieve far more than the destruction of the Bane, Sentek, and easier access to their goods—you go to protect all that you hold dear."

And with that, Baster-kin strides away into the apse, evidently expecting Arnem—who must puzzle over the Merchant Lord's last remark, even as he adjusts to the altered circumstances of his own life—to match his pace toward the tall bronze doors of the Temple.

In Davon Wood, the Specter of the Death . . .

THE MAD LAUGHTER had been unmistakable: it had come from Heldo-Bah, who had crept undetected around and below the entire area of activity on the rocky shelf above the *Ayerzess-werten,* clinging to ledges of wet, nearly sheer stone, then coming up on the flank of the Outrager Welferek. Although Keera and Veloc had been relieved to hear his voice, they had not been surprised by his appearance: it would have been unlike Heldo-Bah to run from such a confrontation or to abandon his closest (indeed, his only) friends, particularly at such a pass. The only remaining mystery had been how he had managed to immobilize the powerful Welferek; and when Veloc and Keera had approached the oak—Veloc to retrieve the Outrager's short-sword, Keera to snatch the dagger from Welferek's waist, along with a quiver of arrows from beneath his cloak—they had found their answer: two marauder knives had expertly pierced each of the Outrager's muscular forearms just below the half-sleeves of his mail shirt, and then plunged deep into the tree. The first blade had been a particularly fine throw, catching Welferek's outstretched sword arm against a stout lower limb of the tree; the second fixed his left arm to the tree's trunk. Welferek had tried to wrench the knives free, but the movements had only caused the double-edged blades to cut further into his flesh and increase his bleeding; and so he had decided to wait, in order to discover the identity of his attacker.

Heldo-Bah now stands on the moss-covered ledge, soaked from head to foot in the waters of the *Ayerzess-werten,* which he tries to shake from himself like some unhappy animal. Keera and Veloc run toward him, Veloc ready with a friendly taunt:

"Heldo-Bah! As timely as ever, I see."

Heldo-Bah keeps his third marauder knife ready, his eyes upon the form of the Outrager, who, from the mossy ledge, is a dark shadow within the larger shape of the oak. "You're lucky I got here at all, philanderer," he says. "I had to climb all round those damnable rocks." He indicates his boots, which are strapped about his neck, and his trousers, the feet of which† are torn away. "With my feet bare, no less—look what it's done to my trousers! There were spots where I had no more purchase than two toes' worth." He nods to the oak. "What do we know of him?"

"An Outrager, although that's obvious," replies Keera. "He claims to be someone called Welferek, Lord of the Woodland Knights."

Heldo-Bah shows a delighted eye. "Welferek? He gave that name?"

"I could hardly dream it up, Heldo-Bah. Why? Do you know him? Great Moon, do you have an active feud with *every* Outrager?"

"No, no, Keera," Heldo-Bah replies, with transparent disingenuousness. "We met once. That's all." He pulls on his boots, somehow making even that simple action seem furtive. "Our bags are still in the rocks— why don't you ready them, and your brother's bow, too, while Veloc and I glean what we can from this 'woodland lord'?"

For an instant, Keera looks as though she will object; but a meaningful glance from her brother tells her that things may now occur in which she will wish to play no part—indeed, that she may not even want to witness. "This knight represents our only chance to determine what is happening in Okot, Keera," Veloc says, taking care not to further alarm his sister. "He will tell us what he knows, that I promise you."

Keera realizes that her brother is correct; and her concern for her family combines with this knowledge to overcome her usual repugnance at the bedeviling of any creature—even an Outrager. "Well, then," she says hesitantly. "Work fast, Heldo-Bah—we've lost enough time here. And if he has nothing to tell us, do not bring divine wrath upon us by so tormenting him that he lies, simply to put a stop to it."

"No, no, Keera," Heldo-Bah answers quickly. "In his case, I'll not need to go so far; nor will I require much time. As for tormenting him—past what I've already done—when have you known me to abuse my enemies? Although the Outragers never stop at such behavior."

"I trust, then, that you will not let your hatred of them make you behave as despicably as do they."

Keera gets a vague inclination of Heldo-Bah's head in return, and remains uncertain of his true intent; but she does not press the issue, and sets off toward the crag, wishing to remain unaware of what may now take place under the oak, and deciding that the chore of organizing the foraging bags may take a little longer than usual. Even so, her ever-keen ears cannot but hear one final exchange between her brother and Heldo-Bah:

"We can't kill him, Heldo-Bah," Veloc says. "We've as good as slain a soldier of Broken already, this night—we can't have Keera mixed up in murdering an Outrager, as well."

For her brother's consideration, Keera is grateful; yet she must confess that there is something in her heart that almost hopes Heldo-Bah will reply as he would on any other night—as, indeed, he does now:

"And who will know that it was we who killed him, Veloc, once the bastard's body is in the *Ayerzess-werten*? No—you leave this matter to me. Whatever we *must* do to find out if Tayo and the children are safe, that we *shall* do." And then, he moves merrily toward the oak, calling out in full voice: "Welferek! Imagine our meeting out here like this. But what's happened to you—great Moon, man, you look like the Lord God of the *Lumun-jani*!"[†]

Keera is relieved by these statements, yet at the same instant feels even more anxious at the mere intimation that her family may be in danger. She moves faster toward the crag, and when she reaches it, she finds that the words of her companions have once again vanished into the thunder of the *Ayerzess-werten:* a fact for which she is grateful.

The next few minutes are difficult for Keera, although not in any physical sense: her responsibilities as the Bane's finest tracker, along with the numerous foraging terms that she has been forced to undertake with her brother and Heldo-Bah, have made her as strong as almost any male member of the tribe. The retrieval of her party's three deerskin sacks is a cumbersome affair, but one easily managed, and she almost effortlessly draws Veloc's powerful bow, in order to sling it over her head and onto one shoulder. She replaces his uniquely well-made arrows in their quiver and straps it to her waist beside the shafts she took from Welferek, after which, Keera is ready to begin the final stage of the homeward run; but she realizes that she must wait, and allow the process of questioning the Outrager to proceed as it was always fated to do, given Welferek's arrogance, his apparent acquaintance with Heldo-Bah, and the latter's fiery hatred of all Outragers.

The specific causes of that hatred are largely a mystery, to Keera, although she knows as much as anyone in the Bane tribe about Heldo-Bah: about his eternal dissatisfaction with and grumbling over all aspects of his existence, and about his powerful yen for violence. Both Keera and Veloc were born in Davon Wood, of parents whose own parents had been exiles; and they are therefore counted among the most respected of tribesmen, the "natural" or "native" Bane (for even a tribe of exiles must have its hierarchies). Heldo-Bah's origins, by contrast, could scarcely be humbler, or more troubling, and it is his place in Bane society, Keera knows, along with how he was relegated to that place, which holds the explanation for her friend's eternal rage.

The secondary, or "fated," class of Bane tribesmen is made up of those who were born in Broken, but exiled to Davon Wood and to presumed death because they were afflicted with what the Kafran priests term "imperfections": weaknesses of body or mind, unusually small stature, the bearing of evil markings at birth, a tendency toward recurring illness—the list is almost endless, and is kept in the Sacristy of the High Temple in Broken. But there is a class of exiles that are viewed as lower even than the fated—the "accidental" Bane—and it was out of these dregs that Heldo-Bah arose.

The ranks of the accidental Bane are regularly replenished, not by the birth of new members, but by misfortune that befalls young children far from Davon Wood. Sold into slavery outside the frontiers of Broken (for the buying and selling of humans is unlawful, in the kingdom of the Tall), such children are brought into the wealthy kingdom by men who pass as "labor dealers," and who offer their young commodities as indentured servants within the letter of Broken law. But the lives of these "servants" are as unrewarding and as devoid of choice as are those of the more honestly styled "slaves" in such great empires as *Lumun-jan*. And, as an uncertain Moon (or, perhaps, a capricious Kafra) would have it, some of these unfortunate children, after being sold, are further revealed as marred by some one or several of the physical afflictions that are intolerable to the Kafran faith; and they thus go from the betrayal of being sold as slaves by their own families, to lies told about them by the labor dealers, and finally, to a culminating sentence of exile to Davon Wood.

Ordinarily, such exile is the last of these misfortunes, and the unfortunates, if they survive the Wood long enough to be located by the Bane, are welcomed into the tribe as fated members. But once in a great while, the most cursed of these children also demonstrate, while in Broken, flaws greater than those of the body alone: flaws of character so flagrant that their punishments, the priests of Kafra say, cannot stop at mere exile.

In Heldo-Bah's case, the physical indication of his unworthiness was stunted growth: a "fault" that he was able to hide for several years by telling simple lies about his age to the First District merchant who held his indentureship, and who enjoyed having the alert boy attend to the horses in his stable. But when Heldo-Bah also displayed, over time, a far greater talent for thievery than for grooming horses, even the merchant could not protect him. Heldo-Bah was doubly cursed by Kafra, pronounced the priests; and as such he was marked, not for exile, but for death. The Grand Layzin of the God-King Izairn—predecessor of the current Layzin, just as Izairn preceded Saylal on the Broken throne—elaborated on this judgment (while making sure that his opinion never reached the ears of Second Minister Caliphestros, who was known to oppose the banishments, especially of children), and declared that only the influence of the malevolent spirits that were still believed to inhabit the lower slopes of Broken's mountain could so pervert a boy not yet thirteen years of age. The remedy? Death by drowning in the Cat's Paw, which, if carefully carried out, would ensure (or so the priests said) that the demons would be trapped in the furious river, once their host was dead.

During the whole of this time, Keera and Veloc continued to enjoy a childhood that contrasted sharply with Heldo-Bah's: passed in one of the small communities to the south of Okot, this childhood included hard work for the whole of the family, without question; but it also offered Keera and Veloc time for exploration and adventure. And it was only through the siblings' curiosity and daring that Heldo-Bah was ultimately saved. For events so conspired as to find the two young Bane one day fishing along a relatively calm stretch of the Cat's Paw, below the *Ayerzess-werten*. The priests and soldiers assigned to the ritual of drowning Heldo-Bah lost the nerve to face those dangerous cascades, and they agreed among themselves to obey the spirit rather than the letter of Bane law, by binding the boy's hands and feet and placing him in a coarse sack, closed with a few winds of rope. They then threw him into the waters east of the *Ayerzess-werten* and departed—not knowing they were observed all the while by a pair of very curious Bane children.

Once certain that the party of Tall priests and soldiers were indeed gone, Veloc and Keera snatched the wriggling sack from the river; and when they cut Heldo-Bah out of his soft instrument of execution, they found that the boy was close to dead from breathing in the cold waters of the Cat's Paw. They carried him home; and for as long as was needed for Heldo-Bah to recover, he lived in Keera and Veloc's home, was fed by their parents, and behaved with gratitude commensurate to their kindness. Even so, after several years, the tug of a mischief-maker's life proved too strong for the boy who was, in truth, neither Tall nor Bane (indeed, Heldo-Bah has never known precisely who his people are; nor has he ever voiced a grain of interest concerning the matter to Keera or Veloc). He accepted membership in the tribe readily enough, and he did not steal from Bane households; rather, his unshakable preoccupation became vexing the Tall in any way he could, and his activities more than once brought real trouble from the soldiers of Broken, not only for the Bane's own soldiers (for the tribe did have an army, in those days, although it scarcely merited the name), but for foragers, traders, fishermen, and hunters, as well.

Asked by Keera and Veloc's parents to leave their home when old enough to see to his own needs, Heldo-Bah took to passing his summers in the Wood and his winters in abandoned huts. And, while he remained fast friends with his childhood rescuers, he was all the while honing his talent for raids across the Cat's Paw, in those smaller Broken villages that served as way stations between the city on the mountain and its principal trading center on the river Meloderna, the walled town of Daurawah. These villages usually consisted of a small collection of earthen houses, stone storage and trading stations, and a large tavern or inn: activity enough to attract Heldo-Bah's taste for mayhem. As he reached manhood, he added gambling and brawling to his recreations, on those occasions when there was nothing present worth simple stealing, or when Broken soldiers presented themselves as victims. When Veloc became a man, he began accompanying Heldo-Bah on these adventures, which grew in scope to include nocturnal forays into Broken itself, raids during which the handsome Veloc seduced lonely Tall women (who had often been told mythical tales of the remarkable physical appetites of the Bane—myths that happened, in Veloc's case, to be true) while Heldo-Bah emptied the distracted mistresses' houses of anything of value that would not slow a hasty escape.

Yet none of this explained the special anger that Heldo-Bah reserved for those "blessèd" men back in Okot who were periodically chosen by the Priestess of the Moon for entry into the Outragers. Heldo-Bah would often speak of that hatred, first to Veloc and, later, to Keera, when she began to slip away from her tracking duties and join her brother and the friend they had known since childhood on their increasingly infamous forays across the Cat's Paw. After Keera married Tayo (a young tanner and butcher who made good use of the game that Keera hunted) and gave birth, in rapid succession, to three children, her participation became more limited, as was natural; but on occasion, she would still find herself drawn into the many arguments with the Outragers that Heldo-Bah and Veloc indulged in wherever they went; and if apprehended, she shared their terms of foraging. Yet through all these years and the many adventures and punishments that the three experienced together, neither Keera nor Veloc ever learned the reason behind Heldo-Bah's hatred for the knights, which rivaled even his loathing of the Tall.

A sharp scream suddenly interrupts the monotonous roar of the *Ayerzess-werten,* along with Keera's remembrances, and causes the tracker to bolt upright from her seat on the rocky lip of the crag. Is it a cry of pain, Keera wonders, or merely of terror? Not that it is of consequence; she has no intention of returning to the spot until her companions call for her. Keera has seen enough of death and blood and strange events, this night, and she will be happy to get home to the good-hearted Tayo and their three playfully obstreperous children: two boys who have, thankfully, taken after their father, and a girl, the youngest, who, just as thankfully, is much like her mother. Keera sits again, listening to the pre-dawn chatter of birds that are nested close by the *Ayerzess-werten* and chiding herself for having once again gotten mixed up in trouble between Veloc and Heldo-Bah and a group of Outragers, and thus securing for herself a place on this term of foraging. She does not seriously believe that either she or Veloc will ever so associate themselves with Heldo-Bah's troublesome ways as to earn lifetime terms of foraging, as he has already done; but such consolation does not free her of the shame and heartache of being absent from her children. How would she feel, she sometimes wonders, if the situation were reversed? If her children ran away, even for a short time, leaving her naught to do save await their return? Keera cannot imagine life without the little creatures of her flesh, who have already begun to learn to hunt, and hunt properly: with respect for the Wood, for the spirits of the game, and finally for those other, far less visible spirits that lurk in the forest. How could she ever exist without the companionship of those pieces of herself?

A bad churning in her stomach, a cold rattling up her spine: the mere notion has frightened Keera more seriously than any of the night's other peculiar events. She remembers, too, that she has not yet reasoned out any adequate explanation for the many soundings of the Voice of the Moon, but has been left with the shapeless dread of some sort of attack on Okot. With these considerations in mind, she decides to brave the short screams that continue to emanate from the direction of the oak, and begins to gather up all her party's goods, ready to tell her brother and Heldo-Bah that she will continue on her way home immediately, whether they accompany her or not. The weight of her bag so customary as to be unnoticed, she seizes the other two sacks and easily lifts what would be a taxing load even for a strong Bane man, then races round the crag and heads directly for where Veloc and Heldo-Bah—both with gutting blades in hand—kneel to some urgent task. A few more steps, and Keera can see that the Outrager Welferek is no longer held to the tree by Heldo-Bah's knives: he is lying on the ground between his two captors, looking quite dead.

Keera feels anger grip her spirit at what she thinks her brother and

Heldo-Bah have done. Arriving at the tree, she throws the pair's sacks to the ground, causing Heldo-Bah to loose a dog's high cry of surprise and alarm; but he quickly caresses the bag, opening it and finding that its contents are safe.

"I thought we understood each other!" Keera lectures, infuriated by the sight of Welferek's motionless, bloody body. "No more killing!"

"Save your scolding, sister," Veloc answers; and for the first time, Keera notices that he is using his gutting blade, not to torment Welferek, but to cut bandages from a length of Broken broadcloth that he has unwound from one of his leggings. "He's not dead."

Heldo-Bah spits once before rejoining Veloc in binding the wounds on Welferek's arms. "Though he'll wish he *was* dead, when he wakes and remembers all this: the damned idiot *fainted*—dead away!"

Keera is still not certain of what she is seeing. "Fainted?" she asks. "And what could you two do to make an Outrager like this one faint?"

"*I* did nothing," Veloc protests, glaring at Heldo-Bah.

"You—? Did nothing?" Heldo-Bah groans mightily. "You did nothing *less* than persuade him that I would carry out the threat!"

"Threat?" Keera demands.

Heldo-Bah turns to her, his face a mask of unjustified persecution. "I would not have done it, Keera, I swear to you—it was only to loosen his tongue! I cut his breeches open, put my knife against his stones, and told him that I would certainly geld him if he didn't tell us—"

Keera nods. "Those were the girlish screams I heard?"

"I drew not one ounce of blood!" Heldo-Bah stamps his feet in protest. "As soon as the blade was on his manhood, he screamed like an ill-used sow, and down he went. He struck his head on that rock there."

Glancing at a sizable lump on Welferek's head, Keera examines the ground beneath it, and finds the rock in question. Heldo-Bah, meanwhile, waits for a further rebuke—and is surprised when none comes. "Then," Keera continues, "he told you nothing about Okot?"

With uncharacteristic suddenness, both Veloc and Heldo-Bah become utterly somber; and as Heldo-Bah undertakes the job of binding Welferek's arm wounds, Veloc takes his sister aside.

"He was nearly unconscious, when he spoke the words, Keera." Veloc is as grave as Keera can remember him ever being: further cause for worry. She waits an instant, then slaps her brother's shoulder.

"And—?"

Veloc's brown eyes stare directly into Keera's blue, knowing what effect his next statement will have: "He spoke of—of plague. In Okot . . ."

The word is nonsense to Keera, at first; but with Veloc's continued hard stare, she allows it as a possibility—and is so stunned that she forgets even to breathe, for an instant, and then must hurry air into her body with a panicked gasp. "Plague? But—we have never—"

"No. The Wood and the river have shielded us," Veloc agrees.

"Which may mean," Heldo-Bah says quietly, with what might pass for tact, "that our luck has held too long. And has now run out . . ."

Keera can say nothing for a moment. When she regains her composure, her mind fastens on practicalities. "Strap your sacks on, both of you," she says, noting Welferek's bound hands. "I'm going to wake him."

"We've tried, Keera," Heldo-Bah says. "It's like asking a log to get up and dance. The man's past distraction."

"We are going to wake him, damn you," Keera begins to shout. "I want to know what he's talking about—there has never been plague in Okot!"

The shrillness of her voice has apparently succeeded where all Heldo-Bah's and Veloc's efforts failed. Welferek's head tosses and he murmurs nonsense for a moment. He then opens his eyes, looking at the foragers, but clearly unsure if he is seeing them.

"Plague—in Okot . . ." Welferek looks down at his bound hands, then at the forest around him, as if these and all other sights are new to him. "There is plague in Okot . . ."

Keera rushes to the man, fastens her powerful hands onto the chest of his tunic and pulls him into a sitting position; then she slams him back against the oak tree. "What are you talking about, Outrager?" she shouts. "What plague?"

Light slowly reenters Welferek's eyes; he recognizes Keera, at last, and then the other two; but precisely who they are and why he is among them is obviously still a mystery. "Do not—return. They're dying—so many are dying." He gasps once, then lifts his arms, oblivious to the pain of his wounds, and puts his bloody, bound hands to either side of Keera's chin, as if he somehow understands her urgency. "Do not return!" he shouts. "There is plague in Okot—*there is plague in Okot!*"

Keera snatches his hands and tears them from her face. Standing, she turns to see that Heldo-Bah and Veloc have fixed their sacks to their shoulders. "We go—*now*," she orders. "Cut him loose—his own men may still be about. If they do not find him, he can make his own way, or be eaten by panthers, I don't care. I will lead."

Veloc touches her arm as she passes. "Keera, we don't know—"

"No," she replies. "We don't. And we won't find out here. Now run, damn you both!"

And, in the time it takes for Welferek's bobbing, slowly clearing head to right itself, the three foragers disappear once again into the deep forest, leaving no trace of their encounter save the Outrager's bandaged wounds and the lump on his head.

1:{*xi:*}

Arnem learns many secrets of his city, and
of the perils it faces . . .

WALKING UP THE CENTER AISLE of the Temple nave, Sixt Arnem has remained a respectful half-step behind Lord Baster-kin, not wishing to presume to equal rank, yet unsure of just what his position has become. He has been named the new commander of the army of Broken; that idea alone would require time for the sentek to take in. But beyond this, he has been unsure of just what Baster-kin needs to tell him concerning the coming campaign against the Bane, and why, if the matter really was and is so urgent, the Merchant Lord has said nothing at all, to this point. Evidently Baster-kin wishes to converse in a place more shielded than the Sacristy of the High Temple; but as to where such a place might be, the sentek can hazard no guess.

As Arnem has continued to follow his lordship through the nave, he has noticed that the east and west walls of that central part of the structure have begun to come to life: the deep indigo illumination of early dawn has begun filtering through tall, wide windows in each of the walls. These windows, like those in the Sacristy, consist of panels of colored glass; but, because secrecy has never been a consideration in the public congregation hall, the panels in its windows were originally made far thinner, which had allowed for them to be leaded together to form enormous patterns of profound complexity[†] that have never failed to awe the many worshippers who, on high holy days, abandon their smaller district temples and stream up the Celestial Way to the High Temple.

Now, as Baster-kin approaches the building's enormous brass doors, which are tended by two priests unfamiliar to Arnem, the Merchant Lord pauses, exchanging a few words with these men outside of Arnem's hearing. The priests nod obediently, then stay where they were as Baster-kin signals to Arnem, telling him to follow into the far eastern corner of the nave. As he obeys this signal, Arnem sees Baster-kin reach for something within his scarlet tunic—an angular object, suspended from his neck on a thin silver chain, which reflects the light of a torch set in a sconce on the nearest of the nave's columns. Soon, Arnem is able to see by that same light that the object is a key of some sort; and, after he has lifted the chain over his head and taken this key in hand, Baster-kin stops before a marble initiation font,[‡] a basin almost three feet wide with a base some five feet square. A small, circular piece of brass[††] is mounted to the bottommost section of the base, and when Baster-kin slides this aside, Arnem can see a finely worked keyhole, also of brass. The Merchant Lord kneels, inserts the key, and turns it, producing clicks: the working of some inner mechanism.

Getting to his feet again, Baster-kin declares, "What I am about to show you, Sentek, are things of which you must never speak to anyone— not even to your wife." Arnem is somewhat taken aback by this reference to Isadora, to whom Baster-kin has only been introduced (so far as Arnem knows) very briefly, during a few official ceremonies; yet there is a vague air of familiarity about this latest statement that the sentek does not care for, and even more ominously, that he fears. *Two things alone can be responsible for it,* Arnem calculates: *ordinary lust, which would be both insulting and ill-considered, and is therefore unlikely; or, full knowledge of Isadora's past—her past, and her activities—which would be less likely, yet far more dangerous . . .* "I have your word that you will maintain such silence?" Baster-kin presses.

"Of course, my lord," Arnem answers. "But I assure you—"

"Perhaps I should not have mentioned it," Baster-kin says quickly; and then he looks away, scowling and annoyed, it seems to Arnem, at his own awkward choice of words. "My apologies. It's simply that, given what we have just observed . . ."

"Yes, my lord," the sentek answers, relieved at the credible statement of contrition. "I understand."

"You are now to learn things you must know, if you are to lead our army—and I think you will appreciate the need for secrecy, once you've seen them." Baster-kin signals to the priests at the Temple doors.

The pair rush to him, seeming to Arnem to require no spoken instruction. Both physically powerful young men, the priests pivot the heavy marble font on the point of its brass locking mechanism, revealing a spiral stone staircase that leads down into utter darkness. The priests stand back, and Baster-kin takes the nearby torch from its sconce.

"These tunnels run between the most important structures in the city," the Merchant Lord explains, leading the way down the steps. "Particularly those that would be crucial during time of siege." As soon as Arnem's head is below the level of the Temple floor, the priests above rotate the font back over the hole, and its locking pivot mechanism makes a rather sharp snapping sound.

Thus sealed into the narrow staircase, Arnem is unable to keep from thinking that this descent into the bowels of the city is not a propitious start to his new command . . .

But, as he reaches the bottom of the steps, the sentek finds a large, vaulted chamber, which offers immediate relief from the cramped stairway. Branching off are perhaps half a dozen roomy tunnels carved through the solid stone, while the chamber itself is filled to brimming with sacks of grain, sides of salt-dried beef and pork, piles of root vegetables—and, finally, enough weapons, Arnem estimates, to arm half a *khotor*.

"We try to replenish the food supplies regularly," Baster-kin announces, his voice uncharacteristically enthusiastic as he moves the torch about the chamber to reveal all of its remarkable contents, "and we do what we can to prevent moisture from rusting the weapons."

"It almost surpasses comprehension," Arnem says, his eyes following the torchlight. "But who instituted this practice?"

Baster-kin shrugs. "It has gone on for many generations, certainly—it was likely part of the original plan of the Mad King himself. I had the full system of tunnels and chambers mapped, when I assumed my office, and created an inventory of their contents—enough to secure the city for months, at the very least, if need be."

Still inspecting the chamber, Arnem finds one thing glaringly absent: "And water?" he asks. "I see no cistern."

Baster-kin nods. "It has never been a consideration—we have always had an abundance of water, from the various spring-fed wells through-out the city, many of which are connected through fissures in the stone summit of the mountain, out of which Broken's walls were carved. That is why we take this matter of the poisoned well so seriously: I've long had a suspicion that the Bane knew how much we would depend on the re-sources that lie within the city walls, during a crisis, and that they might send Outragers to make some brazen attempt to pollute them—as they now have. I can't even be sure that killing the God-King was their pri-mary purpose—it might have been merely a fortunate secondary result. As it turns out, since the damage seems confined to the one well, it suits our purposes more than theirs . . ." The Merchant Lord thrusts his hands into a grain sack, examining its contents carefully, as he continues to speak contemplatively: "I'm having every other well watched, as we speak, of course, in the event that they try again—or, worse yet, that the poison should find its way into other reserves at some future date. But for now . . ."

Baster-kin becomes even more inscrutable, for a moment, his eyes narrowing as he examines his handful of grain; and Arnem finds him-self, while impressed, a little confused. "My lord?" he says. "You seem perturbed, rather than relieved. If I may say so. Do you fear the grain stores have also been tampered with?"

"Not yet," Baster-kin replies, his mind clearly wrestling with the thought. "But we must be ever-vigilant . . ." Shaking himself, he turns to the sentek once again. "You and I, however, are not farmers, to vex our-selves with such matters—and yet now it is *you* who look uncertain."

"Well—perhaps not uncertain," Arnem answers quickly. "But—in the Sacristy, earlier, you did make it sound as though the Bane's sole purpose was to assassinate—"

"Oh, yes, yes," Baster-kin replies, waving the fact off with one hand as he replaces the grain. "As I say, the event has as yet served our purposes far more than theirs: particularly yours and mine. The Layzin's energies are—*overtaxed,* as you saw; and the version of events I relayed to him, and thus to the God-King, was not incorrect. I merely laid more emphasis on certain details than on others, in order to make the case as simple to comprehend as possible. I trust you can see that?"

Arnem knows that much depends upon the nature of his answer to this seemingly harmless question: he is being invited into a conspiracy, of sorts—one with a noble purpose, perhaps, but with consequences that belie its innocent tone. And so he accepts without detailing his complete opinions: "Yes, my lord," he says simply.

"Good. Fine." The Merchant Lord is clearly pleased. "But come—I am expected at the Merchants' Hall. Or rather, beneath it . . ."

Arnem studies Lord Baster-kin's face as they begin to move quickly along one of the many tunnels out of the storage area, soon passing into and out of another vaulted stone chamber. The sentek can see that the Merchant Lord's evident concern for the city, which so often seems obnoxiously zealous in the company of others, somehow assumes a vastly different and more appealing quality, when one is allowed to view its private, even secret, manifestations: its careful inspections and judgments of the materials necessary for the public good in a time of crisis.

"Was Yantek Korsar aware of all this?" Arnem asks, still quite amazed at the extent, not only of the underground maze of expertly carved chambers and tunnels, but of the amount of supplies that are hoarded away in them, and kept replenished for use at any time.

"He was," Baster-kin replies, speaking in an odd manner: not out of harshness or rancor, but rather with something oddly like sad admiration. "But we were under the impression that you *knew* he was . . ."

Arnem needs no explanation of this statement: Baster-kin is plainly referring to Niksar's role as a spy. But he does not say so at once: "No, my lord—the yantek never shared such knowledge with me," he says. "In addition, another commander might wonder at how you can be so knowledgeable about what confidences the—" He is on the verge of saying "the yantek" again, but catches himself, remembering the Merchant Lord's admonition against such in the Sacristy "—what confidences *Herwald* Korsar and I exchanged."

Baster-kin nods, appreciating the gesture. "Another commander would have done a great many things far differently than you have, Sentek. For instance, you're aware that Linnet Niksar spies for us; you've been aware of it for some time. I know it, the Layzin knows it, and the God-King knows it. Yet you have made no protest." When Baster-kin glances back to find Arnem still more dumbfounded, he laughs once sharply—a rare and remarkable event. It produces a sound that is too sudden, too ill practiced to be pleasant: how much worse would the effect be, Arnem wonders, if it happened in a room full of dignitaries? Yet here, in private, the awkwardness of the laughter can be overlooked, and the sentiment behind it valued. "You needn't look so shocked, Sentek," says Baster-kin, his voice becoming businesslike once more. "We knew you were aware of Linnet Niksar's role, as I say, but we also knew that you neither held it as a mark against your aide, nor ceased to place your full trust in him. Thus we, in turn, were given additional reason to trust *you*. That counted for a great deal, I don't mind telling you, with both the God-King and the Grand Layzin. You're an exceptional man, Arnem, and an even more exceptional commander. I'm sorry for Korsar, I truly am— but his time had long since passed, even before he gave voice to heresy and treason. No, this moment belongs to *you*, Sentek—make the most of it. Continued trustworthiness would be a fine first step, along those lines, and if eliminating the pretense with Niksar will help, we can easily arrange it."

Still unaccustomed to such collegiality from his lordship, Arnem simply says, "It will help both Niksar and myself, Lord Baster-kin; I thank you."

The sentek's attitude toward Baster-kin is transforming: Arnem has always respected the Merchant Lord, but now, to walk with him in these secret passageways and learn their equally secret purpose, to talk to him as an equal about the inner workings of the kingdom, and to gain deeper insight into how this man, who is the very embodiment of Broken power, thinks, as well as into how he manipulates even the supreme authorities of the great kingdom for their own good and preservation . . . It is enough to deeply humble anyone, much less a man who was once a troublesome youth from the Fifth District—and Arnem is humbled, indeed: where there had been only sadness for his old friend Korsar not long ago, there is now a profound sense, not only of humility, but of Fate. Fate, which has chosen Arnem to lead the mighty army of Broken in a cause that will bring greater security to the subjects of Broken, and greater safety to the God-King. Yes, humility and Fate: these are the forces driving Arnem's actions.

Or so he finds it comfortable to believe, for the moment . . .

In this way, he soon grows to feel that he can presume—humbly, of course—to voice the most critical question of all: "My lord, if I may ask— you have said that this campaign will have a goal far greater than the destruction of the Bane. What might that goal be?"

As he begins to answer this question, Baster-kin guides the way from the tunnel through which they have been traveling into a secondary, steadily widening passageway, one that soon opens out onto a large stair- case leading up to a formal doorway, into which is set a series of stout oak boards, banded to form a door by thick straps of iron.

"Let me answer that question with another, Sentek. Herwald Korsar believed that the Merchants' Council arranged this campaign simply to make ourselves richer. But am I right to suppose that you do not?"

Arnem does not hesitate. "You are correct, my lord. If all you desired was greater wealth, there are far more efficient ways to gain it."

"Precisely," Baster-kin judges, further pleased by Arnem's answer. "Given the amount of blood, effort, and riches we will have to put into taking the Wood and destroying the Bane, it hardly makes sense as a business undertaking—the expedition will likely not pay even its own costs. But there are deeper questions involved."

As they pass the halfway point of the staircase, Arnem's attention is diverted when he hears water flowing, seemingly inside the mass of stone beneath the steps. "The sewers?" he asks. "Are we really so low?"

"We are lower still," Baster-kin replies. "The city's sewer system in fact runs *above* these tunnels. Look there . . ."

Arnem has reached the top of the steps, and sees that, indeed, one sec- tion of Broken's extensive (and pungent) sewer system runs beneath the landing at the top of the steps, then into an opening above the tunnels he has just left. "It really was a fantastic vision, that of the Mad King," Baster-kin muses in appreciation.

"In truth," Arnem agrees. "And fortunate that he worked in solid stone—for what else could have survived intact for all these ages?"

Baster-kin only nods thoughtfully—perhaps (or so Arnem supposes) even a little worriedly. "Indeed," his lordship murmurs, and then he sud- denly returns to business once more: "However, as we were saying: the destruction of the Bane will likely be an undertaking that will not even pay its own cost. Certainly not in the short term."

Arnem's eyes squint a bit. "And so—why undertake it *now*?"

"Arnem," Baster-kin says, as he pulls the large key over his head again, "when was the last time you were in those areas of the kingdom that lie between this mountain and the Meloderna?"

"It must have been—well, some time ago, my lord. It's the irony of the soldier's life—we join to serve, but also for adventure; yet most of our time is spent in endless drilling and preparing for events that we hope will never come to pass. In the meantime, the world goes by."

"Well—be that as it may, Sentek, you shall have the chance to see some of that world again, and soon." Baster-kin approaches the oak door at the top of the stairs, fits the key into another brass hole much like that in the initiation font, and prepares to turn it. "You will need to gather supplies for your men, and forage for your horses. And when you do, you will see that matters have—changed, in much of the kingdom. There is no reason for me to elaborate now"—Baster-kin gives his key a quick turn, at which a locking mechanism inside the oak planks gives out clicking sounds almost identical to those that Arnem heard in the Temple—"but we face grave dangers, Sentek. Dangers made all the more deadly because so few of our citizens either see or concern themselves with them." Pushing the oak door once, Baster-kin leads the way into the chamber beyond.

Arnem follows, and finds himself in yet another large space with a high and vaulted ceiling—but this one is more familiar. It is the cellar of the Merchants' Hall, which Arnem has been in before. The cellar walls are bare stone, and the vaulting above supports the long, planked floor of the spacious Hall, gathering place of Broken's most powerful citizens, where they sit in council, enjoy meals, and, in honor of Kafra, often spend late nights away from their families in the company of young ladies whose names they scarcely know. Such entertainment is apparently being played out this very night, to judge by the sounds of laughter, breaking glass, and men's and women's voices that echo through the floor.

Baster-kin looks up. "Yes, they are at their favorite form of worship yet again," the Merchant Lord says, with frowning disgust. "Fools. But"—Baster-kin leads Arnem to the far side of the torch-lit cellar—"the Layzin approves of their pursuits, as does the God-King. Revels in the Hall, and games in the Stadium, without respite—and men like you and I to tend to the state in the meantime, eh?"

From out of the half-light, a large opening in one end of the cellar is illuminated by both Baster-kin's torch from below and the steadily if slowly progressing light of dawn from above, both sources of illumination revealing a massive stone ramp that leads to the avenue above. "And now, Arnem, having seen many of our secret strengths, you must be told of our equally shrouded weaknesses: and the largely unrecognized truth, Sentek, is that the present actions of the Bane—even this poisoning attempt—represent less of a threat to both our safety and our commerce than does the very fact of their existence." And then another of his lordship's strange moments of seeming uncertainty, even discouragement, grips him: "We are not, as a people, inclined to concern ourselves with what takes place beyond our own frontiers; it is a tendency that develops among superior societies. But some of us *must* keep such watch. And I tell you, Sentek—we have no reason to feel easy about the world beyond Broken. Indeed, we will, in the months to come, be pressed by would-be conquerors as never before."

"But—why, my lord? Since the Torganian war—"

"A great victory, certainly—but your stand at the Atta Pass[†] was *eight years* ago, Arnem. And during that time, traders have taken tales back to their peoples, tales of how the mighty kingdom of Broken cannot effectively control a population of misshapen, dwarfish exiles.[‡] We begin to appear weak, despite all that you and the army have done. Think on it, for a moment—what conclusion would *you* draw, in their place? Bane traders come and go in Daurawah almost at will. They meet foreign traders, there, and tell them of our weakness, and of how our own citizens breed too fast, for a kingdom our size. Not that they need be told—any foreigner with eyes can see for himself, in Daurawah, how farmers' and fishermen's second and third sons every day give up their families' vital forms of work and come to Broken to seek easy fortunes. We *must* have new land to clear and work, our enemies can see that, as well—and they are well aware of the only region where we can secure such territory with relative ease. But instead, we allow the Bane to survive, even to attack our people." Baster-kin's voice has continued to decrease in volume, Arnem notices, even though he and the Merchant Lord are seemingly still alone. "In short, Sentek, I must tell you that there is much truth to these tales. Oh, not that the Bane represent a direct threat—that's nonsense, of course. But no one knows better than you do, that fewer and fewer young men willingly enter the regular army, and that those who do are increasingly from the Fifth District—men hungry only for regular pay. And I will not even touch upon the difficulty I have in securing good men for my Guard—only look at the specimens I had escort you to the Temple tonight. Bullies, degenerates, near-idiots, some of them; yet better candidates . . ." Baster-kin's eyes stare off at the stone ramp that appears, from his vantage point, to lead up to the peaceful, early morning sky. "Better candidates pass their hours competing and gaming in the Stadium—at best."

"Aye, my lord, it is so," Arnem answers, uneasy at Baster-kin's latest change in mood, and feeling, as well, the uncertainty that nearly always plagues him when talking of weighty state affairs. "But what *of* that same Fifth District? Surely, if we need new space in the city, we should cleanse and restore it. It was not always such a sinkhole, after all—"

Baster-kin smiles. "Spoken as a patriot, and a man loyal to his district. I applaud the thought, Arnem—but you do not understand the difficulty of such an undertaking. For the act of rehabilitation will be, politically, not simply in the doing—we shall need your men, and especially yourself, home to do it. If the people are to believe in the rewards with which Kafra blesses the faithful and diligent, they must also see how he punishes those of faint heart and will; and punish them we shall. Severely enough that the eastern marauders, the Torganians and the Frankesh to the south, and, perhaps most ominously of all, the Varisians to the north with their longboats,[†] will remember the forceful respect we have always made them pay us." Seeing that Arnem is disturbed by such harsh talk about his home district, Baster-kin assumes a reassuring air: "Fear not— nothing will be done without your presence and approval. These are the facts, however, with which we are faced, Arnem, and I enjoy them even less than you do, make no mistake. Yet we have it in us, I believe, to remedy all these situations. So be bold, and be swift. The quicker you destroy the Bane and take control of as much of the Wood as we require, the greater the legend of your conquest will grow within and without the kingdom, and the sooner you can return home to consolidate matters here. That should suffice to convince all would-be enemies that, if they choose a fight with us, they make a very poor decision."

Arnem has weighed Baster-kin's points, and found most of them sound; on only one or two counts does he feel the need for more details, plainly spoken, and so he determines to ask—

But as he does, a sound rises up to challenge the din of the reveling merchants above: it is a scream even more arresting than that Arnem heard earlier atop the city walls—a scream of undiluted agony.

Arnem instinctively draws his short-sword, and steps before the Merchant Lord, half-suspecting that an attack of some kind is under way. But Baster-kin only mutters under his breath, and then says aloud:

"Do not be alarmed, Arnem. It is likely of no consequence. But my Guard were able to lay hands on at least one of the Bane assassins who poisoned the well outside the Inner City. It would appear I am needed—"

Arnem, in a moment of revulsion, cannot help but touch Baster-kin's arm, as the latter starts away: "An Outrager?"

Glancing at Arnem's hand briefly and indulgently, but with indignation enough to make the sentek remove it immediately, the Merchant Lord replies, "Not such as you or I would recognize—a trader, to judge by appearances. Of that smaller stature, and with neither the clothing nor the arms peculiar to the Outragers and their absurd 'knighthood.'" Baster-kin sighs, looking across the chamber half-heartedly. "Every day, the exiles grow more clever—and more deadly . . ." He starts away, saying only, "I will be but a few moments—but you must allow me to . . ."

"My lord!" Arnem calls, intending to keep his words and their tone subdued, but failing singularly. "It was my understanding that the God-King Izairn had suspended all such coercion."

"He did," Baster-kin says. "But only on the advice of his Second Minister, the sorcerer Caliphestros. Our present monarch, having allowed the torture of the acolytes of Caliphestros after the sorcerer's banishment, has continued the practice." Pausing in attempted sympathy, Baster-kin nods. "I know how you soldiers feel, Arnem—you believe that physical torment produces unreliable results, designed to please the tormentor. And that it puts your own men at risk of revenge, should they be captured by our enemies."[†]

"Indeed, my lord," the sentek answers confidently. "The Bane did not create their 'Woodland Knights' until we had tortured enough of what we thought dangerous men and women of their tribe who came to the city to trade—and, I must remind you, no act of treachery was ever proved against any of them. Not until—"

"Until this attempt to murder the God-King?" Baster-kin interjects, his voice even, but his words pointed. "You don't consider that a remarkable exception?" Arnem gazes downward, realizing that his last words may have defeated his cause. "And who knows how many other examples, in earlier years, were not the first stirrings of similar plots? Plots that we exposed early enough to save a Guardsman's or a soldier's life? I remind you, Sentek, that it was Oxmontrot himself—he to whom you and your men look for inspiration and with such admiration—who made the practice of torture, not only acceptable, but *required,* when examining persons of humble or even of consequential status; and that he did so in imitation—as was so often his habit—of the *Lumun-jani.* It is a policy with which even I, who do not share your martial admiration for our founding king, can find no fault." Seeing that his words, while persuasive, are not yet convincing, Baster-kin presses: "Think of the matter just as the *Lumun-jani* have done for so long, Arnem: *without* both the threat and the practice of torture, who knows what additional lies such prisoners would concoct? What incentive does a man who would poison a city well have to speak the truth, save the prevention or cessation of agony?" Confusion replaces stubborn disagreement in Arnem's features, and Baster-kin returns to him. "It is not as though we conduct the practice in the manner of the eastern marauders or the Varisians, Arnem. There is no joy in it, for myself or for the men I have trained in its use; but we have learnèd minds in this city that have made a study of the business. And so . . ."

Baster-kin strides to the area from which the scream emerged, and pounds on what must be a door, from the sound of it—although Arnem can see no such details, in the darkness at the far end of the cellar. Then a long shaft of light appears: the space between a door that is opening and its frame, leading into yet another chamber, another corner of the world within the mountaintop that Oxmontrot may have built, but over which Lord Baster-kin has made himself master. The shaft of light remains visible only for a moment, but it is long enough for Arnem to detect both more cries of pain from beyond, and the Merchant Lord's controlled, chastising voice, speaking indistinctly, but with intent. Then, the shaft of light disappears soundlessly, at which Baster-kin returns, as quickly as he departed.

"I apologize, Sentek," he says. "I had thought we were finished with the man. Evidently not. He confirmed the poisoning plot, but we have been trying to ascertain if he has any further information that might be of use—the location of more Outragers in the city, most importantly."

Indicating the door in the darkness, Arnem says only: "So that chamber is where such—*work* is carried out?"

"Yes," Baster-kin replies, not entirely comfortably. "Along with several more beyond it. Our own, more worldly 'Sacristy,' if you will. With its own sacred implements . . ."

Arnem feels a passing urge to renew the two men's philosophical debate—but there is no purpose, he realizes. Clearly, both Baster-kin and his Merchants' Council, having extracted the information concerning the poisoning of the well through torture, will not listen to arguments against such techniques. All that the sentek feels now is a sudden need to be gone.

"My lord," he says, "I have much to prepare, and little time. Therefore, with your permission—"

"Of course, Arnem. My thanks for your patience. And if it is agreeable to you, I think that a parade and departure in the late afternoon will show your men off to their greatest advantage in front of the citizens."

"As you wish, my lord."

"Would you like my Guard to escort you home?" Baster-kin asks, with seeming earnestness. "I don't imagine you need it, but—"

"You are correct, my lord. I do not. And so . . ."

"Yes. Until tomorrow. Try to get some rest. It will be an exhausting business—these public affairs always are. I'd ask you to come upstairs, where I fear I must make a brief official appearance, but I very much doubt that you'd enjoy it . . ."

"No, my lord," Arnem agrees quickly. "And my wife will be waiting."

"Ah, yes. Your wife. I understand that you have been—*lucky,* in that regard."

Again, there is something in Baster-kin's tone, when he speaks of Isadora, that Arnem both dislikes and fears; but by now, the new commander of the army of Broken is too weary and baffled to pursue the matter, and so answers simply, "Indeed I have been, my lord. These many years."

"Yes," Baster-kin murmurs. "Fortunate, indeed. Speaking of which, we haven't had a chance to discuss your—*family situation.*" Serious purpose fills Baster-kin's face. "It is one of the effects of your great success. Were you a less consequential man, perhaps we might have let it go . . . But, as you are not, the matter will have to be resolved soon, Arnem."

"And I have no doubt that it will be," the sentek replies.

Baster-kin seems to realize he can ask only so much, at so rare a moment. "Yes. Time enough for such matters to be settled upon your return. Which I do not doubt will be triumphant. But keep it in your thoughts."

"It rarely leaves them, my lord," Arnem answers, starting up the stone ramp toward the light of earliest dawn. "And so, by your leave, I will bid you good night."

Baster-kin says nothing, only lifts a hand in acknowledgment; but when Arnem reaches the top of the ramp, he looks back down into the cellar, watching the Merchant Lord's movements—

And he is not entirely surprised to see that Baster-kin does not, in fact, take the stairs leading up, in order to make his appearance in the Merchants' Hall; rather, he goes back to the doorway of the room where the Bane Outrager, Arnem is sure, continues to be tortured.

Turning to face the slowly brightening sky, Arnem breathes deep, glad to be away from the business of state and as confused as he can ever remember being. He will need some time, to assess all that has happened; time—and his wife. His Isadora: *"Lucky, in that regard . . ."* Why, of all the statements that the Merchant Lord has made this evening, is it such a trivial comment that echoes so relentlessly in the sentek's mind? He knows of the rumors that circulate concerning the tragic illness of Lord Baster-kin's own wife—who has not been seen in public for many years—and of the Merchant Lord's heroic efforts to attend to his spouse's every need; is it simply the unpleasant taint of envy in Baster-kin's voice that sparked Arnem's uneasiness? Does the appearance of *any* weakness, in this man who is ordinarily so haughty and self-assured, bring on some unwelcome sense that Broken itself is not so mighty as it appears? Or is Arnem displeased to think of himself as someone who can find room in his spirit, at such an important moment in the life of the kingdom, for base, boyish jealousy at the mere mention of his wife's name by another man of influence and power?

Longing for the comforts of his home, his family, and slumber, Arnem turns to begin walking at a healthy pace down the Celestial Way toward the Fifth District of the city. But as he sets out he sees, through the early mist of a spring dawn, the distant sight of Lord Baster-kin's Plain, and the black mass of Davon Wood spreading away beyond.

It is a vivid and unwelcome reminder, one that will make sleep impossible in the few hours he has until assembly sounds: for, when dawn breaks fully, Arnem's oldest friend, Herwald Korsar—"*Yantek* Korsar," Arnem says aloud, pointedly defying the stricture never to so refer to his comrade again—will be taken to that very edge of the Wood. He will then be tied by his forearms and thighs between two trees, after which two priests of Kafra—using ceremonial knives and axes from the Sacristy, their polished steel blades, engraved brass fittings, and well-turned ash handles making them seem unsuited to so base a task—will sever both of Korsar's legs at the knee. If the yantek is lucky and the priests are skilled, only two swings of the sacred axes will be needed; but whatever the case, he will be left hanging, to bleed to death or be torn apart by scavenging wolves and bears while still alive, after having been literally reduced to the stature of a Bane. It is the ritual's ultimate purpose (along with the suffering that leads to it), for no more ignoble end could be imagined—particularly for so great a soldier as Korsar . . .

Thinking of this, Arnem decides that he will run home, to the comfort that discussion of such subjects with his wife nearly always brings; and his pace, as he sets out, is rapid, indeed.

$$1:\{xii:\}$$

The Bane foragers learn the inscrutability of all
gods—even their Moon . . .

THERE IS NO ONE ALIVE who knows Davon Wood better than do Bane foragers, of whom Keera's party are the most experienced; and, while their lungs may be small, the foragers have developed the ability to maintain fast paces over distances far longer than any laurelled champions of the Tall. Imagine, then, how fast a Bane mother who is also a forager, and who harbors the deepest fears for the fate of her family, might run. Imagine it, increase it, endow it with any superlative you may wish to conjure—and you will yet be unable to describe the pace that Keera has set for Veloc and Heldo-Bah on the dash from the *Ayerzess-werten* to their home of Okot. More remarkable still, the two men behind her have never once complained of that pace, never once asked for respite; nay, not even for a sip of water from the skins they carry. For they know only too well that they are not mere athletes striving to add luster to their names: they are tribe members who have learned that the blackest horror has, after two hundred years of safety, struck their home; and they run to know what price the Death has exacted from their people.

Dawn begins to break, and life to stir, in the vast wilderness; but among the three foragers, it is noted only because the markings along the trail they follow become easier to see. It is a merciless bit of irony that these same markings, which usually impart the happiness of being ever closer to home, now only heighten the agony of the possibility that such joy may be gone forever. Keera's disciplined mind works hard to push aside her mounting fears; but what occupies her thoughts instead is not hope of a happy resolution. Rather, she puzzles with the supreme mystery that eventually befalls every soul that harbors true faith in a divine providence:

How could her deity have forsaken her? How could the Moon have inflicted the Death upon her tribe and her family?

Has *she* brought it on her people, by battling the Knights with her brother and Heldo-Bah, and thus insulting the Priestess of the Moon? It cannot be, for then the punishment would be hers alone. And what of Heldo-Bah's many crimes, and Veloc's too-frequent participation in them? There are no answers, here, either, for Heldo-Bah has paid the price with the loss of his freedom forever, while Veloc, too, submits himself to punishment when he thus angers the Priestess, the Lunar Sisters, and the Groba Elders; and even if he did not, where is the divine proportion in meting out plague to punish a few brawls? Is not the Moon a deity of compassion? And if she is not, then what marks her as superior to the Tall's absurd and vicious golden god, Kafra?

There—in the distance: Keera can see the trees thin, and then, away past that point, the last of the downward grade that ends in the rapid drop of the high cliffs that form the northern edge of Okot. In mere moments, they should be upon—nay: *They are upon them already!* Hidden, in the ghostly light that is the Wood at dawn: huts. Bane huts. Deserted.

And no sign of the fires that should be burning, now, with great-bellied cook-pots atop them, heating the morning gruel with boiled wood-fruits—dried apples, pears, and plums—that, sometimes fortified by a few thin strips of boar's back cooked on a skillet of flat iron, constitutes nearly every Bane's first meal. But here, among these twenty or so thatched huts . . . nothing. Not even the light of fat-lamps within . . .

For the first time, Keera slows, and comes to a halt. As her lungs work hard, she stares about in bewilderment, fearing—not fearing, *hoping*—that she has lost the trail, and stumbled upon some old settlement that has fallen into disuse: the sort of place in which Heldo-Bah spent much of his early manhood. But the markings are just where they should be, prominently cut into large rocks and ancient trees. Now as ever, Keera is on the trail she intended to follow, and she and her companions are in one of the northern settlements that surmount the cliffs ahead: they are, in fact, among the community of Bane healers and their families, who carry on their noble work inside the caves that pock the faces of those same cliffs, the barely accessible retreats called the *Lenthess-steyn*.[†] It is possible, of course, that the healers are in those caves even now, if the Outrager Welferek spoke the truth, and did not concoct a callous lie to spare himself torment at the hands of Heldo-Bah; and yet—

If the healers are in the *Lenthess-steyn*, then where are their families? Where are the signs of daily life? *Where are their children?*

Heldo-Bah and Veloc draw up next to Keera, each man more winded than their leader, and both, like her, staring about in consternation.

"Where—?" Veloc draws in one enormous breath, in order to speak the question that all are asking themselves: "The healers—their wives, their husbands—?" (For women are among the most skilled of the Bane healers.) "Have they been attacked?"

"I've warned them!" Heldo-Bah declares in a gasping roar, putting his hands to his knees and bending over, the better to take in air. "How many times have I warned them? *Move the healers,* I've said, they are atop the cliffs, too far north, they will be the first to go, should the Tall find us, but who listens to a criminal—*yaeeyah!*" The gap-toothed forager squeals in pain as Veloc swats an open hand across the exposed back of his head. Heldo-Bah thinks to retaliate, but a look at Veloc, who nods quickly at the still-silent Keera, reminds him that the only order of business, now, is to discover what can have happened here.

Anxious to redeem himself for his thoughtlessness, Heldo-Bah approaches a hut. "Well, we're not going to learn anything if we don't look . . ."

Keera spins about when she hears this. "Heldo-Bah!" she calls, displaying something as close to panic as she ever has. "Do not enter—if the Death has taken the healers, it will take you too!"

Heldo-Bah knows not to enter, at this moment, into an argument with Keera over whether he is really foolish enough to enter a plague hut; and so he limits his reply to, "Believe me, Keera, I have no intention of going inside!" Heldo-Bah draws to a stop; and then advances on his toes. "These huts have not been attacked," he calls, spying slapdash crescent Moons that have been painted on each structure's door. "They've been abandoned—abandoned and sealed, Keera!" The door to the hut he approaches is shut tight, and across every window opening thick planks have been fixed. Any gaps around the door and between the window openings and the boards have been filled with a thick paste, white streaked with purple: almost a mortar, which has not yet had time to fully dry.

"Stay well back!" Keera commands, now facing each hut in turn, noticing the same purple-streaked white paste about every opening, and retreating as if from some deadly enemy. "Quicklime and meadow bells—it is plague of the bowels, then," she says. "They will have removed all of the families to—"

A new voice interrupts: "Ho! What are you doing here?"

The three foragers close ranks to watch as a Bane soldier emerges from the dawn mist east of the healers' huts. He wears the standard protection of the Bane army: a hauberk, extending from elbow to neck to knee, and composed of iron scales stitched onto deerskin. It is armor far more ambitious in design than it is effective in battle,[†] during which the comparatively broad spacing of the large scales caused by the limitations of Bane metalworking too often allows both spear and sword points to penetrate gaps, while the size of the scales makes movement difficult. Like Welferek, the soldier carries a short-sword in the Broken mold, save that his is an obvious Bane imitation, its steel being of a visibly inferior quality. The same is true of the single-piece helmet that covers his head and nose: the brass fitted to the edges of the iron sections cannot hide the inferior grade of the iron itself.[‡] What he lacks in quality weapons, however, the young man makes up in self-possession: the Bane army—as re-imagined by its leader, Yantek Ashkatar—is a relatively new creation, less than a dozen years old, and the men who fill its ranks hide their in-experience and inferior arms with all the courage they can muster, al-though they disdain the arrogant pride of the Outragers, for whom they have as little liking or use as do the foragers.

"Entry to this settlement has been forbidden by the Groba," the sol-dier says firmly. But, as he comes closer, he notes the hefty sack that each of the newcomers carries. "Ah," the soldier noises with a nod. "Foragers." The lad is still raw enough to feel that he must not allow his lack of expe-rience to show, especially at this crucial hour; and so he buries it beneath a tone of authority. "But I perceive that you are only just returning. You answer the call of the Horn?"

"Oh, admirable," Heldo-Bah answers, spitting onto the ground near the soldier's boots. "You must already have achieved high rank, with that kind of quick thinking—" Veloc delivers a sharp elbow in his friend's side for this, which allows Keera to ask:

"Where have they been taken? The families that lived here—surely the plague cannot have taken them all."

But the soldier's eyes are on the most notorious member of the party: "You're Heldo-Bah, aren't you? I recognize you."

"Tragically, I can't return the compliment," Heldo-Bah replies.

"It's no compliment, friend, believe me," the soldier says, with a sour laugh. He half-turns, and assumes a more respectful tone. "And that would make you Keera, the tracker?"

"Please," Keera says, uninterested in reputations or conversation. "What's happened to them? And what—"

Suddenly, she turns fully about on the toes of one foot, stopping when she faces just north of east. She puts the infallible nose in the air once again, and having sniffed, her face goes pale, as she turns back to the soldier. "Fire," she says, in almost a whisper. "They are burning huts!"

The soldier nods at the huts around them. "And they'll be burning *these,* soon enough. Sealing them has not confined it."

"But what do they burn *now*?" Veloc asks impatiently.

"The northeastern settlement; it was taken first—"

"*No!*" Keera cries, loosening the straps of her bag, dropping it, and dashing in the direction of the smoke on the wind. "That is *my* home!"

Veloc follows quickly, as Heldo-Bah picks up Keera's sack and throws it on his back beside his own. He looks at the soldier, shaking his head and spitting again.

"Well done, fool. Speaking without thinking: continue with it, you'll rise to sentek like a star crossing the heavens . . ."

Heldo-Bah rushes to catch his friends, and contrition enters the young soldier's face; he has enough pride of rank left, however, to call, "But you can't go there—we've surrounded it, they'll not let you near!"

Heldo-Bah, the added weight of Keera's bag scarcely slowing him, bellows back, "We'll just brave that risk!" as he moves on, through the sealed, ghostly huts, and into the shadow world of the woodland morning.

The northeastern is in many ways the most important of the Bane settlements, for it has always been the belief of the Groba that, should the Tall ever determine the location of Okot, they will enter by way of this less direct approach. And so, for several years, the residents of the settlement have been witness to the construction of a stout palisade just beyond the outer limit of their several rings of huts: the Groba's attempt, in pursuit of the Lunar Sisterhood's vision, to offer at least the appearance of a defense. But Okot as a whole is too vast and ill-arranged a community for even its tireless builders to enclose it in one palisade; and so, half a mile to either side of the large gate in the wall that guards the northeastern route into the central square of the town, the fortification simply stops. It has ever been the ambition of the Groba Elders to continue its construction, but both the builders and the current commanders of the Bane army are hard-pressed to see the reason for any more of a show than has already been constructed—and they are confident that the palisade would *be* but a show, should the Tall army ever arrive in force with their engines of war.

Keera reaches the westernmost end of the palisade, covering the mile's distance from the lime-sealed healers' huts in mere moments. But here she hesitates: the upper flames of the enormous pillar of fire ahead are already visible. Her anxious pause allows Veloc and Heldo-Bah to catch her up, and Veloc lays hold of her right wrist.

"Sister," he says, himself filled with anxiousness. "I beg you, let us go in first. If nothing else, let Heldo-Bah go. He knows how to manage these boys that the Groba calls soldiers, and he knows Ashkatar[†] well—"

"Although I'm not entirely sure how much help *that* will be," Heldo-Bah murmurs, making sure that Keera does not hear.

"—and he can prevent any more confrontations that eat up precious time," Veloc goes on, giving Heldo-Bah a warning glance. "He can ensure that we get news without delay. Correct, Heldo-Bah?"

"Of course," Heldo-Bah answers, his gentler tone reflecting a change in his heart. "Keera—I will. I pledge it."

Keera had thought to be the first to the flames; all through the run from the river, she had become ever more determined to confront whoever has control of the disastrous state of affairs. But now, faced with the sight of fire scorching the leaves of the forest ceiling—

For the first time in their lives, her brother sees her lose heart. *This cannot be happening,* says her visage; *and yet it is . . .*

Keera clasps her hands before her face. "But I—" She searches the morning sky for the Moon, the deity who, it seems to her, hides in shame behind the western trees. *"But I was ever faithful!"* she cries, and correctly: she has always been among the most devout of Bane women, outside of the Lunar Sisterhood, and yet now she watches the flames consuming the home that she made in accordance with the tenets of her faith, and in which she taught her children to be similarly devout . . .

Veloc looks to Heldo-Bah, as he puts his arms around his sister. "I will bring her presently," he says to his friend. "Go, and learn what you can."

Heldo-Bah nods, dropping his own foraging sack, along with Keera's, and heading off down the palisade; although his own trepidation makes him approach the scene of evident destruction at half-speed. Even this is fast enough, however, to cause the first soldiers to become visible just as he comes within sight of the burning huts themselves.

At the approach of two pallins (and why, in the Moon's name, Heldo-Bah asks silently, did they feel it necessary to adopt the ranks and organization of the accursèd army of Broken?), Heldo-Bah hears a crack, and sees that groups of soldiers are felling unburned trees to create a cordon of emptiness around the conflagration and prevent its spread: for, despite the moistness of a spring morning in the green wilderness, fire as hot as this is strong enough to spread through any woodland.

"Stay back, forager!" one of the pallins coming along the palisade calls out with authority, trying, like all the Bane army, to keep some semblance of order and prevent such torturous bewilderment as Keera is now experiencing from becoming fully fledged panic throughout Okot. Nevertheless, the unpleasant familiarity of being spoken down to causes Heldo-Bah to reach, imperceptibly, for his knives. He can see that the soldiers are covered in sweat and ash, and that their bodies are burnt, in several spots fairly badly.

"We act on the orders of the Groba!" a second pallin shouts.

Ready to let his knives fly at any moment, Heldo-Bah asks the soldiers: "And what makes you think I'm a forager, you scaly little snakes?" (It is a popular taunt: Bane soldiers are mocked, even by children, for the resemblance of their armor to the scales of a snake.)

"Don't test us," the second soldier says. "The only members of the tribe still returning to Okot are foragers—you're the last of them, I expect. And while you've been running home, we've been tending to the welfare of the tribe."

"Yes, I can see that," Heldo-Bah replies, smiling. "Burning down homes, a most imaginative method." He nods toward the huts. "What's become of those who lived here?"

"Why do you ask?" answers the second soldier, who, though young, is meaty enough to think that he might give this forager a good thrashing— even though he has apparently seen the filed teeth in the newcomer's mouth. "I know who you are, Heldo-Bah, and you've certainly never lived here."

Heldo-Bah nods, and even laughs once. "Which only shows what an infant warrior you are, for all your scaly skin. Answer my question."

"Most are dead," says the first soldier evenly. "Those who have survived are in the *Lenthess-steyn,* being cared for by the healers."

"Have you kept some kind of record of who has died?" Heldo-Bah asks. "Or would that be too inglorious an activity for young heroes?"

A third voice joins the fray, coming from the direction of the men felling trees; a booming, commanding voice, full of a self-assurance that, unlike the younger men's, bespeaks hard years of experience:

"There was no time for lists, Heldo-Bah," the voice says. "The plague kills too quickly—and it spreads even faster . . ."

Approaching the forager is a formidable Bane. Clearly older than Heldo-Bah, his muscles are yet ponderous and tough: not chiseled like an athlete's, but built thick by the vigorous demands of battle. His black beard is inseparable from his bushy, unkempt hair, yet, unlike the younger soldiers, he wears a fine suit of genuine chain mail, and a knee-length tunic bearing the device of a panther charging through the horns of a crescent Moon. In his right hand, he holds a thick leather whip; and at the sight of both man and whip, Heldo-Bah smiles, but not wickedly. Indeed, a hint of genuine affection makes its way into the forager's voice:

"Ashkatar," he says, nodding. "I'd have thought to find you at the Den of Stone," he continues, mentioning the cave at the center of Okot that is the meeting place of the Groba.

"*Yantek* Ashkatar," the impressive Bane replies, reflecting the same trace of comradeship with his own slight smile, and a pleasant narrowing of his dark eyes. "I see your manners are no better than ever, Heldo-Bah."

"And I see you're still playing at soldiers with the children," Heldo-Bah says, angering the larger of the two pallins; but the man called Ashkatar holds a hand up, and indicates the burning huts.

"All right, men," he says. "Back to your posts. I'll attend to this fellow."

The two soldiers reluctantly move along the line of the palisade toward the flames. Yantek Ashkatar looks into the distance over Heldo-Bah's shoulder. "You three are the last home," he says. "You could not have been close. I assume that Keera and Veloc are with you?"

"Yes. And we want word of Keera's family."

"I wish I had it for you," Ashkatar sighs. "There simply wasn't time. We've already burned the dead—are burning them still, in pyres downriver. But as to just *who's* been burned—I honestly don't know . . ."

There are not many in the Bane community for whom Heldo-Bah has any use, fewer still among those that command the tribe; but one of those is Ashkatar, and the respect is rooted, characteristically, in a shared experience of conflict against the Tall. The incident took place when they fought side by side among many other Bane warriors to prevent Broken soldiers from crossing the Cat's Paw and advancing into Davon Wood, an attempt that was the result of the particularly bloody murder of a group of Tall children by several Outragers. Those killings had been a reprisal for the beating of a Bane trading party inside the city of Broken by a group of drunken merchants; a beating that Heldo-Bah and Veloc had witnessed, just as they had witnessed, from a helpless distance, the singularly disproportionate Outrager attack on the children. The two foragers had raced back to Okot, choosing a shorter route than the Outragers knew of and arriving to tell the Groba the truth of the situation before the Outragers had an opportunity to lie about it. Although Veloc played his part in the subsequent effort by the young Bane army to hold the Tall soldiers at the Cat's Paw, it was Heldo-Bah who approached Ashkatar with a solution: after a bloody night, during which Ashkatar's men learned more than one way to kill Tall soldiers without being seen, the officers commanding the Broken force were greeted at dawn by the sight of the three guilty Outragers' heads, placed on spears and smuggled into the Tall camp.

Notes were left with the heads, saying that these were in fact the men responsible for the children's deaths, and that the Bane would consider the matter closed if the Tall did likewise; and so a battle that might have gone on for months was cut short by the tenacity of the Bane commander and the imagination of the tribe's most despised forager. In the years since, Ashkatar and Heldo-Bah have often crossed paths; and it is Ashkatar who frequently defends the forager against attempts by the High Priestess and her knights to run Heldo-Bah out of the tribe altogether; and that is why, when the two meet, it is as if they were only slightly estranged brothers. . . .

Ashkatar cracks his six-foot whip, producing a sound as lethal as the snapping of the falling trees nearby. "Damn the Tall . . . If they want us dead, why don't they face us? Instead, they spread this vile pestilence . . ."

"You think the Tall responsible?" asks Heldo-Bah.

Ashkatar lifts his mailed shoulders. "There are some peculiar reports, from other foraging parties—you'll have to compare whatever you've seen against them." The Bane yantek looks beyond Heldo-Bah once again, this time nodding a greeting. "Ah. Veloc—Keera. Good. The Groba is anxious to see all three of you."

Keera has begun to collect her wits, in the manner of those who have been expecting, for longer than their spirits can bear, to hear dreaded news: unsteadily, but using the ordinary duties of daily life as an anchor. She carries her own sack, while Veloc has the other two hoisted onto his shoulders. As Heldo-Bah takes his, Keera speaks:

"Yantek," she asks quietly. "Have you heard of my family?"

"We haven't been able to keep careful records, Keera," Ashkatar answers, true gentleness in his voice. "Or records of *any* kind." He approaches to take her sack onto one of his own shoulders, and then, tucking his whip into his belt, puts his free arm around her; clearly, Keera finds the press of his weighty limb comforting. "Some survived—but the disease simply kills too quickly to allow us to take note of just who. And it continues spreading, even after the host is dead. We had no choice but to burn the bodies. Those who were exposed but are not yet ill, have been taken to one chamber of the *Lenthess-steyn*—many of the healers lived, thank the Moon, and are attempting to determine why some, like themselves, are unaffected, but others die. The ill are in the uppermost chamber, receiving what care can be given—which is very little. And in the deepest chambers, more healers have been picking at the dead for two days, to know where the plague strikes in the body—the mechanism of how it kills." The yantek stares into Keera's face intently. "More have died than have lived, Keera."

At this, Keera gasps. "May I—go and look for them?"

Ashkatar considers the matter. "Will you not let the healers try to find them? You are our finest tracker, Keera. If I'm any judge, we will need you, in the hours to come. The Groba has asked for you, as I say, specifically."

Keera has been shaking her head from almost the instant Ashkatar began to speak. "I cannot—I cannot meet with the Groba and speak of this as a 'problem.' I must find them, I must know, ere I go mad with the fear of it . . ." She thinks to bury her face in her hands; but she will not break yet; certainly not in front of the commander of the Bane army.

"Then you enter the *Lenthess* at your own peril," Ashkatar replies, nodding. "Should you display signs of illness, you will be kept there. It's all we can do. Come—Veloc, Heldo-Bah, you as well. We go to the square." The four walk past the soldiers who are hard at work with axes. "Linnet!" Ashkatar bellows.

An unusually tall Bane (unusually tall, that is, for a Bane who is not also an Outrager) turns: he has stripped to his waist, and his powerful muscles glisten in the heat of the blaze. "Yantek?"

"Assume command, here. I must take these foragers to the Groba. You have your orders."

"Yes, Yantek—although the fire grows hellish hot, and spreads too fast. If we cannot contain it—"

"I've told you already, Linnet—if you cannot contain it, then *direct* it.

Toward the northern huts. They have been sealed, and want only pitch and oil to draw the flame. See to it."

"Aye, Yantek. The Moon's blessing go with you," the younger man says. He glimpses Keera's terrified face. "The Moon's blessing, lady . . ."

Keera nods in confusion, leaving Ashkatar to say, "And with you— may it go with all of us, now . . ."

Ashkatar leads the way through the forest tangle, emerging on the main path into the village far enough downhill that the group does not run the risk of being struck by burning tree limbs that, when they become fiery embers, break off and hurtle toward the Earth in dangerously large pieces, which burst apart on the forest floor. The flames rising from the twenty-odd huts have now joined, some forty feet above, to form one massive column of flame which seems to be pulled upward—as if some deity is sucking the life from Okot, and especially the northeastern settlement; some capricious, cruel god, Keera cannot help but continue to think, until a more pragmatic fact occurs to her:

"There can be no doubting it, now," she murmurs to Ashkatar, who keeps one heavy arm around her shoulders, even as her brother holds her left hand tight in his. "With so many soundings of the Horn, and now this fire—the Tall will finally see in what part of the Wood Okot is."

"They're probably assembling their blasted troops even as we speak," Heldo-Bah says.

"But let the rest of us concern ourselves with all that, Keera," Veloc says, scowling at Heldo-Bah for his thoughtlessness. "Worry only for Tayo and the children."

"And we *did* consider that likelihood, Keera," Ashkatar adds. "But there was no other course to take—fire stops the spread of the illness, this is virtually the only thing we *do* know."

The group are on the main pathway into Okot now, which is a well-worn cart trail, with clumps of forest grass growing between its two deep ruts. They soon reach the central "square" of Okot (really a circle that the cart path makes around the village well, the only thing in the area that actually *is* square), to find it flooded with Bane of every description. Men, women, children, household and farm animals, all mill about in near-panic, the humans fixing their attention on the northern and southern sides of the square. Towering over the northern gathering ground is the cliff face into which the *Lenthess-steyn* caves are set; while the southern ground leads up to a smaller rock formation, one with a gaping hole between two mammoth boulders: the Den of Stone, where the Groba is now meeting. On the northern side, a group of counter-weighted wooden cages on powerful ropes slowly and constantly rise to and descend from the various *Lenthess* openings, in which the bright light of torches can be seen, and out of which drifts their smoke. Against the walls of the *Lenthess* caves are cast the eerie shadows of Bane healers: men with long, thin beards and ankle-length robes, women in less impressive but more practical shirts and pantaloons, their hair tied above their heads and covered with white kerchiefs. Long lines of anxious Bane wait to take their turn in the cages, trying to find what Keera seeks: news of whether their families are well or stricken, or if, indeed, they are there at all, or have already been burned in the mass pyres near the Cat's Paw.

When they have reached the rock-and-mortar walls that enclose the village well, the foragers note that there are Bane soldiers everywhere, blending in because they wear no armor. Their agitation at this moment of supreme crisis is admirably controlled, given their relative inexperience. Uncertainty as to just how to manage the situation is clear in their faces, but they keep moving, getting tribe members into lines and keeping them there, doling water from the well to healers who fetch it, and guarding the Den of Stone from the villagers' desperate demands for information.

For the ordinarily calm forest community, it is an unprecedented sight; and even Veloc and Heldo-Bah feel their nerves begin to fray, in the face of a scene that looks to burst into mayhem at any moment.

"All right, Keera," Ashkatar says. "I'll have two of my men take you up—" He points the whip toward the wooden cages. "Pallin—yes, you! And the other, as well. Get over here, I've a job for you!"

Seeing whom the voice emanates from, the two young pallins dash toward the Bane commander. Their faces are covered in charcoal and ash, and it is clear that they must have been tending the fire up the pathway, but that this work is being done in rotations to avoid any one man being exposed for too long to the flames and the heat. Both of the pallins, having removed their scale armor, go about their business with their short-swords belted around their soft, quilted gambesons, which ordinarily shield their flesh from the weight and the rivets of their armored hauberks.

"Yes, Yantek?" the first pallin says, as they reach Ashkatar.

"This woman may have family in the *Lenthess*—stay with her until she finds them or you're certain they're not within. Understood?"

The two young warriors hesitate, examining Keera, then Veloc and Heldo-Bah, and paying close attention to the sacks on the backs of the men. The second pallin pauses, leaning toward his commander.

"But, Yantek—" he struggles to say. "She is only a *forager . . .*"

Ashkatar drops Keera's bag from his shoulder, takes his arm from her and snatches his whip from his side; then, in another swift motion, he cracks it once, then wraps it around the youth's neck four or five times. In an instant, he pulls the choking soldier's face close to his own.

"She is an important member of the Bane tribe, boy, and she is a mother and a wife! If I had to snap your neck right now to save hers, I wouldn't hesitate—understand? Never show the pride of the Tall to me, soldier, or the river will know your guts. Now—escort her!"

Ashkatar pulls the whip from the pallin's neck in a hard jerk that leaves burning lines in his flesh, which the soldier grabs at to make sure his head is still secure. The first pallin, having taken Ashkatar's point (which would have been difficult to miss), approaches Keera gently.

"Come, lady," he says nervously, "we will not leave you until we know what has become of your family . . ."

"Correct," Ashkatar says, nodding. "Take her up at once; the Groba wishes to speak to her as soon as she is finished with this mournful work."

"Yes, Yantek," the second pallin manages to wheeze out, his throat nearly as distressed as his neck. "We will guard her with our—"

"*Go!*" shouts the commander, and the soldiers hurry to catch Keera, who is already on her way to the wooden cages. She glances back to her brother and Heldo-Bah once, and Veloc puts his hands tightly together and raises them to her, urging strength and hope; while Heldo-Bah vents his worries for Keera's family on the two hurrying soldiers.

"You heard your commander, bitch's turd!" he shouts, chasing after the soldiers and kicking them to a run. "And if I hear one word of complaint from my friend, be sure that the yantek will be the next to know of it!" Heldo-Bah turns to Ashkatar, allowing a small grin to enter his face.

"Something amuses you, Heldo-Bah?" Ashkatar rumbles.

"Your disposition's improved no more than my manners," Heldo-Bah says merrily. "I thought perhaps you'd actually grown into this 'yantek' foolery; and so, yes, it both amuses and, I must admit, pleases me to know that you can still tend to business as in the old days."

"Hmm!" Ashkatar noises. "Your disposition wouldn't please the Moon, either, Heldo-Bah, if you spent your time defending the tribe, rather than foraging and raising hell with the Tall!" The whip cracks again, causing a passing dog to leap and yelp in fright. Then the Bane yantek turns and, retrieving Keera's foraging sack, marches to the Den of Stone. "And you people!" he calls out to the small but agitated crowd that is still calling for the Groba to emerge and tell whatever they may know. The mob turns as one, when its members hear the whip come alive again. "What in damnation is the matter with you? What don't you understand? It's plague, damn it all! Do you think the Groba and the Priestess are sorcerers, who can drive it from us with magic? Get to your homes, damn you, and let them do their work in peace!" Ordering a few more soldiers to break up the crowd, Ashkatar takes up position just in front of the stone pathway that leads up to the entrance to the Den of Stone, and cracks the whip once more. "I mean it!" he calls to the crowd. "I'd enjoy flaying someone alive, right now—so don't any of you try my patience any further!"

Between Ashkatar's bellowing and the soldiers' less than gentle prodding with long staffs, the crowd breaks up; and as the last of them disappear, an aging, grey-bearded Bane in a simple broadcloth robe appears at the top of the stone pathway that leads into the cave. His bald pate gleams with sweat in the light that seeps through the trees above, and glows orange as it reflects the softer illumination of a torch that is mounted just beside the mouth of the cave. Searching Okot's crowded square, this frail, proud character finally shouts, "Yantek Ashkatar!"

Ashkatar spins about expectantly. "Yes, Elder?"

"The Groba wishes to know if the foraging party of Keera the tracker has returned yet!"

"Two of them are here, Father—Keera herself is delayed."

"Then send the others in to us." At which the wizened old man turns back toward the entrance to the Den of Stone.

"The foragers, Elder?" Ashkatar calls. "Before I have an answer to my request?"

"Your answer will depend on what the foragers have to tell the Groba," the Elder replies, annoyance clear in his voice, a voice that is far stronger than his overall appearance would lead one to expect. "And so, send the first two of them in to us!" Before waiting for another question, the old man shuffles back into the cave.

Ashkatar heaves a worried breath, indicating the cave with his whip. "Well—Veloc. Heldo-Bah. You heard him—you'd better go, damn it . . ."

Both foragers set their bags down near Keera's, Heldo-Bah taking advantage of another moment: "Watch these for us, won't you, Yantek? I hate to ask, but there *is* an order to things, in this life, and while some of us stand sentry, others must attend to—"

"Get *inside*," Ashkatar warns. "And keep your business brief."

Heldo-Bah laughs and takes to the pathway, leaving Veloc to ask, "Just what 'request' were you referring to, Yantek? If I may ask?"

"You may, Veloc. I want permission to lead a small raid across the river. Snatch one or two of Baster-kin's Guard, and see what they can tell us."

Veloc nods judiciously. "I believe we may have saved you that chore, Ashkatar . . . ," he says, following Heldo-Bah along the pathway.

"You—*what*?" Ashkatar shouts as they enter the cave. "What in blazes are you saying? Veloc! And it's *Yantek* Ashkatar, blast your soul!"

But the foragers have already disappeared into the Den.

$$1:\{xiii:\}$$

Within the Fifth District of Broken, a remarkable woman struggles to protect a secret, as well as a child, as her husband takes his leave of the city: at first triumphantly, and then most strangely . . .

ISADORA ARNEM REALIZES that she must hurry, if she is to have a meaningful amount of time alone with her husband in his quarters before the commencement of the Talons' triumphant march out of Broken on their way toward their fateful encounter with the Bane. And so, after being helped on with her cloak by her two daughters, Anje (at fourteen already a wise young maiden) and ten-year-old Gelie, the most theatrically humorous of her brood of five, Isadora rushes to make a few final adjustments to her lustrous golden hair, gathering its thick tresses at the back of her neck with a silver clasp. She then kisses the girls, and calls farewell to two of her sons—Dagobert, the eldest at fifteen, and Golo, a very athletic eleven—who are playing at sword fighting with wooden sticks, having been inspired by their father's parting words to them several hours earlier. Finally, she turns toward the central doorway of their home, a spacious if unpretentious Fifth District building composed for the most part of wood and stucco, and finds herself, unexpectedly but not surprisingly, faced with twelve-year-old Dalin,[†] the last of the Arnem children.

Dalin has recently been selected by the God-King and the Grand Layzin themselves for royal and sacred service; service all the harder to refuse because he is not the scion of the Arnem house, but only its second son. It is a calling that the boy is eager to undertake, an eagerness that has caused the many noisy arguments with his parents, particularly his mother, that have of late driven his father to stand watch on the walls of the city at night. With dark, handsome features that strongly resemble Sixt's, clever Dalin is also the most like his father in his pronounced stubbornness: all similarities that make it especially hard for Isadora to even think of parting with the boy, particularly when Sixt is about to embark on what may be a long and dangerous campaign.

Isadora sighs, seeing that Dalin is blocking her exit and preparing to debate the subject still further. "Don't let's fight anymore, just now, Dalin," his mother says. "I must be quick if I am to meet your father."

But it is wise and very womanly Anje who takes charge of the situation. "Yes, Dalin," the maiden says, dragging her brother out of the doorway. "Mother and Father will have little enough time to themselves, as it is."

"That's right, Dalin," young Gelie adds; but then, at a hard look from her brother, she hides herself within the folds of her mother's blue-green cloak. Peering out just once, she adds, "Don't be so selfish, honestly!" before disappearing again.

"Be quiet, Gelie!" Dalin replies, angered that he cannot resist Anje's strength, and must therefore yield the doorway. "You don't know anything about it, you're just a child—but Mother is perfectly aware that I should have gone into service long ago!"

"We can talk more about the matter when I return," Isadora says, gently if wearily. "But for now, you must let me go and see your father off."

"I know what that means," Dalin says bitterly. "You're hoping I'll have forgotten about it—I'm not a fool, Mother."

"Well," Gelie declares, her wide eyes going particularly round. "You're certainly making a very good show of being one!" And then, at another angry scowl from Dalin, she is back amid the folds of the cloak.

"Both of you, be quiet," Anje commands, now pulling Gelie close to her, even as she maintains her grip on Dalin. "Go ahead, Mother—I'll keep these two from killing one another."

Isadora cannot help but give her oldest daughter, with whom she shares so much more than their similar types of great physical beauty, an amused and grateful smile; and then she says, "Thank you, Anje. But you may let me have one last moment alone with Dalin. I think I shall be safe."

"I wouldn't depend on it, Mother," Gelie calls, as Anje drags her from the hallway into the sitting room nearby. "He's dangerous, truly—I may be killed, after you leave!" As Anje pulls the little one along, Gelie adds, "Although, if I am, I'm sure no one in this family will care!"

Isadora chuckles, and for an instant light comes into her eyes, which are so deeply blue as to appear almost black, at moments. "That's nonsense, Gelie, and you know it," she replies.

Gelie forces Anje to pause. "It is?" she says brightly.

"Yes," says Isadora simply, without turning to the girl. "You know perfectly well that your father would be devastated. So would the cats."

Gelie turns, stamping her feet hard for effect as she enters the sitting room. "That's cruel, Mother—just cruel!"

Laughing lightly at this declaration, Isadora looks to the doorway through which Gelie has disappeared, and murmurs, "I honestly think that we will have to find a king for that one to marry . . ." Turning to find Dalin still unamused, Isadora approaches a table by the entryway, taking from it a silver clasp. Her son knows the object: it depicts the face of a furious, bearded man, one of whose eye sockets is covered by a patch, and on whose shoulders sit two large, crow-like birds.[†] Glancing at the clasp and wondering (not for the first time) why it is not Kafra's face that smiles out from its surface, Dalin senses an opening, which he seizes as his mother fixes the clasp to the gown beneath her cloak:

"Mother—is it true what they say about you?"

Isadora's blood stirs. "People say many things about your father and me, Dalin. Do you listen to gossip?"

"It's not gossip—it doesn't sound like gossip, at any rate."

There will be no avoiding yet another subject that Isadora hopes to avoid, it seems: "And what is it that people say?" she asks.

"That you—they say—" The boy can scarcely form the words. "They say that you were raised by a witch!"

Her annoyance and anger deepening, but still scarcely detectable, Isadora says evenly, "She wasn't a witch, Dalin. Just a wise, odd woman, of whom silly people were afraid. But she was the most learnèd healer in Broken, and she was kind to me—she was all I had, remember, after my own parents were murdered." She faces the boy, filling her words with weight: "Besides, I'd like to think that you are wise enough not to listen to stories like that. You know that empty-headed people say all manner of malicious things about us, because your father is so important, but wasn't born wealthy. Many in this city resent his success. But far more think him a great man—so, when you hear people talking about your parents, have the nerve to dismiss them for the worthless souls they are, and walk away. And now—" Isadora walks to the doorway at last. "I must go. Run inside, and if you don't want to play with the others, then have cook make you something special to eat. Or, why not ask Nuen† to tell you marauder stories, while you practice swordsmanship?"

Isadora refers to the strong, cheerful woman of eastern marauder stock who has lived with the family as nurse, governess, and household servant for some thirteen years: ever since Arnem discovered her, along with several other women of her kind, during a brief campaign along the southeastern portion of the Meloderna valley, being used as slaves (and worse) in the fields and homes of grain merchants, in plain violation of Broken's ban against such absolute servitude.

"All right," Dalin replies, moving dejectedly away from her. "But I *do* know that you're simply avoiding the subject of my service, Mother—and I'm not going to stop reminding you . . ."

As he disappears up the house's central stairway, Isadora watches him go with a smile, the resemblance to his father occurring to her once again.

Finally, Isadora steps onto the stone terrace outside the doorway, and moves through the family's spacious garden, which is surrounded by a ten-foot wall, on her way to a gate in the farthest side of that protective barrier, a wooden portal within a stone archway that gives out onto the Path of Shame.

The Arnem family's garden is unique: the statuary, carefully tended plantings, and orderly pathways that fill the courtyards of the great houses in the First and Second Districts are absent, and disorder by design reigns. Some years earlier, before Dalin developed his troublesome preoccupation with the Kafran church, it had been the desire of all the children to create, within the safety of their garden's walls, a space much like the dangerous but fascinating wilderness that covers the slopes of Broken's mountain below the walled summit. In particular, the Arnem brood took adventurous pleasure from the scenery that surrounds the noisy course of Killen's Run, the rivulet that emerges from beneath the southern walls of the city to make its way to the base of the mountain and join the Cat's Paw, before that mighty river storms its way along the northern edge of Davon Wood.

Sixt Arnem was both amused and impressed by his children's notion: for, as we have seen, he was and is not a man who shares the taste of the kingdom's most important citizens for excessive fineries. And he saw in his children's idea a chance for them to learn about the Natural world outside the city without being exposed to the dangers of panthers, bears, and wolves, to say nothing of those malignant creatures who hunt children whilst walking upright: those troubling citizens of Broken who let their Kafran belief in purity and physical perfection bleed into unnatural lust for the bodies and souls of the very young.

And so, Arnem proudly put the family servants at the disposal of his three sons and two daughters for several days, and the project was undertaken. Cartloads of large, mossy stones, along with smaller rocks worn smooth by the waters of Killen's Run, had been brought into the Fifth District from their original resting places, to the consternation of most of that district's inhabitants. So, too, were imported, in not inconsiderable numbers, those creatures—fish and frogs, newts and salamanders—whose natural home was the waters of the Run, where they sought safe remove in which to breed beneath its larger configurations of stones. The safety of these delicate beings would be increased by the children's plan, although the initial experience of being transported proved to terrify at least a few past their ability to survive the trip; most, however, were safely deposited in the artificial streambed that was cut into the Earth through the whole length of the Arnems' garden. Ferns, wildflowers, rushes, grasses, and young trees were carefully transplanted along the banks and hillocks that lined the new waterway; while, in the greatest offense to those few persons of fashion from the Arnems' class who were aware of the doings in their garden, a very old and, some said, important piece of statuary—a fountain that depicted Oxmontrot's son, the God-King Thedric, vanquishing a forest demon that spat water from its pursed lips—was smashed to bits by the family's two strongest servants, who, like the rest of the Arnems' staff, proved enthusiastic in assisting the children in realizing their vision of a wild mountain stream. Where the statue had once stood, the children oversaw the construction of a waterfall, with the fountain's spring-fed waters tumbling over a group of large, piled stones and into a deep, cold pool.

From out of this lovely and calming collection point flows the garden's artificial *breck*† (as Isadora often refers to the thing, using what she had been told, as a child, was the language of her ancestors); and the *breck* forms several smaller falls and pools as it winds to the foot of the garden. Here the stream vanishes, joining the city's sewer system beneath the gutter of the Path without; but the children made certain at the start to supervise the installation of a series of safeguards: fine metal grates covered by small rocks, supporting a sifting bed of gravel. This successfully keeps any living creature within the stream from being swept away, while still keeping its waters fresh.

As she walks through this unfashionable but lovely setting, Isadora allows the peace of the garden to give her a moment of calm pause, for she knows that, having left the ever-loud and sometimes (in Dalin's case) hurtful activities of her own children behind, she must soon enter the Fifth District, and its busiest thoroughfare, the Path of Shame. Fortunately, it is the quietest time of the day, in the district: the hours when drunkards sleep off their revelries of the previous night, or half-wittedly prepare for their next round. As she steps through the arched door in the thick garden wall, Isadora pauses, attempting to savor the moment. Yet there can be such a thing as too much quiet, even in the Fifth District. For, along with the sounds of adult debauchery and corruption, the comforting sound of children at play—children of an age that would make them suited to enter the royal and divine service—is also noticeably muted. But the diminution of this sound is not a change that varies from day to day; it has been steadily declining for months and even years, although Isadora tries to put meaningless explanations to the change, such as the citizens of her district having become so concerned with intoxication of various kinds that even fornication is losing its place in their schedule of daily activities—

But there have long been other explanations for the change, she knows, explanations whispered even by drunkards: tales that Isadora has assiduously driven from her mind. Now, however, she listens, she must listen, more carefully to these stories of Kafran priests and priestesses, protected by Lord Baster-kin's Guard, coming by night to pay poor couples to place their children in the God-King's service, because the pool of worthier families' children is too small for the royal retinue's purposes—shrouded as those purposes may be . . .

Whatever the reasons behind the momentary and relative quiet in her district, Isadora is forced, on this unseasonably warm afternoon, to hold her breath against the stench of the gutters outside her garden wall, and to hurry along the stretch of the Path of Shame between her house and the district wall. Affairs in this least squalid portion of the Fifth are declining, without doubt, just as matters are growing worse every day in the district as a whole. Granted, they were none too good even during Isadora's childhood, when poverty had been but the first of her troubles. Her parents had been murdered by a thief in the district when Isadora was but six years old: the couple were rag- and rubbish-pickers, gleaning an existence from the enormous, redolent mounds of trash assembled by the nightly practice of running enormous wooden ramps out atop the southwestern wall of the city and dumping the populace's garbage out onto the steep face on that side of Broken's mountain. Whatever usable goods Isadora's parents could wrest from these vast piles they bartered in a small stall that they operated in one of the less fashionable streets of the Third District; but despite the distasteful, backbreaking nature of this existence, the couple were devout Kafrans, convinced that, if they kept faith with the golden god, he would one day reward them with riches enough to grow old in peace—and that, whatever the case, it was better to worship a god who offered such hope in this life than it was to offer prayers to one who asked them to wait until the next reality for pleasure and satisfaction of all kinds.

Instead of such rewards, however, their sole blessing for devotion to Kafra was murder: they were stabbed to death by a drunkard as they returned to their home and daughter one evening, after what (for people of their desperate station) had been a particularly good day of trading. Following this tragedy, the woman who had long occupied the house next to theirs—the remarkably knowledgeable yet often-disagreeable old healer called Gisa†—decided that she would take in the dead couple's spritely little daughter. The girl had often been a visitor to the crone's small, startlingly clean house, the walls of which were lined by seemingly endless numbers of vials, jars, and bottles, each of which contained some magical substance Gisa called *medicines,* medicines that nearly every citizen in the Fifth District (and a great many outside it) knew to be far more effective than the treatments of the Kafran healers.

Gisa offered to make of little Isadora both a ward and a student; and in time, as the child progressed from mere assistant to apprentice, she also came to understand that her mistress's insistence on remaining in Broken's seamiest district was no simple matter of poverty. Her work among the poor of the Fifth was not lucrative, but the secret cases she undertook in the dead of night in other districts (cases in which the Kafran healers revealed the extent of their ignorance) certainly were. Yet a spirit of mercy, as well as a refusal to abandon the old gods of the region that Oxmontrot forged into Broken, all meant that Gisa would never leave the Fifth District. In time, her ward came to adopt similar sentiments and beliefs, in part because she determined to carry on Gisa's medical practice after the crone's eventual death, but also because of the manner in which her parents' murders had been treated by the God-King's servants.

Or, rather, because of the manner in which those killings had been assiduously *ignored* by those same officials. The poverty and disheveled appearance of the victims, their lack of pride and ambition, had marked their deaths, to every Broken priest, as religiously and legally—to say nothing of morally—irrelevant, no matter the extent of their devotion to the golden god in life. In time, Isadora bitterly accepted this fact, enough so that she began to make plans to carry on not only Gisa's work but her ancient faith; and when, as an adult, she further emulated her teacher by periodically answering calls to save the life or ease the suffering of some worthy personage in the wealthier parts of the city, she, too, was very well paid for her efforts—but only, like Gisa, secretly. Finally, the most unqualifiedly happy events of her adult life—her encounters with and eventual marriage to Sixt Arnem, and the subsequent births of their children—were also a result of her decision to forgo Kafran celebrity and beliefs, and to remain in the streets of her childhood: her loyalty to the Fifth District was, through all these events, sealed.

Small wonder, then, that—even as the mother of five children who would be safer elsewhere—Isadora continues to insist on maintaining her family's residence in this place. Certainly, that decision has joined neatly with her husband's similar desire to remain in the neighborhoods of his youth; yet Isadora knows that Sixt would ultimately move the family to whatever part of the city she might choose, if she firmly insisted. But no; for Sixt, but above all for Isadora, who knew love and safety as a girl and a young woman only from persons scorned by Broken's rulers and most powerful citizens, and who rejected all of the fundamentals of Kafran faith and society as a result, the assiduous continuance of her own and her family's lives well out of the view of Kafran priests and their agents has continued to be the chief priority for how and where the family lives . . .

Isadora's thoughts having remained fixed on her husband, her faith, and her children and home, during this walk, the sharp tug at the hem of her cloak is a shock, when it comes. She stops, to find in the dirt of the street a drunkard, much like the many who lie snoring in similar spots up and down the Path; but this fellow is awake, and his bony, filthy hand is capable of a firm grip. He grins, then drops his jaw to release the stench of cheap wine; and when he begins to laugh, the shaking of his body wafts the foul odor of his clothing far enough to reach Isadora's nostrils.

"Please, lady," the man chortles. "A few pieces of silver?"

Isadora does not hesitate to answer: the situation is not new to her. "I have little enough silver. If you seek work, come to my door, or to any good citizen's, and ask for it. But I'd bathe, first." She tries to move on—but also takes the precaution of unsheathing a small knife that she keeps hidden inside the sleeve of her cloak at all times.

It is well that she does so: for the man refuses to release her. "*Work,*
lady?" he says bitterly. "And what work do you do for your silver, eh? This
is a rich enough city to meet the needs of one lost soul!"

"Release my cloak, or lose your fingers."

The man ignores the threat. "Too fine a lady to be wandering in the
Fifth District all alone," he says, attempting to pull her down with real
force. "Maybe I don't need silver, after all. Not so much as I need—"

Isadora would indeed slice a finger from the offending hand, were it
not for the fact that the butt end of a spear catches the drunkard squarely
in the chest, knocking him flat on the street and leaving him gasping
hard for air. Isadora, surprised, turns to find Linnet Niksar, spear in
hand.

Niksar kicks at the drunkard, hard enough to get him to his feet. "Go
on, now—don't make me use the other end!" he calls after the fleeing
man. Then he softens his voice. "Your pardon, my lady," he says, bowing
quickly but gracefully. "I hope I didn't startle you. Your husband dispatched me to escort you, as the hour grows late—"

"Thank you, Niksar," Isadora says, "But I assure you, I was perfectly
capable of handling the situation." She returns her knife to its hidden
sheath. "He was only a drunkard who wanted a lesson." Niksar bows
once again in deference, and Isadora's aspect softens. "I don't mean to
sound ungrateful, Reyne. I confess that I'm not in the best of spirits, at
the moment."

Niksar smiles, making sure the drunkard is retreating. "I'm afraid
there are many more of them," he says. "And they grow more restive
every day. They seem to have it in their heads that silver grows in this
city. We ought to let them have a term in the army . . ."

Isadora smiles. "You sound remarkably like my husband, Reyne.
Speaking of whom, we'd best hurry along."

"Yes, my lady," Niksar replies, matching Isadora's impressive pace.

Within moments Isadora and Niksar have entered the Fourth District,
which is alive with action: two full *khotors* of regular army troops have
been brought in from their camp on the mountainside, to defend the city
in the absence of the *khotor* of the Talons. Hundreds of soldiers are mill-
ing about on the training and parade grounds, some slinging packs onto
their broad backs, some undoing them and smiling, happy to be able to
spend some time in the city barracks, rather than sleeping on the ground

outside the walls. Spearheads and swords are sharpened, horses are made ready, and everywhere there is the laughter and shouting of men preparing for duty, at home as well as in the field.

A few of the men take note of Isadora's arrival, and soon word is spreading about the camp, producing a healthy effect. If Amalberta Korsar had been beloved as the mother of the Broken army, Isadora Arnem is adored as the object of its collective amorous (but always respectful) sentiments. By the time she has reached the steps to her husband's quarters, on the far side of the southernmost drilling ground, crowds of men from a wide variety of units have begun to assemble before the pine log structure, the differing colors of their tunics and trousers—blue for the regular army, wine red for the Talons—for once causing no competition. They have come together for the happy work of sending off the men who are being readied to march—Broken's five hundred finest soldiers (and luckiest, say the men who must stay behind); and each man hopes to get a glimpse of Isadora, as well as a chance to hear Arnem's words of encouragement for the coming campaign. To the west, the sun is just beginning to set, sending the warm light of a spring afternoon to break through the dust kicked up by all the busy preparations: no one could ask for a better setting from which to begin the hard work ahead.

Above the Talons' quadrangle and drilling ground, Isadora finds her husband in close council with the leaders of his *khotor* and their staffs, some ten men, in all, gathered around a rough-hewn table upon which sit half a dozen maps. Each of these men snaps to glad attention when their commander's wife enters, busily saluting and bowing, laughing, rolling maps to be slipped into leather cases, and thanking Isadora for once again making the trip to their district, as well as assuring her of how much it will mean to their men.

As his aide delivers Arnem's wife to him, the sentek calls out: "Thank you, Niksar. And now, gentlemen, if you will all join your units, I need a few moments with my wife, who wishes to remind me, I've no doubt, of how an officer in the field ought to conduct himself."

Well-meaning if somewhat lusty mumbling to the effect of, "Certainly, Sentek—a difficult duty, but an urgent one," goes around the group of departing officers, causing a ripple of equally good-hearted laughter to pass through the small crowd. Arnem scolds the men as he follows them to the door and closes it tight. He then pauses as he turns to his wife, raising his brow and widening his eyes, as if to say, *What's to be done, they are good soldiers, and good men, at heart . . .*

"You are as popular as ever, as you can see," Sixt says aloud, moving over to embrace his wife, who leans back against the table. "And they're right—it means an enormous amount to the men."

"So long as I serve a purpose of *some* kind," Isadora answers.

Arnem tightens his arms around her, putting his lips close to her cheek. "Do you feel your life has no purpose, wife?"

"A purpose for children," she answers softly, turning her head so that her lips meet his. "And I suppose that will have to do. For now . . ."

What man can truly know the heart of a woman who allows her lover or husband to pursue his destiny, even unto death? And what woman can understand the passion that such trust builds in men? To be sure, there is neither any woman, nor any man, whose heart achieves such mutual trust more flawlessly than does the honest soldier's and his equally self-less wife's; and no more instructive instance of their mutual generosity than these times of departure, when the full reality and weight of what may transpire during the days to come, in the home as well as in the field—when just what sacrifices each will incur for the honor and safety of the other—are brought home with a terrible yet magnificent poignancy. And, in the few minutes they have to themselves, both Arnem and Isadora indulge those passions, without removing all or even most of their clothing: for they know the maps of each other's bodies as well as Arnem knows those more traditional charts that were laid out on his table but moments ago. Indeed, they now know them so well, and can satisfy their mutual desire so greatly and knowingly, that they forget, if only for a time, the admiring groups of soldiers who guard their privacy with ferocious loyalty—even as those men continue to make respectful yet enviously ribald remarks to one another, in the most discreet and hushed voices . . .

But in the wake of these transcendently private moments, more immediate and devilish questions intrude, as they must, on the sentek and his wife:

"You've had no word from the Grand Layzin?" Isadora whispers; and it need not be said of what "word" she speaks.

"No," Arnem says, keeping his head at rest on her shoulder. Their gentle intimacy has drawn a soft moistness to the surface of her flushed skin, which makes the more delicate and deliberate fragrances of both her body and the wildflower extracts with which she scents herself more potent; and he breathes all the aromas in deeply, knowing how long these last exposures may have to sustain him. "But I assume the ritual took place," Sixt continues. "Some sort of word would have come, if it had not."

Isadora sighs, her eyes welling. "The poor man," she whispers.

Arnem, too, feels an enormous weight press down on his heart. "Yes. Although they may be right, Isadora, he may simply have lost his mind—certainly, *I've* never heard him talk that way before . . ."

"Mad or no," Isadora answers, "he was our friend, to say nothing of a great man to whom they owed much. How can they have treated him so? And how can we be sure that the same fate will not befall you, should you fail to please them?" Her eyes search Sixt's desperately. "We know so little of it all—the Layzin, the God-King, the priests . . . I understand their need to preserve 'the divine mysteries,' but how should we know, husband, if those mysteries were no more than disguises for terrible lies?"

"We likely would not, my love," Arnem answers simply, recalling his own, similar thoughts. "But—I would be more concerned, had Baster-kin not taken me into his confidence as he did. I tell you, Isadora, I've never seen the man like that. Direct, yes, he's always been direct, even rude, but—he honestly seemed concerned. About *us.* He's an odd man, no question, and often shows his concern in peculiar ways, but—so long as I succeed, and please the God-King, I honestly don't think we have true cause for worry. In fact, I would guess that he will try to protect all of you, while I am gone—certainly he takes an interest in your well-being."

They have too little time before Arnem's departure, as it is, for Isadora to enter into a discussion of why else Baster-kin might take an interest in her and their children. So she gently turns Sixt's head to force his eyes to stare into the small oceans of her own. "Let us pray that you are right . . ." And then she concocts what she conceives to be a helpful lie: "I'm sorry if I sound less trustful than you, Sixt. I suspect the Merchant Lord strikes a good many people as strangely secretive, but that does not mean, as you say, that he does not intend to be of assistance, while you are gone."

"Indeed," Sixt replies hopefully. Then he studies his wife's face again, his hands gently moving over and beneath her cloak and gown, which have already been disarrayed by their encounter. "Who would ever have thought," he murmurs, in amazement that is only partially affected, "that such great wisdom could come from so pretty a head . . ."

Isadora stings his cheek with the flat of her hand, just hard enough to let serious intent show through her playfulness. "Pig. Never let your daughters hear that sort of talk, I warn you . . ." Then she adds, even more earnestly: "Above all, we *must* decide what his posture regarding Dalin truly is."

"I've told you, Isadora," Arnem replies quickly; for on this matter, he believes he has read Baster-kin's words accurately. "If the men and I *do* carry this business off, they will suspend the order—I truly believe it."

"They did not suspend it for Korsar's boy," Isadora replies doubtfully, turning away from Sixt as her eyes again grow perceptibly mournful. "However great the services the yantek performed . . ."

"True," Arnem answers. "And yet, I think that our situation is different—in fact, he nearly stated as much, although, as you say, one in his position will never reveal his true intentions, about this or anything else. But certainly, ours is a more serious case—else why should he have taken me into his confidence as he did?"

Isadora turns her face to his again, feeling the bristle of his beard as it passes her cheek, and tries with all her soul to smile. "And so—I must simply wait for you to succeed, and all will be well?"

"That is the matter entire," Arnem answers, returning her smile. "And have I ever disappointed you?"

She puts a hand to his mouth and presses hard, laughing softly. "I despise your soldierly conceit, and always have."

Pulling her hand from his face, Arnem protests, "There is no conceit in trusting the abilities of the Talons."

"Ah. I see . . ."

"It is plain truth, wife! My officers—following my example, perhaps—have made those young men into a mechanism: my sole responsibility is to set it in motion, then stand away and observe its working."

"*Hak!*" Isadora scoffs, as loudly and rudely as she can manage. "As though you could stand away from anything involving those men . . ."

"Besides—" Ignoring his wife's cynicism, Arnem stands, arranging his armor and the clothing beneath it. He then picks up his cloak and hands it to Isadora. "Five children later is no time to be telling a husband what you do and do not despise about him."

"Well—your children believe your nonsense, at any rate." Isadora stands and straightens her own garments, before she sets to fixing the silver eagle's claws of Sixt's cloak in place on his wide shoulders. "They hope and trust, as one, that you will thrash the evil Bane, and come home soon." Uncontrollably, her arms go around the sentek's neck in a moment of earnestness. "As do I . . ."

"Do they?" Arnem chuckles. He then holds Isadora at arm's length, that he may consume the sight of her in solitude one last time—and catches sight of the silver clasp fixed to her gown. "Oh, wife . . ." He touches the clasp, understanding, as do most in Broken, what it signifies. "*Must* you wear that thing? There is always the chance that some one of my superiors will learn of your past and your . . . *opinions*. It cannot help our cause."

"It could," Isadora replies coyly, knowing that it will irritate her husband. But then, with greater seriousness, she declares, "Come, now—it's only a meaningless keepsake, Sixt. I've only ever really trusted two people in my life, since my parents were killed: *you*"—She pokes her husband hard in the throat, just above his armor—"and Gisa. Am I not allowed that much?"

"Just see that you don't wear it while I'm gone," Arnem answers. "We need no further trouble from the priests—and if you seek to explain any peculiar behavior on Baster-kin's part, his spies reporting that you wear such barbarian idols would more than serve the purpose. Who knows how much of this business with Dalin is spurred by such talk?"

"I don't intend to wear it while you're gone," Isadora replies, undoing the clasp. "I'm giving him to you."

"To *me*?" Arnem groans. "What in the world am I to do with such a thing? Other than make my men doubt my sanity?"

"Keep it close, husband," Isadora says, finding a small pocket in the soft padding of his gambeson, beneath both his leather armor and his mail. "For my sake. I don't like the notion of this war, Sixt—and, whatever you may have thought of Gisa and her religion, this token has always brought me something more precious than luck."

"Oh?"

"Yes. The god it depicts, as you know, traded one of his eyes for wisdom. Such is what it has always brought me, and you shall need all you can muster."

"You know full well, Isadora," Arnem protests, "that I have never said a word against Gisa . . ." He pulls the clasp out and studies it. "But her kindness and her skill as a healer were separate from her faith."

"She would have argued against such a conclusion."

"Perhaps. But I can't very well wear it, that's certain. I could be stripped of my rank, and much worse, simply for possessing such a thing."

Isadora presses a finger to his mouth. "Do you suppose I don't realize that? I do not ask that you wear it." She secures the clasp in his pocket. "Just take it and keep it, hidden but close. As quietly as you can—if that's possible."

"Insults, now?" Arnem shrugs. "Very well, I submit. But I don't know what good a half-blind old man and two ravens are likely to do me."

"It's not your place to know—just keep it close, and see what occurs."

Arnem nods, and then the pair catch each other's eyes: the hour has arrived, and they both know it.

"Come," he says, taking her in his arms again. "We must address the men. You've always been their favorite—and yes, I've always been unhappy about that fact, if such pleases your vanity."

"It does," Isadora replies, kissing her husband deeply just once more; then she whispers into his armor, so quietly that he cannot hear: "You *will* be back." She feels again for the clasp. "*He* will see to it . . ."

Slowly and quietly, save for a few unexplained laughs such as pass between those who together have grown beyond explanations for such, the couple goes to the door. Sixt opens it, Isadora eases onto the platform at the head of the steps—

And a deafening roar rises up from the quadrangle, a sound more unrestrained than any heard within the Fourth District since last the sentek brought his wife to appear before his troops. The spectacle below and about Isadora is an awesome one: the five hundred most battle-hardened, disciplined men in the army of Broken stand in formation, cheering in appreciation. Surrounding these, in every free area, stand still more men, from other units that will not march today, who wish only to celebrate their comrades, their new commander, and, most of all, the woman who is their commonly held ideal of all that they train and march to war to preserve.

Arnem allows the men to continue until it seems they will exhaust themselves, and then takes his wife's hand and holds it aloft.

"Talons!" he shouts, when their roaring lowers to surmountable cheers. "Shall I designate my wife to lead you against the Bane?"

The troops burst out in an ecstatic affirmation that makes even their first mighty effort pale by comparison; and only Isadora herself can finally quiet them, by holding up her free hand.

"I fight a far more ferocious battle at home," she calls out, "against an enemy just as small, yet far more devious!"

It is almost more than the soldiers can bear, particularly the married men: Isadora's words bring thoughts of their own homes and their own children, while she herself becomes the very spirit of *all* their wives; and her words draw a final, ecstatic cheer that is the loudest of all. It is for Arnem, now, to silence them, by banishing his own smile, letting his wife step behind him, and holding his arms up. On the ground, every linnet calls his men to attention, and they are silent, snapping their spears to their sides and fastening their eyes on the man in whom they have placed such trust as few are ever allowed to experience.

"You all know," Arnem begins, when the men have become so silent that the warm western wind can be heard rushing through the yard, "of the fate of *Yantek* Korsar! We shall not dwell on it. Remember his past service to this kingdom, for it is all he would *wish* you to remember, along with the great cause to which he devoted his long life—the safety of this city and this kingdom! We are now charged with that responsibility, and we undertake our duty in dangerous territory. Or so some say. I say that, for the Talons, Kafra has yet to create the ground that is truly dangerous— let our enemies look to the dangers the ground holds for them! And in the meantime, we shall march to the Meloderna, to gather up all the supplies our train can carry. But supplies alone will not steel your hearts. To that end, I say only this: however insignificant the Bane may seem to any of you, they are a vicious people who have tried to strike at the beating heart of this kingdom—the God-King himself. The end of Saylal is the end of all you hold dear, Talons—defend him, defend the name of your legion, defend one another, and above all, defend your homeland, where your families will wait, secure in the knowledge that you will make them proud, and will return to them! Talons—Kafra bless you all, bless the God-King, and bless this noble kingdom! We march *now*!"

Only hours upon years of the most exacting training can hold the men of the Talons in their places at that moment. They shout with renewed passion, while the other soldiers, who are not required to be in formation, leap about, hang from the roofs of the other buildings in the quadrangle, and bounce off one another like wild animals. As if on cue, Niksar appears with Arnem's horse, the speckled grey stallion known throughout the army as "the Ox," in affectionate homage to the founder of Broken. Arnem descends to the ground before his wife and, placing a foot in one of his saddle's iron stirrups,[†] he mounts the restless grey. He then coaxes him closer to the steps, and reaches down to pull his wife onto the saddle in front of him—another gesture that drives the soldiers to delighted distraction.

And thus seated, Isadora stays, as the troops turn at the blare of horn calls from their standard-bearers. The column that marches out of the Fourth District is a joyous one, tempered only when, having ridden with her husband to the Celestial Way, Isadora kisses the sentek once more, then dismounts: the soldiers must now proceed through the city to the High Temple, and what is fond camaraderie in the Fourth District will seem improper before the Grand Layzin and Lord Baster-kin. And so, with the lead cavalry units having been brought their hundred horses (herded up from the greener slopes of the mountain before being saddled earlier in the day), the column starts north once more; and Isadora waits for the whole of the *khotor* to pass her by, waving, it seems, to each of the five hundred men individually, but reserving a thrown kiss for her husband alone, who rides with Niksar at the end of the column, having observed the entirety of the men's march out and made sure that they are truly fit for the coming review. Isadora then accepts the escort of two regular army linnets, and sets off home.

The Talons draw crowds all the length of the Celestial Way. The Second and Third Districts are nearing the end of a long day of hectic bartering: trading stalls are being stored for use the next day, while the proprietors of shops within the buildings along the avenue are closing up early to avoid damage from the frantic spectators—and also to get a look at the review. The soldiers' behavior becomes steadily more serious and precise the farther north they progress; and when they arrive at the Temple steps, they find the Grand Layzin, robed in white, under a canopy held by shaved priests. The men receive their blessing from the God-

King, read to them by the Layzin; but this pious show is for the good of the citizenry, more than it is to the taste of the troops. It is only when the Layzin returns to the Temple and Lord Baster-kin appears on his own black mount that the soldiers feel once again free to fully absorb the ecstasy of patriotism that is consuming the citizenry.

As the troops march back down to the East Gate, they once again pass under the watchful eye of their commander, as well as of Baster-kin. Citizens begin to shower the troops with flower petals, and Arnem agrees with both Baster-kin and the other merchant councilors who, all on foot, soon collect about them: the men are in fine form, and their morale seems appropriately high. When the last of the troops have passed by, Arnem salutes Lord Baster-kin, for whose presence he has been genuinely grateful; and Baster-kin continues to speak with the air of confidential trust that he established the night before.

But is it in that same sense of trust that he delivers his final remarks to Arnem? Or does something more perverse lie behind them?

"Oh, one thing more, Arnem—" The Merchant Lord spurs his black mount alongside Arnem's grey. "I thought you'd like to know—the ceremony went off well. Korsar was a model of discipline to the end."

All the joy of the review drains out of Arnem; and he looks down the Celestial Way and over the walls of the city, to the line of Davon Wood, where his friend and commander is almost certainly hanging still, perhaps in wretched agony. "You—you had reports, my lord?"

"I went myself," Baster-kin replies simply. "It seemed the thing to do. At any rate, I thought you'd like to know that he met his end well. Now— fortune go with you, Sentek. Return victorious!" Baster-kin's heels dig into his mount, and he trots easily off in the direction of the Merchants' Hall.

Arnem does not proceed; and Niksar grows concerned.

"Sentek?" Niksar says. "It's time."

"Yes," Arnem answers slowly. "Yes, of course, Niksar," he adds, forcing himself out of a moment both dazed and pensive. "We go—but Niksar? If you happen to see that old madman we encountered last night—bring him to my attention, will you? I've a feeling he's in the crowd."

"Of course, Sentek. But, if you like, I can take care of him myself—"

"No, no, Reyne. Simply point him out . . ."

As it turns out, Arnem does not need any help from Niksar in finding the old man. When the column of men begins to pass through the East Gate, the sentek and his aide are still bringing up the rear. Arnem can see that Niksar has been somewhat unnerved by the mention of the apparitional heretic; and the commander attempts to calm his aide's restless thoughts with pleasant conversation.

"Your brother serves in Daurawah, does he not, Reyne?" the sentek says. "Under my old friend Gledgesa?"

Niksar brightens. "Aye, Sentek. He is a full linnet, now, though I can scarcely believe it. All reports of his service are excellent."

"You'll be happy to see him. As shall I. A fine lad."

"Yes," Niksar says with a nod. "And surely *you* will be happy to see Sentek Gledgesa? For it must have been years—"

It is Arnem's turn to smile. "True. But Gerolf Gledgesa is much like the immutable stone of these walls, Reyne. I expect him to be exactly as—"

Arnem goes silent as he glances toward the East Gate. It is the briefest flash of fabric, but unmistakable enough for the sentek's ever-watchful eyes to mark it: that same garment. The old, faded robe, which was once, no doubt, kept clean and without rips or wrinkles by the careful work of young acolytes, although not such acolytes as are found in the High Temple. The man stands beyond the regular army guards at the gate, staring into Arnem's eyes. How long he has been there, the sentek cannot say, any more than he *can* say why he indulges a perverse idea:

Arnem reins the Ox in, near the spot where the old man stands. Niksar appears increasingly disturbed by the meaningful but silent looks that his commander and the old cripple are exchanging, and finally calls out:

"You, there—guard! Remove that old heretic—"

Arnem holds an arm out, and orders: "No—stand easy, soldier!" He turns to his aide. "No need for that, Reyne," he goes on, as they are enveloped by a hail of rose petals tossed from the tops of the guard towers on either side of the gate. Arnem would indeed be hard-pressed to say why he is about to carry out a most peculiar plan: was it Baster-kin's mention of Yantek Korsar's mutilation, and the peculiar shadow that it threw over Arnem's previously proud mood? Or was it his wife's confusing insistence that he take her pagan clasp, which is even now pressing against his ribs? The sentek has no answers, but he proceeds with his scheme:

"Niksar," he says, still quietly. "Tactfully instruct that guard to let the old man through. Then I want you to ride ahead, and get one of the spare mounts from the cavalry units."

"*Sentek?*" Niksar says in astonishment, keeping his own voice low. "He's mad, and a heretic, what can you possibly—"

"Do as I say, Reyne," Arnem insists gently. "I shall explain later."

Niksar shakes his head in exasperation; but he is too used to following Arnem's orders not to realize when the sentek is in earnest. He pushes his mount through to the gate, and has the guard snatch the mad, agèd vagrant from the crowd. The old man smiles at this, although he must work his staff quickly to coax his wooden leg to keep pace with the soldier. Niksar tells the "heretic" to go to the sentek, while he sets off at a gallop to fetch the horse Arnem has commanded be brought.

As he stands before the new chief of the army of Broken, the sentry who fetched him having returned to his duties, the old man's lips once again curl into that slight, knowing smile; and, to his no more than mild surprise, the sentek returns the expression.

"*Visimar.*" Arnem holds the Ox steady. "Unless I am mistaken."

The old man's smile widens. "You *must* be mistaken, Sentek—for the man you mention is long dead. Indeed, you, as part of the military escort for the priests of Kafra, were present at his mutilation. I am called Anselm—*now* . . ."

"'Anselm'?" Arnem nods judiciously. "'The Helmet of God,' eh? An ambitious name. No matter. You were once a follower of Caliphestros."

"I was first among his acolytes," Anselm declares, discreetly but firmly.

"Yes—all the better," Arnem answers, as Niksar comes back leading a riderless horse behind his own. "Niksar," Arnem says, with subdued cheerfulness. "Meet a man called Anselm. Anselm, my aide, Linnet Niksar."

The old man inclines his head, as Niksar declares, "I've no need to know the names of heretics, Sentek."

"Oh, but you do need to know this one," Arnem replies; and then he looks back down at Anselm. "Can you ride, old man?"

"Sentek!" Niksar blurts out. "You cannot—if word spreads—"

"But word will not spread." Arnem's tone has the ring of finality, and he stares into Niksar's eyes, exuding uncompromising purpose. "You will see to that, Niksar. You're no longer a spy, you've been told as much.

Now, you act only in the interests of the men. And this will, I believe, serve those interests." The sentek looks at Anselm. "Well?"

"I can ride, Sentek," the old man says. "Perhaps you will even wish to explain my missing leg by saying that I was a cavalryman maimed in battle." Arnem smiles and nods agreement. "But, whether I ride or walk, the course that we must now travel was determined when you found me last night: there can be no question but that I shall go with you." Anselm approaches the horse, then glances about for assistance.

Arnem presses the same guard back into momentary service: "You. Get this man mounted."

The guard makes objection with a sour face; but he knows well enough to follow orders, and quickly forms a sling with his hands. Anselm puts his one good leg into the guard's palms.

"Thank you, my son," Anselm says. "Now, if you would only help me swing this gift from the God-King over the beast . . ." The guard—too humiliated to even make sense of this remark—lifts the old man, then roughly seizes the wooden leg and pushes it across the horse, evidently causing the old man some pain; but it is not enough to diminish the latter's pleasure at the moment. "And, if I *should* at any time complain, or slow you, Sentek," the cripple says to Arnem, getting his one foot into the waiting stirrup, "I hope you will tell me. I've no desire to burden this mission more than it already has been."

"Nor shall you." As their horses start through the gate, Arnem turns a serious face to Anselm. "For your role will be that of a mad fool, brought along to coax good fortune out of our smiling god. You agree, I trust?"

"You have my word, Sentek. Now—shall we see what Fate has prepared for us below the mountain?"

Arnem nods; and, with Niksar unhappily bringing up the rear, these last three members of the column head out through the East Gate.

The men eventually wheel right, heading toward the southern and fastest, if not the easiest, route up and down the mountain. (They could not very well have used the South Gate for their exit, for it guards the far less than glorious Fifth District.) In making this move, they are brought to and over a bridge that spans Killen's Run, where Arnem, accompanied by Anselm and Niksar, rides ahead to take up a waiting position and keep a careful eye on his men as they cross, knowing that Niksar's uneasiness about allowing the old man to travel with the column will at first be shared in the ranks. Yet by showing, from the outset, that Anselm travels at his invitation, Arnem knows that he can counteract this. Indeed, if all goes as well as the sentek hopes, Anselm may soon be perceived as just the bringer of good fortune in the field that he has mentioned. For soldiers are a superstitious lot, and a wise commander makes that instinct work for rather than against him—

None of which truly explains why, Niksar observes silently—as Arnem and Anselm receive the (admittedly confused) cheers of the troops during their crossing of the Run—the sentek has asked this disturbing old heretic along on an expedition of vital importance to the kingdom . . .

The march out of the city has been a lengthy one, however, even given its joyous nature; and no man in the ranks is inclined to dwell on the newcomer's presence, nor to fix any save momentary attention on anything but the trail down the mountain and the adventure that lies beyond it. Were any one of them to persist in such curiosity, and to look, for instance, down at Killen's Run as he passes over it, that man would see there, wedged in among the rocks and drifting sticks, the lower portion of a small human arm. The fetid, decaying skin is jaundiced, and drawn tight over the bones; large sores gape grotesquely in the lifeless tissue; and, as the Run laps at it, small pieces of flesh are torn away, disappearing amid the waters that rush to join the Cat's Paw.

$$1:\{xiv:\}$$

The Bane foragers learn of their people's fearsome hope—
and of the part that they are to play in realizing it . . .

TWO SMALL FIRES BURN in three-foot holes chiseled long ago into the cold, smooth granite floor of the antechamber of the Den of Stone, offering some warmth but, together with a few torches mounted on the walls, far more light. Heldo-Bah and Veloc walk behind the Groba Elder and through a short stone passageway leading into this relatively small area, and they do so none too eagerly: both men are aware that their tale, while important, will as a matter of course be doubted by those awaiting them. Indeed, even before they enter the Den, the Elder turns on them suddenly and says: "I warn you two—the High Priestess sits with the Groba tonight, accompanied by two of her Lunar Sisters." Tugging at his beard as he continues forward, the Elder adds, with a sense of gravity heightened by the crisis at hand, "Let us see how well you lie before *those* esteemed personages . . ." Then the older man pauses, commands the foragers to remain in the antechamber while he announces their arrival, and disappears down a second passageway that is longer and even darker than the first, and that leads finally into the Den.

Heldo-Bah immediately begins to pace in fear. "Oh, sublime," the gap-toothed forager noises. "Perfection! Did you hear, Veloc?"

The handsome Bane is wandering about the antechamber, admiring a series of ancient reliefs that are cut directly into the stone walls: scenes of exile and suffering, which eventually lead to happier images of homes being built and a tribe being formed. And in the background of each depiction looms the image of a fortress-capped mountain, a constant reminder of how consistently the people of Broken have tried to thwart the ambitions of the Bane—without success. Water that drains down slowly from springs inside the stone walls and ceiling has covered the carvings with a light, black-green growth; and the motion of this water, along with the jumping light of the fires, makes the carvings seem alive.

"Did I hear what, Heldo-Bah?" Veloc asks, transparently blithe.

"Don't—do not even attempt it," barks Heldo-Bah. "You heard—the bloody High Priestess is there. We are *dead men!*"

"You overstate the issue," Veloc says, maintaining his false air of calm. "She and I parted on congenial enough terms . . ."

"Oh, certainly—she rejected your application to be the blasted Bane historian out of hand, and sent us out into the Wood immediately! Very congenial!" Heldo-Bah paces anxiously. "It's never made the slightest sense, Veloc. You try to seduce every woman in Okot, in Broken, and in every town between—and when a woman who might actually do us some good asks for you, what do you do? Refuse her!"

"I'm not some prized bull, to play stud to an overbearing young female whenever she goes into heat."

"Absolutely absurd," Heldo-Bah murmurs, shaking his head. "Utterly and completely—"

He is interrupted by the sudden call of the Elder's voice: "Ho, there! Foragers! You may enter!"

The two men walk into the passageway before them, the utter darkness of which is a contrivance designed by the Groba, so that when supplicants enter the main chamber they will be all the more overawed by its dimensions: a ceiling over thirty feet high, with enormous, needle-like formations of rock and minerals seeming to drip down from above, as though the cave were slowly melting. The walls of the chamber are adorned with elaborate suits of Broken armor, stuffed with rags and straw so that they appear alive, even to the smooth white-and-black riverbed stones set into the sockets of human skulls (which in turn rest inside each helmet), so that they resemble the eyes of dead men, staring madly at those who have come through the passageway. Weapons of the Tall also adorn the walls: large collections of spears, swords, battle-axes, and maces, each group bursting out from a Broken shield, any one of which is as tall as a Bane. The chamber is lit and heated by an enormous fire set into one recess in the wall opposite the Groba's council table; and the "chimney" of this fiery alcove is a naturally occurring shaftway that empties out at the very top of the rock formation, along the sharp rise of the mountain slope above. In all, it is a sight that makes a profound impression on nearly every Bane, particularly as most only ever see it once in their lives, when they petition for permission to wed.

For habitual guests of the Den, on the other hand, the inner chamber is noteworthy only because it never changes, save for the occasional addition of some trophy taken from the Tall; but often, even these changes go unnoticed, for to be a frequent visitor is to be an incurable nuisance to the tribe—or worse—and all such tend to train their eyes on the Groba itself, to determine what mood the old men are in, and what chances exist for leniency.

Heldo-Bah follows this pattern, taking in the five familiar faces of the Groba Elders: elected officials,[†] each of whom is, in appearance, remarkably like the next. They all wear identical grey robes, cut their beards to the same middling length, and sit on rough-hewn, high-backed benches. The only differences among the five are the amounts of hair on each head, the length of their noses, and, finally, the fact that the chair belonging to the senior Elder (formally referred to as "Father") has a higher back than the others; and that the top of said back is carved into a crescent Moon whose horns point skyward.

Tonight, however, all is different among the Bane, within the Den as without. At the right end of the table sits the Priestess of the Moon, who wears a golden gown over a white smock. Draped over her shoulders and head is an airy shawl of deep blue, onto which have been embroidered golden stars, which grow more numerous as they approach the front of a golden coronet that holds the shawl in place, and which is adorned with yet another crescent Moon. She is young, this High Priestess, having taken her vows only a year earlier, at sixteen. Before that, she had been merely the most promising of the Lunar Sisterhood, and was therefore entitled, as Heldo-Bah has said, to decide which men from the tribe she would mate with, in the hope of producing more semi-divine female children. Thus, all of the Lunar Sisters, and therefore the High Priestesses, are descendants of those women who originally held the same positions, and their pure lineage gives them enormous power: for, while they are far from a chaste order of female clergy, they are as close as any member of the Bane tribe (whose notion of immoral behavior is usually quite loosely defined) could wish for—or would desire.

It therefore requires men of rare talents to push the boundaries of so loose a system of theology and morality beyond acceptable limits; but Veloc and Heldo-Bah are just such men . . .

The two foragers can see that behind the High Priestess are not only two of her Lunar Sisters, but a pair of Outragers, as well. Evidently, the High Priestess has points she wishes to make about the catastrophe that has struck the Bane tribe, and she wants to make them forcefully enough to command compliance from the Groba Elders, who, if the letter of Bane law is followed (and the Bane have indeed preserved their laws in writing), have principal say over secular matters in Okot, just as the Lunar Sisterhood rules on matters of spiritual importance. Yet, again, laxity of customs allows these divisions to occasionally shift; and every so often, control of the tribe's reaction to a secular threat can be influenced by the High Priestess, a young woman whose only qualification for power over matters of mortal importance is that she is said to possess a unique ability to converse with the sacred Moon.

The Groba Father, a man whose features—sharp, clear-eyed, and tightly wrinkled—seem to indicate an even greater intolerance of nonsense than that which characterized the bald-headed Elder whom Heldo-Bah and Veloc have just followed into the Den, looks up from a scattered raft of parchment documents[†] that litter the council table. His grey hair and beard are distinguishable from those of his fellows only by their streaks of white: badges of honor for having prevailed in a majority of the frequently argumentative sessions of the Groba. And never is the chamber more full of disagreements than when the High Priestess chooses to attend—a fact of which Heldo-Bah and Veloc are only too aware.

"Ah. Heldo-Bah—finally," says the Groba Father, his voice hoarse. "I might have known you'd be the last to return. But it's just as well—your party will have a crucial task, and we have just finished compiling all information that was gleaned in the Wood by the other foraging parties."

"Father?" Heldo-Bah says, with astounding obsequiousness, considering his constant complaints about what he habitually calls "that great collection of stone-brained eunuchs," the Groba.

The Groba Father ignores him. "And Veloc is here, too. Good. Less time wasted explaining." The Father looks down the council table. "You will remember Veloc," he says. "The man who was nominated for Historian of the Bane Tribe last year." The four other men nod, so nearly in unison that Veloc almost laughs aloud; but he becomes somber again, and quickly, at the sharp sound of the High Priestess's voice:

"A nomination that was rejected," she says, the pretty dark eyes in her round face fixed on Veloc, as if she will destroy him with a glance, "because of the corruption that we discovered in his disobedient soul."

Heldo-Bah's eyes open wide, and he bounces a bit on the balls of his feet, looking up at the cave's ceiling and murmuring softly, "Oh, yes, by all means—let's bring *that* up at a time like this . . ."

"You spoke, Heldo-Bah?" the Priestess demands.

Keeping his gaze as wide as an innocent child's, Heldo-Bah replies, "I, Divine One? Not a word."

"See to it that you don't," the Groba Father says sternly, "unless you are spoken to. We have much to resolve—approach the table!"

Dragging their feet and picking at their tunics, which are laden with signs of nights spent in the Wood, the two foragers move to the council table. The faces gathered around that heavy assemblage of split logs become clearer in the light of small fat-lamps that sit upon the uneven surface. Viewed close-to, the Groba Elders display admirable self-possession, both despite and because of the ongoing crisis. The faces of the High Priestess and the Lunar Sisters, by contrast, remain haughty, dissatisfied, and full of accusations, while the Outragers behind them display a much simpler desire to beat the foragers senseless.

"Your current foraging assignment," the Father says, staring down at a parchment map, "should have taken you northwest. Near Hafften Falls and Lord Baster-kin's Plain." The Father looks up, expecting a contradiction. "Did it?"

"Of course, Father," Heldo-Bah answers simply.

"How refreshing to even think of you obeying an order, Heldo-Bah," the Father says, with weary familiarity. Then he takes note for the first time of just who is *not* before him: "But where is Keera?" he says, deeply concerned. "She is the leader of your party, and the key to what we seek from you."

"She searches the *Lenthess-steyn,* Father, to find her family," Veloc answers, his own worry plain. "Or at least, to hear word of them."

For the first time, all the Groba Elders display signs of exhaustion. The Father rubs his eyes hard, and then sighs. "The Moon go with her," he says, and the other Elders murmur assent.

The eyes of the Priestess, however, blaze ever hotter, though her body remains quite still. "She has done little, of late, to earn the Moon's favor." The Priestess concentrates her gaze on Veloc, who persistently avoids it. "Indeed, none of this party has ever shown true worthiness."

The Groba Elders are clearly not in agreement with this statement, at least insofar as it refers to Keera; but they desire to avoid an argument with the Priestess. Into this momentary silence steps Heldo-Bah:

"We cannot all be blessed with your abundance of virtue, Divinity," he says with a patently false smile. He catches the Priestess's eye, but, unlike Veloc, refuses to turn away.

"Do not," the Father repeats in annoyance, "speak, Heldo-Bah, unless it is to answer a question. So—Keera seeks her family, and you have already been fully informed of the details of the plague?"

"Well, we were hardly likely to miss—" Heldo-Bah's comment is cut short by one of Veloc's boots, which catches him in a shin.

"I beg your pardon, Father," Veloc says. "My friend is, for want of a better word, an idiot. To answer your query, we have seen the fire in the northeastern settlement, and we have spoken with Yantek Ashkatar. He said that the pestilence is believed to be the work of the Tall—" Noticing the impatience on the Father's face, Veloc grows silent, realizing he is providing excessive detail.

"We are concerned," says another Elder, who puts his elbows on the table and folds his bony hands, "with what you have seen in the *Wood,* not Okot—assuming that you did, as you say, follow your assigned route. Were there any signs of plague to the north? Unexplained animal carcasses? Dead men? Activity of the Tall near the river?"

"We saw nothing—" Veloc suddenly stops himself, catching sight of the High Priestess's hateful eyes; but thinking of his sister and of what is at stake for the tribe as a whole, he decides that he must abandon caution. "Actually, Elder, that's not true. We saw and heard several things that we could not explain, and that may well have to do with the plague."

The Groba Father folds his arms, and lets out an infuriated snort.

"I am sorry, Father," Veloc says to the man. "But you did say that we must only answer questions."

"All right," the Father says. "Just what *is* your remarkable tale?"

Heldo-Bah looks astonished. "Yes, just what *is* our tale, Veloc?" he echoes, fearing full revelation of their night's activities.

"I'm sorry, Heldo-Bah," Veloc replies, "but there may be importance to it—"

"Importance to *what,* Veloc?" Heldo-Bah murmurs, far more urgently.

"She's my sister, damn it all!" Veloc defends, quietly but emphatically. "Those children are my niece and nephews—you can't possibly expect—"

"I *expect* nothing, Veloc," Heldo-Bah now whispers, pushing his nose close to his friend's, and pointing to the Outragers, "except that we get out of this chamber without having to cut our way through those paragons of viciousness up there—"

"*Enough!*" The Groba Father stands, and walks around the council table to face the silenced foragers. "What are we to do with you, Heldo-Bah?" he demands. "Eh? You remain the first and the only Bane to be condemned to a full lifetime of foraging, yet you still risk bringing the wrath of Broken down on us with your unremitting offenses against the Tall. Do you think that you are the only Bane who wants to see the destruction of that city? We all pray for it. But can you not work for the good of the tribe, rather than constantly seeking to harass the people of

Broken?" The Father steps to his left. "And you, Veloc—far from offending the Tall, you wish to make *love* to them!"

"Well . . . ," Veloc mumbles cravenly. "Not to *all* of them, Father."

The Father balls his hands, speaking with measured fury: "No. Not to all of them. But every woman of the Tall you've bedded has brought retribution from Broken's merchants and soldiers! Can you not be satisfied with a female of your own kind?"

"Are not the Bane men, too, Father?" Veloc asks, his mouth moving with more speed than sense.

"Don't be clever with me, boy," the Father answers, putting one trembling fist in Veloc's face. "You know what I mean." The Groba Father wanders back around the table toward his seat. "And I understand Keera least of all. She is our finest tracker, and has no flaws of character, save an inexplicable willingness to defend you two! *Why?*"

Veloc kicks at the cave floor. "It's difficult to explain, Father. You see, we all grew up together—Heldo-Bah and I, and Keera—"

"A poor excuse for ignoring her responsibilities as a vital member of this tribe, Veloc—to say nothing of her duties as a mother!" The Elder collapses into his seat with another sigh. "Why I should have expected useful information from you three, I don't know . . ."

Silence reigns; and Heldo-Bah, who has been wrestling with the sickly thing he calls a conscience, coughs. "Father—if I may speak?"

The Groba Father looks as though someone has put his thumb in a screw. "*Must* you?"

"Well, Father, you did ask, and Veloc was trying to tell you—that is, you wished to know if we had seen any activity on the part of the soldiers of the Tall. And, while it's true that we did not *see* such activity—"

"Then why waste the Groba's precious time in this hour of sadness and crisis?" the Priestess demands harshly.

"Yes, Divine One," Heldo-Bah says, bowing in her direction, "it's probable that I do waste your time. That is, if you consider the presence of one of the Wives of Kafra in Davon Wood to be insignificant."

The Father's shock is mirrored in the faces of the other Elders. "A Wife of . . ." His voice soon recovers its strength. "When?"

"Last night, Father—just before the sounding of the Horn."

"And where? To the north? Speak, man, for out of your liar's mouth may yet come the true answer to this deadly riddle!"

Quickly, and with embellishment from Veloc, Heldo-Bah relates the tale of the Wife of Kafra and the panther, as well as of the dead and diseased member of Lord Baster-kin's Guard, and the golden arrows that killed him. All of Veloc's storytelling skills go into heightening the drama of his friend's account, and, following the completion of their performance, the Groba Elders whisper among themselves, doing their best to limit the contribution of the Priestess and her Lunar Sisters. Finally, the Father speaks:

"And Keera knew of nothing that could induce such behavior in the panther? Nor of any other cause for the Guardsman's death?"

"She swore that nothing in Nature could explain either event," Veloc replies. "It was surely sorcery of some sort, Father, regarding the beast— and the arrows speak for themselves."

"We need no forager to tell us as much," the Priestess scoffs. "What we do need is to stop dawdling—the Tall have sent the plague through Broken sorcery, and we will only be able to respond in kind."

The Groba Father looks at the other Elders' faces; and, one by one, they all nod assent. "It is agreed," he says. "Heldo-Bah, Veloc, you are—"

The Father cuts his statement short, fixing his eyes on the entrance to the chamber. A figure has appeared in the shadows at the mouth of the passageway; and as it moves toward the table slowly, the Groba, the Priestess's retinue, and the foragers can all see that it is Keera:

She carries her daughter, four-year-old Effi,[†] whose arms hang around her mother's neck. The child has been weeping, and she continues to sob in an exhausted manner. Keera's own face is wet with tears, and she stops when she has covered half the distance to the Groba's table, blankly searching the faces of those arrayed before her. As Veloc goes to her, Heldo-Bah looks quickly to the Father.

"You may approach her," he says. "If the healers have released them, they are safe. Would that we knew why, when so many others die . . ."

With that assurance, Heldo-Bah and Veloc rush to either side of Keera; and both men are slowed and then stopped by what they see. Keera's face, ordinarily the image of confident (if realistic) readiness, has been transformed into a portrait of devastation. Veloc takes Effi from her, at which Keera does not so much kneel as fall painfully, feeling nothing as her kneecaps land hard on the stone floor. But it is the expression on her face that remains the principal cause for concern: her eyes are drawn deep into her skull, her lower jaw hangs in seeming lifelessness. Indeed, Heldo-Bah realizes that he has only ever seen such changes to human features on the faces of those who have been tortured unto death by human hands, or expired amid the terrible cold of the high mountains in deep winter.

"Tayo was already dead," Keera says of her husband, the words scarcely enunciated. "Effi is unaffected, but Herwin and Baza—they will not allow them to leave the *Lenthess-steyn*. Herwin may survive, they say, but Baza will almost certainly . . ." She begins to fall forward: it is only Heldo-Bah's attentive agility—an alertness born of his expectation that the worst in life not only can happen, but usually will—that allows him to snatch her up before her face hits the stone. He holds her back upright, and she stares into his eyes without seeing them. "I did not recognize him . . . Tayo. His face, as well as his body—there were so many sores, so much swelling, so much blood and pus . . ." Tears come when she speaks of her boys: Herwin, eight years old, and Baza, only six. "Baza is barely alive . . . He cried out, when he saw me, and said there was pain— *everywhere* . . . But I was not allowed to touch him. And Herwin looks as though—as though . . . Yet no one can predict—*anything.*"

She looks about frantically for a moment, murmuring "Effi," and then sees the girl in Veloc's arms. She snatches the child away, and together they begin weeping anew, Effi in the same weary manner—for she has been forcibly separated from her father and brothers in the *Lenthess-steyn* for over a day—and Keera with the rigidity of body that is often present before the reality of death has become fully comprehensible: as if physical exertion can will it away. Heldo-Bah and Veloc each put a hand to her shoulders.

"So this is how the Tall kill, now," Heldo-Bah says to Veloc, characteristically attempting to dissolve his own grief into bitterness. "Would that I had put my knife in that witch's heart . . ."

A few silent moments pass, with only the sound of Keera's and Effi's sobbing playing off the walls of the Den, along with the occasional crackle from the fire. Whispers pass from Veloc to Keera, after he puts his mouth close to her ear; and the Groba Elders allow the little group of the foragers and Effi a few minutes before the Father gently calls out:

"Keera?" He stands again, and positions himself between Keera and the High Priestess. If more unfeeling remarks should escape the latter, the Father has decided that he will interrupt and then stifle them, lest they do yet more harm to Keera's already brutalized soul; indeed, the Father determines that he will risk divine wrath by plainly telling the zealous young holy woman to hold her tongue, if he must. But his eyes stay on the foragers. "We grieve with you, Keera, believe that. There is not a member of the Groba who has not lost someone dear—children, grandchildren—"

"A wife of thirty years," says the bald-headed Elder mournfully; and when Heldo-Bah looks at this man—who brought Veloc and himself into the Den without exhibiting the smallest sign that he had suffered so devastating a blow—he feels not only remorse for the old man's loss, but admiration for one who has, in so disciplined a manner, put the tribe ahead of his own suffering.

"Indeed," the Groba Father says, looking back at his fellow councilor. "This pestilence has struck at every part of the Bane tribe, and will continue to do so, if we do not act quickly. So believe that our hearts are with you, Keera, and believe, as well, that you three foragers must now undertake a task that offers our only hope, not only of stopping the spread of this malevolent sickness, but of avenging the dead."

At this, Keera lifts her face and turns to the Elders; then, slowly, she takes her brother's and her friend's comforting hands from her shoulders, and walks a few steps forward, approaching the Groba's council table while constantly clinging tight to little Effi. She wipes at her face with a sleeve, and musters the strength to ask, "But—how is that possible, Father?" And then she adds, with humble skepticism, "We are only foragers."

"Your brother and Heldo-Bah may be nothing more," the Father replies. "But you are the best of our trackers, Keera, a true mistress of the Wood. No one has traveled as deeply into its southwestern reaches as you have—and it is there that we must now ask you to go again."

And for the first time, a faint light of hope seems to dawn amid the wasteland that is Keera's face, and to put the smallest gleam of comprehension back into her terribly deadened eyes.

But it is Veloc who speaks: "Your pardon, Father, but—why? You see what this disease has already done to my sister, to her family—how can you ask her to leave them again?"

"See how he avoids service," declares the High Priestess. "Truly, this is not the party to send. The two men should fight with the warriors, not avoid the dangers yet to come. And the woman should be allowed to be near her children, when they come to face death."

Heldo-Bah, whose eyes have been studying first Keera, and then the Groba, begins to smile. He turns to the Priestess, with a look that would, under other circumstances, provoke combat between himself and the Outragers. "But there *is* no other party to send, O Divine Trough of Lunar Grace," he says, the falseness of his deferential tone now transparent. "Am I not correct, Father?"

The Father nods, then looks to the High Priestess and her Sisters. "Do not think that they escape danger by undertaking this task. Indeed, theirs may well be the gravest danger of all—" He looks to Keera again. "And more important than any battle of armies."

All five of the Elders are examining Keera, Heldo-Bah, and Veloc, in turn; they are pleased to find comprehension in the first two, and are ready to wait for it to strike the third.

Soon enough, it does: *"Caliphestros!"* Veloc declares.

Heldo-Bah's grin widens, as he looks at the Priestess; and his eyes speak eloquently of how badly she has lost this encounter. "Yes," he says, giving voice to his quiet but pointed triumph. "Caliphestros . . ."

"Indeed," the Father declares, giving the Priestess one final glance, as if to say: *And so, be still—there are no other possibilities.* Then, aloud, he repeats the appellation a third time: "Caliphestros . . ."

For several moments, all in the chamber sit still, absorbing the name with obvious dread. The Outragers, in particular, seem swept up in the superstitious fear that has been instilled in Bane children for the last two-score years, that to speak of the man—if man he is!—heightens the chance that he will come to one's bed, of a night, to sweep the unfortunate victim's spirit away . . .

Finally, it is Veloc who brings practical considerations back to the fore: "But, Father—it is true that we once saw his dwelling, or what we thought was his dwelling. But that journey was long, and largely the result of accidents. It nearly killed us, as well, and—"

"And it can be repeated." It is Keera speaking, now, and her voice is regaining strength. "I can find the place again."

Veloc moves up to stand with his sister. "But, Keera—we do not even know if he is alive."

"Perhaps not," Keera replies. "But if there is even a chance . . ."

"And what of the children?" Veloc insists, although it is clearly for Keera's benefit: he does not yet trust that she is thinking clearly, and would not have her commit to an undertaking that will later cause her more grief and guilt. "Don't you want to stay—"

"There is nothing we can do, Veloc," Keera replies. "Nothing, save this. The healers will not let me near Herwin and Baza, and likely cannot save either of my sons. And Effi will be safe—our parents can mind her, until we return." Exhausted little Effi quietly objects to this notion, but Keera calms her.

"Listen to your sister, Veloc," Heldo-Bah says, continuing to smile at the High Priestess. "This is our only hope—to fight the sorcery of the Tall with the Tall's greatest sorcerer."

Veloc has not quite conceded: "But the disease spreads so quickly. How long will we have to succeed, before our efforts become meaningless?"

"Only the Tall can answer that with any certainty, Veloc," says the Father. "We believe they mean to attack, once the disease has weakened us sufficiently; what they have not counted upon is that our healers believe that they can, at least, control the disease's spread, by separating the healthy from the ill, and above all by burning the dead. Hastily." This last word causes Keera to wince; and, seeing as much, the Father continues: "I regret such blunt words, Keera. It is not an easy thought, I know, and I wish I could tell you that time will make it easier. But the only thing that can ease our suffering is precisely what Heldo-Bah says—we must fetch the greatest sorcerer that ever walked among the Tall, to undo the deadly work of the kingdom he once served." The father sits, taking a sheet of parchment and scribbling on it with a quill. "There is no more specific order we can give you. Make what preparations you must, take whatever supplies you need. This—" he rolls his completed document, and holds it out to Heldo-Bah, "will give you full authority. You will want for nothing—but do not abuse the privilege, Heldo-Bah."

"And, in the name of the Moon—" The Priestess, having conceded the point of who will go on this vital journey, feels the need to at least attempt to assert herself a final time: "Try to show greater faith than you have in the past. The life of the tribe may well depend upon it."

Keera's head snaps about, to give the Priestess a hateful glower. "Some of us, Divine One, have already learned that."

It is yet another impertinence, and the Priestess thinks to protest. But a firm look from the Groba Father repeats the warning he must not voice aloud: *You have said enough—be still.* He turns again to the foragers.

"Go, now," he says, "and take our heartfelt prayers with you."

The same Elder who guided them into the Den now rises to escort the foragers back out. Veloc puts an arm around Keera and Effi, and gently tries again to ascertain, as they go through the passageway, whether or not Keera truly has the strength for this undertaking. This leaves Heldo-Bah to walk behind them with the Elder; and it is an awkward moment for the forager. He does not speak the language of polite Bane society, nor indeed of *any* polite society; and yet, for reasons he cannot precisely define, he wishes to express his respect and sympathy for the man. He waits until they pass through the antechamber and emerge into the day. The Elder comes to a halt just outside the cave's mouth, and Heldo-Bah faces him.

"Thirty years," he says awkwardly, scratching at his beard. "A long time, to be with one woman." The Elder's pain becomes apparent; but he also seems baffled. "Long time to be with *anyone,* really," Heldo-Bah continues. But it is no use—he has no talent for saying what he wishes in a proper manner; and so he drops the guise, smiles, and says, "Don't worry, old fellow—" Then he pulls a tunic sleeve over one hand and, inexplicably, rubs the top of the Elder's bald pate. "We're going to find that bloody sorcerer for you—and you'll have your justice!"

"Stop that—Heldo-Bah!" The Elder takes hold of the forager's arm, and pushes it away with surprising strength, staring at Heldo-Bah in shock; and yet, possibly because he understands that some small kernel of compassion lies at the heart of the forager's bizarre behavior, he does not reproach him, other than to say, "At times I do believe you really are mad . . ."

But Heldo-Bah is already hurrying down the pathway to catch his friends, who have stopped to retrieve their sacks—no easy task, as Ashkatar is atop them, stealing some desperately needed and richly deserved snippets of sleep, while intermittently waking to ensure that the crowd of angry Bane does not gather again. He bolts upright when he hears the Elder call out:

"Yantek Ashkatar!"

Ashkatar gets himself righted, with help from Heldo-Bah and Veloc. "Elder?" he shouts.

"The Groba will see you now!"

Ashkatar has not gone half a dozen steps before he stops and turns back to Keera. "You have accepted the commission?"

Rocking Effi, who has fallen into sad slumber, Keera replies, "We have, Yantek."

Ashkatar nods. "Some thought that you would refuse it—but I felt certain that you would not. And I want you to know—about your boys." Ashkatar pulls at his whip. "Don't fear that they will be forgotten, while you're gone. My men and I shall watch over them as if they were our own—and I shall keep your parents ever informed of how it goes with them."

Keera's eyes fill with tears, but she is determined to control her grief and her worry until the journey she is faced with is done. "Thank you, Yantek," she says, with deep respect. Then she begins to walk slowly toward her parents' home, just south of the village center, still rocking Effi from side to side.

"And Veloc—" Ashkatar points his whip. "You and Heldo-Bah take care of her, eh? Especially in the southwestern Wood. Take care of yourselves, too—it's hellish country, and all our hopes go with you."

Veloc nods. "Aye," he says, and then turns to catch his sister.

Heldo-Bah pauses, still grinning. "And how would you know what the country's like down there?" he asks. Ashkatar flushes with angry embarrassment, at which Heldo-Bah laughs once and says: "But it was a noble sentiment, Ashkatar. I'm deeply touched . . ."

Before the commander of the Bane army can reply, Heldo-Bah runs off; nevertheless, Ashkatar shouts after him: "Damn you, Heldo-Bah— It's *Yantek* Ashka—!" But then, out of the corner of his eye, he catches sight of the Elder still waiting, and murmurs to himself, "Ah, the blazes with it . . ." Straightening his tunic, he watches the foragers disappear into the crowds of weeping, shouting, desperate Bane as he starts up the path.

"The Moon go with you three," he murmurs softly.

Then he hurries inside the Den of Stone, to propose the scheme he believes will allow the infant and drastically outnumbered army of the Bane—a force as yet no more than two hundred strong—to defend Davon Wood against the mightiest military machine north of *Lumunjan,* at least until such time as the foragers return.

"And what happens after *that*," Ashkatar murmurs to himself as he catches up to the Elder, "I can't even begin to guess at . . ."

$$1:\{xv:\}$$

Sunset at the High Temple brings strange and
wondrous visitors . . .

ON MAKING THE KAFRAN FAITH the state religion of Broken—and of himself, a deity—Thedric, the patricidal son of the Mad King Oxmontrot, speaking through the first of the Grand Layzins, pledged to create great works in the name of his "true father": the golden god. He quickly completed the High Temple of Kafra (in which Oxmontrot had never shown more than a passing interest), and greatly increased its beauty of design; and through rituals conducted therein, the banishments that Oxmontrot had instituted as a pragmatic method of forging a united people who would be capable of not only creating an impregnable city, but of defending themselves in the field from the conquering hordes that the Mad King had fought during his years of service to *Lumun-jan*, became the unshakable pillars of the new kingdom's faith. Soon thereafter, the Sacristy had been built, above the ground between the Temple's western and the Inner City's eastern walls; so, too, had been the Stadium, where once had stood a second, smaller headquarters for the northern watch of the Broken army; and finally, adjoining the Sacristy, was erected the House of the Wives of Kafra, the second story of which became the Grand Layzin's official residence. A spacious veranda off the Layzin's splendid bedchamber offered an excellent view of the Inner City's Lake of a Dying Moon, as well as the upper stories of the royal palace, while a new, underground passage beneath the House of the Wives of Kafra connected the Temple, the Layzin, and the priestesses directly to the palace and the royal family. But these additions were merely practical, designed to make the secret lives of Broken's rulers and the business of Kafran clerics easier; only the veranda and balcony outside the Layzin's bedchamber had been designed purely as an indulgence, one intended to give Broken's senior priest a view of the Inner City, that he might watch as the setting sun was reflected off the black waters of the Lake.

For the long succession of Grand Layzins, who had neither claim nor pretense to godhood, life within the House of the Wives proved a welcome respite from the often overwhelming responsibilities of giving voice to (and more often than not, creating) the edicts of the various God-Kings, whose removal from the world made their views upon mundane secular matters of somewhat limited utility. The Layzins' burdens were eased, early in the new life of Broken, by the elevation of the head of the city's Merchants' Council to the position of First Advisor of the realm. The most onerous of the Layzin's chores could finally be handed off to a worldly man more suited to dealing with them, and none too soon; for the rise of the savage tribes on every side of Broken, during the first generations of the kingdom's existence, required some very *secular* responses.

The successive Lords of the Merchants' Council proved, thankfully, dedicated men. Indeed, they were so effective (especially when supported, as they usually were, by those peerlessly loyal men who attained the supreme rank of yantek of the Broken army) that the Layzins had time to focus the greater part of their energies on elaborating precise ways in which the sublime quests for physical perfection and the attainment of wealth should govern the daily lives of the people of the kingdom. And no single spot on Kafra's own Earth, these men have ever believed, was or is more suited to such ruminations than the veranda above the House of the Wives of Kafra, where their lofty thoughts have ever been fed by views enveloped in the powerful scent of the wild roses that climb the walls of the gardens that surround the building.

The man now called Grand Layzin has taken particular delight in the simple pleasures offered by the secluded veranda since first taking office; and this evening—as he reclines on a sofa of expertly worked calves' leather that is scattered with down cushions covered in the very softest lamb's wool and silk, and which is so positioned as to give him a wondrous view of both the Celestial Way to the south and the Inner City to the west—his thoughts turn to the gloriously serene early years of his service. They had been full of seemingly unlimited opportunities to guarantee the sustained youth and vitality—indeed, the *immortality*—of his beloved young God-King, Saylal; had been full, in fact, of the promise that not only *his* sacred beauty and strength but those same qualities among his priests and priestesses could be made safe forever from corruption and death, if the Natures of all these qualities and processes could be but better understood and opposed. All this had seemed within reach—*once* . . .

But now, as the Layzin's mind inevitably turns to thoughts of the departure, earlier, of five hundred of the city's finest young men to attend to a problem that the Layzin himself knows to transcend that of the Bane, the exhausted high priest finds himself rising to close one set of the gossamer drapes that hang on the veranda; finds himself, strangely, *obscuring* his view of the Inner City and the Lake of a Dying Moon, and then taking his seat again, to stare at the long avenue down which those five hundred nearly perfect men—commanded by an officer of, if not perfect breeding, at least perfect loyalty—marched on their way out of the city.

And, thinking of all these things, the Layzin sighs . . .

He is still dressed in his ceremonial robes, which are of the softest white cotton available to Broken traders; and he sips the sweet white wine made from grapes native to the valley of the Meloderna. Below him, he can hear the frequent laughter of the Wives and the other priestesses, which should be a perfect accompaniment to the beautiful spring evening. But then, as he looks to the right of the Celestial Way and at the gates of the Inner City (the walls of which enclose no fewer than forty ackars[†]), he spies detachments of Lord Baster-kin's Guard changing their watch; and the pleasure of the roses and the laughter fades. *Yet all is being done that can be done, that is certain,* he tries to tell himself; and then the nagging doubt: *But will it prove enough . . . ?*

To his right, the gossamer drapes catch the sharpening golden light of the setting spring sun: that same light that entranced so many Layzins before him. The drapes diffuse the glare, in much the same way that the wine begins to calm the Layzin's soul; and a light breeze buffets the fabric ever so slightly, then does the same to similar hangings that cover the arched doorway to his bedchamber. Suddenly, through these last drapes, the Layzin sees the silhouette of a graceful servant approaching. He silently prays for the servant to bring no new reports, no new rumblings of still more troubles in the farthest reaches of the kingdom, and, above all, no word of still more poisonings—indeed, the Layzin would be pleased with no message at all.

But he knows that it cannot be so: not at this moment in the life of the kingdom. Thus he is unsurprised when the youth—some seventeen years of age, with a powerful body plainly visible through his own very sheer white robes—delicately steps out onto the veranda, made timid by the thought of disturbing his master.

"It's all right, Entenne," the Layzin says softly. "I am not sleeping."

"Thank you, master," the youth Entenne says. "Her blessedness, the First Wife of Kafra, has returned from Davon Wood."

"Ah." The Layzin sets down his goblet, believing his prayers for good news to have been answered. "Excellent."

The youth wrings his hands in distress. "Apparently there was an—an *encounter,* master. Of which she can best tell you, I am certain."

The Layzin appears pained. "All right. Then let her enter."

The youth slips from the veranda as silently as he entered it; and in moments a young woman with a long, striking sweep of black hair and brilliant green eyes enters. She wears a robe of black edged in red velvet, and moves with confident strides toward the Layzin, her remarkably fit legs appearing through long slits in the robe. Kneeling, she takes the Layzin's ring hand when it is offered, and kisses the pale blue stone, which appears all the paler under the brilliance of her green eyes. She kisses the stone a second, then a third time, after which she holds the hand tightly to her neck.

"Master. I have succeeded. In the name of the God-King, and for his sake. The animal is within the palace. The children are outside."

The Layzin leans down to her. "And this 'encounter,' Alandra[†] . . . ?"

The woman looks up at him, smiling yet momentarily concerned. "A party of Bane foragers, Eminence. Before their Horn had sounded. No harm was done—I believe they suspected sorcery."

The Layzin cups the woman's chin, admiring its perfect angle and size. "And would they have been so very wrong? I sometimes wonder . . ." He stands. "The animal is for tonight. Saylal is most anxious. And the children—their parents agreed?"

"Yes, Eminence. It was only a matter of money."

"And what are the ages?"

"Twelve years the boy, eleven the girl."

"Ideal. We must prepare them at once. The others . . ." The Layzin looks at the guards before the Inner City gates once more: "The others are dying more quickly than we can dispose of them . . . And it grows harder to greet those who replace them, knowing . . ." He rouses himself. "But it must be done—and so bring them to me, Alandra . . ."

The woman departs; and for several disconcerting moments, the Layzin tries, with every ounce of strength, to continue looking out over the city; anywhere, save west, at—

The woman reappears, this time accompanied by two children, who wear clothes of a rough fabric. They are fair-haired, with light young eyes that peer out from pale faces in wonder and fear. Guided by the woman, they approach the Layzin, who smiles gently at them.

"Do you know why you are here, children?" he says. Both the boy and the girl shake their heads, and the Layzin laughs quietly. "Your family has given you in service to the God-King Saylal. What that means is very simple—" The Layzin glances up when he hears the musical rattle of glass, and sees the woman Alandra within the bedchamber, preparing two deep blue glasses with lemon water, the new granulated crystals known as *sukkar*[†] (for a taste of which nearly all children, and many an adult, will do almost anything), and finally a third ingredient, contained in a glass vial. The Layzin looks at the children again. "Whatever you are told to do, you must obey, with pleasure when you can, but above all without question—to doubt is to risk your souls, and those of your families. Kafra rejoices in the prosperity of the God-King, and the God-King delights in the obedience of his servants. Here—drink this . . ."

The Layzin takes the two glasses from Alandra, and hands one to each child. They drink cautiously, at first, then eagerly, when they taste the sweet liquid. "Good," the Layzin pronounces. "Very good. Now—" Tenderly, the Layzin kisses each child on the forehead. "Go along with your mistress," he whispers. "And remember—obey, always."

Looking more confused than they did on entering—but also undisturbed, now, by that confusion—the children follow the First Wife of Kafra out of the room.

"Entenne?" the Layzin calls softly; and the youthful servant reappears. "Run to the home of Lord Baster-kin. Say to him that I am unwell, after the exertions of the day, and will not be able to attend his dinner. Express my apologies."

Entenne nods, and goes down on one knee. "Of course, Eminence," he says, kissing his master's ring and departing quickly.

The Layzin then reclines upon one of his sofas, grimly determined to enjoy the remainder of the sunset. He has suddenly realized that much of his disquiet, this evening, has been most immediately caused by Lord Baster-kin's characteristically relentless insistence that the matter of Sentek Arnem's son entering the sacred service be pressed upon the great soldier's wife at once. *If you feel so strongly about the matter,* the Layzin had finally replied to Baster-kin earlier in the evening, *why not tend to it yourself?*

He might have known it would be just the sort of commission that would delight the Merchant Lord . . .

Several additional moments of similarly irritating ruminations continue to give the Layzin scant relief; and his mood does not truly improve until he catches sight of the youth Entenne departing the House of the Wives and moving onto the near-empty Celestial Way. The pleasant image of his favorite servant setting off at a run, southeast into the wealthiest residential section of the First District, prompts the Layzin to marvel, as he so often has, at the power and grace of Entenne's long, muscular legs; and all thoughts of Lord Baster-kin's aggressively pious preoccupations (which are no doubt patriotic and faithful, at heart, the Layzin eventually decides) dissipate, as the herald vanishes from view. His Eminence then allows himself to recline more fully and rest more completely, as the dusty golden light that fills the city at this peaceful, divine hour slowly begins to give way to equally serene nightfall; and he allows himself to hope—even to believe—that all in Broken will yet be well, despite the shrouded ills that beset the entirety of the kingdom, from the depths of the seemingly serene Lake of a Dying Moon behind the Inner City walls to the farthest towns and villages in the Meloderna valley, into which the loyal soldiers of the God-King are even now making their way. *All shall be well, all shall be well,* the Layzin muses; until he finds that, in his desperate desire to believe the statement, he is whispering it aloud . . .

$$\boxed{1:\{xvi:\}}$$

*Isadora Arnem's children bring her signs of a deadly mystery, one
that only she may be able to understand—and put to use . . .*

Q UIETLY GAZING from one of the tall, open windows of the
sitting room that overlooks the unique garden of her family's
home, Isadora Arnem appears to be both keeping watch over
her children, who have gathered about the stream in their
walled wilderness, and preparing to attend to several of the vital triviali-
ties of a mother's existence: sewing, mending, settling household accounts, and writing letters. And, were her husband merely on duty in the
Fourth District, or had Sixt left the city on some trivial military matter,
such would doubtless be the sorts of activities with which Lady Arnem's
mind and hands would now, in fact, be preoccupied. But this is early evening on the day following the departure of the Talons from the city, and
the commencement of their campaign against the Bane in Davon Wood
has complicated the affairs of Sixt's family ominously: for Isadora has
already received written inquiries from Lord Baster-kin, expressing the
Grand Layzin's desire to know when the priests of Kafra may expect to
receive Dalin Arnem as one of their acolytes . . .

Isadora had not been so foolish as to believe that her husband's departure would actually bring an end to the matter of their son's religious
service. Nor is she entirely surprised that Lord Baster-kin is pressing the
matter: for, despite the sentek's oft-expressed admiration for the Merchant Lord, Isadora has personal reasons to suspect that the latter might
prove . . . troublesome. Yet she had dared to hope that her husband's belief that his own elevation would protect his wife and children was right;
now, however, she sees that precisely his elevation, together with the
convenience of the great soldier's being away on campaign, are the factors that have forced the hands of Broken's rulers. The importance to the
Kafran clergy of preventing the Arnems from becoming a dangerous
precedent for other powerful families who might have doubts about
making gifts of their children to the God-King (especially given Isadora's
known origins as an apprentice to the heathen healer Gisa) must have

superseded any moderating considerations: more and more, Isadora curses herself for not having seen before Sixt departed that this calculation might even have played a role in the orders that sent him from the city in the first place—particularly if, rather than despite the fact that, the royal retinue heeded the advice of the man Isadora once knew as an angry, sickly youth: Rendulic Baster-kin . . .

These thoughts, and others like them, have rushed about Isadora's tormented mind throughout the day and evening; and so it is perhaps not surprising that even this strong-willed woman cannot now find the composure to simply sit and occupy herself with ordinary tasks. Instead, she has decided to stay by the sitting room window that offers the best view of the garden and of her children, and to fix her mind upon the sounds of those children at play: for their daily boisterousness, when released from the restraint of their lessons and into the protected freedom of their marvelous garden, has ever been as consoling and amusing to her as it is to them.

Yet today, even the comparatively small and qualified comfort of her children's enthusiastic games and endless disagreements is denied her: the voices that are carried into the sitting room, as the light of spring at dusk begins to burnish the city with a flush of deep gold, are unnaturally controlled and plainly uneasy. Looking more closely, Lady Arnem sees that all five of her children are drawn together in a close circle, and are talking among themselves quietly. Their attention is closely fixed upon something that Dagobert holds in one cupped hand, and little Gelie has begun to weep: not in an overwrought manner, which is her usual reaction to such typical trials as condescending insults, but out of sadness, such sadness as makes Isadora immediately suspicious as to what the unknown object in her son's hand might be. Lady Arnem knows only too well what creatures inhabit the children's *breck,* and also understands far better than any Kafran how important those creatures are: indeed, the chance to bring such beings into close proximity to her family and their home was an important (if unstated) reason for her having told Sixt that the children's ideas about remaking the garden were healthy ones. And so, demonstrating the extent of her concern, she walks quickly into the front hall, then through the building's stone-framed doorway to the terrace outside.

When she emerges, it is teary-eyed Gelie who catches sight of her first;

and, despite warnings from her siblings, she runs to her mother, who is already on the path that follows the stream through the garden.

"Mother!" Gelie cries, throwing her arms around her mother's waist and placing her feet atop Isadora's, so that Lady Arnem's strong legs lift and carry the girl as she herself walks along the path. "Mother, you must help!"

"Gelie—!" warns Golo forcefully; for, unlike the thoughtful, moody Dalin, Golo is every bit the youngest child's equal in phrenetic† energy. He, too, runs to his mother's side, but walks manfully beside her, staring hard at his sister. "Didn't you hear what Dagobert just said?"

"I heard him, Golo," Gelie says defiantly. "But Mother understands the poor creatures best, so we ought to tell her!"

"We didn't want to keep it from you, Mother," Golo explains. "But we know you've been worried about Father, and we thought . . ." At a loss as to how to continue, Golo looks (as all four of the younger siblings are accustomed to doing, in moments of difficulty) to Dagobert, who—possessed of both his mother's fair coloring and his father's handsome features—speaks with all the confidence of the admirable, resolute Broken youth he has in recent years become:

"We thought that we could solve the problem on our own, and we didn't want you to have to worry any more than you have been."

"We shouldn't be 'worrying' at all," mutters Dalin, who keeps his distance from the others and scowls at his mother. "Paying so much attention to those creatures is a sin—you're acting like *pagans!*"

"Oh, don't take on such airs, Dalin," says the ever-practical Anje, throwing her long braid of golden hair behind her back. "You're angry over being kept from the Inner City, and your anger makes you say things you don't believe—you ought to put that anger aside and help, instead of assuming that your own family has been swept up by some strange desire to commit *sacrilege* . . ."

Although full of curiosity, Isadora takes a moment to nod in great and characteristic appreciation to her elder daughter. "True, Anje," she says; and looking at the faces assembled before her, she asks, "For what have I always told you about making assumptions?"

Dagobert smiles, knowing the answer, but too near to being a man to play childish games that are clearly intended for the others.

It is the decisive finger of impulsive little Gelie that shoots up from within her mother's dress, as she cries, "Oh, I know!" Having brought her body out from her hiding place, the girl assumes a declamatory pose, and recites words that her mother originally learned at the feet of her own guardian and teacher, Gisa: "*'Assumption is the laziest variety of thought, which leads only to weakness and bad habits!'* " Then, with the same rote quality to her words, and her triumphant little finger still in the air, she adds: "But please do not ask me what any of that means!"

Her anxiousness eased a little by this display, Isadora is able to laugh for a fleeting moment: "What it means," she says, lifting Gelie up and groaning at the speed with which the ten-year-old is growing, "is that making assumptions before we have assembled all available facts, and before we have determined the reliability of those facts, is not only foolish, but mischievous."

"But I don't see why, Mother," Gelie answers, folding her arms. "After all, when we visit the temples or do our religious studies, it seems that all we ever learn are more ways of making assumptions without facts."

"Gelie." Isadora's voice becomes stern for an instant, although in her heart she is glad to see that even her youngest child can detect the superstitious essence of the Kafran religion; but, to keep her safe, she must warn her: "Those are matters of faith, not reason. Now—tell me what you've all been doing out here, other than getting yourselves filthy and squabbling."

Dagobert, staring into the pool at the base of the woodland waterfall, says, "It's strange, Mother—we had been trying to determine if the newts have mated yet, because we haven't seen any eggs. And then we found . . ." His words drift, as he studies the water with real concern: "Well, we're not really sure, Mother. They *have* come out, but they—"

"The poor things are dying, Mother!" Gelie blurts out.

"Gelie," Golo scolds. "Let Dagobert tell it, you don't understand—"

"Stop this bickering at once," Isadora says, suddenly and inexplicably grave, "and show me what worries you all so." Dagobert holds out his hand—and his mother is brought back to the true starkness of the dilemma facing her family when she sees:

Two dead newts, lying in the youth's palm. Their skin is dark, near black, as it should be; but at various points on their bodies, as well as upon the crests that surmount their backs,[†] they exhibit raw, bright red sores. The insults are small, as befits the newts' delicate bodies, but have a painful appearance no less shocking for their size.

Isadora is so fearfully apprehensive that her children finally grow hushed.

"When did you find these, Dagobert?"

The youth is puzzled. "They're not the first. And they're not the only things that have died. Some fish, two or three frogs—"

"Dagobert," Isadora insists, "when did you *begin* to find them?"

"The earliest were—a week ago, I suppose. What is it, Mother?"

"Yes, Mother," Gelie says, her manner subdued by fear. "Tell us—what is wrong?"

Isadora only presses: "What did you do with the dead creatures?"

It is Anje who answers: "We burned them, and buried the ashes." The maiden points at a patch of ground where there are as yet no plantings.

"Anje," Isadora says, turning, "did you bury them deep?"

"Yes, Mother," Anje answers; and Isadora gives silent thanks that she has trained her oldest daughter well. "They *did* appear sickly—and you've always said that such creatures, if they die of illness, must be burned, and their ashes buried—especially creatures such as newts. What you call salamanders, Mother."

"Yes, Mother," Gelie says. "Why *do* you call them that?"

Isadora's body trembles, although her gown disguises the momentary quivering even from Gelie, who is moving into her usual hiding place amid her mother's clothing. "Good," Isadora says. "That's wise thinking, Anje; I can always depend on you to be sensible. Now, mark me, all of you—I want you to keep a record, beginning with the first deaths you can recall, and keeping careful count, in the days to come, of how many of each type of dying or dead creature you find, with signs of this sickness. Do not touch or drink the water in the stream—I'll have the servants fetch water from the wells in the Third and Fourth Districts, for now, and we'll use the rain barrels as well. In the meantime, fasten the small nets that your father brought you from Daurawah onto the ends of long sticks, and use them to fetch the creatures out. Do you hear, Gelie?"

"Yes, Mother," the girl says, in whining protest. "But I didn't touch the water, it was Golo who found the dead newts."

"Golo, if you find any more, and a net isn't at hand, use a shovel to take them out. They must be burned, and the ashes buried deep. Do it well; show respect for them, don't play with the bodies or cut them up."

"All right, Mother," Golo says, his voice conceding that he has tampered with one or two of the dead creatures already.

"But are they dangerous?" Dagobert asks, all manly concern.

"Many believed them creatures of great power, once," Isadora says, studying the dead newts. "And some still do. The sickness that is killing them would, if such people are right, seem likely to have considerable power of its own. It's possible, however, that it is an illness of their kind alone. Whatever the case, study your own bodies: if any of you feel ill, or feverish, or if you discover these sorts of sores upon your skin, and it happens that I am not here, then, Anje, fetch a healer from the Third District—they are all indebted to me, and will come. Speed is vital. Do you understand?"

Anje looks increasingly worried, but nods. "Of course, Mother."

"We must burn these two *now.*" Isadora sees the children have built a small fire within walls of piled stones. "You have prepared a pyre, then— good. We must maintain it, and anything that you find dead, whether on the soil or in the water, burn it, respectfully and completely. Then mark the spots where you bury the ashes, so that you will not later disturb those already in the ground."

Golo, the son for whom words come as readily as the grumbling of his belly at mealtime, twists his face into a mask of incomprehension. "'*Disturb*' them? But they will be dead and burned, by then, how will we disturb them—"

A rapping at the arched door in the garden wall interrupts the forthright boy: someone outside, on the Path of Shame, is in distress of some kind, that much is readily apparent. "I'll answer it!" Dalin shouts, taking two quick steps before being nearly lifted off his feet by a strong hand that snatches the collar of his tunic. The boy then turns, with no little shame, to see that it is his sister Anje who has stopped him so decisively.

"Not so quickly, little man," Anje says, heightening Dalin's mortification. "*I'll* see who's there, lest you start telling strangers that your family is acting like 'pagans' . . .." Having pulled Dalin back, Anje completes his humiliation by slinging him into Dagobert's strong grip.

"You just keep quiet, brother," Dagobert says, not cruelly, but with authority against which Dalin cannot rebel.

Anje unbolts the garden door, but only after loudly demanding through the banded wooden planks that the caller identify herself, for a weak woman's voice is the only answer she receives. Opening the entrance to permit a quiet, brief exchange, Anje holds up a hand, asking the woman to wait, and then bolts the door once again.

"Mother," she says, returning uneasily. "There is a woman outside. She's with child, and claims to live off the end of the Path, by—"

"By the southwestern wall of the city," Isadora says, nodding; for she has recognized the voice that came through the seams of the doorway. "Her name is Berthe. I have consulted her about the birth—the child was badly positioned, but I thought we had attended to it. Is that why she—"

"No, Mother," Anje interrupts. "She's come about her husband."

Isadora sighs, exasperation and impatience blending to form the sound. "*Hak.* Another useless drunkard—Emalrec,[†] he's called. Dagobert?" She turns to her eldest son, indicating that she wishes him to accompany her. "As for the rest of you . . ." Isadora glances about, then asks, "Anje—will you take the others in to Nuen, and ask her to get them ready to sup?" Anje nods obediently, and herds her younger siblings to the house as her mother walks toward the garden door. "Let's see what evil foolishness the poor girl has been subjected to, now . . ."

Having quit the garden, mother and son join the waiting woman, who has withdrawn some dozen paces from the Arnems' doorway. Her dress is shabby, even by the standards of the Fifth District, just as her body is sorely in need of a scrubbing. But she is pretty enough that she must have been truly desperate to have braved the Path, on a night such as this one: for there are few drunkards on the avenue who would scruple at marriage or motherhood, once they had determined to ravish a comely young woman.

Isadora approaches the woman, whose face bears the expression of fear common to nearly all honest (or at least sober) women in the Fifth— women who can never be certain whether they face greater danger in the streets or in the homes that they share with drunken, cruel husbands. Berthe's body is covered by a simple piece of sackcloth gathered at the waist, which serves as both tunic and skirt, and is poorly stitched, with no smock beneath it to ease the perpetual chafing of such rough material.[‡]

"Berthe?" Isadora asks, touching the woman's shoulder. "Is it the baby? Or has that husband of yours been at you again—"

"No, Lady Arnem," Berthe says quickly. "The baby has calmed, at last, thanks to your help. No, it *is* Emalrec, my lady, just as you say, but—not in the way that you suppose."

"Is it the drink? Has he brought no food for you and the children? You must eat properly, we have spoken of this—"

Berthe shakes her head. "No, Lady Arnem. He is ill—very ill. I thought it was the drink, at first—he took such a fever, and his head was near to bursting. But he could bear no wine—he spat it up right away, and continued to vomit through the night. Then, this morning, his belly began to swell, and—" Berthe looks about, afraid to finish her tale.

Indicating to Dagobert that he should keep watch, Isadora urges Berthe toward the shadowy garden doorway. "Tell me," Isadora asks more gently. "What worries you so much that you cannot speak of it on the street?"

Berthe swallows hard. "This afternoon, with the fever still on him, he began to show—sores, my lady. On his chest, and soon on his back."

Isadora's face betrays alarm: "Do you suspect plague,[†] Berthe?"

"No, my lady!" the young woman whispers desperately. "I *did* suspect it, until tonight—but the spots haven't spread, and they remain red. Painful, and terrible to look at, but—there is no blackness to them."

Isadora considers, recalling the sores upon the salamanders. "You think it the rose fever,[‡] then." Berthe nods, saying nothing—for the rose fever can spread through a city as quickly as the plague (even if it is not so deadly) and create panic that transforms all too quickly into violence against those afflicted. "Then we must have a look at this husband of yours." Isadora takes Berthe's hand. "For if it is the rose fever, or any of the tens of diseases that resemble it . . ." She signals to Dagobert with just a nod, and he joins them. "Dagobert," Isadora says, taking him a few steps aside and speaking urgently. "Tell Nuen to get some of my old robes out—a few light woolen things, soft and warm, and a smock. Then get some of the clothing that you all wore when you were younger. It's stored below my bridal chest. Also blankets, strong soap—and have cook put aside a pot of the venison stew that I saw her preparing for supper, and wrap it with the lid on tight so that I may take it to Berthe's home."

"Mother—?" Dagobert replies. "What are you planning to do?"

But Isadora's attention has drifted. "If my suspicions about this business are correct, it may offer the chance to bargain from a position of greater strength—or, at least *some* strength . . ." She shakes herself back to immediate concerns. "I will go and see what is taking place in Berthe's home and neighborhood, and try to determine just what it is that ails her husband. It's not so very far from here, although it will plainly be a perilous trip. Still, I *must* be certain of the nature of the sickness, before I attempt the more uncertain venture that will follow. And so—have Bohemer and Jerej† bring the litter here." Isadora speaks of the family's two male servants, who are guards as much as anything else. Massive, bearded *bulger*‡ warriors, originally from the tribes far to the southeast of Broken, the men do perform heavy tasks as required about the house and its grounds; but far more often, they accompany Sixt and Isadora Arnem, and often their children, into the city, the various straps that gird their bodies holding small armories of weapons. "They are to guard Berthe and wait while I pack my healing kit and change my clothing. Tell them that I am going abroad in the city and that they should prepare themselves."

This command brings what is left of Dagobert's patience to its end: "Mother!" he says, sharply enough to finally make Isadora meet his gaze. "*Where* is it that you propose to go? It's already past sunset, and in a few minutes it will be dark—what madness can you be thinking of?"

"As I say, I will go to Berthe's home, first," Isadora answers, as though that notion did not entail entering the most dangerous neighborhood in the city. "And then, assuming all is as it should be—or, rather, as it should *not* be—I will continue on."

Lady Arnem turns to explain to Berthe that she must wait in the doorway for her, and not be frightened by the admittedly unsettling men that will shortly appear with the family's litter; but Dagobert is not yet satisfied with her explanation, and as he opens the garden door, he asks:

"And where will you 'continue on' to?"

"Why, Dagobert," Isadora says blithely, as she walks swiftly into the garden, "I had thought you'd be clever enough to have determined that. I will continue on to the home of the Merchant Lord himself."

Dagobert's mouth falls open, and he slams the garden door from within, bolting it in astonishment. "To the *Kastelgerd* Baster-kin?" he says. "But—"

Isadora, however, has turned and put an urgent finger to her mouth, ordering silence. "Not in front of the others, Dagobert—I will explain it all later. For now—do as I have told you . . ."

Dagobert enters the house close behind his mother and searching for another member of his family: Anje, who stands at the foot of the central staircase, awaiting them. The maiden begins to move toward her mother and brother, explaining that she has attended to her various tasks, and that Nuen is now feeding the other children—yet she has scarcely got the words out before Isadora takes her arm, issuing new requests for assistance:

"Come and help me change my gown, Anje," Lady Arnem says, climbing the stairs quickly. "And I'll need rose water, as well as galena for my eyes and red poppy lip paint . . ."[†] Manly youth though he may be, Dagobert recognizes all such commands as parts of an effort by his mother to ready herself, not for the ugliness of the neighborhood she has said she will visit initially, but for the splendor of her ultimate goal, the First District, and in particular the Way of the Faithful, the finest street in the city, at the far end of which stands the most awe-inspiring residence in Broken: the *Kastelgerd* Baster-kin, that ancient home which, in its complexity of design, is often said to rival or even exceed the royal palace itself.

Dagobert attempts to somehow convey this understanding to his sister by calling after Anje and Isadora, as they continue up the stairs, "I must change my clothing, too, Mother, if *we* are to visit the *Kastelgerd* of the Merchant Lord!" Anje's expression as she glances back shows that she has taken his meaning, and will attempt to learn more of what is at hand as she helps her mother dress. Isadora, meanwhile, sees none of this, and does no more than clarify to Dagobert that she will make the second part of her journey alone; she then reminds him to make sure that the family's litter is readied, along with the men who will carry it, after which she disappears into her bedroom with Anje.

When mother and daughter have finished transforming Lady Arnem's dress and appearance into a powerful echo of the considerable beauty with which Isadora was graced during her own maidenhood, and have returned to the stairway, they learn of Dagobert's full intentions: a seemingly strange man stands at the base of the stairs in leather armor worn over a full shirt of bronze mail, a gently curved marauder sword within a wood and hide sheath hanging from a broad belt at his waist and one hand resting rather imperiously upon the pommel of the sword. A stunned silence ensues, interrupted only by the sounds of the three younger Arnem children's laughing and arguing as they consume their evening meal farther away in the house. After what seems a very long moment, it is Isadora who declares:

"*Dagobert!* And just what do you suppose you're doing?"

But Dagobert has been preparing for just such a reaction, and is not in the least unnerved by his mother's angry astonishment. He steps forward deliberately, holding a scrap of parchment out to her.

"Nothing more than I was instructed to do, Mother," he states.

The parchment that her son holds causes an uneasy quivering in Isadora's gut: she knows that collecting such bits of the valuable writing material, to be used to issue brief written orders during his campaigns, is a habit of her husband's. But only when both she and Anje, who remains beside her, look up from the small missive do they realize that Dagobert has donned not just any armor, such as he might have bought for a small sum in the Fourth District, or traded for in the stalls of the Third, but an old suit of his father's, complete with a faded cotton surcoat[†] emblazoned with the rampant bear of Broken: mother and daughter both know that Dagobert would never have dared put on such a costume, much less have taken hold of the sword at his side (one of many in Sixt's collection), without his father's permission.

As Isadora descends the stairs and takes the parchment note from her son, she further realizes—of a sudden, just as she earlier noticed the fullness of Anje's womanly maturity—how tall and strong Dagobert has become: for his arms and chest fill the shirt of mail that he wears below his leather armor, while his broadening shoulders support the panels of layered leather that cover them in a most handsome manner. Left with no other course, Isadora unfolds the scrap of parchment slowly and reads the message written upon it, in Sixt's simple hand:

> DAGOBERT: IF, WHILE I AM GONE, YOUR MOTHER
> VENTURES OUT INTO THE CITY AT NIGHT, EVEN WITH THE
> SERVANTS, ARM YOURSELF WITH MY BEST MARAUDER
> SWORD,[‡] AND ACCOMPANY HER. I RELY ON YOU, MY
> SON. —YOUR FATHER

For a moment, Isadora does not move her eyes from the message; but just then, the younger children, with Nuen pursuing them, run in from the room off of the kitchen in which they have been eating. Nuen, despite moving with haste, carries a small iron pot covered with a wooden lid and wrapped in thick white cloth; and it is a demonstration of the small, round woman's remarkable agility that she keeps the hot stew within from spilling, even when she abruptly comes to a halt behind Golo, Gelie, and Dalin. They, like Isadora and Anje, are stunned by the sight of Dagobert dressed as a seasoned campaigner, enough so that they forget their games for the moment.

"Dagobert!" Golo cries out merrily. "Are you going to join Father, and fight the Bane?"

"Don't be ridiculous," Gelie adds, with a short laugh that brings a sour look from Dagobert. Realizing that mocking her brother so openly was unwise, Gelie adds: "Although you look very impressive in Father's old armor, Dagobert—where *are* you going, if not to the Wood?"

"Those are matters between Father and me," Dagobert replies, moving his hand further down to grip the hilt of his marauder sword in what he hopes is a meaningful fashion. "Keep your nose in your own affairs, Gelie—little as it is, someone might still cut it off!"

Gelie's hands race to cover her face as if her nose might, indeed, be sliced away at any moment, and Dalin laughs out loud.

"Might someone, indeed?" he taunts. "And is that your notion of how a pallin in the God-King's legions proves himself, Dagobert—by threatening little girls? You will discover differently!"

"That is enough, Master Dalin." Nuen's tone is not impertinent, and she executes a small, deferential motion toward Isadora, one that might seem insignificant, by Broken standards, but which the lady of the house knows would be a sign of extreme respect in Nuen's marauder tribe. The servant emphasizes her meaning by placing the stew pot on a table and moving more speedily than a horse on the open steppe to take Dalin by the back of his shoulders with real force. She leans down, her ordinarily thin eyes narrowing in her broad face so much that they are scarcely discernible, and murmurs, "Would you behave like a teasing, disrespectful brat in front of your mother?"

It is far from the first time that Isadora has been deeply grateful to Nuen (whose own son, but a year older than Golo, marched off with Sixt Arnem's *khotor* the day before, as *skutaar* to the sentek himself), but the act is no less appreciated for its reliability. "Thank you, Nuen," Isadora says, trying with all the composure she can collect to keep her temper; then, scowling at each of her younger children in turn, she declares, "And now, all three of you—upstairs. If you mind me, I may be persuaded to let Nuen tell you marauder stories."

Even Dalin's face brightens a bit—for there are no legends or histories, even in the city library, that can match the excitement of Nuen's terrifying tales of storied battles and rivers of blood, of men who ride their small horses so fast and so hard that they can, it is said, cook meat between their own naked thighs and the backs of the animals, and most famously, tales of the skulls of their fallen and executed enemies piled as high as mountains[†]—and the fact that they are related by such a deceptively docile teller only seems to increase their power to excite, no matter how many times they are repeated.

Aware of how restless such stories will make the younger children during the night, but also aware that her ladyship has, at the moment, larger problems with which she must grapple without the children asking too many questions, Nuen turns to Isadora, arching one of her long, thin eyebrows and making only one inquiry of her own: "My lady is certain?"

Sighing at the inevitability of her own night's lost sleep, Isadora nods. "Yes, Nuen," she says. "I would appreciate the help, just now . . ."

The three youngest children turn eagerly to the stairs, Golo and Dalin quickly disappearing up them. Only Gelie, as she passes Isadora, pauses to comment upon the mystery of her mother's having donned her best green gown and her small but lovely golden necklace, as well as her having applied the poppy-dyed paint that beautifies her lips, and the lines of black galena that make her eyes appear even larger and more mysterious than they actually are. But Anje quickly steps in to take her sister's hand. "You and your questions come with me, little empress," Anje tells her sister. "You can hear all about it when Mother gets home, and if you don't hurry, you will lose your chance to learn of new marauder horrors . . ."

Isadora's pride in her elder daughter swells once again, making her realize how soon an appropriate suitor for the maiden will have to be found: a suitor, that is, who will allow her to establish a household that will, Isadora is certain, be more sensibly supervised than this one in which she has grown up. These thoughts are confirmed when Anje looks at her mother a last time, aware that Isadora has not revealed all of her plans to her, but accepting that she has good reason for withholding them. The maiden barely whispers the words, "Be careful, Mother," before chasing Gelie up the stairs; and for a moment, Isadora's admiration becomes melancholy at the notion of how close she is to losing the daughter she has come to depend upon so . . .

Finally, Dagobert alone is left standing before her; and Isadora's features suddenly darken, although perhaps not as much as she might wish or intend. "Do you have any idea, Dagobert," she begins, "what your father would say and do, were he here to see you in that costume?"

But Dagobert holds his ground admirably: "I imagine he would be pleased, Mother, that I have followed his instructions so closely."

Pausing to consider the entire matter, Isadora at length asks, "And when, pray, did you two concoct this scheme?"

"Yesterday, as he was leaving the house. He pretended to have forgotten Yantek Korsar's baton, the baton of the army's supreme commander, and went to fetch it. When he returned with it, he also handed me the note."

"Very clever . . ." Isadora pauses, silently rebuking herself for having been taken so off-guard; but then she nods in defiance. "All right, then," she says, without enthusiasm. "You shall come, if that is how it must be. But wait in the garden, while I fetch my healing kit from the cellar."

Isadora walks swiftly to a door beneath the staircase, one that leads to the cool confines of the house's lowest chamber, where the family's supplies of wines, oils, herbs, root vegetables, and meat are stored. It is a place that the children are forbidden ever to enter—since it is here, too, that Isadora keeps her supplies of the ingredients for her medicines, and where she mixes those concoctions. Ignorant tampering with such dangerous things, the Arnem children have been taught since birth, could result in sickness and death; and so, unruly troop that they often are, they obey this one household stricture without question.

None of which means that they have not experienced great curiosity about the place; and in recent months, the inquisitiveness of the two oldest Arnem offspring has become most pointed. There are many reasons for this, the most important among them being the continual remarks by children outside the Fifth District about Isadora's having been raised by a witch. And, although the studious Anje has carefully determined that the crone Gisa was nothing like so malevolent a being, she has also become convinced that Gisa *was* an adherent of the old religion of Broken. This proposition has been supported by investigations undertaken by the sharp-eared Dagobert, who has several times laid his head upon the flooring of the hall on the house's main level to gain clues about what transpires below. For while the walls of the cellar are composed of the same raw stone from which most of the rest of the city was carved, the ceiling is nothing more than the bottom of the thick plank flooring of the hall above. These planks are softened and sealed, during the winter, by carpets and skins; but at the first hint of warmer weather, all such coverings are removed, laying bare the floor.

It is thus free of coverings this evening, making it an unusually propitious moment for Dagobert to risk putting an ear to the cracks between the floor planks, in order to see if his mother is merely collecting the bottles and earthen jars of secret mixtures that have maintained her reputation as a healer, or if she is not also about some other work: work hinted at by mysterious recitations, pieces of which Dagobert has more than once heard.

One phrase is common to all of the statements Isadora makes when alone in the cellar, a phrase that, from the first, did not seem to concern medicine—or at any rate, not medicine specifically. Rather, it always seemed an appeal to a deity, one whose high office was and is apparently that of *Allsveter:*[†] the "All-father," a title that, as Dagobert and Anje have discovered during their studies, was often given to the chief of the old gods of Broken, a being called *Wodenez,*[‡] whose image the children have seen displayed upon a silver clasp with which their mother often fastens her cloak: a clasp that Isadora has consistently explained was simply a dying gift from the woman who raised and taught her, the supposèd "witch," Gisa.

And again this evening, with the younger children upstairs struck silent by Nuen's tales of marauder ferocity, Dagobert hears this phrase through the flooring of the hall; this, and one more, one that, although voiced in his own Broken tongue and clearly not the name of any entity, contains some secret that makes it every bit as strange as the other:

"Tell me, great *Allsveter*," the Lady Arnem seems to plead, as cool, dank air brings her words through the cracks in the floor to her son's ears, "what can all this mean? Why are such great spirits consumed by fever, which is precisely the element over which they have mastery, even as they dwell in and near cooling water? What unnatural forces create so terrible an illness, which the runes[††] say portend great danger to this city? What sense can there be to so strange a riddle: *how shall water and fire conquer stone?*"

Dagobert lifts his head, utterly confused; but before he has time to puzzle with his mother's last words, the gentle sounds of final preparation—vials and bottles being capped and replaced in their shelves—carry up from below; and, at the first step of his mother's feet upon the stone stairs that are carved into one wall of the cellar, the youth is up, has taken hold of the pot of stew that Nuen has left steaming on the floor, and is out the door of the house, calming his nerves and pacing upon the terrace in what he hopes is a confidently expectant manner.

His mother soon approaches him, and, with her black box of medical supplies snug beneath one arm, she passes by the youth without a word, her moments of preparation in the cellar seeming to have reconciled her little if at all to her son's secret arrangement with his father. Dagobert follows uneasily, as Isadora leads the way quickly back to the door in the garden's southern wall, which she pulls open in a swift motion, further revealing the strength that she possesses at moments of anger and peril. Darkness has fallen entirely, and, with the Moon as yet unrisen, all light on the Path of Shame is supplied by torches and fires fueled by whatever the drunken residents can scavenge or steal. The sounds of mindless laughter have become noisier and more numerous, by now, as well as more insistent, forcing those engaged in equally senseless arguments to shout their meaningless indictments and insults at each other.

Close by the doorway to the Arnems' garden, the family's modest lit-ter[†] has been made ready. Its light wooden frame and simple bank of cushioned seats are draped with heavy wool, despite the unseasonable warmth of the air, which would usually call for cotton. Such coverings provide plain, effective privacy for passengers within, and the frame of-fers comfort without luxury, being light enough, with one or two occu-pants, to be carried by two strong men lifting thick, twelve-foot bearing poles that slip under brackets on each side of the conveyance. In the Ar-nems' case, this bearing is done by two enormous, black-bearded men, each of whom wears light, weathered armor—predominantly leather, but reinforced, at vital points, with simple steel plates—and both of whom give the constant impression of filth, despite the fact that they bathe regularly.

"Good evening, my lady," calls the giant at the front of the litter, Bo-hemer, in a respectfully jovial manner; then he nods at the youth, who has never looked more like the champion of his clan. "Master Dagobert," he adds, with a smile scarcely visible through his thick beard.

"Lady Arnem," adds the somewhat less powerful man to the rear, Jerej, who speaks through a slightly thinner mat of hair; then he, like his tribesman, offers a knowing grin to Dagobert, which the youth returns with a proud smile of his own—for to be admitted as a fellow by these two is an honor, indeed.

None of which alters the fact that such acknowledgments are, at the moment, unwise: the already displeased Isadora quickly and rightly suspects that the men have been given advance warning by her husband and son of their plans for Dagobert's participation in such nighttime adventures, and her temper snaps. She glares angrily at each in turn, fairly striking them with her words: "Silence—*all* of you!" Isadora knows that Bohemer and Jerej are as ferociously loyal to the Arnem family as is the good Nuen; but she also knows that they, like her husband, no doubt took satisfaction from the notion of bringing Dagobert fully into the ranks of men with this plan. And while she is grateful that they will be present to support her son as the little group descends into the dangerous streets surrounding Berthe's home, she has no intention of revealing as much. Instead, she shakes her head with strained self-possession, and helps Berthe into the litter, taking her own seat as quickly as possible. "All right, then," Isadora proclaims from within the litter. "You know our destination—proceed!"

"Aye, Lady Arnem!" Jerej replies, as he and Bohemer lift the litter in one well-practiced motion that scarcely jostles the women.

"Master Dagobert—?" Bohemer asks quietly; though not so quietly that Dagobert does not take more pride and confidence from the increased camaraderie. "Perhaps you will lead us, to the left and just ahead?"

Dagobert nods with still more enthusiasm, keeping his marauder sword unsheathed just enough to expose its guard, so that it can be quickly brought to bear. His eyes search the crowds ahead intently, as though he were a soldier of great experience, able to distinguish the first sign of threat. Soon the party is moving southwest along the Path of Shame, not as wealthy intruders, but as persons of consequence who are *of* as well as *in* the district: persons whose business must, in short, be respected.

"I will say, young master," Bohemer tells Dagobert, still confidentially, "that I'm pleased you've paid close attention to the lessons your father has given you—because I'd stake a Moon's wages that we'll *need* your sword arm, before this business is done. If not in the poorest part of the city"—Dagobert turns, to find Bohemer speaking with genuine intent—"then in the wealthiest . . ."

$$1:\{xvii:\}$$

An unnoticed departure, a daunting purpose . . .

AFTERNOONS IN OKOT have never been known for their brightness, given the near-impenetrability of the forest ceiling, even where small clearings have been made for huts. In part, this is because of Davon Wood's remarkable power to reassert itself; but just as much, it is by design of the Bane themselves. Any significant break in the Wood's vast expanse of treetops would be visible from the walls of Broken, and so care is usually taken to ensure that the sunniest of mid-days elsewhere is no more dazzling than a moderate twilight in the forest. But there has never been an afternoon quite so dark as this one. It has passed with more deaths, more pyres, and the burning of more huts, all of which have created a cloud of hot, heavy smoke blotting out the sun: the plague still shows no sign of relenting.

The Bane healers have assured the Groba that by morning this will change; and, as if determined to make good on their hopeful prediction, they continue, at twilight, to toil without pause in the *Lenthess-steyn,* as fearlessly as they have done from the start. And yet, by the time the sun begins to touch the western mountains, the only apparent effect of all this determination is that the plague claims still more of these martyrs to knowledge and compassion. Their passing seems to go scarcely noted by their colleagues, who labor on in the most secluded chambers of the honeycomb-like caves, cutting the dead to pieces, trying to uncover some clue as to the origin of the disease's horrific symptoms. They have devised, by now, several mixtures of the herbs that they grow in their gardens with extracts from various poisonous flowers brought back by the foraging parties, and each concoction serves to ameliorate some one from among the several torturous effects of the disease: the sores, the racking cough, the fever, swelling, and pain. But there is still little hope of preventing death itself. The pestilence remains a mystery, wholly unlike anything that the healers have ever treated with their potions and poultices; and with the healers' frustration comes renewed conviction on the part of the Groba and the Bane tribe generally that the plague is the result of sorcery. In the face of this conclusion, still more of those struck by the disease ignore the healers and the *Lenthess-steyn* altogether and, while they still have the strength to walk, choose to end their lives as did the family that Keera, Veloc, and Heldo-Bah observed earlier: by wandering through the forest (ever observed by parties of Outragers), praying that distancing themselves from stricken Okot may bring salvation, and, upon finding that it does not, submitting themselves to the comparatively swift end of the Cat's Paw.

By nightfall, pyres are burning all along the south side of the river. From a high hill just west of Okot, the three foragers—so much more than foragers, now!—can see the smoking glow of these funereal flames forming an ever-longer chain across the dark landscape, as well as the smaller lights of torches near the pyres and the river. One large mass of torches has assembled on the rocky summit of the *Lenthess-steyn,* and is creeping northward: a luminous, coiling sign that Ashkatar's army of warriors has come together in full assembly, and is beginning to march.

Before leaving Okot, Keera, Veloc, and Heldo-Bah gathered at the hut that all three had once called home to prepare for their journey. The parents of Keera and Veloc—called Selke and Egenrich[†]—knowing that their two children and their former ward represented what might be the last hope of the Bane, welcomed the three as if they had left home but yesterday, and, in the case of Heldo-Bah, gave no sign of any lingering resentment or disappointment; for in truth, they felt none. Taking little Effi into their care, Selke and Egenrich pledged to keep her safely away from the most dangerous parts of the village, and to continue to refuse her persistent requests to visit her brothers; in addition, they further pledged, when pressed by their daughter, to take care of all three children, should Keera never return—and should her boys survive. As they watched the three prepare for a journey so riddled with dangers that it was unnecessary even to speak of them, preparation steadily became the sole subject of conversation: the foragers emptied their sacks of all the precious goods collected during the term of the most inscrutable Moon ever to rise over Davon Wood, and refilled them with all manner of implements, of foodstuffs—and of weapons, especially. The three were given their pick of all the arms forged or captured by their tribe, and each took only the best sword, arrows, bow, and knives on offer. They then slipped out of Okot undetected, lest any great hope be attached to their mission by their fellow Bane; hope that might ultimately prove cruelly and tragically vain. The hill on which they now stand is the last spot from which the tribe's village and its outlying settlements can be seen, and all the foragers stare back somberly, knowing that it may be their last glimpse of home.

"They say that Ashkatar has brought together a greater force than was expected," Veloc murmurs, his right hand gripping the hilt of a freshly honed Broken short-sword, and his dark eyes gleaming with the flames of the distant fires. "Women warriors as well. Hundreds, in all. What is his plan? To attack?"

"No," Heldo-Bah answers. "If I know Ashkatar, he will wait. Give the Groba and the healers time to control the plague by inviting the Tall to enter the Wood. Destroy all the bridges, save the Fallen. And if they are foolish enough to come in by that route . . ." He spits at the ground with force. "The odds may not be even, but they will certainly improve."

"But why should the Tall come into the Wood?" Keera asks quietly, leaning on a fresh maple staff and staring at the village with eyes bereft of anything but heartache. "When the plague does their work for them?"

"The pride of the Tall," Heldo-Bah answers scornfully, but with truth born of his many raids into the city and kingdom that once tried to kill him. "They will want a fight, even if the plague has weakened us."

"And," Veloc adds, "they'll want to see for themselves that their vile work is completed."

Keera keeps her eyes fixed on the distant flames. "For Tayo, it has already been completed. As for so many others . . ."

"Completed?" Heldo-Bah echoes bitterly. "No, Keera. Not while there is yet breath in you, in all of us, and revenge to be had." His grey eyes burn more wildly in their sockets than any mere reflection of the distant pyres and conflagrations among the huts could cause. "And with us goes the hope of that revenge. We shall have it. All of them—" He points toward Okot. "They shall all have it. We shall find Caliphestros, and by the Moon, the Tall will know the grief that you have felt this day." Heldo-Bah spits again, as if to seal his compact with the demons that lurk beneath the Earth. "The faster we move, the faster their suffering begins. Follow your trail, Keera, and we follow you. We rest only when we must." The grey eyes narrow, and the filed teeth grind painfully. "And from the Moon's realm, the dead shall see that they have been avenged."

Starting southwest, the three Bane disappear into the Wood; and soon they are cutting masterfully through the darkened vastness, at a faster pace than even they have ever achieved . . .

INTERLUDE:

A·FOREST·IDYLL[†]

[But] what are we to make of the legend's more apparently fantastic aspects? I do not speak, here, of the several references to sorcery and the like, which are addressed in the text itself, and may be dispensed with by noting, as at least two characters will do later in the tale, that the greatest "sorcery" has always been science, while the darkest "magic" has just as consistently been madness. Rather, I allude to such only marginally less outlandish notions as civilized or even partially civilized men scheming to use wasting diseases as weapons of war, as well as to the fact that so relatively advanced a society as Broken's was capable of mutilating and exiling a not inconsiderable number of its own members, out of no loftier motives than to purge the national stock of its physically and mentally defective elements (including, among many others, agents of knowledge and especially scientific progress, which they equated with sedition), as well as to ensure that particular air of divine secrecy, which, almost universally, results in unchecked power and excesses on the parts of some or all agencies of government.

And what, by contrast, of the assertion that animals other than men are graced by the Deity with consciousness, and therefore souls, and so must logically be accorded the same respect that we, who flatter ourselves as having been made in the Almighty's image, demand be paid us alone? Doubtless, such beliefs will appeal to those increasing numbers of young poets and artists in our own time, who claim to seek the dubious enlightenment of the unrefined, untaměd world of Nature, while allowing themselves to flirt dangerously with ideas akin to those that are driving the forces of revolutionary destruction;[†] yet can we, who detect the dangers of those same rebellious forces in precisely the manner that you have detailed so completely in your "Reflections," look beyond such youthful superficiality, and ourselves find deeper meaning in such tales as this "idyll"?

But, *pace:* I run ahead of myself, and assume airs akin to those displayed by the most mysterious and peculiar character to inhabit this account, one whose acquaintance, I confess, I am most anxious for you to make; for he did indeed bridge that chasm between Reason and a kind of reverence for the souls and aspirations, not only of men, but especially of beings other than human, finding, between the two, little if any contradiction at all. . . .

—Edward Gibbon to Edmund Burke

The Old Man and the Warrior Queen

I T MATTERS LITTLE how much the settings of the old man's dreams change, from night to night, for their most important aspects remain consistent: he is forever among friends—or, more correctly, persons he somehow knows to be friends, even if their faces are strange to him—and, whether they gather in a remote village or in the palace of a prince, the congenial group soon find themselves caught up in some entertaining and important business. This activity invariably occasions praise for the old man, who is rarely old, in the dreams, but young and handsome, with the golden hair, slate grey eyes, pronounced bones and thin mouth that once marked him clearly as having come, originally, from a land far to the northeast of both Broken and Davon Wood. And, amid the indistinct but delighted audience, there is always the clear image of a young woman's face. It may be a girl he in fact knew, once, or it may be a stranger; but always, her eyes light with fascination when the old man picks her out from among the busy, talkative group. She blushes and looks to the ground, but soon brings her gaze back up to meet his in silent invitation. He then moves to either acquaint or reacquaint himself with her, and to engage in conversation of the type that leads inevitably to a touch or even a kiss: soft and brief, but still exciting enough to cause soothing tremors throughout his body's web of *neura,*[†] and, ultimately, to create the feeling that the old man's ancestors on the steppes had called the *thirl:*[‡] an excitement so deep and so potent that some crave it as the drunkard craves wine, or as the eaters and smokers of opium lust after their drug.

Lastly, and most importantly, there are the old man's legs: he yet dreams, without exception, that he still has his legs, and can do all that he was once was able to in life. He can run, through palace halls and gardens, up and down castle stairways, and about the world's great forests; he can cavort and dance at festivals and royal receptions; he can brace his body to make love to a woman—and he can boldly ride a horse,

whether through the streets of the great ports his grandfathers and father built, after they were pushed by wave after wave of brutal marauders off the endless steppes[†] and onto the coast of the sea to the north, or
along the caravan routes that his own generation of his clan—and he
himself—played no small part in extending into the strange, dangerous
lands of the far south and distant east. He had traveled these routes on
horseback, on camelback, on elephant and ox: astride, that is, nearly any
beast that could bear his weight, and in this way, from boyhood on, he
had gained a deep affection for and ability to communicate with forms of
life other than his own. In this way, too, he had been brought into contact with more peoples of the Earth by his early manhood than most
men ever heard so much as stories of, in all their years. Such had been a
heady life, one full of adventure, riches, and, soon enough, women. But,
despite such diversions, it had been the great centers of learning that he
saw on his travels that had fascinated him most. And so, when he reached
full manhood, he defied his father's wishes, abandoned the life of a merchant, and chose to do scholarly combat with that most magnificent
question of all: what animates the bodies and minds of the men and creatures who inhabit this world?

It was as a man of science and medicine, then, rather than of commerce, that he had made his mark in any and all lands that he visited, and
particularly in those few places where scholarship and the great advances
it could bring were still understood and respected;[‡] and it is to those days
of glory that his mind now turns, during long nights of sleep plagued by
often bitter physical agony. Sometimes, if the need is great enough, his
mind will go still further, fancifully elaborating upon those memories of
the fame brought by wisdom (memories no less pleasurable, in their way,
than are his visions of lovely young women), by allowing him to dream
that he debates the great scholars who ennobled the towns and cities to
which he traveled, whether they be such masters as lived long before his
own time—the physicians Herophilus of Alexandria and Galen of Per-
gamum, for example—or those scholars who, like the historian Bede of
the monastery at Wearmouth[††] across the Seksent Straits, he was once
fortunate enough to have called his colleagues.

During the first few years that such dreams had come to dominate his
fitful exile's sleep in the most remote corner of Davon Wood, the presence of his legs in his nightly visions had puzzled the old man deeply.

After all, he had spent no small portion of his life as a scholar and a physi-cian weighing the value of dreams as a means to measure the health of his patients, a skill that he had initially learned through careful study of the brief but vital "On Diagnosis from Dreams," a work written nearly five hundred years before the old man's time by that same master of med-icine whom he often dreamed of debating, Galen the Greek.[†] But the old man expanded upon Galen's preliminary work, to such an extent that he had eventually attained the ability to divine the true natures of the ill-nesses of his patients, as well as many details of their private lives and vices, from their dreams.[‡] Such diagnoses were uniformly startling to those patients, and not always welcome. But the old man plunged for-ward with his experiments in this area, eventually determining to his own satisfaction—as well as to the profound shock and disbelief, not only of his patients, but of the various holy men with whom he had cause to discuss such matters—that humans are not the only animals who dream. And with this determination came an even more profound in-sight into how extensive were the sensibilities, not only of those horses, camels, oxen, and elephants who had once carried both him and his clan's goods, but of a far wider range of creatures.

This discovery that dreams were universal among all types and breeds of men and animals, and of the purposes that those dreams served, should have had a practical use, especially during his exile, the old man believed. When the continuing pain of the imperfectly healed wounds inflicted on him by the priests of Kafra during the *Halap-stahla* made vivid dreams of his own a nightly occurrence, they ought to have been dreams (given the loss of his legs) of *falling*: short tumbles, such as to the ground from standing, if the pain of his wounds was light, and longer ones—terrifying plummets from high walls or cliffs—if the pain was severe. Of course, his suffering was *always* severe when he slept, if not during the first hours, then certainly when the dose of opium blended with a judicious amount of mandrake that it was his habit to smoke be-fore retiring lost its hold over his *neura,* and the stabbing sensations re-turned to rouse him. Such drugs were not a cure, and could even become a sickness that he had often observed and treated; yet his dreams, far from offering him any hint of a more fundamental treatment, only grew more pleasant and consoling, as his pain returned. It was as though his mind, rather than rationally applying itself to the problem of a more fundamental course of treatment, became instead an agent of escape from the reality of his condition—became, indeed, an agent of ministration, determining its own remedies, whether he bid it do so or not.

In keeping with this strange counterargument to both Galen's and his own principles, which occurred even on the worst of mornings—if he had stumbled the night before, for example, against the rocky walls of the cave that had been his home ever since the first night of his exile, causing his mutilated legs to throb mercilessly—the old man often awoke smiling, sometimes even laughing, with small tears of simple joy moistening his pale, vexed features. The pain would soon claim his conscious thoughts, of course, particularly during the first months of his exile, when he possessed none but a few drugs with which to mitigate it; and his smiles and laughter would then quickly dissolve into cries of rage and agony, caused not only by the pain itself, but by its relentless reminder of how very much the circumstances of his once wondrous existence had been altered; had, indeed, been *stolen*.

Over time the oaths of bitter frustration and the conscious lust for vengeance that initially characterized his morning hours had been tempered by acceptance of life as it had been remade for him; and the change in his outlook was in part the result, the old man readily admitted, of his cultivation of a pharmacopoeia that would have roused the jealousy of Galen himself, or even of that supreme expert of old *Roma*,[†] the Cilician Dioscorides[‡] (who, like the old man, studied in the library, museum,[††] and academies of Alexandria, when that city was still, despite its conquest and reconquest by the warrior zealots of faiths hostile to true knowledge, the greatest center of learning in all the world). And with this acceptance, the old man gradually came to think less of mutilating his tormentors in the brutal manner that they had employed against him, and to treat his woodland life as a unique opportunity to achieve a greater form of justice. But this was not an attitude born of his own wisdom: for he knew that few if any men, even among those possessed of their legs, could have achieved so seemingly brave an outlook—particularly among the southwestern mountains of Davon Wood, by far the most remote and forbidding portion of the wilderness—without aid in the form of an example. And so, even as he recognized that the work that he was carrying out during his exile was the most impressive, and in many ways the most important, of his life, he rarely congratulated himself on it; because he recognized that there was an even more important reason for his remarkable disposition and achievements:

She had made it possible. *She* had taught him a fundamental philosophical lesson, one that—through a lifetime of journeys, of scholarly study, and dangerous intrigue among kings, holy men, and warriors—had never truly penetrated his soul: she had taught him what true courage comprised. And, even more effectively, she had *shown* him the practical meaning of that quality, and made it plain to the old man that we reveal ourselves as most brave when there is no admiring audience to applaud us. She had imparted this wisdom in the way that all great philosophers have ever acknowledged most superior—by example. For she herself had long lived with as much suffering, of the heart as well as of the body, as he had ever seen any gregarious member of human society endure, much less a solitary forest-dweller such as herself, even given her royal heritage. That much became clear to the old man upon the very first evening of their acquaintance: the night of the *Halap-stahla.*

Barely conscious, he watched her emerge from the Wood, as soon as the ritual party of priests and soldiers left. He was without his lower legs, yet he was bleeding slowly: for it was part of the fiendishness of the *Halap-stahla* that the priests first cut away the principal ligaments within the knees and then removed the *patella,*[†] in order to permit a clean stroke of their axes at the joints, which were opened to such sectioning by the victim's painful suspension between two trees. This positioning, like the crucifixion inflicted on prisoners by the soldiers of old *Roma,* pulled nearly every joint of the body open to the verge of dislocation, bringing on eventual *gangraena,* as well as wretchedness of almost every other variety imaginable. But the Kafrans had gone beyond their Roman predecessors, who are sometimes thought the masters of inventive torment, but who showed at least a trace of pity by ending the misery of the crucifixion with the hard mercy of the *crurifragium.*[‡] The Kafran priests, by sickening contrast, cauterized and tied off the flesh and vessels about the middle leg (but only those parts of the wound) after their severing blows had been struck, to prevent the prisoner's bleeding to death too quickly—robbing their own victims of the sudden end which was granted even those wretches upon the crosses of *Lumun-jan.*

Despite the priests' intention that the anguish of the *Halap-stahla* go on as long as possible, the old man had in fact been near death when the warrior queen approached. When he first detected her, having fallen into a state of agonized delirium, he thought the rustling in the undergrowth of the forest's edge was one of his acolytes, more than a few of whom had pledged to come to the edge of the Wood at nightfall and, if they found him alive, to either save him, if they could, or end his misery, if they could not. (Should the latter have proved the case, the acolytes had pledged further, they would respectfully inter his remains in some anonymous spot, one that no Kafran priests could find and violate.) But when the old man had finally been able to make out who was approaching him—when he saw that she was a female from an infamously warlike forest breed, one about whom he had heard fearful, fantastic tales—he had conjectured that she intended to finish him: a death that he would have welcomed, so great had his suffering grown.

Perhaps, the old man had thought, studying her eyes as closely as the roaring agony permitted, *she means to kill me out of compassion; for, behind the sharp defiance in those eyes, there is a softer knowledge of suffering . . .*

What the old man could not yet know was that the initial bloodlust in the warrior queen's remarkable eyes had been put there, not by his own sanguinary scent, nor by his helplessness, but rather by the mere sight of his tormentors: the priests of Kafra, and still more the soldiers who accompanied them. It had of late become her way to kill any man of Broken with whom she came into contact: for it had been such men who, not quite a year earlier, had slaughtered three of her four children, enslaving the youngest and making the queen herself the last of her royal clan and, more importantly, shattering her spirit so thoroughly that, over the near-dozen Moon cycles that followed, she had scarcely been able to reassemble enough of it to go on living. As a consequence, she did not much care, now, when she happened upon riders who sat tall in ornate saddles atop mighty horses, if they were soldiers, merchants, or priests, like those who had committed this latest act of near-murder: all such men (easily distinguished from the smaller tribe who inhabited the forest, and who had always shown deference to herself and her children, before their deaths and abduction) were representatives of the city that she had so often observed atop the lonely mountain to the northeast, the city that was outlined, at night, by flickering lights, and into which her last living offspring, along with the body of her eldest, had been taken that terrible day, as she, wounded by a spear to the thigh, tenaciously defended the only thing that she yet could: the two lifeless bodies of her other departed yet no less belovèd young ones.

In this way did *all* citizens of Broken eventually become the warrior queen's enemies, to be attacked and killed; and thus did she, in turn, become one of the most terrible of the many legends concerning Davon Wood with which those same citizens unnerved one another and attempted to curb any wayward behavior on the part of their children.

Yet on that night, she had approached the site of the old man's mutilation carefully, and therefore too late to take the lives of the latest band of priests, attendants, and soldiers who had come to the edge of Davon Wood from the mountain. Why? It did not seem to the old man that she was motivated by fear, but rather by some larger purpose: what, then? To finish his suffering for him? Could she truly display such sympathy? He did not doubt it was possible: it was of a piece with his studies of all creatures to know that even inhabitants of the Wood could be moved by such sentiments. And his theory was confirmed yet again as she drew closer, and the old man detected with certainty the full complexity of her aspect: as she studied his mutilated half-legs, dangling awkwardly in the gap between the two trees from which he remained painfully suspended, her expression lost much of the vengefulness with which she had watched the retreating ritual party, and she eyed the old man instead with something very like compassionate curiosity. She detected something unusual in him, he could plainly see that much; and she heard, as well, something noteworthy in the forlorn, agonized sounds that continued to emerge weakly from deep within him.

The old man could not, at that moment, bend his mind to further speculation about her motives; he could only hope that she would end his suffering. That torment was rapidly mounting, in proportion to the steady decline of the effect of such powerful drugs as his acolytes had managed to place inside his cell in the dungeons of the Merchants' Hall, prior to his being taken to the edge of the Wood. In the one loaf of coarse bread apportioned to the condemned by the dictates of the *Halap-stahla*, those brave, loyal adherents had concealed half a dozen small, compressed balls of highly potent drugs derived from both unusually pure opium and the resin of *Cannabis indica;*[†] but the old man had only consumed two doses, while hiding the others on his person, along with other crucial items: long cotton strips that could later serve as bandages were wrapped tight by the old man to hide medical needles and cotton thread soaked in spirits and oil, a ring bearing his private seal, and finally, the remaining doses of his medication, all against the slender possibility that he might survive the ordeal with the help of his acolytes. In the event that they were unable to secure more drugs before coming to his aid, he would need the remaining doses to tolerate his removal from the ritual site, as well as to endure the closure of his wounds with the needles and thread, a necessary means of preventing further bleeding during his no doubt hasty escape. (Later, of course, he would reopen the wounds, allowing all pus to drain from them as they healed, assisted by cleaning and treatment with honey, strong spirits, and the juices of whatever wild fruits he could find.)

This innocent little bundle he folded inside a longer cotton sheet, which could be strapped around his groin to serve as an undergarment, keeping his secret supplies safely tucked behind his scrotum where no priest would be anxious to search. Yet, despite these preparations, the deliverance that he had hoped might appear did not; or, rather, it did not take the form he had expected. Before his faithful students could effect the old man's liberation, the silent, thoroughly wild, but still wise and regal queen had emerged from the Wood; instead of delivering the *dauthu-bleith*[†] that the old man thought inevitable, however, she had extended her unusually long and supple body, like some feral child, so that she could bite through the tightly knitted thongs that bound the prisoner. In her subsequent gentle actions, the old man had indeed been able to detect compassion; and when he took the time to consume one dose of his medicines and then, after the drugs had taken effect, to meticulously stitch up his wounds, she exhibited great patience, as well. Only when he was ready had she helped him onto her back, and carried him to the cave in the mountains that had been her home long before it became his.

Yet why had she done it? the old man had wondered, all the years since that day—for on this as almost all subjects, she remained mute: the silence of those whose hearts have been rent almost past repair, and whose souls have thereby lost their voices. The old man had eventually formed notions about her reasons, and these had grown more detailed and accurate, during their time together; but whatever her past, the old man had never doubted that the agonies of flesh and spirit that had been inflicted on him when he had been cast out of the city of Broken would have utterly consumed him—would have driven him, eventually, to himself finish the job that the axe-wielding priests of Kafra had started—if his years of exile had not been graced by her sublime example.

But they *had* been so graced: she had not only rescued and nursed him, but taught him, as well—taught him the ways of survival in the Wood, both physical and spiritual. And perhaps the greatest miracle of their long forest idyll had been that her every lesson had continued to be embodied in example: brave, silent, instructive example. No member of any of the academies or museums in which the old man had studied and taught throughout the known world and beyond—great talkers, all—would ever have believed it possible; indeed, they would have called it sorcery, as the learned classes and the holy men of Broken had branded so much of the old man's work. But if sorcery it was, he had long since concluded, then the moralizing of priests and the investigations of philosophers since the beginning of time had been incorrect; indeed, the entire development of human ethics had been absolutely wrong-headed, and so-called sorcery was, in fact, the most profound good that any creature could embody . . .

Yet we ought not think that the old man did not experience his own doubts, concerning both his sanity and the circumstances of his survival, during the first few of his ten years with the warrior queen; but the proofs and the reality of her care and her tutelage had quickly become so constant that such doubts, even had they persisted, would also have been speedily rendered moot. In the event, they had *not* persisted; still essentially a creature of adventurous curiosity, the old man had quickly taken all of her lessons and proofs to heart, learning their thousand vital details fairly quickly (especially given the many and considerable factors that could reasonably have been expected, in such a place as Davon Wood, to slow a legless and aging man's progress), but above all paying heed to that initial quality he had seen in her: the bravery with which she tended to the business of her own life, as well as to the needs of his, while always plainly bearing a hurt that never healed, a tragedy that not only underlay the imperfectly mended wound in her right thigh (which caused a slight, imperfectly disguised limp when she walked, though never when she ran), but that kept the deeper wound to her spirit open and apparent. Even at its mildest, the old man could detect this inner pain tugging at the corners of her watchful eyes, and occasionally causing her shoulders to slacken. Slacken—but never submit. She labored through her grief to meet her new life's demands, *their* new life's demands, knowing (and, as always, demonstrating to the old man) that while some suffering could be instructive, a surfeit of heartsickness could kill; that such excess was far from the most profound manner in which to honor either the souls of the belovèd dead or the memory of a life of wisdom destroyed by ignorance and spite; and that, even when apportioned its proper place, such sorrow, such repudiation of the world and one's fellow creatures in it, was a thing not to be superficially indulged, as the old man had seen so many poets play at doing, but was one to be respected, and, finally, transcended . . .

II:

Within and Without the Cave

SUCH TRANSCENDENCE FILLED the pair's life together, as the years grew to many; and as they so grew, the old man determined to ever more assiduously embody the skills of brave survival and defiant achievement that he saw her practice. It was a regimen that, for her, was not simply a testament to the depth of her injuries and her loss, but that kept the spirits of those treasures that she had lost—those four spirited and precious children, murdered or taken as they were bursting from childhood into the first full, daring flushes of youth—alive in her mind. And without the spark of those exquisitely painful memories, the old man came to see, she would not only have quite likely left him to die, on that evening of the *Halap-stahla,* but would probably have laid herself down to quietly await death on the forest floor.

As a result of all this patient study, the old man came eventually to know of what the warrior queen dreamed, when her own sleep turned restless: her mind re-created, he was certain, her family's battle with the deathly party of powerful horsemen from Broken. She did so, not as a means of further tormenting herself, but out of the plaintive hope of a different result to that day; and yet, as was evident in the spasms of her legs, she failed each time to achieve that happier outcome. Seeing as much, the old man began, with care, to comfort her as she did him: with soothing sounds and innocent caresses, balm-like contact that was a reminder both of lost joy and of the fact that joy need not *be* utterly lost, so long as they both lived to dream and to remember.

Among the several effects that this mutual (to say nothing of magnificent) defiance and embrace of tragedy had on the old man, one was preeminent: he set himself, mind and body, to rebuild what he could of his own life and work, both to prove worthy of her greatness of heart and to make her life, if not happier, at least easier; and he started, as soon as his legs had healed sufficiently for simple movements, by improving their primitive dwelling. While she was in the Wood securing their food, he dragged his mutilated body, with supreme endurance, about the rocky, half-lit sanctuary, creating first fire, and then, in the fire, tools: tools wrought from the iron that ran in thick veins through cave and that, more accessibly, bled from the loose rocks that fell from the mountain ledges. With these tools he could fabricate for himself a new way to walk, as well as carve into the cave's stone ledges more comfortable nooks on which they both could sleep, once those surfaces had been lined with Earth and softened with goose down that the old man stuffed into wide sacks fashioned from animal hides. He even built a crude, protective door for the mouth of the cave, one that kept the curious as well as the threatening out, while keeping in the heat of that first fire: a fire that became perpetual, fed by the stacks of dead limbs that were every night snapped from the trees along the ridgeline by the infamous mountaintop winds.

Basking nightly in the warmth of that first fire, he thought he saw his companion allow something akin to a smile to enter her features: a relaxation of the mouth that, while not necessarily an expression of joy, was nonetheless one of contentment—contentment that, if momentary and even superficial, was a precious commodity for two such wounded bodies and souls, in so merciless a wilderness as Davon Wood. But when sleep came, that smile vanished, and the torment returned. Ever mindful of this ongoing fitfulness, the old man developed an increasingly accurate conception of her mind's activity; and as he did, he began to wonder if he might not yet find some way to heal the essential torment of her life.

He began to observe her as often as he was able, and spent long periods of time sketching, on parchment fashioned from the skins of her kills, the expressions that filled her dreaming features, when those terrible visions of battle and murder passed through her slumbering mind; and he did so skillfully, for he had once been an accomplished illustrator of anatomical treatises. Soon, by way of these attempts to understand her dream state, he unexpectedly came to recognize an entirely different aspect that quietly filled her face when she awoke and, without moving her body, lifted the lids of her eyes: her bright, alert eyes, which were of a green like to the bright shade of spring's earliest flora. This expression, he soon understood, was not simply bitter disappointment at the reassertion of her heartsick reality; no, in addition, her face at such moments was a countenance of guilt.

The old man was reasonably sure whence such guilt emanated, for studying the moods and minds, along with the dreams, of royalty had long been a preoccupation of his. And he could state with confidence that what he recognized in her features, at such moments, was her realization—all the more powerful, in its silence—that her own careful instruction in those habits of headlong bravery peculiar to champions of unforgiving battlegrounds (habits that she had learned from her own mother, in her youth, and that she had known, when she bore her own young ones, that they must learn from her), had contributed in no small measure to those children's deaths. What mother—what father, for that matter—could bear such knowledge *without* deathly guilt? After only a few moments of this contrition, she who had survived to rule her region of the great forest alone would half-rise to locate the old man, who would quickly pretend to be at some other activity. Reassured by his presence, she would set off again tirelessly: back into Davon Wood, to walk the boundaries of her domain, to hunt, and to protect and provide, the only wakeful activities that seemed to give her any calm, or to temper her shame and her sorrow.

And that dedication had useful results: venison, fowl, and boar—some cooked, some hanging to age, some above the fire and being cured by its smoke, and some absorbing the preservative salts that the old man eventually discovered in deeper caverns—all hung about the cave's walls, the more so when the regal huntress observed that the old man did not eat the smallest animals that she brought to him, and so stopped hunting them. As to the other needs of diet, the wild plants and trees that grew along the ridgeline outside the cave and in the dales below it, along with the beehives that appeared to fill every hollow tree limb, provided fruit, roots, nuts, berries, and honey more than sufficient for a prudent subsistence; and soon, having mastered the system of supports for walking that he had fabricated for himself, the old man could reach these necessities without aid, and thus free more of her time for hunting and keeping the eternal watch for more riders from Broken . . .

A nearby feeder stream that fell down the mountainside on its way to the Cat's Paw provided water, as well as the icy, swift balm that, in their early days together, had been the old man's speediest relief from pain—although behind this seemingly trivial fact lay another revealing detail of the formation of their bond. It had been she who had originally revealed the merciful stream to him, quite without his cooperation. Alarmed by his howls and screams on the very first of the mornings that she shared her shelter with him, she had done all that she knew how to help; all that she had ever been able to do to ease her own or her children's physical distress, if they were injured while learning to hunt or while playing with each other in too rough a manner. She went to him, and attempted to caress his wounds; and, when he would not allow this, she tried to pull him upright by his tunic, with surprising tenderness. When this attempt, too, failed, she leaned down to show that she only wished him to throw his trembling arms around her neck, as he had done on the evening before, following the *Halap-stahla,* so that she could carry him to the beneficial waters. But he, bereft of drugs and frantic in his agony (and still not certain of her ultimate intentions with regard to him, at that early point in their association), had at first become more panicked. Still weak from their journey up the mountain, he at length lost consciousness altogether. She had then lifted him, very tenderly, onto her back (for, in his new, insulted form,[†] he weighed scarcely more than her children had, when young), and carried him down to the stream, where the stitched flesh that had once been his knees began to be soothed.

This ritual was repeated every day for weeks to come, the old man having quickly realized her benevolent intent; and it soon proved so effective that he was able to turn his attention to the task of locating wild ingredients that might be blended into a remedy more powerful than cold water. With his well-practiced eye, he had immediately noted several: mountain hops, the bitter juices of wild fruits, willow bark, flowers and roots that often proved poisonous, in other men's less educated hands, and those same limitless sources of honey; all these did he gather, in order to produce medicines that would not only reduce pain, but prevent festering and control fever.[†] Eventually, this humble regimen—in the forms of both poultices and infusions—would bring the old man back to something that resembled, if not his former self, at least a welcome companion, and even a watchman when she slumbered through the daylight hours. This duty would prove especially important, the old man knew, should the rulers of Broken ever discover, not only that *he* had survived the ordeal of the *Halap-stahla*, but that he had taken up residence in *her* cave, and that the two now had what the priests of Kafra would have denounced as an "unholy alliance," a demoniacal threat whose whole was more dangerous than the sum of its brutalized parts.

Yet there seemed little chance of such discovery: no Broken cartographers, and only a few Bane foragers, had ever reached the remote mountains that were now home to the old man and his protector. His anxiousness relieved by this knowledge, and his wounds in the last stages of closing (his poultices, medicines, and cotton bandages, boiled first in stone and then iron cauldrons, having done their work), the old man soon cleared sufficient ground outside the cave to establish a garden. Here, he cultivated the wild plants and herbs that he gathered along the ridgeline; and the collections of dried medicinal flowers, roots, barks, and leaves that he amassed in the cave, along with the generally pleasing stenches of the various concoctions that he created from them, indicated even to his companion that he was not only returning to something like full health, but was also imagining a new way of life for the pair, the details of which she could not guess at, but the effects of which she soon learned to appreciate fully:

It came to pass, one evening, that she had difficulty tracking a stag that she had wounded; and that, when she finally did find the creature, the proud beast managed to pierce the skin of her chest with the point of an antler before she finished him. When she returned with the carcass, the old man proved more interested in the wound than the meat, releasing exclamations of concern in one of the several languages that he was prone to speak, none of which were entirely comprehensible to her, and at least one of which she suspected of being sheer gibberish, so guttural were its sounds.[‡] From out of his now-thriving garden, as well as from his stores of prepared ingredients, the old man produced newly blended medicines, balms that had seemed strange and disturbing, to her—until they reduced the pain and sped the healing of her wound.

To the old man, of course, such cures were comparatively rudimentary, especially in comparison to what he might have achieved, were he in possession of his proper instruments, as well as the exotic and far more potent ingredients that he had been accustomed to cultivating in his storied garden in the Inner City of Broken. But in order for him to proceed past such basic preparations and aspire to the creation of what he was certain would be dramatically new treatments—medicines that would blend the forest remedies of which he had learned during his exile with those he had grown and formulated in Broken—he would need to create a new sort of *laboratorium*[†] in the cave, one that would be unlike anything that any scholar, even in Alexandria, had ever seen or imagined.

He would require his instruments, and seeds and cuttings from his garden in Broken, along with his vials of tinctures and jars of crystals, minerals, and drugs, all of which, he was certain, remained in his former sanctum high in the tower of Broken's royal palace. The God-King Izairn, whose life the old man had more than once saved and extended, had not only raised the foreign-born healer to the rank of Second Minister, at the same time granting him leave to come and go as he pleased from the Inner City through those hidden passageways formerly known only to the priests and priestesses of Kafra, but had bestowed rooms in which to live and work, grounds in which to grow his garden, and two royal children to tutor. Surely Izairn's son, Saylal, when he was persuaded by his own Grand Layzin and the then-newly-invested Merchant Lord that his father's Second Minister sought supreme power for himself and ought to be ritually banished to the Wood, had been clever enough to realize that he must preserve the "sorcerer's" materials and books, and had ordered the accused traitor's acolytes to gain mastery over those countless ingredients and concoctions, rather than disposing of it all. And if the minister's acolytes had complied, then the things that the old man needed to create his forest *laboratorium* were yet being cultivated and maintained. But how to secure them?

$$\boxed{\text{III:}}$$

Their Separate Torments, Their Consolation Together

THERE WAS BUT ONE WAY:
Although the old man's most trusted students had not
reached the edge of Davon Wood on the evening of the *Halap-stahla* before he had received salvation from an entirely unexpected quarter, he had many good reasons—rooted in years of loyal service—to believe that they had *eventually* arrived: after all, during the affront to justice that the Kafrans had called his trial, the old man had never so much as hinted that they were complicit in his activities. He even insisted that he had carried out his "sorcerous" experiments without the assistance of the first among his followers, the man known in Broken as Visimar. (And, although this had been a far more difficult claim to uphold, uphold it the old man did.)

Yet, in the event, the acolytes had apparently been unable to repay the old man's protection by coming to the Wood as soon as the members of the ritual party were well on their way back to the gates of Broken. If they had simply been delayed by caution, as the old man believed, they must have conjectured, on their eventual arrival, that their master had somehow frustrated the desires of the Grand Layzin, the Temple priests, and Kafra himself by surviving the *Halap-stahla* without them. And, if they *had* so conjectured, then the old man might now allow himself to hope that, if he could somehow contact them, they would be all the more willing to bring many of the things that he required out of the Inner City and the metropolis and down the mountain to the edge of Davon Wood. But how to get word to them?

It was a measure of the old man's essential decency that he finally decided that, where once he would have employed only guile, now he would attempt trust: trust, not in the power of his own mind, but, rather, in the loyalty, first, of his companion, and, second, of those young people who had sworn allegiance to him. These risks paled in comparison, however, to the last exercise in trust he would have to undertake: he must hazard the return of his instruments and medicines, his cuttings, seeds, and plants, as well as the safe obscurity of the far more precious life he had made for himself with his warrior queen, on the integrity of the tribe of exiles that he knew lived far to the northeast of the cave that was now his home.

That the role of those strange people would be crucial to his plan troubled the old man more than he preferred to acknowledge; and yet, in the event, finding a way to build that trust proved far less difficult than he had supposed. To begin with, he composed a message in the cipher that he had devised and commonly used when, as Second Minister of Broken, he wished to communicate with his acolytes without being spied upon by Kafran priests or the Merchant Lord's Guard. This code had been cited, during the convocation of the corrupt that had presided over the old man's trial, as evidence of his own and his followers' ability to speak in demons' tongues; in reply, the old man had arranged a demonstration that purported to show that none of his assistants understood so much as their own names, when they were spelt out in the cipher. This ruse had only helped to ensure the accused minister's condemnation as a lone sorcerer; but that had been a foregone conclusion, whereas his deception had protected the lives of the loyal, as well as the secret of his shielded set of symbols and letters.

With his new message thus encoded, the old man proceeded to tightly fold and then address the note in the plain language of Broken; at the same time, however, he sealed the document with wax composed of a melted honeycomb tainted by the juice of dozens of belladonna berries, boiled down, and further mixed with the venom of the Davon tree frog: if anyone save the old man's former assistants (who knew of this trick of their master's) attempted to steal a look at the letter, and then touched their fingers to their mouths or eyes, they would die quickly and painfully. He then imprinted the wax with the ring bearing his seal that he had kept hidden in his undergarments throughout the *Halap-stahla;* and finally, he had asked *her,* in the pieces of simplistic language that they had, by then, begun to share, to carry the packet to the race of small men, of whose existence, he had divined, she had long been aware. He also knew, however, that the Bane had always seemed to treat both her and her children (when the latter were still alive and in the Wood) with an almost religious deference, and this fact had given the old man reason to hope that she might not fear bringing the message to and leaving it with the exile race, and that they might, in turn, actually deliver it. With that end in mind, he tucked the epistle into a carefully stitched deerskin pouch, and suspended the pouch around her neck. All that remained was to send her off, stressing the importance of his request, and expecting her journey to last a few days, at the very least.

He had therefore been very surprised when she'd returned the following evening: after only one night away. *She encountered and delivered the note to some especially daring Bane foragers,* he had immediately conjectured, when he saw her coming home bare-necked; *she is far swifter and more clever than even I imagined—*

It was not fear of discovery by any such foragers that gave the old man sudden pause: for he knew (or at least, he believed) that the Bane were—with the exception of the infamous Outragers—a people who adhered to a crude but strict code of honor. But he had been in the Wood long enough to comprehend that these two traits—curiosity and integrity—were not always easy to reconcile. Even Bane foragers, the old man knew, might well (while respecting the note's integrity) have been fascinated and puzzled as to why a message such as his would have been transmitted by a courier such as the warrior queen; and their curiosity might very well have been too great to prevent them from tracking her, at a safe distance, back to the cave, before they returned home to carry out the request in the pouch.

But, even if they have tracked you, the old man murmured to her, as darkness fell on their home and they both continued to watch the forest around them carefully, *will they yet bear out my claim that they possess integrity by answering our plea, and taking the message into the city?*

With these battling hopes and fears in mind, the old man had kept watch for hours, that night; and, although both he and his companion had sensed a human presence, lurking in the forest around and above the ever-expanding grounds of his burgeoning garden, they never saw or found any true sign of visitors; but then, he knew that no one, not even a foreign-born master of scientific arts such as himself, would be able to uncover any trail left by Bane foragers. In the end, catching sight of them (or of evidence that they had been nearby) had not mattered, for the essentially principled nature that the old man had always suspected the Bane of possessing had been demonstrated: a party of foragers had paid an unexpected call on those of the old man's acolytes to whom the packet had been addressed late one night, within the walls of Broken. In return, the foragers received a hoped for but not wholly expected reward; and a small band of the acolytes immediately began to scheme to meet their former master at the spot along the upper Cat's Paw that he named to them.

The old man's companion had carried him there; and, after that first meeting, several more had taken place, each of which saw the acolytes bring more and more of their former master's books, scrolls, plant cuttings, and instruments to the edge of the Wood, until nearly his entire collection had made the journey. Then, each time, he climbed back onto *her* back, much to the never-ending astonishment of the acolytes, and the two, bearing as many of the supplies as they could, would begin the first of many trips up and down the mountain to fetch their bounty home.

There was but one reason for the old man to worry, during the transfer of so much equipment and so many precious goods from the city: each time the acolytes made their trips, fewer and fewer of them appeared, revealing that their ranks were being thinned, not by cowardice, but by imprisonments—and discreet (rather than publicly announced ritual) executions. The God-King Saylal (once the young prince that the old man had tutored from boyhood through youth) had raised up his new Grand Layzin and Merchant Lord; and this young, powerful pair, as the old man knew from his own ordeal, were more than capable of first suspecting and then discovering what the acolytes were up to. Through the use of torture, carried out in the secret dungeons of the Merchants' Hall, the truth—horrifying for the Layzin and the new Lord Baster-kin to hear—of the old man's survival and, far worse, of his companionship with the warrior queen, had been heard. Each time an acolyte was broken, he or she revealed some new detail of the story; but, thankfully, when only one such detail remained—the most important detail of all— it was Visimar who was brought to the dungeon; yet even Visimar could not reveal what he did not know, that is, where the old man and the warrior queen's cave was. Such was the Merchant Lord's wrath, however, that he demanded (with the Layzin's less vicious support) some greater punishment than quiet death for Visimar; and, when that last and most faithful of the old man's acolytes failed to appear at the appointed hour and place along the Cat's Paw, his erstwhile teacher suspected that some typically horrifying Kafran ritual had taken place; yet he dared hope—

because the extent of Visimar's knowledge was, if not as great as the old man's own, nonetheless considerable—that his most brilliant acolyte had somehow survived what he rightly suspected would be the *Denep-stahla;* and, because he and his companion never discovered, during several dangerous trips downriver, any evidence of the outrage, the old man's faith was redoubled.

The sacrifice of his acolytes had only made the old man more certain that he must set aside his deep sadness at the loss of the students, friends, and the ultimately scornful lover he had left behind in Broken, and make certain that his new work in the Wood would be remarkable: worthy enough, at the very least, to vindicate the loss that had made it possible, to say nothing of the dangers that his new companion undertook every day to protect both it and him. With so many modern tools now at his disposal—pieces of delicate equipment, books by the masters he most admired, and seeds of those exotic plants that he had been the first man to bring west from the far eastern mountains of Bactria, and from India beyond[†]—his work proceeded at a pace so increased as to be startling.

After building a proper stone and mortar fireplace within the cave, one that was capable, during winter months, of performing threefold service (as cookstove, forge, and furnace, the last of which could throw enough heat to operate an adjoining kiln), Davon Wood's most illustrious exile proceeded, with all the energy afforded by the more powerful palliative medications that he could now concoct, to fabricate still more implements of comfort. First, a simple system of spindle, hand-driven wheel, and loom, with which he wove fleece that had been harvested from wild Davon sheep[‡] (often found herding near the cave on their way to the sweet grass in the valleys below) and produced simple woolen cloth, to be used first for the creation of new, warmer garments, and soon sleeping sacks that he filled with the downy feathers of the warrior queen's wingèd kills. After the loom, he set about building a proper forge outside the cave entrance, one in which he could not only fashion more complex tools and instruments, but create rudimentary glass and blow it into the shapes necessary both for his scientific experiments and for domestic use.

He could also now continue his investigations into *metallourgos,*[††] a science that had, in part, been responsible for his gaining a reputation among Broken's Kafran priests as a "sorcerer"—for who could so tamper with the minerals and metals pulled from the ground, all to create steel of unheard-of strength, save an alchemical sorcerer?[†] Freed, now, from the constant meddling of those priests, he could again envision a day when he would create the particular variety of steel that had long been his object, and other metals, as well; save that now he would place them at the service of all who sought, not mere vengeance against Broken's rulers, but a grand correction of all that had gone wrong in the remarkable city-kingdom: wrong, not only for himself and for she who had saved him, but for thousands of others, as well—wrong within the very soul of the state, itself . . .

And yet, as he slowly wakes on this particular morning, and observes the especially bright beams of spring sunlight that reach through the open cave door (she having long ago departed on her morning hunt), and as he finds, too, that his half-legs are not quite so painful as is usually the case upon waking, the old man realizes that it is difficult to keep his thoughts fixed on such momentous concerns. He looks toward the fireplace, which still sends small wisps of smoke up from the white ashes that cover the few bits of wood not yet burned, and turns his mind toward the quiet, one might almost say contented, contemplation of all that he has been able to achieve; and he wonders, for a moment, if any of the past masters that he admires could have done as much, in a similar predicament, even with the aid of so formidable (if academically unschooled) an ally. This thought leads him to look beyond the fire, to the shelf that he long ago chiseled out of a deeper part the cave's stone wall to accommodate his most precious books:[‡] his volumes, not only of the original giants, Hippocrates, Aristotle, and Plato, but of the Egyptian Plotinus, who had furthered Plato's work concerning the soul, and so helped to order the old man's instinctive insights into the minds and spirits of beasts; of the Byzantine emperor Maurice, who had assembled (and largely authored) the *Strategikon,* the greatest volume of military principles to have appeared in any age, which the old man had used to ingratiate himself with many a ruler during his travels (not least the God-King Izairn of Broken); of Dioscorides and Galen; of Procopius and Evagrius, the Byzantines who had done much good by correctly chronicling the first years of the latest appearance of the old man's onetime obsession, the Death, when it had broken out in that Eastern Empire, and who had determined that the disease had originated, like all pestilences of its kind, in Ethiopia; of Praxagoras and Herophilus, the anatomists and discoverers of the *pneuma* and *neura;* of Erasistratus, Herophilus's colleague, who defined the workings of the four chambers and the valves of the human heart and followed the *neura* into the brain during the golden age of Alexandria, when dissections of the human body were considered neither illegal nor immoral; and, finally, of Vagbhata, the ancient Indian who assembled so impressive a pharmacopoeia of potent Eastern plants.

Truly, the old man muses, there is now life, love, and scholarship in his life in Davon Wood, a life achieved through enormous effort and sacrifice: particularly on the part of his acolytes, of course, but also through his own determined defiance of all difficulties, and, of course, through the extraordinary partnership of his companion. Yet now—as he struggles to pull himself up, and notes that the full chorus of songbirds has returned to Davon Wood—he wonders if his life is not something other than merely remarkable; if it is not something that he, as a man of science, once argued was a useless term that described a nonexistent set of phenomena, a term that sprang from man's still-vast ignorance: he wonders if it is not a *miracle* . . .

He does not wonder for long. Perhaps encouraged by her example—her early rising to tend to her share of their pragmatic needs—he, having dragged himself upright with his arms, looks habitually to the desiccated tree stump that serves him for a bedside table, noting that the several moderate doses of the same opium and *Cannabis indica* that allowed him to sleep, last night as every night, are in their usual places, ready to make his portion of the morning's tasks in and about the cave easier. Yet, perhaps because of the early hour, with its glare of spring sunlight, or perhaps inspired by the regenerative nature of the season itself, he pauses, and soon decides that he will brave the pain in his half-legs for as long as he can, and enjoy the comparative normalcy of mind that such forbearance brings. He pulls himself to the edge of his cushioned stone bed, and—ever mindful of the painful scars left by the imperfect healing of his knees, and making sure that they do not drag or knock against any bit of his wool and goose-down bedding or, worse, the stone beneath it—he makes ready to first clothe himself and then to strap his thighs to the walking device that was the very first of his exile inventions.

As he does so, his mind wonders at the pain he yet feels, seemingly strangely, in the missing portions of his lower limbs: wonders, because during all his years in the Wood, he has been able to add little to his understanding of such pains,[†] save the certainty that he must ever avoid the contacts that bring them on, and have his medicines always at hand: for, whatever their cause, the pains themselves are as real to him as they were for the soldiers he once treated who suffered similarly from the loss of limbs; so real, indeed, that the old man sometimes issues piteous cries that cause his companion to do her best to gently caress the sites of the wounds—attempts that are yet another phenomenon more powerful than logic might lead one to suspect.[‡]

Because of all this, the old man moves with particular caution this morning, as he pulls his wool nightshirt up and off, then reaches for one of his now-faded robes of office: more thoughtful gifts from his acolytes, brought during their risky visits long ago. After urinating into a glass jar that he crafted with his own hands, he pulls the rich but simple garment over his head, and then reaches down to the cave floor, from which he carefully takes a well-worn, flat piece of wood, some two feet to a side, which has a section of the sturdy, well-aged trunk of a young maple firmly attached to its underside, and leather thongs affixed to its surface. Lifting his two thighs, he places the platform beneath them, then sets about strapping the thongs tightly to the remnants of his legs. His discomfort grows, as he goes through these motions, but his slow deliberateness limits his distress. Then, when he has finished the careful job of strapping and has started to ease the maple pole, the platform, and the remains of his legs over the side of his bed, he jerks his head up—in a quick, alarmed motion that is most out of keeping with the cautious actions that have preceded it—and looks out the cave door when he hears:

Her. She is not far away, and she is crying out a lamentation in a voice as resonant, rare, and beautiful as it is tragic and heartrending. It is often this way with her, the old man knows, on fine spring mornings, when countless forms of life are being renewed and regenerated in the Wood, and she is forced to realize, yet again, that her own contribution to that Natural display—her extraordinary children—are yet lost, and can never be restored by something so simple as the passing of the seasons. Several times each year she cries out—nay, *calls* out—in this manner, as if to say that, if she cannot summon her murdered children home to her, she will rouse their spirits from the same forest floor upon which she, pierced and bleeding, fought so madly and valiantly to save them.

She attended to the two bodies that the attackers left that day with care: cleaning their wounds and their entire forms, as if they were alive; or if the full truth be known, as if she might nurse them back to life. Indeed, bones they became, before she would as much as think of removing them from the clearing where they fell, much less permit their being laid within the Earth. The old man had himself finally gathered those bones, brought them farther up the mountain, and interred them closer to their cave beneath both Earth and rock mounds as best he could, in a desperate attempt to console her; yet consolation was so slow in coming as to seem, at times, impossible. Rage and sorrow burned on within her, long enough for the two mounds of stone to become accustomed features of this part of the Wood, so much so that, in time, every creature in the forest had learned to leave the site be. Which is not to say that she did not appreciate the old man's painfully laborious gesture; and certainly she came to know periods of calmer sorrow in his company; but to this day she will climb atop some mighty tree that has been torn from the ground by the mightiest of the furious winds that lash the mountains in winter, or brave one of the many rock formations that protrude from the mountainside, at this high elevation, and call out to the dead as she does today, summoning them home as if the graves and the thefts had no meaning—as if the four valiant young ones have merely strayed too far, or momentarily lost their way, and require only her voice to bring them back.

The old man stays on the edge of his stony bed, and listens once again to the same lonely song (and how uncharacteristic it is, for one of her breed to sing at all!) that he has heard many times. And as he sits, he scarcely notices the tears that begin to tumble down his wrinkled face and long grey beard: a peculiar reaction, for the old man, who was not, before his exile, one who easily showed such depth of feeling. Over the years of his woodland existence, however, he has become one: at an exorbitant price he has been transformed into a man whose passions, when sparked, are apparent yet deep; and no living creature can stir those passions as immediately or as deeply as can she . . .

Her song stops, after a time; but only when the full chorus of birds has resumed its chattering does the old man resume his morning's routine. He reaches out for a pair of rough-hewn crutches—aged and worn to match the single leg beneath the square of wood that serves the purpose

of the two he once possessed—and pulls himself up, with great but practiced effort, onto the three points that have for these many years provided him with independent movement, compromised as it may be. He
takes a few steps across the cave, each time planting the crutches a short
distance before him, allowing his weight to be supported by them, and
then swinging his body and the third support ahead. It has become, over
time, a routine movement, although he tries never to treat it casually—
for missteps can bring catastrophic pain, even if, as is usually the case, no
new injury results from them.

But his caution fails him this day: as he approaches the stone shelf on
which rest his precious books, he suddenly notices the tears on his face;
and while so doing, he *fails* to notice a patch of morning dew that has
formed on the cave floor, far enough from both the sun's rays and the fire
to have not yet evaporated. Worse still, he plants one of his crutches
firmly—or what seems, at first, to be firmly—upon it. But when that
crutch starts to slide away from him on the stony slickness with terrible
speed, he realizes his error; and realizes, too, that his initial reaction to
the sudden instability that follows—an attempt to brace himself on his
other crutch and his single wooden leg—will not succeed. It is all happening too fast—indeed, in an instant, it *has* happened.

The sole flaw in his system of supports has ever been that, while it
spares the stumps of his thighs contact with aught save air, it exposes
them to whatever surface he strikes when he falls. On almost every occasion, such falls have taken place on the forest floor, which, like the rest
of Davon Wood, is kept moist and (for the most part) soft by the vast pa-
vilion of tree limbs that form its ceiling. As for the stone of the cave, he
has never before fallen upon it, he realizes, just before he does so; and the
first rush of pain reminds him why he has been so careful.

When that initial wave of agony gives way to many more in quick succession, the old man knows that his inattentiveness to the perils of shuf-
fling about the cave has only been the first of his terrible mistakes, this
morning; the second was not to consume his usual medicines. As matters stand, even if he is able to reach those ready doses on his bedside
tree-stump table, he will be unable to do anything but chew and swallow
the bitter substance: the slowest way to commence the action of the
drugs. But this problem may be academic; for when the successive pulsa-
tions come, they are so torturous that he doubts he will be able to move

at all, for some time; to move, to breathe, to do anything but scream, terribly and forlornly.

They are not pleas for help, these cries; not at first. They are nothing so rational: his thrashing and screaming is pure madness, and his reason returns only after moments that his mind has made into hours have passed. The first indication that time has begun to elapse are his hands, which clutch his thighs in an attempt to cut off the pain along with the motion of the blood through his arteries and veins. *"Arteries and veins!"* he hisses between still more wordless shouting, as if concentrating on the discoveries of those great Alexandrians who first described how blood moves through the body, pumped by the heart and carrying the *pneuma* to all organs, will somehow take his mind from his predicament. And it does begin to do so; but it is no more than a beginning. Many more moments are required before he suddenly realizes that he is no longer simply shouting indistinctly—he is calling out a name:

"*Stasi!*"[†]

It is *her* name; or rather, it is the affectionate name that he gave her, long ago. He tried his best, in the beginning, to learn if such a wild forest creature even had a name of her own; but elaborate verbal communication had never been something in which she took particular interest, and he was forced to conclude that he would have to provide a name for her himself. He considered the matter carefully, and tried several possibilities before striking on one to which she responded: *Stasi*, the diminutive form of an ancient name—*Anastasiya*[‡]—given to female children among his people. It had first occurred to him because it was a name implying a return from the dead; thus it seemed fitting, to say nothing of intriguing, that she seemed ready—even pleased—to have it bestowed upon her. Perhaps she had *always* comprehended far more of what he said than her silence inside the cave indicated; whatever the case, she accepted the name, and it quickly became the one infallible means that he possessed of attracting her attention.

Would that she were close enough now, he thinks, to hear him: for his mind turns desperately to the notion of her carrying him down to the small feeder stream, and placing him in its icy waters just as she did when they first met, and has done so many times since. Indeed, whenever he has injured himself within her hearing, they have made this pilgrimage; but she is likely far away by now. And so he must, with only his arms to rely upon, try to free himself of his walking apparatus, and then pull himself across the cave floor to the tree stump by his bed, and to the medicines that lie atop it.

But no matter the effort, no matter his screams and denunciations of whatever god or gods have reduced him to this pitiable condition, it is of no use; and finally, after a timeless, numberless series of attempts, and with his body long past exhaustion, he realizes his defeat, and allows his perspiring brow to fall, finally, upon the cool stone beneath him. He exhales a terrible moan, his truncated body following his head in utter collapse. "I submit to you, cursèd divinities . . . ," he begins to whisper, trying to catch his breath; but regular breathing brings only a sudden return of pulsating pain, pain that had been temporarily masked by effort. The return of such agony makes his predicament, for a moment, too great to bear, and he abandons himself to despair: "I submit to you— *where is the godliness in thus amusing yourselves . . . ?*"

And—not for the first time, when he is in such a desperate state of distress—the old man begins to quietly weep, too exhausted, finally, to either scream or to carry on an angry indictment of the Heavens.

How long does he lie there before fear replaces his distress? He has neither knowledge nor interest; for the fear, when it comes, is pronounced. It is sparked by a rustling, some twenty yards from the cave, and the slight vibration of a heavy step through the stone floor that reaches the *neura* of his face; and it is deepened by the fact that he is utterly vulnerable, now, bereft of either weapons or further strength. And yet, when he quickly confirms the vibrations as being a hasty step that belongs to a creature too large for him to dismiss, the old man's fear is mitigated by a sudden thought:

Perhaps it is time, he muses through the pain. Perhaps he has defied Fate for long enough, and ought to finally allow the great forest outside the cave to claim him. It will do so one day, no matter how many times he may succeed in staving that moment off; why not today? This very morning? In the midst of Davon Wood's great renewal, why not allow some creature to make of him food for itself or its young? It will likely be a far more useful end than that which he has flattered himself he may one day enjoy, should he finally return to human society. He is saddened by the thought of leaving *her,* of course; but will she not be better off, as well, without him to continually fret over . . . ?

The steps come nearer and faster: evidently the creature—moving at something between a walk and a run—has no fear of the scent of humankind. The old man faces away from the cave door, thinking, in his agonized resignation, that he will not even turn. Rather, he will offer up the back of his neck, the most vulnerable part of his spine, to be crushed in the jaws of what most probably—given its lack of stealth, indeed its behaving as if it already owned the den—is a brown bear of Broken, the same beast whose rampant image was chosen by that kingdom's founder, Oxmontrot, to serve as the emblem of all his line and realm. The animal will have recently woken from the long winter sleep, and is doubtless emboldened by the hunger that comes with burning away all the stored sustenance in its body. Such a creature will be more than capable of crushing the frail bones of the old man . . .

But then he hears it: a heavy yet hushed trill of the throat. And when he does, he recognizes the peculiarity of the step: each leg moving independently as they trot. Only two creatures, the old man knows, possess such coordination of movement: cats, both great and small, and horses. Thus, it must be his companion[†] returning unexpectedly, he dares hope for a moment . . .

His head lifts without his consciously willing it, and his agonized face turns toward the sunlight; then, instantly, his expression changes completely, as the newcomer enters into view . . .

$$\boxed{\text{IV:}}$$

The Specter of Salvation

O N ITS WAY INTO THE CAVE is the most dreaded animal in all the Wood, a Davon panther: not *any* panther, but the one known for many years as a legend throughout Broken, not only for the unusual lust it possesses for the blood of certain men, but for the extraordinary beauty of its coat: fur that should, at best, be a gold akin to ripe wheat, is almost a ghostly white, and where the slightly darker striping and spotting should be, there are only the faintest traces of those markings,[†] rendered in a shade that nearly matches the beautiful but mysterious jewelry that the old man was fond of crafting for the God-King Izairn's daughter: an alloy of pure gold, silver, and nickel, all readily available in the mountains along Broken's frontiers. A mature female, and one with the scars to prove her age and experience, the panther is fearless, that much is evident from her quick step and lack of concern with the smell of human flesh and waste that she must have detected long before reaching the cave. The massive paws (for she is at least ten years of age, as well as over five hundred pounds in weight, some nine feet in length, and half that in height, when measured at the lowest point of the long, dipping spine[‡]) make a sound too careless for the hunt, however: they pad along the forest floor before the cave regally, the great and noble head never turning to remark upon the old man's extraordinary garden, or his forge, or any other detail of this miraculous habitation. The large ears, which come to unusually pointed tufts, are turned purposefully forward; and yet, although the tongue is out and panting, there is no bloodlust in the extraordinary brilliance of the light green eyes, eyes that mirror the shade of the newest leaves on the youngest trees surrounding the camp . . .

The old man holds his breath, his eyes filling with tears; but these are not the tears of a man about to leave this world—they are those of a man who has found salvation where he thought there could be none.

"*Stasi!*" he manages to say, in cracks and cries. "But—you were . . ."

But she was not, in fact, so far away, after all. And, now that she is close, the white panther pays the old man's voice no heed; instead, she trots into the cave as quickly as she approached it, and, standing with her head over his prostrate body, glances about, noting his disordered table and the scattered pieces of his walking apparatus as if she comprehends their meaning. And, indeed, in her eyes, as she looks down at him, is a gaze that could be interpreted—if one had the talent to see it, as the old man can—as embodying both concern and admonishment.

"I know it, Stasi, I know it," the old man groans in contrition, still wincing with the cutting waves of pain. "But for now—"

He need not finish his sentence. With loving compassion, the panther lowers her head to rub her nose and muzzle gently against his nose and face,[††] and then places her neck over his arms, extending her forelegs, so that her shoulders and chest also descend. This allows the old man to reach up and lock his arms around her graceful yet enormously powerful neck, which she then twists, with equal ease and agility, in such a way that he can, as effortlessly as his throbbing scars will allow, pull himself atop her shoulders, with each of his thighs resting between her shoulders and ribs. The panther then lifts the hundred or so pounds of mortal flesh with which the priests of Kafra left the old man, so long ago, exerting no more effort than she would if rising unencumbered; and, although the movements cause the old man some additional pains, his relief is sufficient to make these seem slight.

He reaches up, running one hand down the top of her impressive head to her moist, brick-red nose, the lone spot of deep color on her body: apart, that is, from the black lines that frame the remarkably tinted eyes, deepening their effect in such a way that the lines might have been applied with cosmetic paint by one of the women of the old man's homeland on the Northeastern Sea.[†] Then the panther, consolingly, moves her face to greet the hand, and to allow his fingernails to scratch lightly, first at the long crest of the nose, then across the brow atop those strangely exotic eyes, and finally to the crown of her proud head. With tears, not of further anguish, but of the very deepest joy and relief streaming freely and silently down his face, the old man places his mouth by one of her enormous ears.

"The stream, Stasi," he murmurs, although he need not; she has known since entering the cave that this is to be their destination. As she turns to go, she immediately slows her former quick pace to an easy, rhythmic gait, one that she knows the old man has always found soothing: her shoulders ripple, her spine undulates just perceptibly, and her chest rises and falls with her heavy panting. Most of all, she continues the throaty purr that she long ago determined to be of such entrancing comfort to the old man, never more so than when he is in distress and astride her, where he can put one ear to the back of her neck and listen to the steady vibration.

And in this manner is the great sorcerer Caliphestros once again brought back from the brink of despair and death by the legendary white panther of Davon Wood. They are the two most infamous beings of their generation, to the people of Broken, the stuff of more than mere parents' warnings to unruly children, or of those children's nightmares; for their existence, especially together, strikes fear into the royal and sacred clique of the Kafran kingdom itself. Yet one would be hard-put to find greater tenderness and compassion among any two creatures in the kingdom of the golden god, or, indeed, anywhere on this Earth, than exists between the seemingly very different—yet, in their hearts, not at all dissimilar— enemies of the realm of the Tall . . .

The panther had been relentlessly hunted by men of Broken even before she rescued the old man from the inexplicable evil to which she had watched his own kind subject him. The panther hunt more generally had, for generations, been the definitive rite of passage into manhood for eldest sons from such Broken families as possessed the wealth and position (to say nothing of the additional male offspring) to allow them the leisure, the horses, and the servants to engage in so vicious, dangerous, and foolhardy a blood sport. And, because exceptional purity and uniformity in the coloration of panthers was believed by Broken hunters as well as by the Bane to imply great mystical powers (despite the teachings of Kafran priests that such was a mischievous remnant of pagan beliefs), a high value was from the first placed on this uniquely hued female. But when it became clear that no human would likely ever prove brave or clever enough to track and kill her, an only slightly diminished value had been placed upon the heads and hides of the four golden cubs she soon mothered.

The family had never been tracked: the unspoken truth among those who survived the encounter that terrible day was that a Broken hunting party, led by the son of the kingdom's then–Merchant Lord himself, had stumbled upon the young cats at play, under their mother's watchful eye, in an open dale too close to the Cat's Paw. The hunters quickly found themselves faced with a far more desperate struggle than they would have expected from one female and four juvenile panthers: the white mother had been able to kill several of the humans, before being wounded herself by a spear that pierced her thigh and glanced off the bone beneath. Thus slowed, she had been forced to watch and lunge desperately, as three of her brave children had been killed, one after another. The body of her eldest male had been taken off toward the city atop the mountain, along with her surviving daughter, who was painfully herded, terrified, into an iron cage; and then all the intruders and their captives disappeared, off toward that mountain, the walls and lights atop which the white panther so often studies, of a night, now in a seeming attempt to try to comprehend what those distant, glittering movements may signify . . .

Since that fateful battle, sightings of the white panther by hunters of Broken have been few; and she has made certain that fewer still of those brash pursuers have returned to the mountain of lights, and that none have tracked her to her high cave-den. In this way, she has kept secret the location of the sanctuary to which she brought the damaged old man, and in which she has helped him to recover, just as he has warmed her winters, preserved her kills, and healed the wounds of her hunts. And so the old man's name for her—Stasi, *Anastasiya*, "She of the Resurrection"— is more than simply an apt description of her; it is a constant testament to their life together, to the challenges they have met and overcome—and to the great challenge each knows they will one day face . . .

If this tale of dual tragedy and redemption should stir disbelief[†] in any who read it, they may comfort themselves that they are not alone: for, on the very day in question, when the white panther he calls Stasi once again carries the suffering Caliphestros to the cold stream near their cave to soothe him, two observing eyes—hard, tough eyes that have watched from the safety of a tall ash—also widen with incredulity. They are the eyes of a man who, if the white panther had the time, she would gladly dispatch: for she detected his stink, despite the aromas of the old man's herb garden (newly revived by spring), as well as the "hidden" observer's attempts to disguise his stench, well before she reached the clearing outside the cave. Although the intruder is clearly of the small tribe in Davon Wood (who have always respected her), the panther likes nothing about the blended stenches of fear and filth, as well as the stolen scents of other creatures, that mark him. Yes, she would steal upon and finish him, had she not another mission of mercy to perform for long-suffering Caliphestros . . .

High in that ash tree, meanwhile, the man who creates that stench of fear knows full well that the panther would indeed kill him, had she the chance; and he waits a long while, after the beast and her strange rider have disappeared, before he even thinks of returning to the forest floor. He continues to wait, in truth, until that long while has grown a good deal longer, letting the unnatural pair put as much of the Wood as is possible between themselves and his solitary form (which has never felt so small), before he silently makes his way down the ash trunk, and lightly drops to the ground.

Heldo-Bah stands gazing toward the trees and undergrowth through which the panther and the sorcerer Caliphestros have disappeared: and "sorcerer" he must be, thinks the forager, if he not only survived the *Halap-stahla,* but lives with the most dangerous animal in the Wood! Only after several moments have passed without Heldo-Bah's wide, amazed eyes catching any further movement in the forest beyond the clearing outside the cave does he dare even murmur, in his sourest tone:

"Perfection . . ." But Heldo-Bah's sarcasm lacks its usual conviction. "Most supreme perfection!" he tries again; and then (although he knows he could offer the panther nothing even approaching a fight) he clutches his gutting blade at the ready as he dashes back east, toward the camp that he made with Keera and her brother a few hours earlier.

"Let that fool Veloc explain *this* to me!" Heldo-Bah says aloud, when he deems such volume safe. "The sorcerer lives—but with the most feared panther in Davon Wood, a creature that most think a phantasm! Oh, this has been *well* worth three days' run—we can't even approach him, with that monster in his thrall!"

More astounded and merely senseless expressions of bewilderment at the ongoing perversity of his life echo about Heldo-Bah, as he runs—and yet his last statement was nothing if not true:

Although he does not yet know it, the strange vision he has witnessed has been more than worth his own and his friends' desperate dash through Davon Wood over the last several days and nights . . .

PART·TWO

THE·RIDDLE·OF·WATER,
FIRE,·AND·STONE

NOVEMBER 3, 1790
Lausanne

It is my hope that you, among all my friends and colleagues, will understand why I contemplate not only publishing this tale, but associating my name with it. It is not simply that, even as I write, grievous abuses of *Opportunity* (indeed, such Opportunity as History rarely offers to any man or state twice) are being committed by a collection of destructive dreamers, self-serving knaves, and—worst of the lot!—viciously yet brilliantly manipulative men, all of whom now pose as the legitimate legislature[†] of one of our mightiest and most ancient European realms [France]; no, equally tragic are the streams of exiles of every description that are flowing out of that state in all directions. Many have come here, to Lausanne: and I can assure you that they are learning the same lesson upon which you have expatiated so sagely in your *Reflections,* and which the ruling and mercantile classes of Broken also confronted: that wise men, when forced to take up arms against evils that masquerade as "popular" passions, must be careful also to redress such complaints as prove to represent true grievances. Failure to do so will most assuredly lend plausibility to the most absurd and violent rants of the basest scoundrels; indeed, it is by way of this last consideration that we arrive at perhaps the most perplexing philosophical question put by this tale:

How could a human society reach the relative superiority and sophistication evidenced in the great kingdom of Broken, and then, because of a stubbornly and ultimately cataclysmic unwillingness to adapt its religious and political customs to changing realities, *disappear so utterly* that a millennium would pass before the sole surviving account of its existence would again find eyes and ears capable of understanding it? We are, at this very moment, witnessing the reassertion of this timeless quandary; and while, ten centuries ago, there may have been little or no way of foretelling the horrors to which the unyielding yet flawed rites, dictums, and standards of those who held ultimate power in Broken might lead, *we,* by virtue of histories and legends such as this one, ought to know far better—and yet there is every sign that WE DO NOT!

—EDWARD GIBBON TO EDMUND BURKE

I:

Water

{i:}

"AND WHAT ARE your feelings today, Sentek?" asks Visimar, as he brings his mare to a halt alongside Sixt Arnem, who is seated atop the great grey stallion known as the Ox, reviewing the fitness of the Talons as they pass along the Daurawah Road, heading east from the base of Broken's mountain toward the great port. Having had no time to accustom himself to command of his kingdom's entire army before being ordered to destroy the Bane, Arnem is glad to be at his familiar post as commander of Broken's most elite legion. Only the endless questions with which Visimar has confronted him since they departed Broken have disturbed his thoughts; for they are of such a nature that the sentek finds it difficult—even, at times, impossible—to give forthright answers. He has tried every way he knows to distract Visimar: he has even told him the details of the attempted poisoning of the God-King. But all to no avail; for it seems that Visimar's knowledge of that subject, too, somehow exceeds his own.

"Today?" the sentek finally concedes, looking at the bright blue sky that continues to be dominated by a peculiarly hot sun. It is a sky that would rouse little interest in high summer; but during the height of spring, it is unsettling. "Today is no different, old man. This strange heat bodes ill for our undertaking. I should think little of it, had the past winter been a mild one—but such harsh cold has not visited Broken since the winter of the Varisian war. Indeed, we had killing frosts well into early spring. Yet you know all this, Visimar. So, tell me—why does such heat come so early in the year?"

Although evasive, the sentek's reply is relevant to the business at hand: for on this, the second morning of the expedition's steady march toward the port of Daurawah, the sun's continued hammering of the farming dales of central Broken is unobstructed by even the suggestion of a cloud.

The sentek (setting, as always, an example) wears his lightest suit of leather armor beneath a wine-red cloak of cotton, not wool, and forgoes either steel cuirass[†] or shirt of chain mail, ordinarily the prudent uniform of the Talons in the field. But the spring morning is too warm for such precautions, and there are still at least two days of safe marching distance between the Talons and the Cat's Paw—two days that were to have been used to find forage for their horses and supplies for the men in the towns at the rich heart of the kingdom. Arnem does not think his command in true danger of anything more than a skirmishing attack by Bane Outragers, as yet; but his mind is vexed, by the strange weather as well as by the odd gloom of the towns through which the Talons have thus far passed.

There the soldiers have been greeted, not with the gratitude a prosperous people owe their defenders, but with the sullen antagonism (or even open hostility) that a mistreated populace feels for troops who require more food and forage than the townspeople seem able to offer. Arnem, aided by Visimar, has begun to see that the cause of these unhappy confrontations is not ill will toward the soldiers themselves, but resentment of Arnem's masters in Broken. The anxiety that has crept into the hearts of subjects who have always composed the most secure communities in the kingdom has also meant that these same subjects now angrily refuse to trade the valuable fruits of their various labors in the busy markets of Broken: finding prices for their goods in the great city impossibly low, of late, they are instead hoarding their supplies, not only of grain and other foods, but of fabrics and the handiwork of other craftsmen, as well—all apparently for their own use, despite the considerable and even dangerous loss of profit that they will thereby suffer.

Popular anger over this disruption is fixed not only on the merchants in Broken, but also upon those foreign raiders from the North, now turned "men of commerce," who bring plundered stores of goods in their longships to Daurawah and other, smaller river ports. In all these places, agents of professedly uncertain employ purchase and transport such wares up the mountain to Broken, that they may be sold again, still for far less than Broken's own farmers, weavers, and artisans can afford to ask for their goods. It is because of this that the people of the provinces are withholding the fruits of their own labor, and surviving by bartering them locally; and the worry occasioned by this fact, in turn, causes

Arnem to sigh at Visimar's repeated desire to talk of what the sentek calls "irrelevant events from the past":

"You are aware of the intent behind my question, I think, Sentek," Visimar says. "Certainly, I do not seek your opinion of the weather."

Hoping that concession on his part will produce movement on to more pressing affairs, Arnem holds his hands out in resignation and says, "If you are asking whether I have this morning found such words as have eluded me for the last eight years, I can only tell you—as I have for two days, Anselm—that I have not." Arnem refers to his companion by the latter's assumed appellation, lest any passing soldier recognize the legendary, indeed the infamous name of Visimar, which, for close on twenty years, has ranked second only to that of Caliphestros in its power to frighten the children of Broken: children who have grown up to become, in many cases, the sentek's youngest pallins, such as Arnem's companion on the walls of several nights earlier, Ban-chindo. Such young men are scarcely more than boys, at heart, however powerful their bodies have grown during many months of relentless training. And the faces of those youngest soldiers have appeared ever more boyish still, it seems to Arnem, with every mile that the column has put between itself and home.

"I begin to wonder if my aide was not correct, old man," Arnem says, half-seriously. "Perhaps bringing your blasphemous old bones along *was* a mistake."

"I am not quite so 'old' as the suffering inflicted by the priests of Kafra makes me appear, Sentek," Visimar replies. "And, if I may voice the obvious, you are no devout member of that faith, to speak of 'blasphemy' as though you mean it. Was it not your doubts about the absurd faith of the golden god that inspired you to invite me on this march? I believe so— and I believe that you know it, in your heart."

Arnem's aspect darkens. "I warn you, Visimar," he says quietly, after he has made sure that no one else has heard the old man's words. "Try my patience all you like—but unsettle my men, put doubt into their heads, and I shall pack you off to the merchants and priests in Broken, and let them finish their work." The sentek turns to watch the last unit of cavalry pass by, two abreast, and then studies the first of the infantry, who march four-wide: a tight formation designed to keep the *khotor* ready to wheel quickly into the infantry and cavalry *quadrates*[†] that are their standard defensive battle formation, should the Bane be foolish enough to attack so far from Davon Wood. For all the wise caution of the formation, however, it also makes the words that pass between Arnem and his officers, and especially his conversations with "Anselm," more audible to his men; and this is why the sentek warns his guest so quietly, yet so sternly.

For his part, Visimar watches the soldiers pass for a moment; and, having taken their measure, he nods judiciously. "You are right, Sentek," he says, surprising Arnem. "I shall endeavor to be more careful." He seems to genuinely regret that he was briefly provocative. "Too many years of playing the madman in back alleys and taverns have, I fear, made me foolhardy. It is the great danger of disguise—if we play our assumed roles too long, we risk never finding our way back. Do you not think so, Sentek?"

Two days ago, the remark would have startled Arnem, who had not known, as he left Broken, exactly what "role" his impetuously chosen companion would play during this campaign, other than (as he told Niksar) the sort of idiot that soldiers are fond of having about camp. Men faced with the reality of death nearly every day (whether from wounds or from pestilence) can be as superstitious as old women; and one of the most popular superstitions among Broken troops is that a madman's touched mind allows him to make sense of what sane soldiers cannot— the chaos of conflict.[†] It is an ability that transforms such peculiar souls into agents of good fortune, who may increase a man's, and even an army's, chances of surviving the shapeless tumult of war.

Such had been Arnem's outward justification for enlisting "Anselm"; and the older man has played his role well. He has also, more importantly, given not only Arnem, but the sentek's troops, some explanation for the blackness of mood displayed by the farmers, fishermen, and *seksents*[‡] along the Daurawah Road: for their complaints have been voiced, not only to Arnem and his officers, but to the sentek's bemused legionaries. The whole of Arnem's column are now aware that the affairs of the kingdom of Broken are badly out of joint: never a safe thing for soldiers to have gnawing at their minds. The schemes regarding trade might be counted as simply another ploy of the ruthless merchant class of Broken to increase their profits; but such weakening of the kingdom's own industry by illegal imported goods is forbidden by Kafran law. In addition, if the supposèd men who are plying the rivers in longboats are in fact raiders, Northern or otherwise, and if they are conducting business with anyone in Broken, merchants or otherwise, then it represents a serious violation of Broken law, both religious and secular: for the subjects of the God-King are forbidden from dealing with such men, whose motives are purely material and who are not animated by the golden god's emphasis on wealth as one of the fundamental paths to righteousness. Most unsettling of all, reports are rife that the authorities who are entrusted with protecting Broken's commerce from such foreign goods (from the Grand Layzin and the Merchant Lord, all the long way down to local magistrates) are aware of the true origins of many of the shipments of goods with which unscrupulous men line their pockets at the expense of humbler subjects. There are even rumors that these lofty royal servants do worse than ignore these merchant dealings—they *profit* from them . . .

In reaction to the villagers' complaints, Arnem has explained to his officers (at Visimar's—or "Anselm's"—repeated urging, which is supported by the madman's "visions") that the grumblings are fantastic concoctions, designed to explain away the ill fortune of those subjects lacking the nerve to survive in the heated competition of Broken's marketplaces; and each officer has been careful to pass this on to his men. At the same time, the sentek has also explained earnestly to those town elders whom he has encountered that neither he nor his officers have been made aware of any such treasonous shifts in trade practices, and that the leaders of the army possess no authority to address purely commercial issues—the conduct of trade being, within the Kafran faith, ultimately a sacred, not a secular, activity. Nevertheless, Arnem has repeatedly pledged that, when he reaches Daurawah, he will root out all nefarious traders, and will extract from them not only the names of their partners within Broken, but whether they possess the written dispensation they would require to carry on such an apparently sacrilegious form of commerce. And, while this pledge has not been enough to convince the elders in the villages through which the Talons have passed that they should part with any of their supplies of provisions and fodder, Arnem has seen that these stores are meager, indeed: his men will doubtless have better luck at the first really sizable trading town they come to. Counting himself lucky, therefore, simply to have avoided violence between his troops and the disgruntled townspeople and country folk they have thus far encountered, Arnem gives the order to press on toward one of the wealthiest towns between Broken and Daurawah, Eselben, where his men are confident that they will receive both a warm welcome and good food.

And yet . . . Such coolness on the part of subjects who have always been happy to welcome Broken's soldiers as the embodiment of the God-King's love, even for the humblest of his people, has caused a dangerous sort of confusion to begin spreading through the ranks of the Talons. It is, as yet, mild; but it is the kind of uncertainty that feeds upon itself, Arnem knows this only too well. And so, while it occupies a slowly growing portion of his men's thoughts, it must and does command a far greater portion of their sentek's.

"They will see far more unsettling things, when they actually find themselves in an engagement," Visimar muses, echoing Arnem's thoughts. "And should they continue to meet with this ingratitude on the part of the very subjects for whose sakes they will be fighting, and in many cases dying—they may lose the will *to* fight, and especially to die . . ."

With the two men's remove from the troops now safe, Arnem finds that he is grateful to voice and hear voiced the anxieties that have plagued him since the night of Korsar's banishment. He has not dared express such doubts to anyone—not even to the loyal Niksar, or, in full, to his wife—but somehow, he feels safe sharing them with one who obviously (if somewhat surprisingly) comprehends them: even if that one has ever been rumored to have been nearly as evil as the dreaded Caliphestros himself. Indeed, some within Broken consider Visimar to have been the *more* evil of the pair, for while Caliphestros cut up the fresh bodies of citizens killed by violence, execution, or poor health, it was Visimar who supervised the acquisition of the bodies. And the more handsome the corpse, whether male or female, the more eager the creature of the sorcerer was to buy or steal it.

The sentek takes the hem of his cloak and moistens it with a large skin of water that hangs from his saddle, then leans down to wipe sweat from the Ox's glistening shoulders. "I was not aware," he says, dismounting and using more water to clean the Ox's neck and face, "that explorers of the dark arts were also interested in military matters."

"You mock me, Sentek," says Visimar, still good-naturedly. "But I was once given a unique perspective from which to study your mind and heart—as was my master. I know your moods; and I comprehend your devotion to the rites of Kafra—or rather, its compromised nature."

Pain seizes Arnem's body: it is the physical discomfort, not of illness, but of shame. Visimar has brought their conversation—not for the first time—to the brink of a terrible truth the two share: that Arnem had not merely been *among* the soldiers that escorted the *Halap-stahla* ritual party that mutilated Caliphestros, so many years ago, and then, some months thereafter, the *Denep-stahla* that left Visimar in his present condition; no, the full truth is that Arnem *commanded* those detachments. He and his troops played no active part in the repugnant rituals, of course; but they protected the priests from any interference by the acolytes of the sorcerer and his principal assistant, or by the ever-watchful Bane.

Visimar observes what has washed over Arnem's features, even as the sentek continues to lovingly groom his horse. "I only persist in broaching the subject, Sentek," the older man says kindly, "so that you will realize that, if you speak of it once, we need not dwell on it. I could see at the time that you disdained the rituals; and I heard that, after my own punishment, you refused to stand guard at any others—and that your refusal played no small part in the God-King's decision to suspend the practices altogether. I tell you truly that I then felt happiness for you. Not loathing."

Arnem looks up, his eyes dark. "Such understanding would be extraordinary, Visimar. And it cannot have made these years easier."

Visimar tilts his head thoughtfully. "It has not—and yet it has. My body's suffering would have been worsened by perpetual hatred of men such as yourself, Sixt Arnem. You were all—and remain, whether or not you know it—nearly as helpless, *effective* prisoners of the priests and the merchants as both myself and my master once were. Or so he and I have always believed—and, I think, you have begun to suspect."

Much of the darkness lifts suddenly from Arnem's aspect. "You said '*have* always believed'—so the tales are true, and Caliphestros yet lives!" Visimar glances away uncertainly; but he does not deny it. "I have always suspected as much," the sentek continues, with apparent relief.

Visimar smiles at Arnem's eagerness, knowing it grows from a strong desire to be absolved of the shame of having guarded the Kafran mutilation rituals—even if such participation had been compulsory. For the old acolyte also knows that, where matters of such violent moment are concerned, compulsion does not absolve participation, in the mind of the superior military man: instead, he will wonder—if, eventually, he refuses to carry out a repugnant order, and then finds that his refusal leads, not to his punishment, but to a reassessment of the actions ordered—how many other unfortunates might have been spared, had he objected earlier.

"Well, Sentek, I can but say that I *knew* him to have been alive, at least until fairly recently," Visimar replies. "But as to the questions of *how* I knew it, and whether or not he lives still, I can say but little, save that I have plainly been in no condition to seek him out. I *will* tell you this, however: if anyone could have survived for so long, without his legs and in the most dangerous parts of that wilderness, it would have been my master. And so—fear not, Sixt Arnem. If Caliphestros *is* still among the living, then we shall both meet him again, and likely soon."

Just then, the two men mark the sound of a horse approaching at the gallop. The man astride the hardworking white animal is Niksar, returned to them from the column's head.

"Sentek!" Niksar shouts; and even through the young linnet's urgency, Visimar can see that Arnem's aide remains confounded by the manner in which his commander continues to spend private moments in close counsel with an aging unbeliever. "You must rejoin the vanguard. Scouts have reached the next town—one is now returning."

Arnem, reading trouble in Niksar's noble features, shifts his attention. "But this will be Esleben—surely the merchants and farmers of so wealthy a town can offer no such complaints as we have heard already." Arnem studies Niksar closely. "Yet your face tells me that they can . . ."

"Their objections are far *worse,* from the first look of things," Niksar replies, hoping his commander will pull away from the madman at his side—as, indeed, he does.

"Stay well back, Anselm," Arnem orders, as he sets out. "We cannot say when dissatisfaction may turn into something distinctly more unpleasant!"

Visimar nudges his horse with his thighs back toward the marching troops. "True enough, Sentek Arnem," he muses, as his whispering is drowned out by the rhythmic tramp of the infantry. "Neither here—nor anywhere else, in this kingdom. Not on this journey . . ." Knowing he

has a part to play in that journey, Visimar becomes all happy congeniality, as he draws alongside the foot soldiers of the Talons; and they give
loud voice to their satisfaction at his choosing to march for a time in their
company.

{*ii:*}

A T THE HEAD OF THE MARCHING COLUMN of Talons,
Arnem and Niksar gallop past the suddenly and plainly apprehensive lead cavalry units. They are entering a lush, flat expanse of farming fields, beyond which, almost a mile from the head of
the column, lies Esleben: a considerably larger and more well-to-do place
than any of the communities the expedition has yet passed. This is a result, not only of its rich farmland, but of its position at the juncture of the
Daurawah Road and a similarly well-traveled route that spans the kingdom from north to south. It is also the terminus of an impressive stone
aqueduct that brings water from the Cat's Paw to the south: an aqueduct
that powers the enormous stone mills that are the town's chief places of
employment and sources of profit. The mills and the farming required to
feed them have long kept Esleben an energetic community; yet that energy seems fixed, today, on turmoil. Arnem and Niksar can hear, above
the drumming of their horses' hooves, the unmistakable voice of a mob,
echoing among the town's stone-walled, *thatch*-roofed mills, granaries,
forges and smiths,[†] as well as its many taverns.

In order to guard against raids by the Bane upon this wealthy center
of commerce, its garrison of twelve veterans of Broken's regular army,
always commanded by an experienced linnet, is maintained in a strong
stockade on Esleben's eastern limits. The impenetrable nature of Broken's borders means this fortification has never seen any real "battle";
today, however, the rage of the townspeople is great enough to lead to a
most disordered clash of arms. Yet this violence seems to be directed
against any man who wears the distinctive armor or identifying symbols
of Broken's own legions: in addition to seeing two of his mounted scouts
amid a throng of menacing villagers, Arnem sees that the third scout,
who is riding back to the column, is spurring his horse as if his life, and

not simply a report, depends upon it. Arnem and Niksar increase their own pace, and meet the approaching scout midway between the town and the rest of the men. One look at the agitated young soldier, as well as at the lather on the flanks of his mount, is all Arnem requires to understand that the two scouts still in Esleben may be surrounded by more trouble than they can manage on their own.

"Ho, soldier!" cries Arnem, reining in the Ox. The scout's horse rears with a cry of its own, after which the soldier gets a fist to his chest in salute and tries to catch his breath. "Akillus!"† Arnem continues; for he knows each of his scouts by name, as they are the most intrepid of Broken's already daring Talons; and none is braver than their chief, who is now before the sentek. In addition, Akillus is, because of his seemingly inexhaustible good humor, a favorite of Arnem's. "The people of Esleben are even less pleased to see us than their neighbors have been, it would seem," the sentek continues.

The scout pauses a moment to steady his voice, and wipes at the moist brown shoulders of his horse as he brings the mount alongside the Ox. "Aye, Sentek," he answers, his concern for his two comrades still in the town, as well as for his horse, plain in his face, if not his disciplined words. "We thought to contact the garrison, but—the villagers are keeping them penned up inside their own stockade, and have for some time, apparently. And, when we asked the village elders for an explanation . . . Well, Sentek, what we received in reply was a mob of madmen. And may the golden god shrivel my stones if we've been able to learn the cause of it all—"

"Akillus!" Niksar says, though his rank is but marginally higher than the chief scout's own. "Whining villagers are no reason to blaspheme before your commander."

Akillus begins to apologize, but Arnem holds up a hand. "Yes, yes, forgiveness granted, lad.‡ Crowds are tricky things—I suspect that even Kafra will not begrudge your outburst." Pulling a scrap of parchment and a bit of hard charcoal from a pocket beneath his armor, Arnem quickly scrawls a short note, which he hands to the scout. "Return to the column, now, Akillus. Give this to the first *Lenzinnet*†† that you find, and have him bring his unit back with you. We go on ahead."

"Sentek?" says the scout uneasily. "Surely you should wait—"

But Arnem has put his ball-headed spurs§ to the Ox's sides, and is away to the town at a hard gallop. Niksar, sighing in fretful familiarity at Arnem's impetuousness, prepares to follow, saying only, "And make them *good* men, Akillus—I don't like the look of that town . . ."

As he begins to turn his own horse round so that he can carry out his order, Akillus glances at Arnem, who is moving directly to the aid of the two scouts in Esleben. And, as he watches his commander, Akillus smiles—a full, heartfelt smile, one that reveals clearly why Arnem's men love him so: their commander will forgive a blasphemy that many officers might punish with a thrashing, and at the next moment rush off into danger before support troops have even started for the trouble.

"*He's* mad, himself," the scout murmurs, in great respect. Observing for a last time how Arnem expertly handles his horse, riding so low that his body seems merely another muscle in the Ox's back, Akillus quietly adds, "But it's a madness that we would gladly share—eh, Niksar?"

Before Niksar can upbraid him again, Akillus is away, his own horse's pace almost matching that of the Ox in the opposite direction.

As Arnem draws close enough to discern the townspeople's outraged expressions, he can also see the large mills and granaries at the center of the town, which are surrounded by a circular cart path fed by the four roads that approach the town from the cardinal directions. Within the dusty circle stands a large platform with pillory and gibbet, a fair-sized temple to Kafra, and the terminus of the long stone aqueduct, which brings its turbulent waters along a gently sloping stone channel several miles in length. The concentrated flow from this channel powers the wheels of the grinding stones housed in the millhouses, the relentless engines of which pulverize prodigious amounts of the grain that is brought from the fields surrounding Esleben, as well as from distant farmsteads—

Yet on this warm spring day, the water from the pool does not flow, and the great mill wheels do not turn . . .

Upon entering the square, Arnem offers the crowd of what he would guess to be some eighty people no sign at all that he is preparing to slow his charge into their midst. On the contrary, when he is sure the crowd can see both his face and the silver claws on his shoulders, he unsheathes his cavalry sword.[†] Holding this deceptively elegant weapon calmly but purposefully along his leg—where it can be easily used to cut a few throats—the sentek charges toward the townspeople who appear most ready to confront his wild advance; but as the moment of collision nears, the crowd's determination breaks, and they dash in every direction, leaving the two scouts alone near the gibbet.

As the townspeople disperse, Arnem sees what Akillus has described in more than a few of their faces. *In truth, it is something beyond rage,* he determines; *something that bears a disturbing resemblance to lunacy . . .*

Both of the scouts, like Arnem, have their riding blades drawn, but have yet to make any truly menacing move; and, although their horses had earlier been frightened into turning tight circles in the midst of the crowd, once free of the mass of humans the animals quickly regain composure. Arnem rides directly to the soldiers, without acknowledging the retreating mob. Both men salute bravely, and as they do, Arnem can hear Niksar behind him, using his own mount to ensure that the crowd stays back. "Brekt—Ehrn," Arnem says, again calling each of the scouts by name. "It seems you've stumbled into some sort of commotion." The sentek keeps the tone of his voice almost merry, as if the threatening scene is nothing more than a mildly amusing spectacle. "Are there any details that I need be concerned with?"

Both scouts laugh, relieved as much as amused, and the taller man, Brekt, replies: "We don't yet know, Sentek—we haven't been able to speak to any of the garrison. All we *do* know is that this lot"—he indicates the now-splintering crowd—"say that they've had eleven of the men penned up in their own stockade for days, if not weeks—"

"Eleven?" Arnem asks, attempting not to betray the dread he feels. "And where is the twelfth?" For a town garrison to be short a man is ominous: such a loss would ordinarily be reported to Broken immediately, to allow a replacement to be sent out. But if the townspeople have laid siege to the garrison for so long, then the missing man almost certainly means the elders in Esleben have deliberately kept the situation from their rulers. *An evil indication,* thinks Arnem, with another apprehensive twinge.

"We can't get a reasonable answer," says the second scout, Ehrn, a slight trembling in his voice. "Just screaming about a 'crime'—"

With greater confidence, Brekt interrupts, "They claim that one of the garrison soldiers committed a terrible offense, but they won't tell us what."

"Where are they keeping the man?" Arnem asks severely.

The scouts shrug.[†] "They won't tell us that, either, Sentek," Ehrn declares.

"The lot of them simply refuse," Brekt adds. "They want us to get out, nothing more or less. Not the garrison, however; they *will* say that we're to leave them behind, as they've got further business with them—or, at least, with their commander."

Niksar, having ridden up behind Arnem, quietly observes, "That tells us what sort of crime we're dealing with, Sentek."

Arnem nods grimly. "I'm afraid so, Niksar. Either a girl or a death—and likely both, damn it all . . ." He turns to the scouts. "All right, lads. Take up position by the west road—watch for our relief, and then detail three men to guard the main routes in and out of the town."

"But—Sentek," Brekt protests, "shouldn't we stay with you? That crowd hasn't shown any great respect for the soldiers of Broken—"

"It's possible they've had little reason to," Arnem replies. "Go on—we'll get nothing out of them, if we attempt to impress them with only our strength. Hold the roads, and above all, keep an eye out for any Bane, even if they are retreating—*particularly* if they are retreating."

As the two scouts slowly walk their horses to the town's western approach, they cast meaningful glances at the townspeople who had pushed closest to them during their recent quarrel, silently assuring them that only the influence of their commander has stayed their sword arms.

Arnem crosses over to the mob, particularly toward three men who appear to be the town's elders. They are agèd, dignified characters, who have stepped forward from behind the protective crowd. Their wizened faces show as little fear as Arnem's; but when the sentek sheathes his sword and swings his right leg over the Ox's neck, in order to be able to slide from the beast in one agile movement that leaves him face to face with the elders, those older men finally do display some little apprehension, causing Niksar to again shake his head at Arnem's familiar recklessness.

"Honored Fathers," the sentek says, bowing his head respectfully. "You speak for the people of Esleben?"

"We do, Sentek Arnem," says the old man in the center, who is evidently senior to the others. "And, unlike our sons and grandsons in this village, we are not frightened by your rank—all three of us gave years of our youth to the campaigns against the eastern marauders during the reign of the God-King Izairn, when we were stronger men. We do not deserve the breaking of faith we have had from his son, or from those who enforce that son's edicts."

Although he is too cunning to allow it to register in his face, the sentek is shocked and alarmed by this statement. "'Breaking of faith'?" he echoes. "These are strong words, Elder."

"Aye, Sentek," the greying elder replies forthrightly, "and meant to be. We have ever kept faith with those who rule in Broken—yet now, the God-King permits the sapping of our kingdom's inner strength, by allowing foreign pirates to supplant the place of Broken's own farmers and craftsmen, even as he allows his soldiers to defile our daughters, planting wasting disease with as little care as they do their seed. It is time that we say these things aloud."

Such are indeed bold indictments; but, coming from an obviously seasoned, proud old campaigner—the kind of man under whom, during his own youth, Arnem would have been grateful to serve—the sentek neither disputes them publicly nor dismisses them in his mind. Indeed, because of the elder's statement, the nature of the crowd begins to change, in Arnem's eyes—for he is now faced with the honest complaints of that unheralded hero whom he has always respected most: a loyal, tested veteran of the army. Arnem is forced to weigh anew the resentment that the villagers feel toward their town garrison and his own troops.

"Whatever treatment you have received thus far, Honored Father," Arnem says earnestly, "I see that you are wise enough to know who, and what, I am; and I hope you know that I will treat your complaints with the seriousness that your service in the defense of the realm merit."

The principal elder nods, perhaps not warmly, but with the beginnings of appreciation. He turns to either side, as if to confirm that he and his fellow elders were correct in thinking that they would receive better treatment from the renowned Sentek Arnem than has been their lot of late. "Your words are gracious, Sentek," the man continues—but then he grows uneasy again, as panicked rumblings go through his townspeople. More horses' hooves are heard coming from the west: the relief from the main column of the Talons.

Arnem turns to Niksar in alarm. "Get out there, Reyne. Tell them to hold their positions at the town's edge—I want no more complaints from these people."

Once again disturbed by what he sees as Arnem's recklessness, Niksar nonetheless obeys, knowing that any objection he might raise to leaving his commander alone inside the town will only irritate Arnem. As Niksar wheels his horse, the sentek indicates the nearby platform to the elders. "Shall we speak privately, Fathers?"

Enjoying the sentek's deference with silent satisfaction, the men nod, motion to the rest of the townspeople to stay where they are, and cross to the town's center to sit in earnest conversation with a man about whom they have heard many tales, but whose wisdom and fairness they must now judge for themselves. As for Arnem, it is only when he leads the Ox to the platform that his ever-searching gaze can finally catch sight of the small, stout stockade just north of the Daurawah Road:

It is surrounded by a larger crowd, who brandish similarly humble (but deadly) weapons as do their fellows in the town square. Happily, however, this second crowd also seems to be calming with the news of what has just taken place. Such being the case, and with the common touch that has ever made him stand out so in the Broken army, Arnem confidently engages the elders; and it is mere moments before looks of appreciation and even light amusement cross the old villagers' faces. Niksar, watching from a distance, turns away from the conference; but his relief is short-lived, for he spies, among the men at the western edge of Esleben, the mounted figure of the old heretic chatting amiably with the several horsemen about him.

Niksar spurs his mount to a trot and rides up to the former outcast, letting his own horse aggressively butt his forehead into the neck of the old man's calm mare. "What are you doing here, Anselm?" he demands; and then he turns his head to the other men. "Who among you took it upon himself to bring this man?"

"Peace, Niksar," Linnet Akillus says, clapping an amiable hand on Visimar's shoulder. "It was I who brought him."

"Oh? And did you never suspect the possible danger—"

But Akillus is already urging Niksar aside with small nods of his head. As the pair moves a short distance away from the others, Niksar quietly demands, "Well, Akillus? On what authority—"

"The sentek's own," Akillus interrupts, producing a small piece of parchment from his belt. "He seemed to think you would find it amusing . . ."

Niksar takes the note that Arnem gave Akillus just before riding into town; and the sentek's aide quickly reads its few scribbled words:

> BRING THE CRIPPLE, AND SHOW THIS NOTE TO NO ONE,
> SAVE NIKSAR—WHO WILL SURELY ENJOY IT.

{iii:}

NIKSAR'S FACE BECOMES an odd mixture of familiar irritation and something new, something that Akillus cannot quite define, but which is plainly not a sentiment to be taken lightly. "He thinks he's always so bloody amusing," the aide murmurs. "This time, however . . ." Niksar knows his commander can be worrisomely careless about his own safety, which is ultimately his own business; but he also knows that Arnem has never acted upon any whim or flight of fancy where the well-being of his men is concerned. Nevertheless the linnet now holds evidence that his commander has summoned the strange old heretic into these most ominous doings. *Has he taken leave of his senses?* Niksar wonders silently, as he stares at the note while the other riders continue to chat with Visimar. *Or can it be that he and the men are right, and that the old lunatic is truly an agent of good fortune?*

"I didn't understand it, either, Niksar," Akillus says, addressing his fellow linnet confidentially and congenially, having read the look on Niksar's face and trying to ease his mind. "But—he certainly did give me that note, and must have had his reasons. You think otherwise?"

Niksar ignores the question, glances at the heretic, and moves his horse toward him. "And so, Anselm—what possible service can you offer, at so delicate a moment as this?"

"I cannot say with certainty, Linnet—but look there." Visimar points toward the center of the town. "I'd say that we're about to find out."

Atop the wooden platform inside the circular roadway at the center of Esleben, Arnem is waving in a broad motion, ordering the soldiers to finally enter the town. After this, he leaps back to the ground and bows to the elders, as they move off toward a series of litters, each of which is borne by two men. Only when they are not watching does Arnem turn again in the direction of his men, and, in an unmistakable motion, wave a flattened hand, blade like, across his left knee.

"*Hak . . .*" noises Visimar, with a small laugh. "Neither subtle nor flattering—but it seems he wishes me to accompany you into the village."

"Aye, old man," Akillus replies. "And, based on how ugly Brekt, Ehrn, and I have already seen those supposedly peaceful villagers become, I'd say your talents for good fortune and laughter will be of great use."

Niksar finally tries to put his own misgivings aside, given both Arnem's note and the genuine good humor that Visimar has been able to inspire among the horsemen in what is plainly a dangerous situation. "Well, Talons?" Niksar says. "We have our orders: by twos, and at an easy gallop.[†] And you, Anselm—will you ride with me?"

Visimar inclines his head in what seems to the others no more than appreciative acknowledgment of Niksar's offer; but the former acolyte realizes that Arnem's aide, in addition to honoring him, is also signaling some tempering of his enmity and distrust. "It will be my honor and pleasure, Linnet," Visimar replies with true gratitude, as he takes the head of the small column with the golden-haired son of Broken.

In the formation and at the pace commanded, the horsemen ride into the central square of Esleben. At the town's center, where Arnem sits astride the Ox once more, the soldiers find that the crowd is breaking up, if sullenly. One of the three elders' litters—the best-crafted of the group, with soft cushions on its seat and colorful lengths of cotton about its frame—is already moving toward one of the stone storage structures near Esleben's mills. Arnem directs the Ox to follow the litter, indicating to Niksar and Visimar that they should join him. When they have, the sentek grins just perceptibly at his aide.

"Do I detect some vague air of harmony between you two?" he says. "I did tell you, Niksar, that he might have his uses."

Niksar nearly contains a smile before asking his commander, "Sentek—where, precisely, are we going? The garrison's stockade, to say nothing of Daurawah beyond, are to be reached by way of the road *eastward*."

"We have a mystery to solve in Esleben, Niksar," Arnem replies, "before it will be safe to go on—and before the elders will release grain and other supplies from their stores."

"A mystery, Sentek?" Visimar replies. "I think not—rather we have two such, both housed, apparently, somewhere in the town's granaries."

Arnem brings the Ox to a halt, as the chief elder's litter continues onward. Plainly impressed and intrigued, the sentek nevertheless takes a moment to turn and call back into the town: "Akillus! Go with the other two elders to the garrison—you'll have no trouble, now. Tell the men in the stockade that when I return, I want its gates open and their commander ready to give his account of what has happened here."

"Yes, Sentek!" Akillus replies; and as the other two elders issue commands to their respective bearers, he leads the rest of the riders to the eastern road, which will take them in a few moments to the palisaded garrison.

"Sentek," Niksar says, watching in astonishment. "What makes you speak of one mystery in Esleben, while this old lunatic talks of two?" The linnet turns his handsome, worried features toward Visimar. "You understand, I hope, that I use the word 'lunatic' only in its literal sense. I grant that I may have misread your intentions—but about your sanity, I was most certainly correct."

"Ah," says Arnem, smiling. "And so peace of a kind has indeed taken a seat at my little war council—well said, Niksar! And, as to the *mysteries* of Esleben . . ." The sentek resumes the march south. "Allow me to ask, Reyne—what lies at the heart of *all* good mysteries?" Seeing that his aide is tiring of games, Arnem continues, "*Death,* old friend—murder, or so the honored citizens here believe."

At the mention of the word, all three men see the litter ahead of them stop, its occupant apparently having overheard this portion of their conversation.

"Murder?" echoes Niksar; and, given the notion, he is not altogether surprised when Esleben's chief elder peers out from between the rear drapes of his litter and replies:

"Indeed, Linnet—or as good as murder. A young woman—the daughter of one of our most respected and successful millers, and a maiden who was scarcely more than a girl—died horribly, half a Moon ago. The only fact that we have determined certainly, concerning her death, is that she was, without the knowledge of her family, carrying on a carnal relationship with a soldier of the garrison, a young man beneath her family in rank and station, and concerned only with his animal appetites."

"The accuracy of those last facts, Niksar," says Arnem, too softly to be overheard, "I have yet to establish . . ." He raises his voice again, before suspicion can be fostered: "But let me add to the honored elder's statement only that the maiden neither took her own life, when the business was discovered, nor was she struck down by some furious member of her family."

"Why think the soldier involved at all, then, Honored Father?" Niksar calls. "Did she show signs of the pox, or some other—*disease* of like nature?"

"Indeed," the elder answers, displaying angry, horrified grief.

"Very well, then," Niksar says solemnly. "The laws are clear, if it was given to her by the soldier. There should be no confusion, no 'mystery.'"

"There *should* be none," Arnem replies, esteeming his aide's respectful manner, and matching it. "But we have two additional and unfortunate facts to consider, for they lie behind the actions of the young pallin's comrades—and, more importantly, those of their commander. Both the soldier and his maiden insisted, even unto their deaths from the sickness, that they had engaged in no—" The commander attempts to find a gentler word, but cannot: "No *fornication*. Only innocent trysts."

Niksar, however, has fixed his mind on one detail of Arnem's revelations: "'*Their* deaths'?"

"Indeed," Arnem says. "For the pallin also died, soon after the girl."

Out of the corner of his eye, Arnem sees Visimar's wandering gaze fix on the great stone structure that they are approaching: it is a reaction of the sort that the sentek has hoped to provoke. "*Ignis Sacer,*" the cripple murmurs. "The Holy Fire . . ."

"Elder," Arnem calls, as the horses reach the litter. "May I assume that the two deaths, while they may not have occurred at the same time, were of the same—*variety*?"

The elder seems somewhat uncertain of the meaning behind this question, and he hesitates; at which the fearfully fascinated Visimar, perhaps unwisely, steps in: "Of course they were, Sentek. In both cases, death was preceded by a fever that seemed to come and go, each time returning with more force. It was eventually accompanied by small red sores across the back and stomach, as well as the chest and the throat."

"Our own healer," the elder says, "then thought it to be rose fever, which was cause enough for alarm."

"Indeed, Father," Visimar says, nodding and glancing at Arnem as the latter starts at the mention of rose fever. "But very soon, it degenerated further, into a madness that destroyed their minds, as well as an unspeakable rot that ate their bodies away."

The elder's face darkens. "I have never seen its like. Kafra's wrath is terrible, especially when it ravages such young and healthy forms."

Already making Arnem nervous with his apparent inability to choose his words carefully (or silence himself altogether), Visimar presses forward with his description: "Yes—a ravaging sickness, perhaps too fearsome to be accurately described by words, and consuming first their minds and then their beauty: it turned their admirably pale skin—particularly that of the girl's delicate hands and feet—a deep, sickly yellow, then the color of plums, and finally black, after which first the toes and fingers, and then perhaps entire extremities, simply . . . fell away. And the stench . . ."

Ignoring the warning look that Arnem has fixed upon him, Visimar seems to puzzle with his own comments: "And yet—there is something incorrect about it all, Elder . . ."

"Incorrect?" the elder says, distrust sharpening the word.

Arnem attempts to patch the momentary breach: "I am certain that my comrade meant only to say that there is something *amiss,* Elder."

The elder, however, is unappeased: "Of course there is something 'amiss,' Sentek Arnem: the entire business is—"

"Of course, certainly, Honored Father," Visimar says, still lost in thought. "But if the illness were a pox of some horrifying variety, as you claim, what you describe would be its final stages. Yet you have proposed to us that the couple knew each other only a short time, and that the soldier's interest was but carnal and temporary, whatever his or the girl's claims to the contrary. The difficulty being that—even assuming their trysts were so base—it would take months for any known pox to manifest such monstrous symptoms."

The elder's expression darkens, suddenly and considerably: a moment before he had felt unexpected satisfaction at the appearance of the noted Sentek Arnem and his officers, and at the justice he had begun to feel that they had brought with them; now, his blood begins to heat with familiar yet disappointing resentment: "I might have known . . . ," he murmurs.

But Arnem has already lifted a conciliatory, if warning, hand. "Hold, now, Father, I beg you. This old man has been my surgeon in the field for more years than I care to count, and I will admit, he has become somewhat addled in his thinking and loose with his speech, due to all that he has seen." Arnem gives Niksar a quick glance, finding in his aide's face at least some comprehension of his ruse's necessity; and then he tries to warn Visimar once more with his eyes that he must keep silent. "And if he has spoken mistakenly today," Arnem continues, "or simply has put the matter more bluntly than he should have, you must accept my apology—our sole desire is to establish the truth, not to insult either you or your loyal community."

"Fine words and sentiments, Sentek," the elder says, his voice more controlled, yet no less suspicious. "And if that is, indeed, your desire, then you must descend with me to the deepest vault beneath our largest granary. There, the temperature is always cool, even uncomfortably cold— and we have kept the bodies of the dead couple there, lest anyone question our demands to the garrison's commander."

"You have *preserved* the *bodies*?" Visimar says, suddenly shocked. "You have not buried or burned them? But—"

"*Anselm.*" The harsh way in which Arnem says the name silences Visimar, at which the sentek turns a kinder expression on the elder. "Of course you would have had to preserve them, Honored Father."

"Indeed," the elder replies. "For in such cases, as you doubtless know, Sentek, the commander of the town's garrison, if he attempts to shield the offending soldier, is, by law, as guilty of misconduct as the soldier himself. Yet after the girl died, and we learned of the youth's illness, the commander would neither yield the boy up until he was dead, nor put *himself* into our hands for trial."

By now Visimar is staring at the large stone granary, as if the mere sight of it held answers. "But if this be the entire extent of the matter, Father," the old man murmurs, "why, I pray you tell, have you experienced *more* outbreaks of the unidentified pox? For you have, have you not? And why have you not told us of them? Surely you are not suggesting that this one pallin was behind *every* death in Esleben?"

At these words, everyone present is suddenly seized by differing forms of dread: Arnem recognizes that Visimar is not merely speculating, but is certain of his accusations, whereas Niksar is consumed by a new confusion that causes him to grip the hilt of his sword in preparation for a fight; the elder's litter bearers, meanwhile, suddenly release their burden, which hits the ground with a sharp slamming of wood against hard Earth as their faces fill with fearful astonishment. Yet Visimar does not move, as the elder fairly leaps from his conveyance and thunders in accusation:

"Who is this man? I demand you tell me, Sentek!"

Matters only worsen when the elder's bearers begin to murmur the dreaded word: *"Sorcery . . . it must be sorcery . . ."*

The elder silences these men with a wave of one hand, and shouts: "Well, Sentek Arnem? How comes this fellow to know so much of our business? Not only the girl's death, but our subsequent misfortunes! Is he in secret communication with someone in Esleben?" But both Arnem and Niksar remain, for the moment, too stunned to speak. "I demand to know, I tell you!" the elder rails on. "You call him your surgeon, yet he does not wear the uniform of your legion—who, then, by all that is holy, *is* he?"

Although inwardly somewhat satisfied that his suspicion concerning Visimar's usefulness to this campaign has been borne out, Arnem must, because of the cripple's rash statements, continue to affect only shock: "You don't mean to say," the sentek asks the elder, "that he has spoken the *truth* of this business?"

"Truth enough," the elder answers, himself astounded at Arnem's question. "But surely you know it to be, Sentek."

"I know no such thing, Elder," Arnem replies, aware that he is engaged in a dangerous ploy. "If you tell me it is so, I shall not contradict you—but do not mistake this fellow. He is still a competent healer, one who inspires faith in my men, and I have kept him on this march for their sake. But his rants are not true 'vision,' Elder; they are only the noises created by his broken mind, whatever their seeming conformity to any truth." The elder becomes suddenly uncertain. "And, even if he has stumbled upon some few details of events here," Arnem presses, "do not doubt that he yet remains a stranger to reason, the greater part of the time." Drawing his blade slowly, Arnem faces Visimar, but glances at the elder. "Finally, I promise you this—if there *be* any truth in what he says, then I shall discover how he knows it . . ." The sentek steps closer to Visimar. "But that inquiry, as well as my inspection of the bodies in the granary, do not require your presence, Father. For I have seen the dead of all varieties, during my campaigns, and require no guidance—whereas I would not have you witness what may become necessary, during my interrogation of this man. Niksar—" Arnem's aide salutes his commander. "Escort the elder back to his home. Do not allow anyone to bully or threaten him in any way." As Niksar salutes once more, Arnem calls to the elder: "And accept my assurance, Father—you may leave this matter in our hands, and my Talons *will* determine the truth of it for you . . ."

Faced with Arnem's hard aspect, Visimar realizes that he has said too much, and ought to have waited until he was alone with the sentek to divulge his accurate apprehension of the lovers'—and indeed the town of Esleben's—fates. His words have been dangerous, he quickly sees, precisely *because* of their accuracy: the townspeople are plainly interpreting the mysterious illness as some sort of punishment brought down upon their whole community by the golden god as punishment for both the reckless acts of the malevolent young soldier and the disobedience of the commander of the garrison. They do not know, as Visimar believes he does, that a terrible sickness is at work in Esleben, one that is not only impossible to cure or control, but is also of an entirely different nature than the supposèd "poison" with which the Bane (according to Arnem) are said to have attempted the assassination of the God-King Saylal.

In short, there are in all likelihood *two* deadly diseases now at work in Broken: one in the city, and one in the provinces. The first might admit of some cure, if treated as an illness and not a poison; but the second, should it spread, will become as voracious as the fire for which it is named.

Visimar requires but an instant, after this realization, to finally comprehend that he must cooperate with Arnem's deception, and convince the elder and his bearers that his conclusions concerning the lovers' deaths and the fate of the town indeed arose from a disordered imagination. By doing so, he will gain for Arnem the freedom to seek out the commander of the garrison, and then determine if, in fact, the soldiers of that unit are as doomed as most of the townspeople appear to be.

With this end in mind, Visimar quickly affects a long string of nonsensical declamatory remarks, deliberately made within the retiring elder's hearing and concerning the "true" (and "magical") source of his insight. The cripple makes a great show of saying that the birds about Esleben have whispered to him all that they have seen and heard, a ploy—inspired by the work of Visimar's old master, Caliphestros, who often seemed truly able to draw such information from creatures wild and tame—that is effective; and ere long the elder, still peering out through the back of his litter, orders his men to hasten the return to Esleben, satisfied that Sentek Arnem will honestly determine the extent of the old healer's madness, and, should it prove in any mischievous way connected to actual events in Esleben, punish Visimar accordingly.

"But remember, Sentek," the elder calls, as he returns to the assembled crowd, "that the commander of the garrison also awaits the God-King's justice, although I take no joy in it. For we had hoped, when a new commander was appointed—"

Arnem's brow arches. "A new commander?" he calls out.

"Certainly," the elder replies with a nod. "Sent from Daurawah, almost half a year ago. Surely you knew." Arnem feigns simply having forgotten a fact of which he was, in reality, never informed. "And we had hoped he would be worthy of our trust—but a man who locks both his dishonorable subordinate and then himself away from his accusers inspires something very different."

"Indeed, Elder," Arnem replies. "But I tell you again, we are not here to defy our own customs and laws—if what you say is true, you have my word that the garrison commander will hang for it."

It is the first open mention of an execution that has passed Arnem's lips; and it seems to heartily encourage the elder. The drapes of the litter finally close, and Niksar nods to Arnem, signaling that he fully understands his task: to buttress all that the sentek has said with words and actions.

Arnem answers with an easy salute, in appreciation of his young aide's willingness to undertake a less than gallant, but still brave and necessary, service; and when the litter has moved off far enough for plain talk to be safe, the sentek glowers at Visimar, his sword still bared.

"I will tell you but once more, old man. Say what you like to me—but do *not* endanger the lives of my men or their purpose, or I shall hang you *beside* this garrison commander!"

"I admit the error, Sixt Arnem—but I spoke the truth, and you *must,* as quickly as you can, get your men away from Esleben. Deadly sickness is here—indeed, a far more horrifying illness than you have described as being at work in Broken. Its spread in the town can no longer be stopped: and it will begin to kill others with as little warning, or apparent explanation, as it did the unfortunate lovers. And your men cannot be protected from it, save by leaving."

Arnem studies Visimar, deeply puzzled. "How can you know this, old man, before we have even seen the dead bodies?"

"Viewing the bodies is meaningless—indeed, we had best not even enter the granary, lest we expose ourselves to great danger."

"Danger—from the dead?"

"From the dead—and from *that*." Visimar points to the topmost breaks in the high granary walls, designed to allow for ventilation. Through these openings can be seen grain: a great store of it.

Following Visimar's indication, as the two men approach the building, Arnem asks, "And what is that, save grain?"

"*Proof*, Sentek," Visimar replies. "In the form of winter rye, from the look of it: an off-season crop that should have been sent to Broken long ago. Instead, because these people believe that the merchants in Broken are cheating them by buying foreign grain that is less expensive, the townspeople have kept it here, and allowed it to spoil—to spoil in a most subtle manner . . ." As they reach the granary walls, Visimar searches the ground. "Keep a tight rein on your mount, Sentek," he murmurs. "Do not allow him to find and nibble at—ah! there . . ." The old man points to a spot where some of the grain, having escaped through the ventilation gaps, has fallen to the ground. "Do you see there, Sentek—where the kernels have formed a plum-colored growth?" Arnem eyes the kernels as closely as he can, then begins to dismount, in order to reach down and get a closer look. "No, Sentek!" Visimar says, still quietly, but very urgently. "Do not allow yourself the least contact with it."

"But why?" Arnem says, settling himself in his saddle once more.

"Because, Sixt Arnem," Visimar breathes in relief, "should you even touch it, and then bring your fingers into contact with your mouth or eyes, you might well die as horribly as did the young girl and her suitor."

"Visimar," Arnem says, "explain yourself plainly."

"*There* lies your murderer." He indicates the ground again. "The pallin from the garrison was a victim, not a killer."

"And again I ask," Arnem says impatiently, "how can you say as much, without seeing his body?"

"I do not need to see his body, Sentek—and neither do you. The elder's reaction has already confirmed my description of *both* corpses; and we would only be endangering ourselves, if we entered that cellar of death and decay. Any chance contact with the rotting flesh of the pallin and the maid would be as perilous as consuming that rotting grain."

"But what is it? How can mere grain be so dangerous?"

"By giving you a deadly illness that you know well, Sixt Arnem—that is, under very different circumstances," Visimar replies. "Come: let us move to the building's far side, and at least seem to be doing what you said we would do. But in reality, our most urgent task is to get to the garrison, and prevent your men from coming into any contact with this substance."

"'A sickness I know well, under other circumstances'?" Arnem repeats, following Visimar's mare, but not his explanation. "And what would that be? Enough wasting time, Visimar, simply tell me—"

"Very well: I called it *Ignis Sacer,* which means the 'Holy Fire,' in the language of the *Lumun-jani,*" Visimar explains. "You know it as the 'fire wounds.'"†

"*Fire wounds?*" Arnem repeats, his voice very skeptical. "But fire wounds are attained in battle, from wounds that fester!"

"Not always, Sentek," Visimar says, his thoughts occupied with both a patient explanation of the disease and working out a route to the garrison that will allow the two men to make their way to that place unobserved by anyone in Esleben; but he soon finds the dual objects impossible. "Right now, however, I say again, the most imperative task we face is getting your aide and any others among your men who remain within the town *out* of it, and away from the inhabitants—for those unsuspecting people are about to undergo a calamity that will claim many if not most of their lives, as well as those of anyone unlucky enough to tarry here."

"It is not the practice of the soldiers of Broken to abandon the God-King's subjects in their hour of need, old man," Arnem says sternly.

"But they are not 'in need,' Sixt Arnem," Visimar replies, in like tone. "I tell you they are, almost to the last man, woman, and child, *doomed.*"

Arnem would argue the point further; but just then, with disturbing suddenness, a thought—a mere image—appears in his mind: the figure of Lord Baster-kin, standing in the remarkable tunnels beneath the city of Broken, his attention strangely fixed upon the vast stores of grain kept therein. The sentek can recall—quite distinctly, now—that these same small, purple growths upon each kernel had not been visible on the city's grain: a fact perhaps uninteresting, in itself, save for what Arnem now realizes to have been Baster-kin's apparent relief on finding that such was the case. That relief, Arnem comprehends as he fixes his mind on the moment, implied an anxiety that his lordship might have found the grain to be in some other, some far more dangerous, condition . . .

{iv:}

B Y THE TIME that Arnem and Visimar have traveled in the sort of long, furtive route toward the Esleben garrison's stockade that will eliminate any fear of being seen by someone within the town, not only has afternoon begun to give way to evening, but the commander of the Talons has learned a great deal about the two illnesses that his guest believes to be at work in the kingdom, and of the respective ways in which they propagate among men and women. First, there is the supposèd poisoning that took place within the city of Broken, which Visimar believes to in fact have been the first acknowledged (but likely not the first true) case of the terrible pestilence that Esleben's healer rightly dismissed as being at work among his own people: rose fever, a sickness that hides itself in befouled water. The second is a more outwardly chilling rot that savagely attacks by way of any foods or flesh over which it has already taken hold, a malady that the sentek indeed knows as "the fire wounds," but that is more properly identified by the terms "Holy Fire" (for who save a deity could be responsible for its monstrous symptoms?) and, still more precisely, among truly learnèd healers, as *gangraena*. This sickness, as Arnem has said, often appears as a result of the festering of soldiers' wounds; but it can also carve its path using such insidious methods as the commander and the acolyte have just observed. Which of the two is the more dangerous? That is a question to which not even Visimar will hazard an answer; all he can do is continue to urge

Arnem on, and to emphasize the importance of getting his Talons out of and away from ill-fated Esleben and its inhabitants. Before he can commit to that withdrawal, however, the ever-dutiful Arnem requires some more exact explanation of just what has taken place between the men of the garrison and the townspeople.

When the sentek and his fool-become-advisor finally do come within sight of the town's small, formidable stockade, they find that mention of Arnem's name has apparently been, as hoped, enough to prize open the gates of the place, and that members of the small command have emerged, the deep blue of their regular-army cloaks contrasting with the wine-red of the Talons' similar garments. But before the two men can reach the stockade, they encounter some ten to fifteen groups of Talons, each consisting of three to five frontline infantrymen, who, in keeping with Broken military practice, have formed a watchful perimeter about the stockade. These are particularly skilled and veteran warriors, for in battle it is the duty of such men to quickly form the face of each side of the Broken *quadrates,* where they absorb the initial and harshest blows of the enemy, as well as lead the way in unhesitating attack when those *quadrates* shift into offensive or pursuing formations. It is these two equally valiant yet dangerous roles that have given such soldiers their informal name: *Wildfehngen,*† because their disciplined ferocity in battle is believed to be unmatched, certainly by any warriors that the army of Broken has ever faced.

From the *Wildfehngen,* Arnem soon learns how matters truly stand within the stockade: although its gates are open, the men within can give no explanation for what has taken place in Esleben, beyond that already offered by the town elders. As for the commander of the garrison (the sole person, Arnem believes, who may be able to shed true light on the mysterious goings-on in and about the town) he remains barred within his quarters, not, it seems, because of disloyalty or disobedience, but because of illness. This information only makes the sentek more determined to immediately spur the Ox on toward the stockade and greater insight; but before he can depart, Visimar catches his arm, speaking to him as earnestly as he can, while keeping his voice very hushed:

"If the garrison commander is ill," the cripple says, "you must determine the nature of that illness before you approach him. Remember, Sixt Arnem—we have but two goals, now: to get away from here without incident, and to ensure that your own men do not take any of the town's forage or food supplies with them. Nothing in Esleben is to be trusted."

"I shall attempt to remember all such points," Arnem replies, his various frustrations becoming more apparent in his angered words. "But I *will* be given a clearer understanding of what is taking place here— whatever this commander's condition." Once more preparing to speed away, the sentek suddenly catches sight of something ahead, a sight that finally brings some sort of relief to his face. "Well. There's one worry eased: Niksar seems to have escaped the town unscathed . . ."

Niksar is riding at a good pace toward Arnem and Visimar, and the sentek urges the Ox out a short distance to intercept him. "Well met, Reyne," he says, acknowledging his aide's salute. "But before you give voice to the understandable indignation that I detect upon your face, tell me: you weren't, by any chance, offered any hospitality—say, any sustenance—while you were in the town, were you?"

Niksar scoffs. "Unlikely, Sentek. They were only too happy to be rid of me, when I said I had to report to you. I doubt they would have let me eat so much as the grass upon the ground, as at least my horse did."

Arnem studies his aide's mount. "You're certain that's all he ate? No loose grain that might have been scattered about, for instance?"

Niksar looks puzzled, indeed. "None, Sentek. Why, what's happened?"

"We'll explain as we enter the stockade," Arnem says, resuming his progress toward the small stronghold's gates. "It's a tale you may have to employ all your imagination to credit, as well as your newfound trust of our friend here." Arnem indicates Visimar. "But *do* credit it, Reyne, and make certain the men understand that no forage, no grain goods of any kind, are to be consumed in or taken away from Esleben. And, for an even fuller understanding of just what is happening, I'm afraid we'll need the garrison commander, who's evidently ill and barricaded away in his quarters. Hear me, now, Niksar . . ." Arnem draws alongside the younger soldier. "I know you won't like the charge, but once we're in the stockade, help the old man get up the stairs in the quadrangle, will you, while I go on ahead? I must, at the very least, *begin* questioning this man as quickly as possible."

"Sentek?" Niksar says, perturbed; for he can now see that his commander's manner indicates more than mere annoyance. A profound anxiety of spirit is present, as well. "Of course, but I—"

"Questions later, Reyne," Arnem says. "I want some answers, now . . ."

Yet with damnable stubbornness, still more disturbing questions await the sentek when he, Niksar, and Visimar reach and enter the garrison stockade. By now, the first of his long-range scouts have returned from the east, and the news they bring from those towns closer to Daurawah, as well as the rumors issuing from farmsteads within sight of the walls of that sprawling riverfront town itself, are vague and grim. Unrest, varying in degree, has taken hold of the laborers, merchants, and elders of other communities along the way to Broken's principal port; and, perhaps most worrying of all, the scouts have heard that disorder of a far worse variety has taken hold inside Daurawah itself. If such is the truth, it is an unusually alarming fact for Arnem, both professionally and personally: the governing of the port has for several years been the responsibility of one of the sentek's oldest friends in the army of Broken, Gerolf Gledgesa,[†] with whom Arnem had faced the Torganians at the Atta Pass, and to whom the new chief of the army had hoped to pass the command of the Talons when he himself was so tragically elevated to Yantek Korsar's post. But if Gledgesa has allowed matters in Daurawah to deteriorate to such a point, the appointment of his old comrade— always, like Arnem himself, a controversial figure within the army— will be out of the question. The full possible consequences of the scouting reports from the east are plain, then: but none is more ominous than the notion that, even if the Talons can avoid violent encounters with the subjects of the eastern kingdom, those same subjects will continue to surrender the food and forage which the soldiers require for their march against the Bane only grudgingly, if at all—and the men will be able to accept such supplies only if they are found to be untainted. Thus, Arnem may be forced to plan his campaign anew, calculating time, now, as a powerful ally of the Bane, rather than of his own force: ever one of the worst advantages that a commander can concede to his enemy.

As all these possibilities mount, the sentek's temper shortens: *"Akillus!"* Arnem calls angrily, when he finally reaches the center of the quadrangle and spies the chief of scouts laughing nearby amid his own men and several members of the garrison. As Arnem dismounts, the sentek's young *skutaar*, Ernakh[‡] (sole child of the Arnems' nurse and housekeeper, Nuen), appears to take the reins of the Ox, thinking to inquire how long his commander anticipates remaining in Esleben, so that he may determine how much to refresh the steed, as well as whether or not Arnem himself will require quarters. But the black-haired, intuitive youth divines from the briefest study of Arnem's manner that the Talons will not be staying long in this place, despite the sentek's deliberately vague answers on the subject; and Ernakh leads the Ox off to be watered at a trough near the garrison well, so that he will be ready (if not entirely rested) for the force's departure, which may, the young *skutaar* correctly believes, come at any moment. Akillus, meanwhile, hurries along to Arnem, his smile vanishing.

"I understand, Akillus," the sentek says, "that the commander of the garrison is unable to report due to illness—have you determined if this is true?"

"Yes, Sentek," Akillus answers, saluting so firmly that his chest resonates with the impact of his fist. "He is shut tightly away in his quarters, above." Akillus points to the northwestern-most doorway of a dozen such on the fort's upper level, above which the parapet encircles the structure. Another walkway runs the full length of the fort's upper level outside the doors of these rooms, guarded by a railing of cut timbers: all workmanship characteristic of Broken's sappers and engineers. "He says he will not come out, and will speak only with you *alone.*"

"Indeed?" says Arnem, letting out a weighty sigh. "Well, then—his secrets had better be as remarkable as his behavior, or I'll have the hide off his back. And the elders will have his neck. For now—spread the word, Akillus: the men must be ready to resume the march at any moment."

"Aye, Sentek!" says Akillus, never questioning the surprising order; instead, he simply runs to his horse and mounts the animal with his usual, seemingly effortless motion.

Watching carefully, in order to weigh the reactions that Akillus receives from the men as he relays these orders through the clusters of soldiers, Arnem is suddenly startled by a horse snorting, not far behind his head: turning, he once again finds Visimar atop his mare, and accompanied by Niksar. Two *skutaars* appear to tend to the men's mounts, and to help the old acolyte to the ground. Once he has been handed his familiar walking staff, Visimar finds, in addition, that he is being offered a ready and supporting shoulder from Niksar, who follows Arnem's earlier order with a mixture of obedience and emerging compassion. The sentek is thus allowed to rush up the stockade stairs with a speed that, if not enthusiastic, is purposeful; and when he first sets foot on the walkway above, he quickens his pace still more. Only when he gets within an arm's length of the officer's doorway does a sudden apprehension shoot through his bones and prickle his skin, taking nearly all the determination out of him in an instant. It is not a feeling that he can define, but it is one that he must obey: and when he finally raps at the door, he does so but lightly, not knowing whence this hesitation has come.

"Linnet?" he calls, scarcely loud enough to be heard. Then, suddenly, he is made aware of the reason for his wariness: a smell, or rather a stench, the blunt stink of human sweat, waste, and decay, of filthy garments and bedding—in sum, the stink of *mortal illness* . . .

"Linnet!" Arnem states with more authority. "I order you to open this door."

The man within tries to answer, but his words are soon choked off by a fit of moist coughing. When the attack subsides, Arnem hears a weak voice, one that, clearly, was once strong, and with the unmistakable inflections of an officer who, although young, is accustomed to command:

"I am sorry, Sentek—I cannot obey you," the voice says. "But it is not out of impertinence, for I have known you for nearly all of my life, and there is no soldier, indeed no man, that I respect more. But I cannot risk your . . ." The voice trails off; it has, for the moment, no strength left.

And during the pause, Sentek Arnem realizes that, beneath the distortions of sickness, he knows the voice well: it belongs to the younger brother of his own aide, who is—or once was—as vibrant and ideal an example of Broken virtues as is Reyne.

"Donner?" Arnem murmurs, as quietly as he can. *"Donner Niksar?"*[†]

A noise of assent from the chamber's occupant quickly dissolves back into terrible coughing. "Forgive me for not opening the door, sir," the younger Niksar brother says, after his fit has subsided. "But you mustn't come in here—not now. I haven't let the rest of them in since the pallin died. I first detected the symptoms in myself within hours of his death; and, while it is possible that my men have already been affected by the sickness, they may also have escaped, and I won't allow the mess that is coming out of me—that I have *become*—to somehow endanger them . . ."

Just then, Arnem hears Niksar struggling up the stairs with Visimar, and the sentek grows ever more anxious. "Donner, your brother is with me, surely you will wish to talk with him—"

"No, Sentek, please!" comes the desperate reply. "I fear I have only enough time to tell what I must: of these damnable town merchants, with their elders and their plots and poisons . . ."

Arnem's eyes widen. "You think the townspeople tried to *poison* you, Donner?"

"I realize that it sounds like madness, Sentek. And it may well be. But I've good reason to believe it. We meant to interfere with certain of their schemes to remedy their trade difficulties, you see, while at the same time, one of our men had what they considered the cheek to actually court one of their daughters. Their rage was becoming deadly—indeed, as you may have seen, some of them actually seem to be mad . . ."

Arnem is struck by each part of this statement, but none more so than the last—for he remembers well the looks on the faces of some of the townspeople when he entered Esleben. "But, Donner," he says, "what are you doing in Esleben? And what 'plans' of theirs would you have spoiled?"

"I had formerly been serving under your old comrade, Sentek Gledgesa, in Daurawah," young Donner Niksar replies, his voice now so hoarse as to suggest razor-like knives lacerating the back of his throat. "Until he sent me here. The last garrison commander had been caught concluding deals with those river raiders who have been bringing their grain up the Meloderna and into the rivers that feed it, including the Cat's Paw. This was Moons ago, Sentek Arnem, midwinter . . . Before there was any report of disease. Without informing anyone, Sentek Gledgesa called the garrison commander to Daurawah, executed him on his own authority, and dispatched me to take his place. He seemed to know you would be coming, and with you, Reyne; and that you would both believe me, more readily than his other officers."

"But how did this lead to the business of this pallin, and the girl from the town?"

"*That* story began to unfold soon after I arrived here," young Niksar goes on; and it seems that he has found a way in which to speak for longer periods of time, if he keeps the volume of his voice low, making it necessary for Arnem to put his ear directly to the wooden door. "Sentek Gledgesa knew that the commander of the garrison was guilty of the

crimes with which so many had charged him; what he could not determine was what part, if any, the elders of Esleben were *also* playing in the
grain scheme. And despite my taking command, the foreign grain continued to make its way upriver in the raiders' ships, while neither my
men nor I could prove the elders of Esleben were involved—yet such did
not demonstrate their innocence. Then this business concerning the pallin and his maiden was uncovered in early spring, just as we began to
hear of the fire wounds in Daurawah. They were already burning dozens, perhaps hundreds of bodies, every week, all dead from what the
commander was confident, by then, represented a foul new way our enemies had devised to weaken our power—I had by then learned otherwise, however. For the maiden had mentioned to her pallin that the town
elders meant to take the matter of the raiders into their own hands, and
he reported as much to me. I wrote to Sentek Gledgesa, telling him of the
plot—" His words having come too fast, Donner begins to cough terribly
again.

"Slow, now, son," Arnem says, in a voice he hopes is soothing. "Are
you trying to say the *elders of Esleben* meant to oppose the foreign traders?"

"It was after the winter rye had been harvested . . ." Arnem hears Donner Niksar pouring water into his tormented mouth. "The merchants in
Broken—they continued to offer payment that enticed the pirates, being
far lower than anything the farmers and millers of Esleben were accustomed to receiving. Soon, the elders of Esleben decided that, so long as
those long ships were allowed to race up and down the rivers, they would
feed their grain to their own people and animals, rather than accept such
low prices from merchants who were meant to protect Broken's own
commerce, not betray it. They then began to do just that, hoping it would
bring notice from the Merchants' Council or even the Grand Layzin and
the God-King. It did not, but almost immediately, the girl became ill.
Even to myself, the timing of it all seemed—odd . . . And the rage among
the townspeople was implacable. I offered to meet with them alone, to
show the army's goodwill and freedom from further involvement in the
illegal trading that was cheating them of the rightful payment. I was invited to sup with their elders' council, so long as I did, indeed, come
alone—which I did . . ."

Arnem's heart sinks at this news: for he realizes that, alone among the garrison, Donner Niksar had broken what Visimar has told the sentek must be tainted bread with the people of Esleben, unknowingly condemning himself to a hideous death . . .

Suddenly, a small sound of triumph from across the walkway reaches Arnem's ears, and he turns to see that Visimar and the sentek's weary aide have reached the top of the wooden stairway. Arnem waves to the pair urgently to slow their advance. Both are confused, but Arnem cannot concern himself with it: he must hear Donner out, before Reyne does so and, very likely, is driven to violence by his brother's condition.

"Donner, we haven't much time—your brother approaches."

"Reyne?" the younger Niksar gasps. "Delay him, Sentek, please—although there are certain things I must tell him, to ease my family's burden . . ."

"And you shall," Arnem says, a still greater feeling of wretched responsibility settling on his heart. "But first, you must complete your tale—what can the trysting of the pallin and a town maiden have had to do with all these other matters?"

Donner Niksar spits; this time as much in disdain as because of sickness. "Nothing, Sentek." And instantly, Arnem recalls Visimar's words concerning the dead soldier: *a victim, not a murderer* . . . "The notion that we were all protecting one lovestruck member of our company simply offered the ever more unreasonable elders and their followers an easy illustration of their grievances and simple justification for their desire for vengeance: the merchants in Broken were in league with the raiders, and the army was protecting the whole lot, for payment and for the right to occasionally defile virginal country maids . . ." Catching his breath and taking some more water, Donner says, "Were I able to, now, I'd laugh. Kafra knows I did then. But I did *try* to explain the truth to them, Sentek, to make them see the absurdity of what they were asking me to believe, when we met. But they were beyond explanations, by then—at least, explanations that made any sense . . ."

"Yes," Arnem replies. "I have encountered them in that mood."

"Then you know how full of mad rage they can become—" Donner murmurs, before another coughing fit overtakes him. As he listens helplessly, Arnem thinks of one last hope to offer:

"Listen to me, Donner—I have with me a rare man of medicine, who has seen this sickness before. It is possible that he can help you."

"I fear I am well beyond any such aid," comes the plaintive, gasping answer.

"You are not," Arnem declares, as if discipline can overcome disease. "I forbid you to surrender, Linnet."

Still struggling to breathe, Donner assembles a final attempt to complete the task he has set for himself: "Let me only finish my report, Sentek, that I may die in peace . . ." Arnem cannot find it in him to forbid such, and so says nothing, at which Donner tries to marshal his thoughts and words: "I had warning that the elders intended to take some sort of definite action against the illegal river trading. It was a small matter to have them watched. And the madness the townsmen planned was simply that. They believed that they might teach not only the agents of the merchants in Broken, but the foreign traders, too, a lesson. For two nights, they worked in the river's shallowest run, sinking deadly gutting stakes—sharpened tree trunks, their points reinforced by iron plating. As a last measure, the stakes were joined with heavy chains. The longships draw so little draught that they can usually sail or row this far up-river without mishap—but they could not have survived that viciousness. I had no time to do anything save send another dispatch to Sentek Gledgesa, then turn my attention toward dismantling the work of those fools . . . Not because I approved of what the raiders and the Broken merchants were doing, of course, but to try to stop a war with the Northerners—for that would have been the result of it, and the raiders have grown very powerful, through all their piracy and plunder. So I took several men and teams of horses, late on a Moonless night, and went to the river. We fastened our own series of chains to their deadly spikes and undid their trap. That was when we were forced within our stockade by enormous mobs from Esleben and more than a few neighboring villages . . ." Donner's voice pauses; and Arnem can now hear only a wheezing, choking sound, one that is little short of the noises that so often precede death.

"Donner!" Arnem whispers urgently, trying the door once again, to equally little effect. "Unbar the door, son, and let us in to help you."

After regaining enough strength to speak—Arnem fears for the last time—the younger Niksar replies, "Nay, Sentek. I know the lay of things. The townspeople want my death, atop the young pallin's. And I have arranged for all to occur as they wish; for, despite your kind offer, Sentek, there is no art, sacred, black, or otherwise, that can help me—not now. I saw what happened to our young pallin . . ." For a moment, Arnem hears nothing, and his own spirit sinks again; but then, Donner murmurs, in deathly earnest, "You must get your men away, Sentek. I believe I have fulfilled my final commission in the manner that my family, the God-King, and Kafra would have wished, and that yourself and Sentek Gledgesa will approve. Whatever the case, I am dying, and would have my death be of use. I shall not have the strength, then, to tell Reyne—to tell him what I—"

Arnem finally concedes. "Let your soul be at peace, Donner," he says quietly. "I know what you wish him to know—your actions have told me. He is but an instant away, if you can manage the wait—if not, know from me that you are as good a soldier as Broken has ever known, and that I am indeed proud of you, as I know that Sentek Gledgesa will be. And your family, as well." The young officer murmurs his pained thanks, relief finding a way through his suffering; at which Arnem turns, haggard, and signals across the walkway to his aide.

Suspecting some strange development, and making sure that Visimar now stands securely upon his walking stick, the elder Niksar runs ahead; the agèd cripple, meanwhile, watches the linnet's face go pale as Arnem relates some news of evidently shattering effect. Niksar attempts to force the door of the garrison commander's quarters open, fails, and then falls to his knees by it, speaking softly to the planks of wood before him.

Arnem, helpless, moves to join Visimar on the walkway, saying only, "His brother—a lad I knew well," before turning to lean over the railing at his side, almost as if he will be sick. From that position, he nearly fails to notice Linnet Akillus, as the latter charges into the stockade quadrangle and leaps from his horse's back, making for the stairway.

"Sentek Arnem!" Akillus shouts repeatedly, his voice ringing with a sort of alarm that Visimar has not yet heard from the man.

Arnem is angered by the interruption, for Niksar's sake even more than for his own; and he catches Akillus at the top of the stairs. "Linnet! I hope you have some reason for barging in here like a mad dog. What in the name of Kafra's stones are you thinking—?"

But, even as he speaks, Arnem suddenly takes note of his men forming up below, as if some new danger has appeared in Esleben: a danger which the Talons require no specific order to prepare to face. "The townsmen, Sentek!" Akillus says, never for a moment concerning himself with Visimar. "Or I should say, not only the men of *this* town, but others as well, for such are their numbers! And there are women, too—hundreds, armed with farming tools as well as weapons—anything that can be made to kill! They are all moving on the garrison, and they—well—"

"Well *what*, Akillus?" Arnem asks, concerned to see such apprehension in a soldier who has kept his head in far deadlier situations.

"Well, sir," Akillus tries to explain. "It is the *look* of them—like mad, desperate beasts—and moving against *us*!"

{v:}

ARNEM IMMEDIATELY DASHES down the stairs before him, leaving his aide to bid a heartrending farewell to his brother Donner (who continues to refuse any healthy person entrance into his chamber), and requesting of Akillus—a man whose lack of social condescension is as strong as his reliability in a fight—that he bear Visimar upon his back to the old man's waiting mare below to save time. Once upon the earthen quadrangle floor, Arnem finds that his own mount, the Ox, is refreshed and ready to ride, the *skutaar* Ernakh having, as always, anticipated his commander's orders. Soon, Arnem is among his men outside the garrison gates as they continue to group into defensive formations to meet the approaching mob, which the sentek now spies for the first time; and that first glimpse is enough to tell him that his chief scout's extreme alarm was not unwarranted.

What must indeed be hundreds of townspeople, from Esleben as well as surrounding villages, are moving against the stockade: merchants, laborers, and farmers, as well as men of obviously less established station, the greater number of them interwoven with more than a few score of their own wives and older daughters (whose sex does nothing to diminish their fury), are all armed, and moving in a great wave east. The sentek cannot yet accurately determine what their full numbers must be, for they seem scarcely human at all: most wear bandages which are stained and oozing with pus and blood, both fresh and dried. As for their weapons, they matter less than the manner in which they are wielded: even a sickle, or a mere sharpened length of tree limb, can attest to a man's or woman's commitment to their cause, if carried in such a way that clearly displays a desire for blood.

Sixt Arnem is no practiced philosopher: but even he must pause for an instant, in the face of such a sight, to apprehend the apparent irony in the fact that the Natural wealth of Broken—which has been transformed, over many generations, into the formidable bone, sinew, and muscle that enables a legion such as the Talons to become peerless fighting men—has (according to Visimar) somehow been altered, so that it contains an agent that has imbued these townspeople with the equally exceptional, if utterly irrational, conviction required to attack the very soldiers they have long relied on for protection. And Arnem can further see that the coming fight, during which his men must try to fend off and then retreat before these loosely organized lunatics, is indeed reminiscent (as Akillus attempted to express) of some diseased, maddened beast that gnaws at its own flesh, torturously destroying and consuming itself from its tail and feet forward and upward with burning mind and slashing teeth, for reasons that the agonized creature itself does not understand . . .

Although many of the maddened citizens are rushing toward the garrison gate from the south, the main body approach from the direction of Esleben itself. A central group from among the latter (they can scarcely be called a "formation") drive powerful farm animals: oxen and horses, in the main, yoked to wagons that bear still more men and women, as well as larger implements of violence. Atop one aging wagon is an interwoven grouping of smaller logs, branches, hay, and pitch, all of which the several men who assist the oxen yoked to the conveyance in driving it forward are eager to set alight with torches they carry. Yet this is not the most hideous aspect of this crude machine of war:

Impaled upon an iron-tipped stake that still shows signs of the river bottom in which it was lately sunk is the shocking figure of a man: and no young warrior, but a mature, distinguished man of Esleben. Arnem has by been joined by Visimar, who, like the sentek, observes this cart's approach largely in stunned silence—for they realize that the body gutted by the stake is not some agèd tramp or vagabond, nor even some humble craftsman: it is the same chief elder with whom the two men met but hours ago, in an attempt to reach a reasonable, if not an amicable, solution to the conflict between the town garrison and the citizens of Esleben. His body has been driven with such force upon the stake that his ribs have cracked outward and now show bright white amid the darker gore of his body's central cavity, as do bits of his spine, while a jumble of intestine-strangled vital organs hangs from the jagged pieces of bone. His head is cocked at an angle that indicates the breaking of his neck during this fiendish process, while his eyes remain wide open, full of the shock that filled his last moments.

Around the elder's neck hangs a bit of plank, tied with rope, upon which has been painted—in what may be his own blood, if judged by the tint—only a few words:

> FOR ATTEMPTING TO BETRAY HIS OWN PEOPLE,
> BY TREATING WITH DEMONS DISGORGED BY THE
> TRAITORS WHO RULE IN Broken

As the soldiers about him observe the sight in horrified silence, Visimar says, with soft passion:

"*Too deeply . . . The Holy Fire has burned too deeply into this place . . .*"

In answer comes a most unexpected voice: Niksar's. "We were too late," he murmurs, and when Arnem turns, he sees that Reyne has made no attempt to conceal the marks of heavy tears. "Such were Donner's last words, Sentek—that neither the rose fever nor any other pestilence he has witnessed can account for what is happening here. For what happened to *him* . . . And we all, starting with the garrison itself, realized as much too late to even mitigate its spread . . ."

Arnem turns to Visimar, who raises a brow as if to say, "I take no joy in being correct, Sentek—but we must face this as it is . . ." The old man's thought is soon reflected in other, more pragmatic words by Arnem's officers, as the Eslebeners suddenly ignite the wagons that hold pitch-drenched cargoes, intending to smash them into the now fully formed *quadrates* of the Talons:

"Their plan is not so disordered as their reason," Akillus says. "Mobile fire, whether or not they know it, is ever the best means of attack against the *quadrates*, Sentek."

"To be matched only by the *Krebkellen*,[†] Akillus," Arnem replies, citing the Broken army's chief tactical alternative to the *quadrates:* another invention of the supposedly Mad King, Oxmontrot, the *Krebkellen* is a primarily offensive maneuver, but one that serves admirably when the defensive squares are threatened. "And so, Linnet—will you take, say, two cavalry *fausten* and two of Taankret's *Wildfehngen* in among these madmen, and shatter their initial movement just sternly enough to allow us to get away eastward down the Daurawah Road?"

Akillus is both challenged and excited by the charge. "If I could not, Sentek, neither I nor the men should be worthy of our claws!"[†]

Arnem delivers his next orders to the commander of the *Wildfehngen,* an impressive linnet of infantry called Taankret. The sentek orders this aptly named fellow[‡] (whose surcoat and finely worked steel mail are somehow, even on this dusty march, impeccably neat) to take a hundred *Wildfehngen,* and form them into the center of the *Krebkellen,* coordinating the breaking up of the attacking townspeople with Linnet Akillus, who will provide a similar number of cavalry on the flanks.

"A hard order, Taankret," Arnem says, watching the effect of his commands on the linnet, as the latter dispatches messengers to assemble the needed men. "To ask our lads to engage their own countrymen."

"Not so hard as you may think, Sentek," Taankret answers, with passion but no panic. He swipes a bare finger beneath his mustache and smoothes his carefully clipped beard, then pulls on a pair of heavy gauntlets. Finally, he draws the lengthy marauder sword for which he is known throughout his *khotor* and the army itself, which he took from a vanquished warrior of the East many years ago. "The men have had enough time in this accursèd town to gain a healthy disrespect for its ungrateful passions," Taankret continues. "I do not think that they would happily receive an order to massacre, but a chance to spend an hour smacking this mob about with the flat of their blades while the rest of you start for Daurawah?" A smile makes its way into one corner of Taankret's mouth. "That is an order they'll relish."

"Truly," agrees Akillus. "Have no worries on that account, Sentek."

Arnem grins, proud and more than a little regretful that he will not be joining his rearguard commanders. "Very well, then—Taankret. Akillus. But bear that one thing in mind—the flat of your blades, where you can. Cracked heads will be of more use than severed."

The growing sense of happy challenge among the two linnets, who demonstrate perfectly why they have achieved their status in the most renowned legion of Broken, is suddenly interrupted by a sound of shattering wood and glass. It comes from just around the southwest corner of the small fort that was the home of Esleben's departing garrison: from the direction of, among other things, the window of the commander's quarters.

In addition, a short cry is heard (in a voice that both Arnem and Niksar know to be Donner's), only to be quickly stilled by some unknown force.

Arnem addresses his anxious linnets in a humorless voice, now: "You two finish your preparations. Niksar, Anselm—accompany me." The sentek looks to his aide. "And remember, Reyne: our only task now is to get away from this foul place . . ." Niksar nods in reply, apprehensive of what they may find, but no less certain of his duty, at which the three men move at a slow trot round the corner of the stockade, Niksar's sense of foreboding suddenly confirmed by a most unexpected group of agents:

The maddened townspeople have stopped, if only for a moment; and their eyes are fixed, as if they were one enormous, grotesque creature, on the window in Donner Niksar's quarters. They have, apparently, already seen what the soldiers and their guest cannot, yet—that one of their requirements, at least, has been met, if in a manner utterly different from that which they earlier demanded:

The sentek, his aide, and Visimar, proceeding forward, look up at the shattered window of the commander's quarters. The crude glass has been broken from within, the sound and accompanying sight intended to transfix the rushing, furious mob; and the object used to achieve this effect was Donner Niksar's own body, which now sways slowly by a rope, one end of which is securely tied within his quarters, and the other around his neck. No amount of descending darkness can obscure his condition: his head is snapped harshly to one side, and his eyes are still open. Strangely, the horrifying image reminds Arnem of those in Broken society who always believed that Donner, while of slighter stature than his brother, was nonetheless finer in his features. But not this night: even were his tongue not protruding grotesquely from the corner of his mouth, even had he been able to conceal the raw ravages of the Holy Fire from his face and bared chest, and even if, by some impossible effort, he had been able to clothe himself in a new, clean nightshirt, rather than the hideously stained garment that now wafts about his emaciated frame: even if all these things could have been accomplished, nothing could ever compensate for his swollen, tortured eyes, which cast their pained, accusatory stare onto every face that turns to him, reflecting the mob's torches as his body rotates below the window. The message is unmistakable: the townspeople have exacted their revenge. One question remains, and it is Niksar who murmurs it:

"Will it be enough? For these—*creatures*?"

Arnem has been dumbstruck, for an instant; and so it is Visimar who says gently, "I know you think me a mad heretic, Linnet. And I would never presume to intrude upon the grief you feel after so noble a brother has given his life to try to extinguish the fire that is consuming the people of Esleben." Niksar says nothing, but inclines his head slightly, at which Visimar continues: "At the least, he was able to claim for himself a sane and meaningful death. If you look to the west, you will see that no such mercy will be shown to the mob." A small glance at the momentarily confused mob is all Niksar needs to confirm the old man's claim.

"Aye, heretic," the young officer breathes, without resentment. "Whatever Donner lost, he kept his head, and his honor, to the last . . ."

"Just so. As we must now keep ours. Let us honor your brother, Linnet, by securing what he wished us to: the safety of our own and his troops, and the continuation of what has become an expedition less of conquest than of investigation."

Arnem, amazed that the old man can make sound sense at such a moment, claps a gentle hand to Niksar's shoulder. "The old fool is right, Reyne. We must honor that." The sentek turns his narrowing eyes to the east, as the sounds of the crowd's madness mount once more. "Ernakh!" he cries, and the *skutaar* appears, silently waiting as Arnem scribbles a charcoal note upon a bit of parchment. "Take this to the master of archers, Fleckmester,[†] and return with him—quickly, now." Ernakh salutes, hurtling off into the darkness.

Niksar looks to his commander with some puzzlement. "Sentek? We should be away, as quickly as possible—"

"As we shall, Reyne," Arnem assures his aide, even as he makes no immediate move to depart. "But I will not leave Donner's body to *those* madmen."

Visimar has already begun to nod, suspecting what the sentek plans, while Niksar must wait the few moments that it takes for Linnet Fleckmester to appear, running swiftly with several of his own officers. He is a tall, enormously powerful man, who makes his Broken longbow† seem diminutive by comparison. "Aye, Sentek?" he says, saluting smartly.

Arnem indicates the palisades of the garrison structure. "How much fire could your men direct onto that structure as an opening to the coming action, Fleckmester? I want complete immolation, speedily and with intent."

The master of archers takes his meaning perfectly. "More than enough to serve your purpose, Sentek." Fleckmester bows to Niksar. "With the greatest of respect and sympathy, Linnet Niksar."

Niksar remains silent through Fleckmester's departure, and even after the master has gone, he can say no more than, "Thank you, Sentek— my family will be deeply in your debt, as will I . . ." And with that, after a final glance up at what is only the dark shape of his brother, now released from the agonies of both hideous illness and the hatred of the crowd of villagers he had undertaken to protect, Niksar puts his spurs into his white mount and departs, leaving Arnem to study Visimar before he follows.

"I am aware of this latest debt to you, old man," the commander says, "as I am of the others I have incurred, this day. Be assured of that . . ."

Before Visimar can reply, Arnem urges the Ox to follow Niksar, and the old cripple makes ready to follow; but he is suddenly consumed by a sensation of being observed, one that he at first chastises himself for believing is coming from the dead body of Donner Niksar. Looking up before he can dismiss his superstition, he realizes it is not the feeling that is mistaken, merely the identification of its source. Against the dark sky that is illuminated by the rising Moon, Visimar sees enormous wings pass over his head in utter silence, just above the garrison walls. While most of the soldiers might be unnerved by such a vision—for the six-foot span of the creature's wings is greater than the height of some of the troops—Visimar is elated by it.

"Nerthus!"‡ the cripple calls out with a grin, as the enormous owl (for such the creature is) silently circles downward to settle her twenty pounds of weight—so little, for one of her size and power—upon Visimar's shoulder and lifted arm, startling the mare upon which he rides. Calming the horse and trotting away from the main body of Arnem's troops (although still to the west), Visimar explains to the horse, "No, no, my friend, you have no need to fear this bird, although a newborn colt might!" He turns again to the owl, whose neck cranes around and down as only owls' may, shifting the feathery tufts atop her head—tufts that so resemble ears, or perhaps stern brows—and looks for all the world as though she will tear the old fool's nose from his face; but Visimar does not fear the motion, and indeed, the owl only opens her beak to gently nibble and lick at the bridge and nostrils between Visimar's agèd eyes—an indication of the profound trust that can only result from a longstanding, affectionate, and most extraordinary acquaintance. Visimar cannot help but laugh and reach up to run his fingers gently down the bird's mottled chest feathers.

The owl, it seems, means more than pure affection by its motion, and holds one enormous set of talons up to catch Visimar's eyes. "Ah?" he noises. "And what do you carry, that is so urgent?"

In the tight black claws are clutched a bundle of flowers and plants: some deep blue, some bright yellow, others knobby and green, but all, Visimar quickly notices by the cleanly cut ends of the stems, harvested by men no more than a half a day earlier. "So . . ." Trying to calculate the meaning of all this, as he keeps a part of his attention fixed on the advancing mob, Visimar soon reaches a conclusion. "I see," he says certainly. "Well, my girl, off to your master, and inform him, as well—for you must not stay here to be injured by an arrow from one of these provincial fools, nor from the more precise missiles of the Broken archers. I must away after the sentek—but we shall meet again soon, and in far fewer than the many months it has been this time . . ."

As if satisfied with the man's response, the owl again pulls affectionately at a tuft of his grey hair, cutting a little of it loose and bundling it in among the plants. She then spreads her remarkable wings to either side of Visimar's head and makes for the night skies again. The old man, his mood profoundly changed by the several implications of this encounter, uses his one foot to spur his mount on after Arnem and Niksar.

{vi:}

B Y THE TIME the two officers and their crippled companion have returned to the troops who will participate in the rearguard engagement, most of the remaining contingents of the Talons have already started eastward away from Esleben, and the head of their column is well along the Daurawah Road. The ten remaining members of the Esleben garrison have stayed behind with the rearguard units, looking to Sentek Arnem for direction; and Arnem, in turn, looks subtly to Visimar, uncertain whether the men's exposure to either their leader's illness or, in passing, to any grain-based goods in Esleben, should affect his decisions. A subtle twist of Visimar's head tells Arnem firmly that the garrison troops must not march with the main force; and that the sentek must contrive some mission worthy of the men, while keeping them away until time can tell the danger they pose.

"We would join in the fight, if you will have us, Sentek Arnem," one tall, gruff member of the garrison steps forward to say; and general assent to this proposition is proclaimed by the others. Momentarily at a loss, Arnem soon settles on a solution, turning to the man who addressed him.

"I am impressed by this, Linnet—?"

"Gotthert, Sentek," the man replies, saluting, "but I do not have the honor to be a linnet, sir."

"You do now, Gotthert," Arnem says. "I know the look of a man ready to lead; and so, unless one among your company chooses to contest the appointment . . . ?" All that emerge are expressions of agreement with the sentek's choice, causing Arnem to smile. "Well, then, Linnet Gotthert—I have another plan, equally important, in mind for you: under cover of the brawl about to begin, set out for the banks of the Cat's Paw in the area of Lord Baster-kin's Plain, and judge the preparations of both the Bane, and those patrols of the Merchant Lord's Guard who keep regular watch in the area of the Fallen Bridge. Your men can get some well-deserved rest, once there, to say nothing of decent food, and then report to me when I bring the column along in no more than two days' time." Arnem glances at Visimar, and sees that the cripple does not object to his ploy.

"Very well, Sentek," Gotthert replies, both disappointed (for his men clearly wish to play some role in avenging Donner Niksar) and relieved that his unit's ordeal within the stockade is over. Giving his superior a final salute, and receiving one in acknowledgment, Gotthert begins to move toward the southeast, followed by his troops; but Arnem, having observed the look upon Gotthert's and his men's faces, delays them for a moment.

"You shall at least see this chastisement of Esleben, Gotthert," the sentek calls, "which will do double duty as the official pyre for your former commander." Looking to his right, Arnem finds Fleckmester has drawn up a double line of his strongest bowmen. In front of each line burns a shallow trench of pitch and oil, and the men have nocked arrows with large, dripping heads, and all await only the word to fire.

"Fleckmester!" Arnem calls, holding his own sword aloft. "Collapse the eastward wall first, and proceed from there in the necessary order. If any of the townspeople interfere—shoot them down!"

Fleckmester shouts out the commands to light, aim, and loose the fiery shafts: the dried fir logs always favored in the construction of such palisades prove vulnerable to the flames, and in mere moments the whole of the western wall is burning with a fury to give even the madmen from Esleben some pause.

"All right, Taankret," Arnem calls to the *Krebkellen* of infantry and cavalry *fausten.* "You could hardly ask for a more obliging invitation!"

"Indeed, Sentek!" Taankret replies, the marauder blade going high enough in the air for all to see in it the reflection of the raging fire. "Men of Broken—we move!"

Taankret's words are uttered as the fort's eastern wall begins to collapse with loud cracks, sending burning wood aloft amid a storm of sparks, even as the fire spreads to and begins to destroy the southern and northern walls.

"Very good, then, Linnet Gotthert," Arnem says to the new commander of the garrison troops. "The diversion of your antagonists' attention is complete—away with you and your men, and Kafra go with you. We shall meet soon, on the banks of the Cat's Paw!"

Each man of the Esleben garrison salutes both Reyne Niksar and Arnem as they pass; and yet the blue-cloaked troops do not move with full dispatch until they actually see the Esleben fort transformed into a most worthy funeral pyre for a most worthy officer. When the western wall of the structure is pulled down at the last by the collapse of the other three, all the men to the east are privileged to watch as the ignoble rope with which Donner hanged himself finally serves an admirable purpose: whipped by the collapse of the wall to which it is fixed, it hurls the body of Reyne Niksar's young brother high into the air above the flames, even causing Donner's form to lay out horizontally as it comes crashing down upon the now-enormous pile of pine logs below, which glow and flame in shades ranging from red to orange, from yellow to white. Arnem could not have wished for a better execution of the funereal spectacle, and the sentek is quick to turn to the master archer, Fleckmester, and salute him in gratitude; and the garrison men do the same, as they set out at a run.

The sentek marvels, as he has so many times in his long career, at the resourcefulness of the average Broken soldier. Neither Linnet Gotthert nor any of his garrison comrades could even have suspected what their ultimate duty was likely to be, this night; and yet Arnem now observes their willing disappearance into the darkness, as though their actions were the result of a long and detailed council of war. The sentek takes a moment to reproach himself for the duplicity that underlies the orders he has given them; yet he cannot take a great deal of time for such self-recrimination: although the townsfolk of Esleben, and the people who have been drawn in from the countryside, are moving as mobs will—relying on a few individuals initiating each tentative advance—the pain of the disease that is driving them is clearly mounting, and there is only one spur to rash action more potent than lunacy: physical agony.

Even so, Arnem is able to see the mob are strangely moving past pain, almost as if their sickness is destroying their ability to sense that most potent of physical influences. And, faced with this degenerate behavior among what are, after all, subjects of Broken who must have been, until very lately, no more mad than himself, Arnem finds himself spurring the Ox off to some little distance from Visimar and Niksar: almost thoughtlessly, and by the light of a Moon that has now made its way up over the hills and valleys, he searches for the silver clasp that his wife placed in one of his inner pockets before the Talons' splendid march out of Broken. When he finds it, he withdraws the thing, and gazes down at the stern, one-eyed face and the portentous ravens it artfully depicts; then, without considering what he is doing, he actually addresses it:

"And so, great *Allsveter*," he murmurs, repeating the term that he has sometimes heard his wife murmur when contemplating the thing. "Was it you who inspired a brave young man to end his misery thus?"

Replacing the clasp in his deepest pocket, Arnem shakes his head to clear it of nonsense; but then he hears the discreet voice of Visimar:

"Are you troubled enough to address the gods of old, Sentek? Fearing, perhaps, that Kafra has betrayed his own people?"

Quickly looking to see that Niksar has chosen to bury his grief by personally taking charge of the *Wildfehngen* units, Arnem glares at the old man harshly. "Nothing of the kind. The object is a meaningless token from my wife, to whom my thoughts turn before any battle, particularly so strange an engagement. Make no more of it, old fool."

"As you will, Sixt Arnem," Visimar replies; and then he breathes heavily with concern. "But I fear I must tell you that matters in the home you long for may be growing as wretched as they are here. For the rose fever in Broken, it seems, is spreading . . ."

Arnem's face reveals clear bewilderment. "And how come you to know this?" the sentek asks, making ready to join his aide.

"I should almost enjoy telling you that I have employed sorcery," the cripple replies. "But we have no time for childish games. You shall simply have to trust that I know it—and, it may interest you to know, I have at the same time received further proof that my master yet lives."

"Truly?" Arnem replies, his interest showing plainly. "I pray so. For, by the look of things, we shall require the keenest of minds soon."

Visimar eyes him carefully. "Why should the 'sorcerer,' the 'heretic' Caliphestros, have any interest in serving the needs of Broken? And how *could* he serve them, in a way acceptable to the rulers of the great kingdom?"

Just then, however, Arnem receives an urgent call for leadership from Niksar: the mob from Esleben is proving more troublesome than the sentek had originally thought possible. "Let us say that I hope, then," he tells Visimar, as he draws his sword and prepares to ride. "I *hope* that Caliphestros, upon realizing what is truly at work in this land, will offer whatever assistance he can—just as you did, Visimar, and just as any creature with a conscience must!" Then the balled spurs go into the Ox's sides, and Arnem is away. "Reyne!" he shouts. "Ride out to join Akillus on the left claw, and I shall do the same on the right! Let us finish our work quickly, and then push our foes back toward Taankret's men—let the *Krebkellen* be completed!"

As the Ox passes proudly before the infantry *Wildfehngen*—knowing, as such warrior mounts ever do, the importance of the moment and his role in it—the formations of scarred, powerful men afoot begin locking their great, convex *skutem* shields† about the sides of their three *quadrates*, while Arnem continues to call out his orders with such authority that not a man misses a word: "Remember, Talons—although I wish no death to befall these people, my concern for your own lives is far greater; and should you find yourselves in peril, I shall not begrudge you a wounding or even a lethal blow—however diseased your enemies may be!"

A roar goes up from the *Wildfehngen,* who have been unleashed; and the great machine that is the fiercest part of Broken's elite legion sets to work:

High as their emotions are, they never outstrip discipline. Akillus and Niksar's left *fauste* of horsemen makes quickly for the townsmen, who show the ferocity of madmen collected into throngs: there is no order in their violence, only raw rage, and it is not long before the Broken horsemen have encircled and pressed them into the oncoming foot soldiers. Despite these predictable results, however, a wave of surprise runs through the men of Niksar's command: for some of the townsmen—those who appear the most afflicted by whatever illness has taken hold of their community—simply keep coming at the soldiers, even after sustaining wounds that would make seasoned warriors flee outright. A few of them seem to notice these wounds so little that Sentek Arnem's order against inflicting grievous injury must be violated in several cases, so that the maddened townsmen can at least be disarmed—and such disarming, it becomes clear in these several cases, means the taking off of a hand or a limb. Yet even these terrible injuries cause little or no discouragement.

From the baggage train, where he enjoys the youthful protection of the *skutaars,* Visimar sees this development by the light of the Moon; but the sight gives the old man no amusement or solace.

"*Too deep,*" he murmurs, repeating his phrase of earlier in the evening. "*The Holy Fire has burned too deep into them . . .*" Then, aloud, he calls out: "Ernakh!" Turning, he asks of the young men: "Where is Sentek Arnem's *skutaar,* who is called Ernakh?"

Within a few moments, the dark-haired marauder youth is rushed before Visimar, who seizes the lad's shoulders, as if to shake urgency into him.

"Find your mount, son," the old man says. "Get to your master, and tell him this: the disease has progressed too far, and many are insensible to pain. As soon as there is a separation between the townspeople and his men, he must retreat with haste!"

"*Retreat?*" another *skutaar* calls. "You are mad, indeed, old father, to think that the Talons need retreat before such useless fools!"

"Do as I say!" Visimar commands, keeping his attention fixed on Ernakh, and rightly sensing that the youth enjoys a more serious nature than his fellows. "Your master will thank you when all has finally become clear." As the boy leaps atop a nearby horse, Visimar turns to the other young men. "And the rest of you—begin moving the equipment of the *khotor,* even before your commanders return!"

Visimar keeps his still-keen eyes fixed on the white and grey forms of Niksar's and Arnem's mounts on the distant field, and the speeding Ernakh riding fearlessly into the violence—and how expertly, the old man thinks, how naturally and with what seriousness does the marauder boy move atop a horse and among men engaged in a fight that is becoming increasingly deadly! The cripple sees Ernakh reach Sixt Arnem's grey, deliver his message, and receive acknowledgment from the sentek. Almost immediately, the wagons and pack animals of the baggage train begin to move quickly eastward along the darkness of the Daurawah Road, while Visimar remains behind, quietly but desperately urging speed upon Arnem and his men.

It is, in the end, an unnecessary entreaty; for, just as effectively as they have thrashed and herded the townsmen back toward Esleben, the Talons are able to break the *Krebkellen* formation, form into well-ordered lines of retreat—two abreast, now, rather than four, for speed's sake—and return past the spot where Visimar is waiting, all long before their opponents can follow. Some Talons bleed from lucky blows scored by the Eslebeners, but most are simply sweating and bewildered; yet they never slow their double-quick march along the Daurawah Road. Arnem, for his part, draws up beside Visimar, breathing hard and allowing the Ox a moment to revel in his reunion with the old man's mare.

"Well, cripple, Kafra knows how you could tell as much, but they were beginning to seem beyond—or better say *below*—human: the most grievous wounds imaginable, taken as though they were scratches!"

"I would be surprised if your golden god has any sense of why all this is so, Sentek. It will be my unhappy duty to explain it to you—but let us get your men well away from the evil of Esleben . . ."

Arnem will not take to the Daurawah Road until the very last of his wounded—all, thankfully, sound enough to ride and march—depart; and Visimar, for his own reasons, will not start without the commander. The appearance of the eagle owl he called Nerthus has proved beyond doubt to the acolyte that the pestilences at work in Broken have spread throughout (although each in different parts of) the western kingdom, likely for the same reasons that caused their appearance further east, in and about Daurawah; and he must make the sentek see that *all* the towns along the route that they are traveling, where they had thought to find welcome, provisioning, and forage, must now be avoided.

{*vii*:}

DESPITE THE TALONS' DISPATCH of the threat at Esleben, questions about the future of the campaign upon which the legion had embarked have become more nagging as the force marches east to Daurawah. The enemy had been sickened townsmen, after all, Broken's own farmers, millers, and traders, many of them women, fighting at the behest of some madness or even of Death himself, who had forced them to dance his deadly round.[†] Whatever the case, the work there had not been truly fit for such peerless troops as the Talons, and each of them has come to this realization by the time Akillus and his scouting parties report that Daurawah is close; and the mood among the men has grown somber at best. Is this because, after several days of unusually warm, bright weather, the third morning of the soldiers' march looks, to judge by the dim light and a damp chill in the mist, to be strangely muted? Perhaps; but muted, too, are the sounds of Nature's world, and that absence becomes only more pointed as the column nears the Meloderna River, an Unnatural, unharmonious development that even Visimar cannot (or will not) explain.

And as the grey light slowly increases and the walls of Daurawah come into view, it indeed becomes apparent that even the relief and comfort that it was once hoped the port would offer will be denied to Arnem's men: for the western gates of the place, which no man can ever remember seeing closed, are not only shut, but barred from within and sealed from without. The lack of activity before the northern and southern gates, meanwhile, which front the sharp bend in the Meloderna created by the Cat's Paw's emptying into that larger, calmer river, suggests that those portals are similarly sealed—and soon, sounds begin to emerge from within the port's walls that explain why:

They are the sounds of human beings whose bodies may still walk this Earth, but whose minds are already crossing the Great River, or have completed that journey and arrived in *Hel*† itself. Such are mournful noises, as if those who make them have some faint recognition of what has befallen them, and of how irretrievable the loss has been.

It is not, therefore, any fear that the men of Broken's Ninth *Khotor* (the legion that has for over a century guarded Daurawah and the eastern frontier of the kingdom), or some even larger mob of ordinary townspeople, will be disgorged from the tightly shut city gates that slows the pace of Sentek Arnem's Talons as they march steadily toward the walls of the port; rather, it is simple dread of what sights must accompany such terrible sounds as emerge from the place—in greater volume with every step they take—that holds the soldiers back. It is as if Daurawah—sitting, on its landward side, at the end of a long hillside road, one flanked by inexplicably empty pastureland that ends at the thick strips of forest that line the low banks of the two rivers—has become a place entirely unto itself, one which does not even notice the approach of five hundred soldiers, an event that would ordinarily call for great clamor, either of alarm or of welcome. But on this dismal morning, the echoing cries of pain, woe, and confusion continue unabated until the Talons are well along the road leading up to the main gate; yet when they finally halt, it is neither some great increase in the port's uproar nor a sudden silence that stops them. Instead, the wind—which has been out of the west and at their backs since before dawn—abruptly shifts for but a few moments, so that it comes in off of the wide Meloderna beyond Daurawah, stopping each soldier before he has received any such order to halt. For this wind carries with it the smell of burning human flesh: the stink of hundreds of bodies, which no fire could be large enough, if built within the port's walls, to burn quickly—not without risk of setting entire town districts afire . . .

"So many bodies . . . ," Visimar muses through his cloak, which he holds about his nose and mouth. "Matters are already at far worse a pass than even I thought they could be . . ."

He has brought his mare beside Arnem's mount, and on the sentek's opposite flank, as always, is Niksar. "What can we do, Sentek?" the linnet asks. "Daurawah's gates are nearly immune to violation—and the men of the Ninth are unlikely to let us get close enough to try."

"Nor would such an attempt bear any fruit, in all likelihood, Reyne," Arnem replies. "For, as you say, they are much like Broken's gates—the eight or ten feet of oak at the bottom of each is wholly sheathed in iron plate. And so we will wait. They do not seem to have noticed us: we must observe what happens when they do. In the meantime—" Arnem turns to the men behind him. "Akillus. Dispatch parties of your men down to each of the riverbanks. See if anything has transpired there, or in the water itself . . ."

Without a word, Akillus signals to several other linnets of scouts, each of whom takes three or four men and makes with typical speed for the Meloderna and the Cat's Paw at the most approachable points in the steep riverbanks. It requires deft horsemanship, as well as longer periods than the sentek would have thought, for the scouts to return; and few words pass among those who remain as they wait. It is only when they hear the sound of a commotion emanating from one particularly obscure stretch of riverbank, as well as a call to arms being sounded atop the walls of Daurawah, that any general murmuring goes through the officers and ranks of the Talons. When the other scouts reappear, Arnem realizes with aching dread that it is Akillus himself who has raised the alarm; and the commander does not rest easy until he sees his most reliable set of "eyes" finally emerge from the great trees and heavy undergrowth.

Akillus is, as so often, out of breath, and nearly covered in mud and dust, when he arrives before his commander. Niksar offers water from his own skin, which Akillus gratefully accepts before speaking. "The water gate at the base of the main stairway to the river, along with their wharves, are unmanned—unmanned, and destroyed."

"Destroyed?" Arnem asks, shocked. "To what end?"

"To the same end that the Eslebeners sought," Akillus declares, shaken by what he has seen. "The same sickness has produced the same goal—save that the people of Daurawah were able to achieve it. You ought to see the Meloderna, Sentek, just below the city—a place of certain death, for men and ships!"

"But they are burning bodies, from the stench," Arnem replies.

"The bodies of their own dead, yes," Akillus says. "But the crews of the ships—longships, for the most part, but other river craft, as well—to say nothing of . . . well, Sentek, they *seem* to be Bane, but they have rotted into pieces. And long before they saw Daurawah, I would hazard. Nor are they Bane men alone—there are women and children, too, traders and villagers along with warriors. And come down the Cat's Paw, or at least, their bodies are along *its* banks, from what I could see, as well as the Meloderna's . . ." Akillus is visibly shaken, and Arnem allows him a moment to gather his wits. "The wretched mess is everywhere."

"But how?" Niksar puzzles. "Even if the Ninth brought their *ballistae*[†] up onto the walls, they cannot have been so successful with them—"

Akillus shakes his head. "No, Niksar. There are markers that set out the most dangerous parts of the bend in the Meloderna, below the town walls. They simply moved these, and let Nature do the work that traps would ordinarily have done. And the stench—even the lower stretches are littered with the bodies of Northern raiders. The Ninth had apparently reserved the *ballistae* for the caravans from the south—on my return, I saw dozens of dead pack animals, many camels among them, all killed with the great arrows the machines throw: madness has not degraded the Ninth's skill with artillery,[‡] that much is sure. As for the people of the caravans, some must have been allowed to return home, to tell of the fate with which they met—although most lie in great crowds upon the ground."

"Shot by archers?" Arnem asks.

"That is the peculiar part," Akillus answers, genuinely baffled. "Some, yes, shot down—but many killed by hand, primarily the youngest. The Ninth *must* have been leaving through small doorways in the northern and southern gates in raiding parties, likely by night."

"It is the pattern of the illness," Visimar says quietly. "Again, it takes the young first. It arrived here somewhat later, but it did arrive—and when it did, the commander of the legion may have shut all his people, citizens and soldiers alike, into the city; but the madness of the Holy Fire exacted a toll from the caravans, nevertheless. Sentek, did you not say that this commander was an old comrade of yours?"

"I did," Arnem replies, quickly and certainly. "But the kind of treachery you are describing could never have been his work. Gerolf Gledgesa was not capable of it—I've seen him risk his life a hundred times for the honor and safety of Broken and its people, despite his originally having come from a far-off land that lies hard by the Northern Sea, precisely like—" Arnem has been on the verge of saying "your master" to Visimar, in the heat of his indignation, but has caught himself, in part out of tact, in part because of an inscrutable expression that has entered Visimar's face. "Precisely like some of Broken's most worthy citizens."

Visimar pauses, weighing his words carefully. "He may have been murdered, Sentek—whatever the case, you must try to contact whoever now commands the Ninth Legion, for clearly it is being used by *someone* for these murderous purposes. Certainly, Lord Baster-kin did not warn you that we would find such conditions here, did he, Sentek?"

All eyes turn to Arnem, who looks at the cripple in shock: it is precisely the sort of statement that he has warned Visimar for three days' time not to utter in front of the men.

"I beg your pardon, fool?" the sentek answers, with controlled threat that is not unlike the careful drawing of his sword. "Did you dare to bring the name of the Merchant Lord into this, and question his loyalty and honesty? Or am I mistaken?"

"I assure you, you are indeed mistaken," Visimar replies earnestly; and in the old man's still-expressive eyes, Arnem thinks he can read a message: *I do not intend what you suppose—you must reassure the men that this is a local aberration, that their homes are safe.* "My question was honest," the cripple continues. "If Lord Baster-kin said nothing of this, then he can know nothing of it, which means that whoever commands the Ninth, like the elders of Esleben, has sent no warning of his violent intentions to either the Merchants' Council or the Grand Layzin—"

Looking to his men again, Arnem sees that, in their confusion, they wish and almost require Visimar's statement to be true. "Forgive my quick temper, Anselm," the sentek says, attempting contrition. "You are correct, Lord Baster-kin did not even hint at such disruption. And so we can at least reassure ourselves that the problem is contained to the eastern reaches of Broken—"

But then, finally, it comes: contact with the walls of Daurawah. Taankret is the first to spy movement near the western gate, and he points his sword to the spot.

"Sentek Arnem!" he cries. "A sentry atop the walls!"

Arnem turns the Ox toward the port, and calls, "Make way! Make way, there—he seems to be signaling!"

And indeed, the soldier who has appeared—without either helmet or spear—seems desperate to contact the men below, so wildly do his arms flail about and his mouth open and close, giving the impression that he is shouting, yet with no voice to match the manner.

"Ho!" Taankret bellows. "The southwest tower—another man!"

Arnem stops trying to make out the first soldier's meaning when he turns to see that the second soldier is waving some sort of bloodstained banner, which appears to have been, originally, a sheet of white silk;[†] and yet there seems to be little in his behavior to suggest anything concerning surrender. In fact, the two soldiers appear to have little in common, a suspicion that is confirmed when the first soldier takes flight at the merest glimpse of the second. Planting his banner in some sort of bracket inside the battlements, the second soldier draws his short-sword, quickly pursues the first man and, catching him, thrusts the blade deep into the man's side. He then hurls the screaming unfortunate over the battlements; and for the whole of the thirty-foot fall that follows, the badly wounded soldier's shrill cries of fear and agony continue, only stopping when he slams into the bare Earth.

All the Talons are struck dumb—but Arnem forces himself to speak, knowing that confusion and panic have suddenly become his greatest enemies:

"Niksar! Anselm!" He is forced to shake the old man's arm, in order to jog his memory of his assumed name. "Old cripple!" he cries, successfully gaining Visimar's attention. "You, too, Akillus—come with me. Taankret! Stay here and begin to form into *quadrates*—the golden god alone knows why our own men are killing both each other *and* peaceful traders, but they shall not add any man of the Talons to that list." Yet Taankret's ordinarily calm, keen eyes remain fixed upon Daurawah in horror. "Linnet!" Arnem repeats, at which the reliable infantry officer finally turns. "Keep the men busy—eh?"

Taankret salutes smartly. "Aye, Sentek!" And with that, he is off to deliver orders to the other *quadrate* commanders, as Arnem and his three fellow horsemen set out toward the presumably dead soldier lying near the western gate of Daurawah. When they have covered only half the distance to the man, however, they see that his body is still writhing, and they pause—an action quickly revealed as a mistake. With a rushing roar, something approaches from out of the Heavens, and a thunderous crash throws up a mass of sod and dirt before their horses, who rear up, screaming in rare fright as the officers and their companion take in the sight of the shaft of an enormous bolt: eight feet long and yet another in diameter, its iron head has sunk deep into the ground. It is one of the deadliest weapons hurled by *ballistae.*

Arnem looks up at the battlements, enraged and bewildered, to see that the several operators of the engine of war are busily dropping boulders the size of small pigs down upon the man who was attacked by his supposèd comrade and thrown from the walls, and whose little chance at continued life is soon crushed, literally, by men he would ordinarily have had every reason to trust.

"You've come far enough, Sentek," the soldier with the white banner calls, as he joins the crew of the *ballista.* "Do not mistake our intentions by the color of this standard. It was all I could lay hands on, and I thought that the blood that covers it might at least give you pause, if not cause your immediate withdrawal. Given that neither resulted, we were forced to fire. I take it that you *are* Sentek Arnem?"

"I am," Arnem answers, not wishing to display the full anger he feels at the pallin's impertinence, insolence that is as likely the result of lunacy as of disrespect. "I will not ask your name, although I should like to know why a soldier of Broken has lost all respect for rank, if he recognizes it!"

"Oh, make no mistake," the man says. "I have the greatest of respect for you, Sentek. As I did for that man. But we have had a great deal of trouble determining just who has fallen victim to the foreign demons who are stealing the very souls of Broken. That fellow, for instance—we were old comrades, and even older friends. Recently, however, he'd fallen victim to the disease being spread by unholy forces throughout this entire area. As for you and your men, it was impossible to say with certainty. If some of our own legion have fallen victim to it, why not some of yours, as well?"

"Fallen victim to *what*, Pallin?" Niksar asks.

"It is a devastating and yet peculiar disease," the pallin on the wall answers, as if he were discussing a morning's drill. "At first, very painful—the blood, you see, is somehow stolen from the body, and exchanged for molten metal.[†] The pain is horrific, and the sufferer becomes enslaved to whoever can stop it. Which, we've seen, are the agents of foreign kingdoms, the demon traders. The afflicted continually try to open the gates and allow such enemies in. They've even sought the help of the Bane."

All is silence, on the road below; finally, Akillus murmurs, "The man is a lunatic. Plainly, completely—a lunatic . . ."

"Sentek Arnem?" the man on the wall bellows. "Our own commander—an old comrade of yours, I believe, Sentek Gledgesa—has agreed to come out of the city to speak with you. But I warn you—"

"'*Warn*' him?" Niksar seethes. "Warn the commander of the Talons? I'll have the man's tongue out—!"

But Arnem only replies: "You warn us of what?"

"My comrades are, as you have seen, particularly accurate with their weapon. I would recommend you—and your aide, of course—speak to our sentek, alone. Order your men attempt no tricks, as well."

Arnem knows what his answer must be. "Very well, then."

"One final thing," the soldier shouts. "Sentek Gledgesa's vision is gone, but our healers seemed able to stop the degeneration there. His own daughter will guide him out, and what applies to him, applies to her. The girl's speech has been stolen, but our healers have kept her alive."

"A daughter . . . ," Arnem murmurs softly. "Gerolf has a *daughter* . . . ?" Then he shouts: "Tell your commander that he and any dear to him will be safe with me. I believe that he will understand that. I shall meet him halfway between here and the gate."

"You are as wise as your reputation states, Sentek Arnem," the soldier replies, saluting casually. And at that, the echoing sound of heavy iron locks and bars being thrown becomes audible, and Arnem's men look to see a smaller doorway, just large enough for a man upon a horse, opening in the greater structure.

Before moving forward, Arnem turns to Niksar. "If, for any reason, I do not return, Reyne—I shall need you to get the men back to Broken."

"But—" Niksar protests haltingly. "He has told us you are to bring—"

"I'll take the old man, instead; if Gledgesa is in the desperate condition he describes, he will be of more use . . ." Arnem does not reveal his true reason for taking Visimar to meet Gerolf Gledgesa, a reason that he suspects the old man may guess at: for the truth is, the two officers, Arnem and Gledgesa, shared the duty of escorting the Kafran priests during their ritual mutilations, so long ago; and both were present, the day that Visimar's leg was severed and the man himself left to die on the edge of Davon Wood . . .

{viii:}

A S ARNEM AND VISIMAR MOVE up the road toward the walls of Daurawah and the figures of Gerolf Gledgesa and his daughter—on horse and pony, respectively—appear from out of the smaller doorway in the great port's western gate, Visimar remains silent, and slowly reins his mare, against her will, off the Ox's pace, until he is riding some twelve to fifteen feet behind the sentek. The cripple knows what must be going through the commander's mind: for no man of integrity can face the decay and death of a friend, particularly a friend alongside whom he has faced death on a score of occasions, without a deep sense of wretched sadness and of his own mortality. Visimar therefore does not burden the sentek with practical pressures and details at this moment. Time will press, soon enough—in truth it *is* pressing, already; but not so hard that the last meeting of two good men can justly be curtailed or tainted.

The two pairs of mounts finally come to a stop when a space of perhaps ten feet separates them. The young girl next to Gledgesa was a delicate, once-pretty child, Arnem supposes, but one who now wears bandages and scarves wrapped around her neck, as well as from the top of her skull to her lower jaw, beneath which still more clean white bandages are wrapped securely, leaving only the upper part of her face, particularly her lovely, light eyes, open to view. She reaches up to rein in her father's giant, dark stallion to a stop with the lightest of touches; and as soon as the horse has halted, his rider grins beneath two eyes covered by a soft silken bandage. Arnem's heart sinks far deeper when he sees what has become of his old friend: the same signs of living decay that he and his troops have so often observed during their current march eastward cover Gledgesa's once proud, powerful body, beneath his elegantly appointed leather armor.

A formidable warrior sprung from that rare breed of *seksent* that combines handsome features with an equally well formed and hugely powerful body, Gledgesa had originally been a mercenary, who had come from the lands northeast of the Seksent Straits to Broken because he was tall enough to pass for a respected worshipper of Kafra. Arnem had met him some twenty years before this morning, when both young men had been selected, as a reward for valor, to move from the regular army to the Talons. But, although they had risen together—Gledgesa ever the fiery-eyed, intrepid warrior who delighted at being first into any enemy's front line, while Arnem, although no less fierce, was a more even-headed soldier who could comprehend the full range of threats posed to his men—it had always been plain from their complementary natures that, while each was consistently showered with glory, Gerolf Gledgesa had come to Broken for money, not laurels: after all, a kingdom, the patron god of which delighted in the amassing of wealth, had seemed ideally suited to a mercenary. Gledgesa, like many a similar aspirant, had not ultimately found the rumors of Broken's boundless wealth to be accurate; or rather, he had found them to be so only if the aspirant was willing to subject himself to the tenets of the Kafran faith and state. And so, Gledgesa had elected to leave the Talons and take command of the unique Ninth Legion, composed wholly of fast-moving *freilic* troops, most of them light cavalrymen tasked with making themselves available along the entire eastern frontier of the kingdom—where the possibilities for seizing prize monies and goods happened to be most abundant.

During the time that he commanded the Ninth, Gledgesa slowly became estranged from the rapidly rising Arnem, each of the two men explaining the drift by citing their new duties and physical distance; but there was another and far truer cause for the estrangement, one that went back to the beginning of their comradeship before the Torganian war, and that involved a shared duty to which, as time passed, both men found it increasingly difficult to reconcile themselves: the guarding of the Kafran priests' mutilation and exile rituals on the banks of the Cat's Paw. In particular, it was the fiendishly bloody rites that they had been forced to observe being inflicted upon Caliphestros and Visimar that had brought about, not only their resignations from the much-coveted guardianship of the priests, but the beginning of their estrangement, as well.

Neither man had ever been able to state, precisely, why their mutual objections and protests should have driven them apart. It had been for wise Isadora to later explain to her husband how shared shame often eats at friendships so relentlessly that the glories of triumph can do little to preserve the bond. Thus, while in later years the company of a man with whom one has achieved honorable glory will always be welcome, the mere sight of a comrade with whom one has played even an involuntary part in foul actions, can bring the sense of shame back again with full, vivid force.

And for this reason, these two men—whose last glimpse of one another was long enough ago that Gledgesa has had time, in the interval, to father and raise a child who is now, Arnem would guess, some eight or nine years old—face each other on the plain east of Daurawah, each not quite knowing, for all their bygone years of comradeship, just what to expect of the other . . .

In characteristic fashion, Gledgesa's grin widens, or widens as much as his distorted features will allow. "Forgive me for not saluting, Sixt, old friend, as well as for failing to invite you into Daurawah. But the salute might well crack one of my chalk-like bones; and you mustn't try to enter the port—not now. I haven't let any Broken troops in *or* out—not since it became apparent that the Cat's Paw is now poisoned."

Arnem spins to face Visimar, who, for his part, is busy staring at Gledgesa in a manner that tells Arnem he indeed remembers the now-ravaged soldier's presence at his *Denep-stahla.*

"Did you come by the river?" Gledgesa asks. "And see the bodies?"

"No, Gerolf. We stayed on the main road, to forage in and about Esleben."

"Esleben!" Gledgesa attempts a laugh, one that dissolves into a hideous cough: a cough reminiscent of the final moments of Donner Niksar, whom Gledgesa soon mentions: "I suppose you learned the truth about those ignorant, treacherous townspeople from young Niksar's brother, as I hoped you would." He coughs again, at which his daughter reaches up to attempt to put a comforting hand to his shoulder, although she can manage only his forearm. As she does so, she begins to hum a most pleasant and soothing plainsong[†] for her father. Gledgesa gently presses her hand and then removes it, although the effect upon his symptoms of her touch and song has been immediate. "It's all right, Weda.[‡] I will be fine, as will you." The girl continues to hum her plainsong. "But you must meet my oldest friend, Sentek—nay, *Yantek* Sixt Arnem, commander of the Army of Broken, if the heralds from the great city are to be believed!"

Arnem looks down into the girl's tightly swaddled face, or at the upper half that is visible; and if her father's crisp blue eyes and golden hair, which she has inherited fully, are any indication, she is indeed a lovely child, who inspires immediate pity for the suffering she silently endures. Knowing that she cannot speak, Arnem says, "Hello, Weda," and then rushes to add, "Do not try to reply, I know that you are too ill. I have a daughter almost exactly your age—it must be hard to stay silent, even if you *are* unwell."

"You've been told she's ill?" Gledgesa says, his blinded head moving from side to side, as if he might defeat the silk bandage that covers his corrupted eyes by finding a way around it.

"Yes," Arnem replies carefully. "By those extraordinary sentries on your walls." He cannot help but laugh. "You were always talented with *ballistae* and catapults, Gerolf—and you have evidently shared your secrets."

Having brought up a mouthful of phlegm with an attempt at laughter, Gledgesa spits it out; and Visimar sees that its color is so ruby red as to almost be black. "*Those* maniacs," he murmurs in disgust. "We've had enemies enough, without their creating more."

" 'Enemies enough'?" Arnem echoes. "The Northerners?"

"The northerners alone would have been manageable," Gledgesa replies, his voice weakening. "Them, as well as the easterners, we learned how to either treat with or punish long ago. But the armies behind these southern caravans, both the Byzantines and the Mohammedans . . . They've wanted to destroy us for years, and may even have worked out the method, now. And this new breed of river pirates is leading the way. Just who is paying whom, and why, I don't know, but it will gut the kingdom, if it goes on."

"Gerolf—you speak of the poisoning of the river?" Arnem asks.

"I know, Sixt, you likely find it inconceivable," Gledgesa says. "But I've been writing to the council for weeks; sending dead bodies to prove the point. And not simply Bane bodies. The first of my own men to fall, as well. I even sent reports to Baster-kin himself. Nothing's come of it. And now, of a sudden, we receive a message that all this devastation has actually been the work *of* the Bane? And that you're leading a campaign to destroy them?"

"You doubt both points, Gerolf," Arnem says. "Yet to each, I would ask—who else?"

"*Anyone* else, Arnem," Gledgesa responds desperately, his voice fading. "The Bane? Devastation of *this* order? There are too many contradictions. Many of my own men and their people are dying, yet they do not drink from the river—like any garrison, we have our own well. Suppose the Bane *have* tainted the Cat's Paw—how did they manage to despoil *that* reserve? And try to crush them—yourself and your Talons? What do you know of warfare in the Wood, Sixt? What do any of us? And what's to happen when these other foreign armies enter the kingdom while you're fooling about with the exiles? And enter they will: they're planning the end of Broken, I tell you, Sixt—but what's just as clear is that they've had some kind of help from *within* the kingdom. I'm not certain just who—the Council, Baster-kin, the Layzin, even the God-King—or why, or if those internal partners even realize the true danger of what they're about—"

Suddenly, Gerolf Gledgesa's impassioned plea sends him into a paroxysm of coughing. The attack becomes so severe that he slumps to the side of his stallion's neck, then slips off his saddle altogether. He slams to the ground on his shoulder, screaming once in uncontrollable pain. His daughter's face grows terrified, and she quickly dismounts, sliding down the side of her pony and, as she does, loosening the bandages below her chin. With her attention desperately fixed on her father, she does not notice as those bandages fall away—

And when they do, the whole of her lower jaw begins to come away with them. The rot in her body has destroyed those joints altogether, as well as much of the skin of her lower face; but this is not the most astounding thing about the condition, for all its horror. No, even more amazing is that there is no evidence the girl feels what is happening at all.

Arnem, who has rushed to Gledgesa's side, glances up at his friend's child; but Visimar hurriedly limps to the girl, and deftly relocates the jaw, rewrapping the bandages more tightly. Weda herself is no more than embarrassed by this event, and with her hands and a few plaintive moans urges Visimar to help her father. The cripple obliges, seeming no more concerned for the child than she is for herself.

"What are you doing, old fool?" Arnem nearly shouts. "Gerolf has only fallen, but the girl's face—"

"He has not 'only fallen,' Sentek," Visimar answers evenly, his thinking never clouded. "His ribs have begun to collapse, and if he is not rushed to a resting place, he will die in a very short time." Arnem looks to his old comrade, who is barely conscious: so labored has his breathing become that it seems he is being strangled from within. Yet, despite this plain truth, Arnem's own fatherly instincts will not allow him to simply ignore Weda, and he moves toward her, forcing Visimar to roughly grasp his arm.

"Wait, Sixt Arnem, wait!" the old man whispers. "Look at her, *look at her—she feels no pain!*"†

The sentek looks into the girl's placid eyes—and sees that the cripple is correct. "No pain," he murmurs, stunned and saddened. "But, then . . ."

"Aye," Visimar replies. "The fire wounds have reached their last stages." Putting his mouth close to Arnem's ear, the old man whispers urgently: "They will both be dead before nightfall—and we must away, Sentek—look at the soldiers above. They believe we attacked their commander, who I fear may be little more than their prisoner, and are preparing that machine again, and bringing a second up—"

Arnem's reaction is predictable: *"No, Visimar!* I will not allow a collection of maddened renegades to doom one of our greatest soldiers!" The sentek cups his hand: "Niksar! Akillus! A *fauste* of cavalry, quickly!"

Both young officers have been awaiting such an order: for they have gathered a group of hard-looking horsemen, who thunder out onto the plain before the city. Gledgesa grabs at the sentek's shoulder.

"Visimar!" he seethes, choking up blood with every word and breath. "Did I hear that name, Arnem, or have I finally lost my mind altogether?"

"You have not, old friend," Arnem says gently; and then he looks up when he hears the thunderous sound of the long-barred western gate of Daurawah being drawn back. "It appears your men intend to rescue you,

Gerolf," Arnem says, chuckling in what he hopes will be a reassuring way: a reminder of their old campaigns, when it was common to laugh in the midst of great danger. "So I must be quick. I found Visimar, or rather he found me. He was alive, and in Broken—and I brought him along on this campaign, not least with you in mind."

"*Visimar* . . . If only it were possible—there is much I would say . . ."

"It *is* possible, Sentek Gledgesa," Visimar answers, kneeling as best he can by the dying man. "And you have said all you need say, as has Sentek Arnem. I forgive you for any part you played in my torment, and rejoice that you risked so much to oppose the mutilations."

"And you accept my—apologies?" Gledgesa forces himself to ask. "Inadequate as I know they are?"

"I do. And now, you and your daughter must rest, Sentek, and prepare yourselves. You must give her courage as you both cross the river . . ."

"Then you can help us embark upon that journey?" the blind man asks.

"Fear not, Gerolf Gledgesa, for yourself or your daughter. You shall mount and cross the Arch of All Colors that spans the Waters of Life, and Geldzehn the Guardian shall take you both into the Hall of Heroes. *Hel* shall not use the crime against me that you and Sentek Arnem witnessed, when you were both mere servants of the Kafran priests, as a justification for dragging you to her terrible realm—I release you, in the presence of your gods and mine, from that burden."

"River?" Arnem is confused. "But, Gerolf, you said the rivers are—"

"We speak of another river, Sixt," Gledgesa replies, in an uncharacteristically gentle way. "Another river altogether. Visimar knows it . . . And I thank you, old man. Sixt—put my daughter's hand in mine, and put me on my feet. Then *go,* old friend."

"Damn it, Gerolf! There may yet be something Visimar can do, I have seen his healing skills—"

"There is naught, Sixt—no help of *that* sort, I mean . . ." Arnem helps Gledgesa up and Visimar guides the girl Weda to his side, again making certain her bandaging is sound as Arnem puts the girl's hand into her father's. "I trust those are your horsemen I hear," Gledgesa continues. "We ate all but a few of our mounts long ago. So—let me return without your life upon my conscience." The blind man reaches into the air, not expecting Visimar to touch him, but signaling his contentment, and urging the cripple, too, to go. "And thank you again, old man, for removing our part in your torment from my shoulders, where it has weighed heavily for so long . . ."

All that happens next happens too quickly for the grief-stricken Arnem to comprehend fully. Unable to watch Gerolf Gledgesa attempting to mount his horse on his own, Arnem helps his comrade, while Visimar does the same for the almost weightless Weda. Father and daughter begin to walk their horses toward what must be their ends in Daurawah, the city's commander calling out as best he can to his own troops, ordering them to halt. Akillus and Niksar arrive with their determined horsemen to guard the sentek as he mounts the Ox, and to help Visimar get astride his mare. Then the ride back begins, Arnem's face a mask, not only of terrible sorrow, but of contrition.

"I am as ashamed as I can ever remember being, Visimar," Arnem says. "I pray your judgment was correct."

"About this moment, it was, Sentek, although your shame is understandable," Visimar replies. "But for now, you must steel yourself—bend that shame to other purposes. For, when you fully understand the injustices that lie beneath these ugly circumstances—then, Sentek, you will find answers, and *true* justice." He pauses, seemingly awed by the magnitude of the task he himself has described. "Let us only hope," he murmurs in conclusion, "that we survive to witness it . . ."

II:

Fire

{i:}

HELDO-BAH STANDS before an ancient ash tree, the bark of which is so deeply wrinkled and roughly surfaced as to remind him of the dried, grey skin of a hag seeress, to whom he once traded a fine *seksent* knife for what proved to be the woman's utterly worthless assurance that a half-marauder whore with whom he had passed a recent night near Daurawah was free of disease. He allows his rigid body to fall into the bark of the ash's trunk in such a way that his head strikes first: such has been the effect on his mind and spirit of an argument between Keera and Veloc that has raged since he himself ran back into their camp the day before to relate the news of his rediscovery of Caliphestros's place of exile. Keera is convinced that she must go to meet this all-important character on her own, worrying that Veloc and Heldo-Bah will bungle the matter if they accompany her. For his part, Veloc is concerned, not only for his sister's safety, but for her soundness of mind, as well. And Heldo-Bah has by now reached the simple hope that someone—a noble, merciful tree, if needs must—will knock him unconscious and end the wretchedness of listening to his friends debate again and again the same points.

"You have never in your life shown true respect for the tenets of the Moon, Veloc," Keera snaps at her brother, her voice having grown hoarse. "Why, then, do you now show such sudden deference?"

"I've told you twenty times, sister!" Veloc protests.

". . . closer to fifty . . . ," Heldo-Bah murmurs, quietly and uselessly, as his head slams into the trunk of the ash again.

"It is one thing to question our faith among men and women," Veloc declares, paying Heldo-Bah no mind. "I will grant you that I have some-times done so, often for the pure and idiotic amusement of it. But by Kafra's rotting bunghole, Keera, when you introduce the white panther *herself* into this discussion—"

"Fool—you make my argument *for* me!" Keera shouts, her round face now blazing red. "If, in fact, we are contending with the animal who pos-sesses the noblest and most powerful spirit in all the Wood, then she will not be fooled by your momentary airs of devotion and solemnity—indeed, she will only kill us all the more quickly, when you assume them! You may lie as you wish to the women in the towns and villages you visit, Veloc; you may even, on occasion, persuade the Groba to believe your tales; but if you think for an instant that this panther will not sense your untrue voice and words—I tell you, you must not even attempt it!"

"What, then?" Veloc demands, his own voice exhausted.

". . . suicide . . . ," Heldo-Bah mutters, after which comes the dull thud[†] of his head striking the tree once more.

"But do you *seriously* propose that we allow you to go into that place alone, Keera?" Veloc presses once more. "It's madness! We are faced with the greatest sorcerer ever known to the Tall—so great that he has created, in the worst part of this Wood, a garden that Heldo-Bah says has grown to rival, in beauty as well as bounty, any in the glades about Okot, or even in the Meloderna valley—"

". . . far superior, in fact . . . ," Heldo-Bah agrees, now clinging to consciousness, as well as to the ash trunk, by the barest of threads, yet unconcerned with his condition.

"—and in this miraculous place," continues Veloc, "this place that is plainly governed by sorcerous arts of a kind at which we cannot even guess, this master of black arts lives with this—this wild *creature*! All this, I might add, only *after* he survived the *Halap-stahla*—which neither man *nor* demon has ever done! How will you stand up to such a being, I should like to know?"

"*I will not, you idiot.*" Keera bitterly pushes her face close to her brother's. "I will have no need to. Both panther and sorcerer will sense my sincerity, and deal with me fairly: such great spirits do not demean themselves with the sort of petty viciousness you describe, Veloc. And later, after I have explained to them the—the *peculiarities* exhibited by you and our touched friend, over there, who—" Glancing at the last member of their party, Keera stops shouting for a moment. "Heldo-Bah—what in the Moon's name are you doing to yourself?"

"If death will free me from this squabble . . . ," Heldo-Bah says, through lips that are crushed into deep grooves of the ash tree's bark, "Then I swear to you, I almost welcome it . . . Blood of the Moon, Veloc! When, tell me, please, *when* have you *ever* judged a predicament more wisely than Keera?" Seeing that Veloc has no answer, Heldo-Bah moves away from the tree at last and bellows, "And so why, in the name of all that is unholy, are we still *talking* about this?"

"Quiet, fool!" Veloc whispers. "They may hear you—if they really are but two rises away, the sound will certainly—"

"They will hear *me*, cuckolder?" Heldo-Bah interrupts. "Oh, that is a new depth of dishonesty and dim-wittedness, even for you—the pair of you have been shouting at each other throughout the night. There's nary a creature in Davon Wood that hasn't heard you! *Hear me* . . . I *hope* the sorcerer hears me, that he may come and put an end to all this idiocy—

that is, if he's not somewhere around us right now! In fact, he likely is—indeed, he's probably been here the entire time—" Without turning, Heldo-Bah points accusingly at the tree beneath which the three made their camp the night before: a broad, sheltering oak that stands nearby, protected by the coming together of two relatively small but sharp ridges in the slope of the mountain. "Yes—probably right in that damned tree, having himself a fine old laugh at how petty and imbecilic the Bane can be—"

Heldo-Bah stops suddenly, his arm still in the air. *"Ahhh,"* he noises, just as a man might release his final breath. "Your cursèd, endless talk, Veloc . . . *Ficksel* . . ." The word is less a curse, on this occasion, than a statement of submission, even a kind of obscene prayer; and, blood-speckled as the upper part of his face may be, it quickly loses all inner color, while his lower jaw falls open ever wider.

"Heldo-Bah," Keera says. "What is it—have you done yourself actual harm, you foolish—" She moves toward him, producing a small, clean kerchief, ready to mop the blood from his forehead and face. "You look as though you've seen a demon of some kind, come to kill us all—"

"And I may well have," Heldo-Bah says. "But—I *was* wrong concerning one detail. They are not in the oak." Keeping his arm high, he points all the more urgently, now, just to the left of the oak, where, another ten feet along, stands a beautiful elm. Its delicately laced branches, like those of the oak, are markedly undamaged, for its being so high on the wind-swept mountain. "Death and his handmaiden—or is it the other way round? No matter, for there they are—in that elm . . ."

Keera and Veloc turn to follow their friend's indication, and when they catch sight of the cause of his gaping shock, their faces and jaws, too, droop open.

Along the crotch of two long, low limbs of the elm lies a pale, glowing form, draped as one might a luxuriant white cloth upon a table, if one were expecting honored guests, or perhaps as one would bedeck an altar. But the folds of this drape are undulating: because, apparently, whatever is beneath it breathes, and the many lines of its surface are not, in fact, ripples of fabric, but the folds of powerful muscles. Toward the left extreme, two brilliant green orbs shine out, lit as if by the sun—despite the fact that the sun is momentarily obscured by a cloud. Finally, at each end, two long, lazy legs stretch and steady the apparition, while toward its rear, a tail flicks gently, very gently, its languorous movements speaking not of carelessness but of the near-effortless speed with which the creature itself could deliver death, if such a fancy should strike her.

Above this sight, the three foragers can just make out another form; and, once the cloud that has been briefly blocking the sun passes, this figure is clarified. Two human arms rest casually on elm branches as if they were arms of a chair, while the half-legs lie atop the haunches of the lounging creature below. Greyed hair streaked by patches of snowy white is scarcely contained by a faded black skullcap, while the long, hanging beard would seem to have been washed and combed, recently—or perhaps, given its rich fullness, even groomed with a boar-bristle brush. But the eyes, like those of the beast, catch the light of the day in such a way that they seem *not* to do so at all, but rather to radiate their own inner fire: an effect that is increased by the seeming smiles that fill the features of both forms, in the rather disconcerting manner of hungry hunters toying with their next meal.

"Let your arm drop, Bane," the man says quietly, indicating Heldo-Bah with a nod of his chin. Then he pauses thoughtfully, contemplating his own words. "Well—that *is* odd. The first words I have spoken to another human in . . ." He quickly sharpens his wits and fastens his attention on the foragers once more. "Allow the wise young female among you to see to your head. You may indeed have done yourself some small injury, although I blame you not for it. It really was a most inscrutable conversation. Amusing, however . . ."

Keera is the first to recover herself: she thrusts the kerchief into Veloc's hands, and says, "Get him cleaned up." She then begins to walk, slowly and deliberately, toward the elm tree, wanting to examine the visitors but forcing herself to turn her gaze respectfully toward the ground.

"Health and long life to you," she murmurs quietly, angry that she cannot keep her voice from trembling. "Lord Caliphestros . . ."

"I thank you, young Keera," Caliphestros answers, in all sincerity and with a nod of appreciation. "Though the first of your wishes, regrettably, is no longer possible, while the second holds only limited interest for me. But why do you avert your eyes?"

"Is it not done?" Keera asks with some concern. "Upon encountering such superior creatures as yourselves?"

"*Tetch*," noises Caliphestros. "I am no such thing. Although I cannot offer any similar assurance, so far as my companion is concerned. She cares precious little for humans, I know that much—but as for her being entirely of this world, well . . . Though a man of science, I have often had my doubts. But why do you all exhibit such surprise? Certainly, it was you yourselves who, some years ago, came upon our home, after you had received the packet of documents from my friend here."

Her body quivering with sudden realization, Keera turns to Veloc and Heldo-Bah quickly. "The letters . . ."

"So it *was* him," Veloc answers quietly. "Just as you suspected, Keera."

Heldo-Bah closes his eyes. "Thank Kafra's golden stones and the Moon itself that we bothered to deliver the damned things . . ."

"I don't understand," Caliphestros says. "Surely, when you saw who my messenger was, and then followed her to our dwelling—"

"But we never *did* see her, my lord," Keera replies. "We found the leather pouch in the center of our camp, when we awoke one morning. And, while it is true that we followed the tracks of a panther that we thought might be the white legend to what we supposed to be your camp, we never saw either of you. Indeed, Heldo-Bah, there—"

Heldo-Bah looks at Keera as if identifying him with her mere finger has been little short of signing his death warrant; but he feebly raises a hand and bows his head. "My lord," he mumbles, not knowing what else *to* say.

"—he thought that the panther we tracked had likely killed and consumed you, and that such explained why, although your camp seemed perfectly tended, we did not see any signs of life."

Caliphestros laughs, plainly pleased by every aspect of this story. He looks down at the panther, who turns her head up to him and slowly closes and opens her eyes several times in deep affection, seemingly knowing that she is at least one of the causes of her companion's merriment. The old man reaches down to scratch the top of the head that rises, atop the animal's powerful neck, to meet his fingers. "There truly is no end to this one's cleverness . . ."

Bringing his hand back up, Caliphestros indicates the foragers once more. "When she returned so soon, I knew that you, or other Bane as capable as yourselves, were about, and that, being members of a curious and intrepid race, you would not be able to resist at least an attempt to find the lair of what you might well think to be the fabled white panther of Davon Wood, whose tracks would have been near the pouch when you discovered it. And so, we withdrew into our cave, and left you to wonder at all the mysterious circumstances you had encountered. And, let me only say that I owe you great gratitude, for had you not so decently taken the pouch to my acolytes, I could not have survived these many years."

Heldo-Bah thrusts an elbow into Veloc's side. "There, you see? I told you, did I not, that delivering those things without informing the Groba would be both profitable and decent, just as he says?"

Returning his friend's sharp blow in kind, Veloc whispers, "Save that the word 'decent' never crossed your lying lips!"

Caliphestros sees Keera lift her head for but an instant to steal a peek at the panther, then lower her eyes again in deference; and the old man nods in true appreciation, which is augmented when he hears that Stasi has begun to purr. "It would seem that my companion also recognizes her debt to you: she has remembered your scent, and particularly wishes *you* to feel at your ease, Keera. You should feel honored, for she not only does not trust humans, as a rule, but nearly always sets out to kill any with whom she crosses paths."

"Indeed I do feel honored, lord," Keera says, still with great humility. "For she is famed among all our tribe as the most righteous and powerful of woodland spirits—a noble soul with a mighty heart. One of our fellow foragers claims to this day to have seen her kill nearly every member of a Broken hunting party, long ago."

Caliphestros studies the young Bane woman further. "Your homage is well stated, young lady. I have long known of the deference your people show the great cats of the Wood: but in you there is something else— something more than mere fear or deference."

"Yes, my lord," Keera answers with a quick nod. "If my agreement is not unacceptably vain."

"It is not. You are a woman who exhibits graceful strength, integrity, deep knowledge, and compassion. Do not ever apologize for such quali- ties, Keera, for in the vicious, mendacious world of men, they are the finest and most powerful gifts that anyone can hope to possess." Cal- iphestros leans forward, stroking his grey beard and suddenly realizing just how long the thing has become, and how much of that length is no longer grey, but white. "And so, please, bring your eyes up, if you can bear the sight of the deteriorating, mutilated man before you, that we may converse the easier. As for Stasi—if your friends do not hold her gaze for too long, until she has grown as tolerant of their scents as she is pleased by yours, she shall not strike at them. Not so long as *you* are present, at any rate."

Keera, eagerly but nonetheless slowly, turns upward, letting her eyes run the length of the panther and then settle on the green jewels that are set into her proud face; and for an instant, she feels a deep chill of mournful recognition. "I—it is said, in our village, that she is so fearsome because she sprang from the loins of the Moon itself, which gave her such color, brilliance, and almighty power . . ."

"I have heard this tale." Caliphestros lifts his head, ever more intrigued by this small woman of great wisdom. "But you think otherwise . . ."

"I—with all respect, my lord, I believe I *know* otherwise."

"Indeed? And you may simply call me Caliphestros, Keera. It was my name, when there were other humans to use it, and so I suppose it must become such again." A thought occurs to him. "Do you know the meaning of your own name, by any chance?"

Keera quickly shakes her head. "No. Caliphestros."

Watching this extraordinary scene, Heldo-Bah begins to moan, his upper body rocking back and forth. "She has actually called him by his name alone—without his title. We are dead men, dead, dead, dead . . ."

"Stop it," Veloc hisses, cuffing his friend a quick blow to the head.

"You two will be silent," Caliphestros says, more forcefully than angrily—but his tone is nonetheless stern enough that the panther punctuates his remark by eyeing the two small men and letting out the short, low growl that such creatures employ as a warning call to those immediately about them. The old man reaches down to stroke her haunch as his gaze returns to Heldo-Bah and Veloc. "Do not suppose that my gratitude is infinite," he says, "for I know that foraging, while vital to your people's survival, is also employed as punishment, on occasion. And at first blush, the pair of you have the sort of habitually contrite expressions that would mark Bane who have undertaken their foraging under precisely such disgraced circumstances." Caliphestros deliberately softens his aspect and voice, once more, as he looks again to Keera. "Yours is a name from far to the south," he continues. "From the Sassanid Empire, which some call Persia. Do you know of it?"

Keera shakes her head modestly. "No, Cali—" Her voice falters. "I beg your pardon, but may I not call you 'my lord,' for now? I find that I feel impertinent, doing otherwise. Perhaps, with time, this will change . . ."

"Wiser and wiser," replies Caliphestros, as he slowly nods once or twice. "Very well, Keera. It is a beautiful, indeed a fine name, intended for those who are gifted with sight: to see far and truly—in *all* ways. Which, I suspect, you do."

"She does that, my lord," Veloc says, putting one hand to his chest and holding the other arm out before him, assuming his best historian's pose. He then declaims further, and just as clownishly: "There is no greater tracker in our tribe, nor a wiser head—"

"If you wish to keep *your* head, boy," Caliphestros interrupts, "and the throat beneath it, then mind your tongue until your opinion is requested." He gives Keera a rather conspiratorial glance. "Your brother, eh? I heard you mention as much, during your argument—and it would more readily explain why one of your character keeps such questionable company as his."

"Yes, my lord," Keera replies. "But he is not as great a fool as he sometimes sounds. A good man, in fact, but he has long had the ambition to be the historian of our tribe, which ofttimes causes him to take on airs."

"Historian, eh?" Caliphestros echoes. "Indeed? And to what school of history do you belong, Veloc?"

Again assuming the absurd pose of the orator, Veloc asks, "My lord? I fear I do not understand you—what *school* of history?"

"Yes," Caliphestros says, plainly entertained. "History is, among many other things, a long war, Veloc—a war between factions, each of which is as fanatical as any army. So—are you an annalist, for example, like the great Tacitus? Or perchance you seek moral lessons in the lives of great men, as did Plutarch." Reading utter consternation in the handsome Bane's features, the old man tries not to laugh aloud, and queries further, "No? Perhaps you admire the books of the estimable Bede, from across the Seksent Straits. He was once a friend of mine—although I do not know if he yet lives."[†]

"I know none of these names, lord." Veloc's mask of pride, now undercut by confusion, grows naught but sillier. "And I must ask—what has *history* to do with *books?*"

"Ah," noises Caliphestros. "So you *speak* the tales of history, do you, Veloc?"

The handsome Bane shrugs. "What else should a true historian do, my lord? Were history to be recorded in books, why . . . How should we know who put it there? Or where it originated, and what part is fact, what legend, and what mere myth? Only *spoken* knowledge, handed down through the generations from wise man to pupil, over and over, can offer us such integrity—should any of our number speak lies, his fellows will likely catch him at it, whereas the lies of a man who writes books will long outlive him, with no one left to tell of his deceptions!"

Stroking his beard slowly, Caliphestros studies Veloc for a few silent moments. "He is either more intelligent than he sounds and appears," the old man muses quietly, "or wholly unaware that he has grazed a deep truth. And I am not certain which I find the more disconcerting . . ." Coming out of this reverie, Caliphestros fixes his grey gaze on Keera again. "And so, my sharp-eyed girl—you saw something in Stasi's face, before we were interrupted. I believe so, at any rate."

"I may be wrong, of course, lord," Keera carefully murmurs. "But—it is a thing I have noticed, a thing that certain animals, even though they be as different as man to panther, can sense in each other. The loss—the death—of a loved one. Loved *ones*."

Caliphestros's brow ripples suddenly with profound sorrow. "You have lost children?"

"Not—yet," Keera answers softly. "But . . . my husband. The only man I have ever loved." She nods quickly, without turning, in the direction of her companions. "Loved, that is, as a wife should—with affection, admiration, and—"

There follows a pause, which Caliphestros fills for the modest Keera: "And *desire,* my girl. Eh?" At a quick nod from her, the old man elaborates: "There is no shame in it, Keera, nor embarrassment, save for those who have never known such love. Was it the illness that has struck your people?"

Keera's lips tremble, much as the old man's did, only an instant earlier; and in her desperation to maintain her dignity, she lets the fact that Caliphestros seems to already know of the plague in Okot pass. "He—he was taken, just a few days ago. The pestilence has come to several parts of the town we call Okot. Two of my children are also—" Keera fights back the tide of weeping that is rising in her breast and throat; but a lone tear finally escapes, to fall heavily upon her cheek, and drift down it.

The panther sets her pointed, tufted ears sharply forward, and picks her proud head up. But her green eyes fix, not on the forest about the camp, but on what seems to be Keera's face. *Or is it her throat?* Veloc and Heldo-Bah ask each other with quick, worried glances. Then, leaving Caliphestros on his perch, and in one almost impossibly agile movement, the panther almost *pours* herself from the elm to the ground, upon which she begins to walk softly toward the Bane female.

As Heldo-Bah covers his face in panic and horror, Veloc quickly lifts his short bow over his shoulder and nocks an arrow, all his pompous, foolish posturing vanishing as he executes the expert motion. He then draws the bow, aiming at the panther's chest.

"Keera!" he cries. "Move aside—run, I have no shot!"

"Lower your bow, historian!" Caliphestros orders, raising an arm and outstretching a hand in seeming threat. "Such foolhardy aggression can only anger, not harm, both my companion and myself!"

Keera, who has been staring into the eyes of the beast, only nods and holds the splayed fingers of one hand out behind her. "It's all right, Veloc. Put the bow away . . ."

{ii:}

"I WILL NOT PUT IT AWAY," Veloc says, raising his outstretched bow arm to take aim, now, at Caliphestros. "If I cannot hit the animal, old man, then *you* will suffer for it, unless you truly have charms that can stop an arrow!"

Caliphestros sighs once. "I should hardly be much of a 'sorcerer,' if I did not, historian." The old man seems no longer concerned, now that Veloc's arms have moved, despite the arrow's threatening his own life. Seeing this, Veloc's draw on his bow begins to relax. "You have some little bit of your sister's wisdom, then," the old man goes on. "Good. For you have nothing to fear, in this . . ." He keeps the same hand held out, but turns the palm upward as he indicates Keera and the panther.

As he allows the draw on his powerful bow to ease further, Veloc stares in bewilderment at the masterful huntress who is approaching Keera: remarkably, there is no malice or hunger in the animal's expression, and her body betrays no hint that she is stalking. Although confused and a little uneasy, Keera stands her ground well; and when her face is level with the panther's, there being but a few feet between them, she can see that the cat means her no harm.

"You have a way with creatures, I see, Keera—and they with you," Caliphestros says quietly. "Yes . . . a great gift. I know only one other like you . . ." But the old man can speak no more of the matter, apparently; and his jaw sets, trembling just enough to indicate a battle raging inside him.

The panther's nose, deep red and looking as tough as hide, nonetheless is delicacy itself when it moves to a spot just a few inches from Keera's face—close enough for the Bane tracker to hear the surprisingly gentle sniffing and whistling sounds, as well as the short, ever so short breaths of air, that escape from it.

Having found the precise spot on Keera's face where the single tear fell, the white panther sniffs ever more delicately at the small trace of salt and moisture that remain; and then she reveals her rough, pink tongue. Even as her breath speaks of the kills she has made only recently, the barest tip of that long organ licks the tear and its track gently away from Keera's face . . .

Keera trembles throughout her body; but the quivering calms as trust grows along with it, and the beginning of a bond is formed. When the tracker starts to lift a hand, she glances up at Caliphestros, as if to ask his leave to touch the creature.

"I think you will be safe, now," the old man answers, reassured by Stasi's actions that he has been right to trust these three Bane, and especially this young Bane woman.

Keera, meanwhile, runs one small hand along the panther's arching, solidly muscular neck, and then her fingers move up to scratch behind the animal's ear. At that, the panther begins to purr once more, and to lick Keera's face with less delicacy, yet more delight.

"It would seem," Caliphestros says, "that Stasi has understood you precisely, Keera."

" 'Stasi,' " the Bane woman murmurs, smiling in friendship and still caressing and scratching the panther's head and neck. "What does it mean?"

"It means that she is a creature of rebirth," Caliphestros replies. "Of resurrection—as you will soon discover . . ." He laughs affectionately when he sees the panther put one paw to Keera's left shoulder and the other on her right, keeping most of her weight on her hind legs, and still delicately cleaning the Bane woman's face, and then her neck and hair: precisely as she would if Keera were a cub of her own. In the midst of this seemingly impossible moment, only Veloc continues to look momentarily alarmed, but Caliphestros dismisses the Bane's brotherly concern with a wave of his hand. "You need not fear, Veloc," he calls. "She is only making a new friend—and a new friend who doubtless offers far more amusement than the sole companion she has had these ten years."

"Ten years?" Heldo-Bah echoes. "You have been in that cave with this beast for ten years? Scant wonder you're mad, old man."

"Heldo-Bah!" Veloc scolds.

"Oh, calm yourself, Veloc," Heldo-Bah replies. "If he could have transformed us into toads, he would have done so when you threatened to kill him."

"You suppose yourself as cunning as you are repulsive, eh, forager?" Caliphestros calls to Heldo-Bah. "Well, I warn you—put aside any belief that, simply because I am not all the things that fearful, ignorant men say, I am therefore wholly without—*arts* . . ." Heldo-Bah's expression changes with its characteristic speed, back to youthfully apprehensive; but Caliphestros's next words are calculated to put him, as well as the other two Bane, more at their ease: "Although there is no reason that those who shall now become our common enemies in Broken need ever learn anything I have told or will tell you about either my 'arts' or their limits."

Keera glances up at the old man. "You speak of our undertaking a 'common' endeavor against Broken, my lord. If you have been listening to our argument for any length of time, you know that we have come to ask for your help against the Tall, who, it seems, have at last determined to destroy our tribe, through methods as horrible as they are cowardly. Do your words mean that you intend to give us such assistance?"

"Give?" Caliphestros puzzles with the word for a moment. "Certainly, we shall make common cause, Keera. But please—let us undertake further discussion in the home I share with Stasi, or rather, the home which she has kindly shared with me these many years." Making a few clicking, whistling noises, Caliphestros attempts to summon the panther, who by now is on her back upon the forest floor, allowing Keera to softly caress her belly. "Come, Stasi!" the old man calls out. "We have much to do, and you must first get me out of this tree . . ."

Gathering up his various crutches, which have been hidden among the branches of the elm, Caliphestros waits until the panther bounds back to the tree and up into its branches. She positions herself so that the old man can easily regain his customary position astride her back, just behind her enormously powerful shoulders, and then she carefully bears him back down to the ground.

"My compliments, Lord Caliphestros," Veloc says. "You have trained the animal well."

"And you," the old man answers, settling more comfortably onto Stasi's back, now that the astounding pair are on the ground, "are an ignorant ass, Veloc, if you believe that so proud and strong-willed a being as a Davon panther—and most especially *this* Davon panther—can be 'trained' by such feeble creatures as men. Every step, every decision she takes, she determines for herself. There are no masters or servants, here, Veloc—remember that, if you want to survive the great undertaking upon which we now embark."

Heldo-Bah releases a scoffing grunt in the direction of his friend. "You bootlicking fool . . ." He then lifts his chin toward Caliphestros's crutches. "What are those mechanisms you have, old man?" he asks, even a little haughtily, now. "They don't bespeak any great wizardry."

As he straps himself onto his platform and single "leg," then uses his crutches to get upright and stand free of Stasi's support, Caliphestros eyes Heldo-Bah just menacingly enough to emphasize his next point: "I may in fact be old, forager, and half the man I once was; but I do not stink to the Heavens, nor do I assume pompous airs with new acquaintances whose true powers I have not yet divined, and whose help I desperately need. Therefore—call me anything save 'my lord,' from this point onward, and you'll know the less friendly things that a 'sorcerer' and a panther can do . . ."

Hobbling to the spot where Keera stands and appearing momentarily concerned, Caliphestros lifts one hand from a crutch and quickly points at Veloc and Heldo-Bah. "I have much equipment and other supplies, Keera, that must make the trip to Okot with us—but I believe that you and your brother can manage what Stasi and I cannot." Pausing, the old man speaks in greater confidence. "Is it really necessary that we let the fool, there, live? Or, if we must let him live, can we not send him ahead of us to Okot?"

"He will complain, my lord," Keera answers. "But he has the ability to carry both delicate and weighty goods. And, in the event that we meet any scouting parties come out from Broken, or our own Outragers . . ."

Caliphestros nods, not impressed, but acquiescent. "I see—a man of violent talents, is he? And looks the part. Very well, then. Let us at least get a good meal into our bellies, while I pack the necessary supplies, and then a few hours' sleep upon goose down, before we begin. Bane foragers, if I am not mistaken, prefer to travel by night, as does Stasi. And so, we shall depart when the Moon is well up. We have a most important errand to attend to before we make for Okot."

"Goose down and good food?" says Heldo-Bah. "I like you better already, O Lord and Mighty Caliphestros!"

He is about to clap a good-natured hand on Caliphestros's shoulder; but the old man turns, making the foolish forager as stone with but a glance. "Touching my person, along with sarcasm, is to be included among those things in which you indulge only at peril of your life, Heldo-Bah." Looking away once more, the old man murmurs, "An absurd name—I can but assume that the person who gave it to you intended it as a grim jest."

"And most of my life has been just such, my lord," Heldo-Bah replies, at which Caliphestros cannot help but chuckle. He has never suffered fools with grace; but those who, in some deep recess of their souls, know the extent and truth of their own foolishness, can often be a different matter, and he begins to suspect that Heldo-Bah is one such.

Keera speaks with continuing respect, but boldly. "But, my lord, what errand could be so important as to keep us from making directly for Okot?"

The old man reaches into the tunic that he wears beneath his robe, and draws out what seems a collection of flowers wrapped about a shining stick. He urges the confused Keera to approach, but she hesitates: along with her companions, she can see the mysterious gleam of gold among the blossoms and greenery, and Keera knows that sorcerous charms and spells can be cast with far humbler elements than gold and such wildflowers as these. At further and more insistent coaxing, however, the tracker finally draws close to Caliphestros—and is amazed to find that he is clutching a golden arrow precisely like those that the three foragers saw in the body of the dead soldier at the Fallen Bridge, and that around this arrow are entwined strands of moss, as well as the stems and petals of several particularly remarkable and renownèd flowers. The first are tightly formed bundles of yellow-green, their general form like the smallest of fir tree cones, but their texture and color far more vivid and full of life; the second is a small, star-shaped flower of the lightest yellow that grows in ample bunches; and last, there is a group of large, full but delicate flowers on thick stems, with shell-like purple petals and yellow anthers in a tight bunch at their cores.

Keera points first at the arrow. "But—that is—"

"Yes," says the old man, nodding, "taken from a body that, to judge by the look on your face, the three of you came upon, and recently. The moss that my—my *messenger* fetched up with it grows on the rocks and the trees above the Cat's Paw, particularly at those spots where the natural bridges lie, for there, the rock formations are most interspersed with soil to give the trees life enough to grow so tall. I suspect, in this case, that the arrow was taken near what your people call the Fallen Bridge."

Keera nods. "Yes," she murmurs, looking back to her brother, and seeing that he and Heldo-Bah are exchanging worried expressions.

"You need not fear it," Caliphestros tells Keera of the arrow. "The disease of the victim cannot linger upon it, certainly not since I cleaned it in a solution of lye and quicklime. Take it, then, and tell me what the flowers tell you . . ."

Keera grasps the shaft of the arrow, her body tingling; but the sensation stops, and her face grows puzzled, as she studies the flowers. "These two are no mystery." She indicates the smaller flowers: the clustered yellow-green, and then the yellow stars. "The first are mountain hops, which we cultivate in the Wood for trade to the Tall. They use it to brew a special beer,[†] a drink which drives their young men mad: they drink it in the Stadium in Broken, whether they participate in or merely watch the games there—and they crave it so desperately that we have been able to trade sacks of the hop flowers for instruments that our own healers require. These prettier blooms," the tracker continues, her finger trembling only slightly as it points to the star-shaped flowers, "are woad,[‡] which can be used to make blue dye, but also as a medicine for growths, especially inside the body. Only if the healer is wise, however, and knows the amount to employ." Caliphestros's pleasure at Keera's knowledge remains evident—and yet, she notices, something in his expression also indicates that he has expected no less from her; and so she attempts to speak with more confidence: "But these purple flowers—they are meadow bells,[†] and they are not found in Davon Wood, nor along the Cat's Paw, nor indeed anywhere, save the most fertile vales and plains. In Broken, they grow only in the Meloderna valley, that I have ever heard."

"And their properties?" Caliphestros adds.

"They have many," Keera answers. "To ease the pains of women, and to ensure healthy births; indeed, to ease all pains of the stomach and the abdomen, as well as those of the bones, especially the spine; and to treat the most serious fevers."

"All true," says Caliphestros. "A formidable medicinal flower, especially given its delicacy and beauty. Now observe the stems of each plant—what do they tell you?"

Keera carefully studies the stems. "They were taken with a blade, certainly," she answers. "The hops and woad you might have gathered yourself, my lord, here on the mountain—but how did you come by the meadow bells? And the arrow, as well?"

Caliphestros begins haltingly, "I have—*persuaded* an acquaintance of mine to fetch me a new store of the meadow bells, early each spring, which is its season. I received these, along with the arrow, just before I came here today."

"Whoever this acquaintance is, my lord," Heldo-Bah observes, impressed by this tale, "he is loyal and has stones—from here to the Cat's Paw, and to the Meloderna beyond, would be a deadly journey, for a mere collection of flowers and an almost worthless amount of gold."

Caliphestros looks up at the treetops in irritation, then murmurs to Keera: "Does one become accustomed to the interruptions—should we truly not rid ourselves of him now?"

"He has his uses, as I say. But I cannot promise that you will ever grow accustomed to his foolish remarks."

Caliphestros nods in acquiescence. "Very well, then—examine the stems of the flowers. What do the marks of the knife on them tell you?"

"The flowers are too valuable and too fragile to take for mere decoration, or to be cut with scythe or sickle," Keera answers, puzzled at first;

but her consternation is short-lived. "But their main purpose is a healing one—each, in its own way, can play a part in fighting the most serious of fevers."

"And so . . . ?"

"So—there is fever, along the Meloderna—deadly fever, if they are harvesting such plants in large amounts." She pauses, drawing a quick breath. "Is the plague, then, at work in Broken, as well as in the Okot?"

"If plague it be," Caliphestros replies. "Certainly, there is a terrible fever at work somewhere in the kingdom of the God-King—likely in *many* places, if, as you say, the flowers are being harvested in such quantities that my messenger could readily find them in piles."

"And the arrow?" Keera asks. "It tells us the man was killed by the priests of Broken, but not why—and his death occurred far from the Meloderna."

"True. It does not enlighten us as to why he was killed—not completely. But enough for now—we shall discuss all this further, within Stasi's cave. Help your fellows, there, and then join us as soon as you can."

The old man begins to hobble away again, the great panther taking up her watchful position, just far enough behind him to have an unobstructed view of the foragers, who observe the pair's departure with three puzzled faces.

{*iii:*}

"HIS MIND CERTAINLY SEEMS unaffected by all he has endured," Veloc judges, watching Caliphestros and the seemingly magical white panther disappear over the next ridge. "Although I'll wager his talk of not being a sorcerer is a ruse."

"Do you fault him?" Keera asks. "Look what his punishment for that title was, from the God-King and the priests of Kafra."

The conversation is interrupted by a sudden flutter of wings: the small, active wings of a speckled bird that descends onto a branch just above the foragers, clicking its beak and clucking from its throat.

"*Te-kamp!*" the bird blurts, still flapping its wings energetically at the Bane. "*Te-kamp! Kaw-ee-fess-tross!*"

Keera eyes her disbelieving friends. "I think you have a small hint as to his powers as a sorcerer, Veloc," she says. Then, to the bird, she calls, "Tell your master not to worry. We shall not be long!"

But the bird makes no move.

"Oh, splendid . . . ," Heldo-Bah grumbles, as the three foragers set about breaking their camp. "Must I now mind my mouth around every animal in Davon Wood, lest it report back to that old cripple?"

"For now," Veloc replies, "I'd recommend it. And I'd recommend learning a few new phrases of address for him, Heldo-Bah. It's plain we don't know what he actually is, or what power he has over how many and which of these beings."

"True, brother," Keera agrees, kicking dirt atop their smoldering fire and still studying the starling admiringly—for she has rightly begun to suspect that the bird's speech has been the result of long acquaintance, not sorcery. "And did you take note of one thing, particularly? The effortless manner in which he persuades the panther to do his bidding—does it not remind you of someone?"

Veloc claps a hand to his forehead. "That witch of a priestess—she showed precisely the same art!"

"Well," Heldo-Bah says doubtfully. "Not *precisely* the same art. I don't think the old man uses seduction upon—that is . . . Oh, no . . ." As so often happens, the gap-toothed grin of confident skepticism instantly becomes an expression of shocked fear. "Does he?"

"No, I don't believe anything of the sort," Keera says. "The similarity is only in the silent, practiced manner of communicating; and it is no coincidence, I'll wager."

"Exactly so, Keera," says Veloc. "To find one such being is improbable enough, but *two*—and both of the royal circle, in which they must have moved for at least a few of the same years? Why, sister, he said it himself: 'I *know* only one other like you.' Yes, he bears watching, our new friend. Clever as a stoat, for all his being legless."

Keera holds up a hand, considering the matter for a moment, and then finally whispers: "You are right, Veloc—he did not say he *knew* one other with such a gift. 'I *know* only one other . . .' Those were indeed his words."

"You suspect he yet communicates with the Kafran priestess?" Veloc asks.

Keera cocks her head, puzzling with it. "Not as we understand it, certainly. But two mortals who can command the mightiest of forest spirits?

One old, one young—is it not likely that the one taught the other? And if the other is indeed not only a priestess, but a Wife of Kafra . . . I do not like to think it, for I believe he is a good man who truly wants and means to help us. But his soul is as scarred as his legs, and his thoughts have been made obscure by the deceit and treachery of Broken's rulers. Until we are certain of the pattern of their twists and turns, I think we must keep our encounter with the priestess from him . . ."

So great does Keera's preoccupation with these thoughts become that she not only falls behind her brother and Heldo-Bah as they make for Caliphestros's camp, but nearly stumbles headlong into the old man's enormous herb garden, with its rich, almost overpowering blend of aromas, before realizing that they have arrived at their destination. Only as her head is sent swimming by those same scents does Keera hear the calls of Veloc and Heldo-Bah, who are already by the mouth of the cave wherein Caliphestros and Stasi have lived for so long; and, taking a few moments to appreciate the other seemingly impossible aspects of the grounds outside the cave (particularly the forge, with its marvelously engineered chimney of stone and mortar, in which the foragers' host has created, by the look of the area about the thing, many essential tools, as well as fascinating scientific implements, over the years) Keera finally joins the others, her happiness growing, once again, as the panther bounds toward her when she appears at the cave entrance.

Yet no amount of speculation based on what they have seen outside the cave can prepare any of the foragers for what Caliphestros and Stasi have achieved within: for the den's appointments are almost stupefying.

"You could give our Groba a welcome lesson in the comfortable furnishing of caves, old man," Heldo-Bah declares, throwing himself upon Caliphestros's own large sack of goose down, but quickly getting to his feet again when the panther growls low and turns toward him. "But how did you manage it all?" the gap-toothed forager continues, joining Veloc and making no attempt, for a few moments, to dilute his amazement with sarcasm.

"Aye," Veloc agrees. "It is achievement enough for any man, but you, wounded—nay, mutilated!—as you found yourself upon arriving here, how was it, how *has* it been possible?"

Caliphestros indicates the panther, and then begins to hobble toward her, feeling a most pointed confusion of heart and mind that is caused by the unprecedented sight and sounds of other humans moving about settings that have ever been his own and hers alone. "I never could have managed it without the assistance—always given ere it was ever asked—of Stasi. I should never have survived, if not for her help."

As he reaches the panther, Caliphestros scratches behind her tall ears, requesting affection and receiving, without doubt, much; but Stasi also maintains her position by Keera.

"You have made a true friend," Caliphestros muses to the tracker, allowing the slight—and, he knows, somewhat absurd—jealousy that he feels to reveal itself plainly in the tone of his words.

"She honors me, my lord," Keera says. "But such adversities as the two of you have conquered together must surely have marked you as forever her closest friend."

"And here are your vaunted books, my lord," Veloc calls, having reached one of Caliphestros's rough-hewn shelves in the cave walls, upon which sit many of the former Second Minister of Broken's volumes. "Even in a cave, so many—yet have they truly aided the creation of this wondrous home?"

"More than you could likely comprehend, Veloc," the old man answers. "These are but a small part of the collection that I brought with me to Broken, and built upon during my years there. And, with a few exceptions, they were chosen because they had some relevance to my survival in this place, and to the final reckoning with Broken that I first prayed, then later hoped, and finally believed would come: hence, as you see, I have pored time and again over examinations of history and medicine, of science and war, and of the realms in which science and war merge—those of metallurgy and chemistry."

Heldo-Bah, having detected attractive aromas emerging from a large iron pot that sits on the edge of the cookstove's surface, has begun to lift its lid; but at these last words, he drops it noisily. "*Alchemy!*" he cries, glancing from Veloc to Keera quickly. "So—that is why they exiled you from Broken!"

Caliphestros only tilts his head judiciously. "If, by that ridiculous outburst, you mean to say that the rulers of the great city and its kingdom were, in the end, as superstitious, ignorant, and hostile to reason and knowledge as yourself, Heldo-Bah, then you are correct."

"Oho!" the impertinent forager scoffs. "You call alchemy reason, do you? And attempting to transform base metals into gold is evidence of high scientific wisdom, I suppose? Tell me, then—do you also abuse yourself out in the great Wood, spending your seed into holes in the ground and attempting to grow tiny men like vegetables?"[†]

Caliphestros sighs, heavily. "Only imagine the blessèd silence, Keera, were he gone . . . He would feel little pain, I promise you: only the brief stab of Stasi's largest teeth into the great artery of his neck, and his life's blood would quickly and quietly stream away . . ."[‡]

Keera laughs quietly (for she has ceased to believe, rightly, that the old man intends Heldo-Bah actual harm), and says only, "We seem to have far too many things to pack and carry, my lord, to allow the loss of even one bearer. And, as I have said, he can carry a great deal."

"Very well. I shall trust your word, and let the matter rest." Lifting his head to call to the sharp-toothed Bane again, Caliphestros says, "Heldo-Bah, allow me to propose a more practical test of what you ignorantly call 'alchemy': the weapons that you and Veloc carry—I believe that I noted two rather well-crafted short-swords of Broken manufacture among them. Is this so?"

"Indeed it is," Heldo-Bah crows. "Veloc's was taken, just days ago, from one of our own Outragers, who had stolen it, I suspect, while undertaking one of his errands of murder and imagined justice for the Moon priestess. My own, however, came directly from a member of Lord Baster-kin's Guard, whom I myself subdued!" And with that, Heldo-Bah unsheathes the sword and brings it out from under his cloak, holding its unarguably fine blade out toward his host.

Caliphestros nods silently, taking one or two steps toward Heldo-Bah and seemingly impressed by both the blade and its origins. But then it becomes plain that he has stepped less toward Heldo-Bah than in the direction of his own bedding, where, in a quick movement not at all encumbered by his crutches, he reaches beneath his sack of goose down and produces a sword of his own. Though not so elegant as either Heldo-Bah's or Veloc's, especially in the crafting of its hilt, handle, and pommel, the sword nevertheless has a peculiar and impressive effect on the three Bane, achieved primarily through the ripples of cold blue-grey that seem shot through its carefully honed, single-edged blade of moderate length.

"And suppose I were to tell you," the old man says amiably, still holding his weapon out and toward Heldo-Bah, who uneasily but quickly moves his own blade into a position of defense, "that I could offer you something better—far better, in fact? Would you still cling so tightly to your prize?"

Further unnerved by Caliphestros's attitude—which is less one of threat than of confidence—Heldo-Bah says only, "If you think to trick me into some sort of barter for that unadorned slab of steel, old man, I tell you that you would as likely persuade me to put my head in your companion's maw."

Once again, Caliphestros nods with seeming indifference; he then moves his own blade up and down casually, gripping its deerskin-wrapped handle with his right hand lightly—

And suddenly, in a pair of movements that seem to the foragers far too quick for a crippled old man to achieve, Caliphestros releases the pressure of his right armpit on the corresponding crutch, letting it clatter to the cave floor as he shifts all of his weight leftward, onto his wooden leg and remaining crutch. Even as he does this, he raises his right arm and his sword swiftly and brings the strangely tinted length of steel down with great force on Heldo-Bah's blade. When all is still once more, Heldo-Bah stands in precisely the same attitude, save that his eyes have gone wide as they look down to see that the prize he took from the unfortunate young member of Lord Baster-kin's Guard has been severed by Caliphestros's seemingly humble blade. The piercing tip of the Bane's once-proud trophy, along with more than a foot of the best Broken steel, now lie on the cave floor.

{*iv:*}

CALIPHESTROS EXAMINES the cutting edge of his own sword, and frowns slightly. "Hmm—not so clean as I would have liked," he says calmly. "I seem to have nicked the edge of my blade, a bit . . ."

"Truly?" Veloc says in amazed derision. "Nicked it *a bit*? How unacceptable . . ."

Heldo-Bah's head slowly shakes in disbelief, before nodding with envy; and finally, when he regains his complete composure, he casts his diminished sword to the cave floor as thoughtlessly as he stole it. He then fairly leaps to Caliphestros's side, and anxiously indicates the blade that Keera has also moved closer to examine. "May I—Lord Caliphestros, may I have this one? It's only fair, after all, now that you've rendered mine useless."

Caliphestros shrugs. "If you wish," he says. "I have several more like it."

Heldo-Bah takes Caliphestros's sword from the old man and gauges its weight. "So light!" he pronounces. "By the Moon, Veloc—we could sweep through the Tall as though they were so much wheat, had we blades like this!"

"Aye, Heldo-Bah," Veloc replies, "I can already envision the historical epics I shall compose and relate, concerning the swords of the Bane that dealt mighty blows to the Tall and their kingdom."

Caliphestros's tone turns momentarily harsh. "You will be tempted to think you can achieve such feats, as would almost any people who have been maligned and subdued for so long, and who suddenly find themselves offered the chance for forceful redress; but *the weapons are useless unless one learns the proper ways in which to use them.* Repeat that phrase to yourself, Heldo-Bah, from now till we reach Okot; nay, until we find ourselves, one day, before the gates of Broken itself. And if you can believe it, at length, and make your people believe it, then we may, we just *may,* succeed . . ."

Turning to the cookstove and lifting the lid of the pot to find that its contents have begun to softly bubble and pop, Caliphestros fetches several earthenware bowls and spoons, as well as a ladle (the utensils all carved from a tightly grained wood), and then sets the collection of objects on his rough-hewn table. "But before this process can begin, much less be mastered, we must work, eat, and then sleep. My admittedly theatrical exhibition was intended only to hearten your spirits about the struggle to come—not to slow our progress."

"And you have achieved your object, old fellow," Heldo-Bah declares. "Now, let us finish the packing of your possessions, that we may consume this fare—for if you can cook stew as well as you can steel, Lord of Feathers and Fangs, it shall be satisfying, indeed!"

In this way—by the portentous shattering of a single sword—is formed an odd yet fast friendship between the most infamous person in Broken's history and the three Bane foragers upon whom the mantle "saviors of their tribe" rests most precariously.

The stew is, even Heldo-Bah must admit, a most excellent concoction, not least because it is flavored with all manner of herbs and heartened by roots and greens, all taken from Caliphestros's own garden. Of course, the fact that the three foragers have been swiftly running and somewhat madly searching for most of the last three days and nights would make almost any food palatable, at this moment. But so genuinely satisfying is Caliphestros's stew, and so much do his guests consume, that, by the time all the packed sacks have been set by the cave entrance, the three Bane are more than ready to seek out places among the many large bags filled with the down of various birds that cushion the cave's hard rock. Exhausted and sated, the foragers fairly collapse onto these welcome spots to sleep away the few idle hours they have been allowed, ere nightfall signals their departure.

For his part, Caliphestros attempts sleep, as does Stasi, the latter lying on her side at the foot of her companion's bedding, vigilantly lifting her head whenever a sound is captured by her exceptional ears, in order to assure herself that the Bane men are indeed slumbering harmlessly. In time, however, this duty becomes plainly unnecessary, and the great white panther rises, glances once more about the cave, and then walks slowly to its entrance, where three heavy deerskin sacks, as well as two lighter bags, sit waiting for their bearers to rise. Stasi will now sit and stand guard from this spot, and at first, she thinks to do this duty alone; but her wakefulness has brought her companion out of his comparatively light slumber, for they are as alive to each other's restiveness as any two humans who have lived together for many years. Caliphestros drags himself across the cave, using the arms that have grown powerful in the absence of his legs to swing his half-body forward, and reaches the spot where Stasi now sits, her hind legs tucked beneath her, her forelegs side by side in front of her, and her powerful neck holding her head in an easy but alert position.

Caliphestros makes a small, affectionate sound of greeting, one that he is glad the three Bane cannot hear, for he does not wish them to think him overly sentimental. Yet his watchfulness, at this moment, is not a matter of sentiment alone: for often, on pleasant evenings when the pair have found themselves abroad in Davon Wood long past nightfall, Caliphestros has noticed Stasi's wont to climb some log or large stone and fix her eyes on the distant sight of the small lights that flicker atop the great mountain to the northeast. The old man has always been able to see—in the panther's strikingly expressive eyes, in her steady, low growls of threat, and in a distinct tightening of those muscles which all cats, the greater as well as the lesser, employ during their deadliest maneuver, the *pounce*—that Stasi long ago identified those lights as marking the den of her enemies. Caliphestros has usually seized the chance to speak to her, at these moments, and tell her of the day when they must and will scale the distant, shadowy mountain, and fight against the humans in the city that crowns it. And so he believes sincerely, this evening, that the panther understands that the moment when they must undertake their great, shared object has arrived.

The old scholar leans his left side against Stasi's nearest shoulder, and together they sit and observe for what may be a final time the gardens before their cave and the forest beyond them, which are illuminated by the twilight that seems to slice open the highest mountain ridge far to the west. From there, the light is fractured by the countless new leaves that cover the boughs of trees far and near, and finally comes to burnish both the colors in and about the old man's gardens and Stasi's unique coat. The panther's near-white fur absorbs and then reissues the fading sunlight, until she seems to become even more than usually apparitional. But there is nothing otherworldly about her movements. Stasi's head remains up and constantly moving, just as her tail continuously swipes from side to side as she warily glances in the direction of what seems every noise produced by the surrounding Wood, Caliphestros determines that his words continue all the while to sharpen both her alertness and her desire that they at last be on their way, and so he continues his soft yet passionate monologue.

The foragers, however, never wake, making it necessary for the pair at the mouth of the cave to continue waiting, if only for a short while longer. But as they do, and as the old man whispers still more words into the white panther's ear concerning their coming, shared vengeance, Caliphestros suddenly notices in Stasi's expression a new aspect. It is an expression of longing, that much is plain, but longing for what? Revealed in those dazzling green eyes that comprehend all that lies before them and many things far beyond are powerful emotions that burn deep in the panther's heart, emotions that Caliphestros has seen her display during their life together, but never with this suggestion that what she longs for is beyond this cave, this companion, this life, and will give her greater reward than that which is to be had with the mere sight of her enemies' suffering: it will, in fact, restore at least one among the missing pieces of her spirit—

"What is it, my girl?" Caliphestros whispers, his voice full of urgent curiosity. He pulls himself round to face her, and places his hands on each side of her noble head. "You would have more than blood—I see this. More than killing, richly deserved though the killing may be—but what?"

Stasi's steady gaze never breaks, however; and she offers no hint to her companion of what the unprecedented longing he has detected might be.

But this display has not escaped another mind present: for, unnoticed by the old man, Keera has suddenly yet silently woken, and has spent the last few moments using her remarkable ears and mind to listen to and try to comprehend Caliphestros's moment of worried confusion. And, slowly, the tracker realizes that she saw something similar earlier in the day, something in the great cat that the old man evidently has not himself seen, yet, and, even more essentially, *cannot* see; cannot, Keera detects, by simple virtue of his sex, and of his never having fathered children.

The two Bane men finally start from their own beddings, upon the first cry of what sounds like a Davon dog-owl.[†] *Yet this bird must be unusually large, if it is indeed a dog-owl,* Keera judges silently. Just what has prompted such an alarm, the Bane tracker cannot say, the area outside the cave being out of her sight; but she wonders if the as-yet-unknown creature is without, standing guard; and so she stands, herself, to carefully look out the mouth of the cave into the semi-darkness, attempting to see what might be the cause—

"It is always so, Keera, at this time of the evening," Caliphestros says aloud, startling her; for he has made not the slightest move to turn in her direction. "It is fledging season, and the dog-owls are on the watch for ravens and hawks that would take their little ones, or younger owls who would usurp their domains. There is a pair who have returned to the hollow of a large maple tree just above this cave for as long as I have been in the Wood, and the male has only heightened his defiance of all enemies, over the years." For the time, this is the explanation that Keera must agree to; although not without her own ploys of conversation:

"An unusually long time for a male dog-owl, much less a couple, to have survived and bred yearly in the same nest, my lord," Keera says, allowing suspicion to taint her words.

"Blasted creatures," Heldo-Bah grunts, scratching at his groin and arse with one hand and his head with the other, and presenting an appearance that would be merely comical, were it not so vile. "Dog-owls! The most unpleasant way in the world to be woken . . ." He holds a hand up to Keera quickly. "And yet, I know, we must respect all owls, Keera— for they are mystical heralds of the Moon . . ."

"So they are," Keera replies sternly, "and you are wise to withdraw one of your own blasphemous outcries, at last. For the Moon despises those who mock or abuse her night-flyers, and demands that such fools be tormented severely—and promptly."

"You would think that the Moon would have tired of tormenting me long ago," Heldo-Bah mumbles.

Within an hour, the foragers have helped Caliphestros tidy, seal off, and disguise the entrance to what he insists is "Stasi's cave." Heldo-Bah watches as the tracker and Veloc assist Caliphestros in taking his place atop Stasi's back, his own smaller bags over his shoulders. Both man and panther bid a brief farewell to the dwelling and grounds that have for so long been considered both mythical and mystical, not only among the Bane, but among those Tall who have heard the rumors of their existence; and then, the little troop that carries the hopes of the Bane tribe, in the form of books and instruments that the foragers cannot begin to read or comprehend, finally gets under way.

Not, however, at the speed that Caliphestros had insisted to the foragers would be necessary—not initially, at any rate. Instead, the old man explains that one additional leave-taking is necessary. So earnest and even grave is his manner, when he makes this statement, that even Heldo-Bah offers neither opinion nor argument; instead, when Caliphestros requests ignition for a small torch he produces after getting atop Stasi, the gap-toothed Bane quickly produces a flint and his gutting knife, using the blunt side of the heavy blade to strike the stone and, after several attempts, obliging the old man. Then, at no more than a steady if brisk walk, the travelers make their way farther west, to an icy feeder stream that, Caliphestros tells his new allies, has often been his quickest source of relief from the persistent agonies of his wounds; but the old man indicates silence again as the party start downhill in a northerly direction, along a worn path next to the stream, walking for some minutes before they reach a small clearing, where the slope of the mountainside levels for a short distance. Apparently, this is their destination: Stasi takes Caliphestros to a fallen tree on the eastern edge of the level clearing, and gently dips her forelegs and turns her neck so that he can take a seat upon it, without being forced to strap himself back into his walking apparatus. The three Bane, in the meantime, look about, by the light of Caliphestros's wavering torch, in utter bewilderment.

As they do, Stasi slowly walks toward what appear to be two burial mounds at the center of the clearing, while Caliphestros urges the foragers to keep well back. And when Keera asks what is taking place, he begins to tell the tale that he has assembled, bit by bit, of Stasi's murdered children, explaining that the mounds before them are the final resting places of two of her cubs—the pair that were speared and trampled to death by Broken hunters and their servants, in full view of their wounded mother, and left to rot. Caliphestros speaks so passionately, for the first time since meeting the three Bane, that it quickly becomes apparent to the foragers that, if anyone in the seemingly impossible friendship between mutilated man and powerful beast is "enthralled," it is the supposèd sorcerer himself, and not the panther, as the foragers initially believed.

Hearing the hideous tale of brutal murder naturally deepens Keera's profound sympathy for the panther; and when she sees Stasi climb a nearby rocky ledge, and then begin to issue the long, low cry that seems a summons, not only to her stolen children, but to the spirits of those whose bones lie under the mounds of stone and Earth that are now before her, Keera is moved enough to approach the creature (something that Caliphestros has never dared, at such moments, out of respect for Stasi's grief). And then, before the eyes of the three men, some shielded path of communication between the two females, a path that had been indicated earlier in the day, now opens fully, plainly apparent for even Heldo-Bah to see. Keera mounts the rocks, puts her own head to the panther's neck, and with her looks up and northeasterly to see:

"Broken," the tracker announces to the others. "She can see the ac-cursèd city from this spot—as can I . . ."

For long moments, only the night creatures of Davon Wood are au-dible in the little clearing; and despite the impatience of Heldo-Bah, Cal-iphestros makes certain that none of the three men say or do anything to interrupt the deepening of the remarkable bond between what are now the two leaders of the newly reshaped woodland party, Keera and Stasi. Only when that pair descend from the rocks willingly and take up their respective burdens does the group set out again.

{v:}

THE PARTY REACHES the rocky gorges of the upper Cat's Paw before the creeping indigo of dawn has even begun to transform the sky—a sky that is once again fully visible only in broad, Moonlit swaths, between the overhanging branches of the trees that so desperately grasp the rocks on both sides of the ever-furious river. Once on those rocks, both Keera and Stasi slow their steps for the first time, respecting the danger of the slippery shelves of flat, massive stone that, when covered with leaves and moss, set perhaps the deadliest series of natural traps in the already lethal Wood.

This slackening of pace offers a new opportunity for conversation; and Veloc, attempting to impress Caliphestros with his historian's skills, courteously asks the old man to explain the most essential facts of his long and interesting life, that the handsome, ambitious Bane may begin the composition of a *Heldenspele*,[†] the heroic narratives that are passed from generation to generation of Bane historians, to ensure that the tribe never loses its unity, as well as its unique sense of itself. Bane children can best learn their place in the world, Veloc explains, by hearing the songs and stories, not only of the tribe's own heroes, but of those outsid-ers who have occasionally allied themselves with the tribe. Caliphestros is plainly flattered: it has been a very long time since the old man experi-enced the sensation of being appreciated by a society of human beings of *any* kind. And so, he agrees to Veloc's request—despite his awareness that such compliance will open the way for a new onslaught of dubious observations from Heldo-Bah.

And Heldo-Bah does not disappoint. Following the old man's cautiously limited but honest recitation of the start of his long life's tale, the skeptical Bane undertakes to dispel at least some of the aura surrounding the legendary man who travels with them.

"Now, a moment, please, O noble lord," Heldo-Bah calls from the rear of the little column. "You have told us that you originally came from the great northeastern trading lands, home to those tribes for whom buying, selling, and bartering are not mere ruses to make raiding and raping easier, as is the case with their cousins farther north, but a wholly different and more enlightened way of life."

Caliphestros simply smiles and laughs quietly, for he has also come to understand that many of Heldo-Bah's seeming insults, clownish or otherwise, mask a strangely fascinating willingness to do the distasteful work of actually attending to the safety of his tribe, and especially of his comrades, by determining the reliability of newcomers.

"Yes, my small friend," Caliphestros replies, echoing Heldo-Bah's impertinence with muted amusement. "That is what I told you."

" '*Small*'?" Heldo-Bah replies. "If I were without my feet and half my legs, and required the use of mechanical contrivances and legendary beasts to get about, I'm not certain I'd be so free with that kind of language, O Legless Lord."

"Perhaps not," says Caliphestros. "But then, never having had the trust of a legendary beast, I doubt that you are able to appreciate precisely the sense of security that such a bond brings."

At that instant, in a further demonstration of her remarkable intuition concerning human language, Stasi turns her head fully about, looking over her shoulder at Heldo-Bah just as a long, large drop of saliva falls from her panting tongue to the ground.

"Very well," the malodorous forager replies. "Let us stay away from such questions—what I particularly want to know is this: you say you studied, for the most part, in this city called Alexandria, in the grain kingdom of Egypt-land, where they let you cut up dead bodies to your peculiar heart's content; which was not the case in Broken, where you were forced to have your minions steal bodies before they were placed atop funeral pyres. And you became fascinated, you say, by the subject of diseases, and of plagues—and most especially by the Death itself."

"Your memory astounds me, Heldo-Bah," taunts the old man.

"And when the Mohammedans, displaying that infinite wisdom of

men who worship one entirely improbable god, conquered this Egypt-
land, and decided, after a brief period of uncertainty, that all you grave
robbers and body hackers should either go somewhere else or have your
own bodies hacked to pieces, you set out for the capital of still another
people who believe in one god, but who hold that their *one* can actually
be the sum of *three* deities—an only slightly less idiotic notion than that
of one almighty lord creating both all the good *and* all the evil in the
world."

"The Christ-worshippers may indeed hold beliefs that seem to turn
back on themselves, Heldo-Bah," Caliphestros concedes. "But I am not so
certain that they can be dismissed as 'idiotic.'"

"No?" queries the Bane. "Well, listen further, then: I have made a
study of their faith, and even conversed with that fool monk who has for
so long been wandering about from tribe to tribe and kingdom to kingdom. Surely you know of him, great traveler that you are—the lunatic
who cut down the ash tree of the Frankesh thunder god—"[†]

"*Winfred?*" Caliphestros queries, in such amazement that he almost
falls from Stasi's back. "You, Heldo-Bah, have discussed the Christ-
worshipper's religion with this man, who was given the name *Boniface* by
their supreme leader, after he crossed the Seksent Straits to undertake
his work?"

"The very fellow!" Heldo-Bah laughs. "'Vat of Turds'![‡] I shall never
forget his face when I explained to him why so many laughed at his 'holy'
name, in Broken—for it has the same sound, does it not? You know of
him, then, do you, wise man?"

Caliphestros nods slowly, still in profound amazement. "I knew him
quite well. It was before ever I saw Broken—indeed, I first journeyed to
that city in his company. I was living, then, at the abbey at Wearmouth,
across the Seksent Straits, in Britain. My friend—the historian Bede to
whom I have made reference, Veloc—was unusually curious concerning
science, for a Christ-worshipper. He had given me a chamber and a place
in their apothecary, where I worked for the abbey by day, and conducted
my own labors by night." His words coming to a sudden halt, Caliphestros looks at both Veloc and Keera, without seeming to actually see
them. "I have not spoken of all this since . . . by the heavens, for so many
years . . ." His body rattles suddenly, and he returns to his tale: "I met
Winfred there—he was a monk and a priest, seeking funds as well as

companions and followers for the great endeavor of converting the tribes and kingdoms hereabouts as well as farther north to the way of the Christ. I had heard many tales of the kingdom where the Kafran faith ruled, and was deeply curious about it. And so I packed my instruments and books, crossed the Seksent Straits in Winfred's company, and went on to the city upon the mountain. One of Winfred's first objects— although those of his faith called him Boniface, by then—was to convince the God-King Izairn to accept the Christ. He had heard that Broken was a mighty state, where law was maintained and commerce thrived, and that Izairn was a fair man, as indeed he was—"

"*Hak!*" Heldo-Bah exclaims with a laugh. "I did not know he ever attempted to play his holy tricks upon Broken's God-King—although he seemed fool enough to try. The last I heard of him, some few years ago, he was planning to convert the Varisians! Imagine it—those bloodthirsty rapists, attempting to live according to the Christ's babble about loving their enemies. I should like to know if he ever undertook that mad effort, and what became of him, if he did."[†] Seeing that Caliphestros either will not or cannot continue his own tale, for the moment, Heldo-Bah charges on: "At any rate, this fellow, this Boniface, had, as I suppose you know, been booted out of Broken, soon after he first entered the kingdom and city. He was doing his best to get back in, at the time I made his acquaintance. Indeed, I was to provide the horses for his followers, if they were ever allowed to return—although such was plainly unlikely."

"And I'm sure his party would have been safe, under your guidance and protection, Heldo-Bah," Caliphestros mocks softly.

"Indeed he would, for they had far too little gold to—" Catching himself before the indiscretion is voiced, Heldo-Bah declares: "The point that I am attempting to make, my lord, is that he and I spoke, several times, about this idea that three divine entities can be one god, and that the one thus produced should be praised as having authority over all the evil as well as all the good in this world. 'Yet how can this be so?' I asked of him. 'If your god is indeed three deities in one, and the one master of all, then his actions are either capricious, or tell us plainly that his mind remains badly cracked into warring parts.' And the next question I asked him, I will put to you, Lord of Woodland Wisdom: how, tell me, *how* can *one almighty* creature be so unmercifully wanton as to create and spread pestilences such as the Death, on the one hand, and yet, on the other, claim credit for what enjoyments and pleasantness this life offers? The entire proposition is madness!"

Caliphestros laughs quietly again, using a small swatch of cloth to wipe perspiration from his own brow, and then pouring a small amount of water from a skin into Stasi's upturned mouth, before drinking himself. "You Bane have a peculiarly perverse manner of arriving at the truth of things, or rather, at a *kind* of truth."

"Ah! But it *is* truth, eh, Wizard Lord?" Heldo-Bah declares in triumph.

"Let us say that it is," answers the old man, "and proceed to your point."

"Assuming you *have* one," Veloc chides quietly.

"I have made it already," Heldo-Bah scoffs. "See how my genius confounds the wise man! My *point* is merely that the more you learn of these one-god peoples, the more absurd they become . . ." Shaking his head, the forager continues, "And you, old man: what god did you find to worship, who seems to have preserved you during your foolish—but doubtless noble!—pursuit of the Death, only to snatch your legs from you for your merciful troubles?"

"Heldo-Bah!" Keera finally shouts, unable to endure her friend's endless disrespect and mockery.

"I am deeply sorry, Keera," Heldo-Bah replies, "but, sorcerer or no, noble intentions or not, what kind of fool follows the Death about from place to place?"

Keera is red-faced with rage, and Veloc, seeing this, calls out, "Can you not simply discuss the subject, Heldo-Bah, without recourse to insults and altercations?"

"Do not concern yourself, Veloc," Caliphestros says. "And I am honored by your indignation, Keera—but among the endless procession of ignorant assaults under which I have been trampled during my life, your friend's is actually one of the more amusing and even interesting varieties." Urging Stasi closer to Keera, Caliphestros continues to speak to her, but in confidence, now: "And my distraction and indulgence of both Heldo-Bah and your brother has a purpose, Keera. If what I suspect about the plague that has come to Broken as well as the Wood is indeed true, then we may catch the scent—*you* may catch the scent—of still more bodies among the rocks that line the Cat's Paw, as well as along the heights above it. Animal scents, in addition to human. All things dead near this river must be examined carefully if we are to solve this terrible puzzle."

Keera stands straighter as she walks, putting her nose into the westerly breeze. "I understand, my lord; although I cannot say that the task will prevent me from hurling a stone at Heldo-Bah's rude, ignorant mouth."

"You leave Heldo-Bah to me," Caliphestros laughs quietly.

Sighing once, Keera says, "Very well, my lord," and then turns her nose and her gaze in all directions. "We have passed the most deadly rocks, and dawn begins to make the remaining distance safer," she judges at length.

"What in the name of Kafra's foul face are you two scheming at?" Heldo-Bah shouts.

"Calm yourself, Heldo-Bah," replies Caliphestros. "And begin to temper the volume of your voice—for the river is narrowing, and I hardly need tell you who is on the other side. Baster-kin's men may be using the time they have left before their advance to search for those Bane who trussed one of their number and served him up to the wolves."

"Calm *yourself*, ancient one," Heldo-Bah says; yet he eyes the far side of the river uneasily. "Even if the Merchant Lord's men are there, they will likely not have heard me. These chasms do strange things to sound."

"You would stake your own life, and all of ours, on that proposition?" Caliphestros declares. "After all, Stasi and I heard the man's shrieks, and subsequently investigated their cause; and it is entirely possible that the watch atop Broken's walls heard it, as well. Prudence, my defiant friend, may let you keep a few more of your teeth, along with your life."

"Yes, yes," Heldo-Bah answers, waving the statement away. "But do not think that you can continue to avoid my principal question, by so distracting me. I would know this, finally: with all the lands you have visited, and all the great philosophers and kings you have met and advised—why, *why* would you choose to settle in *Broken,* of all places? You must have known of the evil nature of their faith—"

"In fact, I did," Caliphestros replies, still calmly and readily. "For I first observed what is there called the 'cult' of Kafra in Alexandria. It had been brought hence by tribes who live along the upper reaches of the river *Nilus,*[†] which is called 'the mother of Egypt.' I next encountered the faith in several small but wealthy border towns in Broken, during my journey there with Boniface—"

Heldo-Bah cannot help but blurt, "Ha! 'Vat of Turds,'" assuming an air of complete self-satisfaction as Caliphestros continues:

"The faith and its adherents had traveled repeatedly, or so I was told, aboard the grain ships that ply the seas between *Lumun-jan* and Egypt. And that was what interested me, particularly, about the golden god: his path across the waters, throughout the empires to the south, and then to the northern kingdoms, followed exactly the route that had been traveled by every spread of the Death." The old man pauses, and then glances down at the remnants of his legs. "Not unlike the rats that infest those same grain ships . . .† Yet it had never occurred to me that such a peculiar faith could become the foundation of a state, and when I began to hear that it had, I grew fascinated. I had already intended to visit Broken in Brother Winfred's company, to determine if the Death had struck there; and the remarkable news that the place had become not only a functioning but a powerful Kafran kingdom became simply an additional reason to make the journey."

"I feel I should point out, my lord," says Veloc, not without some indignation, "that any Bane schoolchild knows that Kafra came into our own part of the world when Oxmontrot and his comrades, who had traveled south to seek their fortunes in the wars of the *Lumun-jani,* returned home."

A sudden, rather peculiar look of fascination enters Caliphestros's features. "So the Bane know of Oxmontrot?"

"Why should we not?" Veloc queries, still playing the role of offended scholar. "He began the banishments of all those who could not or would not be slaves to the plan to build his great city, after all. And so he was, in one way, the father of our tribe—as the man who rapes a woman and leaves her with child is the detestable but undoubted father of that infant."

Caliphestros is further impressed: "That is soundly argued, Veloc, and with an economy of words. I begin to wonder why your Groba should have refused to name you historian of your tribe."

"If you'd like clarification, my lord," Heldo-Bah interrupts, "simply ask him how many women of the Tall he's bedded—that's but one reason why the members of the Groba doubt him. There is also the small matter of his being often in *my* company—which, I think, they would ignore, save for the additional business of his refusing to copulate with the Priestess of the Moon . . ."

"Is all this true, Veloc?" Caliphestros asks, without either rancor or censure. "But I understood that the Priestess may choose any mate she desires from your tribe—in emulation, say the Kafran clergy, of their own customs—and that none dare refuse her."

"Well, Lord Sorcerer," Heldo-Bah declares, now holding a mockingly proud hand toward Veloc, "allow me to present the only one who ever has!"

Trying to ignore Heldo-Bah's caustic comment, Veloc also attempts to direct the conversation elsewhere: "But how come *you* to know so much of *our* tribe, my lord?"

"I?" the old man says. "It was many years ago—a lifetime, one could say, without exaggeration. I had served the God-King Izairn long and faithfully enough to gain his trust, and he bade me undertake a study of your tribe. Together with my acolytes, I assembled an enormous store of information—a store that would subsequently become very useful during my years of exile."

"Oh?" Heldo-Bah inquires pointedly. "And what has become of that collection? For there are more than a few in our tribe who contend that you carried out your 'study' by dissecting the living bodies of Bane prisoners."

"Can you never cease your childish prattle, Heldo-Bah?" Keera says angrily. "Those were fables, made up by a few Outragers."

"I'm simply asking, Keera," Heldo-Bah says. "You know that I despise the Outragers even more than you, or indeed than any other Bane. I merely wish to know what truth, if any, there is in the tale."

Caliphestros snorts in dismissal: "If you will believe such stories, Heldo-Bah, there is little point to continuing either our discussion or our actions in concert." The old man's features grow momentarily puzzled: "But is it true that you despise the Outragers—and that others in your tribe harbor similar sentiments?"

Keera and Veloc nod in turn, leaving it to Heldo-Bah to say: "Despise them? Why, we as good as left one for dead, not a week ago. And an important one, at that—"

"Heldo-Bah!" Keera commands. "There is no reason to reveal what we may or may not have—"

"Oh, but there is, Keera," Caliphestros says. "If you will pardon my interrupting you. This hostility among the Bane against the Outragers was not a fact that was contained in my study of your tribe. During my years in Broken, I actually tried to rouse similar sentiment against another group of murderers turned sacred soldiers—the Personal Guard of the Merchant Lord, of whom we have just been speaking. Those posturing villains who, after my banishment, tortured and murdered my acolytes."

Heldo-Bah's mangled brows come together in distrust, and his filed teeth again show in the skeptical curl of his lip. "Truly, old man?"

Caliphestros takes in an excited breath, yet he hesitates: he knows that the veracity of his next words, and the greater trust that they will (with luck) breed, cannot help but be crucial to the future of the little band's present undertaking; but as ever, secrets shared make him uneasy. "What I tell you now, I say in confidence. Fate having brought us together in a vital undertaking, I must trust in the sincerity of each of you, and must also be able to trust that you comprehend the need for constant discretion—because that undertaking will require from us all the best efforts and truest belief in one another that we can muster. And so—can you, all three, pledge me that trust and that assurance? And will you believe me if I pledge the same?"

Among the foragers, it is Veloc who nods assent first, quickly and eagerly; Heldo-Bah, not surprisingly, continues to appear uneasy, but also agrees to the compact, after only a few moments' further consideration; but Keera, somewhat surprisingly, displays the most cautious aspect. "If that be so, my lord," she says, "then—in the spirit of the honest alliance you would establish between us—there is yet one thing that we must tell you."

Both Veloc and Heldo-Bah appear suddenly alarmed, as though they know exactly what Keera is referring to, and dread its announcement. Yet Caliphestros—to the surprise of all the foragers—smiles kindly; indeed, almost indulgently. "Yes. I thought there might be."

Heldo-Bah throws his hands toward the branches of the forest ceiling. "There—you see? He reads our very thoughts—undoubted a sorcerer, just as I have always maintained!"

"Hush, Heldo-Bah!" Veloc orders; and then, to his sister, he murmurs, "So long as you are certain, Keera . . ."

Keera keeps her gaze on Caliphestros's gently smiling face. "How did you know, my lord?"

"How could I not?" answers the old man. "I do not know if you realize as much, Keera, but you Bane, inscrutable as your activities may sometimes be, are not obscure, when conversing with one another. And last night, as we were packing my instruments and materials, there was one subject that all three of you seemed anxious to mention—save that every time any one of you came near to it, one of the others would give the careless speaker a boot in his backside, or the flat of your hand across his head."

Caliphestros coaxes Stasi a few steps away from the others, and faces northeast, toward Broken: for the distant mountain and the city walls atop it have now been plainly revealed by the dawn, across the river and through gaps in the much thinner lines of trees on the riverbanks. "So," he says, his voice scarcely audible. "She has been in the Wood again . . ."

The foragers move slowly closer to the spot on which stand the white panther and her rider. "She has," Veloc says. "And you know more about this Wife of Kafra, my lord, than simply her station and rank—as we supposed you must. And, apparently, that she ventures into Davon Wood from time to time. But we *must* be sure—you are *certain* that we're talking about the same witch?"

Caliphestros inclines his head in agreement, but keeps his eyes on the horizon. "A tall woman with coal-black hair that falls in straight, gleaming sheets, and eyes of a darker green than Stasi's, but just as brilliant?"

"The very one," Heldo-Bah answers, clapping his hands to the sides of his head in resignation. "Allow me to guess—she is your daughter? Or are you yourself a half-breed demon, who had your way with some mortal female—and a female of great beauty, she must have been—when you still had legs?"

To the forager's somewhat accusatory suggestions, Caliphestros offers only a small laugh. "You are wrong in every respect, Heldo-Bah. The woman you saw is no kin to me—or no *blood* kin, I should perhaps say. She was—*is*—a princess: the daughter of the God-King I served, Izairn, and sister to that good man's heir, Saylal."

"That cannot—" Veloc stops before he can complete the question, allowing himself time to frame it more cautiously. "I would not have thought that possible, my lord. For the Wives of Kafra, Bane historians have long known, are the God-King's mistresses, as well."

"Fool, Veloc," Heldo-Bah chastises quietly. "Did you truly think that a woman demented enough to seduce a Davon panther would pause at bedding her own brother?"†

Keera alone sees that Caliphestros winces and trembles abruptly at this question. "My lord?" she asks. "Are you unwell? Shall we rest a short while, and prepare some of your medicines?"

The old man smiles faintly at the question. "No, Keera . . . although I thank you. But not even I have medicines to cure such foolishness and tragedy . . ." Again he looks up and through the trees to the northern horizon, as if he can see into the chambers of the God-King's palace itself; and, as he indulges this seeming vision, he murmurs just one name: "Alandra . . ."‡

Keera approaches Caliphestros and Stasi carefully; and when she is beside them, she summons the nerve to ask, "That was—is—what she is called?"

Caliphestros nods again. "It was and is, Keera. A name derived from the legends of those whom the people of Broken know as the *Kreikisch,* and the people of *Roma,* or *Lumun-jan,* call the *Graeci.*†† In particular, the name comes from the ancient tale of another great city that was put to siege—just as we may well be forced, if the next stages of our plan go badly, to lay siege to Broken."

Ignoring a scoffing grunt from Heldo-Bah, Keera says, "I do not wish to reach for conclusions before we have sufficient reason, my lord, but—"

Keera grows suddenly silent, turning toward the northwest with an expression that Veloc and Heldo-Bah know only too well: for it betrays the detection of some new danger. A gust of wind has coursed through the series of long, high gorges that comprise this portion of the valley of the Cat's Paw, and finally made its way to the rock on which the tracker stands with Caliphestros and Stasi; and, almost immediately after turning away to the left, Keera turns back round again, to glance down and see that the white panther has also detected something on the breeze, and that her large, brick-red nostrils are flared open.

The panther's ears slowly go down and back, down and back, until they sink beneath the crown of her head; and she is already growling in both alarm and warning, as well as opening her mouth and taking quick, steady breaths in the quietly peculiar way that cats do at such moments. Caliphestros, in a whisper, explains to Keera that, when employing certain exceptionally sensitive organs found inside their mouths, cats can actually *taste* scents[†] and therefore danger: a most impressive ability that seems, to the uneducated, a sort of magic.

Yet Keera is little interested in academic matters, just at this instant: *"Death!"* she suddenly cries. "Perhaps not *the* Death, but death, all the same, and much of it. I would place it—" Her nostrils again flare, as the cat growls. "Above the point at which we emerged from the deep forest and reached the river; and it comes—" She dashes to the edge of the Wood and climbs a gnarled cherry tree, judging the increase or decrease in the power of the scent from that point. She then returns to the spot where Stasi stands with her rider, the old man knowing enough to let the tracker go about her work without interference. "From very near the river, if not from within the valley itself. Indeed, my best guess would be that it originates along the silted banks of one of the large pools that form where the river first descends. Those calmer stretches, that is, where creatures of every variety come to drink and bathe." Her upper teeth bite at her lower lip, as her confusion and concern heighten: "For there are many varieties of death and decay, within this one stench . . ."

Stasi soon steps to the left, moving onto the more solid ground at the edge of Davon Wood; and there she paces uneasily to and fro, her eyes searching the northwest forest and sky, both of which are still gripped by darkness sufficient to allow her imagination full sway. Caliphestros strokes her neck and urges her to be calm, but with little success: "It was in just such a spot," explains the old man to the others, "that Stasi and her cubs were first spied by the party of Broken hunters and drivers that gave them chase deeper into the Wood."

Keera studies the white panther's motions and the expressions of her face and voice for a few more moments, and finally says, "It seems that Stasi returns to that terrible time even now—as if she senses that those who carried out the attack upon her family are also responsible for the death she now detects; and she desires another chance to settle—"

Stasi suddenly releases her resonant, hauntingly high-toned cry of alarm. She then rushes a little deeper into the forest proper, to a nearby cluster of thick roseberry[‡] bushes that grow out of a patch of particularly soft Earth that is covered by a thick layer of moss. Here, she gracefully but deliberately dips her left foreleg and side, causing Caliphestros to lose his balance atop her and, clutching his twin bags and his bundled crutches, to roll into the patch of almost harmless bushes and, soon, into the thick moss at their base. Then, briefly glancing back to see that the old man has survived without mishap, Stasi dashes away, keeping just within the line of the forest's edge, where the ground is easier to grip, and soon disappearing into the northwesterly wilderness.

"*Stasi!*" Caliphestros cries, before he has even gotten himself into a sitting position. As the foragers rush to assist him, he continues to shout in fear, "Stasi, do not be rash—you must wait for our help!"

{vi:}

"MY LORD!" Keera says, leaping into the enveloping bushes, finding a path through the more widely spaced branches at the base of the thicket, and thus a way to the old man's side, as quickly as we might, by now, have grown to expect of these Bane. "Are you injured?" Keera says, when she reaches him.

Caliphestros grinds his teeth hard, already grabbing at a small deer-skin pouch that hangs round his neck. "No—not injured, Keera," he says, groaning. "It is nothing more than the old pain . . ." This statement bleeds into another groan and more teeth-gnashing: "*Nor is it anything less.* May the true deities who watch over this world damn the golden god and his priests to such eternal fire as is forever mine!"

"*Hak!* Be careful, now," Heldo-Bah laughingly scolds, as he cuts his way through the berry bush branches. "You've spent too much time in our company already, Lord of Wisdom—blaspheming like some cheap Daurawah whore, you shock me!"

"But what happened, my lord?" Veloc asks, his mind, like Heldo-Bah's, fully capable of carrying on a conversation while slashing away at the strong bush expertly enough to avoid the painful cuts that the larger thorns can inflict.

"As I have told you, Veloc, Stasi's actions and purposes are her own," the struggling Caliphestros replies sharply, taking three pressed balls of what Keera can tell, simply by their scent, are powerful combinations of herbaceous medicines out of his pouch, then quickly putting them into his mouth and chewing them, seemingly oblivious to what the tracker surmises must be their terribly bitter taste. "Although I cannot pretend that both my pride and other, pettier feelings of my heart do not suffer when these things happen . . ." Already having revealed far more about this moment than he would have liked, even in friendly company, Caliphestros abruptly ceases such talk and calls out: "Heldo-Bah! I assume you have some quantity of potent drink on your person?"

Much of Heldo-Bah's humorous view of this latest event has been driven out of his mind and manner by sudden and close scrutiny of the terrible scars on the old man's thighs: he responds to this inquiry by reaching inside his tunic and producing what appears to be a fairly small wineskin, made of kid hide and lined with the stomach of the same animal. "You assume rightly, my lord, and you are welcome to as much of it as you need . . ."

Caliphestros nods, takes a deep draught from the skin, and hastens to draw air. "By whatever gods *be* true!" he soon gasps, staring at Heldo-Bah with stunned features, "What *is* that?"

Heldo-Bah grins and lets the old man take another pull at the skin; then he indulges in one, himself, and even he must work to keep it down. "*That* is the one civilized thing to come north with the dark barbarians southeast of the Tombs," he says, sucking in his own cooling gasp of air. "Plum brandy, or so they claim it to be. *Slivevetz,*[†] they call it."

"*Brandy?*" Caliphestros echoes in disbelief. "It cannot be. An incendiary used by their armies, perhaps—I would almost believe it to be *napthes,*[‡] save that I know from my own studies that those tribes are too ignorant to distill such."

Heldo-Bah laughs once, and heartily, as if he has just seen the first evidence he can truly comprehend that Caliphestros is indeed a *man,* as Heldo-Bah understands the word: a person who, whatever his present diminished state, once savored the visceral joys of life. "Yes, I thought the same, my lord, when first I tasted it," the Bane calls in delight. "Save that it does not rob one of life. Rather the opposite!"

Keera has taken the small but weighty bags from Caliphestros's shoulders and set them aside, after which she helps the old man to sit fully up. Caliphestros looks off in the direction of the forest undergrowth through which Stasi disappeared.

"Should we not hurry, my lord, to aid Stasi?" Keera asks. "If you are able, of course."

"We shall," answers the old man, getting his crutches on. "But we need not move *too* quickly. Stasi will attack only if she finds living humans at the site of whatever death has taken place upriver—and the chances of discovering such life, be it animal *or* human are, if I am correct about what is taking place, small. And that is fortunate—for it is the dead who hold the clearest answers to our questions . . ." The old man, gaining strength, glances about. "Yet we must consider that our purposes now seem to lead in two opposing directions."

"These strange deaths upriver," Keera says with a nod, "and the soldier at the Fallen Bridge."

"Indeed, Keera," Caliphestros replies. "Thus we must, for the moment, split our band into sensible pieces. I propose that you and I follow Stasi; Veloc, you go with Heldo-Bah and keep watch over the body downriver, taking every care not to be observed until our return, when we may conduct a more thorough investigation."

"It shall be done as you say, my lord," Veloc replies, again anxious to please the old man. "You may rely upon it, and upon us."

"And," Heldo-Bah adds eagerly, "as yours will be the longer journey—" Without anyone having ordered it, he fetches up Caliphestros's two bags from the midst of the roseberry bush. "Permit me to assume these burdens for you, Lord Caliphestros." Moaning when he lifts the bags onto his shoulders, he removes one and hands it to Veloc. "Who would have ever thought that the day would come when we would be draughting books about the Wood, as if they were blocks of gold or iron ore . . ."

"I very much doubt that anyone would believe it," Caliphestros says quickly, anxious to get under way. "Come here, now, both of you." Heldo-Bah and Veloc obey, and stand quite still as Caliphestros retrieves a few small objects from his bags, and then hands these apparently precious items to Keera, who places them in her own shoulder sack. "Remember this," the old man says, indicating his bags to Veloc and Heldo-Bah. "These books, as well as the instruments you carry, are in fact of far greater importance to our finding the source of the illness, and whether it is indeed a plan set in motion by those who rule Broken, than any of the goods you usually carry. Be careful with them, especially at those moments when you display, as you so frequently do, little concern for your own necks. And so—on your way!"

"If my senses are true," Keera adds, "we can be no more than an hour or two from the deaths Stasi detected. Cover your ground quickly, Veloc, for we should not be far behind."

Veloc and Heldo-Bah sling their larger foraging bags atop their free shoulders. "We shall meet again ere noontime," Heldo-Bah calls as he departs, "at the Fallen Bridge!"

Having watched the two Bane men depart, Keera and Caliphestros soon set off on their own, less certain journey, Keera walking beside the hobbling old man and carefully following the trail that Stasi has evidently made no effort to hide—indeed, that she must have deliberately tried to mark, so much is the path at variance with the very great stealth that Davon panthers ordinarily exhibit. When Keera considers this fact in combination with Caliphestros's strange lack of surprise or meaningful reaction to Stasi's departure, as well as to his having been left rather unceremoniously to the mercies of forest moss and a berry bush, she feels that she is safe in asking:

"My lord—Caliphestros—I am curious: what causes these sudden departures by the great panther?"

Caliphestros smiles. "Yes—you looked as though you might be puzzling that out." He sighs once, any lingering pain in his legs now being very effectively shrouded by the medicines he has consumed. "Stasi has what I would term an instinct for unnatural death. But often, when that admittedly facile explanation seems inadequate, I have followed her to the various streams in our part of the Wood, where we happen upon agèd or mortally wounded creatures who have come to the water to die, and I ask of myself, again and again—*why has she come here?* In virtually every instance, during these investigations, Stasi has approached the dead and the dying with neither alarm nor killing in her thoughts, but as if to determine why they have met or are meeting their ends. I began to see that it is chiefly death inflicted by man that fascinates her. When Stasi—in my presence as well as, I suspect, alone—comes across an eagle, a hawk, or even a raven, that has been pierced by an arrow but is still alive, she neither finishes nor consumes it; not immediately or, in most cases, at all. The same is even more true if she encounters some creature who shares her world of the forest floor: instead of throttling it and consuming its flesh, she will nose about the injurious arrow, seeking the scent—or so I have always thought—of whatever human loosed it."

Putting his own nose into the air, Caliphestros stops short. "*Hak!*—

the stench of death grows more pungent with nearly every step. It must be particularly oppressive, for one with senses as powerful as your own."

Keera nods. "Yes, lord. I did not wish to interrupt, but—we cannot be far off, now . . ."

The rest of their short progress through the Wood is made in silence, for the heightened stench soon makes it necessary to use their mouths only for breathing, after they have blocked their noses. This small task they achieve when Keera harvests the redolent sap of a nearby pine tree, and compresses it into bits small enough to fit into their nostrils.

"So much death . . ." Keera murmurs, anxiously moving ahead of Caliphestros when the path that Stasi has already taken approaches the banks of the Cat's Paw.

"Indeed, Keera," Caliphestros calls after her. "Yet why and how—these become even more important questions." Pulling himself toward the sound of the river, eyes ever on the increasingly dangerous ground, the old man arrives at the silty shore of a broad and relatively calm pool in the river, fed at its far end by a single high waterfall. A thick mist obscures the pool's surface, at various spots, and an enormous rock formation serves as its easternmost bank, a narrow but deep channel of escape having been cut into the middle of it by countless powerful spring floods. Keera stands atop this formation, taking in whatever surrounds her with apparent horror.

"Keera?" Caliphestros says, as he moves toward the base of the rocky mass, which obscures his view of all save the nearest banks of the pool. "What is it?"

Her voice is eerily—indeed, deathly—calm: "Stasi was right about the scent of men . . . but wrong in her concern that they were a threat to us . . ."

Caliphestros comes closer, and soon sees that the tracker is not alone atop the stone rise:

"Stasi!" he calls, at which the great cat bounds down to him. To make amends for her sudden departure, she takes a moment to rub her brow, muzzle, and nose into the old man's lowered face and his side, in what she evidently considers gentle affection, which is still nearly enough to topple him from his crutches; and, when certain that he is both amenable and ready, she lowers her neck and shoulders in the usual manner, allowing Caliphestros to get off his walking contrivances and back astride her shoulders. Though happy to see him, the panther is also in a clear state of agitation, and is evidently anxious that her companion see the object of her unrest as quickly as possible.

"All right," Caliphestros says, as Stasi bounds back up and onto the stone embankment upon which Keera stands. "We can discuss the manner of your departure later. Now, what is it that caused you to—"

But by now, rider and mount are atop Keera's enormous rock, and Caliphestros is able to see the scene in and around the broad pool that spreads out before them. The sound of the fall at the water's far end is muted, in reality by distance and the last of the morning mist—but for a moment it seems that the terrible scenes that line the pool's northern and eastern banks have themselves caused the falling water to quiet its roar, out of solemn respect: respect for the dead, and respect for the irretrievably dying . . .

{vii:}

CALIPHESTROS HAS WITNESSED most of the varieties of brutality which either Man or Nature can display—but he is now forced to admit woefully that he has scarcely ever beheld such unnatural carnage as that which stretches away before him. All stages of death and decay, afflicting nearly every kind of woodland and lowland creature, are represented; and, while there are flutters of movement among several groups of untamed grazing animals, these are greatly outnumbered by the scores of the dead. It is a supremely lamentable and pitiable sight, made worse when one or another of the throng's still-living members—who lie, almost uniformly, on their sides, their ribs revealed so clearly and painfully that it seems they must soon burst through their hides—twitch and occasionally start, trying but inevitably failing to get back to their feet. The dead, meanwhile, are only less horrific for their being, mercifully, finished with life: some lie with abdomens burst open, some with but a little rotted meat clinging to their skeletons, and some with those same skeletons bleached to an almost pure white, but all in the same position, with their necks and heads extended toward the bank of the pool, as if they had expected to find salvation or at least comfort in the cold waters, but were cruelly disappointed. Yet there are other, even more surprising varieties of dead beasts at this place, too: hunters of the wood and the plains, including wolves, and even a young panther, have also come to the cooling waters, seeking relief from whatever it is that sickened and then slew them. There is cause for pity in this, too, for the wolves have brought their young with them, in an attempt to save at least those future members of their indomitable breed; yet those smaller hunters also lie dead and dying, their whimpering providing the most lamentable and strange sound in the small world that Death has built here, over what must have been many days and weeks.

"Look, my lord," Keera says at length, scarce able to contain her sorrow, but suddenly intrigued by one collection of carcasses and half-dead beasts that surround a small, shaded inlet, a cove of sorts, at the very northernmost point of the pool's long bank. "Can it be . . . ?"

"Aye, Keera," Caliphestros whispers, urging Stasi forward on the great mass of stone that provides their vantage point. "Shag cattle—strays, and almost certainly Lord Baster-kin's own."

"It is as if . . . ," Keera speaks softly, and tears have by now moistened her face; and so she sets her jaw and says no more.

But Caliphestros knows her well enough, by now, to finish her thought: "It is as if every sort of creature has been assembled to die in this one place; and finally, in that death, they have become neither hunters nor hunted, but only fellows in their suffering, fellows who are soon, together, to travel to and reside forever in the next existence . . ."

Keera nods silently. "Yes, my lord—and have you noticed one thing more?" Caliphestros makes no reply, and so she continues: "All creatures of this portion of the Earth *are* here . . ." Keera lifts a hand to indicate an ash stand in the northeasternmost corner of the pool. "Even our own . . ."

Caliphestros requires a moment to make sense of the dappled, early morning scene toward which Keera has directed his gaze; but soon he sees that a human body hangs amid the ash trunks, strapped by its arms between a pair of the trees, and missing the lower portions of its legs: a victim, plainly, of the *Halap-stahla*.

"Armor," Keera says, as if unable to quite believe it. "He wears the armor of Broken. And very fine armor it is . . ."

"And, therefore, warrants further inspection by us," Caliphestros an-

swers with a nod, his manner suddenly fretful. "But be careful, Keera—
you must touch neither the body, nor any of the other carnage, here, no
matter how great your pity and sympathy. It is enough that we even walk
through this scene—for the very air may be full of pestilence, for all we
know or can tell . . ." Glancing at the water that flows through the stone
channel beneath them, which is some eight feet across and again as deep,
Caliphestros judges, "Stasi can leap to the other side, with my scant
weight on her back. I can then send her for you—"

"There is no need, my lord." Keera has been searching the surrounding trees, and has found what she desires—a length of thick climbing
vine, which hangs from one especially stout limb of a high, spreading
oak on the opposite bank. Taking up a long, notched branch that lies
among a scattering of dead wood on the rocky surface, she grabs hold of
the vine with it, and has swung across the spillway even before Stasi's
broad paws have leapt from the south to touch the northern side. The
hardest part of their passage to the ash stand on the far side is, however,
yet to come: Keera must exert all her will to keep from looking into the
eyes of the now-close collection of dying animals—for there is, in the
wide, dark eyes of each surviving thing, not only a terrible, bewildered
fear, but a pitiable plea begging relief of any living thing that might pass
by. It is not long before Keera must look away altogether, and hurry to
keep pace with Stasi and Caliphestros. The panther's mind is fixed most
determinedly on the man suspended from the trees, a man who reeks
with the scent of those deadly and despicable men of Broken . . .

When Keera does reach her comrades, she finds them both deep in
contemplation of the scene of ritual mutilation: Stasi's nose moves from
spot to spot upon the ground, able, apparently, to pick up a scent trail.
Caliphestros, in the meantime, twists and turns his head as Stasi roots
through the undergrowth of the forest floor, keeping his eyes—which
have gone from an expression of worry to one of recognition and shock—
fixed on the hanging dead man. Deeply creased skin interrupts the victim's grey and white beard and surrounds the eye sockets (the latter
emptied by scavenging birds, some of them, perhaps, the very ravens
that are now among the dying that ring the pool), all of which betray a
man of advanced years.

"Korsar . . . ," Caliphestros pronounces, lifting a trembling hand to indicate the lifeless half-figure. "But I *knew* this man . . ." He stares deep

into the famed soldier's eye sockets as if searching for the light of mutual recognition, and finding only the gleam of putrid gore.

"*Yantek* Korsar?" Keera asks, herself shocked, now.

"Aye, Keera," Caliphestros answers. "Once, the famed and honored commander of all of Broken's legions. Yet now . . ."

Keera glances at Caliphestros, to take the measure of his sentiment; but she finds an expression impossible to interpret, and so looks again at the sadly mutilated body. "Was he one of those who denounced you?" she asks at length.

"Denounced me?" Caliphestros answers, his face and voice ambiguity itself. "No. Neither did he speak *for* me, but—Herwald Korsar was a good man. A tragic man, in many ways. But no . . ." And at that moment, as his characteristically certain voice trails away again, an aspect enters his features that surprises Keera, perhaps more than the sight of the mutilated body. For the first time during his alliance with the Bane foragers, this master of sorcery, or of science, or of whatever art it is that usually enables him to speak with such authority about so many strange and wondrous subjects, appears uncertain. "I had expected some such horror as this, when news came of Broken's plan to invade the Wood and attack your tribe," he says. "But to see it . . ."

Keera thinks to ask where such "news" could have come *from,* to one alone in the Wood; but the strangely discomfiting moment is shattered by a sudden scream of pain and terror from one of the stray and dying shag cattle that lie in the small inlet on the pool's north shore. As if magically, the beast, a once-imposing steer, rises suddenly from the carcasses around it, stands awkwardly upon strangely misshapen hooves, and begins to buck wildly. Caliphestros and Keera both watch warily as the steer's mad eyes—out of which seep small trails of blood—catch sight of Stasi's brilliant green orbs, which must appear to it as a signal fire in the morning mist; and a clearly malicious intent abruptly taints the steer's every breath and movement. Stasi growls in return, the massive muscles of her shoulders and haunches readying for combat; but, just as Keera prepares to lift Caliphestros's scant weight from the panther's back, in order to allow Stasi freedom for battle, the old man stays the tracker's arm.

"No, Keera!" he cries, locking one arm as tightly as he can about the panther's thick, straining neck, and using the other to cover Stasi's eyes.

"She must not tear the flesh of the diseasèd beast, nor allow herself to be even scratched—your bow, quickly, drop the animal as it charges!"

Keera asks no questions, but lifts bow from shoulder and arrow from quiver, each with one arm and in a practiced set of motions, as she steps out in front of her friends. She nocks her shaft at once, and then—with the shag steer bearing down on them out of feverish madness, charging through bank, mud, water, and finally over stone—she takes careful aim and lets fly. The arrow finds its way to the animal's breast, through scant meat and between bone, and finally into the heart. The steer collapses and slides along the stone upon which Keera, Stasi, and Caliphestros stand, its body made slick by its own sweat, blood, and spittle, so that it comes to a halt all too near the brave Bane tracker. When the creature does stop, Keera finally draws breath once more, and for the first time allows herself to realize what has occurred.

"Impossible," she mutters, as the last rattle of death shakes the pitiable beast before her. "Could the pestilence drive it so very mad?"

"Not the pestilence that you have described to me as afflicting your people," Caliphestros answers, as he and Stasi come up beside Keera. He nods in acknowledgment of the skill of her shot, then says, "But another pestilence altogether was plain to be seen, as soon as the poor creature rose. Observe the ears, Keera, and then the hooves . . ."

Keera takes a few steps toward the beast, and sees that its ears have been badly mauled by some sort of combat; but then she realizes the truth, murmuring, "Nay—they have *rotted away* . . . !" And so, she then sees, have the hooves, whole parts of which are missing, revealing sickly flesh beneath.

"Oh, great Moon," Keera whispers, going down upon one knee before the steer, but careful not to touch it. "What can this harmless animal have done to warrant your fire?"

Caliphestros's head cocks at these words, as Stasi begins to shift to and fro, knowing now that the steer is a mass of disease and anxious to be away from it. But Caliphestros strokes her muzzle and neck calmingly, and asks the tracker, "What say you, Keera—'fire'? You know of it?"

Keera's head slowly nods. *"Moonfire,"* she says. "The fever that maddens and rots . . ."

"Yes," Caliphestros says. "Of course that is what you *would* call it. Moonfire—the fire of Saint Anthony, *Ignis Sacer*—the Holy Fire . . ."

Keera stands and approaches the old man, who has again retreated into a world of unsettling thought. "My lord? What are these things of which you speak?"

"All names that are one, in their essence." Caliphestros sighs deeply, glancing back up at the decaying body of Yantek Korsar. "So we are doubly cursed—doubly plagued . . ."

And then, strangest of all, the old man cradles his forehead in one hand—and quietly weeps. It lasts a mere moment, but the moment is enough: "Lord Caliphestros," Keera says, not at all reassured at the sound of even quiet tears. "Do you not have the skill to face the presence of two pestilences in this place—and perhaps in Okot?"

But Caliphestros, his tears gone, only answers in a tongue that is strange to Keera, and which further unnerves her: "*Ther is moore broke in Brokynne . . .*"

"My lord," the tracker insists, sternly calling him to the moment and its perils. "Has the fire taken *your* reason, as well, then?"

Holding up a delicate, wrinkled hand, the old man steadies himself and says, "Forgive me, Keera. It was a saying, a small jest, with which the monk in whose company I first came to the great city—Winfred, or Boniface, of whom we have spoken—was wont to ease our cares, in his own tongue, when we came to realize the true nature of the place: '*Ther is moore broke in Brokynne, thanne ever was knouen so.*'[†] It meant only that, beneath the surface of its renownèd power, Broken was a far more ominous place than either of us could even say with accuracy. But now—" Again with his eyes fixed upon the old soldier strapped between the ash trees, Caliphestros murmurs, "—now, I know the bitter truth of that 'jest'; and I believe we can begin to see and know the true extent of Broken's malice and corruption. Certainly, it is doubled, at the very least: twice the peril—two pestilences, as you say, Keera, and perhaps still more danger. For we also have this testament"—he points up to the mutilated remains of the once-proud Yantek Korsar—"to another kind of illness, another type of danger, altogether . . ."

Keera can only shake her head in frustration, and then cries, "My lord, you must explain these things! I must know if my children—"

"And explain them I shall," Caliphestros answers, with deep if controlled concern, as he turns away from the ash stand and attempts confident composure, putting a hand to Keera's shoulder. "Not least for the sake of your children, Keera. And, as a way of atoning for any confusion that I may at times inflict upon you, let me say that *all* Bane children, at least, should be in no greater danger, from this second disease that we have discovered; for, although we cannot be certain, the plague you have described as being at work in Okot shares few if any symptoms with the second fever, that which you call Moonfire. That is one thing from which we may take solace. And with that assurance, let us be on our way, and speedily. I have much to explain to your leaders, and on our way to meet with them we might even try to *prove* why the rose fever alone has struck Okot."

Caliphestros quickly urges Stasi back to the deep cleft in the rock formation, and to the noisy waterway at its base; once there Stasi bursts, with the fantastic strength that comes so easily to her kind, over the rushing outlet—

And yet Keera, clinging fast to her vine and reaching the southern bank just after Stasi, can hear the old man still murmuring to himself, over and over, as if it were a desperate prayer, now:

"Ther is moore broke in Brokynne . . ."

So long as Stasi maintains a fast pace, however, down the stone and back onto the trail that brought the three to this place, Keera does not question the old man's strange speech, nor any other aspect of his behavior. Neither does she trouble her mind more than a little over a brief glimpse that she caught, as she swung back over that pool's outlet, of a flash of shining white: a fleeting glimpse of a human bone, being washed quickly through the waterway. She has no cause to let it worry her, she assures herself as she runs: after all, where was found one dead, decaying man whose legs were severed, there would likely be an abundance of such bones, from long ago. And if this one in particular appeared too small ever to have resided within the body of a full-grown human, whether Bane or Tall, well . . . Certainly, it is of no importance to the affairs of the moment; thus, although she knows this explanation to be inadequate to the peculiar sight, she tucks the memory away in the back of her distracted mind and fixes her thoughts upon reaching Okot . . .

{viii:}

BEFORE OKOT, however, must come the arranged meeting with Veloc and Heldo-Bah at the Fallen Bridge. Keera finds, as she does her best to keep pace with Stasi during their morn-to-noonday run, that the memory of their terrible discovery cements the particular bond that the three of them—tracker, scholar, and panther—have from the first been inclined to feel, even as it confirms the full and terrible importance of the journey upon which they have embarked and the purpose that they are now serving; and this sense of importance, the tracker knows, outweighs anything that could have propelled even Heldo-Bah's and Veloc's swift steps: Keera is not altogether surprised, therefore, when—as the stench of the rotting soldier's body begins to cause her nostrils to flare in renewed distaste soon after the enormous, moss-draped form of the Fallen Bridge comes within view some distance down the deep, rocky riverbed—neither of the male foragers are anywhere to be seen. She surmises aloud to Caliphestros that their own speed may have been sufficient to have allowed them to outstrip her brother and Heldo-Bah, who cannot always be counted upon to give their fullest effort or to follow instructions precisely once they are out of both the hearing and the reach of her personal commands and exhortations. For his part, Caliphestros wonders if the two Bane men have not met with some mishap; but Keera assures him that her heart is not vexed by such worries, for Veloc and Heldo-Bah know this stretch of the Cat's Paw only too well; and since neither she herself nor Stasi have smelled the fresh blood that would characterize such violence, she suspects that her brother gave in to the lazy exhortations of Heldo-Bah, once they had run for a good part of their journey and their usual taskmaster was well out of sight, and slowed his pace to accommodate the added weight of Caliphestros's books. Keera therefore suggests that Caliphestros and she inspect the diminished corpse of the soldier while they wait for the two to appear, an activity that proves to take little time: the seemingly sorcerous old fellow is able to judge, even by the maggot-infested mess that the soldier's body has become, that he died of the rose fever alone: that he was not killed by the priests of Kafra (as the golden arrows that seemed to have pierced his body indicated), but was made to appear as if he had been so dispatched, and that the remains are no longer a danger to other living creatures, if indeed they ever were.

"But how can you make such judgments, my lord," Keera asks, her voice rising over the eternally roaring waters of the Cat's Paw, "when the body itself is so very decayed?"

"Most of my conclusions are the result of simple observation," Caliphestros replies. "Keera, have you ever tried to loose one of the Tall's golden arrows from your bow?"

"We have never had reason or opportunity," the tracker answers. "When we discover such valuable items, they are always in the bodies of similarly executed outcasts from Broken, and our Groba insists that they be brought back to decorate that council's Den of Stone, in order to increase the mystical power of the place."

"Well, then," the old man continues, "perhaps now you might examine at least one more such shaft from a practical point of view?"

Bemused, Keera steps toward the mass of decay on the ground; but then she pauses, seeking reassurance. "It—*will* it be safe to touch them?"

Caliphestros smiles gently in admiration. "While I should not be surprised if your healers and other wise men and women were unable to divine the cause of his death immediately, now that you, Keera, know it to be the rose fever, I will wager what is left of my legs that you know its chief properties."

"I—believe so, Lord Caliphestros," Keera answers. "As you have said, the rose fever, unlike some similar diseases, seems to lose its threat with the host's death."

"Indeed," Caliphestros replies. "Although when my assistant brought my arrow to me"—he quickly takes the flower-entwined example that he displayed to the foragers on the previous evening from within his smallest, lightest satchel—"I was forced to take extra precautions. Only when you told me your tale did I realize they had been unnecessary, for both myself and my . . . messenger . . ."

As Keera makes her first informal estimate of the weight of the shaft she took from the soldier, she says, with affected disinterest, "Yes, your messenger—*messengers*—I wonder if we may not discuss *all* the creatures who do your bidding, ere we rejoin the others, my lord . . ." She moves quickly from the body, using the seemingly inconsequential moment required to study and clean bits of decayed flesh from the arrow. "For it is the only thing that you have yet to—"

"Clever, my girl," the old man answers, with a light laugh. "But let me retain one small secret for now, eh? Well then—to the business at hand. What do you note about the arrow?"

Keera's face fills with disappointment as she lets the arrow rest upon her finger. "The balance is wretched. You could not loose this shaft from more than a short distance with any chance of accuracy. And these flights—there is no question of their being able to steady its course, even could you launch it further."

"Just so," Caliphestros judges approvingly. "And what, then, would you guess the likelihood of the best Broken archers killing a man with such arrows to be, even were the condemned close by?"

"Small, my lord," Keera replies. "If it exists, at all."

"Indeed, Keera," Caliphestros says. "These arrows are intended to thus deceive Broken's enemies. And the body itself was meant to spread a disease that the priests of Kafra were unaware could *not* be spread after death. They no doubt thought it identical with the Holy Fire, the pious fools . . ."

"Whatever their thinking, they pressed the deadly heads into the softer parts of his flesh," Keera says, "after he was already dead."

"Excellent." Caliphestros urges Stasi a little closer to the corpse, glancing at it again for as long as he can tolerate the stench. "Thus we can, indeed, conclude that the fever had killed him before he was pierced by such precious ritual weapons."

"Then when we were at that terrible pool upriver," Keera says, "you were adamant about our not touching any creatures, the dead along with the living, because we could not say just what affliction had killed which creature, particularly from a distance."

"Well reasoned, Keera," Caliphestros answers. "Would that I had been able to teach the Kafran priests and healers such logic. My quickly increased alarm was due to my detecting the presence of what you call *Moonfire;* for after the victims of that disease—call it what you will, Holy Fire, the *Ignis Sacer* of the *Romani,* or the name other Christ-worshippers use, Saint Anthony's Fire—die, their bodies release a type of evil vapor or bad air,[†] one that the illness seems to use, to carry itself on to other living beings."

"But, surely," Keera answers, "if one disease can ride undetected upon the air released by the bodies, others—such as the rose fever—would do the same."

Caliphestros lets a deep breath escape him in frustration. "Indeed. It is an inconsistency that I have not been able to resolve, save to think that these pestilences, like other orders of beings, are not all equally clever. Why should one sickness remain dangerous after its host has died, while another does not? Most that call themselves healers—and none worse than the Kafran—cannot grasp the notion that this is a question that *must* have an answer. To nearly all such, it is the will of their god, and that is enough."

Although he is about to continue, Caliphestros, like Keera and Stasi, suddenly goes rigid and looks up, when a loud *"Shhh!"* sounds from above. The panther growls low, looking for a tree to climb as well as the human who has, presumably, made the sound; but she finds neither, until Heldo-Bah's voice continues to whisper, "Can you two not conclude this imbecilic discussion, or must you tease out every little thread of mutual congratulation, to assure one another of your shared genius?"

Not even Stasi can locate the gap-toothed Bane at first, thanks to his ever-reliable trick of keeping his body smeared with the scents of various animals when in peril; and it is unsurprising, therefore, that neither Caliphestros nor Keera can spot him, either. Soon enough, however, Heldo-Bah's ugly mouth and teeth—made somehow even more repellent by their being upside down—appear, along with the rest of his face, when he lets himself slowly hang by the knees from the lower limb of a nearby oak tree, its branches laden with leaves.

"Heldo-Bah!" Keera says. "So you *did* make good time in getting here!"

"And shall remember your unkind words on that subject," Heldo-Bah replies. "The very thought that we would shirk our duty at a moment such as—"

"Get them into the trees, will you not, Heldo-Bah?" comes Veloc's whispering voice, from further up; then, to his sister, he adds, "You are in greater danger than you know, Keera—I would suggest any one of this stand of trees for you, and that rather obliging beech, there, for Lord Caliphestros and his companion, who will find its lower limbs easily conquered."

Heeding Veloc's sense of urgency with no more than whispers and gestures, the old man is able to direct Stasi up and into the nearby beech, which does indeed have several stout lower limbs that grow at odd angles, offering easy pathways upward to the panther's sharp claws and powerful legs. In only a few quiet moments, cat and rider find themselves in the higher reaches of the beech, at about the height of the three Bane, who are nestled into other, more upright trees of different varieties.

"At last," Heldo-Bah whispers. "I did not think that either of you would ever allow us to get a word in, that you might get off the ground and into safety. Great gods, what vain chattering . . ."

Now that Keera is away from the rotting soldier, the scent of men becomes unmistakable, bringing several low growls from Stasi before Caliphestros quiets the panther. Yet it is not the simple scent of one tribe of men, but the complex aromas of at least two, and perhaps more. "Yes— I make it out, now," Keera pronounces. "Our own warriors, somewhere close by. But something else, too—not the honest scent of true Broken soldiers, but the scented, preening aroma of—of—"

"Baster-kin's Guard, sister," Veloc says, directing his chin to the far side of the river. "They imagine themselves well hidden, but even I can pick up the scent and detect their movements. I imagine they await the arrival of some more powerful contingents of the actual Broken army— a fact that would be comforting, were our own men not also proving inexplicably noisy, behind us . . ."

"Behind us?" Caliphestros asks. "You mean to say that we . . . ?"

"Yes, old sage," Heldo-Bah replies scornfully. "You've hit upon it: we've stumbled between two quietly advancing forces, and sudden revelation of our presence may be enough to earn us either outright execution from the Guard, or several mistakenly aimed, poison-tipped arrows from advance groups of our own archers, who are no doubt very, very nervous just now. A devilish predicament . . ."

"But what can your commander be thinking?" Caliphestros says, somewhat stunned. "When stealth and the Wood have always been your people's greatest protections?"

"I believe he intends some gesture," Heldo-Bah replies, "to make the Tall reconsider all their usual thoughts about how our people fight."

Veloc is far from satisfied with this explanation: "And yet it is inexplicable that Ashkatar should make so terrible an error—he is a great soldier . . ." An idea strikes Veloc at that moment, and he turns to face south. "Linnet!" he suddenly says, not in a full shout, but in a whisper loud enough to be clearly detected. *"Any* Linnet, in the Army of the Bane Tribe!"

"Veloc, you imbecile, shut your mouth!" Heldo-Bah commands; and it is well that he does, for almost immediately, an arrow that they both recognize as having come from a sharp-eyed Bane archer's short bow strikes the tree near the handsome tracker's head. "Do you listen to nothing that I say? Do you imagine that Ashkatar's men are acquainted with the *average* forager's methods of concealment, much less our own, and so can know who we are? Fool!"

At the commotion, Stasi growls deeply, looking now to the woodland to the south and its small race of men, who suddenly seem a source of threat: unusual and confusing considerations, for her, an animal who has always respected the Bane enough to spare them from vengeful attacks, just as they have always respected her. Caliphestros whispers words of explanation and reassurance to his companion, stroking her magnificent white coat, but she will not take her brilliant green eyes from the forest, and the fur of her mighty neck and shoulders remains bristling and high, as her tail begins to flick in a manner that would ordinarily mean death for some creature. Keera, observing her fellow foragers' confusion and the discomfort of their new allies with equal alarm, decides that she alone can remove the threat of violence from this turn of events.

"The pair of you!" she whispers loud to her brother and Heldo-Bah, swinging down to a lower branch of her tree. "Make no move. And if you would please oblige me, Lord Caliphestros—I will bring some member of our own forces to our position without useless death. If I can . . ."

With a few more fast, agile movements, Keera reaches the forest floor, and disappears into the undergrowth of the thicker woodland. Her brother offers one quick protest, but Heldo-Bah has a tight hand over his mouth before he can do any more.

Their wait is a mercifully short one. There are few of Ashkatar's officers and men who do not know Keera, at least by reputation; and she manages to find and return with a young pallin who relates that the Bane commander's force has been on the watch for the return of Heldo-Bah's foraging party—along with "unexpected guests," Ashkatar has been careful to say, although he has vouchsafed no more to his men, in the hope that they would not serve their various watches in a state of panic. No warning of Ashkatar's could truly have prepared his men for the approach of Caliphestros: and when the young Bane warrior sees not only the old man but the enormous white panther, as well, descending from their beech tree, he begins to visibly shake.

Keera puts a reassuring hand to his shoulder. "Do not fear, Pallin," she says. "They have proved true friends of our tribe—for many years, it turns out."

"Yes," the young man gasps, his dark features going quite white, "but you must understand, Tracker Keera: since I was a child, I have been told that this animal was but a myth. And the sorcerer was spoken of only when my mother wished to terrify me into complying with her wishes—"

"Well," Heldo-Bah laughs quietly, leaping to the ground from the next-to-lowest limb of his own perch, "now *you* will have something with which to terrify *her,* young Pallin! As is only right and just, the world turning as it does, and all parents who engage in such behavior eventually receiving a dose of their own medicine, when the Moon is playing fair."

"Pay no attention to Heldo-Bah," Veloc says reassuringly; but he realizes his error immediately, for any comfort he might have offered with his manner is removed by his referring to his infamous friend by name, a name almost as fearful to the pallin as is that of Caliphestros.

"*Heldo-Bah?*" says the young man, again turning to Keera. "Then it is true you travel with the murderer—" Quickly realizing his own misstep, the soldier glances back at the approaching forager. "Although I have been told, we have all been told, of the great and terrible quest upon which the Groba sent you, several days ago, and I respect your patriotism, sir—"

"Don't bother, boy," Heldo-Bah whispers cheerfully, showing the filed, irregular teeth in a grin that does little to help the trembling young fellow. "I do what I do for my friends, out of the desire to exact vengeance on the Tall, and because I must—no great nobility involved in it, as you will yourself discover, should your yantek actually be fool enough to take you out across the river and onto the Plain." The lethal eyes search the forest further south. "Where is he, by the way? I rather expected *him* to greet us, after what we've been through."

"Be at your ease, soldier," Veloc attempts, joining the group and leaving Stasi and Caliphestros just a few steps behind, so that they are both partially hidden and shielded by his own and Heldo-Bah's bodies. "You have nothing to fear from any of us, as I'm sure my sister has told you."

"Sister?" the lad repeats. "So you, then, are Veloc, the final member of the party. I am honored—"

"You need to put aside all this being honored and tell us what's happening, little hero in swaddling clothes," Heldo-Bah says, still merrily, but also insultingly enough, now, to make the soldier a bit indignant, despite his fear.

"Ignore my friend," Keera says, wondering just how many times she has *had* to say such things, as she claps the pallin's shoulder hard to bring him back to the point. "Rudeness comes to him as does breathing to most." She looks to her fellow foragers with familiar irritation. "The pallin was part of a small scouting party, when I found him—his linnet and another pallin have gone back to fetch Ashkatar, but it will likely take a few moments, as the yantek is moving up and down the line. Apparently, he does indeed intend the attack that Lord Caliphestros envisioned. It seems we have arrived only just in time to prevent a terrible error."

Very soon, Ashkatar, even more heavily armed than is his usual custom, whip firmly in hand, comes running into the small clearing into which the foragers and their guests have moved with the pallin, another foot soldier and an equally young linnet trailing close behind him.

"Ah—so it's true, then," he says through the bristling black beard, his voice rumbling from deep in his chest despite his lowered volume. "The three of you have returned." Looking over Veloc's and Heldo-Bah's shoulders, however, even the powerful and angry Ashkatar pales a bit. "And have succeeded in your mission—or so it would seem," he adds, his voice losing a good deal of its certainty and confidence.

Both Stasi and Caliphestros draw themselves up proudly, at the appearance of this small but impressive man, for whom authority is an obvious habit, and begin to move slowly forward. The young Bane soldiers move backward in a matching manner, but Ashkatar stands his ground admirably, and even takes a step or two forward to greet the newcomers. "You are welcome among us, Lord Caliphestros. Should I—would it be customary to address your great companion, the noble white panther?" Ashkatar speaks uncertainly, yet also with great respect. "Keera informs us that she understands human communications very well."

This statement clearly impresses and pleases Caliphestros, although he stops short of smiling. "Thank you, Yantek Ashkatar. Your manner does you credit. No, you need not offer any particular address to my friend, although she will be able to sense both your own and your men's intentions and attitudes instantly. They would do well to remember that fact, and to spread the word quickly, so that there are no unhappy misunderstandings as we make for your camp and then for Okot."

"Well, you lot?" Ashkatar barks at his men. "You heard Lord Caliphestros. Return to my camp, quickly, and tell all troops you encounter to make it known up and down the line just who has arrived, and how they are to conduct themselves." Half-turning to see the soldiers too awed to comply, he growls. "Go on, then! And have my staff prepare food in my tent. We shall follow quickly behind." As the young soldiers vanish into the forest undergrowth, the great black beard turns to Caliphestros again. "I should, perhaps, have said that we will return however quickly it is your pleasure to travel, my lord. You will find my men nervous, at your arrival, as you have seen, but you will also find our leaders grateful for your willingness to come to our aid in this time of crisis."

"Just how much aid I shall be, Yantek," Caliphestros replies, still aware of the need for appearances, "is yet to be seen. I must judge the worthiness and intentions of your tribe, although I have never been given cause to doubt either."

Ashkatar nods, clearly impressed by and appreciative of this statement. "Shall we proceed, then, my lord?" he asks, holding his whip out in the direction that the soldiers took to return to their lines, and where Caliphestros can now see a rough trail barely marked out. He senses that Ashkatar expects him to move up and walk by his side, as the highest Bane authority present, and the old man indicates to Stasi to do so. She shows no hesitation in complying, for she has truly taken the measure of this rugged yet proud and impressive man, and found him to her liking. As he passes Keera by, however, Caliphestros brings Stasi to a halt, and says to Ashkatar:

"I should like the tracker Keera to walk alongside us, as well, Yantek Ashkatar. She has already proved most invaluable, both to me, to the discovery of information invaluable to our shared goals of learning who and what lies behind the terrible illness—if single illness it be—that so afflicts the Wood and your tribe, and in the cause of keeping the great being upon whose back I am privileged enough to travel calm and reassured."

"Of course, my lord," Ashkatar says. "Although I fear the other two must follow behind. Veloc and Heldo-Bah are not held in the respect that Keera enjoys, among our tribe, and it would be inappropriate to offer them such honor, whatever their service in the last few days."

Caliphestros lifts his nose in mock haughtiness as he moves forward past the two male foragers, murmuring to Heldo-Bah in particular, "How refreshingly accurate and honest an assessment, Yantek . . ."

"Well, Heldo-Bah," Veloc says, making sure he cannot be overheard by those in front of him. "It's the servants' place for us. As usual . . ."

"Speak for yourself, Veloc," Heldo-Bah replies bitterly. "There will be time enough for us to claim our proper position and respect, once our story becomes known."

"Oh, certainly," Veloc replies, his voice the essence of sarcasm. "But for now—try not to trod upon any panther droppings . . ."

So numerous and rapt in wonder are the Bane soldiers that appear on both sides of the route that the remarkable lead party take south (a path which leaves the course of the river behind altogether) that no one at first thinks to comment on Caliphestros's peculiar request for Ashkatar's tough, game troops to begin digging holes in the ground every one or two hundred paces. The old man quickly becomes immersed in their efforts, and seems satisfied with the results only when the troops' shovels reach water beneath the forest floor. He is especially fascinated when the water thus discovered bears a particular odor, an odor reminiscent, to Keera (whose memory of what she has perceived through her senses is as sharp as those senses themselves), of the dying pool that she visited in the aging scholar's and Stasi's company only hours before. Most of the troops doing the digging cannot help but wonder further at Caliphestros's insistence that all men and women who come into contact with such fluids instantly bathe their hands with strong lye soap, and above all do not drink of their discoveries. His inscrutable behavior in this regard seems only to match both his reputation and overall manner, however, and one thing that is clear is that Caliphestros is not a man to see such efforts as the soldiers expend go wasted. Yet not until the group goes before the Groba will the full significance of these strange investigative activities become startlingly clear . . .

Stone

{i:}

THE WARM, GENTLE BREEZE that blows across the city of Broken from the west on this spring night might be expected to offer some comfort to the greatly admired yet even more feared chief of the kingdom's most powerful trading clan, Rendulic Baster-kin. Such soft, sensual waves of air, particularly when they occur at night, are known as "Kafra's Breath," for the welcome effect that they have on the citizens of the city, who are just emerging from beneath winter's hard-soled boot. This widespread sense of joyous release is perhaps best embodied in the scattered pairs of trysting young lovers that the Lord of the Merchants' Council can even now spy on the rooftops of their various houses in the First District from his vantage point on one of the two highest points in the city: the terrace that surrounds the central tower of the magnificent *Kastelgerd* Baster-kin. Both the terrace (once a parapet) and the tower were originally intended as defensive military positions, from which threats to the family and the city itself could be spied long before they became deadly; but for generations, that function has been unnecessary, and the tower as well as the terrace have served as the private sanctum of the Merchant Lord, a place to which the supreme secular official of Broken may summon any subject—nearly all of whom dread such invitations.

Far below the tower lies the foundation of the *Kastelgerd*, completely concealed from public view and composed of another section of the city's remarkable series of vaulted storage chambers, which, like all the others, is filled to overflowing with weapons and provisions. Above the foundation, the visible wings of the great residence are on a scale, it has often been said (not always with respect or admiration) to match the palace of the God-King. But because the *Kastelgerd* sits hard by the eastern wall of the city, and was first intended to serve the same genuine military purpose as the tower, it is stouter in overall appearance than the sacred ruler's paradise: a forbidding exterior that further cows those who are required to attend audiences within.

Yet throughout Broken's history it has been the tower that has remained the most unnerving part of the *Kastelgerd*. If the Sacristy of the High Temple is Broken's greatest wonder, and the royal palace the kingdom's most beauteous enigma, then the tower is the clearest and plainest statement of raw power within the city's walls. The Merchant Lord may have no religious title, as such, but his might is in no way diminished by the suggestion that it is not governed by sacred codes: quite the contrary. Thus, while most citizens would rather forgo a command to appear in either the Sacristy of the Temple *or* Baster-kin's tower, they would far rather receive a summons to the holier of the two chambers—a fact from which Rendulic Baster-kin cannot help but derive a deeply personal satisfaction. A location that inspires so much fear in others is the only sort of place where this man, whose deepest soul is a strange blend of worldly severity and almost boyish enthusiasms and fears, can feel truly safe.

With his own security, as well as his family's, nearly as well protected as the God-King's, then, it seems odd indeed that Baster-kin—even and perhaps especially as he stands upon the parapet of his tower, this night—cannot allow himself to take any solace in the voluptuous brush of Kafra's Breath. Indeed, the warm air only seems to make the uneasiness that is plain in his features more apparent.

His concern has been caused, first, by the latest in a series of reports that began to arrive during the winter, detailing the particulars of northern raiders bringing cheap grain up the Meloderna and the Cat's Paw to trade illegally with undiscovered partners. Such a story would not, ordinarily, cause Rendulic Baster-kin undue anxiety: disgruntled farmers and traders in some quarter or another of the kingdom are a constant, given the sacred laws and secular codes that govern such activities in Broken. But dispatches over the last several days from Sentek Arnem have reported that more than one trading village has crossed over from unhappiness into open rebellion; and their violence has been unknowingly fueled, Arnem's reports say, by spoilt grain, several kernels of which he has included for Baster-kin's perusal, along with a warning that the Merchant Lord wash his hands carefully after inspecting them. Yet even this combination of provincial reports and those of the new commander of Broken's army would not be enough to alarm Baster-kin, at any other time. But there is a final thread that does stitch these seemingly manageable problems into what may become a tapestry of serious worry: the samples of dangerous grain that Arnem has sent to the Merchant Lord resemble all too closely kernels that the ever-watchful master of Broken's mightiest *Kastelgerd* has, within the last day and night, found in one of the hidden stores beneath the city.

Rendulic Baster-kin's commitment and sacrifices to his kingdom and his office have always been great: far greater, he would rightly contend, than those of not only the other members of the Merchants' Council and previous Merchant Lords, but even of his own father, the most infamously ruthless Baster-kin of all. Certainly, Rendulic believes that he has little in common with the earliest man in his family to be declared Merchant Lord, who had been the most cunning of the mercenary adventurers who accompanied Oxmontrot on his travels about the world in the service of the Western and Eastern halves of the vast yet strangely fragile empire of *Lumun-jan,* and who had brought the creed of Kafra back to Broken. Yet despite these shared adventures, according to rumors too well founded to die, it was not loyalty to Oxmontrot that secured the first Lord Baster-kin a place of prominence in Broken politics and society, but treachery. For his elevation in rank, along with the gift of resources sufficient to build the first wings of the *Kastelgerd* around the family's original tower, had come not from the Mad King, but from Oxmontrot's son, Thedric; and it had been said then, and has been said ever since, that the origins of both the Baster-kins' renown and their wealth could be traced to complicity in the murder of the Mad King. Not many who had known Thedric, after all, had credited him with enough intelligence (or his mother, Justanza, with enough sanity) to have planned and carried out the scheme on their own; and construction of the *Kastelgerd* Baster-kin had indeed begun on the very day that Thedric had been crowned and declared semi-divine. Since then, additions to both the *Kastelgerd* and the elaborate, terraced gardens that wind about it have been almost constant—constant, that is, until the ascension of Rendulic Baster-kin, who has been determined to wipe away all smears upon his family's name through his devotion, faith, and hard work.

In addition, if there have been more than a few unworthy men among his ancestors, Rendulic knows, there have also been several wise enough to merit respect. First among these were the Lords Baster-kin who—

indignant at frequent abuses of power by the Merchants' Council, which periodically sought to take advantage of the royal family's isolation from secular affairs—created and strengthened an instrument of force with which to serve Thedric's heirs: the Personal Guard of the Lord of the Merchants' Council (or, more commonly, Lord Baster-kin's Guard, as no other clan chief, after one or two early and disastrous challenges, has ever held the office). For many generations, the strict mandate of these not-quite-military units was simply to maintain the quiet, secure, and legal conduct of trade within the city. But eventually, being an instrument of secular power, the Guard had been corrupted, not only by rivals to the Baster-kins, but even (or so some voices said) by certain royal representatives, who wished their peculiar yet sacred activities to remain discreet. The Guard also widened its activities to include keeping the peace, a task that became ever more violent and even lethal, as the prevention of thievery and plots within the city expanded to include the authority to arrest, beat, torture, and even execute whatever persons, within or without the walls, the linnets of the Guard found objectionable. True, the head of the Baster-kin clan always retained command of the increasingly unpopular Guard; but command and control have ever been very different qualities. Then, too, while the clan Baster-kin may have been losing its effective grip on the Guard, the fact that its "soldiers" continued to keep careful watch over the great *Kastelgerd* lent to that residence and to its lords something like a regal air, one sufficient to allow the Lords Baster-kin to deny even well-founded charges of degeneracy, corruption, and effective tyranny: abuses, all three of which Rendulic's father had managed to practice within one lifetime.

And so it would be for the man who now paces the terrace of his tower to reassert both his family's honor and its devotion to Kafran ideals, a task that Rendulic has undertaken not only through public pronouncements and rulings, but by way of private methods more extreme than any citizen has ever known of or appreciated. Yet these steps have not brought him peace of mind: no, for one as alert to danger as is Rendulic Baster-kin, even those threats that come in so seemingly inconsequential a form as a few misshapen and discolored kernels of grain must push the pleasure of a mild spring evening from his mind—particularly now. *Now,* at the outset of what will be the most fateful period in Broken's history: a time when the kingdom's ongoing pursuit of the sacred Kafran goals of perfecting all aspects of individual and collective strength must, of necessity, regain primacy. Any lingering doubts or hesitancy among the leaders of Broken concerning both the annexation of the daunting wilderness of Davon Wood and the destruction of the tribe of outcasts who inhabit that cursed but treasure-laden forest should have been put to rest, Baster-kin believes, first by the attempt on the life of the God-King, and then by the mutilation and death of Herwald Korsar. And yet, despite the city's proud, joyous dispatch of the Talons upon their twin missions of conquest, only three people truly know, with any kind of certainty, what actually determined the momentous decision to move against the Wood and the Bane now. The first two of these—the God-King and the Grand Layzin—remain, tonight as all nights, inaccessible to the people of the city and the kingdom, and free to enjoy their particular pleasures. The third, Baster-kin himself, is the only man who is not only aware of but entirely consumed by every consideration that has gone into the decision to dispatch the kingdom's most elite soldiers against the Bane; and so the Merchant Lord stands alone, peerless and friendless, upon his parapet, tonight, brooding over a single kernel of spoilt grain that lies hidden in one of his hands.

Damn Arnem, Baster-kin muses; *a soldier should be concerned solely with unrest in the kingdom, rather than confirming my fears about this strange grain.* Yet the Merchant Lord knows that the problem represented by what he holds in his hand is not so easily dismissed as he would like; Sentek Arnem, in fact, has only done his true duty by making his report. *A pity he will have to pay such a high price for it,* Baster-kin concludes. And yet, is it not Kafran doctrine that one man's loss is another's gain? And, thinking of this possibility—that Arnem's loss might be his own gain—Baster-kin becomes aware, for the first time, of the gentle caress of Kafra's Breath. But he cannot indulge the instant of pleasure; for he must be certain of his next moves, as certain as he has been of all arrangements that have been made this week. Such attention to detail quickly drives him out of the comfort of a spring night's warm breeze and back inside his tower, there to attend himself to the details of his plans: plans that, to the untrained mind, might all too closely resemble scheming . . .

Baster-kin reenters the octagonal tower without ever taking notice that the room's gaping stone fireplace—which is set into its southern wall, with a massive mantel supported by granite sculptures of two rampant Broken brown bears who have been frozen in eternal submission and service—is empty of flame, due to the warmth of the evening. His attention is immediately and wholly fixed upon a large, heavy table at the room's center, its shape the same as the tower itself, and its size large enough to permit meetings of the most important members of the Merchants' Council. Tonight, however, it is covered by maps of the kingdom, over which lie the dispatches of Sentek Arnem, detailing the state of the towns and villages between Broken and Daurawah—as well as the conditions of their grain stores.

But most importantly, atop all these sheets of parchment lies a note from Isadora Arnem, which she left with the second-most-powerful man in the *Kastelgerd*, the Baster-kin family's greying yet remarkably vigorous seneschal, Radelfer.[†] A veteran of the Talons, and possessed of all the highest traits of loyalty, courage, and honor associated with that *khotor*, Radelfer was once the guardian of the youthful Rendulic Baster-kin: plucked from the ranks of the kingdom's finest legion by Rendulic's father, he had spent almost twenty years playing a role that the elder Baster-kin ought by rights to have filled himself. Now, the aging but still powerful Radelfer oversees affairs in his former charge's home; and when Lady Arnem first appeared at the *Kastelgerd*'s entrance just two evenings after her husband's departure from the city, only to find Lord Baster-kin himself not at home, she had asked to see Radelfer, with whom she apparently had past acquaintance. Happy to see the seneschal, and hinting at some urgent business with the Merchant Lord, Isadora had announced her intention to return the following evening, leaving behind a note that said as much. And it is this note that, to judge from its position atop the great table in Rendulic Baster-kin's most private retreat, the Merchant Lord considers more important than all the maps of the Cat's Paw crossings and the dispatches concerning unrest in the kingdom that lie beneath it. As he leans upon the table, he studies the note; not for its few and inconsequential words, but rather for the hand that wrote them, the hand that is so like it was, many years ago . . .

His distraction is interrupted when he suddenly hears a shriek, the human cry that he most dreads—a desperate, pained sound that might once have belonged to a woman, but surely cannot be made by any mortal throat now. It comes from one of the largest bedchambers in the northernmost corner of the *Kastelgerd,* opposite the northwestern face of the Merchant Lord's octagonal tower. Listening to the sound with no more than a passive, even a downcast, reaction, Baster-kin comes to a conclusion: *The heralds of death and rebirth ought to have a voice,* he tells himself, *and no one could deny that such a cry would more than suit their purpose* . . . His own behavior certainly gives little evidence of such momentous change: as the voice shrieks on, only the fingers of his right hand move, slowly and forcefully grinding the fragile seed of grain held within them against his palm, until it has become but dusty bits.

There is little about this scene that can be called new, a fact that does not stop Baster-kin's patience and temper from wearing away, as if the voice were in fact some sort of demon's lash striping his very soul: for it is, in truth, the sound of his own wife's voice, and it continues on and on, echoing through the halls of the *Kastelgerd* like a loosed fury. Assuming an accusatory tone, it screeches just one word over and over—and that one word is his name:

"*Rendulic!*"

But Baster-kin only moves to a basin in the tower room's corner, remembering Sentek Arnem's urgent warning that he wash his hands after handling the tainted grain.

{*ii:*}

HOPING THAT ONE of Lady Baster-kin's ladies or her healer will soon control her screaming, his lordship paces about his high retreat, studying the only ornamentation in the room: four enormous tapestry panels that cover the walls between the eastern and western doorways, all depicting an earlier time in Rendulic's life, the celebrated moment when he had completed his transformation from a slight, sickly youth into the strong, manly figure that he is today: the time when, though only eighteen years old, he had embarked upon a panther hunt. This had been the kind of hunt about which the scions of Broken's merchant families dreamt, in the days before the city's Stadium became their haunt: before, that is, less hazardous sport replaced the dangers of battling wild beasts and pursuing Bane criminals and Outragers into Davon Wood.

During his hunt—which was led by that same tireless guardian, Radelfer, who had ever been the boy's only true friend and counselor—Rendulic, riding ahead of his men, had encountered a group of four adolescent panthers, offspring of no less than the fabled white panther of Davon Wood. Although seemingly doomed to a most savage death, Rendulic had nonetheless demanded, when two of the animals were already dead and their mother disabled by a deep wound to one thigh, that he be allowed to engage the final brace of beasts.

The youth who braved death in what seemed so reckless a fashion that day had long been treated as a disappointment by his exacting father, then lord of the *Kastelgerd*. Rendulic had dared to believe, with a passion that made him so bold as to be utterly unconcerned with his own safety, that the outcome of the hunt would change his father's low opinion of him; and, fueled by such thoughts, the brave young man and ever-faithful Radelfer succeeded in tricking and caging the young female panther, after which Rendulic flatly insisted that he be allowed to battle the last male alone. And alone, with arrows, pike, and finally a long, elegant dagger, Rendulic had indeed fought that animal, in the same clearing beyond the Cat's Paw where the rest of the battle had taken place. Having mortally wounded the young panther with his pike, Rendulic gripped his dagger tight and used it to administer the *dauthu-bleith* to the still-defiant beast—all within clear sight of the animal's living but helpless mother.

Doing thus, Rendulic had made this hunt, the last of its kind, a legend among the people of Broken. Even so, his father had not proved as readily persuaded of his son's worthiness as Rendulic had hoped: a result, the youth chose to believe, of a bout of the pox that was returning to torment the aging lord with ever greater frequency. Then, too, the Stadium's athletics were fast on their way to eclipsing woodland blood sports, and young men and women would, from that time on, turn almost exclusively to such activities for excitement, and as a way to prove themselves to the citizenry. True, their exhausting amusements still included contests against the great beasts of the Wood: but now those animals were captured and safely chained upon the sands of the Stadium, so that death was never a real danger for any young Broken athlete who entered the lists.

But it should not be thought that the tale of Rendulic Baster-kin's panther hunt was forgotten: indeed, its memory would later form the basis of much of his unquestioned personal authority in the city. *And most of all*, he broods as he stares at the tapestries, *it had virtually eliminated talk of an earlier incident in his life, an incident that was rumored to have involved a romantic quest after a young beauty from the Fifth District who was but two or three years older than he, the assistant to a renowned healer who had been summoned to help when, as the first signs of manhood matured in his young body, a terrible malady from which Rendulic had always suffered, that of the* megrem,[†] *had worsened cruelly. This crippling pain in the head and illness of the gut had proved beyond the skills of all Kafran doctors, just as it had, since ancient times, outwitted so many such feckless healers around the world, who knew it by different names. Any such men or women worth their fees, however, could recognize its symptoms instantly: the healer Gisa, for example, had been able not only to name it, but to ease it, with treatments that secretly took place at one of the Baster-kin family's lodges on the lower slopes of Broken, whence one of the Merchant Lord's younger brothers, an uncle who was near alone in having sympathy for the boy, tended to the herds of cattle upon the Plain that bore the family's name. To such a place, Radelfer knew, the lord himself was unlikely to venture; and in this safe and shielded place, the ancient healer who was a legend to most of Broken, but a boon to many others in her native Fifth District, had set Rendulic Baster-kin on the road to a healthy manhood.[‡] But while Gisa prepared the tinctures and infusions herself, keeping the ingredients jealously secret, the actual doses were administered by the soothing hands of the crone's lovely apprentice, the orphaned girl called Isadora. Golden-haired and tall, Isadora possessed a comforting touch that had burrowed its way deep into young Rendulic's heart and mind, and had been the source of his scandalously desperate efforts to find her in the weeks that followed her departure from his bedside. The boy's father, meanwhile, either ignored or threatened to remove all such wagging tongues: and once his latest bout of the pox had passed, the sight of a son growing healthy had made the relentless Lord Baster-kin take horse, and begin the search for a politically advantageous wife for his heir . . .*

Suddenly, Rendulic Baster-kin notices that another figure has appeared in the room: unannounced, remarkably, by any knock or other request for admission to the chamber. In a silent, eerie manner, this figure makes its entrance through a door opposite that to the terrace. He is clad in a black hooded robe of the lightest cotton; but what should be the exposed parts of his body—the hands, feet, and face—are wrapped in white cotton bandaging, continuous save for narrow slits that reveal the eyes, nostrils, and mouth. The brief opening and closing of the door to the high tower room brings the shrieking voice below all the more clearly into Baster-kin's sanctum, and he hears the cruelly suffering woman shout distinctly, *"What is it . . . ? No! I will not, I have told you, unless my husband comes and puts the cup to my lips himself, I will not . . . !"* Then, as the black-clad figure closes the iron-banded oak door, the sound fades somewhat, and Baster-kin sighs in relief, before turning back to the table, obscuring Lady Arnem's note with his hands, and leaning upon the maps and correspondence as if he had been studying them closely.

"Well?" the Merchant Lord says quietly, in a strangely uncertain tone: disdain is present, and brusqueness, too, but something else tempers these harder sentiments, creating an opening for both tolerance and— what is it? Affection? Surely not.

The voice that speaks in reply, although it attempts discretion, is helplessly unpleasant: words poorly enunciated, accompanied by bursts of spittle that escape from one corner of the mouth, and the sound itself hoarse, grating, and displeasing. "My lord," it announces, "the infusion is being administered. The crisis should soon pass, says Healer Raban[†]— although it would pass the quicker, he begs me inform you, should you yourself administer the drugs, and wait by her side as they take effect."

Baster-kin only grunts in ridicule—but it is ridicule prompted by the thought of the traditional Kafran healer called Raban, and not by the messenger who brings it, that much is clear. He continues to stare at the map before him. "I trust you told that idiotic butcher that I am far too busy with matters of state to undertake a nurse's work?" Baster-kin's head remains determinedly still, but out of the corners of his eyes he nonetheless catches, by the light of torches held in iron sconces on the walls, a brief glimpse of the black robes and hood, as well as the white bandaging carefully wrapped around the near-useless hands, their fingers bound as one to oppose each thumb. The creature's feet, as his lordship can more easily see without moving his head, are similarly bandaged, and shod only in soft leather sandals lined with thick lamb's wool; but this is all Baster-kin will even glance at, for he has plainly seen this strange vision, in all its detail, before. He needs, above all, to avoid the bound face, in which the two azure eyes and the mouth are visibly surrounded by bits of deteriorating flesh marked by moist, pus-filled sores and leathery cracks in the visible skin. And yet, the voice that emerges from this pitiable human wreckage speaks, not with an air of criticism, nor even with a servant's obsequiousness, but in a tone much like Baster-kin's: with a certain familiarity, even intimacy.

"I told Raban as much," the voice explains. "But he bid me warn you that, if you cannot find a moment to visit with her, he will not answer for her behavior when the effects of the drugs subside."

Baster-kin draws in a deep, weary breath. "All right. If we can make some greater sense of this business with Arnem, I shall do as Raban requests. But if not, you must simply tell my lady's charlatan to administer *more* of his cursèd drugs . . ."

"Raban says he has already treated her with as high a dose as he considers safe. Any more, he says, and her heart will slow so that death will draw near, and perhaps overtake her."

A part of Baster-kin would like to give voice to the passionate but silent response that is plain on his face: that it might be better for all concerned (and particularly for him) if such death *did* write an end to the unfortunate woman. But then duty and, perhaps, some trace of true concern abolish all such thoughts and set the jaw once more. "Very well," is all that he answers quietly.

"There is more," says the black-clad figure. "Lady Arnem is here, once again. As she said she would be . . ."

"*What?*" Baster-kin finally looks up at the peculiar man opposite him. "But she was not to arrive for another hour. Does Radelfer know that she is here? Has he placed her somewhere—?"

"I have taken the liberty of consulting Radelfer," the slurring, spitting voice answers, "and it was our decision that he show Lady Arnem into the library, and keep all its doors firmly closed. I have also suggested to him that he might entertain her, for they are known to each other, and they seem to have genuine affection for one another. His service in the Talons also coincided, it seems, with at least some of the sentek's early years in those ranks—they may have known one another then. And if any room is safe from the cries coming from the north wing, it is the library, particularly if conversation is taking place. Finally, Lady Arnem has been informed that her early arrival cannot be expected to have more than a slight effect upon your own urgent schedule."

Baster-kin looks uneasy at this statement: another uncommon reaction to draw from him. "And how did she receive all this information?" he asks.

"I would not report that she was pleased," the spectral figure responds. "But as I have said, she trusts Radelfer, and that trust induces her to make every effort to manifest understanding and respect. All should yet be well—or so I would hazard."

A shadow of gratitude quickly passes over Baster-kin's face. "Very wise, Klauqvest,"[†] he says, suddenly and imperiously. "There remain moments when I am reminded why I spared you the fate of the Wood— and yet, when you have so little contact with properly formed persons, how is it, I wonder, that you can be so deft at dealing with them?" The rhetorical question, and the sentiment beneath it, is not meant to be as cruel as it sounds; and if it is received as malicious, the man Klauqvest exhibits no sign of it. But then, beneath so much bandaging, as well as the wafting black robe, it would be nearly impossible to distinguish one response from another . . .

Baster-kin shifts the position of several maps on the table, affecting a control of his own passions that is, for one who knows him as well as this Klauqvest apparently does, plainly transparent: the coming of Isadora Arnem has disordered his confidence. "And does she offer any explanation for the liberty she takes by arriving so early?" the Merchant Lord inquires.

"No, but I suspect you know the reason," replies the moist, scratching voice. "Or, at least, the greater part of it."

Mildly annoyed by the familiar tone of this comment, Baster-kin forgoes reprimand or argument, and proceeds directly to the source of the trouble: "The dispatch of my messages to her home," he murmurs, nodding slowly.

"Yes, my lord," Klauqvest replies. "Although there are other points to be considered, as well." The master of the *Kastelgerd* glances up in mild surprise. "She has, it appears, received some further communication from her husband. And, while she would say nothing precise to Radelfer on the subject, I formed the impression, as I listened outside the library door, that these latest messages touched upon the same subjects as did the sentek's latest dispatches to your lordship." Klauqvest holds a bandaged hand—one that is more like the extremity of a shelled sea creature than it is like a man's, as his name unkindly suggests—toward a series of lines lightly drawn on the most detailed of the maps of the city and kingdom. "Am I to assume, then, that your lordship intends to accede to Sentek Arnem's request for emergency provisioning of his troops at the encampment he intends to establish near the river?"

Whether it is the course of the questioning being pursued by Klauqvest, or simply the man's voice, that has grated too long on the patience of the Merchant Lord, he suddenly slams a hand down upon the table. "You are to assume nothing!" And yet, as soon as he has lost his temper, Baster-kin makes an obvious effort to regain it—another strange action by this man who usually cares little or nothing for the feelings of his minions. "You have informed me of her presence, Klauqvest," the master of the *Kastelgerd* states, through tightly set teeth. "Well and good. Now, with darkness upon us, I suggest you attend to your original task within the passageways beneath the city, and complete your inventory, continuing to pay special heed to both the quantity and condition of the grain stores, as well as the integrity of the sewers. And, given that your appearance forbids your playing any more open or constructive role in the life of this city and kingdom at this crucial hour, I should think you would be anxious to do so."

What seems a long moment of silence passes between the two men: the gaze within Klauqvest's eyes, whatever the state of the flesh surrounding them, remains clear and fixed upon Baster-kin's own, in as close an expression of defiance as anyone would dare attempt before the Merchant Lord; and yet, for all the rage evident in his quivering jaw, Baster-kin neither continues his outburst nor calls for assistance. Rather, and remarkably, it is *his* eyes that break off the engagement first, as he flings several pieces of clearly unimportant parchment from the table, and then allows himself to sigh in something oddly like contrition. But the look in Klauqvest's gaze never changes, as he waits for silence to return before declaring:

"Very well, then, Father—"

It is the unfortunate creature's first misstep; and his eyes reflect vivid awareness of the error. Baster-kin looks back up as if scalded; and then, his eyes displaying less triumph than profound blending of sadness, disappointment, and anger, he strides about the table and stares hard into the strange man's eyes. Klauqvest is fully as tall as the Merchant Lord, although he soon shies away from the older man a bit, and, as if anticipating a blow, stoops to take a few inches from that height.

"I shall see to my wife," Baster-kin says, in an even tone. "As well as to greeting the Lady Arnem. *You* will remain here, for a time, before returning to those passageways beneath the city that are your only fitting home. I want answers to all my questions—" He waves a hand at the maps and charts upon the table, then draws a step or two closer to Klauqvest, who retreats yet more. "And never forget—I let you live solely to devise such answers, when it became clear that your mind was the only part of your body that Kafra had saved from your unholy origins. Yet, in so doing, I may have worsened the madness that was planted in my lady when you entered this world, and she saw, not only your true lineage, but evidence of the curse that Kafra had placed upon her soul. So *never* let that word escape the vile tangle that passes for your mouth."

Klauqvest's head finally bends in defeat. "Of course. Allow me only to apologize—*my lord.*"

"Keep your apologies." Baster-kin turns toward the door, but then catches himself, in the manner of a hunting animal that has found one last way to torment his wounded prey. "But, since you mention the word—I need not ask, I suppose, just where my *true* son is, right now?"

"As you say—an unnecessary question," Klauqvest responds simply. "Just as I hardly need reply that he is in the Stadium, with his fellow paragons of Kafran virtue . . ."

Baster-kin nods, releasing a long, dissatisfied sigh; and then he says, with continued severity: "I shall attend to him, and to the fools with whom he associates, and I shall do it soon—for upon *his* fate rests the only hope that Kafra has mercifully granted for the preservation of this house, this clan, and this kingdom. And you are to remember that the Wood is ever ready to receive you—as it received that misshapen creature, your sister—should you overstep yourself, should your mind cease to be of use, or, finally, should you choose to communicate with the world outside this tower and above the passageways beneath this *Kastelgerd* and city."

And with that, the Merchant Lord strides out of the room, dragging the heavy oak door closed and slamming it resoundingly.

Alone in the tower chamber, Klauqvest allows his bandaged hands to drift across the documents upon the table for a moment, although he can lift them with only his thumbs and the collected fingers of each hand. Then he leans over, closely studying the maps. His movements remain slow and careful as he takes the further liberty of walking around four of the eight sides of the table, and then standing in the spot that belongs to the lord of the *Kastelgerd,* and sitting in the simple military camp chair that Baster-kin himself is accustomed to using. Trying to fit himself to the feel of the hard wooden arms, and the tight leather that is drawn across the seat and back of the frame, Klauqvest soon finds that his raw, painful skin will not allow it. He stands, continuing to study the maps—

And as he leans over them, a droplet of some salty bodily fluid falls from the exposed portion of his face onto the parchment sheets; a droplet that Klauqvest quickly wipes away, before it can leave any hint of having existed.

Satisfied with what he sees on the detailed charts, Klauqvest moves from the table to one of the tapestry panels, studying the scene it depicts: the dramatic moment before handsome young Rendulic Baster-kin— spear in one hand, dagger in another—killed what would forever be known, throughout Broken, as "his" panther. The composition and nee- dlework are admirable, endowing the young merchant scion with fea- tures of exaggerated courage, and giving the young panther—whose body had, in reality, already been studded with and crippled by arrows— an aspect of equally heightened ferocity and power. Klauqvest then glances down from the tapestry to the hide and head that have lain, for as long as he has lived, on the floor of the chamber; and, with pain so severe that he very nearly cries out, he leans over to stroke the beast's lifeless head with one bandaged hand, and what seems great tenderness.

Rising, and relieved to do so without mishap, Klauqvest steps away from the remains of the panther and toward the chamber's eastern door, which leads out onto the old parapet. He opens the door, looks up at the sky, and sees that the Moon has begun to rise. Staring at that wisp of white in the rich blue of the southeastern twilight, Klauqvest then turns and looks back inside the chamber, at a bronze relief that hangs there:

It depicts the smiling, omnipresent face of Kafra, which—unusually, for such pieces—is set atop a muscular yet lithe young body, clad in naught save a loincloth: a body, Klauqvest knows, that was modeled on Rendulic Baster-kin's own, in the days that followed that same panther hunt that dominates all decoration in the chamber. It is the sort of un- usual yet impressive image that would bring sighs of admiration and rev- erence from most of Broken's citizens, should they ever be permitted to see it; but from this black-robed outcast, only scratching, misshapen sounds that might pass for some sort of laughter emerge. Klauqvest's hooded, bandaged head turns from the Moon to the image of Kafra and back again several times; and then he lets his eyes rest on the relief, as his laughter dies away.

"Smile all you like, golden god," Klauqvest says, fluid again rising in his throat to obscure his words. "But *that* deity"—he lifts a hand to indicate the rising Moon—"is having the best of you, outside these walls. And it has only begun to wax . . ."

{*iii:*}

OUT OF THE STAIRCASE that connects his private tower to the hallway of the *Kastelgerd*'s upper story, Rendulic Baster-kin quickly emerges, moving to the top of the broad central stairway of the residence—one of many deliberately overawing aspects of the building that visitors encounter upon entering through the structure's high, heavy front doors. From above, his lordship sees a short, strong woman dressed in a plain gown of deep blue and bearing a towel[†] that has been soaked in water, as well as a clay pitcher filled with the same liquid. Baster-kin suspects that the healer's servant has been moving repeatedly up and down the stairs between the kitchens to the rear of the great hall and the second-story bedchamber in the north wing, wherein lies the stricken lady of the house, all of the evening. Standing by the railing that runs the length of the gallery's edge and offers a commanding view of the marble-floored entryway below, Baster-kin observes as the same servant halts, runs back down the stairs to fetch a large kettle filled with hot, steaming water, and resumes her speedy errand. When she reaches the top of the stairs once more, she catches sight of the lord of the *Kastelgerd,* and attempts to bow deeply, a task made difficult by the many burdens she bears. Baster-kin waves the woman off, detecting that the heated water contains a new infusion. Such is all he needs to tell him that Healer Raban's first medicinal doses were not, in fact, sufficient to quiet Lady Baster-kin: a fact that, while unsurprising, rouses the master of the house's ire. He makes ready to follow the servant, and to sternly chastise Raban for his half-measures: *Nothing,* he had warned his household servants throughout the previous two days, *not a single detail must be allowed to affect or disturb my meeting with Lady Arnem, on the night I have appointed for it to take place.* If this order required an increased amount of Healer Raban's medicines to calm his lordship's wife, then so be it; but instead, Raban has erred on caution's side, and the consequences of that caution become even more apparent when the maid opens the door to her lady's chamber.

Lady Baster-kin was removed to this luxurious but nonetheless remote location when her screaming fits became uncontrollable and unpredictable enough to cause her husband to worry that she might be— indeed, almost certainly *would* be—heard by strollers on the Way of the Faithful; whereas, facing the inner courtyard of the Kastelgerd and her husband's solitary tower, she would torment none but his lordship—a punishment that Baster-kin has more than once wondered if he has not deserved . . .

"No! I will not swallow another drop, lest it be my husband's hand that places it upon my lips! Rendulic! Tell him—"

But then the door closes again, and the screaming becomes stifled, although no less frantic. The sound strikes fear deep into Baster-kin's heart, particularly when he hears footsteps coming from below: with great speed, he again moves behind one of the marble columns at the gallery's edge, and peers out to see who approaches. He breathes with no little relief when he spies not Lady Arnem but his most trusted servant and counselor, Radelfer, walking alone to the stairway, having come from the library that opens off the southern side of the building's great entry hall. Baster-kin walks out to the open area at the top of the staircase and waits for his faithful seneschal, a tall man who still exudes power, even though his shoulder-length hair, his close-clipped beard, and the tone of his skin have all gone quite grey through his many years of service to the Baster-kin family.

"I told that fool Raban to make his doses strong enough, this evening," Baster-kin says, as the older man falls in beside him and they begin to walk up the hallway of the northern wing. "Has her screaming been audible in the library?"

"Portions of it, my lord, but only if one knew what to listen for," Radelfer answers. "Which I did. But Lady Arnem took no heed."

Baster-kin laughs humorlessly. "None that she told you of, at any rate," he scoffs. "She is far too wise to intrude in such matters, when worries about both her son and her husband have brought her here. I assume those *are* her reasons for calling?"

"Yes," Radelfer replies carefully. "Although she has other information to impart—things that she would not tell me. Some business of great importance having to do with the Fifth District."

"Ah, yes," Lord Baster-kin answers ambiguously. "Come, come, Radelfer—what business in the Fifth District is *ever* of great importance?"

"I only convey the message that she related, my lord," Radelfer says, still watching his former charge carefully as the pair reach the thick door into the bedchamber that has been the source of the evening's disturbances.

"Is it a ploy, Radelfer, do you think?" Baster-kin asks. "To strengthen the plea she makes concerning her son?"

"I would not say so," Radelfer answers calmly; all the more calmly, given that he is lying. "She is little changed: guile is no more her art now than it was years ago, and her concern has an unquestionably genuine quality to it." He affects greater confusion when his master does not immediately reply. "My lord? Are you aware of some matter in the Fifth District that she may have stumbled upon?"

Baster-kin eyes the man. "I, Radelfer? Nothing at all. But tell me—you say she is little changed?"

"So it appears to *my* eyes, lord," Radelfer replies. "But remember—I have ever been a poor judge of women."

Baster-kin laughs. "You had judgment enough to know that both she and her mistress could help me, in my youth, when the rest of Broken's healers proved useless."

"Perhaps," Radelfer replies. "But in my own life, that judgment has been less discerning."

"Many are the great philosophers who know the world well, yet almost nothing of themselves . . . ," says the master of the *Kastelgerd*. Then he weighs the matter at hand silently. "Very well—return to her, Radelfer. Engage her further in conversation, lest she detect our larger purpose. When you are certain all sound from Lady Baster-kin's chamber has been quieted, bring her to the base of the stairs."

"Why not keep her safely in the library—?" Radelfer asks.

"I do not have time, now, Radelfer, to explain in greater detail," Baster-kin replies. "Have her there when all is silent—that is my wish."

Radelfer watches his lord disappear into the bedchamber, arching a brow as he realizes: *Yes—have her there, so that when you descend, you may look all the more impressive. You are as you were, Rendulic, at the mere thought of encountering her: a lovesick boy in search of admiration . . .*

The seneschal's manner changes only when he has descended the grand stairway once more, and is alone; or, rather, presumes he is alone. A whispering voice calls from the shadows beneath the stairs, startling him: "Radelfer . . . ?"

The seneschal turns and sees a black-robed man step out from the darkest shadows in the great hall. "Klauqvest!" Radelfer whispers in surprise. "You should not be here—you risk discovery. There is much activity in the *Kastelgerd* tonight."

"Well do I know it," Klauqvest answers, "but Lord Baster-kin bade me issue several private commands to Healer Raban, which I have just done."

"In truth?" Radelfer takes a moment to turn to the ever-troubling matter of relations between Rendulic Baster-kin and Klauqvest: *If my lord wishes so passionately that this pitiable young man remain hidden,* the seneschal asks himself, *then why does he also insist upon employing him in ways that risk further discovery of his existence?* Dispensing with such unanswerable queries, Radelfer asks aloud, "And are you on your way back to the cellars, then?"

"Not quite," Klauqvest replies.

"I should reconsider that statement, lad, and get below at once, if I were you. Best to be safe, whatever your—" Radelfer pauses to choose his words carefully. "Whatever your *lord and master's* willful ignorance of the risk."

"I shall," Klauqvest says quickly, "but as Raban is already here, I wondered if you could not—*coax* some of his medicines out of him, for I failed in the attempt. I do not seek them for myself, but for Loreleh."†

"Your sister?" Radelfer draws closer still to the bandaged face. "Is she ill?"

"Less ill than in pain," Klauqvest says. "But ask her yourself."

A third timid voice, that of a young maiden, now joins the discussion from a spot even further back in the shadows beneath the stairs. "Hello, Radelfer."

"*Loreleh?*" Radelfer moves further into the shadows, and as his eyes become accustomed to the darkness, he finally discerns the form of a girl whom he knows to be fifteen years old. Her face and most of her form are lovely: pale skin, wide, dark eyes, and luxuriant tresses of dark hair lightly tinted with red, all atop a fine form. The only suggestion of imperfection in this beauteous image is a rough-hewn cane that Loreleh carries in her left hand, which directs the observer's eye to the awkward angle at which the foot on that side of her body is articulated at the end of the leg, and to the heavy, specially cobbled boot that covers that extremity: the girl is clubfooted.[†]

"Are you *both* mad, then?" Radelfer continues. "To be out of the cellars when so much activity consumes this household?"

"I am sorry, Radelfer," Loreleh replies. "And please, do not blame my brother. I forced him to bring me."

Radelfer smiles through his alarm and skepticism. "Forgive my saying that I doubt if such coercion was either necessary or used."

"Oh, but it was," Loreleh replies naïvely, as Radelfer and Klauqvest exchange a knowing glance. The maiden then smiles at them both as she drags the clubbed foot a few steps closer to the seneschal. "But do not suppose that I make this request for medicine for myself, alone: Klauqvest has been suffering too, due to how many tasks our—that *his lordship* has demanded he undertake, these last few days."

"Loreleh, I've told you, I am well enough," Klauqvest protests, in an exhausted, weakening voice that belies his words. "We must address your pain first—"

"Just as you always do," Radelfer says, as he kneels to examine Loreleh's left foot, which is yet covered by the unique boot. Finding nothing, he begins to delicately undo the boot's buckles and laces. "Loreleh, did you fall or twist the foot in some way?"

"No," Loreleh answers quickly; but her brother puts one of his bandaged, claw-like hands atop her head.

"Loreleh," he admonishes gently. "It will defeat our purpose if you insist upon bending facts simply to preserve your foolish pride . . ."

Loreleh submits. "Very well, brother," she murmurs. "I did trip and fall," she continues, to Radelfer. "Two days ago. And so, when we heard that Raban would be coming on another errand . . ."

"Yes, I see," Radelfer replies, by now studying the denuded foot. It is horrifically misshapen and turned inward, certain parts having grown too large for the shortened shin above it; in addition to which, it bears the deep crimson and plum shades of recently acquired bruises. "It must pain you badly. With its additional bones, there is far more to break and to bruise than in your right foot . . ." The considerate manner in which Radelfer utters this last statement almost makes the ugly mockery of a woman's delicate foot that is in his hands sound less a source of shame than an object demanding compassion, an attitude for which Klauqvest and Loreleh are clearly grateful, as they have been throughout their lives, during all of which Radelfer has been more benefactor than servant.

"I will offer you a bargain," Radelfer says, standing. "If you will get back to the cellars as quickly as is possible, the pair of you, I shall secure generous amounts of Healer Raban's medicines, before he departs, and bring them to you as soon as I am able. Fair?"

Unable to stand on the toes of her feet and reach Radelfer's cheek, Loreleh contents herself with taking his one hand in her two and kissing it: an action that plainly embarrasses the seneschal. "Now, now—none of that," he says quickly.

"But we are once more in your debt," Klauqvest whispers. "You go beyond the bounds of service, as you have ever done for us. And so we ask only that you yourself take care, Radelfer, on so dangerous a night."

Attempting to shrug off such sentiments, Radelfer motions in the direction of a hidden door beneath the grand stairway. "Go, I beseech you. Lest we *all* be exiled to Davon Wood . . ."

And, as he says these last words, he hears but does not quite see the stairway portal in the shadows open, then close again. When he is sure all is safe, he turns and directs his steps toward the thick door to the *Kastelgerd*'s library, on the opposite side of the great hall. Striding across the hall's marble floor purposefully, he shakes his head, recalling Klauqvest's words in a whisper:

"'So dangerous a night . . .'" And then he muses silently: *A dangerous night, indeed. And may the gods let it pass quickly—for tonight the Moon throws shadows of an equally dangerous past ever longer across this great house . . .*

{*iv:*}

WITHIN THE BEDCHAMBER in the north wing of the *Kastelgerd*, meanwhile, Rendulic Baster-kin has entered. He quietly closes the door behind him, yet remains close to the doorway, trying to take in the scene before him as if it were new; but all elements within are as they have been for the last few days, as well as during crises of similar intensity and duration that have struck every few Moons over the last several years: the upward arching of his wife's body with the worsening of her fits; the desperate restraining efforts of Lady Baster-kin's own marauder maidservant; the maidservant's obvious discomfort with so freely laying hands upon her mistress, even if it is required; the vapors that rise from the infusions and tinctures of Healer Raban's treatments as they are mixed and brewed and fill the chamber with strange aromas; and, finally, the various and increasingly sharp scents of Lady Baster-kin's body, which bring to any visitor's nose the biting tinge of bitter pain, as well as of deep confusion and fear.

Lord Baster-kin cannot keep his thoughts from journeying back to the early and happy days of his marriage to the marauder princess called Chen-lun,[†] an event that he had dreaded, until his father had returned from the East, the princess and her small retinue riding beside him. Chen-lun could sit a mount as well as any Broken cavalryman, and the treaties that Rendulic's father carried in his personal coffers would benefit not only Broken, but the Baster-kin family; and, while Chen-lun could not have been less like the one maiden ever to have captured Rendulic's heart (the lowborn, golden-haired healer's apprentice from the Fifth District called Isadora), the scion of the Baster-kins—fresh from his panther hunt in Davon Wood—had soon found that this made no difference. The eastern princess was well versed in such amorous skills as would make any young man's head swim. And—although Rendulic's father had succumbed to his pox soon after his return to Broken, without ever speaking another word to his son—the new Lord Baster-kin had only become more deeply enamored of his young bride, all the while. He quickly got the wife his father had selected for him with child, before even the dying man had made his journey to Kafra's paradise . . .

Remaining by the bedchamber door for several moments more, and calling to the fat-faced, richly robed Raban, Baster-kin informs the healer that he himself will approach the bed only when the patient has in fact been calmed. The healer nods obsequiously, and then returns by reverse steps to a table by the bed. He quickly prepares and administers to the tormented woman before him a powerful, crude mixture of several of his drugs: opium, *Cannabis indica,* and, finally, ground and properly brewed wild hops† from the mountainside. The effect of this combination is swift: within moments, Lady Baster-kin's pain and seeming madness finally begin to subside, although, in her face, there is no greater apprehension of the events about her than there had been moments before.

A quieted chamber and household is what Rendulic Baster-kin has repeatedly demanded of Raban this evening. Only when the Merchant Lord is sure the effect is not temporary does he slowly approach his wife's bed. He orders Raban and the healer's apprentice out of the room, but exempts Chen-lun's personal servant from this command: he has learned over the years of his marriage and especially of his lady's illness that even attempting to order the ever-silent attendant from her mistress's presence, particularly during such crises as this one, has no effect, and indeed can lead to unspoken yet dangerous confrontations. The woman, who is called simply Ju,‡ has been Lady Baster-kin's shadow†† since long before the striking, black-eyed princess came to Broken. A dark, silent form, lithe of shape and movement (just as was her mistress, before illness struck and began laying long siege to her body), Ju seems ever to keep one hand on the pommel of a large dagger, its scabbard stitched into a belt drawn round her waist.

Only the most warlike marauders, of the regions to the east and northeast of Broken, carry such blades; and the weapon is not merely ornamental, especially in one such as Ju's hands. Upon those few occasions when Baster-kin has seen her wield it, she has demonstrated admirable skill at the close quarters for which it was designed. He therefore treats the woman with far more respect than he would any common Broken noblewoman's handmaiden, just as Ju plainly appreciates the fact that, difficult as her mistress's long illness has been for Baster-kin, his lordship has neither ignored his wife, nor failed to allow whatever healers she desires to treat her, doubt though he may their abilities. Then, too, this strongest Merchant Lord in the history of the Baster-kin family has never lost his temper when Chen-lun, in the grip of fever and pain, has assaulted her husband with maddened fantasies, uttering indictments that Ju knows are often more than unfair.

But finally, and most importantly, Baster-kin and Ju share one terrible secret: the reason that their lady lies so grievously ill upon the bed between them. Ju knows that, in truth, her lady has been truly fortunate to have been tied to so unexpectedly decent a husband, whatever his occasional manifestations of pained disgust at the sickness that long ago destroyed the intimate world that once gave the pair not only pleasure, but unexpected solace, and which now separates them, both physically and as true man and wife, forever . . .

Chen-lun, too, knows how hard her husband struggles to relieve her pain and cure her disease without revealing the secret of its cause and destroying her name in the kingdom she adopted as her home upon their marriage. Indeed, if the full facts were known, they would likely ruin her even among her own people; and the knowledge of her lordship's faith inspires the initially happy (if still feverish) attitude that she takes toward him, once she is indeed certain that her perception of his tall form emerging from the shadowy entryway to the bedchamber is more than the mere effect of illness or drugs.

"*Rendulic,*" she whispers, attempting a smile and some sense of composure; but her face and body offer living testament to the torment she has endured during the hours leading to this meeting.

For his part, Baster-kin does what he can to disguise the various forms of despair, masked by disappointment, that the progression of her disease causes deep in his soul. He tries to concentrate his attention upon her black eyes, which once shone in enchanting harmony with the long sheets of her utterly straight black hair as it fell across her skin and his own during the short time that they found joyous pleasure in each other's embrace. *That all too short a time . . .*

The wedding of the newly invested Rendulic, Lord Baster-kin, to the exotic Chen-lun had seemed an entirely brilliant occasion. Only weeks after the ceremony—weeks during which the upper floors of the *Kastelgerd* were often heard to echo with the sounds of swordplay, in addition to bursting crockery destroyed by flying arrows, as Chen-lun (raised to be a most capable warrior, it should be recalled, in her own tribe) and Rendulic punctuated their long bouts of lovemaking with athletics of a wholly different order—the new lady of the *Kastelgerd* was declared by the family's healers to be unquestionably with child; and a mere seven

Moons later, the couple's first son, a golden-haired boy that they agreed to call Adelwülf,[†] was born. The new scion appeared to be nothing if not a confirmation that Kafra had approved the match of an eastern princess and a loyal new leader of the kingdom over which the golden god had long ago elected to shower his radiance—

And then had come, almost as quickly, another son . . .

Later pressed by the family's healers to recall his wife's physical condition at the time of this child's conception, Rendulic Baster-kin had replied that if some sign of disease or divine disfavor had in fact been present, he had not detected it. Certainly, the conception had taken place very soon after Adelwülf's birth, perhaps unwisely soon; but Chen-lun had not experienced any signs of illness until the later stages of her carrying of the creature—and those had not seemed sufficient to explain the thoroughly misshapen condition of the boy; the mass of pustules and ill-formed bones that seemed to mar every part of his skin and body, and worse, to grow only more numerous and offensive during its first weeks and months of life.

The then-obscure Healer Raban had stepped forward to suggest to young Lord Baster-kin—who every day grew more desperate for an explanation that would remove not only some part of the revulsion engendered by merely gazing at the child, but the terrible sense of guilt he felt when he remembered his own sickly youth, and then gazed upon this fruit of his loins—that the child might not be a Baster-kin at all; that, much as his lord- and ladyship may have passed every night together, throughout the period during which the monstrous child was thought to have been conceived, there were nonetheless *alps*[‡] living in the forests of Broken's slopes who could make themselves undetectable to men of true virtue. Worse still, there were stronger and more artful such creatures inhabiting Davon Wood: enemies of Broken that might well have made the journey across the Cat's Paw and up the mountain, if they were certain that a member of a Broken noble house had taken to wife a woman who was, by both blood and nature, less innately virtuous than a daughter of the Kafran kingdom would have been . . .

At first, this notion enraged Rendulic Baster-kin, causing him to seize Raban by the throat and then use the flat of his short-sword to drive the healer from the *Kastelgerd*. Mysterious as the origins of the infant's vile condition might be, Baster-kin was by now determined to discover them—for he was a man who had had some experience of the strange and painful paths down which it was sometimes necessary to walk, in order to find true cures for seemingly magical or divine ailments. And he had an advisor who was well practiced at traveling such paths with him, at this moment as at an earlier point in his life: the man he had made seneschal of his household shortly after taking the rank of Merchant Lord, Radelfer. In all the years since the seeming end of his preoccupation with Gisa's young apprentice from the Fifth District, Rendulic Baster-kin had never asked his old friend and guardian to find either the maiden or the crone; but now, the young lord did beseech Radelfer to undertake that journey, in the interests, not of his earlier infatuation, but of both his wife and his second child. It was, after all, a near-certainty that he would wish to father more children; and if Chen-lun was, for reasons of this world or any other, unfit to allow him to do so successfully, it was necessary that Baster-kin know.

Radelfer disliked the notion, without question; but he understood the importance of the matter, both to his former charge and to the clan he served. It was never wise for a house of such importance to rest all its hopes upon one heir alone; and so, departing alone at nightfall of the next day, Radelfer ventured into the Fifth District.

Not very far down the Path of Shame, as it happened, Radelfer encountered a fellow veteran of the Talons, and learned that Gisa was in fact living, not in the small house near the southwestern city wall in which she had tutored and raised the orphan Isadora, but in the latter's very fine home nearby. Isadora, it seemed, had become a bride, herself, only a few years earlier, marrying one of the most promising young officers in the Talons, a man that Radelfer had only met once or twice during his years of service: Sixt Arnem.

Finding that Arnem was on guard duty atop the city walls that night, but that Gisa and Isadora were at home and willing to receive him, Radelfer next learned that his luck would not carry him very much farther: both women were adamantly unwilling to involve themselves again in the affairs of the illustrious Baster-kin family. However, Gisa did suggest a solution that seemed, as Radelfer made his way back to the *Kastelgerd,* ever more adequate to Rendulic's dilemma.

Gisa knew of only one healer in Broken whose knowledge rivaled or surpassed her own; and, now that her former patient had become Rendulic, *Lord* Baster-kin, he had every right to call upon that illustrious figure's talents and resources. She was referring, of course, to the Second Minister of the realm, the foreign-born scholar called Caliphestros. Provided the God-King Izairn was amenable, Caliphestros could hardly refuse the appeal for assistance; indeed, everything that Gisa knew of the man suggested that such a request would appeal to his scholar's vanity. With this seemingly sound plan formulated (and truly relieved that there would be no risk of Rendulic ever crossing the path of the crone's former apprentice again, having seen that the maiden Isadora had by now grown into a truly beautiful woman who had thus far mothered no fewer than three irrepressibly healthy children), Radelfer reentered the *Kastelgerd* in fine spirits, and relayed the substance of Gisa's suggestion to a very curious young lord.

{v:}

RADELFER DETERMINED, when making his report that night to his master, to deny ever having seen any member of the Arnem family; and he was quickly given reason to be glad that he had taken such a decision, when Rendulic Baster-kin made it apparent, through a succession of ill-disguised questions, that he had used a series of disreputable spies from what was now *his* Personal Guard to discover just whom Isadora had married and when, just where she was currently living, and even that Gisa was a part of the Arnem household: all facts that, if the young lord's soul had been truly healed, he could have told Radelfer before the latter's departure.

Such considerations, however, were quickly set aside, that the delicate arrangement of a visit from the Second Minister of Broken to the Merchant Lord's *Kastelgerd* might be arranged. From the first, and despite the advice of his trusted old advisor and friend, Rendulic Baster-kin proved resentful, even combative, concerning the entire affair: never mind the fact that it was *he* who was requesting a service of the Second Lord, under conditions of secrecy so strict that most of the household staff, as well as Chen-lun's healers, were successfully kept unaware of the proceedings. It gradually became clear that the success or failure of the meeting de-

pended on the reactions that these two men—now the two highest secular officials of the kingdom—would have to one another. Both possessed
pronounced characters and the same strong unwillingness to suffer argument from any person they dubbed a fool. Radelfer steadily lost his
early enthusiasm for the meeting, the more he considered the idea, realizing that, while there was a chance that Caliphestros's visit to the *Kastelgerd* Baster-kin would offer the young lord and his wife a way out of the
present dilemma, it was at least as likely that the meeting would end in
most calamitous failure.

Radelfer's concerns ultimately proved well grounded. A most discreet,
late-night visit from the Second Minister of the realm was soon arranged;
and on the appointed night, at the appointed hour, a plain litter appeared
at the *Kastelgerd*'s lowest and most hidden entrance. Scorning the protection of Lord Baster-kin's Guard, Lord Caliphestros arrived with no more
significant protection than his litter bearers, men who were less servants
than acolytes, it seemed to Radelfer. Humbly introducing himself to the
Second Minister—whose long beard, scholar's black skullcap, and silver
and black robes of state did not disguise the fact that, while of an age that
matched Radelfer's own, this Caliphestros was also in nearly as vigorous
health—Radelfer remarked that, while he could see that the two bearers
had good sword arms and fine blades at their sides, they nonetheless
seemed a very limited party of protection with which to go abroad in the
city at night. To this, Caliphestros replied that, having calculated from
the Merchant Lord's petition that the fewer persons—particularly
servants—that knew of the meeting, the better for all involved, he had
brought only two of his stronger assistants. Radelfer could find no flaw
in his reasoning and, ushering the litter bearers into the gardens that led
up to the *Kastelgerd* Baster-kin's somewhat overawing main entrance, the
seneschal asked the men to wait there, among the tastefully arranged
fruit trees, flowers, and few pieces of statuary, promising that food and
wine would be brought to them. The two men expressed thanks, after
which Radelfer led Caliphestros, not further up the terraced grounds to
the main entrance to the *Kastelgerd,* but down, through a long tunnel
that eventually ended in one of the building's more remote cellars.

As the builders of the *Kastelgerd* had spared no effort or expense in either the design or execution of the building, so the cellars that they had
constructed beneath the palatial home were wondrous and extensive

creations in their own right. There were many long-since-forgotten chambers and hallways below the residence of Broken's most powerful merchant clan, places unknown even to the *Kastelgerd*'s servants, Radelfer explained: some were even outside the ken of the present master of the house, since so many generations of secretive lords (such as Rendulic Baster-kin's own father) had needed discreet places in which to conduct their less than noble personal affairs, and had destroyed all records of their locations.

Caliphestros followed as Radelfer, having lit a small torch, led the way up narrow, winding stone steps that opened out into a shadowy remove below what proved the main staircase of the reception hall. Radelfer held his dim torch close enough to the illustrious visitor that he might read the Second Minister's reaction, when he saw the great hall for the first time, lit by the Moonlight that streamed through high windows in the western wall that faced the gardens of the Way of the Faithful. What he saw in those aging features was less awe than fascination, of a type that the seneschal found pleasing. Wandering into the center of the hall, Caliphestros glanced about as if to make certain that no witnesses were anywhere nearby; and Radelfer, assessing the older man's expression, quietly announced:

"This night, I have instructed all servants to remain within their quarters, Minister, unless called for, using Lady Baster-kin's distress as my ploy. Meanwhile, members of my own household guard are stationed at various positions throughout the *Kastelgerd,* to make certain that the orders are obeyed, discretion is ensured, and no miscreants can take advantage of the lack of general activity to attempt any crime or mayhem."

Caliphestros smiled, amiably and knowingly. "Yes, Radelfer—I have heard talk of your 'household guard,' as have the God-King and the Grand Layzin. Veteran soldiers, assembled quietly from the moment you became seneschal of the *Kastelgerd?* It almost seems you oppose, even distrust, the activities of the Personal Guard of the Merchant Lord . . . But fear not. We all—Izairn, the Layzin, and I—share your disdain for that force's increasingly troublesome behavior. Indeed, I have yet to meet a soldier or veteran of the regular army who *does* approve of those effeminate, violent louts—and rightly so."

As soon as Caliphestros had satisfied himself that there were indeed no ordinary servants stirring in the great residence, he placed his hands upon his hips, and nodded: less, again, impressed than he was interested. "I have heard stories of the interior of this greatest of all the *Kastelgerde*— yet only being here can make one understand the endless gossip." He glanced about the hall once more. "It is truly a structure worthy of kings . . ."

"I am glad to hear you say so, Minister," came the unexpected voice of Rendulic Baster-kin in reply; and Radelfer realized with some distress that his master must have been listening from the gallery above, for he was now midway down the great stairs. "And to dismiss such idle talk with such excellent dispatch," Lord Baster-kin continued, slowly descending the steps to the hall below—a carefully arranged bit of theatrics, Radelfer silently observed, one that would become habitual, in future years. "It gives me all the more pleasure in welcoming you into my home—and thanking you for coming under such . . . unusual circumstances."

"Unusual, but understandable," Caliphestros replied, bowing slightly— although not nearly so deeply, Radelfer knew, as Rendulic Baster-kin would have preferred. "If your wife's and your son's conditions are indeed as critical as I have been led to believe, it is of great doubt that Broken's own healers would be equal to the task of diagnosing and determining any true cure that might exist. Except, of course, for the truly capable Gisa—who recommended my services, I understand, as a consequence of having had some past business with your lordship . . . ?"

"How very knowledgeable you are, Minister Caliphestros," the Merchant Lord replied. "Which is as well, for the situation seems now to worsen by the day. And so I trust that you will take no offense if I forgo further niceties by asking you to cast your no doubt expert eyes on the troubled members of my family at once?"

He held what appeared to be an inviting hand out toward the stairs: but the gesture was in truth less welcoming than redolent of his intention to demonstrate his greater status and his supreme power in his own household and kingdom. Second Minister Caliphestros seemed incapable of being cowed, however, especially by one so young, and only smiled, joining Rendulic Baster-kin on the stairs and walking with him up and toward the bedchamber then still shared by the master and mistress of the *Kastelgerd*. Radelfer followed some few steps behind: where, he knew, the increasingly confident and bold young man had also expected Caliphestros to walk. Sensing the onrush of some unidentifiable crisis, just as he had once been able to smell the coming of battle during his years as a Talon, the seneschal prepared for it by reaching instinctively for the hilt of a fine raiding sword that had for all his career as a soldier been at his side, but was now gone: in its place, he found only a small jeweled dagger that had become his sole weapon of defense when he became a glorified domestic servant . . .

Shown first into the chamber where Lady Chen-lun lay, Caliphestros had needed even less time than Gisa would have, Radelfer observed, to reach some unspoken conclusion concerning her condition, one that even so experienced a healer and scholar had found shocking. And, once his examination had been completed, he asked to see the stricken child immediately, and was taken to a distant, cramped nursery.

If the great scholar's expression on examining Lady Chen-lun had been one of shock, his countenance on studying the infant was over- whelming sadness. The child had not yet been named; but the latest Lord Baster-kin had already and bitterly taken to calling him "Klauqvest" (with a cruelty, it seemed to Radelfer, which all too closely resembled that of Rendulic's own father) because of the child's fingers and toes, the bones of which had appeared malformed at birth, and were quickly growing ever more fused, like some crawling, shelled sea beast. Asking only a few questions as he examined the boy—whose pain was the true cause of his unending wailing, explained Caliphestros, rather than any fault of character or desire to irritate his parents—the Second Minister next inquired as to how the child was receiving sustenance: for his mother certainly neither wished nor was in any condition to nurse him. Rendulic Baster-kin explained that he had attempted to find a decent wet nurse, but that all such had been too terrified by the prospect. Finally, a drunken hag from the Fifth District had been discovered, who would take on the task, provided she was liberally paid and constantly supplied with wine. When Rendulic Baster-kin had asked Caliphestros if such was a fatal mistake, and in any way the cause for the child's worsening condi- tion, the Second Minister had replied that, while never a particularly sound notion, the use of a drunken hag as a wet nurse, in this particular case, was unlikely to make a dramatic difference: if she at least provided milk, that was preferable to slow starvation—although the latter might, ultimately, have been the more merciful course.

These words caused the Merchant Lord to stiffen noticeably. "And what does the minister mean by such a statement? Are the tales I have heard true, then, and is this—this *child* the result of unnatural relations between my wife and some spirit, some *alp* from Davon Wood?"

Caliphestros could only laugh weakly, as well as grimly. "Yes, such a tale is what the Kafran healers would doubtless have arrived at, sooner or later. Absurd as it is, it would be better than the truth, which they would be too unnerved to tell you . . ."

Rendulic Baster-kin had been standing by the small window in that small chamber in which there were few comforts, as far from the crib of his infant son as it was possible for him to position himself; but when this statement by the great scholar Caliphestros caused him to turn, Radelfer needed no more than little light to see that his face was already filling with, at once, greater sorrow, rage, and malice than he had ever seen the young man exhibit.

"'The truth'?" Lord Baster-kin softly murmured. "You claim to know the truth, Minister—the same claim for which you mock Broken's own healers?"

"My lord," Caliphestros replied; and there was now genuine emotion, true sympathy, in what had before been the face and voice of an impassive man of science. "We can none of us declare, with absolute certainty, that we know 'the truth.' But I must tell you: never, in all of the thousands of afflicted souls that I have observed, have I ever heard a plausible argument made for the interference of magical or divine forces so childish and petty as elves and *alps,* demons and *marehs,*[†] unless the sufferers' healers themselves were too terrified or too ignorant—or, as in most such cases, both—to admit that they did not know the true cause of the illness, and required some inexplicably persecutory intervention by such creatures behind which to hide their ignorance." Caliphestros could see that his words were causing the Merchant Lord's rage only to rise. "It gives me no pleasure to say this, but—"

Rendulic Baster-kin looked up, his eyes having become deep-set, malevolent weapons of their own. Caliphestros took a deep, steadying breath. "My lord—your father, I have heard from certain healers, was a victim of the pox. Is that so?"

Rendulic nodded quickly; Caliphestros had just given voice to the very nightmare that, of late and near every night, woke the Merchant Lord in sweats both hot and cold. "It is so . . ."

"Then," the Second Minister continued, "it is necessary that I tell you that both your wife and this child may well be displaying signs of the pox, as well: your wife, only intermittently, but your son . . . The disease, I suspect, has cast the very form of his being. And it will only become worse as the years go on—although with care he may live, even if both you and he will wonder from time to time if such has truly been a blessing."

Rendulic Baster-kin stepped back as if struck hard. "But—" He had begun to grasp at any other conclusion that his mind could formulate. "Our first son—Adelwülf—he is the very model of health and virtue!"

"And conceived when the disease had scarcely taken root in the Lady Chen-lun," Caliphestros answered earnestly, "as well as born during a period when it had, for a time, retreated. There are many of us who have studied this illness, my lord, who have come to call the pox by another title: the 'Great Imitator,'[†] for its ability to mimic other ailments, until the terrible truth becomes undeniable. And such may be the case here— it may be that what we have called 'the pox,' in the case of your father, your wife, and your son, may be some other disease. But to be safe, my lord—you must not attempt to conceive a child with your wife, until she is healthy once more, and for an extended period of time. You yourself appear to have escaped, as has your eldest son—that at least argues for, not the pox, but a pox-like disease. And it ensures you at least one healthy heir. But you must not risk your safety again, or the safety of a future child. You are simply too important to this kingdom."

But it had already become clear that Rendulic Baster-kin saw only the worst in his predicament: Radelfer watched his young friend and master turn back to the window, as the Merchant Lord said, in a soft, bitter voice, *"Even from beyond the pyre, he strikes at me . . ."*

Radelfer rushed quickly to the young lord's side. "Did you not hear the minister, my lord? It may be some other illness, there may have been no such attempt to curse your life at the last—"

"I knew him, Radelfer," Rendulic quietly continued, shaking his head to deny his seneschal's protest. "It would be precisely his perverse idea of—of *immortality:* to poison his descendants for generation after generation . . . And so, whether he knew it or not, I would stake my life that he believed he was planting the seed of the plague in us all . . ." Without fully turning back about, the Merchant Lord tried to speak with as much composure as he could muster: "My . . . *thanks,* Lord Caliphestros. We have, at least, solved one mystery, I believe: the condition of that"—he tossed his head in the direction of the crib—"that *thing* that was to be my son. And now, I must ask you to give me a measure of time alone. Radelfer will see you out, and arrange all payments."

Caliphestros nodded. "No payment is necessary, my lord—and let us pray that I am wrong, as all healers are, on occasion. I shall take my leave, then, offering only my deepest sympathy—and my most emphatic advice that you heed my words, which are not mine alone, but the sum of knowledge gained by most learnèd men far outside the frontiers of this kingdom . . ."

Not waiting for an answer, Caliphestros moved quickly to the nursery door, where Radelfer intercepted him even more speedily. "Can you find your way back out, Minister?" the seneschal whispered. "I—I confess that I am afraid to leave my lord alone with either this child or his wife, after what you have said."

Caliphestros nodded. "You are right, Radelfer, to take such precautions. Of course, I can look after my own departure. But you must continue to try to make him see that, even if his child and his wife have been so abominably cursed by his own vicious father, he must care for them, and not turn to the punishments which I know are first in the minds of all Broken nobles, when they are presented with such imperfection and perfidy."

Radelfer nodded, urging the minister further along the hallway. "You speak of the *mang-bana*?"† Radelfer asked. "I confess, it is my own fear— for my master is, as you have witnessed, a young man of enormous passions, capable of reason one instant, and of . . ." The aging soldier did not seem able to complete this thought, bringing Lord Caliphestros's hand to his shoulder.

"You are wise, Seneschal," he whispered, "and your master is fortunate to have had your steadying influence. Remain here, if only as a kindness to my *own* conscience." Caliphestros looked into the nursery a last time. "For the *mang-bana* may be the least of what will occur to him, once he has brooded on the subject at length. And with that—I fear I must bid you farewell . . ."

As Caliphestros moved more rapidly than Radelfer would have thought his silver and black robes would have permitted down the grand staircase and toward the front entrance of the *Kastelgerd*—for it mattered not if any servant heard those doors open and close, now—he heard the child within the nursery begin to wail once more, his torment rising again, and looked in to see his master moving toward the crib.

"My lord?" the seneschal asked carefully. "Are you well?"

The young lord shook his head. "Evil has been done, and there must be blame. There must be—*punishment* . . ." As Rendulic continued to stare at the wailing child, he held out a desperate hand. "Do you know—I would comfort him, had I any idea of how to do it. Simply to be touched, said the great scholar of the Inner City, to be taken up and swayed, gently rocked to expel the air and vomit in his stomach, all that a child requires, *this* the child finds agonizing. And so—I cannot . . . I cannot bring myself to offer him such ordinary comforts, if it is at the cost of such severe pain. We must have a drunken bitch of a wet nurse to do it, for his cries will mean naught to her ears and heart, or whatever machine passes for her heart, until the inevitable day . . ." And then another thought, altogether different, occurred to Rendulic Baster-kin, and he looked to Radelfer:

"And yet, what if the great scholar who has just left us is wrong? What if this disease will resolve itself before the child must be left to the Wood? Or, worse yet, after he is thus outcast? Weigh the matter carefully, Radelfer—why should we pay that man Caliphestros greater heed than we do our own healers? He said himself that these are all issues of debate, of opinion—and has *he* arrested the deterioration of the God-King Izairn? No. Why, then, Radelfer? *Why heed him . . . ?*"

The seneschal wished to utter the simplest reason why: that Rendulic Baster-kin knew himself, from personal and bitter experience, that Broken's Kafran healers were fools, and that Caliphestros, while he could not stop the inevitable progression of the God-King Izairn's decline, had at least softened that march of mortality. But, ultimately, the seneschal found that calming his lord was far more important than proving this point: and so, as soon as the drunken wet-nurse appeared, wiping grease from her mouth with the same filthy sleeve that she would shortly use to wipe the face of the unfortunate infant in the crib, Radelfer guided the somewhat stunned Merchant Lord from the room.

And as they went, Rendulic Baster-kin made only one sensible statement: "I can prove it, Radelfer—you think me near-mad, at this moment, but I can prove my assertion . . ."

"My lord?" Radelfer replied, wishing simply to get the master of the house abed.

"*Another child,*" Rendulic Baster-kin replied; and at that, Radelfer was forced to pause in the hallway.

"But my lord, we have just heard—"

"An *opinion,*" the young master replied, with the fire of inspiration in his eyes. "The great Lord Caliphestros said as much, himself. Well—I have formed my own opinion: if my wife and I can conceive another child, one that resembles Adelwülf rather than that horror we have just left, then, *then* I shall know the truth. And then there shall be punishments enough to slake even *my* wrath . . ." Walking unsteadily, Lord Baster-kin moved toward the bedchamber where Lady Chen-lun now lay alone, attended constantly by the marauder woman Ju. "Fetch Raban back here," Rendulic Baster-kin said, pausing by the chamber's door. "Send for him. I would have my wife well enough, at least, to conceive, and he shall accomplish it, if he wishes to live. Tell him that I have determined his tale of the *alp* from Davon Wood having invaded this house and violated my wife to be correct. We shall have a priest to purge this *Kastelgerd,* and protect it from such beings in the future. And then . . ."

{*vi:*}

THE LADY CHEN-LUN'S HEALTH did improve sufficiently for childbearing, for the most part because of Healer Raban, or so the lord and lady of the house believed; in reality, it was because of liberal reliance on various instructions which Lord Caliphestros had, Radelfer later learned, left behind with the marauder woman Ju, the only person in the great house who knew what had actually transpired between her mistress and Rendulic Baster-kin's father, and therefore the only person, as well, who knew the truth of Caliphestros's statements concerning Chen-lun's illness.

The birth of a baby girl brought immediate joy into the home of the greatest of Broken's ruling secular families, joy that lasted half a dozen years unabated. The beast-child Klauqvest remained exiled to the maze-like cellars of the *Kastelgerd,* along with a new and kindly nursemaid. By

Kafran rites, Klauqvest should have been exiled to Davon Wood, a fate he escaped only because of the increasingly vexing nature of his brother, Adelwülf. While still a young boy, that publicly acknowledged scion of the clan Baster-kin had become so much the delight of the women of the household, and had learned how to use their adoration to achieve his every young desire, that he had grown spoilt and intellectually lazy, facts that often irritated his father; yet Klauqvest paid undivided attention to learning and development of the mind, achievements that were ever made clear to Rendulic Baster-kin by Radelfer. A taste and talent for knowledge could not, however, overcome the utter disgust his lordship felt upon simply looking at the boy; and so it was that the youngest child of the group (who believed Adelwülf to be her only sibling) became the joy of the family, embodying enough of both qualities—loveliness and true quality of intellect—to make her father constantly proud.

Early in her life this happy creature exhibited a joyous, almost ethereal talent and taste for dancing about the halls and rooms of the *Kastelgerd;* and yet this inclination did not cause her to ignore the studies that she was tasked to undertake early, and that she would need, should she ever in fact find herself leader of the clan Baster-kin. In addition, she was undeniably lovely, with beautiful, thick hair and the wide, dark eyes that made visitors—especially male visitors—innocently indulge her with gifts; although her father was delighted when she sometimes informed these acquaintances, quite earnestly, that she had not achieved enough that day to merit reward, and put off acceptance of such tokens. Thus did Baster-kin become ever more certain that, even if his eldest son became a useless wastrel, his daughter would never do so, and the clan would be secure. Keeping all this in mind, and still feeling most fortunate that the legacy of illness and despair that his father had intended to inflict upon Rendulic's children had not, in two of three cases, materialized, the lord of the *Kastelgerd* had determined that he would name his young daughter Loreleh. When he explained to his wife the well-known myth of the beautiful spirit who was to be the child's namesake, a siren said to stand on a large, rocky protrusion in the storied river *Rhein,*[†] drawing river sailors to their crashing doom with her irresistible beauty and peerlessly beautiful voice, the yet superstitious Chen-lun believed the tale to be true. She found it a recklessly impertinent name to give a child who had, only by divine grace, escaped the terrible fate that had befallen the now-unmentionable creature that had emerged from her womb, and whom, Chen-lun believed, her husband and Radelfer had long ago left in the wilds of Davon Wood. Whatever god or gods one worshipped, she pleaded with Rendulic, why tempt them by flouting such a myth?

Rendulic Baster-kin was only mildly irritated by his wife's continued clinging to marauder ignorance; for had not all his prayers to Kafra been rewarded by the lovely girl's birth? The golden god had forgiven and rewarded the Baster-kin family, after punishing it for sins that Rendulic did not wish to mention, he told Chen-lun. And, in the end, Chen-lun's guilt over the "sin" of which her husband had spoken forced her to submit to his reasoning. In addition, their daughter's beauty, as well as her affinity for singing and her almost spirit-like ability to dance—both not only displayed from an early age but quickly developed by tutors of such arts— even convinced her mother, after a time, that her husband might have been right: his golden god Kafra just might have been more powerful than all other deities. And so, Loreleh became the child's name; and if Adelwülf represented the clan Baster-kin's public hopes, so Loreleh represented its private pride, joy—and security.

In all this, Rendulic was encouraged and comforted by an exceptional Kafran priest (whose name has been lost to history, with his eventual elevation to Grand Layzin); and among the many subjects upon which the two maturing men found they agreed completely was a fundamental disdain for the Second Minister of the realm, whose advice to Lord Baster-kin had been so foully wrong. In addition, the priest, although he could speak only in pieces of the matter, indicated that the God-Prince Saylal had been given good reason not only to rebel against, but to find moral fault with Caliphestros—particularly so far as his royal sister, the Divine Princess Alandra, was concerned.

This maiden had evidently fallen under the Second Minister's influence and become his disciple, not only in matters of healing, but in the study of all of Nature's wonders: and the perfection of and delight in the human form that Kafran tenets idealized seemed to hold no place in such learning. Rendulic Baster-kin urged the priest to tell the young God-Prince that, should the day ever come that he or his sister might need "practical" assistance (for it remained clear that their father, the God-King Izairn, was wholly in the thrall of Caliphestros's undeniable intellectual refinement and power), he could depend upon the full weight of the clan Baster-kin being brought to bear in support of his cause . . .

Here, then, was a portrait of a family that seemed to have righted the ship of its fate long ago; and yet on this night, the Merchant Lord kneels at the bedside of his wife to find that her ailments of mind and body are only worsening—and becoming, to him, ever more repellent.

Yet how can we have reached such a pass? Lord Baster-kin wonders, for an instant uncertain if he has murmured the words aloud. *What was our sin? We lived pious lives; and when the God-King finally died, we followed the will of his son, Saylal, not only in ensuring the investiture of a new Grand Layzin, but by working for and bringing about the downfall, exile, and mutilation of that blasphemous minister, Caliphestros, and his acolytes, as well. Where, then, was the grievous error? Why should we have been so reduced?*

But Baster-kin knows full well the individual steps that have led his family to this crisis, and he feels, in some private portion of his heart, enough pity to want to sit—for a time, at any rate—by Chen-lun's side, to comfort and above all quiet her. At the same time, however, he inwardly knows his true *practical* reason for visiting his wife: in his heart, he has grown—until only the last day or two—to despair of any hope for the future of the clan of which he remains chief; indeed, of which he may well be the last unchallenged leader. *And there might be justice, if I were to suffer that ignoble fate,* he muses. But the recent news from the provinces has brought something like hope, if a dark sort of hope, to the *Kastelgerd's* master; and so, as Baster-kin watches the pompous but well-bribed Healer Raban gather his calming and palliative drugs, he makes sure the greedy, ambitious Kafran man of "medicine" also conceals the additional ingredients that Baster-kin has contracted with Raban to slowly mix into her ladyship's medicines. The healer then silently leaves the room, leaving his lordship to glance again at his wife, still writhing upon the bed, and then at Chen-lun's sole remaining personal servant, the marauder woman Ju, who, as always, stands as if made of stone in the shadows of one corner of the room, comprehending few of the words, but much of the behavior, of the people of Broken. And, as he goes to his lady's bedside and waits for her to acknowledge him before taking her hand, Baster-kin silently determines:

Nay, I can no longer lie to myself about these things; for if condemning my second son to the near-perpetual darkness usually suffered only by prisoners in dungeons, as I did when Klauqvest became a youth wise enough to be of use as an advisor, was an act made more bearable by Kafran tenets, I cannot help but wonder if the order concerning my third child has not placed me beyond the pale of any true forgiveness or peace. And even if it has, what of my "merciful" intentions toward my wife: am I so certain that they are the righteous course?

And who is there who could argue with the man's doubts on these subjects? For Baster-kin broods, in the first instance, upon his long-ago yet constantly remembered order that Radelfer take his daughter Loreleh—that same Loreleh who was once the greatest joy of her father's life, but who had begun, late in her childhood, to show tragic signs of the onset of physical deformities all too close to Klauqvest's—into the deadly wilds of Davon Wood, and abandon her there. The *mang-bana* had been forced upon the girl that Baster-kin saw as his greatest hope simply because the city and kingdom were aware of her, and could see the deformity growing. As for his second cause of self-torment, Baster-kin struggles over the deadly course he has lately embarked upon regarding his wife: a woman who, he has been told, no longer has any hope. Yet even if he counts his deadly plans for her a mercy, will his god judge them thus, as well?

"*Rendulic,*" Lady Chen-lun says, seeing him at her side, and then feeling his touch on her own hand. "I heard Raban," she almost whispers. "Speaking in the hallway. Someone said that you might not come, but Raban said that you must; and I knew you would. But—here is the strangeness of it, Rendulic—" Her eyes suddenly grow wide with emotion and she arches her back in torment as she says more urgently: "*I knew who he was speaking to; I knew the second voice!* It *seemed* I did, at any rate—and it was *him*—our child, Rendulic. But it *cannot* have been; I *know* this, husband, for I know that you saw to his exile; I know that he is no more, that he was taken by the Wood. And so, it must have been . . . someone else . . ."

"Calm yourself, my lady," Rendulic Baster-kin says softly, holding her right hand tighter. "It was but Radelfer, whom I earlier ordered, as I ordered all of the household staff, to speak in whispers, so that you will not be disturbed."

Nodding her head nervously, wishing to preserve this moment of peace and affection, Chen-lun responds, "Yes, husband. No doubt it was just as you say. Would that you could always command my mind to be so still . . ."

"But you *do* grow still, now," Rendulic says, as soothingly as he can manage. "Raban's medicines make you so—you must allow them to do their work."

"Yet I would not have it so, Rendulic—I would remain awake, to be with you, to *lie* with you, to be the wife I once was—"

"We are none of us what we once were," Rendulic answers with a small smile, putting a hand to her brow and using his fingers to comb the long, moist strands of her black hair back on her head—and pretending, for the moment, that he cannot see that the ulcerations in the skin of the neck, as well as the lumps beneath the surface of the chest, are daily growing larger.

Wiping at drops of sweat that have appeared on her brow without being aware of the movement, Chen-lun answers, "The night is so warm—*all* nights seem so warm, this year; yet not so warm as the nights we passed in this bedchamber, when first we were betrothed."

"Indeed, wife," Baster-kin says, moving to get to his feet. "And if you are a calm and obedient patient, that warmth may someday fill this chamber once more . . ."

Chen-lun looks suddenly alarmed at the thought of Rendulic's leaving. "You return to your duties, my lord?"

"I do," Rendulic replies, now standing and releasing her hand. "With the greatest reluctance . . . But you must have peace, my lady; and the enemies of this kingdom never cease to plot against us."

Chen-lun's countenance grows a bit more pleased. "They say you have dispatched an army against the Bane, at last?"

"We have, wife," Rendulic answers, surprised at the question. "And with Kafra's aid," he says, stepping away and toward the door, "their defeat and your recovery will come at one and the same time. And then, we shall indeed know happiness, once more. Therefore, be calm—and sleep, my lady; *sleep* . . ."

Chen-lun only nods for a moment; for the drugs she has been given are by now overwhelming her senses. "But do you never wonder, Rendulic?" she murmurs weakly, as Ju appears again, to neaten her bed coverings. "If all that we have endured in the years since has not been a result of *it*—of sending a second child to the Wood? She was so young . . . and had been so beautiful . . . *Loreleh* . . ."

Standing in the doorway, Rendulic Baster-kin watches as his wife is overcome by slumber: a far more dangerous slumber than she, or Ju, or anyone, save her husband and Healer Raban, knows. And he can feel his own features harden as he replies silently, *Yes, Loreleh was beautiful—until she was no longer . . .*

Finally free of his duties of state and family, Rendulic Baster-kin leaves his wife's bedchamber, pulls a pair of black leather gauntlets from his belt, and strides purposefully toward the great staircase of the *Kastelgerd*, pausing briefly when he passes a large mirror. Satisfied with the image before him, he proceeds, pausing once more behind the first column of those that run from the front edge of the gallery to the ceiling it shares with the great hall, and peers downstairs:

She is here, he realizes, as two figures come into view at the base of the grand staircase; *actually here, within these walls . . .*

Rendulic Baster-kin finds that his blood runs faster and hotter as he begins his descent, and the fine, healthy woman in the gown of green comes into clearer view. In her arms she holds a cloak, of the same color that she was accustomed to wearing when she and Gisa were treating him; and one that (as Baster-kin did not know then, but is aware now) he could insist she cast off, if he were to be scrupulous about Kafran law. For it is the dark blue-green cloak with which healers of the old faith, in Broken and surrounding kingdoms, identified themselves to the people. Of course, it could be pure coincidence that Lady Arnem favors this color; but ignorance of the God-King Saylal's deep strictures against any hint of the old ways among his people is no excuse for flouting them . . .

"Lady Arnem," his lordship calls, in as courteous yet commanding a tone as he can manage, still pulling on his impressive gauntlets; although he fears that his voice betrays too much excitement, when he does say the name, and he tries hard to calm both his heart and his voice as her face—that face about which he has wondered for so many years—turns up to meet his gaze.

By Kafra, he declares to himself in the half-light; *how beautiful she still is . . .*

"I hope you will forgive my delay in greeting you," he says, still worried about the tone of his voice. "Unavoidable matters of state and household . . ." Reaching her, he takes her hand, kissing it more lightly than he would like.

And, in an instant, he realizes that his plan, his great hopes and secret arrangements, will be far more magnificent than even he had dared dream. She has aged, without question; the maiden who was just reaching the height of her charms when he knew her so many years ago has matured, as the mother of five should, and wears small amounts of face paint to hide this fact.

"My lord," Isadora says, bending her knees and dipping her body in a most graceful manner, then standing again to face him. "I can only imagine, given all that is happening, how busy you must be—and I thank you for taking the time to see me." Then she smiles: it is the same radiant smile that she possessed as a maiden, that much has not been changed by the intervening years. And she even laughs gently, quietly, just once, with what he takes for affection. "Forgive me," she says. "It is—a shock, that is all. But a happy one. To see, so closely, that you have become—"

"The man you hoped, I trust," Rendulic replies, pleased with the control of his own spirits and voice, the sense of careless good cheer, that he now achieves, and offering Lady Isadora his arm. "For you were instrumental in that formation. And so if you are *not* pleased"—he turns his head to one side in mock severity—"you must look to yourself, I fear."

"No, no," Lady Arnem replies, taking his arm and tossing her head lightly, so that those still-golden tresses float away from her head, as if they are wisps of some magic, celestial fire. "No displeasure. I am impressed, that is all, and that credit you must give to yourself. And to Radelfer"—she indicates the seneschal, who walks several paces behind them—"who always guarded your safety, as well as my own. *And,* in addition to all his other services," she continues, more unsteadily, yet hopefully, "he has put my fears to rest, concerning any *difficulty* that there might be upon our meeting."

"I should not have thought that you would have required *Radelfer* for such assurance," Baster-kin replies. "But that is only one of many things that we can and ought to discuss . . ." Ever more delighted that the meeting is going so well, Rendulic adds quickly, "Among them your own concerns about your family, I understand. Come—let us return to my library, where we can determine all."

Lady Arnem, however, stops before the imposing doorway to the silent library, and her face suddenly turns far more grave, as she looks to Rendulic Baster-kin. "Although I have been much impressed, my lord, by that chamber and its contents during the time that I have awaited your

arrival, may I suggest that we instead discuss all such matters as we proceed to the remarkable and alarming discovery that I have made along
the southwest wall of the city? For I believe that I can say, with no exaggeration, that there is no precedent for either it, or for the danger it may
pose to the safety of Broken itself."

Baster-kin's smile shrinks, but not out of displeasure: he had expected
the former nurse and healer's apprentice who had played the key role in
his own recovery as a youth to speak immediately of his recent communication concerning her son, and of her worries concerning his entrance
into the royal and sacred service; yet instead she has spoken, first and,
apparently, most urgently, of the safety of the city, as he would expect the
best of patriots to do. So impressed is he by this unexpected arrangement
of priorities, that he is immediately inclined to oblige her request—just
as Radelfer, when Lady Arnem originally told him her story, had thought
his master would be.

As for Lady Arnem herself, she in fact *is* most vitally concerned with
her son Dalin's fate. But when Isadora followed the woman Berthe to her
squalid home deep in the Fifth District earlier this evening, to determine
the nature and cause of her husband's illness, she not only discovered a
danger to the city: she found a tool with which to sway and, if necessary,
coerce the Merchant Lord into delaying any determination concerning
Dalin, at least until Sixt returns from his campaign . . .

"I see," Lord Baster-kin at length replies, in slow appreciation of what
he believes is taking place. "Your husband's faithful nature and service
would seem to have healed much of the anger bred by the fate of your
own parents that I recall your expressing, so many years ago. Commend-
able, Lady Arnem. Radelfer?" The Merchant Lord turns toward his
friend and counselor, still seeing, to his amazement, that Radelfer's expression of amused disbelief is yet present. "Have a litter brought round
at once, *Seneschal,* for Lady Arnem and myself. We must determine just
what it is that has roused such creditable alarm in her spirit. And assemble four or five of your most able men, as well. It has become difficult
enough to get the supposed Merchant Lord's Guard to even enter the
Fifth District, much less to rely on them for protection."

"I shall be pleased to accompany you in your litter, of course, my lord,"
Isadora Arnem says. "Although I have my own outside, manned by two
of my family's guards, as well as my eldest son, whose father insists he

accompany me on any nocturnal business I may need to conduct in his absence."

A telling look of disappointment passes across Lord Baster-kin's features, but he is quick to replace it with somewhat forced enthusiasm: "Splendid! I shall be pleased to meet the scion of what I understand to be quite a large and spirited family." Rendulic regrets the statement almost at once; for he has betrayed a longstanding interest in the clan Arnem that he had not wished the Lady Isadora to think existent. And, equally unfortunately, he need not turn to sense that Radelfer has detected the same concern in his lordship. "Your son may follow in your litter, then, while, perhaps with Radelfer walking beside for safety's sake, you and I use the time in my own conveyance to investigate the full range of your concerns—safely surrounded by a larger number of guards." As Lady Isadora nods gratefully, Baster-kin turns to Radelfer. "Well? You have your orders, Seneschal . . ."

{vii:}

WHEN LORD BASTER-KIN EMERGES from his *Kastelgerd* at Isadora Arnem's side, they pause for a moment at the top of the wide stone stairs that lead down from the building's portico to see Dagobert—in his father's armor and surcoat—engaging in harmless but instructive and quietly amusing swordplay with, by turns, the family's two *bulger* guards, who, in their black-haired and bearded enormity, make a particularly unlikely sight, here at the terminus of the Way of the Faithful.

"That is your eldest?" Lord Baster-kin asks, regarding Dagobert with an admiring, almost wishful aspect.

"Yes," Lady Arnem replies, surprised at how kindly his lordship seems as he watches the scene below him. "Wearing his father's old armor, I fear, according to the pact that he made with my husband concerning my safety in the city."

"Why 'fear' such a thing?" Baster-kin asks. "It shows every admirable virtue, for one of his age. Does he frequent the Stadium?"

"No, my lord," Isadora answers uncertainly. "His father's influence again, I fear—Dagobert would rather spend his free hours in the Fourth District, among the soldiers."

"Count yourself lucky," Baster-kin replies. "Too many of our noble youths forgo their duties in the army for the false thrill of playacting in the Stadium. May I meet him?" His lordship starts down the stairs, then pauses, again offering Isadora his arm.

"I—of course, my lord." Isadora then calls out: "Dagobert! If I may interrupt your clowning about—" And, at the sound of her voice, the guards take up their positions at the litter, standing at most respectful attention when they see whom their mistress is with. Dagobert, for his part, sheathes his marauder sword, does his best to order his armor, sur-coat, and hair, and then climbs the stairs as her mother and her host de-scend them, so that the three meet somewhere in between top and bottom; her son's every move, Isadora observes, seems modeled on her husband's, as if he would live up to the responsibility of wearing his fa-ther's kit now more than ever.

"Dagobert," Isadora says evenly, "this is Lord Baster-kin, who has asked to meet you."

Dagobert snaps his body absolutely rigid, and then, to his mother's profound shock, brings his right fist to his breast in sharp salute. "My lord," the youth says, just a little too loudly to reflect true ease with ei-ther the gesture or the situation.

"I appreciate your respect, Dagobert," Lord Baster-kin says, continu-ing to escort Isadora down the stairs. "But you may rest easy. I am not quite the fearsome beast that some make me out to be. You do your fa-ther's armor justice, young man—how long until we can expect to see you actually in the ranks?"

Dagobert turns his eyes, ever so briefly, on his mother, and then faces the Lord of the Merchants' Council again. "As soon as I am of age, my lord. My father would have me train and serve for a time, and then take a junior position on his staff."

Isadora's eyes widen with anger: this is another fact of which neither her husband nor her son has bothered to inform her.

"Excellent, excellent." Baster-kin catches sight of his own, much larger and grander litter approaching, carried by four of Radelfer's youngest household guards. "Have your men fall in behind my litter, Dagobert," Baster-kin says. "For if there is trouble in the deeper parts of the Fifth, I would have my men face it first—I can always find more guards, or my seneschal can, while your family seems"—Baster-kin gives the *bulger* guards a slight smile—"quite attached to these apparently capable men . . ." At that, Dagobert watches his mother and the Merchant Lord step through the rich fabric that curtains the well-cushioned seating of the litter.

Within that larger and far more comfortable means of transport, his lordship does his very best to play the pleasant and concerned host, grateful for Isadora's help in the past and now concerned with whatever threat to Broken it is that she has discovered along the southwest wall of the city. She will offer no specifics, saying that the sight of the mysterious occurrence will speak far more eloquently than any description she can give. She is also very clearly anxious to first discuss what arrangements the Grand Layzin and the Merchant Lord are making for the resupply of her husband's force of Talons, which she insists must be carried out before he is headstrong enough to commence an attack against the Bane without all the supplies he needs. For his part, Rendulic Baster-kin offers comforting statements, one after another, assuring Lady Arnem that if the other merchants of the kingdom will not support the attack, he himself will authorize use of the central amounts of supplies that are contained in the vast array of secret storage supplies that lie beneath the city.

Isadora is genuinely mollified by all these assurances, believing, for the moment, that Rendulic Baster-kin's boyhood romantic preoccupation with her has transformed into a deep sense of adult gratitude, something she had not expected; but Radelfer, as he walks beside the litter, is growing increasingly uneasy, a feeling that began when his master and Isadora met in the *Kastelgerd;* for the extent of Rendulic's disingenuousness has gone far beyond playacting during this meeting, and smacks more of a man who believes he can use the present difficulties to some advantage. But what "advantage" that might be, Radelfer has yet to determine.

The party's journey into the worst part of the city begins when they pass through the gateway in the stone wall that separates the Fifth District from the other, more respectable parts of Broken; and their further trip toward what is certainly the most terrible neighborhood in that already vile district begins as well as any such undertaking can be expected to, primarily because the mere sight of Lord Baster-kin's litter—common enough in the other districts of the city, but remarkable here—followed by Isadora's well-known conveyance, signals to even the most addled minds and depraved citizens along the Path of Shame the beginning of momentous events in the Fifth. The presence of so many armed guards, meanwhile, provides a seemingly absolute check against the inclination to mischief that is always rife among the more enterprising, if criminal, souls who lurk in the darkest recesses of the district, particularly as one moves away from its stone boundary and toward the dark shadows cast by the city walls. This inclination toward thievery and murder is one that runs as deep in such minds as does their fellow residents' appetite for dissipation, fornication, and the production of filth, all amply revealed in the gutters and sewer grates of the Fifth's every street. These sickening rivulets are the source of a stench that every minute grows ever more offensive, and the pieces of refuse that block those streams and prevent their serving their purpose become steadily larger and more hideous. Among these terrible sights one can find objects so sickening and foolish as to seem remarkable: sacks of vegetables and grains, rotted and worm-ridden enough that not even starving souls will touch them; enormous piles of every form of human refuse and waste, bodily and otherwise; and, most horrifying of all, the occasional cloth-bound package that bears the unmistakable, bloody shape of a human infant, either miscarried close to its time or disposed of in the simplest manner possible, and perhaps mercifully so: for it will be spared, first, the privations of the Fifth District, and later, entry (by no choice of its own) into the increasingly mysterious service of the God-King in the Inner City, where, even among the residents of the Fifth, the seemingly inexhaustible need for young boys and girls is the subject of steadily greater, if quiet, speculation . . .

"It seems strange to me," Lord Baster-kin says, glancing through the break in the curtain on his side of the litter as he holds the edge of his cloak to his face, blocking as much as possible the stench rising from the gutters close beneath the litter, "that, after all we went through in a very different sort of place than this—"

"If you mean your lordship's lodge below the mountain," Isadora comments, "it was indeed a lovely spot, particularly in comparison to so much of this district."

"And yet you choose to live here still?" Baster-kin queries.

"Like me, my husband was born here," Isadora answers. "And wished, as he wishes, to remain." Now it is her turn to glance outside, with an air of some slight despair that Baster-kin finds oddly encouraging. "I do not know that I could have lived my entire life in *this* part of the district, which was my home until I met him."

"I cannot pretend to comprehend how dismal a place it must have been for a child," Baster-kin says slowly. "Nor why you and your husband would have chosen to stay—particularly now, when the sentek has been promoted to the leadership of the whole of the Broken army, and you could live in any part of or residence in the city that you might choose to request of the God-King."

"Look about yourself once more, my lord," Isadora says. "Many of these people are victims of their own perfidy and vice, but many others are merely unfortunate victims of circumstances that made this district an inevitable home. Citizens, for example, whose ill fortune is not the result of dissolution or of ill intent, but of the loss, many years ago, of the head of their family to war, or of a limb of that family elder to those same conflicts. It is a cruel and unjust truth, my lord, that many Broken soldiers, having left the army and returned to the district, are unable to find work that would allow them to leave, while some cannot even afford shelter, here, and so haunt these streets night and day, begging and stealing, many of them, and forming a new sort of army: an army of ghostly reminders of the occasionally cruel ingratitude of kings."

Baster-kin holds up a mildly warning hand. "Be careful, my lady, with the words you choose," he advises earnestly.

"All right, then—of the ingratitude of *governments*," Isadora says, with an impatient nod of her head. "Then, as well, there are workmen—masons, builders—who have suffered crippling injury during the continual construction of this city's and its kingdom's houses of government, worship, and wealthy residency, and who are similarly left with no choice but to bring their families here, to the Fifth. You shall meet some such men when we reach our destination—but I ask you now, do not such people deserve at least one capable and honest healer to assist them, and does that not justify my staying and trying to help?"

"They deserve more than that, Lady Arnem," Baster-kin replies. "And the worst residents of this district deserve certain things, as well—and, before long, all shall receive them, you have my word." Despite the ap-

parent charity and condescension embodied in these statements, it occurs to Isadora that there ought to be a sharp difference in quality
between Lord Baster-kin's first and second uses of the word "deserve."
She has no time to dwell upon the subject, however, as Baster-kin suddenly draws the curtains of his litter wider apart. "By Kafra, where can
we be? A place of rare evil, if even the stars offer little light."

"We approach the southwest wall, the shadow of which grows ever
longer," Isadora replies. "Deeper into the district than even I will venture, any longer—although I did as a child. It was my happy habit, then,
to investigate most such neighborhoods, sometimes at foolish risk. But I
learned much . . ."

"No doubt." Lord Baster-kin looks to Lady Arnem and studies her face
for a moment. *And that,* he muses, *is what will make you such a superb judge
of what this city and this kingdom will require, in the months and years to
come . . .*

"And one thing I learned, above all," Isadora says, completing her
thought. "There are at least some citizens in this district who recognize
that the original planners of the city—"

" '*Planners*'?" Baster-kin interrupts, a little less enthusiastically than he
has sounded, to this moment: "You mean *the* planner, don't you? For
there was but one—Oxmontrot."

Isadora deflects the man's critical tone with a charming smile. "Forgive me, my lord," she says; and Baster-kin, of course, cannot help but do
so. "My husband has told me of your great dislike for the founder of the
kingdom, and I did not wish to tread upon your sensibilities. But, yes,
Oxmontrot, whatever his other faults, preached habits of personal and
public cleanliness—if you will remember, my mistress and tutor was
wont to speak of them, during our time together, by the name the Mad
King originally gave them: *heigenkeit.*[†] Yet how could the Mad King"—
and here Isadora ventures to actually touch Baster-kin's gloved hand and
laugh lightly for effect, seeing that she is drawing her companion
in—"particularly as he was, for all his wisdom, apparently going mad
even then—how could he have known that what were, in his time, necessary and rigorous policies, such as the creation of the Fifth District for
his agèd and injured soldiers and laborers, would one day become of far
less concern to his heirs? Heirs who, having become divine and removed
to the inviolable safety and sanctity of the Inner City, were forced to de-

pend all the more on advisors, too many of whom—unlike yourself—were district officials and citizens with less than sound or honest ends in mind, and who thereby helped to create, unintentionally, of course, this—this *disgrace* that we see about us now?"

"Admirably expressed, Lady Arnem," Baster-kin says, turning to look again on the street about him, so that his true enthusiasm for both the thoughts and their speaker will not become obvious in his face. "I doubt if I could have put the matter any better, myself." At that, he searches their immediate surroundings again, as if suddenly more surprised by their appearance than he is by Lady Arnem's thoughts. "By Kafra," he murmurs, "I do believe that this neighborhood is actually taking on an even *more* dismal aspect . . ."

Dissatisfied to see and hear that her brief outburst of opinion and feeling has apparently had so little effect, Isadora also looks outside: *Is it possible,* she thinks, *that he truly has lost the deep, the consuming affection that he had for me, however childish, when he was but a youth?* For, ironically, much as she had once feared that boyish and diseased form of devotion—a sickness that Gisa had called *obsese*†—she had been depending upon some part of it still being alive, in order for her plan of this evening to succeed. But she remains calm, knowing that she has another stratagem in mind with which to achieve the same goal.

{*viii:*}

THE TWO LITTERS STOP before what is undoubtedly the worst of several abominable houses on a block of the street lying in closest proximity to the southwest wall. Baster-kin's imperious bearing upon stepping out and into the midst of the human traffic that fills the neighborhood about them cannot help but suffer some small diminishment, as soot-encrusted groups of residents and indigents immediately begin to gather about his own and Lady Arnem's litters; but the quick drawing of no less than eight well-oiled blades, ranging from the shortest (Dagobert's marauder blade) to the imposing length of Radelfer's raider sword, soon persuade these crowds to, if not disappear, at least move farther off. It is with some sense of quickened purpose that Isadora, Dagobert, Lord Baster-kin, and Radelfer's guards head toward the miserable hovel that can scarcely be called a house, while the *bulger* guards remain behind to protect the litters.

So strange has been, first, the ghostly gathering round of the neighborhood's residents, and then their sudden dispersal, that those in the visiting party who have not yet been to the neighborhood are visibly shocked when a ravenous, maddened hound bursts forth from behind a large piece of half-burnt, unidentifiable wooden furniture that had simply been flung from the house into the yard before it at some past date. The beast bares its enormous teeth while hurtling toward one of the shorter of Radelfer's men, its bestial and unending threats, along with its scarred but pronounced muscles, momentarily creating the impression that the chain by which he is secured will give way; an impression that causes more than one guard to raise his blade.

"Do not!" comes Baster-kin's sharp order; but this stay is ordered only when it has become clear that the chain will not in fact break, strong as the animal may be. "Are you children, that you need a good Broken short-sword to fend off a chained dog?" Baster-kin angrily asks Radelfer's men, and Isadora is gratified to see that the question is not posed to impress her, but is in fact a genuine sentiment. The scarred beast retreats and grows calmer when Isadora tosses him a bit of dried beef she has brought for the purpose; and she then urges the men behind her through the front doorway of the house, after having taken hold of the table that blocks it.

"Spare yourself, my lady," Radelfer says, deftly stepping in front of her. A hint of his youthful strength, which must have been considerable, is offered by the manner in which he effortlessly picks the heavy, unwieldy slab of wood from the ground and quickly shifts it to one side. "I meant no insult," Radelfer adds with a smile, remembering that the young Isadora was always loath to have men perform tasks for her that she was capable of undertaking, herself. "But I must precede my master into this dwelling, as it is, so why not make one task of two?"

Isadora does no more than nod proudly to this logic, casting his action in a different light: "You at least speed our visit, Radelfer—in a neighborhood such as this, to be remarked upon is unremarkable: the silence now surrounding us shows that many are waiting to discover our purpose, and if we can achieve it and be away before they have gathered again, all the better." The group forms four parties—Radelfer and two of his household guard to the fore, Isadora, Lord Baster-kin, and a proud Dagobert next, and finally, Radelfer's last two men, their eyes ever on what and who follows behind.

The squalor within is no great shock to Isadora, who long ago grew used to such sights, during her childhood with her parents and Gisa. The hovel's floor is granite strewn with Earth and dust; a sack filled with hay evidently does for a bed for some five terrified children across the chamber, while the sack before the fire is occupied by their ailing father, with the oldest of the children using a filthy, moistened cloth to wipe at his forehead. The woman who lives there, Berthe, quickly rushes to Isadora, terrified by the sight of the men around her, and most especially by the gaze of Lord Baster-kin, which has gone harder, not softer, at the unpleasant sight of these impoverished surroundings.

"Apologies, my lady," Berthe whispers. "I had intended to try to order affairs here at least somewhat less offensively—"

"Lady Arnem—what is it that you have brought me here to see?" Baster-kin asks imperiously. "For I am acquainted with failure and disgrace, in nearly all their forms."

Isadora gives Berthe a sympathetic smile and clutch of one arm, then urges her back to her husband's side. As the woman goes, Isadora turns a gaze to match Rendulic Baster-kin's own on him. "Such harshness is hardly necessary, my lord, given the circumstances that are plain enough, here."

Berthe has returned to the duty of wiping her husband Emalrec's feverish brow. He gives off the powerful stenches of rotted teeth and food, human waste, and sweat; but none of this slows Isadora, who urges the Merchant Lord on. "Come then, in the interest of the kingdom, if no other," she says, at which Baster-kin covers the lower portion of his face once more with the edge of his cloak, and watches as Isadora pulls away the light, filthy shirt that covers the groaning Emalrec's neck and trunk, just enough to reveal his chest. "It is all right, Berthe," Isadora says, seeing that the woman's terror has only grown. "These men will do him no harm, I promise you . . ." Picking up the barest end of a candle that is seated in a shard of pottery nearby, Isadora indicates the patient's exposed skin to Lord Baster-kin—

And he need see no more. Not wishing to spread his concern about the house or the neighborhood, he urges Isadora toward the back of the next room, and even manages a smile for the huddled, filthy children, as he passes them by to a rear entryway. Further along, there is a small square outside, a long-lifeless patch of Earth shared by three houses. A latrine— its walls long since fallen away, and its four-holed granite bench concealed, now, only by near-useless curtains suspended from similarly degraded ropes and poles—stands in the center of this yard, the holes in the bench leading directly down to the city's sewer system.

Dismal as this picture is, however, Lord Baster-kin's mind is still fixed on what he saw in the room. "I do not pretend to be an expert such as yourself, Lady Arnem," he says quietly, not even wishing his household guards to hear the words. "But, unless I am badly mistaken, that man is stricken with the rose fever."

"You are remarkably well informed," Isadora answers. "Not many could detect its markings so accurately—or so quickly."

"Thank you; but returning to the illness—" Baster-kin's face is now a mask of pure responsibility. "It spreads among people, particularly in areas lived in by such large numbers of people, as fast as the Death, even if more survive it than do that worst of all illnesses."

"Quite true," Isadora answers, now becoming a little coy: a dangerous game to play, at a moment such as this.

"And am I right in suspecting that you have some insight into the method of its spread, on this occasion, my lady?" Baster-kin asks.

Isadora continues her bit of playacting, praying that her fear does not bleed through it: "There are theories, of course, but there are always theories, from healers. All we can be certain of is, if that man is stricken by it, it will soon appear in many, perhaps most, houses in this neighborhood: quite possibly in this district. And from there . . ."

"But what of *your* theory?" Baster-kin asks, in considerably less pleasant or patient a tone.

Isadora urges Baster-kin farther back, into the small, dusty yard. "My lord," she begins, "you knew my mistress Gisa and, unless I am very much mistaken, you knew her to be, whatever her private beliefs on the subjects of the spirit and religion, a healer without equal in this city."

"You are not wrong," Baster-kin answers. "Gisa knew her place in this kingdom, and never sought to advance herself past it, nor to betray its fundamental laws."

"So, then," Isadora continues, drawing a deep breath. "You would be inclined to believe suggestions that originated with her?"

"You were a wise and kind minister of her cures," Rendulic Baster-kin says. "But I was ever aware that the cures were hers. And so, yes, I would be inclined to believe her, and now, *you*, above nearly every other pretender to the office of 'healer.' But what has any of this to do with matters in *this* house, and this district?"

"First"—Isadora works hard to still the tremor in her voice—"allow me to show you an extraordinary display of patriotism further from this house and these *Plumpskeles* . . ."†

"Lady Arnem!" Rendulic Baster-kin calls, as she begins to walk even further from the house, down a narrow pathway that his lordship, his eyes having grown accustomed to the darkness, can now see leads to an only slightly wider alleyway beyond. "I would rather you remember yourself, as I am sure your husband would, than to revert to the behavior and language of this—*place* . . . !"

"Why, Lord Baster-kin," Isadora says without turning, and now smiling just a bit: for she has rattled this supremely confident man. "Do not tell me that this situation unnerves you? But come . . ." Then, in a supreme bit of theater, Lady Isadora holds her own arm out, to wait for the now-familiar resting perch of his lordship's own. "Time and plague bear down upon us . . ."

Baster-kin obliges without answer; and as he does, Isadora's steps become easier.

The alleyway into which Isadora leads her "guest" eventually terminates in the mighty edifice of the city's southwest wall, which looms over everything beneath it. Confronted by the dark mass before him, the Merchant Lord pauses at the alleyway's head, and says, "You pile mystery upon mystery, my lady—and to what end? I have already said, I would be inclined to believe you in this matter."

"To believe is hardly to witness," Isadora calls. "Come, my lord. You need not wait for your men—for we shall have guards enough, upon our brief journey . . ."

Before it can reach the great edifice near its terminus, the narrow alleyway down which the pair walk leads into that broad military path that runs about the entire base of all the walls of Broken, and is kept constantly free of any form of congestion so that the soldiers of the city may always move freely to and along that critical route to their positions.

Thus, the alleyways adjoining it must be kept as dark and clear as the greater path itself. These highly secluded spots in a very questionable neighborhood, when used by persons not of the army, are places where transactions of an illegal nature take place: the buying and selling of stolen goods, unlicensed whoring, or, as ever and perhaps most common of all, robberies and murders.

How strange then, that each doorway of this particular alley leading to the imposing southwest wall of the city—a wall which is easily twice or three times as high as the largest of any of the shacks below, and still bears the clear marks of enormous, long-handled chisels and wedges—is apparently guarded, by two long lines of sentry-like men on either side of the passageway: not particularly young or healthy men, but men, most of whom are wan with age, sometimes supported by canes or crutches, yet all still possessing an essential military demeanor that cannot be manufactured; and, oddest of all—to Lord Baster-kin's eyes, at any rate—it is the single most agèd and crippled of these figures, a thin, balding wisp of a man with a crutch, who is at the head of the alley, and in apparent control of the rest. He holds a Broken short-sword in his free hand, while staring at the Merchant Lord with a peculiar smile.

Blows and wounds seem entirely possible, although it is not clear between whom—instead, however, the ancient man on the crutch sheathes his blade, and hobbles toward Isadora and Lord Baster-kin.

"Lady Arnem," Baster-kin murmurs quietly, to Isadora's further satisfaction, "what, in the name of all that is holy, have you led me into . . . ?"

{ix:}

"WELL, LINNET KRIKSEX,"† Lady Arnem says happily, before she can answer Baster-kin's question, "so you have made good on your promise."

"Aye, Lady Arnem!" the old soldier answers, in a voice that is as rough as a large piece of stone being dragged across a quarry floor. "We were not certain when to expect you, but I told the men that your return was promised, and that it would take place. The wife of Sentek Arnem would never offer assistance and forget the pledge, I said!"

"Well done, Kriksex," Isadora answers. "And now allow me to present

Lord Rendulic Baster-kin, master of the Merchants' Council and first citizen of the city and kingdom of Broken."

Kriksex takes one or two steps toward Baster-kin, who, in a rare moment of humility, rushes to meet the hobbling old fellow more than halfway between them.

"My lord," Kriksex says before delivering a sharp salute. "Linnet Kriksex, your lordship! Pleased to be of assistance to my kingdom, once again."

"Kriksex?"

Another voice has joined the conversation, this one Radelfer's; and Baster-kin and Isadora turn to see the seneschal stepping forward from his guard detail. "Is it really you?"

Kriksex looks past the great Lord Baster-kin, his face going first blank, and then joyous with recognition. "Ah, Radelfer, you have truly come!" he cries out, again flailing the crutch about as he moves quickly to meet what is apparently an approaching comrade. "So the stories were all true, and you did indeed remain with the clan Baster-kin!"

The two older men embrace, although Radelfer is careful with the seeming sack of bones and scars that was once his own linnet.

"But how are you still alive, you bearded, ancient goat?" Radelfer laughs. "It was enough that you survived the campaigns we undertook as young men, but—to find you here, among all this strange business, with what appears your own small army—it seems incredible!"

"Radelfer," Lord Baster-kin says, not sternly, but rather with the tone of one who has had enough mysteries, for one night. "Perhaps you will be good enough to explain to me just who this man, who these *men,* are, and what they are doing seemingly guarding a decrepit alleyway, for no apparent purpose."

"Your pardon, my lord," Radelfer says. "This is Linnet Kriksex, who commanded my *fauste* when I joined the Talons, many years ago. And a more faithful servant of the realm you would be hard-pressed to find."

"Indeed?" Baster-kin asks, looking at Kriksex and not quite sure of the explanation. "And I suppose this is the basis for your authority over these other assembled men, Kriksex, who also look to be veterans of various campaigns?"

"These are loyal men, my lord," Kriksex replies, "here to protect the God-King's name and laws in this district. An able core of veterans keeps the residents in this neighborhood free of both crime and vice. But the ominous occurrence that appeared again recently, the—the riddle that I showed Lady Arnem a few nights ago—went, I fear, beyond the power of men to either create, or to control. And so we determined that we must keep the situation exactly as we have periodically found it—spring is usually the most common time—until we determined whether or not we could persuade someone of greater consequence than ourselves to inspect it. My lady's visit here was by chance; but then, Kafra be praised, you agreed in short order to accompany her back!"

Baster-kin looks up and down the alley with an uncertain expression, as he follows the agèd veteran. "I fear you confound me, Kriksex," Baster-kin answers.

"The smell tells much of the tale, my lord," he says. "But if you will only follow me to the southwest wall, I believe the peculiarity will become apparent quickly enough. It will be preceded by a worsening of that same stench, in all likelihood, one noticeable above even the usually delightful aromas of the Fifth."

Baster-kin takes a deep breath, holding his forearm out to Lady Arnem once again. "My lady? May I assist you, as we follow this good man, that I may see what the difficulty is?"

"Your attention is much appreciated, my lord," Isadora answers, placing her hand upon his lordship's arm; she signals to Dagobert, who steps forward and moves on his mother's free side further down the alleyway and through the lines of veteran soldiers, each of whom salute in turn.

Kriksex maintains the lead of the guard detail that surrounds the three important visitors, and he often turns to watch the intrepid Lady Arnem with his same smile, no less genuine for its lack of teeth. As the moments mount, however, he seems to find some emotion uncontainable, and he lags back a few feet to whisper toward Lord Baster-kin's left ear: "Is she not a fit lady for Sentek Arnem, my lord? Fearless!"

Baster-kin nods, making his way into the deeper darkness. "Indeed, Kriksex," he agrees, in an equally quiet voice that Lady Arnem—who is increasingly engaged by those she passes by, despite young Dabobert's attempts to keep her way clear—cannot overhear. "A finer woman could not be found in all of Broken. But, for now—to the business at hand. For, unless I am losing both my sense of smell and my mind"—the noble nose wrinkles, and a sour expression consumes the face—"something—perhaps many things—seem to have *died,* hereabouts . . ."

"Aye, Lord—many things, if we judge by that stench," Kriksex says. "And yet you will find neither rot nor offal to explain it; only a seemingly ordinary, even innocent source . . ."

It takes but a few minutes to reach the southwest wall of the city; but before the interlopers have done so, Lord Baster-kin's disgust only grows. "Kafra's great holiness. You say there are *no* dead bodies in this area?"

"Several citizens *have* died in recent days," Kriksex replies. "But they are not the source of it, for their bodies were burned by the district priest, according to all proper rites and methods, eliminating their remains as a cause. Young, they have been, most of them, as have been the others who have recently died in the district." Lord Baster-kin casts a quick glance at Isadora; for he knows that the rose fever attacks the young before all others. "A terrible pity and waste, it has all been," Kriksex continues. "But no, my lord—what you smell is a more inexplicable thing, and yet still, the cause will appear simple enough—nothing more than a small stream of water."

Yet that seemingly innocent statement is enough to make Baster-kin pause for a moment. "But there is no water that flows above ground in the city—even the gutters that empty into the sewers are moved by collected rain. Oxmontrot saw to as much, to keep his people safe from the evils that open water of unknown origin can bring."

"Just so, my lord," says Isadora, who by now is standing on the pathway that runs at the base of the massive wall. From somewhere behind Baster-kin, a group of torches seem to simply appear, carried by Kriksex's men, and they light the scored city wall, as well as the pathway beneath it; and when the noble Lord Baster-kin turns, he sees that by now every alley and nook, every window and rooftop of any house that offers any kind of a view of what is happening in this place has filled with the faces and jostling bodies and heads of curious citizens of the neighborhood, who must, by now, have heard who their visitors are. This eerie scene is, for a man such as Baster-kin, a glimpse into another world, almost into the mouth of *Hel* itself, and he has no wish to prolong it any more than he need do.

"Lady Arnem?" he calls out, in a somewhat unnerved voice, turning to notice that she has seemingly disappeared. "Lady—Linnet Kriksex!"

the Merchant Lord demands, and Kriksex immediately lends him guiding aid:

"My lady is farther up along the wall and the stream, my lord," the hobbling soldier says, appearing as from the darkness and pointing. "In the same area that interested her when first she came here, where the water first appears."

Baster-kin nods, hurrying along to where Lady Arnem crouches. There, a delicate trickle of odoriferous water does, indeed, seem to spring from the base of the massive city wall itself: a trickle that soon grows, and that should, according to Oxmontrot's plans for the city, have been intercepted and fed into the underground sewer system long before it ever reached this open spot. It appears to run some hundred or hundred and fifty yards, hugging tight to the wall, until it finally disappears as suddenly and inexplicably as it now bubbles up beneath the lord and lady.

"How can this be?" Baster-kin asks incredulously.

"I have been puzzling with that since being shown it," Lady Arnem says, inspiring his lordship's momentary admiration—for he had truly believed that her ends in this journey had only to do with her husband and her second son's service in the House of the Wives of Kafra. Now, however, it would appear that patriotism numbers among her motives. "And yet," she continues, "its appearance is not the most disturbing part of the matter."

"No, my lady?" he says, mystified.

"No, my lord," she replies, shaking her head. "There is this matter of its coming and going, especially during the rains. And there is also this . . ." With which, she opens her hand, and holds it up to the torchlight.

The Merchant Lord sees several objects that have an all too familiar appearance; and, looking behind him to see the same crowding faces and bodies, Lord Baster-kin places himself between Lady Arnem and the citizens, holding his elbows square so that his cloak drapes her revelation.

Isadora notes this movement with satisfaction—his worry is real indeed.

"Are those . . . ?" His lordship begins to ask the question, but he cannot finish it: whether out of worry over the crowd or his own concern over what she holds, Isadora cannot say.

"*Bones,*" she replies, in a pointed whisper. "Taken from the bed of this—whatever it may be, stream, spring, or something wholly new."

"Yet—so small," Baster-kin says with a nod. "What variety of bones, then, my lady? Have you been able to determine? Some seem not even human—"

"And they are not."

"Yet others—they would seem—"

"Almost from a Bane, a few of them," she says. "And yet they are not."

"No?"

"No. They originated with our own people's children; such bones are far different than those of grown Bane men and women. And there are these, here," she continues. "The several that are not human—first, the bones of small but powerful forest cats: again, not young panthers, but their adult cousins, the Davon wildcats. These others, however, are simply the smaller bones of the larger panthers."

"Lethal Davon cats, all." Baster-kin nods. "And you believe *all* the bones came from this running ditch?"

"I know it," Isadora replies. "For you may find more, if you wish, by digging deeper. The more you do so, in fact, the more you will discover. Yet these objects certainly do not *originate* here—nor does the water. We have the opinions of the residents as to where they *may* come from, but the accounts conflict, and the source of each will swear to the accuracy of his or hers, no doubt expecting to gain some small favor—wine, silver, food, anything—for in many households, you will find small mouths to be fed, as we have just encountered in young Berthe's. And yet those children shall not linger in such houses long—for their parents are also, like the stricken Emalrec, only too ready to sell them, and far too hopeful of doing so."

"*Sell them?*" Baster-kin echoes, in some disbelief, yet remembering who it is that speaks, and knowing her reliability.

"Indeed, my lord. A grave crime that has been regularly committed." Isadora begins to walk slowly along the bank of the strange little streambed that she has been investigating, dropping the bones she holds, and then producing both a small block of soap and a similarly small skin of what appears clean water from beneath her cloak. She offers them to Baster-kin first. "My lord? I would recommend it."

Baster-kin looks at her, with both a smile and a sharp eye. "You seem quite prepared for this eventuality, Lady Arnem—and I appreciate the gesture, although I do not understand it."

"Suffice to say that, if my mistress were alive and with us, she would insist that you do it."

"Inscrutable, at times, she most certainly was that—though never wrong, that I knew of," Baster-kin says, cupping his hands for water, then lathering them with the rough block of soap. "But the various subjects— the rose fever, this water, these bones, the possibility of such serious sacrilege as buying and selling children—what can they have to do with one another?"

"I have not had as long as I would like to consider it, since this particular proof appeared," Isadora answers, as she begins to walk south again. Having reached a safe bit of shadow along the wall, she turns to his lordship, her face full of purpose. "But, as you have asked the question: all I can say with certainty, now, is that I have seen certain things with my own eyes, and heard enough stories to allow me to tell you that the children we speak of are not disappearing into slavery, nor outside of the city." She turns, attempting to meet Baster-kin's gaze full on, reminding herself that this man was but a boy, once, a boy whose weaknesses she knew only too well, and hoping that those weaknesses have not changed.

Gisa had taught Isadora to be rigorous in the exercise of her mind, never to guess or to gamble—but how could one form a considered opinion, when one had only incomplete facts? The method did not exist; at moments, inevitably, every living soul *had* to gamble. Her husband had taught her that by his example, over and over again, with his exploits in the field—and she had even seen Gisa take risks, although the crone would have denied it, especially on occasions when a life hung in the balance . . .

And with this final thought in mind, Isadora Arnem now looks north, and takes one deep breath: "The course of the stream would seem to indicate that it originates somewhere to the north—this is what concerns me most . . ."

Baster-kin, too, turns north; and then, after several moments, his face goes pale. "Lady Baster-kin, even the suggestion of such a thing is heresy . . . You cannot possibly think that this disease could originate from within the Inner City? Why should it not come from the sewers?"

"It runs *above* the sewers, my lord. In addition," she asks quietly, "was there or was there not a recent attempt on the life of the God-King? One involving the poisoning of a certain well just outside that same Inner City? And is the Lake of a Dying Moon not the only standing water source in that direction?"

Baster-kin's face fills, not with anger, initially, but with shock, and then concern. "Lady Arnem, I must warn you: there are only a few persons who know the details of this matter. And yet, since you seem to now be one of them—I assure you, plague can be as much the work of sorcery as of more ordinary paths of disease. And the men of my Guard who died of that sorcerous poisoning had symptoms far more horrible than the ordinary rose fever that your *seksent* in that house exhibits."

"Your pardon, my lord," Isadora says. "But, among many other uncertainties, we do not yet know what kind of symptoms that man may ultimately exhibit."

"You think—" Baster-kin is further shocked. "You think both could actually be victims of the same attack?"

"You captured one of the Bane assassins," Isadora says, holding Baster-kin's eyes with her own. "And tortured him for days on end. *You* would have a greater idea of the extent of the danger than I—whatever their means, they *could* well have released plague of some sort, rather than simple poison. And then there are further aspects to consider, concerning such an explanation."

"Which are?" As she has been expecting, a sudden hardness finally enters his lordship's features; but she presses on:

"Which are," she breathes, "to begin with, the fact that many mothers I have spoken to in this district—including young Berthe in there—have seen at least one or two of their children sold to priests and priestesses from the First District, who are accompanied by those creatures who claim your patronage and name: *Lord Baster-kin's Guard*. Indeed, so lucrative is the trade that certain particularly useless men—such as Emalrec, the man you have just seen on the bed in that house—have begun to depend on the birth and sale of such children as a substitute for honest labor. And now, for his sins, perhaps, the rose fever visits him. Strange, is it not?"

Isadora tries to maintain her composure as his lordship's features only harden and darken further: "Lady Arnem—even if such were the case, you and I cannot pretend to understand the workings of the Inner City, of the royal and sacred family, or of their priests and priestesses. You know these truths." He draws closer to her. "And yet you pretend to be mystified by all of it. But you know the answers, do you not, to the secret of that water, to the poisoning and the rose fever and the plague, to how it all touches upon these royal and sacred persons?"

"Yes, my lord. I believe I have determined all these answers. Some you may suspect—and some would shock you. But all would work to the unrest of this district, and perhaps the whole of the city, were they to become widely known. For the Inner City *cannot* contain or feed so many children as are taken, to say nothing of the wild beasts that they are said to have captured. Nor does disease simply appear as an act of any god. Plague, be it of poisonous or ordinary origins, has broken loose in this city, to threaten *all* citizens. This district is not the cause—it is the victim."

Baster-kin now takes a step away from Isadora. "And yet, you—you, with all this knowledge, have not yet made as much known, even in this district—have you?"

Isadora breathes deeply. "No. Not *yet* . . ."

"And in fact, you will remain silent," Baster-kin says, nodding. "For a price."

"Yes," Isadora finally says. "A price. Perhaps too heavy for the rulers of this kingdom to pay, and certainly beyond your power alone to grant. But you can carry the message: for I would have it stated—in writing, atop the royal and sacred seal—that neither my children, nor any others, will, in the future, be required for the royal and sacred service, save those that go of their own will. Without payment to their parents, and without the escort of Guardsmen who wander the streets under your name."

Baster-kin nods slowly: he is the image of a man whose fondest dream is coming unraveled—yet not in such a way that it takes him entirely off-guard. "And the plague . . . ?" he asks quietly.

"If you bring what I ask, and the city's builders do as I ask, I can control the plague here; and then, in time, it will die at its source—*wherever that might be.*"

"Yet you *know* full well where it is," Baster-kin says.

"Do I? Perhaps." As Isadora continues, her boldness returns: "One thing is clear: for all your theatrical torturing of that Bane, *you* are not certain. Yet I shall not speak of it: there will be no need, if the priests do as I say."

"And if they do not?"

"If they do not, my lord . . ." Isadora lifts an arm, indicating the whole of the city. "There are forces within these walls that have ever wanted only direction and leadership, to put their plight to the ears of power. And they have that ability. Some among the kingdom's powerful may have thought they were eliminating such a capacity by way of this plague; but they have, in fact, only given it greater force . . ."

{x:}

LORD BASTER-KIN HOLDS his ground in the face of this confident threat: *threat,* a variety of behavior that he has never before seen Isadora Arnem exhibit. Of course, that particular part of his mind that has always been prepared for threat from any quarter had said she might turn to it, this night. And so he feels no danger in admiring her strength for a moment, for he believes there is no reason to fear her demands and warnings—he has already calculated his response, which he now elaborates in statements that are perhaps even more shocking than were hers:

"Are you sure, Lady Arnem, that such men as these"—he indicates the streets about him—"can hope to defend this district against my Guard, whatever the shortcomings of that latter organization?"

"I never said as much," Isadora replies. "But I have sent dispatches to my husband that indicate the state of affairs in this city, and, when he returns to us, not only the Talons, but the whole of the Broken army—of which you have placed him in charge—will be more than enough to rescue the fate of the Fifth District."

"It would be," the Merchant Lord agrees. "It is perhaps unfortunate, therefore, that by the time he returns, the Fifth District will no longer exist, at least in its present form, while its residents will either have fled the city or have been killed." Baster-kin pulls his gauntlets from his hands with deceptive lack of concern. "That is, of course, assuming that your husband ever *does* return to the mountaintop."

Isadora's face goes helplessly pale; for she has known for most of her life that this is not a man who gives voice to idle threats. "Ever *does* return . . . ?" she echoes, before she has had time to select her words more carefully. "Has my lord heard of some misfortune that has befallen the Talons in the field?"

"I may have," Baster-kin replies, moving closer to her as he senses his ploy is succeeding. "But first, consider this: without your husband—who may, for all any of us know, be dead already—the Talons will not act against the God-King and his city; and without the Talons, the regular army will make no attempt to similarly intervene against the destruction of any part of their homeland. Then, failing any such intervention, the Fifth District will be cleansed by fire, and remade as a fit home for truly loyal citizens of Broken, citizens willing to give their wholehearted devotion to the God-King."

Isadora's sudden uncertainty consumes her for a long moment; but then she almost forces her confidence to return, in just the manner that her former mistress, Gisa, would have exhorted her to do: "My lord— you know full well the nature of plague. Whether it comes from a god or from man's poison, from the Bane or from the mountain itself—for who knows what other cracks in its stone summit have appeared or shifted, over the years?—such pestilence can and must spread, if treated only through ignorance and superstition, as it will be, should you leave it attended to by Kafran healers alone."

"Any *other* healers, particularly in the Fifth District, being somehow beholden to you," Baster-kin replies. "There is no reason to deny it, Lady Arnem, my own inquiries have proved as much, over these last many weeks. But this is no reason for you to concern yourself." To Isadora's repeated look of silent consternation, the Merchant Lord delightedly takes a few steps forward, and places her hand upon his own. "You and your children need feel in no danger. I shall personally take you out of the district, and offer you shelter in the *Kastelgerd* Baster-kin. As time passes, the memory of this place, like your memory of your husband and your children's memory of their father, will fade, and you shall envision a new future, a future devoid of squalor, poverty, and all the other ills of this place."

Isadora nods slowly. "A future much like the one you imagined for us long ago, when I attended to your *megrem* in your family's lodge at the base of the mountain; but now your father is no longer alive to object to the scheme, nor has Radelfer the power to prevent it."

"Do not think me so entirely selfish, my lady," Baster-kin replies; and there is a note of genuineness in his voice that even Isadora cannot deny. He places his second hand atop the one of hers that rests on his first. "I know how information travels among communities of healers in this city; I know that you must be aware of the . . . *shortcomings* of my own sons, and of their origins. Do not deny it, I beg you. But neither you nor I are past the age of bearing new children. Children who could take the name of Baster-kin, and bear it into another generation—a generation during which they could ensure the continued greatness of my clan, by assuming the leadership of this city and kingdom."

Isadora shakes her head slowly, then finally whispers, "You are *mad,* my lord . . ."

Remarkably, Baster-kin only smiles. "Yes. I anticipated such a response from you, initially; but when the fires begin to blaze in the district, and when word comes of spreading disease among the Talons, and the citizens of these neighborhoods begin to either die or flee—will I seem so mad, then? When the safety of your children is at terrible risk, and you have but one way to save them—will this plan seem like such lunacy to you?"

Instinctively drawing her hand back in a sudden tug, Isadora looks at the man who, she suddenly realizes, is indeed still very much the boy she once treated for a crippling, maddening illness; and she shakes with the realization, not that his mind may be disordered, but that his power and his strange logic may make him frighteningly correct. "Your entire premise proceeds from two assumptions, my lord," she says, not so haughtily as she would like to. "First, that my husband will, in fact, die—"

"Or may be dead already," Baster-kin replies.

"And second," Isadora continues, a deep shudder making itself visible in her body, much to the Merchant Lord's satisfaction, "that the disease that is making itself manifest in the strangely recurrent stream of water at the base of the southwestern wall will suddenly and simply disappear."

"As it will," Baster-kin answers confidently. "For you yourself have told me that you know the secret to making it thus disappear. And make it vanish you shall—shall, that is, if you wish your children and yourself to escape the inferno that will soon engulf this district."

And with another shudder of recognition, Isadora realizes that she has been, at least for the moment, outwitted, and that Rendulic Baster-kin has at long last gained the upper hand he longed for as a youth.

"None of these are propositions or notions that you can attempt to address now, my lady," Baster-kin says, turning to signal the very curious Radelfer, and ordering him to bring the litter they arrived in to the spot where he stands. "And so, wait. We have both, it seems, cast our dice on gambits of extraordinary stakes—results over the next few days, or even weeks, alone will allow us, and particularly you, to come to any heartfelt decisions. Bearing that in mind"—as his litter bearers and his seneschal rush to where he stands, Baster-kin notices a new, stronger element of doubt creeping into Isadora's features—"we shall, indeed, wait . . ." Pulling back the curtains of his litter, Rendulic smiles in a manner that Isadora has not seen since he was a youth. "But as you wait, think of this—your husband is a great soldier, who was perhaps always destined to die in the field, one day, campaigning against Broken's enemies. And, should that death have already come, or were it to come now, would you truly have wished or wish now that your children perish amid what is a necessary and unstoppable change within this city? Is your loyalty to the squalor where you spent your own childhood really so extreme that you would allow that? I leave you with those questions, my lady—and with a quick demonstration, soon to come, of the God-King's deep commitment to not only remaking Davon Wood, but to restructuring the Fifth District. My thanks for your guidance, and for your explanation of what is, I have no doubt, causing the deaths within the city walls." He turns to his seneschal, who had expected that, by now, his master would be overcome by frustration, rather than strangely calm, even serene. "We go," Baster-kin declares. "And Radelfer will maintain contact with you, my lady, in the event that you should require anything during the days to come—although that contact will have to be initiated, of course, by way of the city walls."

"The city walls . . . ?" Isadora says, increasingly confused.

"My meaning will become clear very soon," the Merchant Lord replies. "Good night, my lady." Baster-kin then vanishes into his litter, leaving Isadora none of the defiant—almost naïvely defiant, it seems now—satisfaction that she had thought the statements with which she had first presented her onetime patient would bring.

Radelfer turns to Isadora briefly, as confounded as she that he finds no expression of quiet triumph upon her face. Although he cannot say the words aloud, being too close to his lordly master, Radelfer would ask Isadora why this is so: why do her features not reflect the same expression that he had already perceived in Kriksex's, the silent pledge that, *When next we meet, we shall be on the same side of the storm that rises . . . ?*

Given this strange aspect upon Lady Arnem's face, when Radelfer turns and sees Kriksex offering a final and distant salute of comradeship, the seneschal, suspecting that the kind of devious manipulation of which he knows Rendulic Baster-kin to be a master is at work, can only return the gesture half-heartedly. Then he suddenly begins to bark harsh orders at his household guards, who move at a near-run in order to get their master safely back out of the squalor of the Fifth District. But the seneschal does not move so quickly that he fails to notice that Kriksex's men keep their blades drawn, as the Merchant Lord's party passes: suspicion yet reigns—indeed, has been heightened—between the two groups of veterans, although neither can say why . . .

"And so, my lord," Radelfer murmurs quietly, attempting a gambit of his own, "did my Lady Isadora fulfill your expectations?"

"Not yet," comes Baster-kin's surprisingly friendly reply. "But she is close."

"Indeed, my lord?" Radelfer answers quickly. "Close to abandoning both the district of her birth and the husband of her children?"

"I realize that you may have thought as much impossible, Radelfer," his lordship says. "But here is a fact that life has never taught you: set any obstacle between a mother and the safety of her young, and you will always gain an advantage—even if that obstacle be her own husband's fate." He glances briefly outside the curtains of the litter. "Are we passing back through the district wall at the head of the Path of Shame?"

"Aye, lord," Radelfer says, suddenly less confused than he is worried.

"And all the elements that I called for are in place?"

"The crews and their masters are assembled, along with detachments of your Guard to oversee their labor; which, I presumed, was to take place in the Fifth—"

"I know what you presumed, Radelfer. But now know my order: they are to close and seal the gateway."

"My Lord? I do not understand—"

"Nor need you, Seneschal. For my part, I must go to the High Temple at once, and assure the Grand Layzin that what was planned begins to take shape." Baster-kin sighs heavily: with weariness, to be sure, but to an even greater extent with satisfaction . . .

At the base of the southwestern wall, meanwhile, as soon as Baster-kin's litter has disappeared, Isadora feels her legs go a bit weak; and from somewhere in the alleyway, her eldest son rapidly appears to support her. "Mother!" he calls. "Are you unwell?"

His mother makes no reply, at first, but takes a few silent moments to control the rate of her breathing, knowing that if it races as quickly as her heart, she will likely faint. In this state does Kriksex find her, as he rejoins mother and son; and his face, too, fills with concern. "Lady Arnem!" he calls out, struggling with his crutch as quickly as he can. "What has taken place? All seemed to go just as you had planned!"

"Just so, Kriksex—it *seemed* to," Isadora gasps. "But I have ever been able to sense the soul of that man, and the conclusion was too abrupt, his departure too swift and sure—no, he has not done with us, this night . . ."

The woman Berthe, having observed her ladyship's distress, has rushed to fetch a small, well-worn chair from a friend's nearby house. "My lady!" she calls, as she stumbles out the doorway of the house with the stick of furniture; she also exhibits the self-possession to immediately dispatch her eldest daughter with a pitcher to the wells at the head of the Path of Shame, where the girl can fetch clean water for the brave woman who seems to have brought the beginnings of dignity to the Fifth District.

Meanwhile, as Lady Arnem waits for this relief, Kriksex stands over one of her shoulders, having guessed that negotiations with Lord Baster-kin will be protracted and producing a rough map of the manner in which he intends to deploy the main body of their veterans during the coming interval. Dagobert looks over his mother's other shoulder at the scrap of parchment, while the rest of the men who have guarded Lady Arnem's party hold their torches aloft in a semicircle, to illuminate the study and the subsequent discussion that takes place—

And then the moment that had seemed, to all save Isadora, to offer some kind of hope, is shattered by a child's voice: it is Berthe's daughter, who screams in alarm . . .

Down the alleyway the girl comes, followed, strangely, by the *bulger* guards, Bohemer and Jerej, whose expressions are not altogether devoid of the horror that fills the young girl's face; and as the three draw closer to the group beneath the wall, the child's words become distinct, although they seem to make little sense:

"Mother!" she cries. "Men are at the wall—*they are closing it!* We will be trapped!"

Weeping, and spilling water from the pitcher she so nobly attempted to fill, the girl throws herself into Berthe's arms, handing what little water remains in the vessel to Dagobert.

"It's true, my lady," Jerej says, catching his breath. "Masons lay stone as fast as it can be brought to them, protected all the while by the Merchant Lord's Guard."

"The good Lord Baster-kin," Bohemer adds, bitter sarcasm in his voice. "He must have had most of the city's masons assembling, even as we were distracted here."

Dagobert looks down in alarm. "Mother . . . ?"

But his mother is already murmuring in reply: *"So that was his meaning—'by way of the city walls . . .' "* Then, never one to allow a moment of crisis to stun her for long, Isadora looks up, encouragement in her features. "But it must make no difference. It must be treated as a sign that we have struck close to the hearts of those who have committed the various outrages within this district."

Having done what she can to embolden those around her, Isadora takes a few steps off on her own, and is allowed to do so by her comrades, who sense her exhaustion. Looking up at the city wall once more, she whispers:

"Forgive me, Sixt. But we who have remained in our homes must see this business through to its end—just as you, belovèd husband, must safely navigate the dangers you face on your campaign . . ."

She is about to issue more commands aloud to those who stand about her; but then sounds still more alarming than the screaming of Berthe's child echo through the streets: it is the hard pounding of leather-soled boots against the granite of the walkway atop the walls, and then the voices of soldiers calling out orders to their men. Moving back from the wall, Isadora and the others look up, their men with torches spreading out so as to cast light in a wider upward arc—

And they are there. Not men of the Merchant Lord's Guard, this time, but soldiers of the regular army, their cloaks of rich blue and their numbers forming a near-continuous line atop the wall. In addition (and most frighteningly, for the residents below), they bear regular-issue Broken bows. Before long, an almost ritual wail begins to rise from many men and women in the streets and houses below—but not from the local children, who flock to aging, stoical veterans, rather than to their near-panicked parents, and who try as best their young hearts will allow to adopt the old soldiers' dispassionate demeanor.

"You men above!" Isadora calls to the soldiers, with real authority and effect. "You know who I am, I daresay?"

"Aye, Lady," says one particularly wide, bearded sentek, who needs not shout to be heard. His face is well lit by the torches his own men carry, and it is vaguely familiar to Isadora. "You are the wife of Sentek—or rather, *Yantek*—Arnem, our new commander."

"And you are Sentek—"

"Gerfrehd,"[†] the man replies. "Although I can understand your unfamiliarity with it. For as my cloak indicates, I serve in the regular army. But rest assured: you are well known to me, my lady."

"Good," Isadora calls back. "And, while I do not expect you to disobey orders that doubtless bear the Grand Layzin's seal, I do think you owe me, as wife of your commander, an explanation of your appointed task."

"Certainly, Lady Arnem," replies Sentek Gerfrehd. "We have been told of insurrection in the Fifth District—but we do not come to engage in any precipitate action."

"I should hope not," Isadora replies. "For this 'insurrection,' as your own eyes can tell you, is largely one of children."

"I have determined as much," the man answers, nodding. "And will report it to the other commanders of our other regular legions, who will doubtless wish, like me, to know more of just why we have been dispatched here."

"And your immediate instructions?" Isadora presses.

"Are simple enough: citizens of the district may exit the city through the South Gate, but no one is to be allowed to enter the city through it. Nor to interfere with the completion of the wall at the head of the Path of Shame."

"You realize," Isadora replies, "that your actions could be seen as those of enemies, Gerfrehd—not of fellow subjects."

The sentek is slow in answering, finally doing so with a rather inscrutable smile. "I am aware of as much, my lady. Just as I am aware that *yours* could be seen as the actions of rebellious subjects, rather than loyal ones."

But for Isadora, after a lifetime of close contact with soldiers, the smile is not difficult to understand at all; and she holds out a hand to the children that surround her aging veterans, standing at their best approximation of attention. "Well, Sentek—I say again, here are your 'rebellious subjects.' There will be little glory in subduing them."

At this, Sentek Gerfrehd almost seems to chuckle quietly, and he replies, "No, my lady. Any more than there is such glory to be had fighting alongside the Merchant Lord's Personal Guard."

"And so?" Isadora asks. Her boldness in speaking thus to a sentek of the regular army has made many of the terrified adults about her ashamed of their fear, and they begin to move forward to surround her and stand by their children.

"And so we will wait, my lady," Sentek Gerfrehd calls. "For we take our orders, as you know, from the God-King, the Grand Layzin, and your husband, in such order. The merchants are not our masters."

Isadora nods once, approvingly. "And so we, too, will wait, Sentek," she says. "And see what actions your superiors force upon us."

"It would seem we await the same things, then, my lady," Gerfrehd replies.

"Indeed," Isadora states; and with that, she nods and moves away from the wall, subtly leaning upon Dagobert for support, and offering as much encouragement to those around her as she can.

But that effort is mitigated by one question that will not leave her mind, as she walks back to her home, despite the fact that she cannot voice it to the citizens around her: yet as she looks above those citizens, above even the soldiers on the wall, and, soon, from the safety of her second-floor bedroom, toward the edge of Davon Wood, as it becomes faintly visible in the far distance, she murmurs:

"And what orders or signs will *you*, my husband, understand as offering the same evidence that matters are far from correct or well at home, and require your return to put them right . . . ?"

{xi:}

SOON AFTER ORDERING the city's masons to work through the night to finish the work of sealing the Fifth District off from the rest of Broken by walling in the gateway at the head of the Path of Shame, Lord Baster-kin orders his litter to return to his *Kastelgerd,* while he and Radelfer journey humbly afoot to the High Temple. Radelfer waits without as his lordship enters the Sacristy, for it is here that Baster-kin must brief the Grand Layzin on the most recent developments concerning what are in fact his own *and* the Layzin's plans for the seemingly ill-fated Fifth District: plans that represent the second part of a long-schemed strategy to reassert and ensure the kingdom of Broken's strength in the years to come. (The Layzin is unaware of Baster-kin's private intentions concerning Isadora Arnem, which the Merchant Lord considers every bit as important to the health of the state as the destruction of both the Bane and the Fifth District.)

The intelligence that the Merchant Lord brings to the Layzin is encouraging: the prospect of besieging the Fifth has brought out in his Guard an unexpected enthusiasm, if not discipline, particularly now that the regular army is in disarray, with its commander and elite troops gone and no standing orders from Sixt Arnem that might interfere with Baster-kin's plots in place. The Guardsmen's enthusiasm has been further enhanced by the Merchant Lord's having revealed, prior to his departure from the Fifth District gate for the High Temple, a written order giving both the sealing of the wall and the ensuing siege of the district royal sanction, sanction demonstrated by the appearance of the God-King's personal seal upon the document. And, now that he effectively controls all official correspondence flowing in and out of the city (including and especially Isadora Arnem's), Baster-kin believes that no future orders contradicting this rare and extraordinary royal edict can or will be received by the commanders of the home *khotors* of the regular army; and they will therefore have no choice but to obediently (if, in some cases, less than enthusiastically) support the undertakings of Merchant Lord's Guard. In the eastern provinces, meanwhile, the Talons will be at first weakened and then destroyed by the illness that is being carried down Broken's mountain and toward the Meloderna, first by Killen's Run, and then by the Cat's Paw: an illness that Baster-kin believes he has coerced Isadora Arnem, by using the lives of her children as a weapon, into working with Kafran engineers to eradicate within the city, thereby eliminating it throughout the kingdom (although that eradication will, tragically, occur too late to change the fate of the Talons and their commander).

Thus, to hear Baster-kin tell it, this evening has been full of developments that offer hope to his kingdom, his ruler, and his faith—as well as to his clan, although this bit of triumphant news the Merchant Lord must continue to keep private. But open expression of any such triumph is unnecessary: the Merchant Lord has so much encouragement to offer the Grand Layzin, as he stands upon the latter's dais in the Sacristy and explains in detail just what all the commotion within the city signifies for Broken's royal retinue, as well as for its most eminent citizens, that he quickly assumes an almost heroic aspect, one that he feels he must temper:

"It had been my hope, Eminence," Baster-kin ultimately declares, with false regret, "that if I gave Lady Arnem an honest account of how the pestilence that both she and we have discovered to be at work in the Fifth District, as well as locations as far east as Daurawah—a sickness that remains, almost certainly, the work of the Bane—she would urge her husband to return home at once, in order both to organize a defensive force to take the place of Sentek Gledgesa's doomed Ninth Legion and to oversee the cleansing by fire of the Arnem family's portion of the city. Yet such remains her strange allegiance to her district, as well as her bizarre apprehension that the priests of Kafra are purchasing or simply abducting its children, that she places the safety of its residents—for in truth, one could not call them citizens—above any concerns for her husband. To be frank, I believe that she has grown used to a position of power in the district, and will not surrender it until she is sharply reminded of what she owes to both the God-King and to Broken itself. In short, she *can* be brought back to a useful life, Eminence, of this I am certain, but not until she has been thus humbled."

"And you are willing to undertake the task of forcibly returning her to the path of obedience and faith, my lord?" the Layzin says, removing the clasp that holds his golden hair at the back of his neck. "The God-King would not demand it of you, for you have already been tireless in stemming the waves of misfortune that have descended upon our people."

"I suspected such royal and divine generosity, Eminence," Baster-kin replies, working hard to keep his eagerness to "humble" Isadora Arnem from becoming plain. "Yet the woman is too important to this undertaking, she possesses too many strengths and gifts, to allow less than careful treatment—I know this from the experience I myself had with her as a youth. And so, I will undertake it. In the case of the Talons, however . . ." Baster-kin holds his arms aloft in seeming helplessness, piling deception upon deception. "Their laudable zeal to continue their campaign to destroy the Bane, despite my most recent warnings to Yantek Arnem of the newfound dangers they face—warnings that have still yet to be answered—confirm the tragic irony that they are men condemned by their own zeal. They will die soon, if they are not in fact dead already; and so, I believe we must look to our commanders within the city to train a new force for the East, and proceed with our plans to reward them, as well as any senior officers of my Guard who may distinguish themselves in the action to come, with new *Kastelgerde* and smaller homes within a rebuilt Fifth District."

The Layzin passes a hand through his loose-flowing hair. "It seems that there is no problem to which you have not turned your considerable energy, my lord."

For a moment, as he realizes he may achieve all for which he has long schemed, Baster-kin's heart feels a passion it has done without for many years; yet he knows that, for the sake of those schemes, he must control such joy. "It is little enough, Eminence," he says evenly. "Given the manner in which our God-King and his ancestors have always favored the clan Baster-kin."

"Perhaps so," the Grand Layzin replies; and the softness of this response makes it seem as though his thoughts are distracted in some obscure manner. For an instant, Baster-kin fears this distraction may betray dubiousness, perhaps even a comprehension of his own shielded designs regarding Isadora Arnem. But the Layzin's next statement lays such fears to rest: "Above all, we must ensure that any attempts at communication between the good Yantek Arnem and his wife are intercepted, for theirs is the sole partnership that might rouse truly popular following within the city and the kingdom."

Baster-kin smiles just perceptibly: what he had taken for skepticism was in fact the Layzin's tacit approval, as he could not have asked for an order more in keeping with his own plots. "Rest easy, in that regard, Eminence," he says. "All correspondence of *any* kind is interrupted at the city gates by my agents—our control of all aspects of life within Broken is as complete as we could wish for."

With these words, Baster-kin takes note of the sudden appearance of a Wife of Kafra from behind the drapery at the rear of the dais. The young woman, if judged by her nubile body, has only recently been elevated from novice to the higher order of priestess: and she arrives so quietly (as do all such young priests and priestesses within the Sacristy) that she seems to materialize out of the very air in the chamber. But her gown of the sheerest green-golden fabric makes plain the very real feminine perfections beneath it, confirming Baster-kin's impression, not only of her youth and inexperience, but of her almost intoxicating physical reality. As the girl hands an evidently much-needed goblet of light wine to the Layzin, the Merchant Lord cannot help but turn away from her, as if to even feel lust for anyone save the object of his complex plans would be a betrayal.

"Will you take some wine, my lord?" the Layzin condescends to ask.

"Your Eminence is kindness itself," Baster-kin says. "But this night yet holds crucial tasks for me to undertake: if, for example, we are to send one *khotor* of my Guard in the place of the Talons to destroy the Bane, I must find and enlist a new set of officers for the task—for those who now command those troops are hardly adequate to the task. And the best place to recruit such young men, who must be both versed in combat and sprung from families who are wealthy enough that we need feel no compunction about requiring them to offer their male offspring for service, will be in the Stadium, where my own son spends a great deal of his time, as do the grown sons of so many noble houses."

The Layzin considers the matter, and then nods approvingly. "Yet another sound plan," he judges. "But surely you could first grant yourself an hour or so during which to pursue some purely selfish diversion? For example, I saw the look that came into your face when this young servant of Kafra entered the Sacristy. Why not enjoy her flesh for a time, before entering the Stadium and reminding the young men of Broken's wealthiest households of their duty—a thankless task if ever I heard of one? After all, the continued failure of Kafra to grant the God-King Saylal with an heir weighs heavily upon my own thoughts—yet I can assure you, having done all I can do, this day, to try to entreat a change in the royal fortunes, I know that I must attend to my own needs, later this night, lest I go mad with vexation."

Lord Baster-kin returns a conspiratorial smile that has entered the Layzin's features, and allows himself to glance again at the body of the young Priestess of Kafra that is so scarcely hidden by her sheer robe. "And in your case, the reward is richly deserved, Eminence," Baster-kin replies, still playing the part of slavish servant, never wishing the Layzin or his creatures to suspect that his own desires can be satisfied solely by the one woman who will offer him (as she did when he was a boy) true peace; and that he will achieve that peace once more when he has so arranged matters that both he and Isadora Arnem are free to bind their lives as he believes they should have been bound so many years ago. "But for a far humbler servant such as myself, neither time or energy must be diverted, for the First *Khotor* of the Guard must be ready to march out of the city as soon as possible."

"Is it that she is a girl?" the Layzin says, seemingly incredulous that Baster-kin will not take the opportunity to enjoy the physical pleasures that can be offered only by the denizens of the High Temple and the House of the Wives of Kafra. "For this one has a brother, just within, a youth her equal in unspoiled beauty, if this evening your tastes run—"

But Baster-kin is already shaking his head, effectively disguising his own peculiar sense of revulsion at this latest offer. "There will be time enough, as I say, for servants such as myself to take our ease and our pleasure, Eminence," he replies. "For now, duty must be our master."

The Layzin sighs and smiles, surrendering his argument as he offers his pale blue ring for the Merchant Lord to kiss. Baster-kin does so, trying hard, now, to keep his eyes from the young priestess; then he turns to finally leave the Sacristy, moving as quickly and forcefully as is his seemingly eternal habit.

Not until an attendant has closed the Sacristy door tightly after the Merchant Lord departs does the Layzin speak again. Apparently without guests, now, he dismisses the young priestess, who vanishes back through the curtain at the rear of the dais, and then leans back against his sofa, tilting his head toward that same drapery.

"You heard all, Majesty?" the Layzin asks.

The voice that responds is filled with a languor to make the Layzin's own seem energetic, by comparison. Yet there is pride in the voice, too, and an easy tone of authority:

"I heard all," the voice states, not without comprehension of Baster-kin's loyalty and self-denial, but without any apparent admiration for either. "And I recall a saying of my mad ancestor's: 'Easy lies the master whose hounds' teeth are sharp, and their bellies empty . . .'"

"*Saylal,*" the Layzin says in toying admonishment. "You must not call his lordship a *hound,* O Brother of God . . ."

"Must I not?" the voice replies.

"No," the Layzin replies. "You must not. Even if his manner does, at times, suggest something of the sort. But his ideas on how to protect you, Gracious Saylal, have almost a profundity to them . . ."

"You misunderstand me, Most Loyal of the Loyal—I have known clever dogs, in my life. Very clever dogs. As has Alandra, of course . . ."

"Alandra *makes* her dogs clever, Sire," the Layzin adds. "Though not so clever as her cats. But the comparison with a mortal is unfair."

"Hmm," the voice behind the curtain grunts. "Well, I know this—even the cleverest of dogs would not refuse such beautiful young creatures as the two of you have sent me. And I would have them both *now,* before my regal sister returns from the Wood and tries to snatch them away to be her own playthings."

"It is fortunate, then," the Layzin replies, "that I was able to rely on Baster-kin's unending sense of duty and self-denial to make certain the pair would be intact. But we owed him at least the offer of such flesh. Yet, Saylal, now that we *have* the girl intact, I beg you, if not for the dynasty, then as a boon to ease my mind, fix your energies first upon her." The Layzin's face and voice suddenly grow more solemn. "But are you truly ready, Holy Majesty, for another attempt?"

"These gifts from my Divine Brother Kafra *make* me ready, I believe."

"I see . . ." The Layzin claps his hands twice, at which another attendant in a black robe edged in red appears from one of the side doors of the chamber. "Summon the Sacristan," the leader of the Kafran faith calls out, making sure that the curtain behind him is fully closed. "Have him open the vestry and prepare my robes of fertility, and his own."

"Of course, Eminence," the attendant replies.

"And you may see to the honing and polishing of the thinnest and smallest of the sacred blades yourself, before he blesses them—quickly!

The organs must be harvested while the blood is hot, and before the opium has begun to lose its effect. I shall speak the prayer of succession myself, as we begin . . ." Leaning toward the curtain once more, the Layzin asks, "How long will you require, Majesty?"

"Not long," struggles the reply. "If, that is, you assist me, old friend . . ."

"Yes, Divinity," the Layzin answers; and then, to the attendant, he calls urgently: "Be quick, and get the Sacristan!"

"Eminence!" the attendant says in compliance, rushing from the room; and only then does the Layzin himself hurriedly disappear behind the curtain.

And, before another day has passed, the often foul yet seemingly mystical stream of water beneath the southwestern wall of the Fifth District will run a little higher, a little faster—and its stench will carry a little farther than it did on the night before . . .

{*xii:*}

THE ORIGINAL PURPOSE of Broken's Stadium, promulgated by one of Oxmontrot's more thoughtful descendants, had been to demonstrate that those who piously followed the tenets of the Kafran faith would be rewarded not only with wealth, but with health and vigor, as well. Yet over the years a change has taken place at the northern extremity of the city: the two worlds, Temple and Stadium, have grown apart. The Kafran faithful say that this separation is the result of a rebirth of the consuming taste for gaming that was so dominant among the tribes that made up Broken's first citizens. Others more quietly assert that the capture of many of the fiercest, most impressive beasts in Davon Wood—panthers, bears, wolves, and wildcats—and their repeated torment by the athletes of the Stadium has angered the old gods of Broken, who are punishing the city as a whole and thus calling into question Kafra's long-asserted supremacy. Certainly Oxmontrot himself, a worshipper of the old gods, never intended for such noble creatures to be trapped, safely secured by heavy chains to concrete posts rising out of the sands of the arena, and made to serve as opponents that can do little or no harm to the children of Broken's merchant nobility; and in this

Lord Baster-kin shares the Mad King's feelings. But his disdain cannot stem the rising popularity of such displays among the future heads of the kingdom's ruling clans: in ever-increasing numbers they come, day and night, not only to display their prowess in the arena, but to indulge in what are, to the Merchant Lord, the even more mindless and loathsome activities that take place in the endless rows of benches and private stalls that surround that sandy stage: gambling, of course, but also drinking to excess, as well as fornication that has no bearing on the arrangement of marriages or the strengthening and preservation of clans.

All of these would together represent cause enough for Baster-kin's hatred of the Stadium. But, as always, there is a personal sentiment hidden behind his purely moral objections: for among the young men most active in the Stadium's amusements is his lordship's own eldest son (and his sole acknowledged child), Adelwülf. Indeed, had Adelwülf never shown any interest in the amusements that take place inside the thick, elaborately carved walls of the Stadium, Baster-kin would likely never have set foot inside it; but, given his son's persistence, his lordship must occasionally visit the place, if only to chide the athletes and audiences, and remind them all—Adelwülf most of all—of the damage they are doing to Broken's future by thus squandering their lives.

These occasional descents by his father are more than a mere embarrassment for Adelwülf: over the last several years especially, the Stadium has become a place in which the handsome young man's unquenchable appetites for besting others in wrestling matches and battles of wooden or blunt-edged steel swords, facing the many chained beasts that are on offer in the cells below the sands, and finally drinking and fornicating in the stalls above the arena have grown to equal his distaste for going home to his own clan's *Kastelgerd*. When he sees his father enter the Stadium, therefore, he considers it a violation, of sorts, of the only place in Broken that he thinks of as *his* home. For the sake of gaining stature with his associates, Adelwülf usually attempts to laugh off his father's intrusions and patriotic rants, confidently and caustically: for he knows well the story of Rendulic Baster-kin's famous panther hunt, undertaken when his lordship was Adelwülf's own age, and he cannot help but find a good deal of hypocrisy in his father's indictments. And indeed, Baster-kin has never, in his storied life, come closer to a battlefield than that single instance of blood sport; yet that one exposure was a world away from what he now views . . .

And, if truth be spoken, Adelwülf, this golden-haired, finely sculpted paragon of Kafran virtue, actually burns less with sarcasm, at his father's arrival, than with shame: shame and hatred, the latter a passion born out of his enduring resentment for his father's having driven his mother mad (or so it seems to the youth) and his sister Loreleh into exile. Adelwülf had known Loreleh only too briefly; yet during that time he had come to think of her as the only sibling he had ever known or was ever likely to know, since all awareness of Klauqvest had ever been kept from him; and a life alone in the great *Kastelgerd* with a lunatic mother and so arch a father had become no life at all. Loreleh had been his temporary respite; and the reasons cited for her removal had never seemed any more sound or just to Adelwülf than they had to his mother.

On this night, however, there will be no exhortations by the elder Baster-kin, and no typical complaints from the younger: for, as his lord-ship arrives at the Stadium gate and begins to hear the sounds made by the crowd within, he realizes that he truly needs to convince any of the young men amid that throng who possess a genuine talent for violence that they have no choice save to march alongside his Guardsmen into Davon Wood, and to participate—in commanding roles, if possible—in the final destruction of the Bane. And he believes, too, that he has finally conceived of an action that will be striking and decisive enough to shock such play warriors into becoming true soldiers. It is an action, not sur-prisingly, that will also play a crucial role in bringing his plans concern-ing Isadora Arnem to full fruition; yet despite the very real advantages it may garner, it is a measure of the plan's extremity that even Baster-kin himself wonders if, when the moment comes, he will possess the steadi-ness of purpose to carry it out . . .

He does not wonder for very long. As he passes under the Stadium gate and stands at the edge of the arena, his eyes and ears are assaulted by sights and sounds that are as wildly intoxicating as ever to those young men and women who either participate in or observe them. The combat that takes place in the arena is, to all present, a most splendid display of the ideals of Broken youth, power, and beauty, all the more arousing for the knowledge that it will never result in the death of a human being, but risks only the lives of those powerful woodland beasts that are brought up from the dungeon-like cells in chains. So extreme is the activity at this late hour, both in the arena and in the rows of seats that stretch into the sky about Baster-kin, that he feels his hatred begin to surge anew, and his momentary qualms to subside. Radelfer, who has followed his lord into the arena, can detect as much: he has seen this man, both as a youth and in his present middle years, with death stalking his features, and he sees as much again when Rendulic studies the Stadium crowd this night.

"My lord?" Radelfer says, the concern he felt for his master's soundness of mind when they departed the Fifth District still very alive. "Are you well? It has already been a long night of difficult undertakings—should we not return to the *Kastelgerd*? You can leave the chastising of your son for tomorrow."

"Concerning that matter, you could not be more mistaken, Radelfer," his lordship answers. "These people must finally learn their duty, and understand the consequences of ignoring it; and they must be taught such lessons *tonight*."

As soon as the crowd in the Stadium begins to take as much notice of him as he already has of it, Baster-kin is appalled to see the usual wave of petitioners moving toward him, each looking for some favor that will allow him to serve in civil government without having to undertake precisely the sort of military service for which the Merchant Lord has already selected him. At the same time, as good fortune would have it, Baster-kin sees that Radelfer has taken the precaution of ordering some eight or ten members of his household guard to report from the *Kastelgerd* to the Stadium, likely by runner while his lordship was in council with the Layzin. The men are arriving now—yet the only thanks Baster-kin offers his seneschal is to say:

"Have your men keep those people away from me tonight, Radelfer. My business is far too important." He pauses, searching the various combatants in the ring before adding, "In every way imaginable . . ." Glancing at the supposèd acts of bravery upon the sands ever more keenly, Baster-kin at last determines: "I do not see my son exercising his talents out there—but find him, Radelfer. Bring him to me. For he has always trusted you more than he has his father. I shall await you—" Baster-kin continues to eye the arena. "There." He points to one concrete pillar near the center of the sandy oval, to which is anchored a chain that restricts the movements of a large Broken brown bear, preventing the confused, enraged animal from injuring any of the several young men who are proving their "courage" by tormenting him with spears and swords, evidently to the crowd's satisfaction.

As Baster-kin makes his way to the concrete pillar he has indicated and is recognized by ever more of the crowd, a strange hush falls over those participating in the various activities in the arena as well those among the audience. It is not a hush inspired by affection, of course, although it certainly contains a large measure of respect. When he nears the concrete pillar to which the brown bear is chained, Baster-kin takes aside one of the enormous, scarred Stadium attendants—the men who do the inglorious work of moving animals and racks of weapons from the arena to the scarcely lit iron cages and storage rooms below—and orders the man and his fellow workers to remove all the animals to their cages, and disarm all combatants. It is a command that would draw jeers, were it issued by any other official: but now, no voice among the assembled athletes and spectators is brave enough to express the disapproval that all feel. Such is the effect of the hard glare that the Merchant Lord moves from face to face about and above him; such is the effect he has long cultivated.

Only when his eyes settle on Radelfer, who stands outside a curtained stall that is one of a group approximately a third of the way up the Stadium benches, does Baster-kin stop studying the crowd. Then, when he takes more specific note of the expression upon his seneschal's face—one of genuine regret for the very public family spectacle that he believes is about to take place—his lordship jumps down from the pillar's base and, issuing a final order to one of the animal handlers, moves at a quick pace to join Radelfer before the more (if not completely) sympathetic seneschal has a chance to warn Adelwülf of his father's approach.

When Baster-kin closes in on the stall, he begins to hear the sounds of fornication emerging from it; and when his lordship arrives, he rips the curtain away, to find his son fully engaged with one young noblewoman, the pair of them having bothered to shift their scant clothing only enough to allow him to enter her, while a second young woman laughs and holds a wineskin, alternately pouring its contents into Adelwülf's mouth and pressing her ample breasts into that same hungry maw. At the sound of the curtain being torn, the two young women shriek, for they are able to see the man responsible; Adelwülf, however, only begins to turn, disengaging from the widespread girl beneath him as he shouts:

"*Ficksel!* Which of you idiots dares interrupt my amusement—?" He grows silent when he sees the figure behind him, and quickly tries to straighten his tunic as he exclaims, "Father! What are you doing here—"

"I assure you, Adelwülf," his lordship replies, putting his fists to his hips, "I am not here for my pleasure or amusement. Our kingdom is in chaos, our bravest young men are daring death of every variety in the provinces and beyond, and you lie here throwing curses more suited to a Bane's filthy mouth at your father while consorting with such as—*these* . . ." Baster-kin quickly nods to the two young women. "Get out," he says to them. "I do not want to know your names, nor those of your clans—for I should have to tell them how their virtuous daughters pass their evenings, and if they have an ounce of patriotism in them, they should exile you to Davon Wood, out of the shame if naught else."

"Just a moment, Father—" Adelwülf says, trying to recover some ground.

But Baster-kin's fury is not spent: "Do not use that term in addressing me, just now, you useless sack of meat—I am your 'lord,' until I give you permission to call me anything else!"

As he tightens a simple belt around his tunic, Adelwülf keeps his blue eyes fixed on his father, with an injured intensity that would burn some sense of uneasiness, perhaps even sympathy, into most onlookers. At the very least, most witnesses could not fail to appreciate the unfortunate nature of the moment; but the hurt and anger in the son's young eyes do nothing to soften the severity of Baster-kin's aspect, and Adelwülf soon murmurs, "Very well—*my lord,*" in resignation, as he gets to his feet. Standing on the bench above the man who has tormented him in like fashion for much of his life, Adelwülf rises higher than his father, and would seem to have the physical advantage; but the air of fear that shows through his rage nullifies any such superiority of position. "Now that you have spoilt yet another of my few enjoyments in life, what would you have me do?"

Baster-kin steps up onto Adelwülf's bench, in order to look him more closely in the eye. "What would I—" the father echoes, with more genuine anger than the younger man can possibly manage. "You really have no idea, no sense of any duty, do you, whelp? Well, then—" With frightening suddenness, his lordship lays tight, painful hold of his son's left ear, pulling him first out of the stall, and then, stumblingly, back down the rows of benches. "Let us have it your way, for a few moments! Let us engage in the enjoyments of this foul place—*clear the arena!*"

Adelwülf would like to argue, but the struggle to keep from crying out at the pain in his ear and the difficulty of staying on his feet in front of his friends below are together too great an effort, and he finds himself saying only, "Father! *My lord*—I beg you, can we not settle this matter at home?"

"*Home?*" Baster-kin shouts. "You *are* home, whelp! Let us, then, enjoy the *true* entertainments that your hospitality has to offer!"

Because Adelwülf is no longer in fact a child, whatever his father's indictments, Baster-kin's maintaining a secure grip on his ear requires keeping a clamp-like, even violent hold on the entirety of the appendage, soon causing its skin and gristle to tear away from the skull at one spot; and, like all similarly minor cuts to the head, the wound begins to bleed profusely enough that by the time they have reached the lowest benches that surround the arena, a stream of the precious fluid covers portions of Adelwülf's face, neck, and upper chest. Catching sight of this seemingly grievous injury, the young man loses all concern with maintaining a courageous demeanor in front of his friends:

"My lord!" Adelwülf pleads desperately, as Lord Baster-kin, again surrounded by Radelfer's men, roughly forces his son out onto the sand of the arena, in full view and hearing of the others in the Stadium. "Please! I am bleeding, let me depart the Stadium, at the least, and spare me this humiliation before my comrades—"

"'Comrades'?" Baster-kin replies. There seems something in Adelwülf's appearance and pathetic manner that gives him a deep satisfaction. "You call these play-warriors 'comrades'?" As he continues to drag his son across the now-empty arena and toward the concrete pillar on which he stood moments earlier, Baster-kin raises his voice and addresses the crowd that stands outside and above the sand-strewn oval. Few of the young men and women present have departed the Stadium, so compelling is the scene being played out before them; and this fact makes Radelfer, who has joined the ranks of the spectators along with his men, profoundly uneasy. "Do you *all* think of each other as 'comrades'?" Lord Baster-kin calls to the Stadium's crowd. "As soldiers in some peculiar conflict that neither risks nor takes any of your lives, yet is somehow of enough importance that you merit the same ranks of friendship and honor as do the young men who fill the ranks of Broken's legions?"

For a long, very strange moment, the Stadium knows something it has rarely if ever experienced, in recent years: silence. Not a member of the crowd watching what takes place between the two Baster-kins, father and son, has the courage to venture an answer to the older man's question, however much they may disagree with what he says. Even Radelfer is uneasy that he is about to witness a scene of violence such as his mind—never so strangely or even terribly ingenious as his master's—is incapable of conceiving. But, although impressed by Rendulic's ability to hold the attention of the drunken crowd about him, it is when Radelfer looks to his own household guardsmen that his uneasiness becomes simpler dread: for he sees that they, too, are struck dumb by Lord Baster-kin's ability to keep the false warriors of the Stadium not only silent but in a state of terror; and these are men who, unlike the youths in the stands, have seen much of true violence, and have developed the ability to know when horror is approaching.

All the greater, then, is Radelfer's admiration for Adelwülf when, seeing that his father has caused his friends, his "comrades," to become thus silently fearful, the youth finally frees himself from his father's grip, takes a few steps from the concrete pillar, and spits into the sand, declaring loudly:

"Yes—*Father*! And why should we *not* declare ourselves the equals of such men? What would you know of it? When have you ever faced the dangers of the arena, perils undertaken without the armor and heavy weaponry your precious legions take with them whenever they go into battle? You bully my friends and me with your position and power, but what do you know of mortal danger, as you sit in your tower and count our clan's money, plotting new ways for *other* men to see to the safety of this city and this kingdom? I have endured this humiliation long enough—give me some proof that you yourself are the equal of those legionaries of whom you speak, and perhaps I will listen to more; but if you cannot, put an end to this endless dissatisfaction with those who risk their safety and honor upon these sands, as Kafra's priests long ago taught them was a righteous way to prove their devotion to the tenets of the golden god!"

A few daring members of the crowd about the arena dare applaud this defiant and unprecedented outburst—until, that is, the Merchant Lord again turns his deathly stare upon each section of the benches and stalls. As for Radelfer, his satisfaction at Adelwülf's daring is quickly extinguished by the strange look of satisfaction that enters his lordship's face.

There is no admiration in the gaze, no sense that Rendulic Baster-kin has finally provoked a manly response from the son who has so eternally disappointed him; rather, it is the aspect of a man whose final lingering doubts about a course of action he has been debating in his own mind have been silenced.

"Well," Baster-kin says, in a much more even yet no less menacing voice. "Perhaps I have been mistaken, then. Perhaps all of you are more than capable of taking your place among the ranks of men who must, at this hour of need, defend our kingdom. And yet . . ." The Merchant Lord takes a few steps away from Adelwülf, then raises a hand to signal to the attendant with whom he had spoken earlier. "I shall require, I fear, some demonstration of courage and valor greater than words, before I can accept you"—he glances at his son, then up into the crowd—"before I can accept *any* of you, as actual warriors."

A commotion becomes audible from one of the doorways that lead down to the maze of cages and storage rooms beneath the arena; and before long, the attendant and two of his fellows appear, each holding the end of a separate length of chain with one hand and a spear in the other. The three long sections of chain all meet at a common end: a heavy iron collar, one that surrounds and (from the look of the missing fur and the irritated skin beneath) has long surrounded the neck of a large Davon panther.

The animal is a female, one who has grown mature but far from defeated during many years of imprisonment within the Stadium. She attempts occasionally to lash out at one or another of the handlers, if he lets his section of chain go too slack, but has become wise enough to avoid the prodding spearheads that are thrust forward in response to these outbursts of anger. That she is unusually large is easy to determine; less so is the true color of her coat, given the filth that she has been forced to live in for so long. To one with an experienced eye, able to see through such discoloration, it would yet be possible to determine, from the parts of her body that she can and does clean with care, that the fur is unusually golden, perhaps even containing a silver or white tint that makes it catch the light of surrounding torches and braziers in an unusual way.

One identifying characteristic, however, is plain for all to see: the unusually light, even brilliant, green of the eyes, which seem to peer directly into the heart of whichever human she fastens her gaze upon.

"So," Adelwülf says, as the animal becomes visible. "I might have known. The eldest of our panthers. It is the female that you brought from Davon Wood, years ago. Or so we are told."

"Yes," Baster-kin says, taking several steps toward the animal as it draws close to the concrete pillar. "And how have you treated a beast that had more heart than you possess now when she was but young? Locked her away in the cells beneath this ridiculous theater, and allowed her to be attended by such men as these—although, whatever their *seksent* shortcomings, they are likely superior to the useless children of wealth who surround me now . . ."

Adelwülf is only paying partial attention to his father's latest tirade, for he has noticed a curious thing: the panther, always known among the Stadium's athletes as one of the most dangerous and bloodthirsty of the beasts kept therein, seems to recognize the Merchant Lord, even these many years later, despite his infrequent trips to the place; more remarkable still, she shies away from him when he draws close. It is not the sight of any weapon that frightens her, for Baster-kin, while he keeps his right hand upon the pommel of his short-sword, does not draw it; no, whatever fear his lordship inspires is caused by his steady gaze and his voice, which seem to create in the panther's mind the idea that the tragedy he inflicted upon her family in Davon Wood so long ago will somehow be replayed in this very different place these many years later.

"Chain the animal!" Baster-kin orders the attendants, who begin to fix their three lengths of iron links to one great loop of similar metal that is sunk deep into the concrete of the pillar. The men then dash off as quickly as they can, each pausing only long enough to catch one of the three pouches of silver coins that Baster-kin tosses to them. "And you, whelp," Baster-kin says, turning on his son. "Select your favored weapon—for if I am any judge, you will need it, and soon . . ."

Adelwülf smiles at this comment, for he apparently believes he is to be tested by the Stadium's usual standards, against a beast of great power whose chains will prevent her from doing him any real harm. Seeing this, several of Adelwülf's "comrades" dare dash out onto the arena's sands, each bearing a different weapon—the long spear of the southernmost tribes, the usual Broken short-sword, a single-headed axe of the northern variety—that he believes their friend must use to impress his father, not only with his own abilities, but with the prowess of all the athletes in the Stadium. Adelwülf, however, only smiles in appreciation to these young men, taking little note of their weapons; rather, he waits for one young woman in particular, a singular Broken beauty, who bears upon her upturned hands a gleaming blade of the later *Lumun-jani* style: longer than the short-sword by a hand or two, with a tapered blade. As Adelwülf accepts the weapon and exchanges words of affection with the woman, Lord Baster-kin walks with purpose to the edge of the arena, a look of the same unhealthy delight upon his face. He seeks out Radelfer, whose own face, his lordship is happy to see, still displays deep apprehension.

"Seneschal!" Baster-kin calls, with the same false brand of merriment. "Did you recognize our old foe from the Wood, when those pigs brought her up from below these sands?"

"I did, my lord," Radelfer answers, with increased concern. "Although I thought the animal long since dead—"

"With *her* pedigree?" Baster-kin replies, chuckling slightly. "Did you really think the young of such a mighty animal as was her mother could be so easily dispatched by—" Baster-kin throws a hand in the direction of the patrons of the Stadium with obvious disgust. "By such as these? Or by my own eternal disgrace of a son? No, Radelfer—such scum as patronize this place may—*may*—be good enough to fight the Bane; but the greatest of all the Davon panthers? You know full well that such an idea is nonsense." Looking once more at the concrete pillar to which the panther is secured, Baster-kin seems to brighten further. "Ah! I see my son is ready to test himself; and by doing so, to represent all these young warriors." With a motion the threat of which is at odds with his tone of voice, the Merchant Lord quickly draws his own blade. "Let us see how he fares . . ."

Radelfer, now confirmed in his suspicions, dares to move to his master and lay a hand upon his forearm, in an attempt to stop the madness he believes is approaching. "My lord!" he says urgently. "I have known you since you were a boy; and I often thought that the great preoccupations of your mind had been put aside, for goals that would serve your clan better. But do you imagine that, using that lifetime of knowledge, I cannot fit the pieces of this evening's activity into a coherent whole? I know what you intend, my lord, for yourself, for Lady Arnem, for the kingdom—and I beg you, abandon this scheme! Life may not have played fair with you, on several points, but you cannot let that justify such—"

Staring down at his arm, his expression gone back to one of utter mercilessness, Baster-kin grips his sword tight. "Radelfer," he says calmly. "If you wish to keep that hand, and the arm above it, remove it from my person. Instantly." As Radelfer resignedly follows this instruction, Baster-kin warns him further: "'On several points,' you say? Life, Radelfer, has placed such obstacles in my way as might well have stopped me from going on with it, save for a few intervening hands. It has pleased me to think you one of them—and if, now, you understand what is to take place as well as you claim, then you know full well why it must; and you know, too, that there is justice in it. *All* of it." Radelfer's face turns to the ground in resignation, and Baster-kin speaks more gently; though only slightly so: "If you cannot bear what is to take place, then return to the *Kastelgerd*—but leave me your men. I shall not be far behind."

"I . . ." Radelfer is at a loss for what more to say, save, "Excuse me, my lord. But I will accept that offer. That boy is not the cause of your life's travails."

Baster-kin glances back out onto the arena. "The cause? Perhaps not. But he is merely another product of the dishonesty and disease that have cursed my existence. And I now have the chance to change all, at what I flatter myself is a profound stroke. Even the Layzin and the God-King have endorsed my undertaking. Who are you, then, to question it?" As his seneschal cannot find it in him to make further reply, Baster-kin merely says, "Go on—I shall not hold this faintness of heart against you, Radelfer, although I would have wished for more stalwart support. But go. I have business here . . ."

The two part, Radelfer ordering his men to remain behind and protect their lord while he himself attends to urgent matters at the *Kastelgerd*. The seneschal then seeks out the fastest route away from the ugly tragedy that he believes is approaching, as Baster-kin rejoins his son, whose mood has improved immensely, along with that of the crowd in the Stadium. Regaining a false, lighter air himself, the Merchant Lord endures the cheers of that crowd, which they offer when father and son stand alone on the sand with the panther once more; and then Baster-kin holds his hands aloft, indicating that he wishes to address the collected young men and women.

"It is my understanding," he calls out, "that most of you enjoy wagering on the results of these heroic contests!" At this, the crowd cheers louder, delighted that Lord Baster-kin suddenly seems to have adopted a far more friendly attitude toward their activities—and themselves. "Good!" Baster-kin continues, as Adelwülf prepares himself for the encounter to come by going through a series of impressive but absurd motions of mock combat. "For I have a wager for all of you—at least, for the young men among you—and I am afraid its terms are not open to negotiation. Should my son triumph against the beast chained here, I will leave this building, never to return." Now, laughter mixes with the cheers that go up from the crowd, as if Baster-kin has just made some sort of an amusing remark. His next words, however, remove all amusement from the crowd's reaction: "But should he lose, each of you that is found, either by reputation or by my men, to have proficiency with a blade, will agree to march out against the Bane in the company of my Guardsmen within the next few days—and any who refuse will share my son's fate."

A hushed confusion now reigns among the benches and stalls of the Stadium, while in the arena, Adelwülf looks at his father with similar bewilderment. "Father?" he says. "My 'fate'? And what fate is that to be?"

"Whatever fate you make it, Adelwülf," his lordship answers, walking to the concrete pillar and leaping upon its base. Once again, he experiences no fear, for the chained panther shies away from him; he is thus free to continue, although he speaks to his son only, now: "You have ever been a disappointment to me, Adelwülf: that much you know. But you do not know all the reasons why. I am aware that you consider my treatment of your mother unjust, and more; yet let me inform you—and, perhaps, offer some additional motivation for the contest you are about to face—that I had nothing to do with your mother's illness: that it was the result of her own degeneracy, long kept secret from me, but discovered, in the end. She is no more than a whore, boy."

Anger enters Adelwülf's face. "You cannot say that . . . Father or no, lord of the *Kastelgerd* or no, you cannot say such things about my mother!"

"Yes, your mother," Baster-kin replies. "To whom you claim such devotion, yet who sees your face but once in a Moon. So let us dispense with that supposèd reason for your hatred of me. In truth, your unnatural contempt is a product of a disease, rife within your mother's womb, that was planted there long before your birth. Yes: your mother was and remains a whore, boy, and as a result you are a lying reprobate, unworthy to call yourself my son. But fear not"—Baster-kin lowers his voice still more—"it is my intention soon to have *new* sons . . ." As Adelwülf struggles with these seemingly insane statements, his father again addresses the crowd: "I am pleased to see that you accept the terms of my wager without serious objection! You do so almost certainly because you believe this contest will be as much an unequal piece of theater as are your usual amusements—but allow me to correct that misapprehension." Turning to his son a final time, Baster-kin calls out: "Prepare yourself, Adelwülf—let us see if you and your 'comrades' are as prepared for the dangers of the Wood as you believe!"

The Merchant Lord—still, evidently, unafraid of the possible dangers to himself—raises his sword high. With a sound that pains the ears of all about him, he brings his fine steel blade down upon the crude iron chains, as well as the anchor that holds them. Swiftly, the restraints break free of the concrete pillar; and then, as the chains slip through her collar, the panther finds that she is more free on the sand than she has ever been. Still utterly confused by and fearful of Baster-kin's inscrutable actions, as well as by the blade he holds in his hand, the panther looks swiftly about for an easier object upon which to vent her rage; and there on the sand stands Adelwülf, so frozen by fear that he takes no note of the sudden cry of alarm that goes up from the crowd.

"You will finally engage this animal on equal terms, my son!" his lordship shouts; and then, still displaying reckless disregard of the panther, he leaves Adelwülf to his fate, returning to Radelfer's men to issue a final set of orders, which proves somewhat difficult, as they, too, are so stunned by what has happened, and so certain of what must now take place, that they scarcely hear him.

"Father!" Like everyone else in the Stadium, Radelfer's men hear Adelwülf's cry, as he holds his sword before him and grows increasingly aware that it will now be of no use. "The animal is loose!"

"As are the Bane, whelp," his lordship answers. "And so let us see how one of the champions of this great arena conducts himself in a true contest—surely, you are unafraid? As are your comrades? After all, in a matter of days—" Now it becomes clear that Baster-kin is speaking to the rest of the young men in the Stadium, and to his son only as a matter of form. "—days, perhaps even *hours,* you will assist the men of my Guard in following the Bane army through the Wood to Okot, that village for which we have searched so repeatedly and fruitlessly. And there, you shall destroy that accursèd tribe, finally opening the riches of the Wood to our kingdom, and its lands to clearing, that we may have new fields in which to grow the grain that our people so desperately need. And so— show me, Adelwülf, that such responsibilities have not been placed upon unworthy shoulders, and that you athletes can undertake it!"

The outcome of the encounter on the sand is so seemingly foreordained that Adelwülf cannot help but cry out, "Father! You have no right to do this!" as the panther begins to slowly circle him, her spine and neck lightly undulating. As she fixes her green eyes ever more tightly on Adelwülf, something that all present would swear is a true smile curls her mouth more and more; while the younger Baster-kin, for his part, simply and tremblingly continues to hold his sword in her direction all the while, almost as if there is actually a possibility that he will be able to use it to control the feelings that have grown close to panic within him.

"Well, my son? Let us see the bravery in attack that your days ahead will require—and let us see it *now!*"

But it is wholly unnecessary for Adelwülf to demonstrate anything at all: with the frightening swiftness and power that is common to all the great cats, the panther sees the young man begin to take his blade back in preparation for a thrust, and then she lunges forward with all the power of a bolt dispatched by a *ballista*. Unhindered by keepers, locks, or concrete, now, the panther bursts full force into Adelwülf's chest, knocking the wind from his lungs, the sword from his hand, and his body to the ground. All those on the benches—who have risen to stand, some trying to comfort each other—shout and scream in horror, seeming certain of the slow, agonizing death that their friend is about to be subjected to. But the panther is not so cruel as are her captors: once Adelwülf is upon the ground, she easily turns his stunned body so that he lies with his face in the sand, then quickly, without much of a sound, sinks her upper and lower canine teeth into the exposed rear of his spine at the neck, at once making all movement, especially breathing, impossible. The unfortunate Adelwülf, who has soiled himself with fear even before this moment, begins to twitch involuntarily with his death throes; and in an instant, perhaps out of habit, the *seksent* keepers have reappeared, to at least spare his being torn to pieces.

"Stay where you are, pigs!" Baster-kin commands them; at which the panther, evidently feeling some sense of, if not safety, at least prolonged freedom, begins to gnaw and rip at various parts of Adelwülf's lifeless body, producing a quick, almost noiseless series of tearing sounds, so great is her power. She does this, her terrified audience notices, not out of any particular enjoyment of the meat found thereupon, but rather to desecrate this human who has, evidently, so often tormented her.

"And so, whelp . . . ," says Baster-kin, quietly and evenly. Then he turns to the crowd behind him, raising his voice: "You young men of the Stadium—look! For this is the sort of fate that will greet you in Davon Wood, unless you steel your nerves now. My men, here, will remain behind to determine how many of you can truly be entrusted to march with a *khotor* of my own Guard on the Cat's Paw—and, by order of the God-King and the Grand Layzin, should you try to escape this responsibility by acting at incompetence just as you have acted at bravery for so long, you will be executed here, and lie by my own son's side."

Baster-kin then steps forward toward the panther. "*Seksent* pigs!" his lordship calls to the keepers. "Bring new chains, and secure this animal."

"*Now?* But, my lord, the beast is free, and has just tasted—"

"Do not fear it," Baster-kin replies, his eyes still tightly fixed upon those of the panther. "As long as I am here, it would not dare turn on any who walk with me."

The panther has finally moved away from Adelwülf's lifeless body, and, true to Baster-kin's pledge, she submits to being fitted with new chains, so long as Baster-kin has her fixed in his gaze. As she is led away, Baster-kin studies the young men and women in the Stadium a last time.

"You all despise me, at this instant, do you not?" he says. "For what you think I did to your 'comrade'? Well and good. *Use* that hatred, then, to steel yourselves for what is to come. For I was speaking in earnest, just now: you will need every possible source of true skill and courage that you can summon, during the task that lies ahead of you. For what awaits you in the Wood is beyond your imagining . . ."

And, never bothering to glance at the last public remains of what he thinks his old, failed family, Baster-kin strides from the Stadium, his mind fixed on the new future he believes he has finally constructed for himself.

PART·THREE

THE·RIDDLE·PUT
TO·POWER

And so, my dear Gibbon, it is neither *entirely* my revulsion at this story's more lurid aspects, nor my impatience with your historical prurience, as you may think, but rather my concern for your gifts and legacy as a Great Intellect and a Great Author, an Historian whose work will prove not only popular but seminal, that compels me to return the manuscript you have "discovered," and urge you to destroy it at once; or, if your pointed interest in such strange subject matter, and in the ultimately disturbing and distasteful conclusions toward which the tale propels itself, force you to keep it, at least conceal the thing in a place where it cannot be discovered, and above all do not publish it, certainly not in any form that can be connected to your good name.

And if you will make an honest attempt to apprehend my concerns, I will in turn confess to my own personal prejudices: First, against the irreligious Nature and Lessons of such tales, with their Obscure and Vulgar Vices and their effective glorification of a kind of barbarism, all of which have been made the more offensive by the manner in which vain but clever men such as M. Rousseau[†] have popularized them; and, Second, against the ultimately unverifiable Nature of the tale, particularly the ambiguity concerning both the identity of the narrator and the time at which he composed the thing.[‡] It seems to me that if we follow the only "logical" (a gross torturing of the word) paths in trying to determine any such identity, we are left with absurd choices: Was he a lunatic prophet, raving in the manner of the founder of this "kingdom of Broken"? Was he an equally implausible and tormented memoirist, "recalling" details of which he could not possibly have been in possession? Or was he, as seems most likely, simply a fatuous contemporary swindler, someone who had you, personally, in mind as the victim of his scheming—a plan which evidently succeeded, given your purchase of the manuscript?

For these and still more reasons, I ask you finally to think, now, of your own life, and its Parallels to this tale you have unearthed: such shared themes as Competing Religions, young men's difficult relations to strict and sometimes Cruel Fathers, and the manner in which a forcedly Solitary Life can agitate one's interest in perverse hedonism.[†] To most of your friends, and certainly to me, all these things make your attraction to this "legend of Broken" more than understandable; but these are the private circumstances of your life, which never should (and with wisdom never will) affect the Larger Publick's conception of you as a Great Man of History, one who I remain proud to call colleague, nor of your masterwork, which, like your fame, will never be equaled or diminished—unless you yourself so detract from it, through such compromising fascinations as this.

—EDMUND BURKE TO EDWARD GIBBON

Still more discoveries await the Bane and their Guest,
as they make for the Den of Stone . . .

THE JOURNEY TO OKOT of the party led by Yantek Ashkatar and Caliphestros (the latter traveling, as ever, atop Stasi), with Keera, Veloc, and Heldo-Bah close behind, had fast become a much more crowded procession than might have seemed necessary, once the column started south through the long, wide portion of Davon Wood that lay between the Cat's Paw and the northernmost settlements of the Bane's well-hidden central community. Word of the newcomers' approach had spread among Ashkatar's surprisingly numerous force; and it seemed that nearly every Bane officer or soldier wanted to get a look for her- or himself at the mutilated old man and the powerful beast atop whose back he rode, not as master, but as one half of a strange and mystical whole.

Not until the remainder of the night—or, more properly, of the earliest morning—of their first meeting has passed, does interest among the soldiers in the activities of the foraging party and Lord Caliphestros begin to wane; and this is only because the "sorcerer" continues to insist upon the peculiar practice of stopping every few hundred yards or so to dig (or rather, to have some few of Ashkatar's soldiers dig) another in the series of holes in the Earth, in order to discover the nature of the ground or the rock beneath the surface of their route, and particularly of any and all signs of water. The old man still exhorts the digging parties not to make use of the small, clear underground pools and streams they find for drinking, or even for washing; and Heldo-Bah, of course—exempted from this labor by his part in finding and enlisting the aid of Caliphestros (although Keera and Veloc choose to assist in the effort)—cannot resist the opportunity to torment the toiling soldiers at every turn.

"You know," he says at one hole in which Bane warriors dig, his mock earnestness particularly infuriating, "you people really should consider yourselves lucky. Fighting the soldiers of the Tall, or digging a hole for this ancient madman? I, personally, would take the latter, upon every possible occasion. As to what he looks for, why bother asking? He does *not* look to see your guts spilled upon Lord Baster-kin's Plain, which should be reason enough, in itself, for obedience. And so, dig—dig, and be happy in your digging!"

As the work goes on, and early evening descends upon the forest, the northernmost huts of Okot begin to take shape in the scant, glowing light of the rising Moon. Ashkatar—curious about the digging from the start, but unprepared to question Caliphestros's orders—finally forces his own uneasiness down his gullet, and approaches the white panther and the grey-bearded man who sits upon her shoulders, the latter patiently and carefully studying the work of one group of soldiers in the newest hole before him.

"My lord Caliphestros?" Ashkatar asks, as he goes down on one knee before the panther.

"Hmm?" Caliphestros replies, drawing himself out of some deep reverie and turning slowly. "Oh. Please—Yantek Ashkatar, do not feel the need to bow before me, nor before Stasi. I know, and she knew long before I did, that you are not a lesser tribe of men and women—quite the contrary. I pray you, then, speak freely, and as an equal."

"Thank you, my lord," Ashkatar replies, standing and assuming his far more characteristic position of proud command. "I only wished to know if you might be willing to share with me the purpose of all this activity concerning the water. For we are consuming much time, and my men were prepared for a fight, when you happened upon us: as I am sure you know, it is difficult to keep troops, particularly inexperienced troops, in a state of such readiness under *any* circumstances; and this obscure labor is sapping them of it. The goal behind all your searching, then, must be vital, indeed—" But Ashkatar is interrupted, at that moment, by two or three diggers in the newest pit, who make up one of several alternating crews that have by now become conversant with the agèd sorcerer who directs them. The interruption comes, at first, in the form of a whistle and then a low moan, at which Veloc shoots his filthy face and head up and over the lip of the hole. "There it is again, Lord Caliphestros— that occasional smell that reminds us of the fecal pits that the Groba fathers and the healers in the *Lenthess-steyn* have us dig and then slowly bury with lime outside Okot—" Veloc instantly silences himself when he suddenly notices his commander standing next to Caliphestros. "Ah! My apologies, Yantek Ashkatar—I did not see—"

"Veloc," Ashkatar says sternly, "do you really think that it is appropriate to speak about fecal pits to Lord Caliphestros, whether I am present or not?"

Caliphestros himself steps in to settle the problem, as, on a rock some distance away, Heldo-Bah roars with triumphant, almost childlike laughter. "Please, Yantek," the old man says, "it was I who told these diligent men and women—including my old friend Veloc—that they must be free with their language when addressing me, as it will be the quickest way of determining just what we are dealing with, in these waters that flow beneath Davon Wood."

"I see," Ashkatar replies; but, not yet settled in his mind, he cracks his whip once hard and shouts, "And you can stop your idiot's laughing, Heldo-Bah, at once! I grow sick to death of it."

"My apologies, Yantek," comes Heldo-Bah's only slightly less giddy response. "But, truly, I have not observed so comical a scene since—well, I cannot recall the last time I did!"

"Doubtless it was the last time you attempted to fornicate with a woman who was not *blind!*" Ashkatar shouts, forgetting his own decorum in the presence of Lord Caliphestros. The whip, too, snaps again, but this second time is one too many for Stasi, who begins to growl uneasily, making such moves as she would if preparing to spring upon some one of these little men. Seeing her unrest, and then watching Caliphestros almost magically calm her, Yantek Ashkatar takes a deep breath, turning to his guest. "I am—appalled, my lord, by my own behavior. Please find it in you to pardon me."

"*I* will pardon it readily," Caliphestros replies, with a gracious and respectful nod. "But do be careful with that whip of yours, in Stasi's presence, Yantek. Memories in panthers—as in most animals, every bit as much as in humans—remain most vivid when they are associated with tragedy and loss; and when she hears that particular sound, especially when it comes amid other noises and sights of armed men, she is reminded of just so tragic a loss—that of her children."

"'Children'?" Ashkatar repeats, somewhat confused.

"Yes. For they were as much her children as human offspring are to those that have them. And Stasi lost all of hers—three to death, one to capture. It was, so far as I know, the last great panther hunt conducted by those you call the Tall in Davon Wood—that of the young man who would one day become, and yet remains, Lord Baster-kin. A story, I am sure, with which the Bane are only too well acquainted."

"*Baster-kin?*" Heldo-Bah shouts, all amusement gone, as he suddenly jumps down from his rock and joins Caliphestros and Ashkatar. "*That* bloodthirsty pig? You did not tell us, old man, that it was *he* who caused your friend such heartache!" And both Keera and Veloc, along with Ashkatar and Caliphestros himself, are surprised when the gap-toothed Bane—whose strange mix of odors Stasi has by now begun to identify as his in particular—approaches the panther quietly, and gently strokes the fur of her neck, murmuring into her large, pointed ear, and causing the small black tuft atop it to twitch, as if she, too, understands the oddity of the moment: "So it was the great Lord Baster-kin who put that terrible song into your soul," the forager says, remembering the sound Stasi made when she stood on the mountainside, just after the Bane's first departure from Caliphestros's cave. "Well, then, great panther, you shall join the ranks of those who will have vengeance upon the rulers of that foul city—and if I have anything to say about it, you in particular shall make him pay for his savagery!"

The great beast's brilliant green eyes narrow, her throat begins to purr deeply, and then she turns to take two light swipes at Heldo-Bah's hand with her rough, moist tongue. The most infamous forager appears quite shocked by this undeniably affectionate and tender action; yet he steps away only a little, letting his hand linger on Stasi's neck just a moment longer.

"*Baster-kin,*" he says again, even more softly, but no less fiercely. "Imagine it. As if his list of crimes was not long enough . . ."

Caliphestros is also pleased by Heldo-Bah's sudden display of sympathy and affection for his companion; but he is only allowed a moment to consider it, before Ashkatar speaks again: "As I was saying, my lord, this constant digging of holes and inspecting of wells and springs—we need to return to the Groba as quickly as we can, and if I could but know why we slow our passage, what intelligence you mean to present to them, I might be able to assist you in forming a plan as to how best to do so."

"Did you not just hear, Yantek?" Caliphestros answers, pointing at the diggers in the hole. "Another spot at which the water that flows underground does not have the scent it should—that *any* water should, if one hopes to use it safely. And yet, at still other locations, apparently inoffensive water can be found. I am marking the courses of all these various natural pathways"—Caliphestros pats one of his bags, from which he removes a bound set of parchment sheets—"in *this,* because I seek to remember all we learn about the causes of your plague, in order to place such knowledge alongside those theories I have concerning a like illness that Keera and I have determined has now erupted in Broken."

"In *Broken?*" Ashkatar echoes, astounded. "And yet, it was our opinion that the Tall brought the plague upon *us* deliberately."

"And their opinion, no doubt—or at least, the opinion of many of them—that *you* brought it upon *them,*" Lord Caliphestros replies; and then he holds another demonstrative hand out to the hole in the Earth before him. "And to provide the answers to all such questions, *water* is the key. Or water which carries fever. Now, then—would I be correct in assuming that, as a general practice, the north and south sides of the town do not draw their water from the same sources?"

Ashkatar looks perplexed. "Aye, my lord. The southern parts of Okot take water from wells and streams fed by the mountain to the south— while the north—" And suddenly, in many faces at once, there is a look of comprehension.

"Yes," Caliphestros says with a smile. "I thought it might be so."

He looks to Keera, finding in her face, as he had hoped he might, the first real look of hope that she has yet manifested: not hope for her people, or any such expansively noble feeling, of which the old man knows the tracker to be capable, but personal hope, for the fates of her own children.

"*I should have seen it,*" Keera says, gazing at the ground with purpose; and even Caliphestros is forced to admire her new determination. She then lifts her gaze to cast it upon Ashkatar again, and continues, "It is, indeed, the water, Yantek. The northern parts of Okot are fed, at least in part, by those waters that drain from the Cat's Paw. But we never would have conceived, as Lord Caliphestros's mind has been expansive enough to do, that an entire river might become—*contaminated . . .*"

Ashkatar, in the meantime, his mind fixed on the statements that Keera has made, is suddenly startled, as are all those around him, by a cry of what seems discovery from one of his soldiers digging inside the nearby hole: "My lord!" the dirty-faced warrior then shouts coherently. "Yantek! See what we have come upon!" And in an instant, the warrior is up and out of the hole, several small objects in one hand.

"Be careful, there!" Caliphestros calls, producing a piece of rag and handing it along a chain of hands to the warrior, so intent on this task that he only now notes that the dirt-smudged courier is no youth, but an athletic, powerful young female warrior. "Wash those hands with lye, girl, when you have finished, and even burn your tunic, if you have in your hand what I fear!" The warrior takes Caliphestros's bit of rag, wraps the objects in it, and walks determinedly to the old man, who, before he has even viewed what she carries, pronounces, "Although I may be able to tell you what most, if not all, of them are, Yantek." He then turns again to his traveling companion. "As can Keera, I perceive."

Keera is already nodding her head. "Aye, lord. *Bones*," she murmurs. "Or rather, at this point, *bits* of bone. And, it may even surprise you, Lord Caliphestros, if I say that I doubt they are only the bones of the animals we saw dead and dying at the pool upriver—there may be some small fragments of human bone, as well. But they are all diseased, this much we know, and truly, they must be handled more cautiously even than the water in which they were transported."

"But—" The young female discoverer twists her features in confusion. "Are *they* the cause of the plague, then? Or are they part of some curse that has been worked by the priests and priestesses of the Tall, during their visits to the Wood to commit their many strange and evil acts—"

Caliphestros makes a small, slightly chastising sound. "We must all make one agreement, before we reach Okot," he says, less with the berating of a pedant than with sympathy and warning. "Keera, what was it that I told you, when we discussed this very subject of curses and priests?"

Keera pauses to recall the words precisely: "That the only true 'magic' is madness," she repeats by rote, but with intent and understanding. "Just as the only real 'sorcery' is science. My lord." She moves through the crowd to gain a look at the objects that the warrior holds.

And they are just what both the tracker and Caliphestros had feared and predicted: *The bones, Keera knows in her heart, of the smallest parts of children.*

Taking in this look of comprehension in his young friend's features, Caliphestros says: "So—*you* saw them, too, eh?"

Keera looks up at Caliphestros. "Yes, lord. As we left the pool. They were trapped in the outlet stream. But I admit that I did not think that *you* had seen them."

"I was waiting for just this sort of moment to discuss the matter," Caliphestros replies. "To see whether or not you would make true sense of the sight, as indeed you have."

Veloc steps forward to put a proud and comforting arm about his sister. "If I am not mistaken—" Veloc says, turning his handsome features to face Caliphestros, "we not only may, but *must* obey Yantek Ashkatar's imperative immediately, and return swiftly to Okot—but even before that, we must send runners ahead, must we not, Lord Caliphestros? To warn that no one in Okot take water from the questionable sources on the northern slope of the town?"

"You share your sister's blood, Veloc, that much is evident," Caliphestros replies, not quite so enthusiastically as the historian would have wished, as the old scholar replaces his various possessions in the small bags about his neck. He then looks to Ashkatar. "For now, however, Yantek—the tirelessness and diligence of your troops have made possible the answers to all immediate questions: anything that is left to explain should be discussed, I submit, in the place your tribe calls the 'Den of Stone.' And so, if you will alert your troops, as Veloc says, to send runners—"

Without thinking, the anxious Ashkatar raises his whip, which Caliphestros catches just before the black-bearded commander can bring it down again, silently giving the yantek an admonishing reminder, and looking to the now fully alert panther beneath him. "Avoiding all acts of foolishness," the old man says, "now that we bear such precious evidence, which is the most accurate and valuable form of knowledge—and persuasion . . ."

"Send runners to the Groba!" Ashkatar orders, busily turning his attention to immediate matters, in part to hide his own embarrassment. "Let them know that more explanations will follow with us—but that they must heed our warning concerning the water in the northern wells!"

"Well said," Caliphestros judges. Casting his eyes about the increasing darkness, and seeing a nearby hillock that is crowned with thick, obscuring undergrowth, he gives Ashkatar a nod. "Now, Yantek, I shall withdraw and attend to the needs of an old man's body, and rejoin you in but a few minutes."

"Very good, Lord Caliphestros—I shall have our escort ready to march by the time you return!" Moving back into his much more comfortable role of admonishing and administering commander, Ashkatar begins to sound out more orders, to both the units that will remain behind on guard and patrol, and to those who will go ahead to Okot. Caliphestros, meanwhile, urges Stasi toward the hillock—

At which Keera notices something odd: the old man has his eyes fixed, not on his destination, nor on the objects he carries, nor even on the powerful companion beneath him. He hurries Stasi along: a natural enough thing, if his old man's need to relieve himself is as strong as he has suggested. Yet, Keera decides, there remains something not quite correct about his behavior . . .

Thus, with darkness now falling in its characteristically rapid fashion, in the springtime hours between bright day and Moonrise within Davon Wood, and with Ashkatar's troops assembling their torches south of the hole at which the foragers, Caliphestros, and the Bane yantek have only just been standing—and most of all, knowing full well that her small scheme may lead to a moment of profound embarrassment between herself and the aging scholar she has come to so admire and trust—Keera puts caution aside and, backing slowly away from the others as they ready themselves for the last stage of the journey south, quickly and silently slips up the trunk and into the branches of one especially thick elm tree. The higher reaches of this gnarled giant offer connections to still other thickly leaved forest sentinels—maples, oaks, and firs—all of which ultimately lead up and over the hillock behind which Caliphestros quickly disappears.

$$3:\{ii:\}$$

One secret unraveled, another made more complex . . .

I T MAY SEEM IMPLAUSIBLE or indeed impossible, that a man or woman, however skilled, should be able to move through treetops every bit as stealthfully as those animals practiced in that form of undetected movement: birds, squirrels, and tree kittens.[†] And yet, with the wind on Keera's side—blowing, as it so often does, in from the west and pushing both her limited scent and any excessive sounds of movement back toward Ashkatar's noisy group of warriors—she is indeed able to achieve this feat, despite the added danger of Caliphestros's continuing to search the branches above him, evidently looking for something or someone with whom he intends to meet.

The discovery of just who that someone is, when it comes, nearly destroys all Keera's clever, silent tracking in the treetops. She hears the quiet chatter and quickly beating wings of a starling flying at night, and, correctly guessing who is on the way, turns about and smiles at the same speckled, rainbow-tinted bird that the three foragers encountered what seems a long time ago, when they first followed Stasi and Caliphestros back to the pair's cave. The bird flits about the spot Keera currently occupies, in the middle of an oak limb, then alights on the limb next to her, staring intently upon the tracker's human features. Keera is delighted to once again hear the starling's approximation of Caliphestros's name, which the bird chatters to her proudly; however, she is also deeply nervous that Caliphestros himself will spot the bird and thereafter lock eyes on her, and so Keera urges it along:

"Quietly, now!" she whispers, as softly as she can. Cupping her hands, she tries to urge the starling down the limb, but, as if in a moment of indignation, the feathered fellow simply flaps noisily into the air a few feet, and then lands directly atop Keera's head. Now utterly at a loss as to what to do—for the bird is no longer making any sound, but rather settling in, as if he means to stay for a bit—she sits as still as her unnerved condition will allow: for Caliphestros has by now heard the starling, and is more quickly turning from one direction to another, imitating the sounds of the bird in an effort to persuade him to come down. When the speckled messenger finally does stir, however, neither of the humans present causes his action; rather, it is the sudden, utterly silent, yet swift and somewhat threatening passing, above, of an enormous pair of dark, gliding wings, which come close enough to the starling to make it shriek once in alarm and then flutter down to Caliphestros in a nervous dart, alighting upon his shoulder.

"Ah!" the old man says, turning to face the starling's wide eyes. "What was all that business? And where is your associate, if I may ask?"

But the starling's "associate" is otherwise engaged, for the moment, having swept down to take up the smaller bird's position on Keera's tree limb; the difference being that this creature—the same great eagle owl that has been only very occasionally and briefly visible, from time to time, in Caliphestros's wake, as well as visiting with Visimar—stands every bit as tall as Keera, when she sits upon the limb they share. The tufts of feathers† that appear at once to be her ears as well as her stern eyebrows, and which ordinarily sit in a lower and more critical position than do those of the smaller males of the species, rise high above her enormous and severe golden eyes, for the moment, in the presence of this strange human who has ventured into the bird's realm.

Upon hearing Caliphestros chatting with the starling below, however, the owl evidently feels that she has made whatever point she intended to impress upon Keera, and suddenly half-opens her wings, falling and then gliding in wide circles, with startling simplicity and silence, down toward the section of an ancient log upon which the great master of Nature and Science lectures his frenetic young student of language and diplomacy.

Only when the owl has left Keera's tree limb does the tracker see that the great hornèd ruler of the air clutches tightly within one talon the same group of plants and flowers that Keera herself discussed with Caliphestros upon their return from his cave: again, not so long ago as events make it feel. *Wild mountain hops, meadow bells, and woad,* Keera considers silently; *and, although I cannot now see, I would guess that these, too, were harvested by a sharp blade—does the fever then spread inside the frontiers of Broken?*

As if in answer to this inward question, Keera hears Caliphestros begin to talk to both of the birds—whose arrival, she suddenly notices, has not raised the least reaction from Stasi.

". . . and so," Caliphestros says to the pair of birds, who are now perched upon two half-limbs that point skyward from a fallen maple trunk which lies close in front of their master's seat. "It will be for you two to find them—" His expressions become much simpler and more deliberate: "Soldiers—with horses," he says, repeating the phrase a few times more, until the starling suddenly cries:

"Sol-jers! Hors-es!" And then the little creature turns to the owl to add, *"Ner-tus!"*

If the two birds were children, it would be a clear baiting of the larger but less intellectually skilled sibling by the smaller and quicker of the two; and the starling darts from Caliphestros's shoulder to the top of his skullcap, and back again, seeming almost to laugh. The owl's glare, meanwhile, becomes the more severe, as if to warn, *Do not gloat, little man, about your chatter, or I shall swallow you up!* Caliphestros, sensing all this, inserts himself in the middle of it, placing a gentle hand around the starling, holding him before his face, and saying, "That is enough of that, Little Mischief"—for such, apparently, is his affectionate name for the starling—"and I have told you as much before. Taunting will get you eaten, and then where should Visimar and I be, eh?"

"Viz-ee-mah!" Little Mischief just manages to squeak out in defiance of Caliphestros's grip, and the old man cannot help but laugh at his diminutive persistence.

And in the tree above, however, Keera's face has gone puzzled: for the name Visimar is as well known in Okot as it is in the kingdom of Broken. Is the mysterious scholar's acolyte, then, a part of his plan that he has not yet chosen to share with his Bane allies? And if so, why has he chosen to keep it a secret? For some sinister reason?

"Remember, now," Caliphestros resumes, below: "It is required that you work together, you two, and so this bickering must stop! Visimar knows of the fever in the countryside and in the city, but he must now know of it in the Wood, so that he can tell Sentek Arnem." All this elaborate talk again proving largely useless, Caliphestros stares at Little Mischief and says, firmly, "Fever—Wood."

"Fee-vah Wood! Wood fee-vah!" the starling replies, now struggling to get a wing free of his human companion, who is finally satisfied that he will speak the correct words at the correct time, and releases Little Mischief to sit upon a nearby branch.

"Which leaves but one thing more," Caliphestros says, reaching into his bag—

And from it he withdraws another golden arrow, indistinguishable from that which he and Keera took from the dead member of Lord Baster-kin's Guard. The enormous owl immediately flies toward Caliphestros's shoulder, shocking the human with her speed, then hovers a few inches above him in order to allow those talons that do not carry the flowers—and which are fully as large as human fingers—to snatch the arrow away from him: once again, no instructions would seem needed, but Caliphestros looks to the starling again, if only to be certain.

"The arrow, Little Mischief," he says. "Also to Visimar."

"*Viz-ee-mah! Awhoh!*" the starling repeats, again comically enough to cause Caliphestros to cradle his head in his hands and try to stifle a bout of chuckling, lest the birds think him anything but resolved and serious in his instructions to them.

As both Keera and Caliphestros will shortly be missed by the rest of their traveling party, she is happy to see Caliphestros wave his arms and send the birds off. They circle the little clearing behind the hillock where they have received their latest instructions, and then finally straighten their path of flight so that they head in the direction of the Fallen Bridge over Hafften Falls and, beyond it, the most likely place for the forces of Broken to make camp before any sort of engagement with Ashkatar's army. Caliphestros then shifts his robe in order to relieve himself (his nominal purpose for coming to this removèd place) without shifting from the log, and finally urges Stasi to stand close by and lower her neck, so that he can slide from the log onto her shoulders easily. Keera takes the first indication of the old man's personal actions as her signal to move back along the treetops that she traveled to reach her perch. In a matter of only a few seconds more, she hears her brother and Heldo-Bah calling her name, a distinct sense of worry in Veloc's voice.

Even for the famous Keera, the marvelous manner in which she manages to move back through the treetops is a wonder; and it is not long before she is once again among the men and women who have collected for the last leg of their march, and coolly lying to her brother and Heldo-Bah by saying that, as Caliphestros had taken the opportunity to see to his private business, she thought that she would, as well.

"You might have told someone, Keera," Veloc chides.

"Great Moon, Veloc," Heldo-Bah bellows, "you would be a thousand times more likely to be taken off by some forest beast than Keera ever would—I really don't know why you persist in playing this idiotic game of being the responsible brother. It's almost as feebleminded as your insistence on your being an expert historian."

"Do not go so far as *considering* a return to that subject, you two," comes a new voice; and the three foragers all turn to see Caliphestros and Stasi appearing from the darkness. "The time for idiotic blather has passed," he continues; but his orders cannot stop Veloc from trembling just a bit as he notes to himself what a truly ghostly apparition the white panther is, in this sort of rapidly fading light.

"Great Moon," Veloc whispers to Heldo-Bah, "it's truly no wonder the Tall fear her as they do—the animal appears as out of the night air!"

"Ah, *ficksel*," Heldo-Bah answers calmly. "And you dare call *me* the superstitious one?"

At which point Yantek Ashkatar steps forward and declares, "All right, then—to those of you continuing on: I intend to be within the Den of Stone in two hours—and Heldo-Bah, if we fail to make it in that time, I shall know whose back my whip will cut, in return!"

"Brave words, when you have an army behind you, Ashkatar," Heldo-Bah answers, nonetheless falling alongside the middling-long column of soldiers to keep pace with them. "But neither the Bane nor the Tall have yet made the whip that will cut my skin, I promise you that . . ."

Once again walking beside Stasi and Caliphestros as they move to catch up to Ashkatar, Keera shakes her head. "I promise you, my lord— there really *are* Bane tribe members who are not so devoted to bickering as are those two. Or three, I suppose, if you number Yantek Ashkatar among them, these three—"

"Oh, I am certain of it," Caliphestros interrupts, an enigmatic smile entering his features. "Indeed, I have seen those among your people who can be almost silent—even as they dance along the treetops . . ."

$$3:\{iii:\}$$

Arrival on Lord Baster-kin's Plain presents
Sentek Arnem's Talons with an eerie silence . . .

ON THE MORNING that Sixt Arnem marches his full *khotor* of the Talons onto the section of Lord Baster-kin's Plain north of the Fallen Bridge, he finds no evidence that the men from the Esleben garrison, who were to have met him there, have survived one or the other of the pestilences that Visimar has been able to determine are at work in Broken, during their march to the Cat's Paw. Similarly, but far more surprisingly, there is no sign of the detachment of Lord Baster-kin's Guard that has always been assigned to the northernmost boundary of the great family's most arable and strategic piece of land; yet neither is there any visible token that these men met with some calamity. Instead, as the Talons make their way through the rough, high grass at the edge of the Plain and then south into the rich pastureland that has been chewed to a short and almost uniform length by the Baster-kin family's renowned shag cattle, they encounter what is, in many ways, the most unnerving circumstance for soldiers who are on the march, full of questions, and far from home:

Nothing.

True, the cattle graze in their ordinary manner (or rather, most of them do, for there are clearly more than a few missing), and take little notice of the newcomers, save to move off to a safe distance; yet none shows any obvious sign of disease. Nevertheless, Arnem's men are all aware that units of the Guard *should* be patrolling this part of the Plain: and so where are they? Arnem knows that action is the only cure for his own as well as his men's bewilderment: thus, after ordering the establishment of a central camp, the sentek orders his scouts to employ their keen talents for detection as far as a dozen miles up and down the northern bank of the Cat's Paw, reminding them, along with the rest of his men, that no water from the river is to be consumed, either by themselves or by their mounts, save from the several collecting ponds for rainwater that the Baster-kin family has constructed throughout the Plain over the last several years. Arnem's central camp is hard by one such pool; and as his tent is erected, the sentek orders the establishment of an observation post near the southernmost of these small sources of safe water, a post that, situated closest to the Fallen Bridge, offers a commanding view of both the river and the Wood beyond. Tents are pitched, there, campfires lit, watches scheduled, and the men are ordered to be ready at a moment's notice.

As the sounds of the other *fausten* preparing their own tents around Arnem's begin to resonate through the midday air north of the bridge, the sentek, Niksar, and Visimar move their horses ever closer to the rough border of the Plain that lines its southern edge, Arnem's eyes alert for any sign of Akillus or his men returning with news, and particularly for any sign of the missing members of Baster-kin's Guard. The mood throughout the Plain grows more grim if determined with the passage of each hour, as does the bitterness over the advantage that the soldiers who were supposed to have been already positioned in the area might have offered.

"*Damn them,*" Arnem seethes softly, and neither Visimar nor Niksar have any trouble understanding who is the object of his ire. "I did not expect to find those brass-banded dandies alert and at their posts, but somewhere in the vicinity of those positions might have been of some use."

"Would you expect jackals to become wolves, then, Sentek," Visimar asks in reply, "simply because an air of danger presents itself?"

Niksar nods slowly. "He speaks truly, Sentek," the linnet murmurs. "Given that this would be the first prize that the Bane would likely attempt to seize during any attack on the kingdom, we might have expected that the Guard would have withdrawn. The sole questions being, in which direction, why, and under whose authority . . ."

"'Authority,' Niksar?" Arnem asks. "You think that they had *orders* to remove themselves from the field? Such orders, I trust you realize, could only have come from one source."

Visimar desires with all his heart not to be the one to respond to this statement, and so is delighted when he hears the handsome young linnet reply, "Sentek—I do not intend this as anything other than what it is: an observation of what I see as undeniable facts, as well as an attempt to honor my brother, and to question the peculiar way in which Donner's plight was consistently ignored by our superiors, our *civilian* superiors, during his time at Esleben; surely this situation suggests that Lord Basterkin, whatever your former respect for him, is not the man you have so often trusted him to be."

"Perhaps, Niksar—*perhaps*," Arnem replies; then, after consideration, he adds, "Although I can but hope that you understand how wary we must be of even considering such conclusions. I do realize that we have not yet found a common thread that runs through all that we have seen, experienced, and *felt*. But the suggestion that such a thread is treachery on the part of the Merchant Lord—I am not at all certain of as much. The officers and men of the Guard share more than enough perfidy and cowardice to explain what has happened—and we must, I fear, leave matters at that. At least for the moment."

At this rebuff from his commander, Niksar—his brother's death still fresh in his thoughts—rides further south alone for a moment, while Arnem and Visimar grow silent once again, Visimar studying the commander of the army of Broken for some few moments before quietly asking, "When did you last sleep, Sentek? Properly, that is?"

"When did *any* of us?" Arnem replies, not sharply, but still with some irritation. "The men need to establish a schedule of watches and rest, the horses need some similarly sustained hours of feeding, or at least of grazing on decent grass such as will fill out their bellies, and sleep, to say nothing of grooming . . . And Kafra's stones, the *skutaars* look as though they will all be felled by exhaustion at any moment. Can I rest before I know that all of these—men, animals, youths—are safe enough from either fatigue or pestilence to undertake their task? Tell me how, sorcerer's acolyte, and I shall put my head to my bedroll as fast as any man who marches with us. For of one thing I am certain—" The cool, steady eyes scan the southern riverbank, and Davon Wood beyond it. "The Bane have been watching all that we have been through. From afar, perhaps, but . . . They are out there, and know at least a little—and likely far more—of our troubled state."

It is not until hours later, when daylight is growing golden with late afternoon, that Arnem is informed that the first of the scouts—not surprisingly, the ever-reliable Akillus—has been sighted rushing at a great speed back to the Talons' camp.

Indeed, by the time Akillus's mount thunders across the Plain and reaches Arnem, the lately returned Niksar, and Visimar, Akillus is still riding so hard that he overshoots the three, and must circle back, bringing light laughter from the sentek, his aide, and his advisor—until they see the grave expression upon the rider's face.

"Akillus," Arnem says in greeting, when the scout finally reins up alongside the other three men and their horses. "Something, I gather, is too important for you either to wait for this evening's council, or to wash off the mud of your long ride before you make your report."

Looking down at the dried brown splashes that cover his flesh, tunic, and armor, Akillus does not laugh or so much as smile in the manner that he so often displays, even in the most dangerous or embarrassing situations—which is Arnem's first hint that the scout has gathered intelligence from his mission which is sinister, indeed. "You have seen something, then," Arnem says. "Along the riverfront?"

"I—I was not alone in seeing it, Sentek," Akillus answers unsteadily. "Every scout, regardless of whether he was in a party that went upriver or down, glimpsed the like."

"Well, Akillus?" Niksar says, his face again attaining some of the gravity it exhibited at Esleben. "What is it that you have seen?"

"A scene to rival Daurawah?" Visimar asks, anxiously and knowingly.

"Aye," Akillus replies, "just so—but far greater in scale, although I would not have thought such possible." Finally looking up at his commander, Akillus bravely attempts composure, and states, "You would think that some sort of battle had taken place upon the river, Sentek, save that we have never known the Bane to use ships, nor to attack the river traders. And certainly, the number of unarmed women and children among their dead does not speak of a conflict—not a formal one, at any rate. But they are all there together, along with the missing patrols of Baster-kin's Guard; the dead of every age and both sides, and those not quite dead, as well—although they wished us to grant them death, so painful were their conditions."

" 'Conditions'?" Visimar repeats. "You mean, they displayed signs of *both* of the sicknesses that we have witnessed: on the one hand, the rose fever—"

"And the fire wounds, as well," Akillus continues, "which have spread among the animals seen by the scouts further upstream. Sentek, the Cat's Paw has become a river of death, from one end to the other!"

"Steady, Linnet," Arnem says, quietly. "And you could find no one free of disease?"

"But one," Akillus replies. "A young member of the Guard, wandering alone. Strangest of all, he was as terrified of the possibility that we might be his own comrades as of the thought that we might be the Bane. He says he was left behind by the main force, to keep watch over those of Lord Baster-kin's cattle that his detachment usually guards, in the northern part of the Plain—but when the hour grew late, and then an entire night passed, he went to see what progress his comrades had made, and found—just what we have found. He is half-mad with fear."

"You have him in camp?" Visimar says, alarm bleeding through his words.

"Just outside," Akillus replies. "He appeared to be untouched by disease, but after what we have seen . . ."

"Wise, Akillus." Arnem breathes in relief, glancing at Niksar. "As ever."

"But—" Visimar is still puzzling with an earlier statement. " '*What progress his comrades had made*'? Which comrades? And in what endeavor?"

"An ambitious one," Akillus replies. "Involving far more than the usual patrols on the Plain. A full *khotor* of Guardsmen, it seems, were dispatched from the city while we were on our way here from the east, tasked with entering the Wood before we would be able to, and destroying any and all Bane that they discovered."

Arnem reins the nervous Ox to a stunned halt. *"What?"*

"Aye, Sentek," Akillus replies. "Most strange, as I say—for this was to be *our* mission, we all knew that. But apparently, Lord Baster-kin—"

"Baster-kin sent them?" Arnem says, again looking to Niksar, but now with an aspect of apology. "But why? Why send us to finally destroy the Bane and then send his own men to do the job separately?"

"Because," Visimar murmurs discreetly, "it was not anticipated that the Talons—and especially you, Sentek—would *survive* their trip east. Baster-kin is attempting to use the terrible events in those provinces as a path by which he may consolidate his control over *all* instruments of force in the kingdom: in order for the regular army to become his instrument, the Talons and their commander would have to be removed, and what tidier way to make this removal seem accidental—or better still, the work of the Bane—than to deliberately send them into that portion of the kingdom that is rife with disease?"

Akillus has evidently seen enough along the river to find Visimar's explanation plausible: "Indeed, Sentek. To judge by what this Guardsman has said—and you may ask him about it, yourself—it was the tenor of your own reports that made the Merchant Lord believe that he must send men more . . . *personally* loyal to both himself and the God-King to undertake the conquest of the Bane, in the event that we either never reached the Wood, or chose not to attack once we did."

Niksar says nothing, but casts his commander a look that says he, too, has reached the same conclusion.

"And there is more, Sentek," Akillus says, his voice now growing even more uneasy. "It would seem—according to this young pallin—well, it would seem that rebellion has broken out in the Fifth District of the city."

Again, a look which indicates that Visimar already knows the answer to his own question enters his face as he asks, "Aye? And who leads this 'rebellion,' Linnet?"

Appearing more reluctant than ever, Akillus says, "Perhaps it will be better if you question this man yourself, Sentek . . ."

"I am questioning *you,* Akillus," Arnem replies, quietly but darkly. "Who leads this 'rebellion'?"

"He says—" And finally Akillus simply utters the words. "He says that it is Lady Arnem, Sentek. Supported by veterans from throughout the district, in addition to—well, in addition to your eldest son."

This news, again, does not come as such to Visimar; but Niksar draws back in no little shock. "Sentek Arnem's wife and son? *Hak*—this is nothing but malicious gossip, being spread by members of the Guard."

"Such were my thoughts, Niksar," Akillus replies. "But the boy does not seem to have been in the Guard long enough to have quite become—*infected* by their behavior."

"But—Sentek! The Lady Isadora and Dagobert?" Niksar questions, bewilderment in his every word. "What can have led them to such actions?"

Arnem himself is far too confused to make any reply; and so it is for Visimar to say, "If I am not mistaken, they have been left no choice, faced with just the sort of death and disease that we have seen, and having now heard still more of . . ."

"Aye, Sentek," Akillus answers. "The cripple is right about that much. They say that plague is loose in the district, and that, when Lady Arnem's appeals for help to Lord Baster-kin and the Grand Layzin went unanswered, rebellion was the result."

"Such—would not be a unique cause of such events," Niksar says, still puzzling with the report, but at the same time provoking a scowl from Arnem, who tries to maintain the evenness of his voice, even as he answers with no little anger:

"It would be unique if it involves *my family,* Niksar . . ." The young aide can only swallow hard; and then, working hard to regain his full composure, Arnem continues, "But let us leave this subject, for now, until we have this Guardsman before us. What of the rest of this business? Dispatching a *khotor* of Baster-kin's own men into the Wood—he gave you no further details of what lay behind this action?"

"He gave us such details as he *believes* he knows," Akillus replies. "Which were precious few. The most important being that the men from the city and the patrols on the Plain together rushed headlong across the Fallen Bridge, apparently, as soon as the *khotor* arrived. Which means, it would seem, at night."

All the faces of Akillus's audience darken: for such would be almost inconceivably foolish arrogance. *"Nay,"* Arnem whispers. "Even the Guard cannot have been so stupid."

"But were, it seems," Akillus replies. "You can imagine the result. The force was cut to pieces by the Bane, and their wounded, along with their dead, thrown to the mercies of Hafften Falls and the *Ayerzess-werten;* although most of those wounded had their suffering ended by the *dauthu-bleith* before their bodies were thus dispensed with."

"Sentek," Niksar asks, both genuinely bewildered and attempting to repair some of the ire brought out of his commander by his last remark. "What can it all mean?"

"I am not in the least certain, Reyne," Arnem replies, "and I suspect that we shall *all* remain uncertain, until we have a chance to question this Guardsman. And so—lead us to him, Akillus, and then get to my tent, and tell the officers that this evening's council will be delayed some little time. Or perhaps longer . . ." Arnem looks ahead in the darkening evening. "For I fear this story may take some time to tell . . ." The sentek is about to spur the Ox on up the incline of the Plain, when Akillus says:

"There is yet another fact that I suspect you will find accounts for this man's terror, Sentek." Arnem pauses, and Akillus rides up beside him.

"Although it is a difficult tale to credit. He claims . . ." And once more, Akillus finds it difficult to choose his words carefully.

"Well?" Arnem demands. "Out with it, Akillus."

"Yes, sir," the scout replies, finally dispensing with any attempt at tact: "Apparently, last evening, while looking for any trace of his comrades, the Guardsman came across a most extraordinary sight lit by the Moon: the First Wife of Kafra, sister to the God-King himself, moving north toward Broken through the Plain—without a stitch of clothing upon her, and leading a large male Broken bear by a golden cord. The animal be-haved as if it were no more than an obedient dog. The lad said that he knew her features because the Guard has sometimes been called upon to accompany her out of the city and down the mountain."

Arnem looks to each of his companions in turn, finding comprehen-sion only in Visimar's face. "It is indeed possible, Sixt Arnem," the cripple says. "For my master maintained that he knew only one person who could so enthrall such beasts—and my master, you must recall, was an expert in understanding those same creatures. But the sister of the God-King Saylal—Alandra, she was called—had a more mysterious, even un-settling, ability to reach them." Visimar clearly knows more of this tale, but he withholds it, waiting for a time when he will be able to speak to Arnem alone.

As for the sentek, he has turned his face up to the sky. *"Kafra's stones,"* he murmurs. "What is happening, in this place . . . ?" Suddenly, Arnem spurs his great mount forward: "Well—we shall not find out here," he says, urging the others on, obviously desperate to learn what lies behind the incredible stories that he has heard—and how much danger his own family is truly facing . . .

$$3:\{iv:\}$$

Caliphestros, Ashkatar, and the Bane foragers
at last reach Okot . . .

I T IS WITHOUT DOUBT true that the sight of the legless sorcerer
Caliphestros riding into the Bane town of Okot on the shoulders of
the famed white panther who had long roamed the mountains
southwest of Okot, inspiring both respect and fear in the tribe of outcasts, would ordinarily have caused astonishment bordering on panic in
the central square. But their arrival in Okot on this occasion, however,
had been preceded a full half-day by Ashkatar's messengers, who had already warned the tribe that the plague that had struck their people was
not the result of magic or a curse inflicted by the Tall, but was a poison
contained in the water of the wells on the northern side of the community. This warning had almost immediately arrested the progress of the
disease, and even lessened its terrible impact. No secret had been made of
the fact that it was Caliphestros who determined the details of this problem and its solution—although, as the old man insisted on saying from
the moment he reached even the most outlying parts of Okot, there were
no divinations or visions involved in his calculations, but rather purely
scientific investigations. Such was an explanation that was difficult for
many Bane to understand, although most in the town remained grateful,
whatever the degree of their comprehension; it was not until the returning heroes and their guests made their way through the crowds gathered
at the town's center and entered the Den of Stone to meet with the Groba,
as well as with the Priestess of the Moon and her attending Lunar Sisters
and Outragers, that they were met with anything like stern or skeptical
questioning.

Ashkatar led the way through the long, dark stone passageway, with
its carved reliefs of important moments in Bane history, which Caliphestros paused to admire: not for their accuracy, in every case, but for the
skill of their execution. Veloc, meanwhile, used the time to quietly urge
Heldo-Bah not to rouse the ire of the Priestess of the Moon, a sentiment
echoed by Keera, who rejoined her friends only when she had made cer-

tain to quickly dash to her parents' home after first arriving in Okot. There she had discovered to her wild joy that all of her children were well or recovering, little Effi having been reunited with her brothers, Herwin and Baza, after the boys were released from the *Lenthess-steyn* following a quick recovery—a recovery made possible by the information brought by Ashkatar's runners.

"Beautiful carvings, are they not, Lord Caliphestros?" Ashkatar asked the old man, indicating the walls of the passageway.

"Indeed," Caliphestros answered, attempting scholarly detachment as Keera passionately embraced Stasi out of both joy and gratitude, not daring to do the same to the panther's companion. "Most residents of Broken," the old man continued, "would think them quite beyond the abilities of your tribe's artisans."

"Yes," Veloc agreed, his voice growing more hushed as the group approached the entrance to the Den of Stone. "Of course, the tales most of the reliefs tell are as much nonsense as the great tapestries in Broken. But they are no less attractive to look at."

Caliphestros laughed, briefly and quietly. "Is there *any* part of the city on the mountain that you have not dared enter, Veloc? You haven't, for example, penetrated the *Inner* City, I trust?"

"Oh, no, of course not, no," Veloc quickly replied.

"Although, based on the form of that First Wife of Kafra," Heldo-Bah added, "the woman you called Alandra, I rather regret that we did not . . ."

Keera quickly noticed, even through her joy, that Caliphestros not only failed to reply, but displayed the same pained expression that he did when the woman's name was first mentioned at the outset of their woodland journey: pained, and something else as well. "Heldo-Bah, you imbecile!" she hissed. "Have you no sense of—"

Further discussion was cut short, however, when the three foragers, along with the rest of their party, heard the sharp voice of the Groba Father:

"Yantek Ashkatar! The Groba invites you and your esteemed guests to enter!" And then the Father added, in far less enthusiastic words that Veloc knew referred to himself and to Heldo-Bah: "Along, I suppose, with the rest of your party . . ."

Veloc had expected that the faces of the Groba, the Priestess of the

Moon, the Lunar Sisters, and the Outragers would likely display suspicion when Caliphestros and Stasi, accompanied by Ashkatar, the foragers, and their guiding Elder, entered the Den of Stone: but the handsome forager had *not* expected that the ten faces before him, which had always been supremely confident when dealing with the likes of himself, Keera, and Heldo-Bah, would be so full of uneasiness bordering on fear when the party made their entrance, a reaction that delighted both himself and Heldo-Bah.

Veloc made the perfunctory introductions, and the Groba Fathers all bowed their heads in great respect to Caliphestros, while the Priestess of the Moon, her Lunar Sisters, and the two Outragers standing in the shadows beside them were far less deferential in their silent greetings. Seeing this, Heldo-Bah began glancing about the Den with a look of dissatisfaction that seemed directly aimed at the Priestess, although his words addressed the head of the Groba:

"*Must* it always be so dark in here, Father?" the sharp-toothed forager asked with no little impertinence. "You see, it makes Stasi—our friend, the panther, here—a little nervous. Am I not right, Lord Caliphestros?"

Caliphestros recognized what the gap-toothed Bane was attempting to ensure: that a correct order of relationships be established, from the start.

"Indeed, Heldo-Bah," the famed scholar lied (for in truth, Stasi was a creature of the darkness); and then, to the man in the tall chair at the center of the Elders' table, he continued, "Perhaps, Esteemed Father, one or two of these gentlemen"—and without looking at them, he indicated the Outragers—"might be persuaded to fetch another torch or two. Their presence is not required for our conference, and so they will not be missed."

"I beg your pardon?" the Priestess of the Moon said incredulously. "Those men happen to be my personal servants, members of the Order of the Woodland—"

"Of the Woodland Knights, Eminence, yes," Caliphestros interrupted, pleasantly enough. "Although they have other names, in other places—names perhaps more befitting their activities. Then, too, I have never actually *seen* one of them in the 'Woodland.'"

The Priestess eyed Caliphestros with a resentful stare. "The correct terms to use when addressing me, *sorcerer,* are either 'Divine One' or 'Divinity.' Please note it."

"Perhaps if one is of your faith," Caliphestros replied evenly, "such are the correct terms. I, as it happens, am not."

The Priestess looked more shocked than ever. "We have allowed a *Kafran* into the Den of Stone?"

But the old man held up a hand. "Nay, Eminence. I assure you, my hatred for the Kafran faith could not be more obvious." He indicated his legs. "But my own faith is, I suspect, not one which I could explain to you quickly. Suffice to say that my own correct title, whatever your faith, is *scholar.*"

The Groba Father weighed the matter for a moment. "My lord Caliphestros speaks truly, Divinity. His actions have proved the faith he keeps with our people, and take precedence over titles and words, as well. Thus, he may call you 'Eminence,' and to you he will be 'scholar.'"

"But, Father—!" the Priestess objected.

"That is my decision, Priestess!" the Father declared.

"A wise decision, too," Heldo-Bah said.

"Do *not* make me regret it, Heldo-Bah," the Father declared. "Now—" The Father deliberately looked past the Priestess, and gave a sharp order to the Outragers: "One or two more torches, and get them in haste." He pulled a collection of parchment maps close and, beginning to study them, said, "We have much to do, and with so many more participants, we can well use the additional light . . ."

Knowing that he was risking serious conflict, Heldo-Bah added quietly to the Outragers as they passed, "And perhaps a few more sticks of firewood, as long as you're going. She does like to bask in the warmth of a good fire, does this panther . . ."

The Father nodded at the departing Outragers impatiently, and they, looking furious, proceeded upon their servants' errands.

"Now, then, my lord," the Father announced, indicating that Caliphestros should draw nearer, which the old man did, sliding from Stasi's shoulders with the foragers' help, and then into his harness and crutches. "I do not know just how much Yantek Ashkatar has told you of our intelligence concerning the Tall's planned attack into the Wood, but—"

"He has told me much," Caliphestros said, studying the rough but accurate Bane maps. "And almost all of it, I think the noble Yantek will concede when he hears what I have to say, is inaccurate. Although understandably so. My own and Keera's investigations, together with communications I have exchanged with several . . . *associates* of mine, indicate that the Talons are embroiled in terrible matters between Broken and Daurawah, matters concerning their kingdom's internal integrity—to say nothing of their own lives. They are only now turning toward the valley of the Cat's Paw, whereas the troops that are presently bearing down upon you are, in fact, a *khotor* of Lord Baster-kin's Guard."

To a tableful of blank faces, Caliphestros reached over to pull a crude tracing of the course of the Cat's Paw from the pile of parchment, then turned when the Outragers reentered the Den. "Ah, good. We need the light. Place the torches here, by the maps, Outrager—"

"He is not your servant, to be ordered to perform such menial tasks," the Priestess of the Moon almost shouted. "Nor is the term 'Outrager' a recognized form of address!"

"Well, Eminence," Caliphestros replied coolly. "Perhaps if they spent less time butchering Broken farming families, it would not be, but I can assure you that outside this chamber, it is only too common—"

It was for the Groba Father to step in again: "With all respect, my lord, further bickering will gain us nothing." And then, to the Outragers: "Set the torches near the table, one of you, while the other feeds and stokes the fire. Then return to your mistress, that we may continue learning what is happening near the Cat's Paw."

"You need only look at what is happening *in* it, Learnèd Father," Caliphestros replied. "Members of your own tribe choosing to end their lives, terribly, in the very waters that made them ill to begin with—yet more, besides. Surely your own foragers have reported large numbers of dead and dying animals, especially upstream—for Keera and I saw as much, ourselves."

"Yes, our people have seen these things," the Father replied, watching in wonder as Heldo-Bah led the great white panther to the hearth before the great fire, stroked her neck and whispered in her ear, and at last urged her to lie down on the warm stones. Then, with no trace of fear, he himself lay beside her, his head upon her ribs. "But," the Father continued, astounded and only half-aware of what he was saying, "we thought it simply part of the same plague that the Tall had loosed upon us . . ." Regaining his dignity and composure, he turned back to Caliphestros, "We shall *all* do our best to cooperate in whatever endeavor I sense you are about to propose to us."

"Your reputation for wisdom is deserved, indeed, Father," Caliphestros said with a nod. "I *do* wish to propose a plan, to yourselves and to Yantek Ashkatar; a plan that may allow us, not only to turn the disease in the Cat's Paw to our advantage, but to entrap those men of the Merchant Lord's Guard who, I believe, will shortly cross into Davon Wood. And, by so doing, we will forestall any need to engage the Talons in combat, once they arrive, and can invite them to parley under a flag of truce, instead."

The Groba Father was momentarily at a loss for words; and it was for another Elder to speak further: "Your—*goals* are without question desirable, Lord Caliphestros," the Elder commented. "Yet they seem, at the same time, extreme, and to contradict themselves. If the rose fever has indeed struck across a broad region of Broken, for example, why should we think that *they* do not know its source, when *we* now know it, ourselves?"

"It was my understanding that age brought wisdom, in this chamber," Heldo-Bah called out. "Use your eyes, Elder, if your mind is of no help—you're *looking* at the reason the Tall do not know the source of the disease, and why our own healers *do*. Lord Caliphestros is a master of the sciences that have given our own healers the advantage—the same sciences that bred such great distrust of him among the Tall that they took his legs."

"*Science?*" said the Priestess disdainfully. "If we are to be delivered from this crisis, it will be faith, and not science, that will be our salvation. Science is no more than the blasphemer's term for sorcery."

Yantek Ashkatar looked first to Keera and then to Caliphestros in some embarrassment "With all respect, Divinity," the gruff, bearded soldier said, never daring to engage the Priestess's gaze. "I fear that your statement may be . . . incomplete—"

"May be *idiotic*," Heldo-Bah murmured quietly, causing the Priestess to slam her young fists down upon the Groba's table and cry:

"That is more than I can tolerate—!" But another low growl from Stasi, who this time lifted up onto her forelegs, as well, was all that was needed to quiet the sacred maiden; and, while this silence was of a sullen variety, it was also continued. Heldo-Bah, in the meantime, coaxed Stasi back to the stones of the hearth by stroking the rich fur of her neck and whispering into the enormous, pointed ear that faced him:

"Save your anger, Great Cat—she is not worth the effort. The time for killing will be upon us soon enough. And so—save your anger . . ."

And again Keera was amazed that Stasi complied with Heldo-Bah's suggestions, the two seeming to have, against all probability, developed not only some newfound affection, but a means of communication.

"Let us hear Lord Caliphestros out," the Groba Father announced at length. "We owe him at least that much, and no one in this tribe, however high or low, can say they are exempt from that debt." General agreement to this appraisal having been reached once more, Caliphestros pressed forward:

"I do not wish to discount the role that faith will play, in the coming days," the old man conceded graciously, although his words did not mollify the High Priestess as greatly as they should have. "For in times of war, such faith is a great comfort to those soldiers and common folk who are made to suffer most. In our own case, Yantek Ashkatar has told me that, whichever forces of Broken arrive on Lord Baster-kin's Plain in the hours to come, it is his desire to draw them into the Wood, where they will be unable to execute their maneuvers, and will instead become confused and terrified, and therefore may be defeated piecemeal—perhaps even annihilated. An admirable opening move." The old scholar studied the Groba Fathers in turn once again. "But there are ways in which the fight can be further weighted in the Bane's favor—if you will but avail yourselves of methods I have developed."

"Methods of science," the Priestess declared distastefully.

"That's the limit," Heldo-Bah suddenly pronounced, rising from his place at the fire. "Don't even try to explain, Lord Caliphestros—one demonstration will do the work of hours of argument."

As he crossed toward the Priestess and the Outragers who stood behind her, Heldo-Bah drew the blade that he had been given by Caliphestros in Stasi's den, causing the two Woodland Knights to suddenly move in front of the young woman. At this, the panther got to her feet, growling deep within her throat again, and letting her teeth show for a moment in a quick snarl.

"Heldo-Bah!" Keera said as he passed her by. "Be careful what you begin!"

"I begin nothing," answered the angry forager. "Instead, I will *finish* all this useless talk." Then, to the Outragers, he challenged, "Go ahead, either of you—or both. Hold your blades forth, try to thwart me."

The Outragers moved farther in front of the woman whose life they were sworn to protect, their blades yet before them, as Caliphestros and Keera moved to restrain and calm the panther. The Priestess looked supremely confident, seeming to believe that she was at last on the verge of witnessing the impertinent Heldo-Bah's death, when suddenly:

With two resounding clashes of metal upon metal, Heldo-Bah left the Outragers holding mere pieces of their blades; and the expressions on their faces were even more awed than Heldo-Bah's had been in Stasi's cave.

"There," said Heldo-Bah, sheathing his blade, wiping at his forehead, and returning to Stasi. "I don't know what you'd like to call that, Priestess, but your 'knights' carry blades taken from Broken soldiers—this much is known. So you go on explaining how we can ignore such advantages, if you must—or let us proceed, in the name of your precious Moon, to go about the business of exploiting them . . ."

Hobbling back to his place before the Groba, Caliphestros pronounced, "Heldo-Bah's methods are perhaps crass, but his conclusion is wise. This *is* the sort of result that my scientific arts can offer you—this and more, if you will only allow me to assist you."

"But—" The Groba Father was still staring at the Outragers, who were in turn staring at the pieces of blades in their hands. "But *how?*" the Father asked at length.

"I can explain it," Caliphestros replied, "although I would recommend that we do so as we undertake the work of preparation." Glancing at the cave walls about him, which were so much like those in his own long-time home, Caliphestros continued, "These chambers of yours contain internal passageways that will be ideal for the work that we must do—and, if my experience is any guide, the chambers atop the mountains higher above us will suit our purposes even better."

"You believe you truly can produce this superior steel in our mountains?" the Father asked, with an urgency none of the foragers had ever heard him employ.

"Within their highest caves," Caliphestros replied, "as I learned to do during my years of exile far to the west. For we will be harnessing the winds that blow and are channeled through the passages in these stone walls, just as they draw the smoke of your fire instantly from this chamber. Not even the great bellows that power your Voice of the Moon can direct such prodigious winds onto any one specific point."

The Groba Father shook his head. "These matters are quite beyond me, as I daresay they are beyond all of us—though perhaps you will tell the tale of their discovery as we begin our work."

Caliphestros nodded in grateful relief. "I shall be pleased to—*as we work*. But work we must, and quickly. As it is, we shall not have time to so arm *all* of your warriors—Yantek Ashkatar must choose his very best troops, and even at that, it will be a close-run affair."

The foragers and Caliphestros began to rise, Keera helping the old man to remove his walking equipment, so that he was able to pull himself onto the white panther's powerful shoulders as she dipped her neck to receive him.

"It seems to me," the Priestess of the Moon declared, "that we are being asked to put faith that would better suit a god than a man in 'Lord' Caliphestros."

Veloc bravely stepped forward, a trace of uncertainty nonetheless present in his words. "We ask you only to believe the words of a man who has made as much of a study of these matters as you have all made of the power and workings of the Moon." There was no member of the Groba who was able to protest to this, and Veloc was encouraged to press on: "And now, I would ask your most honored and revered persons to allow us to withdraw and to host Lord Caliphestros at our family's home. Keera has had but a few minutes' reunion with her children, and my lord Caliphestros has had a most arduous journey to Okot—"

"A fact to which I can attest," Yantek Ashkatar said, nodding certainly. "The journey of Keera's party has been an arduous one, indeed—why, even Heldo-Bah—"

But Ashkatar was interrupted, and further explanation was made unnecessary, when the loud sound of Heldo-Bah's snoring came from the direction of the hearth of the enormous cavity that was the Den of Stone's fireplace. The moment might have been cause for still more argument and insult, and the Priestess of the Moon looked ready for both; but the Groba Father quickly stepped in to offer Veloc a moment to go and kick his friend awake, and to let the troublesome forager gather himself for departure, as the man who occupied the chair surmounted by Moon horns inquired:

"Are you certain there are no more splendid quarters we can offer you, Lord Caliphestros? Keera and Veloc come from good, honest stock, who were generous enough even to have taken so troubling a boy as Heldo-Bah into their home, for many years; yet they are humble people, as is their home, and we can certainly arrange—"

"It shall not seem humble, to me, Father," Caliphestros replied. "For it has been ten years since I knew such surroundings, and longer still since I knew such company. Besides, Stasi and I will sleep out of doors, as is our custom during these months, and therefore we shall not frighten the children too much, nor keep the others awake with the strange hours we keep." He glanced at Keera quickly. "Better Stasi feel safe among such a family than that she feel excessively honored. And I might say the same for myself—"

At which Heldo-Bah's tired voice growled, "I am *awake,* damn you, Veloc, and ready to leave this place, I assure you—so stop kicking me!"

"Perhaps a quick departure for a night's rest, Father," Keera suggested, "would be best after all."

"As you say, as you say," the Father replied, with a wave of his hand.

As the party turned to go, Caliphestros paused to mention only one thing more to the Priestess of the Moon: "And, Priestess, such remove from the great activity of the center of Okot will give me further chance to consider a problem with which, I believe, yourself, the Fathers, and all of the Lunar Sisterhood have been struggling."

"Oh?" the Priestess said doubtfully. "And what might that be?"

Caliphestros paused, studying this remarkably prideful young woman, and determining that had he, like Veloc, been summoned to her bed, he, too, would certainly have refused. "You have, unless I am mistaken, been casting the runes in connection with this crisis."

The Priestess scoffed. "There is no great revelation in that—it is our way to cast the runes, to assist in any troubles that face our people."

"Indeed," Caliphestros replied carelessly, turning Stasi toward the exit to the Den. "Then perhaps I am wrong—perhaps you have determined just what 'the Riddle of Water, Fire, and Stone' is, and are aware of how its solution may very soon aid in the struggle against Broken."

For the last time during this audience, the faces of all at the Groba table reflected utter confusion. "How—?" the Priestess managed to express in alarm; and then the Father asked, in a more coherent expression of concern:

"My lord Caliphestros—how can you know of the Riddle of Water, Fire, and Stone? And what can you tell us of its meaning and use?"

"Little more than you yourselves can—just yet," Caliphestros called over his shoulder, raising a hand as he departed. "But it is good to know that we are all indeed concerned with the same problems, is it not?" Caliphestros and Stasi, without any encouragement, continued on their way out of the Den, seeming weary with the place. "I bid you good night. Tomorrow begins our great work, and we must be rested and ready . . ."

Keera and Veloc turned to issue more formal and acceptable words of departure to the Groba, while Heldo-Bah, like Stasi herself, simply wandered toward the long stone hallway that led out of the Den, scratching at his head and various other parts of his body.

"If you do not mind, Lord Caliphestros," he could be heard to say in the stone hallway, "I shall sleep with you and your friend under the trees and stars, tonight. They are good people, Keera and Veloc's family, but I would rather be in the place that suits me best, and worries me least . . ."

"And you are welcome, Heldo-Bah," Caliphestros answered, his voice now fading altogether. "But do not keep Stasi awake with your snoring, for it is one of many human sounds she detests . . ."

Back in the Den of Stone, the Groba Father looked up and down the great table at his fellows. "Well—what say we: sorcery or science?" Then he gazed at the stone hall once more, as he answered his own question with another: "Or does it really matter at all, when we consider the forces that are even now bearing down upon our people . . . ?"

And to that query, not even the Priestess of the Moon had an answer.

$$3:\{v:\}$$

Upon the mountains south of Okot, Caliphestros and his surprising new
order of acolytes create an inferno as fearsome as Muspelheim; *while Keera,*
for the first time, begins to wonder if the old man's passion holds danger
for her people . . .

T HE THREE BANE FORAGERS had long since learned that
both Caliphestros and Stasi had the capacity to almost instantly
distinguish between persons of quality and compassion and
those more common humans, ungenerous and cruel in nature. And
among the most reliable and generous of people to be found in Okot (or
anywhere else) were certainly Keera's family—not only her own and Veloc's parents, Selke and Egenrich, but the tracker's children: the still-
recovering boys, Herwin and Baza, as well as the storm of energy,
curiosity, and youthful wisdom that was the youngest, Effi, so like her
mother in many ways, although more circumspect, and now having
been exposed to the kind of tragedy and sadness, brief but scarring, that
teaches wise children not to be bitter or selfish.

The morning after Caliphestros, Stasi, and Heldo-Bah slept outside
the welcoming family's home, Keera followed Caliphestros's instruction
to assemble every miner, ironmonger, and smith that lived in the central
and outlying settlements of Okot so that they could listen to the requirements of a plan that, in a matter of days, would so arm the central corps
of Yantek Ashkatar's troops that they could hope not only to defeat even
the soldiers of Broken, but to do so at a point far north of Okot, thus keeping the exact location of the long-hidden community safe.

Because of this, ancient mines dug into the sides of the mountains
above Okot that had long lain sealed and dormant were now reopened,
in order that they could join those few that were still active, as well as
allow the Bane to more easily gain access to veins of a special iron ore
that had been propelled from the night sky into the Earth countless ages
ago. In addition, the miners digging into the mountainside were told to
bring their day's or night's gatherings of coal (the main substance with
which the unique iron ore would be smelted) to Caliphestros, before any

thought was given to using them to fuel the new, smaller but far hotter and more numerous forges that the old man designed. The fiery effect of the forges was increased by the thousands of torch lights that lit the way into and around the mines, creating an ever-expanding impression that the Bane had bargained with their old gods, and been allowed to tear open a terrifying gateway into their underworld: the dreaded *Muspelheim*.[†]

But why, some workers could occasionally be heard to ask, was any deep coal mining necessary at all, when the mountains were already so covered in young and old trees of all varieties—trees that could easily be used to fuel the old cripple's forges? That the city of Broken itself needed coal was not difficult to understand: the summit of Broken mountain was, as has been seen, primarily composed of stone, and been shorn of nearly all its readily accessible stands of heating timber during the kingdom's early generations, as had the plain north of the Cat's Paw. Indeed, it was well known that direct control of new supplies of wood and coal, along with all metal ores found in the great forest (primarily iron and silver), were two of the chief reasons that Lord Baster-kin so coveted Davon Wood. Yet Caliphestros not only insisted on coal, but on personally examining every piece of it that was brought out of the mountains, surrendering much of the little nightly rest that it was his custom to take and instead relentlessly searching through the cartloads that Bane miners, with blackened faces and bleeding hands, dragged under his practiced eye. He was seeking a type of black rock that was marked by certain qualities, qualities that took the miners long days to recognize in the darkness beneath the ground, but that they eventually learned to identify by the light of day quickly enough: qualities of weight and texture, all of which made it well suited to transformation by fire into yet *another* variety of fuel, related but not identical to coal, that was vital to the creation of Caliphestros's near-miraculous grade of steel.[‡]

But in truth, for all the talk among the Bane townspeople of the mines and forges above Okot resembling, to an ever-increasing extent, some sort of terrible entrance to the most fiery of the Nine Homeworlds,[††] a passageway that would eventually disgorge those agents that would cause the end of the old gods and perhaps of the world, Caliphestros privately told Keera that all such tales were but myths, while the work that he was directing on the mountains above Okot, whatever its sinister nighttime appearance, was in fact, like all undertakings to which he applied himself, based on such scientific learning as had been developed and carried on by men and women like himself for hundreds if not thousands of years. These refinements, which so closely resembled sorcerous transformations to the ignorant, were carried out upon the mountains that brooded over Okot not because the spot had been appointed as the site at which the end of the Earth or the imminent arrival of infamous demons would take place, but because the position of the caves within allowed the Bane metalworkers to capture the only winds in the area strong enough to heat the coal and charcoal in Caliphestros's furnaces to so great an extent that they could do the work that must, at this critical hour, *be* done.

One particular mountaintop cave, meanwhile, became both Caliphestros's private new forge and the scholar and Stasi's temporary home. The panther herself slept above the cave, as much as she did within, during these days, for the old man worked long hours, producing (or so the Bane thought) additional weapons in order to keep some vague pace with the Bane smiths to whom he had taught many of his secrets. During these restless hours, when Caliphestros turned his mental and physical efforts to ever more arcane experiments, Keera became the old man's sole assistant; and such only after she swore not to reveal what he was in fact doing. The work in the Bane mines and the mountaintop smithies multiplied daily: Caliphestros knew that the Bane had always been extraordinarily clever and imitative people, who, once shown how to do a thing, required little repeated instruction to achieve their object. All the special coal and special charcoal they created did, indeed, create sufficient heat to allow Caliphestros to himself smelt what the Bane workers came to call the "star iron," because the iron ore itself was brought from deep in the mountains and the mines where it had presumably been embedded hundreds of years ago, after hurtling down from the heavens. That iron was combined, first and above all, with the remarkably high quality charcoal that Caliphestros had taught his smiths to create, a combination that produced a steel capable of not only attaining but holding an edge of fearsome sharpness. Some Bane smiths swore that there were traces of other elements in the ore, a tale that reinforced the other-than-Earthly origins of the "star iron," although none among these same smiths could even guess at what those other elements might be.[†] This new style of heating and smelting, brought back from the East via the Silk Path by Caliphestros during his youth, allowed even the highest grade of ore, what the Bane called "the star iron," to be heated to so uniform a consistency that it could be masterfully united with another iron—one of equal purity but also of greater resistance to fracture or breakage—with the object of giving the blades both mighty durability and at the same time astonishing cutting power. After this, the combination was folded and refolded, worked and reworked, pounded together by smiths until there were hundreds of layers in each uninterrupted strip that became a weapon; and any one of these weapons was capable of becoming higher in both strength *and* sharpness even than that which Heldo-Bah had demonstrated to the Groba, and far superior to anything manufactured outside the realms of the East.[†]

For, while the occasional daring seeker of a European trading fortune, or traveler of great renown as a swordsman, might journey far to bring back examples of this remarkable steel from the most distant realms of the East to the markets of their homelands, Caliphestros alone had understood the formula for the *manufacture* of the steel well enough to record it, during his travels on the Silk Path. He had then brought it back west with him, and awaited the day when the loosing of this seminal substance would create weapons that would change the very rank of power among kingdoms in the West where they were used—just as they had already done in the East.

And yet, even as Caliphestros made a gift of the knowledge of how to create the star iron to Keera's tribe of diminutive outcasts, Keera herself—perhaps the most perspicacious member of her tribe—remained far from easy about all the reasons why he might be doing so. His obvious motives—revenge, for himself and for Stasi, contempt for how the Broken state had changed since the death of his former patron, the God-King Izairn, and the desire to end the dangers of disease that seemed not to be *invading* the city on the mountain, but rather to be emerging *from* it—were apparent and easily understood; although Keera nonetheless wondered, at certain moments—moments when the old man's blood and ire were truly racing—if it would ever be truly possible for her or anyone else to comprehend the inner feelings that drove a man who had lived as long, colorful, and mysterious a life as Caliphestros.

As it only could have, the vital portion of the explanation of the mystery that Keera had built in her mind around the old man and his behavior came without any spoken question on the subject, one night when the winds atop the mountain ridge were building to what seemed an especially portentous fury. With ever more days of massive effort by increasing numbers of Bane laborers piling one atop the other, the southern horizon above Okot had never seemed to crack open with such great and purposeful fire; and, being as the mountaintops upon which the Bane forged the weapons with which they hoped to blunt any aggressive moves by the Tall army or Lord Baster-kin's Guard stood at an even higher elevation than did the point upon Broken's mountain where the Inner City, the House of the Wives of Kafra, and the High Temple were all located, it seemed only too likely that the God-King and his family and minions (to say nothing of the average citizen of the walled city) could not help but look out at that southern horizon and wonder what was taking place. Was their own god, Kafra, preparing some divine punishment for the Bane, one that would make the sacrifice of Broken's young men, whether in the Guard or in the army, unnecessary? Or were, indeed, the demons of the old faith's fiery Ninth Homeland preparing to enter humanity's realm, and punish the subjects of Broken for having abandoned them in favor of the strange deity brought back by the followers of Oxmontrot from the world of the *Lumun-jani,* by first weakening the unfaithful with plague and then releasing their own demoniacal powers upon the kingdom north of the Cat's Paw?

Keera's secret work assisting Caliphestros in his private cave, guarded against all prying eyes by Stasi, only heightened this air of mystery; for the truth was, as she soon learned, Caliphestros was not producing a marginally additional number of spearheads and dagger and sword blades within that cave, but something altogether different. Every few nights, the forager, the old man, and the panther would journey to bog pits among the mountains above and below Okot, the existence of which Keera had never thought anything more than a danger to passing travelers. From these, the old man would extract buckets of a strangely pungent liquid, lighter and thinner than pitch as well as more inflammable, and then they would bring these back to his cave, where he would combine them in various mixtures with strangely colored powders and extracts from the very Earth, always working toward Keera knew not what, save that he produced a broad array of foul-smelling, combustible half-liquids and fluids, all of which he would speak of, at times, but none of which he would fully explain. Only when she returned to her home and her children, Keera believed, did Caliphestros complete these experiments; and in this fact she found reason for uneasiness as much as amazement.

Still, knowing that the Tall in Broken, from the lowliest worker to the God-King, might well be viewing all the fiery activity in the mountains of Davon Wood with real dread and fear was cause for ever greater joy; just as it was when—with the wind rising to a particular fury, creating especially plentiful fire, and with the heat and sparks of the now dozens of exile forges rising in great upward showers—momentous news arrived from those units of Ashkatar's army that patrolled the barrier of the Cat's Paw: a column of Broken troops were advancing on the river. It happened that, when this intelligence came, Keera was outside Caliphestros's cave, beside Stasi at the jagged mouth of the place, a spot where the panther often sat, ever ready to spring forward, as her human companion within brewed and mixed the strange substance that absorbed him so.

It was, predictably, Heldo-Bah and Veloc who brought the news of this march to the old man's cave, the pair being the only Bane, besides Keera, who had the courage to approach Caliphestros when he was laboring at his seemingly mad doings therein.

"Great man of science!" Heldo-Bah called as he reached the cave's entrance. "Come with us! Come and see the column of men that approach on the main road from Broken to the Plain, with torches lit in the night to show us just where they are!"

Caliphestros emerged from the cave, his skin smudged with the smoke and ash of his work, his face sweating as he pulled himself along upon his walking platform with his crutches; and it seemed, even to Heldo-Bah, amazing that a crippled man should be capable of such difficult labors of the mind and body. The wind was continuing to blow with true ferocity, causing the old man's robe to drag directly across his body, and his beard across his face, as well; but his skullcap remained in place, and an expression of wilder emotion than any of his forager friends had ever seen him exhibit soon came into his features.

"So soon?" Caliphestros said, staring only briefly at the winding points of lights on Lord Baster-kin's Plain before moving to a large, naturally formed basin in the outer rock of the cave's entrance, one that was full of rainwater. A small cake of the same soap that the old man had insisted the Bane diggers use during their march to Okot lay on the basin's edge. "Then they cannot be the column of Talons that is on its way from Daurawah," he said, as he began to scrub himself clean of the coal dust and other black patches on his skin that had formed during the smelting and smithing processes earlier in the day.

"Not if they behave so stupidly as to light their path for us to see plainly," Veloc replied. "Although how you could have known that the Talons went to Daurawah in the first place remains a mystery to me, Lord Caliphestros."

"It was the only logical direction to take, if they needed to collect supplies and forage for their horses," Caliphestros answered with a smile. "Besides, did not your tribe's Outrager spies observe them taking the eastern road as they departed Broken?"

"Yes," Heldo-Bah said, spitting on the ground. "But to trust in the reports of the Outragers is folly—and even if one accepts that they were right, it does not explain your insistence that the plague was also active in the Tall's port, Lord Caliphestros."

Caliphestros glanced again at the swaying treetops, and smiled slightly. "You must allow me a few secrets, Heldo-Bah."

But Keera, also glancing at the loudly rustling branches above, knew the secret of the old man's wisdom concerning this subject, even if she could not, at that moment, see either the starling called Little Mischief or the enormous (and enormously proud) owl named Nerthus.

"So—if it is not the Talons, the question becomes, Who is it?" Having voiced the question, the old man moved on his single wooden leg and crutches to stand beside Heldo-Bah, who was scratching at Stasi's thick coat. Leaning against her other shoulder, the old man removed his walking device, then bundled the wooden leg and crutches, and slung them on his back. Climbing with little difficulty onto the neck and upper back of the panther, he settled himself as Stasi stood fully upright again, and Heldo-Bah took a step back "Well, whoever it is," the old man continued, "Yantek Ashkatar must make his preparations—with all crossings over the Cat's Paw save the Fallen Bridge destroyed, he must position his best men amid the Wood on this side of that pathway, so that he will, from the first, force these Broken soldiers to fight on the Bane's chosen ground, and according to the Bane's most practiced dispositions and maneuvers. Has he been alerted?"

"Yantek Ashkatar is even now about the very activities you have mentioned," Veloc replied. "He has obeyed your counsel wholly, in preparing this first battle, my lord, despite the objections of the Priestess of the Moon."

"And he is to be congratulated for that bravery," Caliphestros judged with a nod. "For myself, I would observe the proceedings from the large rocks I took note of on our journey to Okot. You know the place of which I speak, Keera?"

"I do, my lord," Keera replied, somewhat unnerved at the mention of the very spot where the foragers had left behind the arrogant but deadly Outrager, Welferek. "We had an—encounter near there, at the beginning of this business."

Heldo-Bah and Veloc exchanged looks, Heldo-Bah's merry but Veloc's somewhat sheepish.

Caliphestros stared hard at the tracker. "And I am certain that your brother will join me, Keera, in urging, even insisting, that you join me there—you are the only parent your children possess, now, and they need you far more than does Yantek Ashkatar."

Keera looked quickly to her brother, who only nodded sternly. "He is right, Keera," Veloc said. "And, if it offers you any consolation, I anticipate being ordered to join the two of you, that I may be able to prepare records for a saga recounting the tale of this battle."

"So I go alone to draw Tall blood?" Heldo-Bah said, at once proud and a little uneasy about losing his comrades. "Well—I cannot argue your reasoning, Lord of Science, and still less can I condemn yours, Keera. And, as it will no doubt infuriate that little vixen, our Priestess, I suppose I must accept even yours, Veloc. Finally, the truth is, this will be hard and bloody work, best undertaken by those who truly relish the opportunity . . ."

As if to confirm Heldo-Bah's statement, a sudden, single sounding of the Bane Voice of the Moon was heard, telling all who had been laboring on the mountain ridge or anywhere else outside Okot that the time had come to gather for battle. The blast was short, for the enemy was near and growing nearer.

A certain light entered Caliphestros's eyes, once more, and he urged

Stasi to climb to the top of their temporary cave, which offered a fine view, not only of far-off Broken mountain and the city atop it, but of the Cat's Paw in the middling distance, and Lord Baster-kin's Plain just beyond that waterway. The three foragers scrambled to follow, fighting both the steep, slippery slope of the cave's rock and the mounting wind, which was creating the haunting notion that there was a *mareh* behind every tree, inside every cave, and ready to strike from behind every rock.

So much the stranger was it, then, that when the foragers at last joined Caliphestros and Stasi, they found the old man with a look of terrible joy upon his face, and the panther snarling with enthusiasm to descend from the mountain they were perched upon, and make for the enemy that was approaching and, even more importantly, for those ever-burning lights beyond the walls of the city in the far distance.

"They are actually doing it," Caliphestros called to the foragers when they reached him. "See there!" He pointed to the long line of torches as, in the manner of a stream of liquid, the soldiers left the safety of the Plain and began a careful crossing of the Moonlit river's last remaining bridge. "The fools enter the Wood without pause! Baster-kin will risk the lives of what looks to be a full *khotor* of his own Guard in order to eclipse the power and prestige of Sentek Arnem's Talons, and the regular army as a whole—he would secure the land and riches of the Wood for the merchants and the royal faction alone! Never has he been so foolish."

And with that, the party began a run, first to Okot, so that Keera might briefly take leave of her children, and then to the rocks that overlooked the southern side of the Fallen Bridge (and, in the middling distance to the southeast, the *Ayerzess-werten*). Their dash took a number of hours, although far less, as always, than it would have taken any ordinary forest travelers at night. The length of time might have been still less, had they not paused for an unforeseen interruption; an interruption that would not so much solve the enigma of Caliphestros, to Keera, as leave old questions answered, and new ones posed . . .

$$3:\{vi:\}$$

Somewhere on the trail between Okot and their destination, the foragers,
Caliphestros, and Stasi stumble upon a remarkable sight . . .

I T WAS, OF COURSE, the white panther who sensed the presence first, although it was not long before Keera did so, as well. When the grade of the swiftly moving group's path began to slowly flatten, indicating that the valley of the Cat's Paw was growing closer, Stasi stopped, so suddenly as to almost hurl her rider onto the ground before her. To Caliphestros's repeated inquiries concerning the cause of her refusal to move forward, the panther only put her nose high in the air, searching the wind that continued to blow from the west; and, once she had determined the definite direction from which the scent she detected came, she continued forward, although not along the same direct course toward the riverbed that she had previously been following. Caliphestros turned to the tracker, who continued to run beside them.

"Keera!" he called. "Stasi will not respond to my direction—this has never happened before, without her first leaving me behind! Have you sensed anything that would make her behave so?"

A strange expression entered Keera's features, Caliphestros noted, one to match Stasi's behavior. "I fear I have only too good an idea of what she is about, my lord," the tracker replied, tilting her ear rather than her nose into the same breeze that seemed to have agitated Stasi so, as she continued to match the panther's pace. "I can just hear a male brown bear making the sounds and performing the dance of mating[†]—yet the female scent that provokes him is strange: artificial, or, rather, carefully collected and placed, and confined to far too small an area. Along with which, the scent is accompanied by that of—"

Caliphestros had begun to nod his head, his expression darkening. "Of a human female," he finished for the reluctant Keera. The anticipation that the old man had felt at watching a *khotor* of Lord Baster-kin's Guard receive the punishment it so richly deserved seemed to suddenly disappear. "And, I will wager, a human female you have detected before . . ."

Keera glanced at the old man, as concerned by his expression as by the strange mix of emotions in his voice. "Aye, lord. Just so. The Wife of Kafra—on the strange occasion of which we have told you. Save that it was a panther's scent with which hers was mingled that night, rather than a bear's."

Caliphestros nodded his head. *"Well, then . . ."*

"My lord, we should avoid this, if we can," Keera warned. "Battles between brown bears and panthers can do grievous harm to both combatants."

"Fear not, on that account, Keera," Caliphestros replied. "It is not the bear that draws Stasi on."

"What is happening, you two?" Heldo-Bah said loudly, from behind. "We have strayed from the most direct path to the rocks you spoke of, Lord Caliphestros—and you know as much, Keera."

Before further discussion could be pursued, Keera indicated silence to her fellow foragers; and it was not very much longer before the party had reached the edge of a small clearing, where the tracker indicated to her brother and Heldo-Bah that they should take their customary positions of observation in the branches of several high trees. When Veloc questioned with his eyes why they were not being joined by the white panther and her agèd rider, Keera simply held up a hand, indicating patience—

And very soon, that patience on the foragers' part was rewarded: seemingly unaware, now, of the behavior of their three traveling companions, the old man and the panther stepped onto the edge of the clearing, in the middle of which the foragers could now see a familiar yet dreaded human woman moving in a strange, seductive manner, urging on a large male brown bear, who would ordinarily have attacked her long ago:

It was the First Wife of Kafra, once again, her robe as yet clinging to that same remarkably long-legged body, and her long strands of black hair slowly moving with the western wind while her remarkable green eyes—neither so brilliant nor so beautiful as Stasi's, but similar in color— held the confused bear in place, just as they had done to the male panther, on a night that now seemed, to the foragers, very long ago.

From where he sat in the treetops at the southern edge of the clearing, Heldo-Bah glanced at Keera and her brother. "The old fool *is* mad," he whispered. "He should get that panther up into the trees, lest that witch see him and cry out to the forward units of the Guard."

"Heldo-Bah, when will you make up your mind?" Veloc countered. "Is he a fool or an all-knowing sorcerer?"

"He cannot be both?" the gap-toothed Bane questioned in reply.

"Quiet!" Keera commanded, softly, but in the manner that always brought immediate compliance from her fellow foragers.

In the middle of the small clearing below, the First Wife of Kafra—sister to the God-King, the very embodiment of radiance in the Broken conception of life—had begun to slip one perfect shoulder from beneath her black gown, causing Heldo-Bah, once again, to salivate almost visibly through his filed teeth. "Oh, great Moon," he whispered.

Caliphestros had urged the white panther to continue forward, and up onto a stout rock; then the pair stopped, although their presence had evidently been noticed already by the Wife of Kafra, despite the fact that she had not turned to face them. Her green eyes remained fixed upon the black orbs of the bear, and she said calmly:

"We had heard rumors that you might have survived the *Halap-stahla*, Caliphestros . . ." Finally she turned to face the old man, and a sudden look of disappointment—even bordering on revulsion—entered her beauteous features. "Though none of those rumors had mentioned the condition you might be in—and I confess that I was not prepared for it . . ." She studied him more closely. "You have . . . *changed*, haven't you?"

Keera studied Caliphestros's reaction carefully: she knew him well enough, by that point, to see the injury that he tried to cover with pride.

"And what condition did you imagine you might find me in, Alandra? After my treatment at the hands of your priests, and so many years in the Wood?"

The Wife of Kafra shook her head slowly. "I do not know," she replied softly; and, although Keera looked and listened for it, she could find no real trace of remorse, only of disappointment, in either the woman's face or her words. "But not this. Not this . . . You have grown old. But there is more. The evil for which you were condemned has made its way out from inside your body—your demon side is loose, truly."

Caliphestros continued to nod. "Yes. I remember well that you had to condemn me as such an absurd creature as a 'demon'—how else to prove the equally nonsensical notion that your brother was sibling to a god?

You have always required a villain in your life, Alandra, to justify the perversions into which both you and Saylal descended. And when your father—who was in fact a good man, whatever lies the pair of you told about him—died, I suppose I was the next logical choice."

The First Wife of Kafra nodded toward the panther. "And what of this creature? You ride the great mistress of the Wood. Is that not evidence of demonic behavior?"

"I do not ride her," Caliphestros answers. "She offers me conveyance. Just as she offered me life, after your brother agreed to condemn me to what I am sure you all thought would be death."

Suddenly, as if she were able to weigh the emotion of the moment, Stasi issued one short but especially angry—even lethal—snarl at both the woman and the brown bear; and the bear, though not at all pleased about doing so, made a few movements from side to side, then backed out and away from the clearing, eventually moving quickly east.

"Oh," the Wife of Kafra said in disappointment, pulling her robe back over her bared shoulder. "That was not at all kind of your—well, what *do* you call this creature with whom you consort, old man?"

"Her name is not for you to know, Alandra," Caliphestros said. "Nor will any other citizen of that foul city on the mountain ever learn it."

Suddenly, the woman called Alandra adopted a coy, almost flirtatious manner with the legless man before and just above her. "You did not always find it so foul," she murmured with a smile.

"And you did not always find *me* so," Caliphestros replied.

"True," Alandra agreed. "But I was only a maiden, then; and you had been my tutor. An unfair advantage for you to enjoy—when I grew old enough, I came to see the truth, and to prefer . . . other company."

"I assume that by that remark you mean that you came to prefer your own brother's bed to mine."

In the treetops above, Veloc released a slow, near-silent oath: "*Hak—* the old man was once the *lover* of such a beauty?"

"And why not?" Heldo-Bah replied. "There are women among the Tall who have endured *your* touch, Veloc . . ."

"Silence, both of you!" Keera ordered once more. "This is, although I would not expect you to know it, a terribly delicate moment . . ."

In the clearing below, Stasi stepped forward again, once or twice, causing a look of uncertainty even in the supremely self-confident priestess. "But let us not alter facts," Caliphestros continued. "I may have been your tutor, and you a maiden, when we first met—but years later, when *you* came to *me* with your desire that we become more, you were a woman. Certainly enough." With the Broken bear's departure, the old man felt easy enough to lean forward upon the panther's shoulders. "And well you know it, whatever tales you may have since told to make me seem more a demon to your people than they were already inclined to believe. Yet you say that you had heard rumors of my survival, Alandra," he continued. "I take it such came from Lord Baster-kin's torture of my acolytes?"

The First Wife of Kafra smiled in a way that Keera found most repugnant: beautiful, but nonetheless cruel. "Only in part," she answered. "For Baster-kin has never put his full effort behind such methods. We could not be *truly* sure until reports reached us of Visimar's traveling with Sentek Arnem."

Stepping forward herself, Alandra seemed to make a point of exposing her long, enticing legs through the slits on either side of her black gown.

"I am sad to see your tastes for intrigue and plots grown so strong and ugly," Caliphestros replied. "Unlike the rest of you."

"Ah, scorn once more," Alandra said, shaking her head. "I can remember a time when my intrigues did not trouble you so. When I stole away from my rooms, that we might lie together in your high chambers in the palace."

And again, Keera thought, she could see an expression of deep injury hidden beneath the old man's stern efforts to affect disdain. "Was it all deception even then, Alandra? Did you deceive *me* with talk and acts of love?"

"Mmm," Alandra noised, with the first hint of something other than maliciousness beneath her outward manner. "Perhaps not. But that time was so long ago—who can honestly remember?" Seeming to rouse herself from some not unpleasant memory, Alandra continued: "And what does it matter, any longer? You are the enemy of our kingdom, and of my brother—a shadow, as I say, of what you once were. And so, with that, I will leave you to your *new* mate . . ." She turned to depart, but her every movement was suddenly arrested by a stern note of authority in Caliphestros's voice:

"*Alandra!*" The First Wife paused, almost against her own will, but did not turn fully back about. "It is not I who consort or mate with the beasts of the Wood, my girl—although I understand that you cannot make the same assertion. And the heavens only know what your brother amuses himself with, these days. But let that be. Take only this message to Saylal—"

"Do you mean," the First Wife asked, feigning indignation, "to the God-King of our realm, brother to Kafra, the Supreme Deity?"

Caliphestros shrugged, seeming to have suddenly gained the upper hand in the exchange, and to have realized as much. "Call him what you like. To me he is simply Saylal—the frightened, malicious little boy who was taught by priests to lust after his own sister. But whatever the name: tell him that his armies enter Davon Wood at their certain peril, and probable doom. A doom that will be demonstrated tonight . . ." And, as if he had foreseen the moment, Caliphestros looked to the north, as did Alandra, when the sound of a Broken battle horn was heard sounding an alarm. "And tell him," Caliphestros said, smiling now, "that I alone have solved the Riddle of Water, Fire, and Stone."

The First Wife of Kafra turned to the old man suddenly, fury now plain in her face. "That riddle is a myth."

"Oh, it is no myth," Caliphestros said, still smiling, his injury and tentativeness now seemingly erased, and his mastery over the conversation unquestionable. "And its solution will mean the shattering of Broken's impregnability. And so, go, now, by whatever route it is you use to return to the city—for your return will not be possible very much longer. Therefore get back to your life of cruelty, bestiality, and incest, and continue to believe that it is a faith. And remember only this—" The old man raised an accusatory finger. "My age and my decrepitude were inevitable—*as are your own*. A fact that you shall discover, soon enough. Indeed, now that the Moon rises higher, I perceive that you may have begun to discover it already." Alandra's hands suddenly reached for her face, as her eyes searched the skin of her arms and the exposed parts of her legs. "Go, Alandra. In the name of what we once shared, I shall not hand you to the Bane Outragers, despite the advantage their tribe should gain from your capture—although I doubt that you would show me the same courtesy, were our positions reversed. *Go on, then!*"

And, with no more cleverness or cruelty to offer, with nothing at all remaining, save a look of simple fear, the First Wife of Kafra turned and moved swiftly out of the small clearing toward the south, glancing back only once, with what seemed to Keera, now, an expression of not only resentment, but, perhaps, regret, as well.

As soon as she had disappeared, the three foragers quickly leapt down from their high perches to tree limb after tree limb, until they were upon the woodland floor once again. Each was plainly full of questions; although Keera and Veloc could see that the encounter had drained Caliphestros—despite his final posture of defiance and anger—of too much energy to allow any possibility of immediate reply, and so brother and sister were silent. Heldo-Bah, of course, exhibited no such delicacy, and no such manners:

"*You,* old man," he said, stepping closer, "have a great deal of explaining to do . . ."

"I suppose I do, Heldo-Bah," Caliphestros replied, his great store of exhaustion finally making itself audible in his voice. Keera and Veloc both rushed to each of his arms, fearing that he would fall from the panther's shoulders; but he indicated that he was able to travel unaided atop Stasi with a quick lift of his hand. "For now, however—let us get to our destination, before the fighting begins . . ."

"Demons take the fighting!" Heldo-Bah replied. "I have seen much fighting, in my time—but never have I seen so strange an encounter as that one. No—I will remain with the rest of you, to learn what lies behind all this."

Caliphestros nodded, urging Stasi forward once more. "And learn it you shall—but I am not yet ready to speak of it."

It was not long before the group approached the high rocks that offered a broad view of the trees and ground on the southern side of the Fallen Bridge; and, in the distance, the flickering lights of the torches being carried by Lord Baster-kin's Guard could just begin to be seen. Before long, their laughing, triumphant voices, aided by wine, mead, and beer, began to become audible: a clear demonstration that they believed the complete lack of resistance they had thus far encountered was an indication, not of any trap or stratagem on the part of the Bane, but of the terror with which they had filled their enemies' hearts.

$$3:\{vii:\}$$

*As the battle between Ashkatar's men and Lord Baster-kin's Guard rages
about them, the foragers learn the deeper truth of what they are
witnessing . . .*

T HROUGH THEIR OWN and Stasi's ability to move with unmatched swiftness, Keera, Veloc, and Heldo-Bah managed to
compensate for the time lost during the strange but enlighten-
ing encounter that had left Lord Caliphestros racked by turmoil and a
weariness of the spirit, and to reach the high rock formation that had
been their original destination before hostilities erupted. Here they positioned themselves behind stony barriers in time to observe the lesson
that would soon be taught to the soldiers of Broken (even if only to the
Merchant Lord's Guard) about war: not war as it was taught to or practiced by the officers and men of that kingdom, but war as it was best understood and fought by the Bane.

"But I do not understand the distinction of which you have often spoken, my lord," Keera said softly, looking out amid the ground lying to the
south and east of the misty crags overhanging Hafften Falls and the
Fallen Bridge, across which the forward units of Lord Baster-kin's Guard
had already made their way, and were now trying, with almost uniform
failure, to drag their *ballistae,* nearly all of which slipped from the surface
of that giant tree, only to crash into pieces in the rocky waters below. "A
hammer or a blade is not different when used by different peoples,"
Keera continued. "Is not war the same? Why should there be one variety
of war for the Tall, and another for the Bane?"

"Because war is not a thing separate from the mind, like the hammer
or the blade," Caliphestros replied quietly, his head ever turning to make
out the forms of Bane swordsmen, spear carriers, and archers who had
already taken up positions amid the northernmost part of Davon Wood,
while more of Lord Baster-kin's Guard continued a march that they presumed would take them closer to the enemy. "It is an *expression of* the
mind," the old scholar continued, "one used to achieve a certain object,
yes, but one that bespeaks the nature of the *collective* mind of that people."

"Yes, yes, all very interesting, I'm sure," Heldo-Bah interrupted. "But now, Lord Caliphestros, if we may return to the small matter of what we saw take place between yourself and the First Wife of Kafra—"

But Heldo-Bah was silenced by a quick warning blow to the ribs issued by Veloc.

"*Aiee*, Veloc!" Heldo-Bah noised, quietly but urgently. "Are you mad? There are not Tall enough entering the Wood, that you think you must attack one of your only friends?"

"Let Keera be the one to ask about such things, Heldo-Bah," Veloc replied, as he took several sheets of parchment and a bit of writing charcoal from a small bag at his side. "You have all the tact of a shag bull."

Heldo-Bah, ready to argue further, was distracted when he noticed just what his friend was doing. "And what does all this mean?" he asked, indicating the parchment and charcoal.

"I shall make a few notes," Veloc answered, "that I may remember all that his lordship says without error."

"*You?*" Heldo-Bah said. "The man who believes that his precious history can only be accurately related by the historian to his audience through spoken words, whereas writing provides opportunity for lies?"

"And so do I believe still," Veloc declared. "These are, as I said, but notes, used to remind me of certain details that, when I speak of it later, may be useful in recalling the whole with greater accuracy."

"With even *more* lies, is what you mean," Heldo-Bah judged.

"Hush, now," Veloc said, with great self-importance. "Let us learn what his lordship would have us know . . ."

The conversation between Keera and Caliphestros had not ceased, during this interval, and the old man was continuing to explain his same theme: "Had Yantek Ashkatar kept to his original plan," he said, "then he would have committed an error of enormous proportions. The Bane have not the training to face soldiers of the Tall, or even of Lord Basterkin's Guard, in an open field, nor have they the weapons or the physical stature. They should have been cut to pieces. Now, however"—and at this, Caliphestros held his hand out to the moving shadows on the forest floor, hundreds of them, marching without any organization at all, due to the trees that everywhere prevented any such order—"it is the Guard who have made the terrible error of attempting to fight their enemy upon his ground, and according to his methods."

Keera looked curious, but far less confused, having been given these thoughts by so expert a mind. "You must have fought in many wars yourself, my lord, to know such principles."

"Myself?" Caliphestros shook his head. "Not at all. Oh, I have witnessed many battles, true, but only as a man of medicine in the employ of one side or the other, who gave his service to heal the wounded, and to ease their pain. But to understand such things, truly? There are great minds, Keera, who have practiced warfare—generals, kings, and emperors—who have gathered their own and others' knowledge into books of instruction, which are available for any to read, and which I used in offering my advice to Yantek Ashkatar. And in this sense, we have been fortunate."

"Fortunate, old man?" Heldo-Bah echoed. "How is it 'fortunate' to find a full *khotor* of the Merchant Lord's Guard entering Davon Wood? Amusing, perhaps, but . . ."

Although Veloc once again shoved at his friend for daring to interrupt, Caliphestros turned and spoke to Heldo-Bah without anger or rancor: "Because it is now plainly evident that neither the Grand Layzin nor Lord Baster-kin has deigned to read any such books, whereas a truly wise soldier—such as Sentek Arnem, who is even now marching his *khotor* of Talons toward the Cat's Paw—would never have made such a mistake. It violates everything he was ever taught by his own tutor, Yantek Korsar, or by his own experience in fighting such tribes as the Torganians and the eastern marauders. He would have waited, and drawn Ashkatar out onto the Plain—and, as I say, despite the fact that the steel we have spent these many days forging is superior even to that carried by the Talons, the manner in which they fight, their discipline and organization, is something that requires years for large groups of men to learn—and its absence among the Guard shall prove as important as any grade of steel."

"Leaving only the small flaw," Heldo-Bah murmured, also, now, listening to the sounds of passing Guardsmen beneath the rocks atop which the three foragers and the pair who had become their traveling fellows were carefully hidden, "that the Guard are a vicious group of murderers, able to do more than a little damage to our warriors on their own."

"Some, perhaps," Caliphestros answered, with a shrug of his shoulders. "But in the end, for the few wounds the Bane may receive, these Guardsmen will trade their lives—and when Sentek Arnem does reach the Cat's Paw, he will be met by a scene of death and horror, of hundreds of Tall bodies in the Cat's Paw amid those poor Bane souls who took their lives in the river before we were able to determine a cause and a method of preventing the rose fever. And that horror will make him pause, unwilling to trade the best troops in his kingdom for a highly uncertain outcome. And then, we may find him ready to treat with us. But hush, now . . ." The old man brought his face in contact with the fur of Stasi's neck and cheek, burying it sidelong in that rich white coat, as if it gave him some sort of deep, even mystical comfort to do so: not only, Keera believed she could see, because of the danger that was so close about them on all sides, now, but because of the lingering yet still-unexplained hurt done to the old man's soul (nay, she thought, to his *heart*) by his encounter with the First Wife of Kafra, the woman called Alandra. "Let us be silent, or as silent as we can," the old man continued. "Further talk can only threaten our being discovered, and, as Heldo-Bah has said, even if these Guardsmen lack order and insight, they do not want for bloodlust."

Perhaps cheered at finally having his thoughts recognized as valid by the old man, even if in a somewhat less than direct or congratulatory manner, Heldo-Bah half-rose, producing the sword he had carried since meeting Caliphestros in one hand, and his gutting blade in the other. "Well, as to that," he whispered, "rest assured, you shall all be safe—I may not wander out into this madness, but the Moon help any Guards-man, or any five Guardsmen, who wander too close to these rocks. Stay low, all of you." He looked directly into Stasi's eyes. "And that includes you, my lovely," he said, before disappearing into the shadows only a short distance away.

Veloc turned in sudden shock. "Heldo-Bah!" he hissed, as loudly as he was able. "Don't be a fool—"

"Do not bother, Veloc," Caliphestros murmured; and when Veloc turned to the old man, he found to his surprise that the old man was smiling in true admiration. "You were right, Keera, in this as in most things: a profoundly irritating man, but possessed of great courage . . ." Stasi growled lowly at the disappearance of the third forager, and Cal-iphestros ran his hands deep into her fur, stroking and scratching and trying to calm her. "Take your ease, Stasi—this is one task for which our filthy friend is best suited—whereas *you* must remain here with me."

And this last statement, it seemed to Keera, as she lifted her eyes to determine the position of the Moon and thereby the time of night, was more a plea than a command . . .

The Moon had not traveled very far from where Keera first glimpsed it before the battle began. The encounter started where Caliphestros had said it likely would: near the Cat's Paw, thus ensuring that, once the whole of Baster-kin's *khotor* were in the Wood, they would not be able to flee back across the Fallen Bridge. Indeed, the foragers and Caliphestros would later learn that Ashkatar had ordered that any Tall given the responsibility of remaining in the rear of their force to hold the southern end of the bridge be dispatched first: this was not to be an encounter in which prisoners would be taken or cowards allowed to flee, but one of complete destruction, which would, therefore, not only allow the Bane to indulge their special loathing for the Merchant Lord's men, but serve as a warning—again, just as Caliphestros had said it would—to any other troops from Broken who were on their way to Davon Wood with the purpose of attacking and destroying the exile tribe.

Thus, the cries that echoed from the southern bank of the Cat's Paw, indicating that actual combat had been joined, were especially horrifying, produced not merely by wounded and dying men, but by the screams of those who were thrown down from the rocky heights into the violent riverbed below. This horror, of course, was no accident, but rather a key part of Ashkatar's plan, designed to make those Guardsmen in the Wood lose whatever small ability the forest had left them to organize their numbers into coherent ranks and conduct an effective resistance; and it served this purpose completely.

Of course, there were other varieties of horror with which the doomed Guardsmen were forced to contend; indeed, there were few if any that they escaped. It is the peculiar nature of the forest, and of primeval[†] forests such as Davon Wood in particular, to change in aspect as soon as night falls, and threats are heard, seen, or felt, into a place of infinite danger; and hard on the heels of this change, the interloper who finds himself stranded in what is without doubt the realm of some other force, realizes the extent of his error. Even the foragers atop the rocks had not truly realized the extent to which Ashkatar's painted warriors had established their presence in every part of the Wood; but following the first terrible screams that echoed up from the chasm beneath the Fallen

Bridge, and the subsequent drone of a Davon ram's horn being blown, every tree, rock, bush, or shadow seemed to disgorge one or more such brave souls. As always, unlike the forces of the Tall, the Bane fighters included women, more than ready and trained to inflict deadly punishment upon their enemies; and their cries, being the higher in pitch, quickly drove the men of Baster-kin's *khotor* into a kind of fear that bordered on madness.

And once this confused and unstable (indeed, given the darkness of the Wood, to which the eyes of the Guardsmen were not at all accustomed, this *nightmarish*) condition had been established, almost anything seemed possible. First, of course, Ashkatar's constant emphasis on vicious war cries from both his male and female warriors made it impossible for units of Broken soldiers to relay orders or to take any accurate measure of how many enemy forces were actually involved in the fight. In truth, the Bane were badly outnumbered; but terror is a mighty method of nullifying such imbalances of power. This effect was only increased by the fact that any attempt by a soldier of the Tall to call for aid instantly marked both the man in distress and those who dared raise their voices in response for death. Fear, again, is whipped into panic if a soldier fighting for his life on foreign ground feels that he cannot even communicate with his fellows without immediately being confronted with the image of an enemy whose body is painted to match the leaves and bark of the surrounding wild plants and trees, or, worse yet, the fur and teeth, feathers and beaks of the deadliest night creatures, and whose immediate attack, therefore, quite aside from being incomprehensibly loud and savagely noisy, is wild and almost bestial in its appearance as well as its violence. Such terrifying methods, if carried off with the skill of which the Bane were masters, could go a very long way toward counteracting differences in numbers, if those differences were not utterly overwhelming.

And then, of course, there was always the bloodshed itself, simple yet supremely effective gore, which Lord Baster-kin's Guard liked to think they understood, as a weapon, but which they had never truly seen demonstrated until that night. The sights, smells, and sounds of comrades being torn open and apart, dismembered and otherwise disfigured and dispatched, sapped the Guardsmen of what little real understanding they had of combat. When the forest floor became wet with blood in the middle of the night, as well as when the curiously horrifying colors and visions of human guts laid open to Moon- and torchlight were encountered, and a soldier was almost certain that the gore was that of his fellows, the man's usefulness in combat (especially if he was unfamiliar with the sight, as was nearly every Guardsman) was quickly cut down to almost nothing, and his primary concern shifted from inflicting punishment to somehow trying to make sure that his own blood, guts, and limbs were not added to the heaps and rivulets that had been loosed by swords, gutting blades, spearheads, crude iron halberds and axes, and daggers.

One can often hear it said, among posturing fools such as those young men who have long spent the better part of their lives in the Stadium in Broken, that some peacetime activity is "like a war," or even "is war"; but such only serves to demonstrate how far they have ever lived in remove from any true battlefield or other place of large-scale violence: for war, like all human activities related to the creation or termination of life, is unique, unique in its pain and fearfulness, of course, but unique, perhaps most of all, in its loneliness, as well as in each participant's terrible lack of certainty—unimaginable until the moment has arrived—of whether or not she or he will survive.

In this case, the sudden realization, felt as a group, that the Guard were in fact *not* more than a match for the Bane, and that their allotted time on this Earth and in this Life had abruptly expired, added an additional note of horror to the shrieks that increasingly escaped the men of Lord Baster-kin's creatures that night; and it was a type of cry that made even Stasi, who had seen so much terrible death in her comparatively short time upon the Earth, draw closer to Caliphestros, Keera, and even Veloc, as much to comfort her own soul as to make sure that her friends did not leave their positions and attempt to enter the fray that was taking place in the darkness of the woodland beneath the rocks that sheltered them all.

Finally, the Guardsmen's religion, their all-important faith in Kafra, failed them at the last. The soldiers of Lord Baster-kin's Guard had received special sanction from the God-King and the Grand Layzin of Broken before this particular undertaking—sanction not only represented by the beaten bronze bands that they wore clamped to their upper arms, but manifested in their grossly overconfident behavior as they marched into the Wood. Kafra, the priests had already assured the men of the

Guard, would provide them special protection and special power. And yet here they were, now, themselves, with death striking at them from out of the darkness at every turn and along every path—including and especially from above. The Bane tactic of dropping down to slash at the throats and other essential parts of their enemies' bodies in an even more sudden and shocking manner than could be managed from their very effective hiding places on the ground was wholly new and especially frightening, for Baster-kin's men; yet no matter how the latter called out to the god whose smiling countenance was depicted on the bands that encircled their arms, Kafra remained deaf to their pleas. The number of deaths among them—either from wounds or from being hurled over the cliffs above the Cat's Paw, below which their skulls and bodies would be shattered and mangled upon and overwhelmed by the deadly rocks and rushing waters of Hafften Falls or the *Ayerzess-werten*—mounted with astonishing speed, and this one relatively confined area of Davon Wood grew ever more littered by and soaked with the bodies, entrails, and blood of soldiers of the Tall.

In short, the encounter proceeded far more successfully than any member of the Bane tribe had dared wish for. For Caliphestros himself, along with Keera and Veloc, nothing demonstrated the triumph and even joy of the Bane troops more than did the heightening, almost mad laughter of Heldo-Bah, who quickly turned from simply keeping watch around the edges of the rock formation upon which his friends and the white panther lay hidden to merrily falling upon any passing Guardsman, whose weapons he delighted in overmatching or even cutting and breaking into pieces—just as Caliphestros had done to him when first they entered the old man's cave. Never was the file-toothed Bane's lust for revenge against the servants of Lord Baster-kin, the man he saw as the embodiment of all that was evil in Broken, that city that had used him so ill during his childhood, more amply displayed than during the night of the battle by the Cat's Paw, when his rage mounted to ever more reckless and gleeful heights. After each quick attack, Heldo-Bah would disappear back into the crevices in the great stone formation that sheltered the others, his lustful merriment almost impossible to contain.

It was hardly likely, given their complete and increasingly triumphant concentration on their slaughter of the Guardsmen, that any Bane would have noticed a lone pair of eyes and ears watching and listening to what was taking place on the woodland side of the river: but the young Guardsman to whom those eyes belonged, a member of the regular watch that patrolled the richest portion of the great Plain, who was as well an inexperienced youth who had been left behind by the larger column because he dared question the wisdom of marching all the other soldiers of the Guard into the Wood for a night attack, soon made his way back north through the grazing ground; and without knowing it, toward Sentek Arnem and the oncoming Talons . . .

$$3:\{viii:\}$$

Sixt Arnem, having gleaned all that he can from the terrified young member of Lord Baster-kin's Guard, receives a bewildering array of visitors . . .

I T HAD BEEN Sixt Arnem's firm intention, upon riding to and then beyond the eastern perimeter of the central camp that his Talons were continuing to establish on Lord Baster-kin's Plain, to take a very stern attitude while interviewing the only surviving member of the First *Khotor* of Lord Baster-kin's Guard; but when the commander of the army of Broken sees the condition of the youth he cannot help but relent from this posture. The Guardsman was but a few years older than Arnem's own son, Dagobert, and although he must ordinarily have been larger in stature than the sentek's boy, what the lad had seen and heard had made him draw into himself in every manner. Thus vividly reminded not only of his son, but of his wife and the strange peril he has been told that both she and Dagobert face in the Fifth District of Broken, Arnem crouches down to look the terrified youth full in the face. "Where *is* your home, son? Do you wish me to send word of your survival back to Broken along with my next packet of dispatches?"

The fearful youth shakes his head vigorously and fearfully. "I would not have my family know that I was not willing to follow my commander into the danger that lay across the river. I would not have them think me so disobedient and cowardly."

Arnem puts a hand to the boy's shoulder. "You are neither, Pallin. Discipline is a vital thing in an army; it can also be a deadly one. More often than not, I would agree that your speaking out was irresponsible. But in this instance?" Arnem looks down toward the line of the trees on the southern border of the Plain, now almost invisible in the growing darkness. "I cannot find it in me to call it so. For to have taken nearly five hundred drunken men into Davon Wood, when he also had every reason to believe that the Bane were fully aware of our people's intention to invade their homeland, was a decision that now places the blame for the disaster on your sentek—not on you. Although I sincerely doubt that the fool yet lives to assume that responsibility. Come, now—on your feet." The pallin obeys the order, slowly but in what passes for a soldierly manner. "Step closer to the light, and let my friend, here, who is a talented healer, examine you." Arnem indicates Visimar, and the cripple steps forward.

Visimar makes several satisfied sounds as he goes about inspecting those parts of the pallin's body that would be first to display any sign of either the rose fever or the Holy Fire, and each murmur seems to embolden the Guardsman, so much so that, after several moments have passed, he says:

"If you would not mind, Sentek Arnem—I should much rather march with your men than return to the city."

Arnem shakes his head, immediately and definitively. "There are many soldiers that would like to march with the Talons, Pallin. But our reputation is not based upon pride or arrogance. There are maneuvers that you must know, and through long training be able to execute quickly and unhesitatingly. Men's lives depend on your knowing such, as has already been demonstrated on this march. I understand your reluctance, but—as I say, I will give you notes vouching for your behavior, to be delivered to both your family and Lord Baster-kin. Be easy in spirit—there will be no recrimination. In addition, I will offer you this, Pallin—we'll tilt the table just a bit, so that the knucklebones† will be certain to roll in your favor. I shall state in my report that upon our arrival we were able to rescue you, and only you, from a rearguard action your *fauste* was conducting. I may even add that we were forced to pull you away from the combat, so heated was your blood. I think that should suffice."

The pallin looks to the ground uneasily. "If you will but hear one additional fact in confidence, Sentek, at some distance from these others, I shall do as you say, if you still think it wise."

Looking to the others and shrugging, Arnem indicates to them that they should remain where they are with a gesture of his hand, then walks off to the edge of the small world of light created by Akillus's torch.

By the time Arnem and the young Guardsman return, the older officer has apparently managed, whatever their secret conversation, to convince the pallin that his return will take place without punishment, if he will follow Arnem's original plan. "But I shall ask one favor of *you,* in return, Pallin," Arnem says, as he moves toward and then mounts the Ox. "Remain outside camp, while I go to my tent to secure you a mount and compose the dispatches we have discussed. My men will know the truth of what has taken place in the Wood soon enough—I do not want more rumors than I can manage flying about camp. Akillus, remain here with the pallin, and I shall send one of your scouts back with the horse and the reports, along with whatever rations they have prepared."

Akillus salutes, reluctantly but without question, and the pallin quickly does the same. Arnem offers them both a nod, and tries to smile reassuringly to the Guardsman.

"The soldier's life is not the Guardsman's, Pallin," the sentek says. "Particularly when you leave the walls of Broken. There's little enough use on the frontiers for making arrests and cracking skulls, to say nothing of watching over cattle. I am sorry that your first taste of large-scale action had to be so horrifying—but remember these truths the next time you feel tempted to castigate yourself." He laughs once, cajolingly. "And consider a change of services upon your return to Broken . . ." Arnem turns to his chief of scouts. "And don't go badgering the boy, Akillus," Arnem declares.

"Aye, Sentek," Akillus replies. "Come, Pallin—let's see what scraps of wood we can collect to make this torch something other than a source of light. It will help to keep the wolves back, even if the evening is warm . . ."

It is a generous attitude to adopt, of the type that Arnem and Niksar have long since learned to expect from the gregarious Akillus. Visimar, however, having been helped onto the saddle of his mare by Niksar, is impressed. "Akillus is indeed a rare man—you are to be congratulated for elevating him, Sixt Arnem."

"He is my left arm," Arnem agrees, smiling at Niksar as he does. "Now that Niksar has suspended his spying duties and become my unquestioned right . . ."

"Sentek!" the linnet protests, until he realizes that his commander jests.

Arnem smiles, wearily but genuinely, to his friend and comrade, and in moments the three riders have passed over the spiked ditch and similarly bristling eastern gateway in the protective barrier about camp that has been constructed with astonishing speed by the engineers of the Talons during the hours since the *khotor* arrived on the Plain. The officers' wine-red cloaks are lifted behind them by the western wind as they trot into camp, a martial image that is made all the more impressive when placed in direct contrast to Visimar's faded black and silver cloak. But even the latter is somehow strangely comforting, in its heightened implication of a perhaps arcane but no less lucky influence: for the old man has undeniably demonstrated both the power of the good fortune he brings to the troops, as well as his wisdom.

Arnem's tent, imposing from the outside, is perhaps more spare and severe within than one might expect from a man of such rank. Thick, quilted walls and modest personal quarters are to the rear, furnished only with a camp bed, writing table, and oil lamps, all of which are curtained off by warm, silencing hides that offer privacy from the tent's front section. That area is dominated by a large table that serves as both senior officers' mess and council center: all in all, a highly mobile structure that is all the commander needs, and more than he ever expected to be awarded, as a young man. He has no illusions—as do, say, the eastern marauders—about creating a traveling den of pleasure to serve as his home while campaigning. He is therefore unsurprised when he enters to find those same senior officers (save Akillus) all in attendance, talking quietly and respectfully among themselves, then standing to salute as he joins them: this is the principal purpose of his tent, to the sentek— professional—and the sooner the business of his men can be planned and executed, the sooner he may gain what little rest he will allow himself; and the sooner, too, will his assigned tasks be completed, and he himself be allowed to rejoin his family, high on Broken's mountain—

And yet, on this night, his usually reassuring thoughts of home are usurped by what he has been told concerning both his wife and his children by, first, Akillus, and, later, the young member of Lord Baster-kin's Guard: a most bizarre set of what the Guardsman referred to, not as rumors, but as confirmed facts, concerning some kind of a rebellion in the Fifth District, and of Isadora's and Dagobert's participation—even more, their leadership—of the uprising; and these are tales about which he intends to know far more, before he will make any move against a Bane enemy that cannot help but be in the full flush of victory over the most despised arm of their enemy . . .

Arnem waves a hand to his officers, urging them to sit. "I shall require a moment, gentlemen," he declares, never breaking stride as he heads for his personal quarters. "Therefore, be as you were, but make certain your reports are ready."

Once behind the curtain that screens his quarters from the council area, Arnem pauses to wash his face and hands in a plain brass basin of cold, clean water that the ever-silent, ever-reliable Ernakh has made sure to have ready. Running his hands through his hair, more to keep himself alert than for appearances, Arnem towels off any lingering water, places the moist, cool piece of cloth about his neck, and turns to lean over his camp table, taking two pieces of waiting parchment and a nub of charcoal and quickly composing the notes to Lord Baster-kin and the Guardsman's family that he promised the youth. Instructing Ernakh to have a scout deliver these reports, as well as to relieve Akillus, that the latter may represent his own men at the council table, and making sure that Ernakh orders the scout to take some of the food that is being prepared outside the tent with him, Arnem dispatches the *skutaar* out the back of his tent, and finally returns through the hide curtain to sit in the lone camp chair that occupies the head of the council table. At last allowing himself to breathe deeply with some small relief, he then eyes the expectant faces around him, noticing first his chief archer.

"Fleckmester," he says, with a slightly surprised although approving tone. "I take it your ability to attend this council means that you are satisfied with the defensive dispositions of your archers at the Fallen Bridge?"

"Indeed I am, Sentek," Fleckmester replies. "I do not doubt that the Bane still have silent eyes in the trees along the southern bank, observing our every move; but any attempt by them to cross the bridge into the Plain now would be as foolish as was the Guard's original march into the Wood."

"Hmm," Arnem noises. "I wish I could say that I doubted you, and that there might in fact *be* an easy way for our men to get across the Cat's

Paw and achieve our object as originally stated; but the Bane have proved even more than usually clever, during this action." Preparing himself for the announcement that he is about to make, Arnem takes the towel that is about his neck and grips it tight, as if it will support an overburdened mind, and says in a louder voice, "I'm certain that by now you all know what one or two of you have learned firsthand, and several others have surmised; the true identity of our guest on this march."

The sentek holds out a hand to the cripple, who sits to his left, at the first seat on that side of the table. Noises of general assent make their way from officer to officer, but few if any are either surprised or uneasy in nature.

"Aye, we have discovered it, Sentek, and have been discussing it," says one Linnet Crupp,[†] with whom Arnem has seen long service. The sentek holds this scar-faced man in high regard, not only for his mastery of *ballistae,* but for the fact that he has ever shown as little true fervor for the faith of the golden god as has Arnem himself. "Can you *truly* be he?" Crupp continues, smiling, now, as he turns to Visimar. "The same demon-man with whose name I once frightened my children into obedience on nights when they were especially unruly?"

Visimar is sipping a cup of wine and kneading his leg, which has begun suffering from a special pain that, he long ago learned, was and remains a signal of the distant onset of a rain.[‡] Given the generally warm, dry conditions of this spring, it is a sensation he has not felt for some time, and would readily have done without for a good while longer: he cannot yet know (despite all his seeming prophetic power) that the rain's arrival will actually be of vital use to his own and his former master's secret efforts to undermine the kingdom of Broken.

"I would gladly have had my name never gain such notoriety, amusing as it may now seem, Linnet," the old man says, as congenially as his discomfort will allow. "If such would have meant living without the decade of pain that I have endured."

Light laughter—most of it easy, some of it guarded—moves about the table, at which the forward opening of the tent is pulled aside to allow the entrance of several pallins, who bear wooden platters upon which sit roasted joints and slabs of beef, surrounded by various mounds of fire-baked root vegetables and stacks of unleavened, rock-fried pieces of bread. The sight is sudden and welcome, bringing immediate cheers of gratitude and anticipation. Such is the clamor that Arnem must shout to make himself heard by the lead bearer:

"Pallin! You are certain that these roots and this bread consist solely of our own supplies, and have not been gathered locally—and that none bore the marks of which Visimar warned you before they were prepared?"

The pallin nods his head with the kind of smile that has proved a rare sight, on this campaign. "Aye, Sentek," he replies. "But we dared not keep the stores any longer, given the time we have been on the march and the molds that our *guest*"—the young soldier inclines his head in Visimar's direction—"tells us are more likely to form with coming changes in the weather. We in the baggage train have been waiting for the right moment to make use of them—and with camp made secure, this seemed as good a one as any."

"You see, fellow Talons?" Linnet Taankret announces with a broad grin, wiping his carefully sculpted mustache and beard further from his lips, so that they will not become tainted with food and the grease of the beef, and tucking one corner of a large kerchief beneath his chin, that the piece of fabric may protect his ever-spotless tunic. "We no sooner have confirmation of Visimar's true identity, than we can enjoy more than dried meat and rock-hard, flat biscuits—I always knew that this old madman, whatever his name, was a breathing and benevolent talisman!"

"I hope that your good humor will last the meal," calls Arnem, "for there are yet more remarkable facts to be revealed, Taankret. For now, however—let us eat. No more than one cup of wine or beer per man, however!" he adds, pointing to the serving pallins who have begun distributing the drinks to each officer.

"A *deep* cup, I hope, Sentek," says Akillus, as he enters the tent to the shouted greetings of the other officers, and takes a place at the bench that runs along the foot of the table.

"Aye, deep I will allow," Arnem replies. "But the men will have their wits about them, tonight, and I have no intention for my officers to be in any worse condition."

One linnet-of-the-line, an engineer called Bal-deric,[†] whom Visimar has noticed and spoken to more than once on this march (largely because the man is without most of the lower portion of his left arm, lost to a mishap during an excavation that employed large, oxen-driven machinery, and has substituted for it an ingenious assembly of leather fittings, sections of hardwood tree limbs, and steel wheels and wires),[†] now signals to the older man, then leans back to use his good right hand to pass Visimar a small piece of cotton containing a tightly packed ball of herbs and medicines. Under the sound of the other officers' conversation, Balderic congenially says to his fellow in suffering, "It is the approach of rain, is it not, Visimar? My arm behaves in just the same way. Break this into pieces and swallow it with your wine. A concoction of my own, developed some years ago—I'm sure you will be able to guess its ingredients, and will also find them most efficacious. But by the heavens, do not let any priest of Kafra know that I have given it to you!"

Visimar smiles and takes the packet gratefully, then leans behind the intervening men to say, "I thank you, Bal-deric—and perhaps, if we come out of this business alive, we may discuss the construction of some better substitute for my missing leg than the admittedly crude support I carved myself, after the first year or so of my changed condition—for I have long admired the device you have created to take the place of your arm."

Bal-deric smiles and nods, and Visimar turns back around, relieved to note that Arnem does not appear to have caught any of this exchange.

As the very last of twilight turns to utter darkness outside the tent, the officers within, most still expressing words of surprise and congratulation to the ever more contented Visimar as they at the same time voice their complete satisfaction with the provisions that have been placed before them, inevitably begin to lose interest in the food, and turn instead to debates about the best and fastest way for their campaign to proceed. Arnem has intended for this to happen; it is the reason for his having limited each man to one cup of drink. And yet, even he, the confident and ever-resourceful commander, finds himself perplexed as to precisely how he will reveal the next portion of his plan—for it does not involve the action desired most by his officers, direct military confrontation, but something very different indeed. Eventually, knowing that he cannot put the matter off, he slams the pommel of his short-sword on the table, and begins to demand reports from each of his officers about the dispositions and moods of their respective units.

"I assure you, Sentek," declares Taankret, "when you have decided precisely how to take the Talons into Davon Wood, they will be as prepared for the task as they were to fight their way out of that madness in Esleben—and the *Wildfehngen* will be no less ready to lead."

Arnem glances for an instant at Visimar, who gives the slightest indication with a movement of his head that the sentek must proceed along some course that is, apparently, known only to the two of them. "That 'madness in Esleben,' Taankret, is precisely the point. You may wonder why I ordered the establishment of what would seem so forward a position on our own ground, rather than waiting until we crossed the Cat's Paw."

"None among my scouts has wondered as much," Akillus declares solemnly. "Not given what fills that river. I do not know what black arts the Bane are practicing, in their defense, but . . . we will need a sure sanctuary on our own soil, for this campaign."

"Assuming that there is to *be* any more of a campaign," Arnem announces, to the sudden consternation of all present.

"But Sentek," Bal-deric declares. "It was our understanding that such were our orders. It was well known throughout the streets of Broken, before we departed, that these were our objects: the final invasion of Davon Wood, and the destruction of the Bane tribe . . ."

"Yes," Arnem replies. "It was well known—by those who had not seen what we have seen on this march."

"But—Yantek Korsar gave his life precisely because he *refused* such an order," Niksar says carefully.

The sentek nods. "And I confess that I did not know why, at the time, Reyne," Arnem replies. "But on this journey, much has been revealed—much that provides us with answers to that as well as other questions. Certainly the horrific fate of the *khotor* of Lord Baster-kin's Guard tells us why the yantek did not wish us to enter the Wood: in that wilderness, our superior numbers apparently mean little or nothing, so well have the Bane mastered combat within the forest."

"But—" A young linnet sitting next to Akillus is, like most of his comrades, puzzling with the dilemma determinedly. "But the Bane also attack outside the Wood. In terrible ways."

"The Outragers do," Visimar replies. "But the Bane army? We have no evidence that they do so, or that they ever have."

"Then do they not deserve chastisement, for allowing the Outragers such vicious liberty?" comes another voice.

Arnem answers quickly: "Do all the subjects of Broken deserve similarly stern treatment, for the equally foul behavior of the Merchant Lord's Guard, or for the behavior of a few nobles who excuse their murderous pursuit of the Bane under the title of 'sport'?"

The sentek takes a few steps away from the council table, toward his own quarters; and for the first time, his officers notice that an additional, large, reversed piece of hide has been hung from the heavy curtain that separates the two areas. He tears away a light covering of fabric from this hide, to reveal a detailed map, not only of the northern side of the Cat's Paw, but of much of Davon Wood—enough to show, after generations of searching, what appears to be the general position of Okot.

"Sentek . . . ," breathes one round-bodied, and equally round-faced, officer called Weltherr,[†] Arnem's chief mapmaker. So fascinated is the man that he cannot help but rise up and move toward the image, lifting a hand to touch it, almost as if he believes it unreal. "But this map includes not only locations of communities, but features of topography, as well. With such a rendering, we could easily complete our original task: the invasion of Davon Wood, and the destruction of the Bane and Okot."

"I do not believe so, Weltherr," Arnem says, returning to the map. "Yantek Korsar, I have come to see, was not only speaking of physical features of the Wood, in his final warning—he also referred to the *tactics* of the Bane. Remember what happened to Lord Baster-kin's men, after all—they were destroyed on ground with which we have long been fairly familiar, within sight of the Cat's Paw. It was the manner, not the location, of their action that was their undoing. And I do not mean for the same to happen to the Talons."

"Sentek," Akillus says, quietly fascinated. "You still have not told us how you were able to compose such a map."

Arnem breathes heavily once. "I did not compose it—but to hear who did, I must exact a special pledge from all of you: nothing that you are about to hear will ever be repeated outside our company. If any man feels he cannot abide by such an oath, let him leave now." Allowing the men a moment to absorb this statement, Arnem eventually continues, in an even quieter tone, as he slowly strides around the table: "I shall not ask of you anything that could be construed as genuinely treasonous; but as we all know, strange things have taken place during this campaign, and it may be that their explanation will implicate persons in high places in Broken. Therefore, remember that our oath as soldiers is to our kingdom and our sovereign. And keeping faith with that oath will likely lead us, now, into territory more unmapped than the most distant corners of Davon Wood, if we follow the plan that I will suggest. We begin with questions, to be followed by facts: did it not strike any of you as strange that the Merchant Lord should have dispatched a full *khotor* of his own Guard to reinforce the patrols on his Plain, much less attack the Bane within the Wood, just when, by my calculation, we had learned the truth of matters in Esleben and the other towns on the Daurawah Road, and were on our way to that latter port, where we would find even worse conditions prevailing? Almost as if he did not *want* the army to play the crucial role in Broken's attack on the Bane?"

"Aye," Taankret replies, a little ruefully. "Although I would not have been the first to speak of it. Could he have been ignorant of what we were discovering, Sentek?"

"You know my habits, Taankret," Arnem answered. "I sent dispatches to the noble lord throughout our march. And Niksar's brother, the unfortunate Donner, had been sending pleas for help for weeks. All unanswered. And then—" Arnem reaches into a pouch in his leather armor, and produces a small handful of kernels of some kind of grain. "—there were *these* . . ." He tosses the kernels into the middle of the table, and at once, each officer half-rises to get a closer look. "Do *not*, any of you, touch them!" the sentek says, going to wash his own hands.

"What can they be, Sentek?" asks a young junior linnet, who is clearly disturbed by the turn the conversation is taking. Arnem, returning from his basin, turns to his left. "Visimar?"

The cripple is confident in his answer: "Winter rye. Such as is stored in almost every town and village in Broken, and was evident in abundance in Esleben."

"But," Bal-deric says, puzzling it out, "winter rye? We are well into spring. Why should the Eslebeners still be hoarding winter rye, when it was likely needed in the city, if not the provinces, during the last and most severe winter?"

"A question that perplexed me, as well," Arnem answers, "until my conversation with the unfortunate Donner. But our own farmers and merchants are no longer, it seems, the sole source for winter grain, nor even the principal source—northern raiders are bringing it into the kingdom, having plundered it in far-off lands, and selling it to factors of the Merchant Lord: including, I regret to say, Lord Baster-kin himself, who believes that our provincial farmers and their representatives have begun to ask prices too great for the treasury of the kingdom to bear." Soft murmuring again circulates around the table, until Arnem goes on: "Akillus—you saw the raiders' ships, or what was left of those vessels, in the calmer portions of the Cat's Paw, as well as in the Meloderna—correct?"

Akillus nods certainly. "Aye, Sentek. And it did not seem clear precisely what the Bane had to do with their destruction."

"The Bane had nothing to do with such," Arnem replies. "Our own people destroyed them when they became aware that the merchants in Broken had found illegal, even treacherous ways to frustrate their attempts to raise prices. This grain, when spoilt, produces a poison that brings about the same disease that we identify after battles as the fire wounds—"

The murmuring at the table turns suddenly more fearful, yet Arnem pushes on: "Yet these are not kernels of the grain recently brought into our kingdom by our enemies. These are taken from the storehouses of towns such as Esleben. Supplies which those unfortunate townspeople and citizens have themselves been consuming, because they refused to underbid thieves in the competition for the grain that goes on to feed and guarantee the security of the city of Broken."

"And so," Fleckmester says, slowly reasoning the matter out, "it was the *fire wounds* that drove the people of Esleben mad—the fire wounds, or whatever name the poison takes in its other forms—"

"*Gangraenum,*" Visimar says quietly.

Fleckmester nods to the cripple, comprehending the term not a bit, but knowing that, if Visimar says it is so, it must indeed *be* so.

"The fire wounds," Arnem explains further, "are but one form of a disease that has many names. The *Lumun-jani* call it the *Ignis Sacer,* the 'Holy Fire.' To the Bane, it is 'Moonfire,' the cause behind the most terrible forms of death among humans and animals—as your men saw up and down the river, Akillus."

"But this," Fleckmester continues, drawing out the logic of the argument, "this means that some of the most important things that have made our kingdom strong are now—because of the stubbornness of the people of the provinces, in combination with the avarice of the Merchants' Council—are now *weakening* it . . . ?"

"That is the predominant fact, Linnet," Visimar replies. "In so many parts of this tale . . ."

"And it is now clear," Arnem says, "that this weakness is afflicting most if not all of the provinces. Not simply because of what we observed outside Daurawah, but because, Visimar assures me, supplies of the only known medicines that Nature offers for the disease are being harvested in great quantities throughout those same regions. Furthermore, I have received *written* reports from several sources that the disease is thus rife."

"But," Weltherr says, his voice trembling with newborn fear, "we have been told that the plague was a weapon, placed in Broken's water by Bane spies and agents."

"And yet, were this so," Niksar answers slowly, "would we now know that not only are *two* diseases at work in Broken, but that one of them afflicts the Bane, as well as ourselves?"

"But are we so certain that one of these same diseases is at work in the Wood?" Taankret says.

Visimar glances uneasily at Arnem, who, not wishing to show any sign of the uncertainty he indeed feels, at this moment, nods his head once. The cripple then reaches down to the right side of his chair, to a pouch he has long been carrying; and from it he withdraws all the objects that were entrusted by Caliphestros to the great eagle owl, Nerthus. Placing them on the table, he identifies each in turn (although many present need no introduction to the golden arrow of the priests of Kafra) and further explains the revealing manner of each plant's harvesting, its function in first identifying the origin of the current troubles and its role in the treatments for the diseases that are loose.

"This is all very well, Visimar," Bal-deric says, when the old man has finished his statement, "but how come you by such knowledge, when you have been marching with us these many days?"

"From the same source as came this map," Visimar replies.

Bal-deric eyes them both. "And you, Sentek?" he continues, coming dangerously close to impertinence. "How can you know so much of what is taking place in the city, if no royal or merchant couriers have been observed bringing information?"

"No 'royal or merchant' couriers, Bal-deric," Arnem answers. "But I *have* received private couriers—from Lady Arnem."

"*Lady Arnem?*" Taankret bellows, throwing down a chop of beef and pulling his kerchief from his chin as he stands defiantly. "Has someone dared offend your wife, Sentek?"

"I fear so, Taankret," the sentek replies measuredly, not wishing to allow the passion of the council to run too far before its purpose. "In fact, we have just learned that Lady Arnem has been accused of leading a rebellion that has flared up throughout the Fifth District—accused by none other than Lord Baster-kin himself. I was as reluctant to acknowledge such behavior on his lordship's part as was anyone. But we have since discovered that the district has been sealed off, and is under effective siege, with veterans of our army leading the younger men and women in resistance."

Arnem quickly learns that he has calculated correctly: like Taankret, nearly all of his officers dispense with their food and drink, stand in indignation, and begin to utter loud condemnations of any such actions. Isadora is, the sentek has correctly reasoned, the one figure whose fate could cause such a reaction; and it is their reaction, once Arnem has quieted his officers, that will dispose them to hear even more shocking intelligence.

"I assure you again, gentlemen," the sentek says, "no one has been more disturbed by all these revelations than have I." Arnem remains seated, attempting to display courage even in a situation that threatens his family and therefore himself. "But there is more. The dispatches from our city do come from my wife, but these pieces of evidence"— he holds a hand out toward the withering plants and the golden arrow—"these have been entrusted to us by another source entirely. A source whose continuing existence, I daresay, many of you will not credit as possible."

"If the honor of Lady Arnem, as well as that of our own veterans, is being questioned," declares Weltherr, "then I assure you, Sentek, we shall credit *anything* as being possible."

Silence again dominates the interior of the tent, as Arnem glances at Visimar one last time; then the commander leans further toward the center of the table on his right elbow, and all his officers lean in toward him. Finally, in a hushed whisper, the sentek says:

"We have received this aid from none other than . . . *Caliphestros* . . ."

Arnem's officers recoil as if each has been struck in the face by some invisible hand; yet before any of them can utter so much as a shocked echo, loud cries of alarm are heard from without the tent, and one of the pallins who served the officers their meal rushes through the quilted entrance.

"Damn it all, Pallin!" the sentek declares, now rising to his own feet in indignation. "You had better possess vital intelligence, indeed, for you to burst in on a closed council of war unannounced!"

"I—that is—yes, I think I do, Sentek!" the pallin says, standing straight as he can and saluting. "Warriors have been observed by the men in our outposts, approaching camp!"

"*Warriors?*" Arnem says. "More of Lord Baster-kin's Guard, perhaps, come down from the mountain to see what has befallen their comrades?"

"No, sir," the pallin says. "Only one wagon approaches from the north!"

Arnem looks suddenly annoyed again. "Well, then, why all this shrieking about 'warriors'—"

"The warriors approach from the *south,* sir!" the pallin says. "A large body of Bane infantry—and under a flag of truce!"

"Truce, Sentek?" Taankret says, his skepticism plain. "The Bane understand as little of honorable truce as they do of mercy."

Visimar now gets to his one good and one wooden leg, gripping the table for support. "I really must disagree, Linnet Taankret. These are myths, told by the Merchants' Council over many generations, until honorable men like yourself believe them. The Bane *do* understand truce, and mercy, as well."

"How can you know this, cripple?" Bal-deric asks.

"By the same means I have come by these pieces of evidence, Bal-deric," Visimar answers. "From my onetime master, who rides, now, with the Bane. It is he who has arranged this truce; he has sent me word of as much, and that the Bane have been willing to comply with it—some reluctantly, some less so. These are the facts of which I can assure you."

"Oh?" Taankret says, still unconvinced. "And how have you been able to learn these supposèd facts, Visimar?"

"Through methods and messengers that, again, you shall scarce credit, ere you see proof of them," comes the cripple's answer. "But be assured of this: no 'sorcery' or otherworldly power has been employed."

Taankret's demeanor softens. "True enough, old man—for if you truly possessed such powers, you would likely have used them in our, or at least your own, defense before now."

"I am glad to hear you apply such logic to our predicament, Linnet,"

Visimar answers, relieved. "There is much I could and would have done to aid your brave comrades, were I what the Kafran priests claim. But I, like my master, can nonetheless use the knowledge and abilities we *do* possess, to help our cause—and so I beg you, receive this flag of truce, and let us speak with the party that approaches."

"That, we shall do," Arnem announces; and yet, despite his decisive words, his manner appears genuinely perplexed. "What troubles me most immediately, however, is this single wagon that approaches from Broken. Pallin!" The young trooper who has brought the information straightens up, once more fearful of another berating. "You know nothing further of what this conveyance carries, and why?"

"No, Sentek," the pallin answers. "Our information was only—"

At just that instant, another young scout enters the tent, as respectfully as some apparently momentous news will allow. He spots Akillus and, despite being covered in dust that has become mud by its mixture with horse and human sweat, moves to his commander at once. They exchange a few apparently astonishing pieces of information, and then Akillus dismisses the man quickly.

"Sentek," Akillus says, "I have now learned the identities of those in the wagon, which evidently departed Broken with the greatest secrecy." Akillus pauses, steeling his nerve. "It is your own children, Sentek."

"My—own . . . ," Arnem whispers. And it takes him many moments more before he can continue: "*All* of them? *Without* their mother?"

"The scout counted but four," Akillus says, his heart now heavy with the pain he has inflicted on the man he most admires in all the army; indeed, in all the world. "And your wife is not with them. In fact, their guardian, the driver of the wagon, is perhaps the most peculiar choice it would be possible to imagine. It is the seneschal of the *Kastelgerd* Basterkin, Sentek—the man Radelfer. And, as I say, he displays no threat toward the children. Rather the opposite. He seems to be protecting them."

Looking up suddenly, Arnem tries as best he is able to regain his composure. "Well—we face a crucial meeting, gentlemen; and my own difficulties must be left out of it." His voice grows stronger, and he stands. "Each man to his command, and quickly, but be certain that each of your men understands that he is both ordered and obliged to observe the formal terms of truce, until he receives my personal order releasing him from those duties."

Arnem's officers all stand to attention, salute smartly, and depart the tent. The sounds of commands being shouted and units being marshaled begin an ever-louder but always ordered chorus, outside the tent, as Visimar remains behind to study Arnem's continuing reaction to the momentous intelligence he has received. Finally, Sixt Arnem murmurs only, "Kafra's stones . . . ," and almost immediately afterward stands and shouts: *"Ernakh!"* Before the briefest instant has passed, the *skutaar* appears from Arnem's private quarters in the rear of the tent, and presents himself to his lord with almost as much bearing as the officers who have just departed. "You heard all that has taken place?"

"Aye, master," Ernakh replies, eager to serve.

"Then ride north to meet the wagon," the commander says, "and guide it here—*directly* here, to the rear of my tent. The children know and trust you, and even if this seneschal does not, their trust will bring about his compliance. Am I clear?"

Nodding rapidly, Ernakh salutes, then runs out of the tent to his waiting horse.

Turning to Visimar after the boy has departed, Arnem says, "Well, cripple—here is a development about which neither your master nor his faithful birds could have warned us."

"No, Sentek," Visimar replies, having felt it expedient, some few days before the evening on which this evening's council of war took place, to tell the commander the truth of Caliphestros's remarkable avian allies, so that Arnem might know just how the old man was receiving messages from his onetime teacher. "My master had a remarkable ability to communicate with creatures other than men, when I served him. And I would wager that ten years in the wilderness have done nothing save add to it. But as to why this lone wagon should be coming—at such speed, and with the passengers and driver it bears—no creature, I suspect, be it man, bird, or other, could or can guess. Not until its arrival . . ."

"You may be right," Arnem says, pulling back the rear entrance to the end of his tent and gazing into the dark northern landscape. "Certainly, *I* cannot yet say—but before this night is done, I will determine what, by *Hel,* is taking place here . . ."

┌─────────────┐
│ **3:{ix:}** │
└─────────────┘

The initial and extraordinary meeting of enemies and friends in the
camp of the Talons, and the arrival of unexpected guests . . .

THE VISITORS WHO WALK under a broad white banner of truce stop in a wide line some fifty paces from the southern entrance to Arnem's main camp; and at this distance, the Talons—who have prepared themselves for a fight, if a fight is to be offered—can discern that their opponents are not so many in number as was first reported; it was merely the order of their march that made them appear so impressive, as well as certain almost unbelievable participants in it.

At their center, the legless "sorcerer," Caliphestros, rides astride the shoulders of the most legendary animal, not only in Davon Wood, but in Broken, as well: the famed white panther, who escaped the last of the great Tall panther hunts, that of the present Lord Baster-kin. On this astonishing pair's right, proudly holding no more seemingly lethal weapon than an impressive whip, is a man that Visimar knows to be Yantek Ashkatar, commander of the Bane army. Yet no *khotor* or even *fauste* of troops encircle this renowned leader for his protection: only a dozen of what any experienced soldier can see are his senior officers walk behind him, and all keep their weapons sheathed. At the end of this side of Caliphestros's apparent escort are three more faces, the male pair of which the Talons know only too well: they are the ever-troublesome, ever-enraging, yet ever-formidable Heldo-Bah, as well as the handsome but heavily resented Veloc, who has cuckolded more than a few Tall soldiers who now stand safely behind their spiked ditch, as well as their hastily but expertly constructed palisade. The female figure at the end of this wing, meanwhile, is the renowned tracker Keera, looking not only wise, but also impressive, even formidable, and therefore, perhaps unexpectedly, like the perfect anchor for the left side of the assembly.

On the opposite side of Caliphestros and the white panther are, first, a group of humbly dressed, elderly and bearded men who exude wisdom, and must, Visimar therefore reasons, be the Groba Elders, and then less than a *fauste* of Bane warriors, male and female, whose swords are sheathed and who, it can only be supposed, are the Elders' only official escort.

For long moments, this delegation must remain where it stands, for Sixt Arnem is still within his tent, awaiting the arrival of the cart that carries his children from the north before he will join the conference: it being always best to know the true disposition of one's own countrymen and allies before attempting to negotiate with one's enemies. This being the case, it becomes the duty of Niksar and Visimar to play chief emissaries, and to depart by foot from their camp to greet their visitors, followed by Taankret, Bal-deric, Weltherr, Crupp, Akillus (who feels it only right to stay in his saddle, in order to balance the scales of the meeting just a bit), and a few other linnets, all of whom have been placed under the strictest orders to bring only minimal weapons, and to keep even these sheathed or slung so long as there is no trouble. This does not prevent Fleckmester and his men from keeping their arrows secretly nocked and at the ready as they observe from the bristling ditch, of course; but the master archer issues this order on his own authority, for neither Niksar nor especially Visimar believes it will in any manner prove necessary.

Nevertheless, the representatives of the kingdom of Broken (if such they truly are, any longer, after all they have heard and seen on their current campaign) approach the line of Wood-dwellers and their allies cautiously, particularly when they see the utterly fiendish expression on Heldo-Bah's face, try as the gap-toothed forager may to exhibit his most somber behavior. When the two lines of opposing representatives are some ten paces apart, Niksar holds his hand up, and all become still where they stand. Searching the group before him, Arnem's aide says, not without some admiration:

"I see no Outragers among you—a gesture, I wonder, or a deception?"

The Groba Father turns to Caliphestros, indicating that the latter will be best suited to speak for their delegation, and the legless old man says, "A gesture, I assure you—for none you see here have any great affection for that particular group of the Moon priestess's servants." Turning quickly to his onetime acolyte, Caliphestros cannot repress a smile, tinged with sadness as it may be. "Well, old friend—the years have been as kind to you as they have to me, I see."

Visimar returns the smile. "But have not swayed my loyalties, master," he says. "I am glad to see you, in *whatever* condition."

"And I you, rest assured," Caliphestros replies. "But what of Sentek Arnem? Surely we cannot proceed without him."

"No," Niksar says, his eyes even more transfixed by the white panther (as indeed are all those of the officers of Broken) than they are by the man who was Second Minister in their kingdom when most of them were children and a heretical sorcerer by the time they became young men. "But he should not be long. He has received new intelligence from Broken that may affect this parley. From the seneschal of the clan Baster-kin himself."

Caliphestros's eyes go suddenly wide, and a smile of an entirely differ-ent sort—one that unnerves Niksar, who knows nothing of the infamous outcast's past dealings with the Merchant Lord and his servants—makes its way into his features. *"Radelfer?"* the old man asks. "Is this true, Visi-mar?"

"I myself have not seen him, master," Visimar replies. "But while we wait for the sentek's arrival, he suggested that we might pass the time with preliminaries."

"Well?" Heldo-Bah suddenly queries, falling flat upon his back. "Who's for knucklebones?"

"Heldo-Bah!" the Groba Father says. "There are protocols to be fol-lowed!"

"Well, Father," the troublesome forager replies, bringing himself up on his elbows. "I'm simply saying, if we're going to sit out here in the sun wasting time, why not cast a few rounds? What *other* sorts of 'protocols' for simply marking time do you suppose we might discover that we have in common?"

Veloc claps a hand to his forehead. "Each time I think he has reached the limits of appalling behavior," he announces to both sides in the nego-tiation, "there is some new offense. And I, as his friend, must apologize for it . . ."

But, because no other suggestions as to how to mark the duration of Sentek Arnem's absence are offered, the two lines of representatives con-tinue to face each other stone-facedly for a few moments more, listening to Heldo-Bah rattle the set of bones he keeps in a sack looped to his belt, until finally, Akillus and several other Broken linnets take the forager at his word, and a game of knucklebones breaks out over the objections of both the Groba and Niksar. Yet these more senior representatives are in turn quieted, in the first instance by Caliphestros, and then by Visimar, each of whom has seen the chance for informal good relations to be opened by the game. So strange does the sight become that Fleckmester's men, a little out of envy and a little out of greed, begin to look back toward their sentek's tent, in an effort to see if they might not be granted permission to join in the gambling. This causes the ever more bewildered Fleckmester himself (who in truth would join in the game himself, if he could) to glance back to Arnem's tent, as well, where, he sees, an ordinary laborer's wagon has appeared at the back entrance.

"Eyes forward, boys, eyes forward," Fleckmester tells the troops who man the camp's southern fortifications, be they archers or no. "We must continue to ensure that, however things may look upon the Plain, the safety of our comrades is guaranteed. As for what is taking place in the sentek's tent, however . . ." He glances at the quilted walls once more. "That is not our concern, nor is it possible for us to imagine . . ."

What is taking place within the sentek's tent is, on the one hand, a wholly ordinary and domestic scene—a man being reunited with all, save one, of his children—and on the other, an extraordinary one: for the fact that Radelfer has been the children's guide out of the city would seem to indicate that something not only unusual but, perhaps, treacherous has taken place within Broken's walls. The seneschal of the most powerful clan in the kingdom should not have to flee like a criminal from those confines, any more than should the offspring of the kingdom's supreme military commander: yet this appears to be precisely what has happened. Arnem's children have already related to their father (for the greater part through Anje's words) the tale of how their mother attempted to alert the Merchant Lord to the source of the rose fever in the Fifth District, and was met in return with ultimatums, siege, and talk of criminality. Throughout this account, Radelfer has stood at attention near the closed rear entryway of the tent without comment: Arnem knows that the seneschal, despite his current employment by Baster-kin, was once a member of the Talons; and that he must have formed, given the two posts, opinions as to what is happening. The sentek rightly suspects that Radelfer's momentary reason for keeping sentinel is primarily to ensure the safety of the sentek and his children, as well as to prevent any besides Arnem himself from hearing the strange story told by the children.

"But Mother was *right*," Anje declares. "The strange water under the southwestern wall of the city *was* the cause of the rose fever, and once the people in that part of the city stopped using it, the fever ceased to spread."

"It's true, Father," says Golo. "But, instead of being rewarded for helping the people, Lord Baster-kin said the God-King and the Grand Layzin had decreed that Mother, and anyone who had or continued to assist her, should be outlaws—even Dagobert!—and that our district should be cut off from the rest of the city and destroyed."

"Wait, now, Golo!" objects the pious young Dalin; and then he turns to Arnem. "We do not know that these orders came from the God-King and the Grand Layzin themselves, Father."

"Your son speaks truly, Sentek," Radelfer says, quietly but firmly, from the shadowy rear of the tent. "We know no such thing . . ."

Emboldened, Dalin continues: "Only Lord Baster-kin himself visited the place where the unhealthy water flowed, only he argued with Mother, and only his men played any part in cutting the district off from the rest of the city. The sentek of the regular army who usually watches over that section of the walls—Sentek Gerfrehd, he told us is his name—is a good and obedient man, with whom Mother speaks, from time to time. And he knows that he is not allowed to attack his fellow citizens of Broken, even in the Fifth District, simply because the Merchant Lord wishes it. That is a command that must first come from the God-King, *and* have your own approval—and it has not been given either of these things."

"Gerfrehd," Arnem muses quietly. "Yes, your mother has written to tell me of their conversations, and I was pleased, for I know the man well—as honorable an officer as has ever held high rank in the regular army . . ." The sentek then quickly and silently glances up to Radelfer, who simply nods once in return, as if to say, *Yes—it is as complex and bizarre as it seems* . . .

"Which is why I do not understand why we were forced to leave home, like common criminals," Dalin complains.

"Oh, most *un*-common, surely, Master Dalin," Radelfer offers with a small smile, raising the sentek's estimation of the man. "Allow yourselves that much, at least."

But the attempt at friendly humor is lost on Dalin: "I don't care!" he states emphatically. "I only know that I have been forced further away from my duties to the God-King."

"*Dalin . . . ,*" Sixt Arnem warns, trying not to be too stern, but having heard enough.

Young Gelie has stayed on her father's knee since she and her siblings arrived in the tent, and now declares, as emphatically as is her custom, "Mother was doing much good for the district, Father, but the entire situation really did become frightening—Lord Baster-kin's men built their wall so quickly, I was afraid that we would be captured forever! If it had not been for Radelfer—"

"And that is another thing," Dalin says, not a little suspiciously. "Why should the Merchant Lord's own seneschal have defied his orders and made himself an outlaw, simply to help Mother?"

"Oh, don't be such a clever little brat," Golo says. "Wasn't it obvious that the situation was quickly becoming far more dangerous?"

"It's true, Dalin," Anje says, putting her hands to her hips—much as her mother might do, Arnem observes with a melancholy smile. "Even you should have been able to see *that* much. As to anything else, we ought to allow Radelfer, who *does* understand the matter fully, to explain it to Father."

"Though one thing is plain enough already, Father," says Gelie. "You would hardly believe how much Mother's help and instruction, along with the work of the old soldiers, have made life better in the district." Her young face screws up in puzzlement. "And yet, that only seemed to make Lord Baster-kin's men *angrier*—you would think it would be the other way round, wouldn't you?"

Arnem's eyes turn up to meet Radelfer's, and he nods. "Yes. I would, Gelie. And so . . ." Arnem lifts his youngest child up and sets her on the woolen floor of the tent. "There is a great table full of freshly roasted beef and vegetables in the next room, my young ones; why don't you all go and have something to eat while Radelfer and I talk about what has happened?"

A general chorus of enthusiasm—one that includes even Dalin's voice—rises up from the children, making it clear that, whatever other improvements Isadora may have effected in the Fifth District, supplies of food to that beleaguered section of Broken have not increased of late. Golo and Gelie lead the dash through the heavy curtain partition, with

Anje urging all of her younger siblings to slow down and behave themselves. But Arnem's eldest daughter pauses at the partition; and, making sure the other children are engrossed in the food, she returns to the sentek and Radelfer despite her own hunger.

"That is not all I was to tell you, Father," Anje says, now appearing more plainly worried. "Although Mother did not wish the younger ones to hear it."

"I suspected as much, Anje," Sixt Arnem says, holding his oldest daughter tightly, as if it will give him some reminder that his wife still lives. "Tell me, then."

Anje—ever her mother's most sensible child—speaks in a remarkably controlled voice. "Lord Radelfer can tell you of it far better than can I. If he will be so kind."

As Arnem continues to keep one arm around Anje, Radelfer says, "I am only too happy to oblige, Maid Anje—if you will promise in return that you will eat, for you are exhausted and have been without proper food for too long."

To this, Anje only nods. "All right, Lord—"

"I am no 'lord,' Maid Anje," Radelfer says. "Although I appreciate the honor you do me by calling me such. Now—get yourself some food."

Anje nods again, and then follows her siblings. Radelfer turns to Arnem, his face displaying both unease and admiration. "Your daughter is brave and wise, Sentek," he says, "just as her mother was at her age."

"You knew my lady even then, Seneschal?" Arnem asks, amazed.

"I did—and I shall tell you more of that in a moment," Radelfer replies. "As well as of the miraculous changes she has brought about in the Fifth District, assisted by your son and by an old comrade of mine that you may remember—Linnet Kriksex."

"Kriksex?" Arnem replies. "Yes, I recall both the name and the man—he was with us at the Atta Pass, among many other engagements, before he was grievously wounded."

"Not so grievously that he has not protected your wife, in the company of other veterans, from the terrible change that has taken place—"

Radelfer stops speaking when he grows aware of a presence; and, turning, both men see a young face poking through the rear entrance of the tent: Ernakh's.

"Excuse me, Sentek," the youth says quietly, "but I was wondering if I might ask the seneschal a question?"

"One question only, Ernakh," Arnem says, increasingly anxious to know what is happening to his wife and eldest son. "Then go and join the other children, and get something to eat."

At this, Ernakh enters the tent fully, making sure to close its flaps tight behind him, and turns to look up at Radelfer. "It is only—" he says haltingly and fearfully; "My mother, sir—why did *she* not come out with the sentek's children?"

Radelfer smiles, and puts a hand to the boy's shoulder. "Lady Arnem urged your mother to leave, Ernakh," he says. "But she would not abandon her mistress. Yet there was probably greater danger in the journey than in staying behind, so you may put your young mind at ease."

Ernakh smiles with relief, then nods once as he says, "Thank you, sir." Turning to Arnem, he repeats, "And thank *you,* Sentek—I only wanted to be certain." The *skutaar* then runs out into the council room, where he renews his friendships with the Arnem children.

The sentek turns to Radelfer. "What is the truth of the matter, Seneschal? Would my children have been safer in the city, and was my lady merely being exceedingly cautious by sending them out?"

Radelfer sighs, then takes the cup of wine and the seat that Arnem— who also sits and drinks a little, out of uneasiness, if nothing else—offers him. "I wish I could say that I had been entirely truthful, Sentek," Radelfer begins. "In fact, the situation in the city has grown vastly more dangerous—especially for Lady Arnem because of my master's past feelings for her, which seem to have returned, if indeed they ever truly departed." The seneschal pauses, staring into his wine. "Although I suppose I must refer to the Merchant Lord as my *former* master, now—and I am not at all certain that such is a bad thing . . . But the peril to your lady, as well as your district? That, I fear, is truly heightened, which is why I have come. Never, in what has been his troubled life, have I seen Rendulic Baster-kin so full of anger, so possessed by schemes that have driven him wild with passionate desire and a murderous determination."

Arnem feels the steady pain of dread growing in his heart. "You say the situation in Broken has changed, Radelfer," he replies. "Is that why I have received no written word from my wife, of late, when previously she had been writing so regularly?"

"Aye, Sentek," Radelfer says. "Lord Baster-kin has closed all avenues of communication between the Fifth District and the rest of the city, as well as the rest of the kingdom. No food enters, and few citizens escape. I only passed into the area and then back out, because of the Guard's knowledge that I am the seneschal of the Merchant Lord's household: I could therefore hide your children in the wagon I took from our stables."

"The Guard?" Arnem echoes. "But my wife's last dispatch, as well as my own children, reported that Sentek Gerfrehd and the regular army were atop the walls."

"As they were," Radelfer answers with a nod. "But, just before our departure, his lordship was able to convince the God-King, through the Grand Layzin, to order the regular army to confine itself to its own Fourth District, because they would not participate in the planned destruction of the Fifth. The second and last *khotor* of Lord Baster-kin's Guard now man the walls above that unfortunate district on all sides, and are preparing, after they have starved its inhabitants, to burn it to the ground. Therefore, if you now plan to march back to Broken, as I suspect you do, you cannot expect to be welcomed. For his lordship has also convinced the God-King—again through the Grand Layzin—to declare both the Talons and the residents of the Fifth to be in league with the Bane."

Arnem's face fills with an expression of both crushing betrayal confirmed and even more terrible fears realized: for what Radelfer has told him is no more than the logical continuation of the conclusions he has already been forced to reach, at Visimar's insistence, concerning Lord Baster-kin's intentions regarding the kingdom's most elite troops; yet he had not thought that such a charge, in all its deadly absurdity, would ever be extended to his wife and eldest son, to say nothing of the people of his native district.

"In league with the Bane . . . ," the sentek repeats, in no more than a dreadful whisper. He stands and begins to pace, running a hand through his hair roughly, as if he will drag comprehension from within his skull. But after several moments of silent bewilderment, as well as being alerted to the full extent of the danger by the laughter of his children and Er-nakh from behind the thick, rich hides that compose the partition inside his tent, he can conclude no more than, "Madness . . . He cannot be in his right mind, Radelfer!"

The seneschal shrugs, having already had at least some time to adapt to the terrible turn that Rendulic Baster-kin's mind has taken. "On the contrary, Sentek—I have known his lordship since he was but a boy, and

I have rarely seen him speaking and behaving so seemingly lucidly." Pausing, Radelfer drinks deep from his goblet, and looks up at Arnem. "I doubt very much that you have heard he not only witnessed but presided over the death of his own son."

Arnem spins on the seneschal in horror. *"Adelwülf?* He allowed him to die?"

"He arranged it," Radelfer replies; and there is a sadness beneath the even tone of his words that he is very obviously working hard to suppress. "In the Stadium. As good as served the lad up to one of the wild beasts, there—he explained that he wished to frighten the wealthy young men who frequent that place into serving with the *khotor* of the Guard that has just marched on the Wood."

"And been destroyed to the last man by their arrogance and utter lack of professional understanding," Arnem says, in an angry reply.

Radelfer takes in this information with the same labored steadiness that has marked the whole of his conversation with Sixt Arnem. "Have they?" he murmurs. "Well . . . then his lordship might have spared the boy so horrifying a fate, and let him die fighting our enemies."

"If indeed they are our enemies," Arnem says quickly. Radelfer's features become confused, but before he can ask the sentek's meaning, Arnem has set his fists heavily on the table before Radelfer and—in a voice measured enough that his children will not hear, but no less passionate—demands, "But why let his own son, his *heir,* die in the first place, much less arrange for it to happen?"

Very carefully, Radelfer stares into his goblet, and states with thinly veiled meaning, "He intends to have a second family. With a woman who, unlike his wretched, dying wife, is someone of strength, someone he has long admired—a woman who will, he believes, give him sons that will be true, loyal, and healthy servants of the kingdom." Pausing to take a quaff of wine, Radelfer finally says, "Just as she has given you such children, Sentek . . ."

Once again, Sixt Arnem is momentarily stunned by how much more elaborate Lord Baster-kin's plotting has run than he or even Visimar suspected. "My wife?" he eventually whispers. "He intends to steal my wife?"

"It is not theft," Radelfer replies, still with remarkable control of his emotions, "if the former husband is dead. And his lordship has been daily expecting confirmation that both you and your men have died from the pestilence that is ravaging the provinces." Staring into the distance, the seneschal reflects: "But instead, you are all still here, and the First *Khotor* of the Guard, along with the sons of most of the prominent houses in Broken, lie dead in the Wood . . ."

"And what of my children, Radelfer?" Arnem demands. "What was to become of them?"

Turning his head to the rough wool beneath his feet, Radelfer muses, with his first real display of remorse, "Your children would simply have been declared unfortunate casualties of the destruction of the Fifth District. Your insistence on remaining in that part of the city, even when you have attained command of the army, has always caused widespread consternation among the royal family, the priesthood, and the merchant classes in the city. The deaths of your children would have been laid to your own inscrutable stubbornness, rather than at the door of his lordship . . ."

Arnem is silent for a few moments, scarcely able to believe what he has heard. "But—*why*? Why, Radelfer, does the Merchant Lord turn on his own people in this manner? Or on my family? I have never voiced anything but support for him."

"I can tell you what lies behind his actions, Sentek," Radelfer says. "But in order to explain the situation fully, I must first tell you things that no one in Broken knows, save myself. The one other who even guessed at the truth paid the most awful price imaginable, simply for his attempt to be truthful and of assistance to the clan Baster-kin."

Arnem ponders this statement for a moment. "Radelfer—would that 'other' have been, by any chance, Caliphestros?"

Radelfer looks up, wholly surprised. "Aye, Sentek," he answers. "But how can you have guessed that?"

Sitting back and taking a deep sip of wine, Arnem says, "It may interest you to know, Seneschal, that Caliphestros not only survived the *Halap-stahla*, but is at this moment less than a quarter-league outside the southern perimeter of this camp, in the company of various Bane leaders, all of whom await my arrival under a flag of truce."

Radelfer, stunned for a moment, eventually murmurs, "I see . . . The tales that the Bane merchants spread are true, then . . . It does seem almost too fantastic."

"Not so fantastic," Arnem replies, "as the mount it is said he rides: none other than the legendary white panther of Davon Wood. Apparently, she is there now, as well—amazing nearly all of my Talons."

Radelfer considers the matter for a long moment, then grows far more restless. "Sentek," he finally says, "if the Bane and Caliphestros are in earnest about their desire to parley—and I pray that they are—then we have greater cause for hope than I had dared believe . . ."

$$3:\{x:\}$$

The seneschal's tale, and the continuation of the truce . . .

THE SENESCHAL GOES ABOUT finishing the full tale of young Rendulic Baster-kin and the healer's apprentice once known only as Isadora, as the sentek's children and Ernakh eagerly laugh and fill their bellies beyond the tent's partition. By the time that Arnem and Radelfer take horse to join the meeting south of the Talons' camp, the sentek, having made certain that the children will be properly guarded in his tent during his absence, has also made certain that he has allowed the surprise and shock that he first felt upon Radelfer's revelations to wane, so that they will not dominate his behavior during the parley to come. Yet now the sentek has been made aware, not only of how far back the history between Isadora and the Merchant Lord reaches, but of the very intimate and dangerous nature of it, as well as of a good many more previously unknown facts concerning Rendulic Baster-kin's life that finally worried Radelfer enough to risk his own life in an effort to save, if not Isadora herself, then at least most of her children, as she asked. By the time they ride toward the southern gate of the Talons' camp, Arnem has become as convinced as is the fugitive seneschal that no good can come of events as they are presently configured in the city. Broken's greatest soldier will need to convince his own officers to march, not into Davon Wood, but back up Broken's mountain—and he will need, as well, to plead that the military arm of the Bane, along with the legless sorcerer Caliphestros and his onetime acolyte, Visimar, support them in their effort, and embrace entirely the changes in outlook and, perhaps, loyalties required for any such scheme to succeed.

It is therefore no omen of success (or is it?) that, as the Ox and the mount with which Arnem has provided Radelfer storm out of the Talons' camp and thunder toward the meeting place of the truce between the two opposing lines of leaders, the principal sound that they both hear and see from afar is that of a certain notorious, file-toothed Bane laughing as he presides over an apparent game of some sort, one being played among Arnem's own officers and many of the Bane leaders. Unnerved by the strangely inappropriate activity, Arnem rides on, unnoticed by the bone-casters ahead.

"I ask you, Linnet," Arnem can hear the infamously ugly Bane he knows must be Heldo-Bah shouting in derision, as the Ox draws closer beside Radelfer's mount. Heldo-Bah has recognized Niksar's rank by the silver claws, the color of his cloak, and the air of authority he projects over his men. "Is this any way for the senior representative from your accursèd city—well, the most senior *yet* present—to face the most important encounter between your own and our peoples since the days that your Mad King began throwing the less than perfect in body and mind down off your mountain full of *marehs* and *skehsels* two hundred years ago? By not honoring his gambling debts?"

"I have told you," Niksar says, "I will honor them, it is simply that my own store of silver is back within my tent—"

"Ah, Linnet," Heldo-Bah replies airily, "if I had a piece of gold for every time I have heard an excuse like that . . ."

Now it is Caliphestros's turn to erupt uncontrollably, declaring for but an instant, "Heldo-Bah! Will nothing stop this idiotic exchange of—"

Then comes the sound of hard-pounding horses' hooves; and the old man looks up to see Sentek Arnem and Radelfer bearing down on their position with ever-greater haste. "Ah!" Caliphestros judges, allowing himself a smile that might be taken for a smirk, in a lesser being. "Well— apparently there may be. Let us see how greatly you feel like disrupting this all-important occasion when faced with both the commander of the Talons and the seneschal of the clan Baster-kin, Heldo-Bah, you impossible student of perversion . . ."

Himself turning to see the same impressive sight, Heldo-Bah's face goes a little pale: he straightens himself into something resembling a martial posture, and immediately grows silent. Throughout both sides of the parley lines, men return to their place of rank and draw themselves upright, silently leaving the knucklebones and the monies involved in the game untouched.

Even through his attempt at dignity, Heldo barks out, "No one touches the goods!"

Further comment from the most irrepressible of foragers is silenced, however, when Sentek Arnem bursts through to the spot where the game had been taking place. Sixt Arnem rides first to face Visimar, then crosses half the gap between the lines to study Caliphestros and the white panther in amazement. "So it is true, Caliphestros," the sentek says. "Your former acolyte's claim that you survived your punishment was more than fable. I confess that I did not fully credit it until this moment."

"Understandably, Sixt Arnem," Caliphestros says, his face a mask of inscrutably complex emotions: for the last time the legless old scholar had set eyes on this soldier, he had been a full man being cut to pieces. "Although I am not certain which of us is, right now, in the more unenviable position . . ."

Arnem can only nod grimly.

"Radelfer," Caliphestros says, with a nod. "I confess to some satisfaction that you are here. It at least proves my suspicion that you were ever a man of honor, who has come to realize his moral predicament."

Radelfer nods back at the compliment. "Lord Caliphestros. I, too, am pleased that you somehow survived your ordeal, for the charges against you were baseless."

"Indeed," Caliphestros says. "But that is the heart of this entire matter, is it not?" Radelfer nods again, although Arnem's features become puzzled. "What I refer to, Sentek," Caliphestros explains, "is the nature of the most dangerous men in Broken—perhaps the world. Do you know to whom I refer?"

Arnem shrugs. "I should think to evil men."

But Caliphestros shakes his head. "No. Evil, when it truly exists, is far too easily detected to be of the *greatest* danger. The most dangerous men in the world are those who—for reasons of their own—put their names and services at the disposal of what they see, at the time, as good causes.

The greatest, the truest *evil,* then, is that undertaken by *good* men who cannot see or, worse, will not see the wickedness they serve. And there is one such man in Broken, perhaps the last of his breed, whose power and motivations have long made him a source of profound concern."

Arnem nods grimly. "You refer to me."

But Caliphestros seems surprised. "To you, Sentek? I do not. But more of such philosophical matters at a later time. We have pressing business to discuss, without delay."

"Indeed—I see that you have called for truce, Caliphestros," the sentek replies. "May I safely assume, then, that you, like your former acolyte, have somehow found it in your soul to forgive my participation in your torture and intended abandonment to death?"

"You may *assume* nothing, Sentek," Caliphestros replies. "For it is not I who have called for truce."

"No?" Arnem asks. "Well, it cannot have been the member of your party who was presiding over the game of knucklebones as I approached, surely."

"No," Caliphestros says, leaning over, stroking the white panther's neck, in a motion both vague and clearly threatening toward his opponents, and glancing at the now-fearful Heldo-Bah with a deep anger. "It would be neither my place nor his to assert such authority within the Bane tribe, nearly all of whom were as ignorant or uncertain of my continued existence as were you and your people, until a matter of days ago. You must address yourself to the Groba Father and his Elders, who alone speak for the Bane. Were it up to me . . ." And at this instant both the old man and the panther look up as one, Caliphestros's slate grey eyes and Stasi's brilliant green orbs seeming to contain an inscrutable sentiment: "Were it up to me, I might well have allowed every soldier in the Broken army to enter Davon Wood, to share in the fate already met, and so richly deserved, by the *khotor* of Lord Baster-kin's Guard." But then Caliphestros's manner softens. "Although that is likely my half-legs, and not my mind, speaking."

Arnem nods knowingly. "I believe so," he says, his tone contrite. "For of all people, I suspect that you know that to speak of Lord Baster-kin's Guard and the true soldiers of Broken, especially the Talons that face you now, as if they were in any way similar, does neither my men nor your wisdom justice."

"True," Caliphestros replies. "And that is the only reason why I am here . . ."

Still attempting practicality, Arnem nods and states, "Your attention to protocol is wisely worded, and I shall heed it." He then looks at the man who, by his slightly superior appearance and bearing, he takes to be the Bane leader. "You are the Groba Father, then?"

The Father, who more than makes up in courage what he lacks in height, takes one or two steps forward. "I am, Sentek," he says with great courage, earning him respect among members of both lines of the truce. "And perhaps it would, as my friend Lord Caliphestros intimates, be the most honest way to begin this discussion by telling you that the Merchant Lord might have sent emissaries, rather than his personal Guard, to us, and together we might have addressed the terrible ailments that we now know afflict your people as well as, at least in the case of what Lord Caliphestros calls the rose fever, our own. But instead, he chose our moment of weakness to attempt to achieve the long-cherished, inexplicable desire of your God-King and the Kafran priests to destroy our tribe." Taking one deep, steadying breath, the Father finishes: "Which, I gather, was *your* original reason for leaving the walls of your foul city, as well."

"Not our reason, Father," Arnem says grimly. "Our orders. But know this—that same order cost me both my teacher and my oldest friend—"

The Groba Father nods. "Yantek Korsar."

"As well as Gerolf Gledgesa," Caliphestros adds solemnly.

Surprised, Arnem looks for a moment to Caliphestros, and then at Visimar. "Well—whatever 'science' you two practice, I continue to learn why it terrified the priests of Kafra so. For this is not knowledge I expected you to possess."

Caliphestros shrugs. "In the first instance, simply an accident of discovery, Sentek," he says. "In the second, a communication from Visimar. There was no great mystery in either case. But please—proceed . . ."

Arnem resumes, still a little unnerved by Visimar's and now Caliphestros's ability to state matters of fact before the sentek himself can reveal them, "That order not only cost myself and my kingdom such men, but was issued long before we knew of *any* diseases at large throughout either your or our own people, or of any attempt to remake the city of Broken itself by use of violent force. Had these facts been known to me in advance . . . I can say that I should not have been willing to play a part in them."

"Some would say that you ought to have questioned such orders, nevertheless," Caliphestros declares flatly. "Yantek Korsar certainly did—and I have seen his body hanging along the banks of the Cat's Paw, as a result."

Arnem blanches considerably, before murmuring, "Have you, indeed . . . ?" Then he uses his commander's discipline to try to recover his composure, and looks to the Groba Father. "And would *you*, sir, also have expected me to thus disregard orders? It is well and good for exiles and men of the shadows to talk thus—" He glances at Caliphestros. "But could *you* forgive such impertinence from the man I now suspect to be at once one of our most formidable and most honorable opponents, over the years—Yantek Ashkatar?" Arnem lifts a respectful finger to indicate the stout Bane commander with the coiled whip, who, in his turn, draws himself up more proudly.

Considering the question momentarily, the Groba Father replies, "No, Sentek Arnem. We likely could not. Very well, then. We shall accept your answer in the spirit of this truce and this . . . *negotiation*. But the Groba will ask you an equally direct and crucial question, in return, one that I hope you can answer in the same manner—" Now stepping further to the nearly precise midway point between the two lines of negotiators and the spot where stands the Ox, with his rider sitting high above, and earning still more respect among the officers of the Talons for doing so, the Groba Father locks gazes with Arnem fully before asking:

"Will you, Sentek, agree to having your eyes and hands bound, and in that condition, to accompanying our party to Okot, there to observe the full effects that the fever with which your people have poisoned the Cat's Paw have wrought, and to discuss what our forces may do *together* to bring a halt to the crisis, both for your people's sake and for our own? Lord Caliphestros seems to think that you will—but I confess to my own doubts. You see, as a younger trader, I once spent a very long night beneath the Merchants' Hall in Broken . . ."

Arnem sits back in his saddle: plainly, this not a question that he has anticipated.

"It is the simplest way in which to demonstrate to you how at least the one disease—the rose fever—is spread," says Caliphestros. "As well as how and where both it and the *Ignis Sacer*—the Holy Fire—may be originating within the city and kingdom of Broken: which, I believe I have determined, is indeed their source—a determination that your own wife, I suspect, has made, which is part of the reason she is now so persecuted."

"My *wife?*" Arnem echoes. "You have been in communication with my wife? And you know where the fever originates, Caliphestros?" Arnem says, shock following upon shock. "For we have already determined, with Visimar's and, I suspect, your aid, that the rose fever taints the waters of the Cat's Paw. How can you know its origin more exactly?"

"In good time," Caliphestros responds. "Finally, the journey to Okot will also give me a chance to show you how the fabled walls of Broken may at last be breached and the Merchant Lord defeated, should you deem it right—or, more to the point, necessary—to do so. For you see, after many years of study, I have at last discovered the meaning of, and the solution to, the Riddle of Water, Fire, and Stone."

Arnem's face betrays shock, once more, and this time it is a shock shared by the Broken commanders behind him. "Truly, old man? Then that riddle was not merely one more fancy of our founding king, Oxmontrot—whom men such as Lord Baster-kin insist on calling 'mad'—in the years before his death?"

"The longer I live, Sentek," Caliphestros replies, "the less I believe that any of Oxmontrot's thoughts were 'fancies'—or that he was mad, at all." The old man sits back on Stasi's shoulders. "Well, Sixt Arnem—will you agree to the Father's proposition, and come to the place your superstitious citizens call the center of all that is malevolent?"

"Sentek—no, you cannot!" Niksar whispers urgently, and the other officers of the Talons murmur like warnings.

"Don't listen to *that* man, Sentek," Heldo-Bah quickly interjects. "He still owes me money!"

"I have told you, forager," Niksar replies angrily, "the money is in my tent—"

"I shall of course stay within the Talons' camp," announces Ashkatar, taking a step forward of his own and attempting to quash this momentary, foolish squabble. "As a guarantee of Sentek Arnem's safety. So shall the foragers who brought Lord Caliphestros to us, in the first place."

Heldo-Bah's eyes suddenly look as if they will burst. *"What?"* he fairly screams. "I will be damned if I will do any such thing!"

"You will be damned, whatever your actions!" Keera declares, quietly but passionately. "Which is why we thought it best not to consult you on the matter." She turns and takes the few steps needed to put her angry face in his. "In the name of our people, in the name of my family that saved you, in the name of my children, who, for whatever innocent reasons of their own, love you as they would any true uncle, you *will* do this thing, Heldo-Bah!"

Realizing that he has already been utterly outmaneuvered, Heldo-Bah allows his face and shoulders to sag with displeasure. "Very well," he at length replies.

"It will at the least allow you to collect your silver from Linnet Niksar," Veloc says tauntingly.

"And so—bring forth a blindfold, Visimar," the sentek says, glancing at Caliphestros. "But I will make one request: may we make our visit as brief as possible? For it has been brought to my attention that you are correct in assuming my wife is in grave danger, Lord Caliphestros, and my men and I must march at once to her relief—a march upon which I should be proud to have the Bane army accompany us." Arnem turns his eyes to the Bane leader. "Father?"

"We may be brief," says the Father in reply, impressed by Arnem's courage and invitation, both. "So long as we are thorough, as well."

Arnem agrees with a silent nod, and looks again at the remarkable man atop the equally remarkable panther. "I assume your former acolyte will be accompanying us, my lord?"

Caliphestros smiles, now: the true smile of a man who has begun to be restored. "You assume correctly, Sentek . . . ," he says, at which Visimar brings forward a strip of clean cotton that Niksar has reluctantly produced for him.

"Must I, too, bind my eyes, master?" Visimar asks Caliphestros.

"You need not," the latter replies with a small laugh. "But you must stop calling me 'master.' If I have learned nothing else from the last ten years, and from this noble tribe that has survived in so harsh a wilderness, it is that such titles, while they may belong within the kingdom of Broken, have no place outside it."

"Then bind my eyes alone," Arnem repeats, as the Groba Father issues a last set of quiet instructions to Ashkatar and Keera, and they then begin to make their way to the line of the Broken soldiers. "And do not despair, Niksar—for you must command, now, and that will be worry enough." The sentek smiles briefly. "That and—paying your losses . . ." Arnem studies the faces of his "captors," then dismounts the Ox, steps forward, and bids his mount farewell as he prepares to submit to the binding of his eyes.

At this moment, Caliphestros allows Stasi to stray somewhat closer to Arnem. It is not the Ox's being led back to the line of the Talons by Niksar that causes the legless old philosopher to so approach: for both Arnem and the Ox know that, if plunged into a fury, the panther could take down even so impressive and mature a Broken warhorse as Arnem's, and likely would: the last time Stasi saw such an animal, after all, was on that terrible day that her family was lost to her, seemingly forever. Rather, the old scholar desires a moment of confidentiality with the man he long ago and correctly surmised would be the only possible choice to fill Yantek Korsar's position as commander of both the Talons and the army of Broken: "Again I urge you to remember one thing, above all, on this journey, Sentek," he says. "The actors in this drama may all be playing far different roles than you have been trained to believe. Keep your mind open to the full range of possibilities, for such is the only true path to knowledge. Of any kind."

Arnem smiles: a genuine and conciliatory expression of hope that the two men may soon be reconciled. "Ever the pedant, even without your legs, eh, Caliphestros?" he says, in such a way that the panther's rider cannot but laugh again at his own manner. "Well, fear not," Arnem adds. "I am prepared to heed your advice, I assure you."

With Arnem's sight securely if temporarily taken from him, all parties to the truce begin the processions—one short, one longer—back to their respective safe territories, when Arnem suddenly stops and turns back toward his own men.

"Radelfer," the blindfolded sentek calls. "Will you tell my children where I have gone, and that I have every expectation of returning tomorrow?"

"I shall, Sentek," Radelfer responds. "And, I believe I can now tell them that they need not fear for your safety—that you travel with an honorable people."

And it is in this mood of perhaps promising confusion that the meeting under the snapping sheet of white cotton concludes, and the development of events that will only be more decisive commences.

"Feel and smell the breeze," Arnem says, being led away by Visimar behind Caliphestros and Stasi.

"I have done so for quite some time, now," Caliphestros answers, turning toward the Broken commander as they reach the members of the Bane Groba.

"It heralds rain," the Groba Father comments, as the procession back toward the Fallen Bridge begins. "Will that interfere with what you have planned, Lord Caliphestros?"

A deeply satisfied smile enters the scholar's features. "Only if it arrives too early, Father. But that it *will* arrive?" The old man seems for a moment almost anxious for events to unfold. "On *that,* I am relying—on that, the solution of the Riddle of Water, Fire, and Stone in our favor absolutely depends . . ."

$$3:\{xi:\} \; \dagger$$

The "Battle" for Broken

1.

DURING SENTEK ARNEM'S BRIEF VISIT to Okot, when that good man and great soldier did indeed learn that the members of the Bane tribe were neither demons, degenerates, nor defective human beings bent on betraying the current truce in order to further prepare their own assault on Broken, the wise and cunning Caliphestros had not been idle. Working, for the time being, without the assistance of the three Bane foragers upon whom he had come to rely, but with the once-familiar aid of his partially crippled acolyte, Visimar, as well as among a people who had come to accept his presence and give him whatever help they could, he had located the two largest carts in the town, as well as any and all brass pots, jugs, amphorae, and other containers that were available or could be made so. The latter were stacked and cradled inside the beds of the former, and the whole lot drawn up to the agèd scholar's cave laboratory: drawn, that is, by powerful Bane warriors, for the Bane had no oxen or cattle or horses of their own. Once there, each container was filled by Caliphestros and Visimar with one of several, usually foul-smelling substances: the true and mysterious fruits of the peculiar labors that Keera had, from time to time, observed Caliphestros undertaking during his time among her people, ingredients which together formed the mysterious answer to the Riddle of Water, Fire, and Stone, an answer whose components needed to be treated gently, Caliphestros emphasized, during the journey back to Arnem's camp on Lord Baster-kin's Plain.

Despite the two old scholars' inscrutable activities (the true explanation of which, Caliphestros had told the Bane again and again, would best be supplied when the results of the experiment took form before the gates of Broken), Sentek Arnem's visit and behavior had established such an air of surprise and open trust in Okot, and so quickly, that it was a foregone conclusion that the Groba—when they met with him on the morning after his arrival, before his return to his camp—would indeed order Yantek Ashkatar to take as many of his men as Arnem deemed fit and place them under the sentek's command, to be a part of the force that would now march back up Broken's mountain to determine what, precisely, was the truth of the situation inside the city. There had, of course, been some argument from the Priestess of the Moon, who objected to there being no role in the campaign assigned to her Woodland Knights; but, when Sentek Arnem had assured both her and the Groba Elders that feeling in Broken against the Outragers ran every bit as high as did the Bane's toward Lord Baster-kin's Guard, and that their presence would only complicate and perhaps defeat the purpose of the endeavor, the Groba Father had decreed absolutely that the Outragers would not participate, even if only in a rearguard action to ensure that no troops from Broken slipped past the Talons and Ashkatar's attack, to launch another assault on Davon Wood.

When the Bane commander had asked his counterpart from Broken how many of his tribe's warriors Arnem would require to support his two *khotors* of Talons, the sentek's answer had perhaps been predictable:

only so many as could be armed with weapons forged from Caliphestros's amazing new metal (which the sentek had climbed the mountain behind Okot to observe being made, with the greatest interest and satisfaction). The number had been placed at only some two hundred and fifty of the best-trained men and women in the tribe; for without such weapons, Arnem assured the Groba Elders, no Bane warrior dared participate in the coming attack on the mighty, granite-walled city. With these final issues decided, the return to Arnem's camp had gotten under way. It was a march made far more arduous by the need to delicately handle Caliphestros's carts, and to transport the contents, container by container, across the Fallen Bridge: each container was tightly sealed, that the fumes emitted by the various contents might not overcome its carrier or carriers—yet even at that, there were one or two near mishaps high above the Cat's Paw. Once reassembled in the carts on the Plain, however, and with horses rather than men to draw the conveyances, progress moved at a much faster pace; but nothing could stop soldiers of either the Bane or Broken armies from wondering what could possibly be in the containers that might create such an effect.

This air of mystery only deepens, now, as the Talons strike their camp: for, with the full combined force of Bane and Broken warriors beginning to move up the southern route of ascendancy toward the great city, a ring of mist begins to form about the middle and upper reaches of the mountain. Pure white, the mist is nonetheless remarkably dry; and there is a fast-spreading tendency among both the Bane and the Talons—who have come to regard each other as allies with remarkable speed, a sentiment urged on by each of their trusted and even beloved commanders— to view the mist as some sort of a blessing from their respective deities, since it will make their movements far more difficult to detect from the walls of the city. (They cannot know, as you do, readers who encounter this Manuscript many years from now, that what they believe their unique and divine gift was, in fact, the first appearance in the mountain's history of that same misty halo by which Broken has since become known, and by which it shall likely continue to be marked until the end of time.[†]) Matched with the general enthusiasm for Caliphestros's steel, which both Bane and Talons are experienced enough warriors to recognize is indeed an unqualified boon, the mist creates an air that further promotes the heartiest of feelings between former enemies.

The mist, meanwhile, is having an entirely different effect in Broken: as Arnem had hoped, it is indeed making it almost impossible for the men of Lord Baster-kin's Guard who are manning the walls of the city to determine just what direction the allied[†] armies are approaching from. The realization of this confusion, relayed by Akillus's stealthy scouts, causes an increasingly congenial atmosphere to overtake the expedition below: for the Talons and the Bane both know full well that they will require such compensatory advantages. Say what one will of Baster-kin's Guard, they shall now be fighting, not in the dark, foreign terrain of Davon Wood, but from behind Broken's seamless walls and mighty oak and iron gates: a position whose superiority is almost impossible to measure in numbers or comparative skills. Certainly, however, odds of less than two warriors to one—which the Guardsmen will be facing, if they not only fight soberly, but organize their positions and their system of response to assault so that it is quick and effective—should not, under ordinary circumstances, be sufficient to cause any defenders of the city alarm, any more than they should bode well for the attackers. Thus Arnem and Ashkatar are inclined to view every favorable development or disposition with even greater encouragement than they usually would, and are forced to turn indulgent ears and eyes to the several and often amusing situations that grow out of the Talons and the Bane warriors becoming acquainted with each other's ways during the march.

The need for this indulgence is only reinforced when they consider the probability that the Guard's exacting and often quite terrifying commander will himself be at his men's backs: the Merchant Lord, no doubt driven on by the consuming desire for a new wife and family, which he has sacrificed so much to gain, as well as by the defection of his seneschal, will press his men toward a rugged defense, one that they may well be capable of achieving.

"What think you of this, my lord Caliphestros?" Arnem calls merrily as he gallops back to the baggage train from his usual position at the head of the column. "A nearly dry mist? What does this herald for your certain prediction of rain?"

Caliphestros is still tightly clinging to Stasi's shoulders, as the panther walks next to the first of the two carts, in which rides Visimar as Keera drives, making up for what she lacks in physical strength by her ability to communicate with the two horses that pull the conveyance through her manipulations of their reins and harnesses. Stasi, for her part, makes it ever clear to the beasts that only strict obedience to their mistress will be tolerated, without actually frightening the horses so greatly that they bolt. Veloc and Heldo-Bah manage the reins of the second cart, and in the beds of both vehicles, pairs of the Talons' rearguard men make certain that the tie lines which secure the brass containers are neither too tight nor too loose, but offer just enough flexibility to both secure the apparently precious cargo and absorb whatever unseen jolts in the road the carts themselves cannot.

"I realize fully the military advantage of this strange phenomenon," Caliphestros replies, eyes ever on the beds of the two carts. "And I am glad that it brings with it no moisture—yet. But when the time comes, Sentek, we shall require rain—a good, driving rain, and as I now have no clear view of the night sky, I am less sanguine than I was that we shall get it. Certainly, the wind from the west that was earlier so promising has died down—and that is not something that pleases me."

"Well, if you would but tell me *why* you require such a rain," Arnem replies, hoping that his roundabout attempt to pry will not sound so heavy-handed as its statement feels, "then I might dispatch several of Akillus's men either farther up or down the mountain, to a position where they could more clearly attempt to divine the approaching weather."

"And I might oblige your rather obvious ruse, Sentek," Caliphestros replies, "if I thought it truly possible for your scouts to do so. But the dying down of the wind, together with the surrounding hills and mountains that both obscure and channel patterns in the weather, make it seem unlikely that their reading from anywhere on this trail would be accurate . . ." The old man nods once. "But I will offer you this, in reply: send Linnet Akillus—for I know he will never be able to pass up such an opportunity for adventure and the gaining of intelligence—as well as whatever men he requires on this errand, and if their news is good, I shall agree to explain what I can about what we carry in these carts."

"Thus you trust Akillus fully," Arnem says with a smile, "but myself only reservedly . . . *Hak,* in your scheme of 'good' and 'bad,' I cannot tell which of us thereby makes the better man . . ."

The old scholar is unable to keep from returning the soldier's smile. "So you have thought upon my words, eh, Sentek? And, I suspect, understood them."

"Studied, yes, but understood?" Arnem shakes his head, then turns to notice that both Keera and Visimar are listening intently. "Who, I still do not know, is the one good man in Broken who does evil in the name of what he perceives as good?"

"Truly, you have not divined as much, Sentek?" Caliphestros answers, surprised. Urging the sentek as close to his side as the Ox will bear, given Stasi's presence, the agèd scholar strains his body as far toward the commander as its compromised state will allow, speaking in a whisper: *"It is Lord Baster-kin, himself."*

Keera gasps suddenly, in a manner almost audible to the eternally inquisitive drivers of the cart behind them. Arnem, for his part, pulls away, stunned. "Lord—!"

Caliphestros hisses silence. *"Please, Sentek*—I tell you this in all confidence. It must remain shielded, especially from that noisy sack of verbal and physical obscenities who drives the cart behind us. So let us speak no more of it. You shall study upon it, now, as you studied upon my earlier statement, and come to comprehend my meaning, in your own time."

Still stunned, somewhat, from what he has heard, Arnem can only reply weakly, "I fear that time will be too short, my lord. We are not so far from the South Gate of Broken as you may think, and the time it takes to reach it is all I can give to such contemplation."

"But this is not at all so," Caliphestros replies. "Did *you* yourself not say that we shall need to pause at the open, roughly flat meadow upon which your cavalrymen train, just south of the city, before we reach the walls? Your purpose was, as I recall, to allow your engineers to begin the construction of the various *ballistae* that I requested from the wood of the surrounding trees, as well as to determine how many horses have escaped Lord Baster-kin's efforts to capture them and thus supply additional stores of meat for the city's population during the coming siege?"

"I did," he answers. "And it will take some time—for those mounts have been trained to avoid capture by such clumsy, untrained hands as those of the Guard, and will likely be scattered. In addition, I don't know why you continue to insist on any 'ballistae' at all—for you know as well as I that both the granite of Broken's walls and the dense oak of her gates are impervious to such weapons. In addition, the building of such devices will take the better part of a day and a night, even for such skilled craftsmen as Linnets Crupp and Bal-deric and their men."

"Perhaps my explanation for wanting the machines, when you hear it, will alter your point of view," Caliphestros replies, knowing that he dangles bait that the sentek cannot resist. "So it would seem you have time and reason enough, then."

"And it would seem that I've been outmaneuvered by *you* again," Arnem comments, without rancor. "I know, now, who taught Visimar that skill. Very well, then—*Akillus!*" The sentek, his mind back upon affairs at hand, spurs the Ox forward, and the others can still hear him shouting for his chief scout long after he has vanished back into the strange, surrounding cloud.

"Well," Visimar comments, with a small laugh. "That was deftly managed—your skills at such negotiation have not suffered during your years among the denizens of the Wood, my lord."

"Perhaps, Visimar," Caliphestros replies, "but one thing I said was simply and unarguably truthful; we must know what change in the mountain's weather this strange mist portends, if any change at all."

"We shall, would be my guess," Visimar says. "Akillus has a shrewd eye for details, as well as the ability to gather them quickly."

"Precisely my impression," Caliphestros rejoins. "We shall not have long to wait, then."

"No, not long," Keera adds softly, from her seat beside Caliphestros's former acolyte. "But, perhaps, time enough—and distance enough from any ears save your own and ours, my lord—for you to explain, without fear of rancorous interruption, what took place in the Wood, just before the slaughter of the First *Khotor* of Lord Baster-kin's Guard . . . ?" The statement apparently comes as no surprise to Visimar, making Keera realize that Visimar and Caliphestros must already have discussed the latter's encounter with the First Wife of Kafra. Keera is taken aback when Visimar turns to face the cart behind them and calls:

"Ho! Heldo-Bah! Veloc! Come help me down, that I may be certain your containers are properly secured. Not that I distrust your assistants— but neither they nor you have ever handled such materials as you now bear."

"What makes you think we need the help of a man with one leg and half a mind?" Heldo-Bah replies. "Worry about your own cart, acolyte!" Stasi turns to Heldo-Bah and gives him an admonishing look, which, although a brief one, is sufficient to its purpose: "Oh, all right, go get the one old lunatic, Veloc . . ."

Veloc trots forward briskly, and, as the two wagons halt briefly, gives Visimar a shoulder and two good legs to lean upon, so that he can take his weight from the worn piece of wood and leather that has for so many years been strapped to his once-whole body.

"Let us get back under way as quickly as we can," Caliphestros commands, at which Keera gets her horses moving once more and he speaks to her privately. "For I would be finished with this tale, ere we reach the meadow Sentek Arnem and I spoke of, when Akillus and his scouts will return . . ."

Heldo-Bah is soon preoccupied enough with the business of getting Visimar up and onto his cart's bench that he cannot so much as try to listen to the conversation that unfolds in the conveyance ahead. Once his horses are pulling again, however, the gap-toothed Bane leans to his side and says to his new passenger:

"All right, acolyte—I will make my friendship easy for you: tell me what those two are talking about."

"Why should you wish to know, Heldo-Bah?" Visimar says, in a congenial but firm fashion. "Even if I told you, it would be as a language deeply foreign to you: mere nonsense-speak that would only conflict with your outlook upon the world."

Heldo-Bah's eyes widen. "You know me so well that you can say this with certainty?"

"I believe so," Visimar answers. Then he turns to the third forager, who walks beside the wagon. "Am I wrong, Veloc?"

Veloc laughs. "You are not, Visimar." He looks to his gap-toothed friend, and says proudly, "They speak of love, Heldo-Bah, if I am right."

"Oh," Heldo-Bah answers. "And so I know nothing of love? Or of loss?"

"I did not say that," Visimar answers. "Simply not of the type of love that they are discussing."

"Believe what you like, you two," Heldo-Bah says, attempting to rise above the insult with rather absurd pride. "But at the same time, return to our story—I want to know how that clever relic we've been traveling with"—he points to Caliphestros—"ever coaxed that supreme beauty into his bed."

"And why need he have been the one who did the coaxing, Heldo-Bah?" Visimar demands.

"*That* argument again," the sharp-toothed forager grunts. "Leave such ideas to fools like Veloc, old man—they are beneath you, if you are half the mystical scholar the Tall once believed you."

His predicament obvious, Visimar shakes his head once. "Not so— and if Veloc will aid me in the occasional translation into your own unique language, Heldo-Bah, I shall relate it." Immediately, Heldo-Bah nods in firm agreement, not realizing he has been roundly insulted; and the tale continues. "Well," says Visimar, "I warn you, Heldo-Bah, what I have to say will not be what you have in mind, in *any* way. You desire a story rife with lasciviousness, but the truth runs in quite the other direction."

"Whatever the direction," Heldo-Bah replies, "I desire to know how that old man achieved such a feat as taking that beauteous creature to bed."

"You will be disappointed," Visimar repeats. "For, as I expect my master, or former master, is now telling Keera, it was Alandra who took *him* . . . And the results were—devastation. For both of them . . ."

2.

THE LARGE CAVALRY training ground of which Sentek Arnem spoke is bounded by short, cliff-like faces on its western and southern edges, so that the trail from below enters on its eastern edge and then continues upward from its northern. The last length of pathway that the two carts must cover to reach it is not long, but because of the plateau-like formation of the field the approach is steep, and special attention must be paid to the heavily laden carts; yet even such care for calm and quiet cannot prevent the horses from announcing their approach, for they are familiar with the place, having spent much time upon it training for battle; and they find the experience of dragging heavily laden carts toward it confusing and irritating. The remainder of the trip, then, is a tricky one, which only gives Heldo-Bah more time to harry Visimar with questions about the romance between Caliphestros and the First Wife of Kafra called Alandra. Not that Heldo-Bah has any difficulty understanding the basic facts of the tale: it is perfectly easy to see how a man like Caliphestros—then ten or more years younger, his body whole and fit, his experience, wisdom, and manner worldly, and his prestige with the God-King Izairn and the latter's retinue so great that he was given chambers and a laboratory within the high tower of the Inner City's royal palace itself, and the unprecedented position of Second Minister—could be seduced by the charms of a young woman such as the First Wife of Kafra, given her entrancing green eyes and her shimmering, straight lengths of coal-black hair, to say nothing of a form that to this day embodies all the attributes that the Tall admire. Caliphestros had indeed been tutor to Izairn's royal offspring, from shortly after he arrived in Broken: throughout the period, that is, that he was also murmured to be the leader of a group (chief among them Visimar) who snatched dead bodies, performed profane experiments upon them, and dabbled in black arts of all kinds, while at the same time performing their royal duties. Which of the offenses was the greater, his accusers eventually asked, sorcery or the supposèd "guidance" of a young girl into becoming his lover? The last was certainly an odd question, to be put by a society whose god and priests called for physical indulgences of all varieties, and between all sexes and ages (and in some cases species). And so the second indictment might never have carried any weight, without the first, which was why Caliphestros's enemies in the Kafran priesthood—who first suborned the young Prince Saylal—knew that they must also gain the backing of the Royal Princess, if their dream of expelling the influential but no less blasphemous foreigner and his followers was ever to take shape.

And yet, the problem presented itself again and again: in a world where priests not only allowed but ritualized every physical excess, how could a romance (and, Visimar emphasized to Heldo-Bah, it was first and foremost a romance) between two people of merely differing ages, even greatly differing ages, be considered some sort of "perversion"? The only way to convince Alandra that she had been taken, rather than had given herself to Caliphestros, was for the priests to convince her that sorcery had allowed him to enter her very mind when she had been his pupil rather than his lover, and had filled it, not with sacred teachings, but with blasphemous science—and desires.

"Great Moon," Heldo-Bah breathes when he hears this: for he is, as he has protested, not so unversed in the ways of both love and lust that he cannot comprehend such ideas. "I knew that those priests were scheming devils, and the people who followed them no more than shorn sheep, but . . . So you have no doubt that she *did* truly love him, once, Visimar?"

"I saw it in her," Veloc answers, before the old cripple can speak.

"Oh," Heldo-Bah groans. "Of course *you* saw it, historian. You see all, that you may one day sing of it to our children . . ."

"I did not say that I *understood* it, Heldo-Bah," Veloc whispers in protest. "But I saw *something*. And Keera saw it, as well, and *she* understood it, and explained it to me, later. The pain in his eyes, and in the priestess's, too, if only for brief instants. Intermingled with all their bitter statements . . ."

"Yes, bitter," Visimar says. "For, as has often been observed, there is no bitterness like that which results from love willfully destroyed. And the happiness that my master and Alandra knew *was* willfully destroyed; its death was plotted, just as surely as was the murder of Oxmontrot, and carried out just as cruelly. And if she had any doubts, all the priests needed do was use her own ambition to exploit them: after all, they said, had he shared his *deepest* secrets, his greatest knowledge, with her, even if such sorcery was blasphemous? Was that love, to give less than all he knew to her? In truth, my master was only protecting Alandra, for he knew the role she had been born to play in Broken: had he involved her fully in his work, she might well have been mutilated and almost certainly murdered on the edge of Davon Wood, as well. Yet from the moment that she began to believe he was keeping powerful forces and knowledge from her—secrets that she saw, not as 'sorcerous,' but as magical—his indictment was only a matter of time. We could all see it, and begged him to leave the city. But he would not go. You see, he never acknowledged that Alandra craved power more than she loved him; and, as I say, if denied the full range of *his* power, she would take the more vulgar form (however 'sacred' it might be portrayed as being) offered by the priests, and view him, not as protecting her, but as ever more determined to hold the position of superiority between them. Thus did he seal his own fate, first with the priests, and then with her; and even more painfully, for him, she began to see him more and more as simply a wicked, even blasphemous old man, who had tainted rather than adored her."

"*Hak* . . . ," Heldo-Bah whispers; but there is sympathy in the oath, now, something like what he displayed to the white panther when he discovered that it was the young Rendulic Baster-kin who had killed her cubs. "The poor old fool . . . Well, it only demonstrates that you can travel the world and learn the ways of the great philosophers, and still make the mistakes of a Moonstruck village boy who has never seen so much as the next town, where women are involved . . ."

Visimar turns for a moment, to study the filthy, foul driver of the cart with some surprise. "That is a remarkably apt statement, Heldo-Bah."

"Do not expect them at regular intervals," Veloc comments with a smile. "But he *does* make them . . ."

Heldo-Bah quickly moves for one of his knives, but Visimar, just as quickly, stays his hand, with the same surprising strength of one who has had to manipulate a staff and crude wooden leg over many years. "None of such foolishness," Visimar says. "Heed me closely, both of you, for we are only now arriving at the most interesting part of the story."

"We are?" Heldo-Bah replies, relaxing his arm and urging his horses on. "There is something of greater interest than bedding the First Wife of Kafra?"

"Indeed there is, Heldo-Bah," Visimar says quietly. "For the last time I met my master in the Wood to bring him supplies, shortly before the priests took me away for the ordeal of my *Denep-stahla,* his mind was still in pieces, great as his affection for the white panther obviously was. He knew that, once Alandra had taken the decision to condemn him as a monster and a demon, she would only cultivate the feeling. And that cut into him deeply. Yet now, that wound has been almost wholly healed. In some way, that great beast has lived up to the name he gave her— *Anastasiya*—in that she brought him back to life, when resignation to death would have been the easiest path. Not only brought him back, but changed him, somehow: she has taken away much of the arrogance he once possessed, and that led him to his ultimate crisis concerning the priests and Alandra. How does an animal, however powerful, accomplish this? Can neither of you tell me, after so many years in the Wood?"

Both Heldo-Bah and Veloc appear somewhat embarrassed by their inability to give Visimar the answer he seeks; and finally Veloc says simply, "It is my sister who knows of these things, far better than do we."

"Well," Visimar sighs, slightly dumbfounded. "There must be *some* explanation."

"There is," Heldo-Bah mutters, almost seeming, for a moment, self-reproachful for speaking of such things. "And, while Veloc is correct, and we cannot supply you with the details, old man, there is one basic fact of which I have become aware, and from which, I suspect, the details spring." He points ahead, to the figures of Caliphestros and Stasi: two beings who seem, in the approaching twilight, to combine into one creature. "There are times when one's own race of beings is the last sort of creature that can or will help or care if you live or die. But if a great heart, like that cat, *does* so care, *chooses* to so care—chooses, in short, *you*—it fills a place that no human can occupy. No mere human, no potion, no powder, no drug—and believe me, I've tried the ones he creates to ease his pain, and they're very effective. But not effective enough. Nothing is, save another great heart. And the reverse is true, as well: Stasi's soul has been mended by a human's. I have seen it between them." Spitting over the mountainside, Heldo-Bah shakes his head. "And so, if that old man is still sane and still capable of doing what he now seems to be doing—seeking knowledge and justice—that is the only reason why. Don't ask me to tell you *how* it happens—talk to Keera, as Veloc says, for that. I know only that it does . . ."

Once again—silently, this time—Visimar studies Heldo-Bah for just an instant, impressed by the forager's words, and then looks to Veloc, who but shrugs his shoulders.

"And so, Heldo-Bah," Visimar asks, "what 'great heart' kept your soul alive, when you were cast out of Broken? For my lord Caliphestros and I have been told that story, as well." Heldo-Bah shoots an icy look at Veloc, who simply shakes his head emphatically. "No, it was not your friends," Visimar says quickly. "It was their parents, Selke and Egenrich, when my master and I returned to your village to prepare these carts. They are truly kind people, Heldo-Bah, and yet you returned to your old habits, even while living with them."

"*That*," Heldo-Bah says, "is because a different type of fire burns within *my* soul, Visimar."

"Ah," the cripple replies knowingly. "Vengeance."

Heldo-Bah nods. "A very different spirit that can fill the heart. I do not pretend the effect is as great," he says quietly. "But it is far more deadly . . ."

Again, Visimar turns to Veloc; but this time, the handsome historian simply smiles, dismissing Heldo-Bah's last statement as bravado.

It is an awkward silence that follows; but then, of a sudden, the horses blow out their frustration and weariness in great snorts, and the carts suddenly heave and then level out; and just that quickly—and precariously—the two teams leave the tree- and brush-lined path and find themselves on the cavalry training ground, which is far larger than Visimar had anticipated, and where many of Sentek Arnem's cavalrymen, as well as the few scouts who are not off determining what weather approaches, are racing about the broad field, chasing down the army's remaining horses, who have been left largely unattended.

"Baster-kin did take a few into the city, Lord Caliphestros," Sentek Arnem says, as he again rides toward the carts, which, between the mist and the near dark, are not easy to find, halted as they are in the shadows of several large fir trees. "But this appears to have been simply to satisfy the sentiments of the most powerful of his fellow merchants and their families, to whom the horses must belong, for he has also taken several of the wealthier children's ponies—"[†]

At that moment, Arnem is interrupted by the sound of quicker, lighter hooves approaching out of the half-darkness and the mist, and everyone on or about the carts turns to witness the appearance of Yantek Ashkatar, riding a small, tan-colored mount with a nearly white mane and tail. The animal's unusual size causes Stasi—who suspects it is merely a young Broken warhorse—to widen her eyes and twitch her tail with thoughts of hunting; yet, as Caliphestros calms her, even the panther realizes that this is no foal, but a creature fully grown: a puzzling discovery, for her and at least some of the Bane alike.

"Look at this little devil, Keera!" Ashkatar calls out. "Have you ever seen the like? He bears my weight as easily as one of his larger cousins would, yet I can ride him with complete control."

"Yes, I have seen the like, Yantek," replies Keera, who nonetheless smiles and laughs at her commander's joy.

"Anyone who has ever been to Broken has seen the like, Ashkatar," Heldo-Bah calls dismissively, as he gets to the ground. "The Tall breed them for their children, and a few rougher varieties to pull carts and wagons up the mountain—for they are indeed as strong as they are strange."

"Well, *I* have never *been* to Broken, as well you know," Ashkatar replies. "And so I am both surprised and pleased to find them. There must be fifty or so, on this field, along with even more horses. Baster-kin apparently does not fear our approach."

"Aye," Arnem says, dismounting from the Ox, "would that he rather did not *expect* it. But, as the scouts have already told us—" Handing his mount's reins to the ever-ready Ernakh, Arnem approaches the lead cart, and eyes Caliphestros, keeping a wary distance between himself and Stasi. "He watches for the first sign of our reaching the mountaintop. And so, it will be for *you* to punish him for having left so many mounts to us. That—and so many other crimes and mistakes, my lord. To punish him with this—with *whatever* is in these containers." As he stands over the bed of Keera's cart, Arnem gets a full breath of the odor arising from within, and steps back. "Kafra's stones, that is a stench! I hope it bodes something unusual—for the gates of Broken, as you know, will not submit to *ballistae,* nor even to ordinary flames."

Suddenly, the mountain trail echoes with the magnified sound of fast-moving horses' hooves, along with a cry of *"Get to the side of the road!"* repeated again and again. Heldo-Bah leaps back aboard his cart, to steer it to the left side of the trail's inlet into the training ground, while Keera moves her own conveyance to the right.

"It's that fire-brained scout of yours, Sentek!" Heldo-Bah shouts. "To judge by the sound of his voice and his horse's pace—whatever he is about, I should move, if I were you—the man would ride down his own mother to achieve his purpose!"

"Which is why I rely upon him," Arnem replies; but the commander, Ashkatar, and Niksar nonetheless comply with Heldo-Bah's suggestion, and then stare down the rutted trail, waiting for Akillus's face to show. But before it does, more horses' hooves resonate from the north, entering the training ground from the relatively short stretch of remaining trail that leads to the ground before the southern and southwestern gates of Broken. *"Where is Sentek Arnem?"* comes a shout from the second scouting party earlier sent in that direction by their commander, and, having been quickly told his location, they descend on the crowd about the carts quickly, reaching it at almost the same instant that Akillus does.

"Sentek!" calls the linnet-of-the-line who leads the northern group. "The sky is clear, once one reaches the open ground above—there is yet a violent storm amid the hills to the west, to be sure, but it is difficult to tell, in this light, how quickly it shall bear down upon Broken, or *if,* indeed, it shall at all!"

"Our own reports confirm this, Sentek," Akillus adds. "All is uncertainty!"

Arnem nods coolly, turning again to issue orders to Ernakh. "Inform Linnets Crupp and Bal-deric that they are to consult Lord Caliphestros on the types of *ballistae* that he wishes made, and to begin building them straightaway. We shall spend no more than one day and one night more upon this ground, before advancing on Broken." Ernakh leaps up on his own small mount and is off, at which Arnem turns to Caliphestros.

"Well, my lord," he says, no little uneasiness in his voice. "The moment has come: you must brew your answer to the Riddle of Water, Fire, and Stone, and the rest of us must make our own preparations."

"Do not look so troubled, Sentek—if only for your men's sake," Caliphestros answers with a small laugh. As he dismounts from Stasi's shoulders, the old man accepts Keera's help in strapping his walking device to his thighs, then takes his crutches from her. "Unity will be as necessary to our endeavor as will force itself. Baster-kin, remember, believes he has righteousness on his side—he thinks he fights the good fight, and he will resist so long as he can. Our only friends remain speed and hope—the hope that, thanks to this mist, he does not yet know our exact position."

"Very well, Lord Caliphestros," Arnem says, turning the Ox to cross the training ground and begin the organization of his attack. "I shall heed these reasons for encouragement—but I nonetheless wait to see what miracle you will draw out of those containers!"

As the various officers' forms fade again into the mist, Caliphestros looks up the mountain, even though, from where he, the foragers, and Visimar stand, only the glow of braziers and the very tops of the walls and guardhouses of Broken can be seen. "No miracle, Sentek," he says softly. Then, in a louder voice, he addresses his former acolyte. "No miracle, eh, Visimar?"

"Oh, no?" Heldo-Bah says skeptically, as he starts to unbind the containers in the carts, with the aid of the other foragers. "What then, old man?"

"Tell me, Heldo-Bah," Caliphestros replies. "You are a more worldly man than most in this camp; did you ever hear mention, among the traders and mercenaries who frequented Daurawah—or anywhere else, for that matter—of what the *Kreikisch* called the fire *automatos*?"[†]

Heldo-Bah stops his work, and stares at Caliphestros with a combination of awe and disbelief. "You haven't . . ."

"I have," Caliphestros answers, as Visimar laughs lightly at the Bane's wonderment.

"But the fire *automatos* is a myth!" Heldo-Bah protests, his voice controlled, so as not to spread what he thinks will be panic, but his feet stomping like a child's, as is his habit when presented with something that is too much for him to bear. "As much a myth as your 'Riddle of Water, Fire, and Stone'!"

"*What* is a myth?" Keera and Veloc ask, almost in unison.

"Oh, Moon—!" the gap-toothed Bane says, with the same hushed urgency.

But Keera interrupts him. "Heldo-Bah—I have warned you about your blasphemies!"

"Blasphemies?" Heldo-Bah replies. "What do *blasphemies* matter? Keera, these two old madmen have rested our entire endeavor upon a *fantasy*!"

Yet Caliphestros and Visimar continue only to laugh quietly, as the former instructs the latter on where each canister should be placed. "Neither the Riddle nor the fire *automatos* are myths, Heldo-Bah," Caliphestros says, still chuckling. "In fact, the fire is the *answer* to the Riddle . . ."

Heldo-Bah attempts no argument, but only nods his head in resignation. "Oh, I am certain it is—and so, go ahead, laugh, you fools," he says. "When you should be praying—praying that you get your rain!"

"It will come," Caliphestros replies; and then, in a slightly more serious voice, he adds, "But will it come with enough violence? No matter, right now. Heldo-Bah, if you know of the fire *automatos,* you must know that we will need every breakable container in the cooks' wagons and the baggage train—rather than weeping, why don't you start to gather them?"

Heldo-Bah makes no further protest, but wanders off meekly, still nodding obediently and speaking in a voice that sounds remarkably like a moaning infant: "Dead men . . . we are all dead men . . ."

3.

TO SEE THE *KHOTOR* of Sixt Arnem's Talons, as well as the two hundred and fifty of the Bane tribe's best warriors, put their full commitment to the task of preparing an attack on Broken, under the direction of subcommanders so expert in their various trades that their like could not be found for hundreds of miles in any direction from the city on the mountain (as well as from Davon Wood), is to watch men and women assembled and readying themselves to do in the best manner possible the most fearsome work, the most awful work, that humankind ever undertakes. For, as Caliphestros explains to those about him, it is only when the essential violence of war combines itself with the arts of *learning,* of construction and experimentation, of the conditioning and steeling of the body *and* the mind—as well as with that finest of arts, *discovery*—that war connects itself to that in Man which is, in truth, both superior and moral. Are these qualities not better attained through other activities? On the greater number of occasions, quite probably so; indeed, this may perhaps be a universal truth. But, like the rain for which Caliphestros waits so impatiently yet confidently on the Broken cavalry training ground, as he mixes his strange brew of materials taken from bogs and mines deep within the Earth, war will visit the lives of all men and women, eventually. And it is in the question of how closely each armed force does or does not labor to connect its practice to those other, nobler studies, rather than allowing it to be confined to mere bloodshed, that will determine any army's true if relative morality (or lack thereof).

Such connections have rarely been in evidence so completely as they are during the relatively few (but ample enough) hours that the Bane warriors and the Talons spend on the cavalry training ground below the southern walls of Broken, during the first night, the following day, and the second evening following their arrival, in preparation for their advance, under cover of darkness, on the walled city. The men's and women's activities would not seem, to those who have witnessed or read of various great clashes of arms through the ages and around the known world, particularly exotic: those Bane (and they are not the majority of their contingent) who have at least some experience on the backs of horses are taught by the Broken cavalrymen to handle the smaller ponies with ease, and to coordinate their movements with larger Broken cavalry *fausten*. This group is led by a restored Heldo-Bah, never so cured of doubt as by action. Together, Bane and Tall riders will provide the attacking army with that single element that besieging forces too often ignore and lack: *mobility*, the ability to test the enemy for points of strength and retreat from and report on their positions, and doing the same if they find weaknesses that can be exploited rapidly. Yet it is in a third role, that of a diversionary force, that cavalry plays perhaps its greatest role during any siege; and Caliphestros lectures Heldo-Bah until the latter cannot stand to hear another word from the old man's mouth on just what part the allied and especially the Bane cavalry shall play, along these lines.

The overall task of the horsemen, in short, is to breed in the enemy from the start a constant sense of imbalance, unhappy surprise, and, in general, the confusion that destroys coherence of command and movement. As for those Bane who will remain afoot, they study how to integrate their own actions into the attack under the overall tutelage of Linnet Taankret: how to play a part in the Mad King Oxmontrot's famed *Krebkellen,* which, like the movements of the cavalry, would seem to less imaginative commanders than Sixt Arnem to have no place in a siege; but, as Yantek Ashkatar is quick to see (much to the satisfaction of both Arnem and Taankret), it can, if its deployment is reimagined.

Nor is it only as students that the Bane have important contributions to make to the great enterprise they will undertake with their former enemies. For, as we have already seen in the annihilation of the First *Khotor* of Lord Baster-kin's Guard, the Bane have their own methods of confounding and deceiving an enemy, ways long considered deceitful and illegitimate by the soldiers of Broken, in that they did not rely on the direct confrontation of warrior against warrior, army against army. Yet they are far from such baseness, as Taankret, Bal-deric, Crupp, and even Arnem himself (to say nothing of the rest of the sentek's officers and men) now learn, primarily—in this as in all such matters—through explanations offered by Caliphestros and Visimar. And once more, it is Akillus—ever willing to modify the tactics of his scouts, and in many ways the cleverest of Arnem's contingent chiefs—who can see the one-leggèd acolyte and his legless master's point that the *khotor* of Baster-kin's Guard that holds the city against only half again as many besiegers may be vulnerable indeed, if any and all "tricks," or more properly, *deceptions,* are employed against Baster-kin's *deceits*. Such deceptions are not at all debasing to the attackers, the attacking force is taught, whereas deceit serves only to dishonor those who stoop to its use; in this case, the Merchant Lord's willingness—even determination—to conceal the many troubles facing his kingdom, as well as his own desire to achieve dishonorable goals, personal and otherwise, under the guise of safeguarding the realm.

After all, Akillus argues during Arnem's first dinner mess on the cavalry ground, one need only consider how many truly disreputable deceits Baster-kin has already employed during this campaign: for how "honorable" was it to send the Talons into an area he had every reason to believe stricken by at least one deadly disease, and then dispatch his own Guard's First *Khotor* into what was thought a safe, perhaps the last safe, region of Broken's southern province, to attack the Bane and steal any glory that Sentek Arnem and his Talons might have gained from their original task of attacking the Bane? These are not the actions of a truly honorable man, Akillus insists; and soon, all of Arnem's staff are forced to agree. (And this is why I, your narrator and guide, have written here of the "Battle" of Broken, marking off the word *battle* in a manner that may seem mocking, but is meant only to warn: to state plainly that to expect, in what remains of my tale, the kind of blind and brutal clash of arms and men that most readers associate with the word *battle,* rather than an example of an employment of wits to cleverly remove the unjust from power, would be a grave mistake.)

Yet how, then, can Caliphestros, who has more reason to despise Lord Baster-kin than does anyone in the allied camp (with the possible exception of his companion, Stasi), call the Merchant Lord "the last good man in Broken"? Because, as he explains at this same meal, in a very real sense his lordship has been and remains just such: even his willingness to arrange the death of his own feckless son Adelwülf, to say nothing of his plans to destroy the Fifth District and the Talons, as well as take Isadora Arnem to wife, have grown, in his lordship's mind, out of a true belief in his own patriotism and desire to strengthen the kingdom by strengthening the clan Baster-kin: the two are one and the same, an assertion that, as matters stand, is hard to deny.

It is this realization that begins to eat into the deepest part of Sixt Arnem's soul when, during the last hours of his own and Ashkatar's combined forces' time on the field below Broken, he listens to Caliphestros, Crupp, and Bal-deric explain the final stages of their construction of their unique group of *ballistae*. Some of these are fairly ordinary machines of war, easily built; but some are such devices as no Broken soldier has ever before seen, designed less to simply batter and destroy than to deliver, in a deceptively gentle manner, Caliphestros's equally remarkable missiles: missiles made, not of stone, but of humble clay containers, which are now filled with that legendary ingredient that the ever-gloomy Heldo-Bah has declared both a myth and the future cause of the now-fully-coordinated allied force's undoing: the fire *automatos*.

By this point, the greater part of the force is already moving north-ward, up the last stretch of mountain path and toward the walls of Bro-ken, in the very dim light of approaching dawn: a dawn that is occasionally augmented by shards of lightning, which is accompanied, at shorter and shorter and shorter intervals, by loud claps of mountain thunder. And if it should seem strange that, even in the midst of all such activities and achievements, Arnem's mind should be so preoccupied with thoughts of Lord Baster-kin's apparent treachery, it needs be re-membered that more than the lives of the sentek's wife and eldest son are now threatened. So, too, is the principle that allowed the sentek to order his once-troubled life, and to make sense of all the fearsome violence that he has both engaged in and led during the years since he first joined the army of Broken: the soldier's code of duty, no small part of which is the unquestioning faith that his superiors' wisdom and morality need not only never be questioned, but *must* be worthy of trust.

However, the sentek soon does force himself to shake free, even of such confusing thoughts; and again fixes upon his goal: "There is no changing course, now," he tells his assembled officers. "Nor am I un-aware or ungrateful of all that each of you has sacrificed, both for this undertaking and for my wife and son, who, for all I know, may be in Baster-kin's custody—or worse—even as we speak. Therefore, let us away to our men—or rather, to our men and women . . ." Taking on a more congenial tone as the two men depart the field, Arnem inquires of the former seneschal of the clan Baster-kin, "Have you noticed, Radelfer, the great ease with which certain of the Talons intermingle with the women warriors of the Bane?"

"I have noticed, Sentek," Radelfer laughs, glad to see Arnem take heart. "Although I would scarce have believed it possible, had anyone merely told me. We are on the verge of strange and powerful changes to our world . . ."

4.

W E HAVE OBSERVED, then, that it has become Sentek Arnem's firm intention, influenced by Caliphestros's lectures in the history and weapons of warfare, to make the siege of Broken, not a drawn-out, dismal affair, but a quick and decisive struggle. Odds do not favor him, as we have also seen: Lord Baster-kin's single *khotor* of Guard troops would have been no match for the sentek's similar number of Talons and their Bane allies in the open field, but with the granite walls and iron-banded, foot-and-a-half-thick oak gates of Broken to protect them, the Guardsmen present a formidable challenge, a foe whose chief weaknesses—inexperience and the unprofessionalism that is ever its consequence—Arnem will have to exploit, not with the usual brute weapons of the siege, but with that most difficult type of operation to conduct, a *grand deception:* a deception that is based not simply on a single device, nor upon the actions of one unit in one phase or area of a battle, but a deception that is coordinated and conducted by an entire army in *every* part of the field, and is carried through without recourse to savage force.

We observers can best understand this strategy as it unfolds, not by attempting to comprehend every order given by those who have constructed it. Rather, by taking to the skies, once more, as we did at the outset of this tale, we shall make for the walls of Broken, where we will watch the great ruse unfold below us. Now, however, we fly in good and Natural company: that of Caliphestros's two allies, the enormous owl he gave the name of Nerthus, and the small but daring starling he calls Little Mischief. It is not difficult to find them, as both birds are in the air above the great city, scanning its streets for any sign of unusual trouble, trouble that they will quickly call to the attention of the remarkable man who is their unique friend. But we immediately see that we have taken flight during the first dismal light of day, which reveals storm clouds still moving on Broken from the horizon to the west. Their speed threatens the city with rain violent enough to match the thunder and lightning that has flashed and rumbled through the night: but will it be rain that serves Caliphestros's strange purpose, the answer to the Riddle of Water, Fire, and Stone, and serves it in time?

The alarm horns of Lord Baster-kin's Guard sound above the main gate of Broken, the East: the point at which any enemy concerned with capturing Broken's richest districts would attack. And if we swoop down upon the streets of the First District of the city, along with our feathered guides, we soon see a tall figure emerging from the *Kastelgerd* Baster-kin, wrapped from neck to calves in a cloak of black velvet, with a cowl of the same luxurious material covering his shoulders, neck, and head. It is the lord of the *Kastelgerd* himself: and when he quickly enters a waiting litter, we hear his distinctive voice shout a command, telling its bearers to make for that same East Gate of the city. We follow the quick progress of the litter, and soon watch as the tall, black-clad man disappears into one of the two ingeniously engineered towers that guard the portal. No one of the city's gates (all of a piece with the great granite walls, and therefore able to support entryways of a thickness and weight far more prodigious than any other city has ever been able to boast) is stronger than the East, simply because of the successive waves of marauders that have appeared from that direction over the centuries, only to be beaten back or convinced to bypass Broken. And so, Lord Baster-kin ascends the worn but seamless steps within the northernmost of these towers without fear; and if we, like Nerthus and Little Mischief, take a perch at the top of a wealthy merchant's home nearby, we can easily observe the exchange of words that takes place between Baster-kin and the Guardsmen stationed at this crucial position.

"There, my lord!" cries a Guardsman, pointing to the spot where the eastern road takes a slight turn to descend the mountaintop, before disappearing from view. "Only see the dust—there must be thousands of them!"

A great cloud of dust such as would, indeed, ordinarily be raised by so large a number of approaching troops is rising from just under the last section of roadway that those on the wall can see; and yet Baster-kin's answer is calm. "Quiet, you fool." He pulls back the hood of his cowl, revealing the topmost portion of a coat of the finest chain mail. Then, looking up and down the wall to see that some thirty or forty men have gathered to observe the ghostly cloud that seems all too close to the gate, he calls out, in a voice now filled with anger: "All of you! Find your spines, and quickly! The traitor Arnem and his unholy Bane allies do not have so many as a thousand troops to bring against us—this dust is simply an indication of how dry the approaches to the city, like our own streets, have become in recent weeks. But look to the west and see the great storm that approaches! When it descends, this cloud of dust shall disappear like the deceitful apparition it is. However"—Baster-kin's eyes narrow as he turns them to the eastern approach and the dust cloud once more—"this most certainly *does* indicate that Arnem has decided to make his first thrust against this gate, without question in the hope of seizing our most sacred centers and persons of power, and then forcing the release of his wife and the other rebels in the Fifth District. Well, we shall deal with Lady Arnem and her friends presently. For now, however, assemble our most powerful *ballistae* upon this wall and within this position, along with the main portion of our men. Do not abandon the other gates, but leave only small watches at each. Position men and machines in such a way that, if the sentek achieves what no marauder leader ever has, and somehow gains entrance through this mass of oak, iron, and stone, he and his followers will be cut down as soon as they enter the city. Move, all of you, we have little time!"

At which the men of the Guard are sent scurrying, their officers trying to call out coherent and coordinated orders—and Lord Baster-kin silently bemoaning the quality of the men with whom he has been left to defend the city. But his faith in its walls and gates, especially the mighty East, is absolute, for he has himself seen to its constant strengthening and restrengthening during his time as Merchant Lord. He has even ignored many of the great stone city's other original yet less visible structures, and allowed them to fall into disrepair, beginning with the Fifth District . . .

Nerthus and Little Mischief may now return to the sky, having seen the great activity that has begun to take place on the walls beside and in the streets below the East Gate of Broken. The owl and the starling (and we ourselves) can see from the sky that the approaching force that lies just under the eastern line of sight from the walls of Broken is *not*, in fact, Caliphestros and Arnem's main force. Rather, it is a detachment of the smaller humans from Davon Wood. And, as the birds arrive above this group, which is led by several of the small men on the strange little horses that the owl and the starling have recently seen added to the army moving up the mountain, we can all attest to the limited number of this group that has separated itself from Caliphestros and Arnem's main force, apparently for the sole purpose of creating the enormous cloud of dust that now fills the sky above the eastern approach to the city.

Indeed, no more than fifty of the men and women from the Wood, riding their small horses, are at work on the road and in the large, dry patches of ground about it, dragging large limbs hacked and torn from nearby fir trees, the needles of which cut into the parched earth almost as violently as do the hooves of the horses, whose movements seem somehow more active, even more frenetic, than are those of their more familiar cousins, just as the smaller humans seem more lively, even wild, than do their larger relations. It is a strange sight, which both Nerthus and Little Mischief understand but little; however, the birds nevertheless follow their instructions to descend upon the familiar and ever-friendly figure of Visimar, and see what instruction he offers next.

They find the old man sitting atop his mare on the edge of the broad area in which the men and women from the Wood are raising their ever-greater dust cloud. Next to Visimar is that same small woman whom both birds last encountered in the treetops just above their meeting with Caliphestros in Davon Wood. These two—Visimar and the small woman—seem to be attempting to command the activity of the others before them; but it is clear that actual authority rests with a man far more fitted, in appearance, for the job: a filthy little man that the birds would consider to be stricken by one of the diseases that, were he one of their kind, lead to pecking and tearing at one's own feathers, as well as to speaking in nonsense chatter.

More remarkable yet, this small man on a small horse has strangely sharpened teeth plainly visible; and yet, for all his mad peculiarities, this atrocious-smelling human never fails to get the most active behavior from his fellows, and so makes the authoritative tasks of both Visimar and the woman next to him almost unnecessary. Thus, Little Mischief feels no compunction about alighting upon the top of Visimar's head; while Visimar, for his part, merrily calls out the starling's name, then quickly extends his arm, seeming to know that the small bird's companion, the enormous (and enormously proud) queen of the night, Nerthus, will soon be swooping in to clutch his wrist and fist, which, along with his other hand and forearm, Visimar has thankfully thought to encase in a pair of leather gauntlets. These leather coverings offer some relief from the talons of the great owl—even if that relief is less than complete.

"*Viz-ee-mah!*" the starling atop the old cripple's head blurts out, punctuating the name with those clicks and crackles that can often make the starling such an annoying bird, especially in the early morning hours.

"My lord!" Keera says, half-delighted and half-mystified. "These are the same birds with whom I observed his lordship having most extraordinary congress during our march to Okot."

"They have been the messengers between Lord Caliphestros and myself for years, since long before this undertaking," Visimar answers, "although never was their service more vital than in recent weeks." Still holding the great owl, he indicates to Keera that she should extend a pair of fingers. "All right, Little Mischief," he says. "Leap upon the fingers of a new friend: *Keera.*"

The bird's head swivels and bobs upon his ever-active body, and he soon leaps down upon Keera's hand, his small feet creating a trembling, vital sensation throughout the forager's hand and body. That sensation is as nothing, however, to when the starling looks up at the Bane woman with his black eyes and declares, "*Kee-rah!*"

"My lord—!" the tracker exclaims softly.

"Oh, it's nothing to do with me," Visimar replies. "One of the many successful experiments, based on previous years of the study of bird as well as other animal life besides our own, that my master conducted in the Wood and elsewhere. Little Mischief—for such is the name Lord Caliphestros gave him—will now know you forever. I cannot pretend to understand how or why; but I do know that it can be of great use . . ." Visimar's eyes fix on the starling's intently for a moment, and he says, "Little Mischief—you go with *Kee-rah*—just to the top of the hill. See what the men on the walls of *Boh-ken* are about, and in what numbers." Visimar looks up. "Keera?"

Keera is too entranced by the magic of the moment to think of hesitating at the order. "Aye, Lord Visimar!" she replies, turning her pony to the east, and making for the crest behind which her fellow Bane have been so hard at work to create their illusion. The trip of woman and bird is a short one, however; in just a few minutes Keera races back to Visimar, enthusiasm in her features. "They do just as we hoped, my lord!" she calls. "Men line the walls between the guardhouses, and bring heavy *ballistae* up to assist them."

Visimar nods knowingly. "Oxmontrot was wise, to make his walls wide enough to support such engines of war," he says. "Although, in this case—as in so many—his descendants will, it appears, make a weakness of his wisdom." Attempting to stare once again into the eyes of the starling that perches upon Keera's fingers, Visimar is forced to purse his lips and whistle sharply; for the bird is still entranced by Keera's features, just as he was in the treetops of Davon Wood.

"Hear me, now, Little Mischief!" Visimar says, with urgency; for the sound of his whistling has finally attracted the starling. "Go to *Kaw-ee-fess-tross,* and say this:" He uses words that Little Mischief—who richly deserves his name, Keera has decided—understands: *"So-jers. So-jers, so-jers, so-jers, Boh-ken, eees!"*

The repetition of the first word, Keera supposes, is intended to indicate that there are *many* soldiers; the last, that these soldiers have gathered at the East Gate. When she sees Visimar detect a gleam, if not of comprehension, then at least of correct memorization, in the starling's black eyes, Keera watches the old man pull a bit of parchment from his robe, and, with his free right hand, place it upon his thigh and print a strange symbol upon it with charcoal.

Catching sight of her interested expression, Visimar explains, "It is merely a coded method that my master and I had of relating meeting places and enemy movements, when he was in the Wood and I in the city, before our communication was severed by my *Denep-stahla* . . ." Having completed the brief scratch of charcoal, Visimar holds it up to his Bane friend; but Keera must ask, "Are they wholly of your own invention, then? For they are not the same as those that appear on the ancient rocks we use for mapping trails."

"Not wholly our own," Visimar explains. "But this is also a runic way of writing, although one not quite dead: merely borrowed by my master from tribes to the north, so that there was little chance that the Kafran, who take little interest in those kingdoms and nations about them, would comprehend them."

Folding the parchment carefully, Visimar produces a string, with which he clearly means to tie the simple message to the talons of the waiting Nerthus; but the great owl takes this as something of an insult, in one motion batting the string away and then using the same talon to clutch the parchment tight, as if to tell Visimar that she no more needs binding to achieve an important assignment than does the starling that is her constant source of irritating (if often affectionate) company and competition. A somewhat chastised Visimar takes the owl's meaning perfectly:

"Very well, then, Nerthus, carry your message to Caliphestros freely, just as Little Mischief does—but hurry, great and beautiful lady. For time now presses, as the storm approaches the city . . ."

And so, with Heldo-Bah, Veloc, and their detachment of Bane warriors continuing to delightedly raise as much dust and noise as they can about the eastern road to Broken, the two birds take flight. Watching them go with a smile, Keera asks a final question: "One point still puzzles me, Visimar: why does Lord Caliphestros wait for the rain to begin before our main assault?"

"Because the rain will *spark* the fire *automatos*," Visimar replies. "The most fiercely burning flame known, even in the mightiest kingdoms—and all our subsequent plans depend on that ancient fire."

Keera grows bewildered. "*Water* will spark *fire*, my lord?"

Visimar shakes his head. "Again, I do not pretend to understand it, Keera, any more than I understand the Riddle of Water, Fire, and Stone. I can only tell you this: that my master's science has never failed, to my knowledge. And so, yes, when the great storm begins, I will wager that we shall see a most remarkable and shocking sight . . ."

5.

NOT MANY MOMENTS LATER, at the crest of the trail that connects a patch of ground south of Broken's walls with the larger, lower plain upon which Sentek Arnem and Yantek Ashkatar's allied force received its final training and orders, loud sounds of amazement—some amused, some awed, but by now, all accepting—can be heard emerging from the sentek's newly reconstructed tent.

Arnem has established his main headquarters for the attack upon the city at the terminus of this trail, so that his tent, like the rest of his camp, is at least partially protected from the eyes of the sentries upon the southern walls of the city by the few stands of firs that have withstood the rocky ground and centuries of wind upon the summit of the mountain. But the sounds of consternation within that tent are not sparked by the plans for deployment of the main part of the allied force, but by the silhouettes of the two birds that can be seen flying away from just outside the shelter, to seek safety among the nearby trees. For these birds—Little Mischief and Nerthus—have brought to Lord Caliphestros what he claims is positive assurance that the deception being supervised by Visimar and Keera below the East Gate of Broken has been a wholehearted success; and that, therefore, the second stage of the allied action must commence immediately.

After handing that assurance over to Sentek Arnem, Lord Caliphestros chose to move atop Stasi to a point nearby the commander's tent, so that his presence would not unduly influence any reactions to the idea of intelligence coming from such a source as birds. And now, as the various commanders emerge from their latest council and move off to prepare for the second and third phases of the attack, Caliphestros remains at that nearby, shadowy spot, keeping his companion—who senses the coming climaxes, both in human affairs and in the weather atop the mountain—calm; and it is here that Arnem finds the pair, gazing almost wistfully off toward the great shadow that is the South Gate of Broken.

"I shall say this, my lord," Sixt Arnem announces, as he watches his trusted commanders move off toward their various tasks, then joins the legless old man. "Your years in the Wood have taught you endurance, but they have also made you forget how remarkable many things that you have come to take for granted must appear to men from either Okot *or* Broken. New realities or notions are not so easy to accept; and the facility with which you have brought myself, Yantek Ashkatar, and our respective officers to accept and appreciate the new realities with which you have acquainted us is to be commended—with no little awe, I might add."

"The sentek speaks truly, Lord Caliphestros," Ashkatar says, his characteristic laugh rolling up from his powerful chest as he follows Arnem. "No one shares your hatred for the men who rule in Broken more than we Bane; yet there were times when, even as I believed that you offered us hope, I could not understand—and, I will admit, even doubted the sense of—your orders and actions: the endless digging on our march home to Okot, after our initial meeting, or the very identity of your companion, the white panther, one of the great legends of our people . . . Once explained, of course all doubt was put away; but every day, every hour, every moment, it has seemed that not only our officers but our men have been asked to accept strange or incredible notions—yet they do so now as if they were the most common of commands. And here the sentek and I stand, by way of profound example, prepared to gamble the timing of the stages of our attack on communications brought by messengers who have feathers rather than feet!"

"This all may be true," Caliphestros says at length. "But had I not happened upon men and women prepared to believe in all I have learned, any 'new realities' of my own would have been explained in vain. And now—but one more 'new reality' left to prove . . ." Straightening up, he searches the officers who move away from the tent. "Are Linnets Crupp and Bal-deric here?"

"We are, my lord," Crupp answers, as he and Bal-deric step forward.

"And our various *ballistae* ready to take up their positions?" Caliphestros then indicates the roiling clouds that continue to darken the light of early morning. "For we *must* be ready when this storm strikes."

"And we shall be, my lord. Please do not doubt that." It is Bal-deric who now speaks. "The first group of machines reached their positions before this council dispersed. As for the others—" Bal-deric indicates the trail up from the training ground, alongside which sit not only Arnem's command tent, but the second collection of Caliphestros's *ballistae*. "We await only word from the Southwestern Gate, as well as any movement by the Guardsmen themselves, at which time we shall wheel them into both place—and action."

"You must not make your actions too dependent upon such messages and signs," Caliphestros replies, with more urgency than any officer present has seen him exhibit before. "The *rain*, gentlemen!" The old man leans forward to take up a nearby piece of fir branch and then wave it before Stasi's jaws, at which the white panther begins to playfully yet fearsomely gnaw at the section of wood and needles. "When the rain strikes, the South Gate must be coated—" He points the branch toward the *ballistae*'s carts and their beds full of clay containers, each ready for launching. "And if indeed it is, you shall see something never before witnessed upon this mountain." At last allowing Stasi to take the fir branch from him, that she may continue gnawing upon it, Caliphestros adds only: "I have said enough, I'm certain you will agree. Sentek Arnem—I leave the rest to you . . ."

While Caliphestros proceeds, as he has so often done on this march, to seek solace in the company of the white panther alone, Sixt Arnem declares, "Well, then, Bal-deric—finish the installation of your *ballistae* at the Southwestern Gate, and begin your bombardments. And with luck— we shall soon know you have completed the job properly by the cries of terror among Lord Baster-kin's Guard!"

Happily, those cries do soon come, in good time for Linnet Crupp and Caliphestros to be prepared to move their second set of *ballistae* to join the others well before the rain climbs up the slopes of Broken. Preparations are nearly complete: what Lord Baster-kin sees as an ill-disciplined attack—one first striking at the East Gate, then at the Southwest— conducted by allies who know little about each other (and trust less), has in fact, to this point, been an elaborate performance carried on precisely to lead him to such a conclusion. How wrong or right he will have been to trust in his native prejudices, in the beliefs and disbeliefs handed down to him by generations of haughty but undeniably effective predecessors, must now be put to a mortal test. But the point of true attack shall not come at Broken's East Gate, its strongest, nor at its Southwest, where Baster-kin has now been induced to have men and machines waiting, as well; rather, the assault will be launched, as it was always intended it should be launched, at the South Gate, another formidable portal before which it is particularly difficult to assemble a large host with supporting machines, and above all, a spot which Lord Baster-kin, who would never have been likely to expect such an assault, has been carefully convinced to think the allied force has struck from its list of candidates.

But, as is known to those who have studied war in the East, the greatest generals do not attack where their enemies are, but where they are not: a thought that would seem obvious, save for the incredible frequency with which commanders violate it. In addition, those same eastern military teachers exhort that battles are played out in the minds of those who conceive them long before the first screaming clash of arms takes place; and they are won ere the opposing commander ever offers his sword or his head in subjugation. These are all factors of importance, because Caliphestros is a man who has been as far to the East as anyone not born there, and he has studied these theories and practices of war well. Thus, it is his vision above all that plays out in the "Battle" for Broken, which is indeed a nearly concluded affair by the time that Linnet Bal-deric's conventional *ballistae* begin to hammer the Southwest Gate of the city with enormous pieces of ancient granite: stone once cleared from within the walls of the city to allow its creation, but that never found its way back within to facilitate the construction of proper homes for the residents of the Fifth District, and which serves instead, now, to give force to the left claw of Sentek Arnem's massively reimagined *Krebkellen*.

Despite the superiority of the allied force's battle plan in Caliphestros's mind, he is, by his own admission, no commander of men in the field; and it is thus for Sentek Arnem and Yantek Ashkatar to ensure the resolve of the warriors under their command once true battle has been joined. So far as the Bane fighters are concerned, Ashkatar knows that he need not concern himself with the contingent at the East Gate of the city: his men upon ponies had been tasked with but one responsibility—the creation and maintaining of so much mayhem that to those within Broken it would appear a fearsome company of horses and men were moving into position to attack. Such was and remains an assignment perfectly suited to the talents of Heldo-Bah, Ashkatar long ago determined: Visimar and Keera might have overseen its proper initiation, to ensure that it did not descend into the kind of ecstasy of madness on Heldo-Bah's part of which the file-toothed Bane is more than capable—and this they have indeed managed to do, with the somewhat less effective help of Veloc, whose soul remains perilously balanced between the glistening heights of philosophy and the tempting depths of depravity. Yet the true rallying and spurring on of the eastern deceivers has been the work, above all, of the irrepressible and constantly screaming Heldo-Bah.

Back where the work of truly preparing an assault is being done, both Ashkatar's and Sixt Arnem's styles of inspiring and motivating their troops are once again on display, just as we have observed them so before in these pages. Ashkatar's remains that strange combination of affectionate encouragement and harsh warning, punctuated by hard cracks of his ever-reliable whip, which keeps the men and women who form his ranks in motion. Yet, with the greater portion of the Bane horsemen at work to the east, what exactly are the rest of the Bane warriors responsible for, as the tasks of Sentek Arnem's *ballistae* do the main work of the battle's opening phase? We shall come to such matters soon enough: suffice to say now that Bane axes (new axes, forged for them by Caliphestros from the steel that the tribesmen believe comes from the stars and is a gift from the Moon) can be heard within the mountain's highest stands of trees, resounding as they strike the trunks of the mighty, lonely fir giants. It is not surprising, given all this activity, that Ashkatar's already thunderous voice, made even more terrifying by the manner in which it resonates up from just below the peak of the mountain, is full of oaths both profane and affectionate—so affectionate, that the occasional Bane warrior takes no offense to seemingly insulting references to such things as his or her parentage:

"You, there!" he might bellow at a member of a felling crew. "I will not see such fainthearted effort from a whelp of mine!" And then the whip will crack, making a sound as harsh as the first cracks of the tree's felling; and, finally, the commander's voice sounds again: "Oh, you are no offspring of mine? Wipe that look from your face, soldier, there's many a Bane on this mountain today to whom I am more than Yantek! Ha! Swing that axe as *I* would, you lazy pup!"

And the wonder is that the warriors under his command actually take heart from such perhaps absurd but nonetheless endearing berating. Ashkatar's treatment of the female fighters of the Bane tribe, meanwhile, is not tempered by any belief that women possess more fragile souls than do men: if they did, he is quick to remind them, they would have done well to have stayed home. Far from being no less demanding of his women, Ashkatar's whip sometimes cracks more often in their company; and, when, as Arnem and Caliphestros have predicted, the thunderous pounding upon the Southwest Gate caused by Bal-deric's *ballistae* causes a sudden panic upon the eastern walls, and Lord Baster-kin is heard to shout his own commands (equally loud, but far less endearing) that more than half his artillery be shifted to the Southwest Gate, it is the women archers of the Bane who are ordered forward to harass the movement, under cover of stout blinds assembled by all the bowmen of each people's contingent, as well as under the great shields of Taankret's *Wildfehngen*.

But it is the insults and derision thrown at the men of the Guard as they pass from the East to Southwest Gate by the Bane women warriors that are especially disheartening to Baster-kin's inferior soldiers. For to take an arrow, to such men, is terrifying or deadly enough—to take it to the loud sounds of women in a seeming constant state of uncontrolled laughter, is quite another. Yet when one linnet of the Guard has the temerity to suggest to Lord Baster-kin that some of the Guard's few bowmen be moved to address the problem, words are heard raining down from the Southwest Gate (for it is to this position that Baster-kin has himself moved, to supervise the *re*-construction of many of the *ballistae* that he had only just succeeded in getting his men to fully assemble on either side of the East Gate) that are as something more than music to Bal-deric's ears:

"Silence, you idiot! These unnatural women are only meant to make your legs weak and your minds confused—as indeed they are doing! I have told you: one of these two actions, that at the East or that at the Southwest Gate, is intended as a ruse: but what good is a ruse, when see how even the most weighty rocks make little or no dent in the oak and iron of the Southwest! By Kafra, if this is all the traitor Arnem has to offer us, then we can have every expectation of success—provided sniveling cowards such as yourself find their manhood, and are not shaken by a collection of mad but harmless hags in armor!"

Word of this remark is immediately sent by runner to "the traitor Arnem"; who knows that now, he must exhort his own main force to prepare for the truly critical assault, the unique attack that will follow the work of Caliphestros's *ballistae* at the South Gate. For it is not simply that the legless old philosopher has pledged the destruction of that gate at the commencement of what increasingly resembles a tempest; that is merely the *third* deception that composes his plan. There is a fourth deception that completes the great design; and it is that deception for which Arnem's men, especially his horsemen, must be prepared to move quickly and decisively.

And so, just as the first of Caliphestros's strange and comparatively few war machines—the construction of which was made possible only by the experience and comprehension of Linnet Crupp—is finally rolled into position on the small open space before the South Gate, Sentek Arnem begins to ride up and down every position that his men hold, preparing them for an act that seems far less natural than it does to his allies: an assault upon the city that is the heart of their own kingdom.

Preparatory appeals such as this, whatever legend may tell us, are seldom effective if they have not been preceded by years of experience, respect, and near-constant reminders that a commander has never asked his men to go into action without attending to every necessary preparation to ensure their success, as well as complete willingness to share their danger. Arnem's words now are therefore few:

"There is little more that I can tell you, Talons," he calls, still an impressive figure, after so many days spent primarily in the saddle, atop the great grey stallion named for the Mad King. "Little more, save that of which I have attempted, until now, not to speak; but speak of it now I must. We all stand to see our families beyond these walls, if we indeed have any, at the very least shunned, likely censured and perhaps far, far worse for our part in today's action. Your loyalty in refusing to allow this to weaken your dedication, even once, speaks for itself; and if it did not, what should I say that would make up the lack? But I have withheld one fact from you, because I did not wish that same steady dedication that you have shown to revert into undisciplined zealotry: Lord Baster-kin will see me punished, should we fail, with as much injustice and cruelty as he once levied against Lord Caliphestros, who courageously returns to this city with us to see his former enemy chastised. But it is not any venom that the Merchant Lord may direct toward me that chills my soul. No, rather it is the sickened desire, tainted by anger, that he directs toward Lady Arnem—toward *my wife*—that has so frightened me that I have not been able to speak of it, until today: for the Merchant Lord has—for many years, it seems—*coveted* Lady Arnem!" Murmurs of astonishment that rapidly become the beginnings of rage spread through the Talons. "Nor is that all!" their commander continues. "In order to make possible his sickened fancy, he has knowingly ordered not only myself, but all of our *khotor* into parts of the kingdom he knew to be diseased! If we lived through this ordeal, supposed his lordship, we would but die in the Wood, with either result suiting his purpose—but if neither eventuality came about, this would suit his design, as well, for, besides declaring us traitors to the Grand Layzin and hence the God-King, the Merchant Lord has, these many months, been poisoning his own diseasèd wife, under the guise of treating her, in order that he may be free to take *my* lady to his side, and produce new sons for the clan Baster-kin—sons more fit for leadership than his own scion, whose death his lordship has been mad enough, only recently, to oversee in the Stadium!"

And this news, as the sentek had hoped, brings the full anger and determination of the Talons to the fore. Despite their always strong loyalty to their commander, more than a few have been confused, in the most shielded parts of their souls, by much of what they have seen and been ordered to do, on this strangest of marches. But even an intimation of harm to—and worse than harm to, violation of—Isadora, the woman who Arnem has rightly claimed is more the beating heart of their ranks than he is himself, is simply too much for the men to bear. Combined with their deep worries for the fates of their own kin, this revelation causes protestations to erupt from every direction, and every kind of pledge and oath is declared: there will be no further need for the sentek to urge the men to find their mettle.

All that is left for him to do is demonstrate to the Talons, and to all the army, that access to the Fifth District, and the city beyond, is possible. For this is, in fact, the final deception embodied in the allied plan: not to bring the citizens of the Fifth District *out* of Broken, but to take possession *of* that district, and use it as a base of operations from which to destroy Lord Baster-kin's Guard. And so, with his men still roaring their angry defiance of the Merchant Lord, as well as their passionate defense of the Lady Arnem, to say nothing of their long-standing hatred of the Guardsmen, Arnem gallops to the position that Caliphestros and Crupp have taken up before the South Gate.

"Well, Sentek," Caliphestros announces, "it seems improbable to me that the moment will ever be more propitious."

"Indeed, my lord," Arnem replies; and Caliphestros can see that the sentek's passion has been no mere performance designed to exhort his troops; now that he has spoken of it publicly, Arnem's fear for his wife and his son has risen to the surface, and he is impatient for what is to come.

"Tell me, my lord—what in the world *are* those things?" Arnem questions, as Crupp commands the men who crew the *ballistae* to load the first of the clay containers that hold the old man's devilishly foul substance into the cradles that sit at the back ends of lengthy, greased ramps. The ramps themselves are secured through adjustable gears of elevation atop heavy wheeled frames, but the angle of flight they are meant to achieve is clearly higher than any device the men commanded by either Bal-deric or Crupp himself would usually be able to achieve; yet Crupp and his men are experienced with all such weapons, and unlikely to commit obvious errors. Rather, it is the *ballistae* themselves that appear, for all the world, less like the usual variety of torsion-driven battering machines, such as Linnet Bal-deric continues to use at the Southwest Gate, than they do enormous bows placed upon their sides.

"I first designed and experimented with such devices when I dwelt for a time in the land of the Mohammedans," Caliphestros explains, "before they, too, declared my presence 'offensive.' But they soon decided—with apologies, Sentek, but just as you did—that the weapons could have but little use as devices for battering, and were therefore a mere folly. Having already encountered, in Alexandria, the formula for the fire *automatos*, I had been thinking from the first of how such machines could be adapted for the delivery of the substance: a longer span for the two bow wings, a gentler force of release, to be compensated for by a higher trajectory." Turning to the western sky, Caliphestros, along with the rest of Arnem's force, feels a new mist—this one very damp indeed—creeping up and over the mountain. "We have little time. Yantek Ashkatar has signaled that he is ready. Sentek, it is for you to give the order."

"I do not think the order was ever truly mine to issue, Caliphestros," Arnem replies. "But insofar as it may be, you have it."

And with that, the great experiment begins . . .

6.

WITH STRONG BUT CAREFUL BLOWS of great wooden mallets, Linnet Crupp's men release the restraining blocks on Caliphestros's strange machines. The first of the clay vessels slide almost noiselessly (for they, too, have been greased, like the rails upon which they ride) up and into the sky, staying aloft for what seems an impossible period of time. Not a sound is heard from any member of the attacking force, although cries of sudden alarm do go up from those members of the Merchant Lord's Guard positioned above the South Gate.

"My lord Baster-kin!" these men shout. "Still more *ballistae*, at the South Gate!" Within moments, Baster-kin has himself become visible, even before the first of the clay containers has reached the end of its flight.

"What in Kafra's name . . . ?" he blasphemes, his furious gaze watching the vessels sail to what must surely be spots short of the gate. But he has not reckoned on Linnet Crupp's mastery of the art of such arcs; and although the vessels land on the lower half of the gate, land they do, smashing to bits and coating appreciable areas of the stout oak with a remarkably adhesive substance, the odor of which he cannot yet identify.

But when Crupp orders quick adjustments to the *ballistae*, raising both their bows and the ramps upon their frames, and then commands a second launch, the next flight of vessels find their way to the top of the gate with expert precision; and from here, it is impossible for any man upon the walls to mistake their strong stench.

"*Incendiaries*, Sentek?" Lord Baster-kin shouts derisively. "This is why you tied your fortunes to the sorcerer Caliphestros, who has clearly gone soft in the head? Ha! Only look at the western slope of the mountain, you fools—within minutes we shall be pelted with a driving rain, and what of your 'incendiaries,' then, you traitorous dolts?"

Arnem views the black figure on the wall with the thin-eyed, smiling hatred of a man who believes he will shortly deliver the decisive blow to his enemy. "Yes, driving rain," he murmurs. "Eh, Lord Caliphestros?"

"You are yet too confident, Sentek," Caliphestros replies. "Crupp, be quick! We have the range, now—in less time than you would have thought imaginable, that gate must be coated. *Coated!* Fire, *fire*, and above all, continue firing!"

The coverage of the remaining surface of the South Gate takes less time than is required for Crupp's expert loaders to loose all the containers from their bindings inside their carts; and such is a good thing, too, for, just as the first containers have achieved their work, Arnem, like every other man on the mountain, is momentarily blinded by a series of lightning strikes brilliant enough to cut through the foggy morning, and then shaken by a clap of thunder louder than any he can ever remember hearing. The rain, when it comes, is all that Caliphestros has predicted, hoped for, and relied upon; and in its wake, those before the South Gate, as well as those atop it, become witness to something that no one among them (save the old sage himself) has ever before encountered, and that many, particularly atop Broken's walls, will wish never to have seen even this once:

It is announced by Heldo-Bah, who left his own contingent of riders to continue their work below the East Gate once he felt the first drops of rain fall; at that point, having made sure that the Bane riders knew only to stay in their position so long as the rain permitted any dust to rise, he joined Keera, Veloc, and Visimar in riding wildly for the South Gate. None of them wished to miss Caliphestros's promised creation of an event that Heldo-Bah has repeatedly called a fantasy. But despite the noisy Bane's doubts, by the time the four arrive on the spot, none are disappointed, nor are the hundreds of Bane and Broken troops who have moved forward to see living proof of:

The fire *automatos.* When the windswept rain strikes the South Gate, that portal is completely coated in Caliphestros's slowly dripping concoction; and, to the amazement of all, the thick oak between the iron bands of the gate is suddenly consumed in a fire completely strange, one that seems something out of a vision, or perhaps more rightly a nightmare. It is a fire that the awed Heldo-Bah, as only he can, declares:

"Kafra's infernal piss . . ."[†]

The first and most arresting aspect of the fire is its brilliance. For while the others in Arnem's force have expected, at best, to see a traditional fire that has somehow defied the falling rain, this is a conflagration primarily blue and especially white in color—and, most remarkable of all, it has not been extinguished, but *ignited by the rainfall.* Furthermore, the harder the storm pelts down upon the gate, the more fiercely the fire burns. Nor does it do so *atop* the great oak blocks: rather, its fierce, destructive heat appears to burn ferociously *into* the wood, as though it were a living, burrowing being, anxious to reach some point within or beyond the oak itself. In addition, its action is swift: the whitest parts of its terrible flame hiss and snap to match the pelting waters that drive it on.

All among Arnem's force are anxious to brave the few archers of the Guard who have remained atop the South Gate (to do what good it is impossible to tell, for they are greatly outnumbered by the superior Talon and Bane bowmen who are covering the actions of Crupp's *ballistae*), and to take turns feeding Crupp's great machines: for, as Caliphestros continually cries out, the fire *automatos* must be constantly replenished, constantly *fed,* that the blue-and-white-flamed creature may continue to sate its feverish appetite to move inward, ever inward, as if it is a being not only voracious but single-minded:

And its sole goal, it seems, is to reach the opposite side of the oak before it, and reduce the mighty iron banding that binds those prodigious wooden towers to a pile of glowing scrap that the Broken horsemen will be able to pull away with comparative ease.

For all these reasons, and despite every word of doubt that he has ever voiced concerning both the Riddle of Water, Fire, and Stone (for who can doubt, now, that water and fire have indeed come together to defeat the mighty stone walls of Broken?) and the fire *automatos* itself, Heldo-Bah races about in mad ecstasy upon his pony, until he has clapped eyes upon the legless old man he has so often mocked. When he sees Caliphestros, sitting proudly—but still without complete satisfaction—on the back of the white panther, Heldo-Bah dismounts and races for the pair of them, first pushing his face in the pleased panther's neck and burrowing as far into her wet, pungent fur as he is able, and then insisting on removing the old philosopher's skullcap and kissing his balding pate.

"Heldo-Bah!" Caliphestros protests, although even Stasi cannot take his protests seriously enough to attempt to defend him. "Heldo-Bah, there is yet work to do, and you are behaving like a child who has become disordered in his mind and senses!"

"Perhaps so," Heldo-Bah declares, taking a seat upon Stasi's powerful back and coming as close to embracing the distinguished gentleman in front of him as Caliphestros will allow. "But you have made good on your promise, old man!" he cries. "And in doing so, you have made every other portion of this attack seem possible!" Carelessly replacing Caliphestros's cap and tweaking his bearded cheek, the forager returns to the ground, and loudly kisses the muzzle of the great cat, who, while mystified by the action, is no less understanding of its intent, and in sheer joy, opens her mouth to let out that curious half-roar that is her method of communication.

And yet, Heldo-Bah thinks to himself, this is not the mournful sound that he has heard her make in the past; quite the contrary. The forager therefore turns to Caliphestros, who is busy fixing his skullcap with no little annoyance, to ask, "Lord Caliphestros? Is this joy at the humiliation of those who took the lives of her children? Or some other happiness that I do not understand?"

By this time, Caliphestros notices that the entire previous scene has been observed by Visimar, Keera, and Veloc, all of whom sit upon their mounts with wide grins, as Heldo-Bah retrieves his own pony and remounts it. "Nay," Caliphestros says. "This is a specific happiness, I have but lately learned. When Lord Radelfer came to our camp, he brought me most extraordinary news: the sole cub of Stasi's who was taken alive, all those years ago, by Baster-kin's hunting party has been *kept* alive, for the amusement of the athletes in the great Stadium. As 'alive,' that is, as any animal can be kept in the dungeons below that place of sickening spectacle—"

The old philosopher is interrupted by a single noise: the first great, thunderous crack of the oak planks of the South Gate. The attackers before the gate can suddenly make out, above the deteriorating portal, the figure of Lord Baster-kin, who is returning from the southwest wall: the site at which, the Merchant Lord had become certain, the main attack on Broken would actually come.

And although this much more may be impossible for those on the ground to perceive, Baster-kin's proud face suddenly sinks into utter despair, as he realizes that his calculations have been incorrect; that whatever sorcery (and he persists in believing it so) the outcast criminal Caliphestros has used to create this fire that has been ignited by, and burns so terribly hot in the midst of, a rainstorm, it is the fire itself that may well prove his undoing.

"Very well," he mutters bitterly, running his hands through his drenched hair and smelling the stench of his rain-soaked velvet cloak that clings to his armor. "But if my world is to vanish—then I can yet take pieces of yours with me . . ." Glancing about at the sky, and realizing that his long-held plan to burn the Fifth District has also been undone, Baster-kin feels his bitterness run deeper; and his only thought, now, is for vengeance. "For if my triumph can be stolen—then you will yet find, all of you, that yours can be turned to ashes in your mouths . . ." He glances at the Guardsmen immediately about him. "Three of you—now! We go upon what may be our last errands of blood!" And then, making his way into the nearest guardhouse, Baster-kin descends to the Fifth District, below, a long and lethal dagger appearing from within his cloak.

It is a dagger, however, that will be stricken from the Merchant Lord's hand almost as soon as he exits the guard tower, just as life is immediately stricken from the unlucky Guardsmen who accompany him. And as he glances about, ready to inflict his wrath on whatever unlucky resident of the Fifth District may have committed the act, Baster-kin discovers a terrible fact that instantly changes the outlook of his entire existence. By now, the South Gate of the city has begun to glow with the destruction of its inner side, and by this light, Baster-kin can see clearly, circling him:

Some ten enormous, powerful attendants from the High Temple, all armed with terrible, seven-foot sacred halberds, well-kept blades that reflect enough firelight upon their gathering for Baster-kin to realize that these are not attendants that he has ever seen before. Their smoothly shaven heads also reflect the light of the gate that will soon collapse in flame—and they wave the Merchant Lord toward the Path of Shame.

"Rendulic Baster-kin," one of them states, in a tone as impressive as is his long, gilt-edged black tunic. "Your presence is required by the God-King Saylal, as well as by the Grand Layzin. And I suggest we move with haste, ere what was entrusted to you as one of the impregnable portals to the sacred city comes crashing down about our heads."

"The *God-King*?" Baster-kin repeats; and for the first time, this supremely powerful man feels the same terror he knew as a boy, when called into the angry presence of his tempestuous father; but, now as then, he attempts initial defiance. "Why do you not address me by my proper title?"

"You no longer have either title or rank," the attendant replies, a strange joy in his eyes. "But you *have* been granted that rarest of gifts—a journey to the Inner City."

Baster-kin's very guts fill with dread; but he will not show this collection of fearsome priests the same terror he once allowed his father to witness. He somehow finds the strength to draw himself up to his full height and attempt his haughtiest posture, and then says simply, as he points along the military pathway, "Very well, then—lead on, that I may finally perceive the visage of my most gracious and sacred sovereign. For I have no reason to fear an audience with him, having only ever served his will."

As the former lord steps forward, however, several of the sacred halberds cross to prevent him. "Not that way," says the same attendant, his voice answering pride with disdain. "You shall ascend the Path of Shame."

The Merchant Lord is momentarily taken aback. "But the Path of Shame has been walled off from the rest of the city."

The attendant nods. "True—and the God-King would ask you about that. As it is, an opening has been made in your illegal barrier. Wide enough to allow our coming—and our going. Shall we, Rendulic Baster-kin?"

"My 'illegal barrier'?" Baster-kin echoes; while silently he realizes, *So that is to be the way of it . . .* But aloud he utters not another word, as he begins what he is all too certain will be his final walk through the streets of the great city.

Soon, however, he is detained: a small group of elderly military veterans—one of whom he vaguely recognizes, as the old soldier hobbles upon a crutch of truly fine workmanship—step out from the Arnem home, near the head of the Path of Shame. The men surround a woman, the lady of the house, Baster-kin can easily see: she for whom, and yet in spite of whom, he has undertaken so many of his recent endeavors. The Lady Isadora Arnem. With her eldest son close by her side, she walks out of the family's garden door; and while both mother and son appear more gaunt than when he last confronted them, they are far more healthy than the greater number of those citizens past whom it is now Baster-kin's destiny to walk, in other districts of the city.

"My lord," comes Isadora's unfailingly kind yet strong voice that instantly reminds Baster-kin of the strangest and, in their way, happiest days of his life. "Rendulic," she continues, taking what would seem an unheard-of liberty; yet none of the royal and sacred attendants so much as makes a move to either prevent her approach or upbraid her manner. Isadora looks to the man who leads the increasingly ominous group. "May I, Attendant?" her ladyship continues.

The man fills his face with a facile smile. "Of course," he replies. "The God-King would have us show every deference to the family of the great Sentek Arnem, out of consideration for the perfidious confusion that has somehow come to dominate the kingdom's treatment of that great man, and of all those he holds dear."

Baster-kin merely nods bitterly, glancing at the attendants again, and then fixes his gaze on Isadora once more. His words, however, are yet addressed to his escort. "Please inform the Lady Arnem that I have nothing to say to her at this time."

But before the leading attendant can respond, Isadora has stepped forward, with a sweetness of urgency to which only a man whose heart has been embittered over long years of loneliness and disappointment could fail to respond. "Rendulic, please, you must try—" Isadora says, unsure of what message she is attempting to communicate. Nor can Baster-kin comprehend her meaning or aspect: would she have him escape? he wonders. Unlikely. Or is it that *she* has finally been reminded, if only for a moment, of what he has remembered vividly for so long: the closeness they shared when he was but a sickly youth and she a maiden, apprenticed to the cronish healer who aided him?

Wishing to believe the latter, Baster-kin would have her speak no more, a wish granted, at that instant, by the sound of the last of the South Gate being shattered by an enormous, wheeled ram, the building of which has been the object of the fevered work of the Bane warriors during the hours leading up to the assault. The gate crashes to the ground, and then the loud clanging of the gate's fiery-hot iron bands being pulled away with chains and hooks from the now open portal into the city by the fearless warhorses of the cavalry units of the Talons resounds throughout the streets of the Fifth District.

But Baster-kin never turns from the countenance of the woman before him. "Do not trouble yourself on my account, my lady," he says, with what seems genuine concern. Finally, he turns away for an instant, to glance at the sky. "For in this matter, as in so many things, today, the wind has blown in your family's favor . . ." He turns back to her once more. "Do not question it—for all the good that could be said between us was said long ago . . ."

And then Baster-kin's face suddenly darkens, and becomes a mask of all the evil he has done in the name of his golden god and the same God-King who has now, apparently, abandoned him; the change in his features is startling enough to take young Dagobert—who had thought the Merchant Lord's resignation and conciliation genuine and even honorable—by such surprise that he quickly grasps the hilt of his father's marauder sword and moves in front of his mother. Smiling just slightly in a cruel manner, his lordship keeps his eyes fixed on Isadora's. "Besides," he says quietly, "I am not dead, yet. Not quite yet . . ."

Without ever softening his look of lethal intent, Baster-kin turns and indicates to the attendants that they may continue onward. Isadora is left to watch him disappear through the widening hole that has been created in the wall at the head of the Path of Shame—by the same masons who built the structure—before losing sight of him for what she hopes, for her children's sake if not her own, will be the last time.

"Mother?" Dagobert asks, sighing with relief. "He seemed almost—a man, like any other, for an instant. I even felt sorry for what those attendants from the High Temple seem bent on doing to him. But just as quickly, he grew—*evil* . . ."

Putting her arms around her son's shoulders, Isadora declares, "Evil . . . I am not at all sure that we poor humans can ever comprehend that word, or know its qualities, my son . . ." A sudden shudder runs through her body, and then she declares, "Now, Dagobert—Kriksex, all of you—we must make ourselves ready for the sentek's arrival. If I am any judge, he—"

And just then comes the sound of thundering hooves, moving up the Path toward the Arnem house and growing closer by the instant. Veterans and the sentek's wife and son alike prepare for the approach of Broken's greatest soldier, who has so precipitously been restored to his former glory—though he himself still knows it not.

Just as the group step further into the Path to await the arrival of Sixt Arnem and his triumphant force, however, Isadora, Dagobert, and their surrounding guardians are forced to move back again at a sight far more apparitional and fast moving than the sentek's cavalry:

It is the legendary white panther of Davon Wood, speeding up and toward the same hole in the wall through which Lord Baster-kin has been taken. The animal requires no guidance: it is all that the legless old man who sits astride her can do to remain there. Nor will she require any direction, from god or man, when the pair dash up the Celestial Way, moving toward the city's Stadium . . .

7.

WHEN THE ADVANCE RIDERS of the Talons' cavalry come within view of the Arnem house at last, both Isadora and Dagobert cannot determine what precisely it is the soldiers are about: for their relatively slow pace does not match the immense noise that they have been producing, while the first six horsemen pull between them, by way of ropes attached to the pommels of their saddles, some crude yet fearsome wheeled device. Isadora is also somewhat surprised, after having carefully listened to as many of the shouted messages that earlier passed between Rendulic Baster-kin and his Guardsmen during the attack on the South Gate as she could safely manage, to see that no Bane warriors accompany her husband's soldiers; but, as she will soon learn, the Bane, after smashing through the glowing, bound towers of burnt or burning wood that were once that same "impregnable" portal with their prodigious, expertly constructed ram, have refused to advance any farther. As ever, they do not trust that some group among the God-King's subjects will not attempt to chastise them for taking part in the assault upon the city, and have decided to wait outside its walls until Sentek Arnem can assure them absolutely that the Tall will not seek such vengeance upon the tribe of outcasts for whose destruction the citizens of the city had until lately clamored—and may, in their hearts (for all the Bane know) still wish. With this consideration in mind, Ashkatar has granted control of the wheeled battering machine to Arnem, for use against the wall at the head of the Path of Shame, which the sentek has every reason to believe still stands intact. Ashkatar and his warriors, in the meantime, withdraw back into the stands of trees on the high slopes of the mountain, to await word that it is indeed safe for them to set foot within the city. Only Visimar and the three foragers with whom he has become fast friends will brave the question of just who holds what power within the granite walls of Broken before the issue has seemingly been decided; and even they move with great caution.

The sharp-eyed Kriksex can soon explain to Lady Arnem that the Talons' riders move slowly and noisily because of their unusual burden, a device the like of which the agèd veteran has beheld many times before. Moments after receiving this explanation, Isadora and Dagobert are relieved of their greatest anxiety when, moving at the fast pace with which the Talons' mounted contingents are more typically associated, not only the *khotor*'s commander, but his aide and several of his scouts appear from behind the riders that work to pull the great ram through the now-softened surface of the Path of Shame. Having glimpsed the dismantling of the barrier at the Path's head soon after entering the city, Arnem has determined that Lord Baster-kin's treachery has been found out by the God-King and the Grand Layzin; and the sentek cannot, thereafter, be prevented from proceeding with all haste to his home, where he receives the cheers of the veterans who surround his wife and son. But his own eyes are fixed on those of his lady, most immediately, and then on the image of his son, who wears the armor Sixt entrusted to him before departing, and carries the best of the sentek's marauder swords. Like Dagobert himself, both blade and armor have plainly seen combat of some sort in recent days, a fact that causes Arnem no little concern; however, he is yet the leader of a force that must be prepared for still more treachery of the kind that has haunted his men since they first began their march. Thus, before obeying his deepest passion and rushing to his wife and son, he cries out over his shoulder:

"Akillus! Inform the advance force that they may abandon the ram, and see to the safety of their own families, if they wish. It would seem the issue has been settled, and that the day is ours—but they must yet be wary of any attempts by the Merchant Lord's Guard to either attack our units or commit some other murderous outrage in their efforts to escape the city and the God-King's justice."

Then, at long last, Arnem leaps from his saddle and hurries to embrace Isadora, holding one arm free to draw Dagobert close to him. Tears of joy and relief well quickly in the eyes of both the commander's wife and his scion; and it requires all the discipline that the sentek can muster not to himself weep before his men. On closer inspection, however, Arnem is unable to prevent his own happiness from being curtailed by unpleasant surprise at the somewhat drawn aspect of both his wife's and his son's features. Isadora, who is as ever able to comprehend her husband's thoughts, puts a hand to his face and, smiling more gently, says, "It is nothing, Sixt—we shared what food stores we had with those most in need, that is all. Nor have we suffered as much as have many . . ."

Arnem kisses his lady with a passion augmented by pride at her bravery, and then turns to his son. "And you, Dagobert?" he says, tightening his grip on his son's shoulder. "It seems to me that my old armor and marauder sword saw more than ornamental use."

"Your son took his place among us, Sentek," Kriksex answers, seeing that Dagobert is too modest to boast in front of the collection of brave veterans who surround his parents and himself. "When defense of the district was necessary."

Arnem's expression becomes suddenly ambiguous. "And were you forced to kill, my boy, during these actions?"

"I—" Dagobert's face, too, becomes a mask of uncertainty. "I did what we were all forced to do, Father. I cannot boast of it, for it was . . ." The youth's voice trails off, and his eyes turn toward the ground. "It was necessary—and terrible. Nothing less—or more . . ."

Arnem leans down to meet Dagobert's eyes intently. "And that is war, young man," he says quietly. "For you are no longer to be counted a 'boy'—by myself or anyone else. That much is plain . . ." Standing and turning to the old veteran who rests upon his crutch, Arnem speaks aloud once more: "And *you* are Kriksex—a few wrinkles cannot disguise that much. I know that you will forgive the concern for my family that prevented my greeting you at once, Linnet. But do not doubt my awareness of how very much I am indebted to you: for my wife made it clear in her letters to me that you have spared no effort to ensure their safety."

"Despite the many strange things we have seen of late in the Fifth District, Sentek," Kriksex answers, "my loyalty to the Talons, to you, and to your house has remained intact. Like your son, I did my duty, and nothing more—although with no little happiness, in this case, for your lady and Master Dagobert both share your courage and your own devotion to all in Broken that is truly good and noble."

"And for that, I shall see to it that you are rewarded by the God-King and the Grand Layzin with more than a crutch—even a well-worked crutch," Arnem pronounces. "For it appears that our rulers were as much taken in by Baster-kin's mad schemes as were many of us."

"But, Sixt," Isadora says, her joy suddenly mitigated by worry. "I do not see the rest of the children—"

Arnem turns to indicate Radelfer, who rides with the advance force of his cavalry. "Fear not, wife," the sentek says. "Radelfer more than fulfilled the commission with which you charged him: the other children wait, fed and safe, within my tent outside the city."

Isadora looks at the former seneschal of the clan Baster-kin, regaining her ordinarily noble outward bearing. "Thank you, Radelfer," she says. "I, of all people, know how much your change of allegiance and your safekeeping of my children have cost you, not only in rank, but in the realization that Rendulic Baster-kin's heart had not, in the end, survived the torment he had endured as a boy."

"True, my lady," Radelfer says softly, riding closer to the garden gate and nodding respectfully. "Even so, the cost was not so great as the dishonor of refusing your request would have been. And may I take a moment to add"—he turns to Kriksex—"that I am glad to find that *this* old comrade of mine has also managed both to fulfill his pledge to you, as well as to keep himself alive. Although I am not sure that there has ever existed a member of the Merchant Lord's Guard who could have put an end to such a man."

Kriksex shrugs the one of his shoulders that does not rest upon his crutch. "There existed some few who made determined attempts, Radelfer," he replies. "Although I am happy to say that they no longer draw breath . . ."

Turning about, Arnem and Radelfer both see that most of the Talons' advance force, recognizing that their commander would as soon be alone with his family, have either taken advantage of his permission to disperse in order to attend to the safety of their own kin, or have begun the task of hunting down the remaining units of Lord Baster-kin's Guard: men who seem to have made every attempt to disappear amongst the population of the city, for there is no sign of any organized resistance on their part. And yet, seasoned commander that he is, Sixt Arnem takes little comfort from this seeming fact, as yet—for the Guard, he suspects, will prove every bit as treacherous in defeat as the sentek has now learned that their commander has been since the beginning of the Talons' campaign.

"I am glad to hear it, Kriksex," Arnem murmurs, eyeing the streets. "And yet—there is something so utterly strange about what has taken place within this city, in so brief a period of time, that I cannot help but wonder if forces other than the sword have been at work." He turns to Isadora with a slight smile. "You have not taken to conjuring, have you, wife?"

"Had I but been able," Isadora replies, bravely returning his smile as she softly lands a fist upon his chest, "there are one or two qualities about certain people I would have changed. No, if this was magic, then it was someone else's—for as soon as it became apparent that the South Gate would fall, orders began to be issued from the Inner City and the Sacristy of the High Temple. We still do not know the wording of most of them, but—at least half the Merchants' Council have been arrested, and their properties confiscated. No one in the first three districts is certain, even now, of what fate may await their own families, but all citizens were ordered to remain in their homes, until the conclusion of the 'present unpleasantness.' Yet no statement has yet been made as to what the 'unpleasantness' was, or to who was responsible for it—although just a few minutes ago, I observed Lord Baster-kin being escorted to the north, by a group of armed attendants from the High Temple. And, soon thereafter, I observed a man I believe to have been Caliphestros himself, astride what could only have been the white panther of Davon Wood, making his way toward the High Temple. I might suspect the sorcery to be his, save that I learned long ago that he has never believed in or practiced the sorts of dark arts for which he was condemned. Sixt—what can it all mean? How did that poor man come to return to Broken by such remarkable means? And what of our children, now that all this has taken place—would they not now be safer here, with us, than in your camp?"

Despite his lingering soldier's worries concerning the missing members of the Merchant Lord's Guard, Arnem can perceive, when he studies Isadora's face an instant more, that—relieved though she may be at his return, and determined as she may also be to display the confident demeanor that his men have come to expect from her—she will not be truly easy in her mind until all of her young ones are brought home. With this in mind, he addresses the former seneschal of the great *Kastelgerd* that is, apparently, no longer the center of Rendulic Baster-kin's power.

"My lady and I have asked much of you, Radelfer, in recent days—do not doubt my awareness of that," the sentek says. "But I have one last service—nay, call it rather a request—that I would make." Arnem faces the Path of Shame, where only his two most trusted linnets, Akillus and Niksar, remain in attendance. "Akillus," he says. "Accompany Radelfer back to our camp, and let it be known that our main force may return to the city, under the cautions I previously declared. And Radelfer, if you will accompany my officers, you can perform this final favor: my children have grown to trust you, and if you will bring them here to their mother and their home, in the same wagon that transported them safely out of Broken, Akillus will escort you with a half dozen of his best men." Radelfer shows every sign of being pleased to be entrusted with this task, and he wheels on his mount, quickly joining Akillus as the latter sets a rapid pace for the now utterly reduced South Gate.

"And Niksar?" Arnem continues. "Ride, if you will, to the Fourth District. Inform Sentek Gerfrehd—or any other senior officer who is currently commander of the watch—that we have returned, and are beginning our pursuit of the Merchant Lord's Guard. They may join us or not—but as we have had naught but favorable signs regarding our undertaking from the Grand Layzin and the God-King, they should feel no sense of divided loyalties. After that—proceed with the undertaking in the First District that we have previously discussed."

"Aye—*Yantek!*" Niksar says, pleased, like the others, to be entrusted with an important mission that will, it seems, begin the process of healing divisions within the city and the kingdom. His impressive white mount rears once to great effect, and then both horse and rider are off toward the palisade of the Fourth District.

Kriksex, meanwhile, nods to his own men, and then faces Arnem a final time. "Well, Yantek," he says. "I have not grown so old that I cannot perceive your family's desire to be reunited in privacy—a natural enough wish. Therefore, with your permission, my men and I will begin the hunt for the fleeing members of the Guard—"

And then, suddenly, Kriksex's face becomes frozen, as do those of the several veterans who remain in a rough circle around the three members of the Arnem clan who are present. At first, Arnem himself is somewhat mystified by this change in aspect; but Isadora is not deceived for a moment, and the hand that does not hold her husband goes to her mouth, to stifle a cry of grief. It is only when Dagobert cries out to him, however, that Arnem realizes the truth:

"Father!" the youth says in alarm, immediately drawing his marauder sword. *"Guardsmen!"*

The veterans surrounding Arnem's party fall slowly to the ground, each crying out in pain as the point of a Broken short spear crashes through the front of his well-worn armor and tunic. With the collapse of Kriksex and the other staunch defenders of the Fifth District and the Arnem family, a new group of faces are revealed: crouching low, the men hide under broadcloth cloaks, and only when they are sure that their far worthier victims are dead do they release their instruments of cowardly attack, and then stand to throw off their cloaks, revealing their well-worked armor, as well as tunics bearing the crest of Rendulic Baster-kin. Arnem realizes that his son was correct, and that his own instinctive uneasiness about the treachery of the Guard has once again been proved reliable: for, when he looks toward the South Gate, now, he sees that a *fauste* or more of these supposèd soldiers—perhaps some sixty in all—have gathered to use numbers against the skill of the relatively small number of Talons who have been left behind to guard their position at the gate. No longer supported by their Bane allies, the Talons have been left, like their commander and wife and son, in a seemingly perilous position by the zeal of their comrades, who have enthusiastically taken to the job of hunting down the Guardsmen throughout the rest of the city: for experience dictates that those overdressed, over-painted dandies should be running in the direction of the gates at the other end of Broken, in order to avoid a fight as they flee the city. But instead, this one unit of "soldiers"—who are little more than ruffians and murderers, as they have just proved once again—have doubled back on the Talons' point of entry into the city, correctly calculating that they would find their enemy unprepared for such a counterattack.

Arnem stares at the linnet who leads the band before him, then says, as he draws his short-sword, "For once, the Guard shows something approaching cleverness—although your cowardly methods remain miserably consistent." Pushing Isadora and Dagobert back toward the family's garden gateway as he draws his own sword, Arnem continues, "I assume that your group broke off from the rest of your *fauste* simply to undertake the task of revenging yourselves upon my family, before you rejoin your fellow fugitives?"

"You assume correctly, Sentek," says the Guardsman to whom Arnem has spoken. "Although I would hardly call it a 'task'—rather, a pleasure. And we are hardly fugitives, yet—for this action may turn the battle. Our master may be taken, and yourself praised throughout the city; but those positions may still be reversed, should you fall, along with your family and the traitors who have followed—"

Arnem has been relying upon the Guardsman's typical inability to refrain from gloating: as the man prattles on, his intended victim suddenly pushes his wife and son within the family's garden, and then just as quickly bars the door within the gateway. At once, the Guardsmen begin to beat upon the wooden planks of the door with fists, feet, and the pommels of their swords. The weakness of the Arnems' position quickly becomes plain, even to Dagobert:

"Father—they shall be upon us in a matter of moments!"

"And moments are all that we now require," Arnem answers calmly, bracing his shoulder against the gateway door. Then, taking Dagobert's marauder sword from the young man, he tosses it aside. "Akillus and his men, and perhaps even soldiers from the Fourth, should be here soon. To meet the challenge that faces us until their arrival, however, *that* blade will not serve you best."

"Sixt," Isadora says, with quiet urgency. "What can you be planning? You saw what they did to poor Kriksex and those other men—they will not hesitate to treat us in like manner, once they have broken down that door."

"And that, wife, will be the moment at which I observe how much our son has truly learned during his afternoons in the Fourth Quarter, as well as from his comrades of late," Arnem answers, pulling Isadora to him, kissing her once again and then, with his shoulder still hard against the rattling gate, nodding toward the house. "Get your mother inside, Dagobert: see to it that she locks herself in that basement that none of us are supposed to know she frequents as often as she does. Then, get upstairs, and get yourself a decent Broken short-sword. One of my best, along with the largest of my shields."

"Truly?" Dagobert replies, swallowing his own fears and trying to match his father's confidence as he pulls his mother toward the house.

"Truly," Arnem calls after them. "You recall the first rule of Broken swordsmanship?"

Dagobert nods. "Yes—'the slash wounds, but the lunge kills.'"

Arnem acknowledges the statement with a proud smile. "As the eastern marauders, with their curved weapons, have so often paid with their lives to discover. Go on, then: it's a new, straight blade for you, and one decent shield for us to share—for it's a great deal of lunging that lies ahead!"

"But, Sixt," Isadora insists, "come with us! Defend the house, if you must defend anything, for the two of you cannot possibly—"

"Isadora," Arnem counters, "the two of us cannot possibly do anything *else*. If they trap us inside, we shall all be consumed by flames—and your beauty was not created to suffer so ugly a fate. Hurry along, then, my lady. Two good Broken soldiers have always been worth any ten Guardsmen—a simple statement of fact that Dagobert and I will now demonstrate to you, as well as to those murderous pigs outside!"

As the Guardsmen's blows upon the gateway door begin to crack its boards, Sixt Arnem lowers his shoulder ever more, digging his boots into the wild terrain of his children's very unorthodox garden as he watches Isadora and Dagobert vanish into the house at its opposite end.

8.

THE WHITE PANTHER and her extraordinary rider have reached the entrance to Broken's Stadium with extraordinary dispatch: for the Celestial Way, from its southern to its northern extremes, has remained empty of all save the most furtive souls, and even the few of those that Caliphestros and Stasi spy cry out in alarm upon observing them, and hurry ever faster in any direction that will take them away from the otherworldly sight. Yet it has not been fear of panther, sorcerer, or any other attackers alone that has kept the inhabitants of the great granite city within their homes. Soon after Stasi had begun her run north, Caliphestros had begun to see public notices fixed to all windowless sides of buildings—homes, markets, and district temples—and eventually to the great columns that have for so long commanded many of the garden gateways of the First District. At first, Caliphestros had not been able to make out their meaning, so intent had Stasi been on hurtling north toward the enormous ovular structure behind the High Temple that the old man had long since come to suspect was her destination. Eventually, however, the returned exile had stopped even trying to slow his companion, for he found that the content of the proclamations was identical, and that he could read a section of the order as he passed by each copy—and the command he soon pieced together had proved most singular, indeed:

This unique quality had not simply arisen out of the fact that the order bore the rarely seen personal seal of the God-King Saylal. Rather, its most curious quality was that it had not committed that sacred ruler to either side in the civil unrest that had broken out in and around the Fifth District and at the South Gate of Broken, and which by now, Caliphestros had rightly presumed, was spilling over into the other districts of the city. Lords and citizens alike were commanded to remain in their homes and carry on no commerce during "this time of confusion and crisis"; yet neither one nor the other of the obvious adversaries in this "present un-pleasantness" had received royal endorsement. Such had been a clever ploy, indeed, Caliphestros had realized: for not only could the God-King and the Grand Layzin treat the matter as one of secular politics, but they could quite truthfully claim, later, to have always favored whichever side emerged victorious.

Yes, clever, Caliphestros had thought, as he had struggled to stay astride Stasi's powerful neck and shoulders: *almost perversely clever, just as Saylal himself has always been . . .*

When the pair arrive at the entryway to the Stadium, Caliphestros breathes easier for a moment, as Stasi pauses for the first time: the struc-ture's portcullis—an almost insignificant (by any military standard) ex-panse of crosshatched boards that serves as more of a warning than a true barrier—has been shut, for the first time that Caliphestros can ever recall its having been. But, while the grating may itself be less than im-pressive, it has been fastened at its base with a prodigious iron chain and equally impressive lock to an iron loop that was long ago sunk into the granite of the mountain. A smaller chain has been strung through a sec-tion of the crosshatching some five feet up from the base, and its two ends are fixed to a large slab of wood that bears Lord Baster-kin's com-mand that the Stadium will remain closed until the young men of Bro-ken have bested the Bane.

Staring at the lock upon the ground and recognizing its basic mecha-nism, Caliphestros begins to rummage through one of the small sacks that he has kept slung over his shoulders.

"Fear not, Stasi," he announces. "I have a set of tools that will allow us, eventually, to—"

Just what his devices will allow him to do is never announced: for Stasi, evidently, knows the sound of her companion's rummaging and studious voice, and decides that she will settle the matter of the portcul-lis herself. Before Caliphestros can coherently object, the panther takes several long strides backward and, lowering her head so that the thick bone of her forehead faces the entryway, begins a hard run that makes her intention unmistakable.

"*Stasi—!*" her rider scarcely has time to call out, before realizing that nothing he will say can prevent her attempt. With this in mind, he low-ers his seating and increases his hold, closing his eyes as he does. Almost before he can comprehend what has taken place, he hears an enormous sound of shattering wood, of which only harmless pieces fall upon his back, so quickly is the white panther continuing to move. Once inside the gateway, Stasi pauses to look back with satisfaction at her work: a gaping hole in the portcullis to one side of the intact chain and lock, and an impact so extreme that the largest pieces of wood that have been blasted away are only now settling to the ground. Smiling and smoothing the fur upon the panther's neck with one hand as he rubs her forehead with the other, Caliphestros determines: "You were right, my girl—a far superior plan. On, then!"

And, understanding his words entirely, Stasi turns, seeming to know her way about the Stadium (although it is scent alone that is driving her, Caliphestros knows), and makes for the doorway that leads to the dark stairway that winds down to the cages beneath the sands of the arena.

Only here do the travelers finally encounter a human presence: one of the keepers of the beasts in the iron cells. He is a filthy man in equally dirty clothing; and despite the fact that he holds a spear before him, he beholds the approach of the white panther and her rider by torchlight with both amazement and an appreciative awe.

"Kafra be damned," he says, throwing his spear aside. "I will not stand in the way of such wondrous determination, to say nothing of a sight that defies all that the priests have taught us."

"A wise decision," Caliphestros answers. "But where are the other men who work with you in this"—the old man glances about—"this little piece of *Hel?*"

"Gone," the man answers. "As soon as Lord Baster-kin ordered the Stadium locked and abandoned, my lord Caliphestros."

"So you know me," the legless rider muses, with a mix of satisfaction and disdain. "It would seem that I am not entirely forgotten in Broken."

"*Forgotten?*" the keeper echoes in wonder. "You are a *legend* in Broken—as is the panther you ride upon. Although it was not known until very lately that you traveled together."

"'Travel'—yes, and a good deal more," Caliphestros answers. As Stasi turns her head from side to side, her unstoppable determination is suddenly confused by the many scents and increased cries of the beasts in the cells around her: cells that are lit only by long stone openings in the top of each wall that catch pieces of sunlight from barred openings in the base of the Stadium walls, as well as by the torches that burn in sconces outside each place of confinement. The former Second Minister of the realm tries to calm his mount as he attempts to gain more information from the keeper. "You say the rest of your ilk are gone. Yet why did *you* stay, if that be so?"

"The animals, my lord," says the keeper. "They would have slowly starved. As it is, I have had difficulty procuring even spoilt meat to keep them alive."

"And why take such pains to preserve what Kafra and his priests have long taught are mere beasts, to be used and abused as man might see fit?"

"Because, my lord," the keeper responds, "savage as they may be, I have grown to know these creatures, a little, and to know what they have endured at the hands of Broken's idle wealthy: young men and women who have used *me* ill as well, in my time. To simply leave them to die, especially the wretched death of want, would have been— *inhuman . . .*"

Caliphestros's expression softens. "And so mercy finds its way even into this place. For that statement, jailer, you may leave with your life. But first, surrender your keys."

The keeper gladly takes from his belt an iron ring which holds the many keys to the cells about them, and tosses it at Stasi's feet. "Thank you, my lord," he says, and then, before the "nefarious sorcerer" has a change of heart, he turns and flees.

Urging Stasi to bend and allow him to the ground, Caliphestros groans as he rolls to the hard floor, then immediately reaches into one of his sacks for several balls of his various medications, which he places in his mouth. He begins to chew vigorously, despite their bitter taste, that their effect may ease the pain of his trip through the city all the faster; and then he slips his walking apparatus from his back and straps it to his legs, beseeching he knows not what or whom to allow the powerful drugs he has eaten to take hold of his senses quickly. Once they have, he grasps one of the iron bars of the cells and tries to pull himself upright. The task is beyond his capabilities, however, and he is grateful when he feels Stasi's muzzle, and behind it the force of her mighty neck, gently lift him upright. He places his crutches under his arms and, as he feels his medicines take full effect, he announces:

"Now, my constant one—let us find she that you have for so long dreamed of freeing and bringing home. And as we do so, let us free the rest of these unfortunates—although I would be grateful if you would prevent any one of them who mistakes our intentions from tearing out my throat . . ."

As the white panther and the man who walks like no other man the beasts have ever seen begin to move through the passageways between the cells, Caliphestros pauses to unlock each door; and he is happy, although not altogether surprised, to discover that each animal—wolf, wildcat, bear, and more—would rather make for the stairs and what they all obviously sense is freedom than they would kill such strange and unworthy prey as he must seem. Yet the liberating pair's quest is peculiarly long: the cells are many in number, the terrible yet exhilarating sounds of the freed prisoners are confusing, and the pathway grows ever darker as they wind on and on through a maze of iron.

Finally, however, panther and man come to the last of the cells, and Stasi's motions become ever more anxious and agitated. Within this last place of filthy imprisonment, Caliphestros can now see, paces she whom his companion has sought: a panther much like herself, if slightly smaller, far leaner, and displaying a far more golden coat, one that is smudged by the dirt of her cell. With all the other animals already departed, Caliphestros feels safe in allowing Stasi to approach the cell first as he stands unguarded to one side, observing yet another of the miracles of which his companion is, it seems, infinitely capable.

Stasi moves slowly to the bars: a strange slowness, when one considers the ardor and speed with which she made for the Stadium. But Caliphestros is not confused: for he knows her expressions by now, and there is an air of contrition about her face and movements, as she steps forward to put her nose between the shafts of iron, where it touches that of the younger panther within. As she moves to lick the muzzle of her long-lost child, that offspring at first snarls quietly, as if to ask, it seems to Caliphestros, why Stasi should have left her in the place of misery for so many years. Only when the white panther looks back at her human companion does he move forward upon his crutches and single wooden leg to unlock the door of the cell. Stasi quickly enters, enduring the two or three swipes of a strong paw that has been kept quick by Broken's wealthy youth: actions that are clearly meant, not to genuinely injure, but to register deep anger at so long an abandonment. Stasi endures these motions without reaction, and then again moves forward to begin to lick the filth of the cell from her daughter's fur. When the child has finally submitted, and begins to return what are, in her case, touches of affection with her own tongue, the feeling within the cage loses its momentary sense of unease; and before long, both panthers are purring with extraordinary volume.

Just how long this ritual goes on, Caliphestros cannot say: for his own sense of rapture, combined with the full effect of his medicines (augmented by a few sips from a wineskin that he has found hanging from a wall nearby) make time utterly irrelevant. Nevertheless, it is a delicate moment for the old man: for he does not yet know if the two reunited panthers will allow him into their company, or even if his own relationship to Stasi will remain unaffected by her discovery of the child to whom she has called, on so many evenings, from the mountainside far, far beyond the granite city.

Soon, however, Stasi does turn to Caliphestros, with an expression of utter kindness. Her daughter's face, too, bears no trace of malice: in all likelihood, the old man realizes, because (as in the case of the other imprisoned animals) he is so utterly unlike any other human she has encountered during her long torment. Far from brandishing a whip or chain, Caliphestros does not even present legs; no man could be less threatening, he realizes, and for the first time in his life he finds himself, if not grateful to have lost his legs, at least momentarily relieved at his mutilated image. He is, as he has hoped he might, being asked to join mother and daughter: somehow Stasi has imparted to her child that he is to be accepted, perhaps even that he has made this reunion possible; and with a sense of reverence beyond anything he has ever known, the old man enters the cell and approaches the two panthers. Understanding fully when Stasi first nuzzles his face and then bends her front legs, indicating that he is to climb upon her back once more—showing her daughter both how they have survived and lived, for so many years, and that they must now leave this place that embodies the worst of human behavior before there is any new attempt to imprison them all—Caliphestros quickly removes his walking apparatus, again slips the three wooden pieces through the straps upon his back, and pulls himself onto Stasi's shoulders. And, as he stares into the eyes of his companion's daughter, he announces:

"And so, my two beauties, let us be done, altogether and at last, with the places and affairs of men . . ." The white panther appears to understand his meaning completely, and guides her child, first out of the cell, then toward the staircase down which she and her rider came. "Let us return your daughter to the Wood, Stasi," Caliphestros continues, "and let us speak or think no more of this wretched, cruel place, or of the kingdom and such humans as would be capable of building it . . ."

With that, the three are upon their way, following the tracks of the other freed animals back toward the smashed portcullis and the Celestial Way beyond, which remains as empty as when they arrived. Their escape would seem assured; yet even so, Caliphestros knows that there is one task that both of his companions would gladly attend to, had they the opportunity. Freedom is certainly more important, at this moment, especially when it appears to be waiting without obstruction, but both mother and child glance about quickly, less in fear than out of seeming desire—

And Fate does not cast the panthers—to say nothing of their legless companion—among the foolish or the undeserving: not on this day, at any rate. On the contrary, it has decided at this moment to be kind (or that which ever passes for "kind," when one speaks of Fate) to all three of the fleeing figures: for, just after they pass the open court before Broken's High Temple, a group of men appear in the middle distance ahead of them. It is not a large group: one man in the center, who appears unarmed and wears a heavy black cloak, surrounded by three blood-soaked members of the Merchant Lord's Guard, all of whom who hold their gory blades by their sides. The men look at the approaching rider and panthers with near disbelief; while Caliphestros, Stasi, and her newly freed daughter eye the men with a mix of challenge and satisfaction, as they draw to a sudden halt.

"I had heard you were in the city once more—and atop the white panther I once nearly killed," calls the voice of Rendulic Baster-kin. "I must confess I did not credit the report—*why*, I wondered, if the great Caliphestros *had* managed to survive his punishment, would he return to Broken, merely to liberate a simple, vicious beast?"

Taking a moment to ensure that his response will be steady, Caliphestros calls out: "As to their viciousness, under the correct circumstances, I can certainly attest—as can you yourself, I have heard, Baster-kin." The old man slides from Stasi's lowered shoulders once again, even before he has had a chance to arrange his walking equipment. "But as to their simplicity," he continues, while the panthers proceed to snarl, pace, and coil their powerful muscles. "I believe you will learn that they possess almost every quality, save that . . ."

Baster-kin looks about him to observe the mounting fear of the three Guardsmen who form his escort—and who have just committed the great sacrilege of murdering an escort of unsuspecting attendants from the High Temple (for they do indeed know that their only hope of survival is to save their lord and kill those who lead his enemies)—and, with a harshness unusual even for him, he shouts:

"Why do you quake, you miserable dogs? They are but two panthers, and both afraid of the sound of my voice. Hold your blades forth, as I do"—at which the Merchant Lord suddenly produces a blade from beneath his cloak and assumes a stance that would indicate his every intention to battle Stasi and her daughter—"and prepare to kill the beasts, before we finally finish the crippled old heretic who rides with them, using sorcery to direct their actions!"

But Rendulic Baster-kin, whose judgment of such situations is usually sound, is mistaken about this moment, in two critical ways: Caliphestros, as we have often seen, does *not* direct Stasi's actions; and it is therefore even less likely that he controls her daughter's. Even more importantly, only *one* of the noble creatures fears the sound of Baster-kin's voice. Stasi's daughter does indeed hear and view the onetime Merchant Lord with both hatred and hesitancy, as she did in the Stadium during the events that led to the death of Adelwülf; freed from the restraints of the Stadium's chains, however, she at least can smell the fear rising off the three Guardsmen, and her green eyes go cold as she eyes them. And for her part, Stasi feels not the slightest worry at the sound of Baster-kin's barking: she is consumed only by a craving for vengeance that has finally been unleashed, after so many years during which the possibility of its realization has been delayed, leaving her to languish in sorrow. In her mind, now, she returns to the patch of forest where her family was taken from her; but her leg is no longer wounded, nor are any such mounted Broken spearmen as inflicted that original, disabling hurt to be seen. She fixes her gaze on Baster-kin with a rage such as she scarcely ever exhibits, even in the wilds of Davon Wood.

What Caliphestros observes next would make most men pale with horror, fear, and revulsion. But the agèd exile has also had many years to allow his desire for this moment to outpace such emotions. As he drags himself to a nearby gateway, insisting on pulling himself into as upright and dignified a position as he can in the few brief minutes that the contest before him will take, he feels neither compassion for what he once would have called his fellow humans, nor repugnance at the sight of what ensues:

The panthers slam into the three Guardsmen that face them before the latter can even fully raise their sword arms. One of the murderous humans is sent into the air and lands a remarkable distance away, his body lofted and his throat torn out by a fast movement of the right fore-paw of Stasi's daughter; and although the man gasps desperately as blood spurts from a gaping series of long, parallel wounds in his neck, it is to no avail, and he dies within moments. A second member of Baster-kin's escort, meanwhile, has received the younger panther's head fully in the chest and ribs, the bones of which shatter and are driven into his heart. To ensure his death, the daughter's enormous, piercing teeth soon close upon his neck, nearly severing the now-useless ball of bone and flesh that once sat atop his shoulders from his body.

Stasi, in the meantime, has dispatched the last of the Guardsmen with equal speed and skill, enfolding him in her ripping claws and throttling teeth when he makes a foolish attempt to protect his leader. She has been careful to carry the man, with the force of her attacking leap, out of the reach of Baster-kin's blade: a blade, the force behind which has been momentarily weakened by the realization that the white panther does not in fact fear him at all: that it was only her wound that held her back, so long ago, during their encounter in the Wood. Soon enough, Baster-kin's third murderous escort has also left the realm of the living, when Stasi's great frontal killing teeth pierce his skull and instantly bring death. Now, both panthers turn upon their old antagonist, uncertain as to which will undertake the task of sending him to join his hirelings.

As Caliphestros watches what he believes is the approaching doom of his own tormentor, he expects the former Merchant Lord's pride to finally crumble. Even at such a moment, however, Baster-kin somehow regains his defiance: a defiance born of years of suffering his own father's drunken diseased abuse, and of having risen above that abuse to become the most powerful and, it is true, the best of all the Merchant Lords in Broken's history. He begins to shout senselessly, urging the panthers to come for him; and whether such is true courage or madness brought on by the moment, Caliphestros cannot say. But he *can* see that it causes still another moment of hesitation in the younger panther, a moment that, given Baster-kin's own physical strength, could be perilous. Rightly turning to face the white panther first, Baster-kin stands his ground, as if he is actually ready to accept her initial charge: a charge that, at the last instant, he uses his powerful legs to deftly avoid, turning quickly to make sure that Stasi has tumbled to the ground beyond him before he rashly and viciously pursues her, his blade held high. Caliphestros calls out a warning, and Stasi is able to regain her feet; but when man charges panther, this time, the peril of an unhappy outcome all too similar to that which took place in the Wood (whether death or another grievous wound) is enough to strike Caliphestros dumb with terror. Yet just as it seems that Baster-kin may indeed inflict a cutting blow to Stasi, the man whose might was once unquestioned in his realm is suddenly thrown forward, his mouth open as if he would cry out in pain—that is, had he not been struck in the back with so great a force that his spine is shattered, stilling his tongue. His hand loses its grip upon his sword, and he clutches for long moments after it, unable to recover the weapon or even to move his lower body before he sees the sky above him blotted out by the head of one of the panthers.

Stasi's daughter has indeed been inspired by her mother to overcome the uncertainty caused by so many years of terror at the sound of Baster-kin's voice; and at the last instant she has found the courage to charge and cripple her tormentor, and then throw him into the air with such force that he now lies upon his back. Stasi joins her child, wishing to at least share in the finishing of this life that has for so long broken their lives; and as Baster-kin feels the white panther's teeth slowly grasp his body and turn it over, he quickly catches sight of another image previously unknown to these most sacred streets of Broken:

It is that of three Bane, emerging from the opposite side of the street adjoining the Celestial Way down which Baster-kin and his men had hoped to make their escape. The three have the rough manner and appearance of Bane foragers, or rather, two of them do—the third, a woman, is neither so covered in light mud (mud that was, Baster-kin realizes, not so long ago the dust that he believed was a sure indication that his enemies meant to attack at the East Gate of the city), nor so seemingly bent upon revenge as are her companions. She runs quickly to Caliphestros's side, slinging the old man's right arm about her neck and helping him keep his mutilated body, suddenly further weakened by the thought of losing his companion, upright. Looking back at the two Bane men, Baster-kin sees one staring at him with a grim look that perceives naught but justice being done; the third, however, smiles with a set of filed and broken teeth.

"It is only fair, *my lord,*" says this man, his words delightedly bitter in tone, and his manner no less fiendish for his size. "Try to fight her now as she once tried to fight you—unarmed, wounded, and unable to move . . ."

But Baster-kin has no chance at reply before the jaws above him—which belong to Stasi's daughter, although he cannot see her—close upon and crush his spine, sinking in far enough to bring blood gushing from the great vessels of his neck. Next, he sees the white panther slowly envelop his skull with her mouth, preparing to use those same stabbing, killing teeth to drive directly into his brain: a death far more merciful than the onetime Merchant Lord granted many a man and creature. As the younger panther joins the white to watch the instant of her tormentor's death, Baster-kin has only enough life left in him to hear the same Bane forager call out, as he moves with the second male in the party toward Caliphestros:

"And now, my legless lord—would you mind telling us just exactly where you were in such a hurry to get to, before we arrived opposite those pigs on the ground?"

They are strange words to be the last I hear, particularly when they come from such a creature, Baster-kin thinks, as the white panther's jaws close; *but then, the golden god has determined that much of my life should be strange— and so perhaps this, too, is only of a part with his design . . .*

9.

IN THE GARDEN of the Arnem household, violence of equal savagery, but very different in kind, has been taking place. Having quickly found one of his father's good short-swords, along with a shield that is nearly as tall as he is, Dagobert has rejoined the Yantek of the Broken Army outside. Arnem swiftly inserts his own, more practiced left arm into the leather straps that are riveted into the back of the shield; and, seeing how much more easily his father wields the thing, Dagobert realizes that his true moment to join the army has not yet come, that he must allow both his body to grow and his arms to learn their trade still more before he can be called a true soldier. But, whether true soldier or apprentice, other matters soon command his attention, as the garden gate finally gives way before the pounding assault of the Guardsmen outside it.

"Stand close by me, my son," Arnem says, with no trace of condescension, but the respect he feels must be shown to a warrior, however young, who has acted in the defense of his mother and his home for many days, now. "These shields are so contrived that one will protect us both, if we use it correctly. Your blade goes where?"

"Above the shield, Father," Dagobert answers, proud that, even through his fear of the oncoming group of Guardsmen, he remembers the soldiers in the quadrangles of the Fourth District practicing the correct performance of the position to be taken by two men who have but one shield. He moves his arm quickly so that the point of his blade extends just up and over the protective expanse of layered metal, leather and wood, which leaves room for Arnem to stand that much closer to him.

"Precisely so," the yantek answers, as he places his own sword in a like position. "I see that you did not neglect to wear your *sarbein*[†]—good. They will be enough, on the chance that these men are even less experienced than I believe, and attempt to come at us below the shield, exposing their necks. In that case, I shall—"

"You shall quickly use the shield to drive them into the ground, Father, that we may lower our blades on their necks," Dagobert recites by rote, using repetition of the basic rules of Broken infantry training[‡] as a way of calming his nerves.

Glancing about as he nods in acknowledgment, Arnem quickly surveys the garden as if seeing it for the first time. "It happens that, from a military standpoint, you and the rest of my clever children have built this garden well. The Guardsmen"—Arnem now looks above his shield to see the first two of the wary killers approaching slowly, then resumes his survey of the ground about him—"will stay to the center path, rather than brave the stream or the mounds of trees and wilderness you have created about us. They will never have seen such a place within the walls of Broken before, I'll wager—"

"Father!"

Arnem turns forward once more at Dagobert's cry, in time to see the first two Guardsmen coming even faster up the garden path, closely followed by a third and fourth. Arnem instantly perceives that their tactics—if indeed they can be called such—are weak: the first pair will come high, as expected, while the second are crouching and will attempt to slip beneath the shield that Arnem holds. The moment has come for him to truly discover if Dagobert has learned not only the terms used in the tactics of combat at close quarters as taught by the army of Broken, but their practice, as well—

And it takes little time to see that he has. As Arnem quickly raises his shield just high enough to force the first attackers to raise their heads as they try to leap above it, the better part of both father's and son's swords suddenly extend with brutal force such as one might expect from Arnem, but that in Dagobert's case is surprising—and all the more impressive. Without hesitation, Dagobert finds the throat of the Guardsman on the left, while his father drives his sword through one eye and then into the brain of the man on the right. Both father and son are sprayed with the blood of these first two enemies, but that does not stop them from quickly retracting their swords when Arnem shouts:

"Below!"

The yantek lowers his shield with speedy force, so that it catches the next two men on their shoulders, driving their faces into the moist Earth of the garden path as they attempt to swing their swords. There the intruders die as quickly as the first two Guardsmen, with the long, tapering points of two Broken short-swords wedging into and then through their spines from the back, just below the head. Seeing the brutal yet efficient manner in which Arnem drives his second opponent's face deeper into the ground with his foot in order to withdraw his sword more quickly, Dagobert matches the motion, and then hears his father order:

"Withdraw—two paces only, Dagobert."

Moving to ground as yet unstained by blood and unencumbered by bodies, and leaving the remaining opponents, now, with the additional obstacle of their own dead in the pathway, Sixt and Dagobert Arnem resume their ready stance. Seeing that the Guardsmen, thinking to have learned a lesson, intend now to charge three abreast, Arnem orders his son back yet another long stride, which their enemies take as a sign of full retreat, and from which they derive enough enthusiasm to increase the pace of their onslaught.

But Arnem has already noted that, from where they now stand, Dagobert and he will have two trees of middling but stout enough width on their flanks, to effectively increase their protection from those directions. "We block the man in the center," Arnem says, noting that this group of Guardsmen is not immediately followed by the remaining three. Among these last few is the blustering leader, whose inability to refrain from proclaiming his own plans, and those of the Guard generally, enabled Arnem and his wife and son to escape in the first place. Now this man urges the oncoming group forward with threats and oaths, all of which are unnecessary. The three attackers, when they arrive before their seeming victims, reveal what they evidently think a most cunning plan: the two men on the left engage both Arnem and Dagobert, but do not hurl themselves upon their position; rather, their role is simply to ensure that the man and youth before them are unable to move from their position, while the third Guardsman, after feigning an attack on Dagobert's left, hurries around the tree to his side and breaks off from the fight, making directly for the door of the Arnem house. Momentarily surprised by this, both Dagobert and his father glance quickly back to watch this man, which allows the Guardsman on their right time to similarly dart about that position for the door. Once there, both men raise their legs and begin to alternately kick at the thick wood and pound upon it, not with the heavy iron butts of the short spears that they have foolishly left in the bodies of Kriksex and the other veterans they have murdered, but again with the far less effective pommels of their swords.

Suddenly realizing the pair's intention—to split the Arnems' strength by posing a threat to the house and Isadora within—Arnem shouts, "We

do not break the concentration of our force, Dagobert. First, this man!"
At which he lifts his shield, swiftly hacks the sword arm of the Guardsman who was in the center of the path off below the elbow, then pulls the
piteously screaming man forward so that Dagobert—who has divined
his father's purpose, and raised his own blade into a side stance with both
arms in preparation—can and does deliver the killing blow, driving his
sword under the flailing, partially severed arm of the man and deep into
his chest. It could almost be called a *dauthu-bleith,* for the speed with
which it puts an end to the man's suffering, were it not for the murderous
intent that had spurred the attacker on in the first place. "Now for the
other two," Arnem orders, stepping forward to snatch the sword from
the severed hand and arm of the dead Guardsman. "Quickly, Dagobert,"
he continues, turning and bounding toward the house. "Before those
that remain at the gate realize their momentary advantage!"

To realize such an advantage, however, the Guardsmen would have
had to have gained experience of such combat, and against such opponents, on at least a few earlier occasions, rather than spending nearly all
their time bullying citizens of and visitors to Broken, and occasionally
doing such murder as has served the purposes of their now-fallen (though
they know it not) commander. And so the leader of the small group and
his two remaining lackeys remain at the garden gateway, watching as
the latest of their contrived assaults is foiled: Arnem, when he is still several steps from the terrace outside the door of his house, hurls the dead
Guardsman's sword with prodigious force into the back of the kicking,
hammering attacker directly before him, and the flying blade catches the
man in the left shoulder, nearly penetrating to the front of his chest but
not completely disabling him. Arnem therefore cries out:

"Engage the wounded man, Dagobert—leave the other to me!"

Father and son quickly exchange positions upon the terrace, Dagobert
taking the right and striking at the man who is reaching for the blade in
his back, but who is quick, nonetheless, to lift his own sword with his
intact right arm to meet Dagobert's initial blow. In an instant, all the
training he has witnessed and been allowed to take part in during drills
upon the quadrangles of the Fourth District moves directly through the
youth's thoughts and into his limbs, and he finds that, although the
Guardsman's physical power is prodigious, even given his wound, he
simply has not the skills that Dagobert has learned through long hours of

practice. Dagobert more than stands his own—but soon grows worried, as, glancing at the garden gateway, he sees that the remaining assassins have gathered their courage and are making for the engagement outside the door of the Arnem house.

"Father—?" he just has time to say, before his opponent has the opportunity to raise a leg and plant it in his chest, knocking him back upon the terrace. Dagobert has the presence of mind to keep hold of his sword, and fends off his wounded opponent's first attack; but he will have to struggle to regain his footing, a fact not lost on Arnem, who quickly dispatches his own Guardsman, using several blows struck with all the fury of a father, not a commander. Yet he is nonetheless forced to leave Dagobert to continue to contend with his own enemy, and to rush back into the garden pathway, blocking it with his shield and preparing to meet odds of three to one: ominous, he knows, whatever his earlier claims, even when one is facing unpracticed killers.

But face them he does, just as Dagobert gets to his own feet and regains a fighting stance against his own Guardsman, who is growing weak through the pain and loss of blood caused by the sword in his shoulder. Yet the two fights remain stalemates, at best: Arnem levels his forearm so that his shield faces the three healthy Guardsmen horizontally, which fends two of them off, if only for the most part: the yantek takes a cut to the upper portion of his shield arm, but it is not deep enough to stop him from keeping the two men at bay, while his sword goes to work on the third. Dagobert, meanwhile, struggles hard to hold his ground, yet cannot quite gain the decisive position against his opponent. The moment has come for the two defenders of the Arnem home to receive some kind of aid—and it comes from a most unexpected source:

The door of the house, which Sixt and Dagobert have worked so hard to keep closed, suddenly flies open, and—with a cry that is reminiscent of the women warriors of her own, once-powerful northern people, most of whom are long since dead or scattered, by now—Isadora drives a northern raider's sword (also taken from Sixt's collection) through the back of the man facing Dagobert with her own right arm. In her left hand she carries a Broken wooden-shafted long spear, which she tosses into the air just above her head and right shoulder, snatching it with her right hand as if she, too, knows the ways of Broken's best soldiers, and then hurls it with impressive force at the Guardsman who is engaging her husband's sword arm, and therefore stands clear of her husband's shield and is the easiest target. The spear catches the man fully in the chest, knocking him back several feet and to the ground, where he lies in a momentary, dying attempt to regain his footing, before coughing out his last, bloody breaths.

Dagobert pauses only an instant to gaze at his mother in bewilderment, before she cries: "Well? You two may have thought me useless in this fight, Dagobert, but I refuse to be—now, go and assist your father!"

And with his own warlike cry, Dagobert propels himself over most of the terrace and into the man on Arnem's left, who has not expected such assistance from either the youth or the woman. Initially as bewildered as was his son at Isadora's fearsome appearance, Sixt nonetheless loses no time, now, in dispatching the man on his right, outdoing his swordsmanship (if any Guardsman can truly be said to possess such a skill) with several terrible strokes of the sword arm that have brought him such fame from the eastern frontiers of the kingdom to the Atta Pass. After knocking the Guardsman's blade from his hand, it takes the yantek but two mighty strokes down on either side of his enemy's neck to nearly hack the man's head and neck off by slicing through each of his collarbones. Without pause, Arnem turns to assist his son: but finds that Dagobert has become determined enough by the assistance of his mother not to require such help from *both* of his parents to face the last of the Guardsmen, the leader and braggart who had been tasked with the murder of the three people who now stand still alive. Driving his sword in a final moment of screaming rage into the fool's gaping mouth—a most fitting final thrust—Dagobert pulls his blade free as the man falls to the ground, instantly dead. The eldest Arnem son then finally crouches upon one knee, working hard to catch his breath.

Upon seeing the blood that now flows, more freely than dangerously, from her husband's arm, Isadora loses her momentary fury and resumes her more familiar role as healer. Tearing a sleeve of her own gown free to use as a bandage, she wraps it around Sixt's wound, and then looks over her shoulder at her son.

"You are not hurt, Dagobert?" she calls, firmly but nonetheless with a mother's care.

The youth shakes his head, still working hard to get air into his lungs. "Only winded, Mother—nothing more. See to Father . . ."

"Oh, I shall see to him," Isadora replies, and as she turns back to Sixt she suddenly pulls the bandage she has applied painfully tight, bringing a cry of pain from the yantek. "Oh, hush!" she instantly commands. "The bandage *must* be tight—and you have a great deal of gall, to cry out like a girl when your son might be lying dead upon the threshold of our own home!"

Arnem, his pain forgotten, issues a grunt of indignation. "This is wifely gratitude, is it, woman? When all I have done—"

"All you have done you could not have done without me," Isadora says firmly, jerking the bandage yet one painful pull tighter. "And that is the last I wish to hear of any of it. I've told you before, Sixt, your soldierly vanity is often more than I can bear, but to crow at a moment like *this*—"

Isadora would go on, but her attention is suddenly drawn, like that of both Sixt and Dagobert, to the destroyed garden gate, where Akillus has appeared with several of his scouts. The newly arrived Talons survey the butchery in the garden with wonder and awe, before rushing toward their commander and his wife.

"Sentek—" Akillus manages to say with great concern, before Isadora commands him:

"*Yantek,* Akillus! Call him by his true rank, if you intend to appear *after* your presence is required."

Humbled by Isadora's harsh tone, which he has never before endured, Akillus nods in her direction. "Forgive me, my lady. It is only—well, we ran into the rest of these murderous swine at the South Gate; Niksar, of course, cut short his mission to the Fourth District, wishing to take some men and assist Radelfer in moving the rest of your children to a safer spot, while my scouts and I cleaned up the—problem." Akillus glances about, observing the blood-spattered, heavily breathing form of Dagobert, who stares back at him with the gaze of a soldier who has just seen his first true action: not gloating, not proud, even, but knowing full well that he has done, as he said earlier, what needed to be done. "We achieved that purpose. And do not worry—our men are now in control of most parts of the city. I have dispatched one *fauste* of cavalry through the East Gate to pursue those remaining Guardsmen who managed to flee the city, as well." To Isadora's now-worried expression, which plainly displays that she is too fearful to ask, Akillus smiles and says, "Rest assured, my lady. Niksar has reentered the city, while Radelfer and the children remain just outside, awaiting your arrival. Their passage shall be unimpeded by danger—of this, I believe, you may be certain."

Arnem nods, then thinks to ask, "And what of Lord Baster-kin?"

"Dead, Yantek," Akillus answers, in a strangely confused voice.

"*Dead?*" Isadora whispers, as she and Sixt are finally joined by their exhausted son. The word escapes her, not with any satisfaction, but with something that her husband would almost take for relief tinged with regret.

"At the hands of the priests who took him?" Dagobert asks.

"No," Akillus answers. "Those priests are dead to a man. Killed by more of Baster-kin's men, who thought to turn the battle through your death and his survival. Those who were responsible for his death, and their present intentions—well, that is a matter that may require your intervention, Yantek. That is, if your wound will not prevent you from such duty—"

"My 'wound' scarcely deserves the name, Akillus," Arnem answers, walking with his wife, his son, and his chief of scouts toward the open gateway to the Path of Shame. "But I would like your men to get these damned bodies out of my children's garden before they return home."

"Of course, Yantek!" Akillus replies promptly, ordering his men to the task, which they undertake with an amazement that matches their chief's.

"All right—tell me, then, Akillus," Arnem says. "What other killers took Baster-kin's life, if not the priests? And where are they now?"

"Just within the South Gate," Akillus answers. "Halted while attempting to make their way back to Davon Wood."

"To Davon Wood?" Dagobert says. "Then it was *Bane* who killed him?"

"Actually, several Bane are attempting to *stop* those who killed him from leaving," Akillus says, still, apparently, amazed by the tale he tells. "But I will allow you to judge the situation for yourselves. For, if true, it is—most remarkable. Most remarkable, indeed . . ."

10.

T HE FIRST SIGHT that Sixt, Isadora, and Dagobert Arnem encounter as they make their way back onto the Path of Shame is that of still more Talons, who cheer their emergence with unaffected enthusiasm. The bodies of Kriksex and his treacherously slain veterans have been removed, and upon asking, Arnem learns that pyres appropriate to their loyalty as well as their struggle are being built just outside the city walls. This fact satisfies the yantek, but does little to ease the sorrow of Isadora and Dagobert, who had come to know and rely upon the men with the utmost confidence and affection during the siege of the Fifth District. Having seen this same look in reaction to fallen protectors many times during his military campaigns, Arnem does not even attempt to speak words of sorrowful comfort to his wife and son, but tightens the hold he has on each of them with his two arms, ignoring the pain of his wound in favor of giving the only consolation that experience has taught him will, for the moment, have any effect.

Fortunately, the moment for such undiluted sorrow is brief: as the three follow Akillus into area before the South Gate, which is strewn with Guardsmen's bodies and smoldering sections of collapsed oak, a human confrontation comes into view that is just what the chief of scouts had said it would be: most remarkable. Remarkable, and fairly confounding, since the participants in the disagreement seemed to have become fast comrades during the march on Broken. Those who are attempting to leave the city are Caliphestros, riding the white panther Stasi, who travels, now, alongside another, more golden beast—the white panther's lost daughter, Arnem concludes, knowing well the famous tale of Lord Baster-kin's panther hunt in Davon Wood. But in front of these three, and blocking their every move to escape with the speed and fearlessness that the sentek has come to expect from them, are the Bane foragers Keera, Veloc, and Heldo-Bah, the last of whom issues indictments of the onetime Second Minister of Broken that almost seem intended to provoke an attack. Observing this strange scene are still more of Arnem's Talons, who are not at all sure what role, if any, they are meant to play in it, and who are glad to observe the approach of their commander.

"Listen to me, old man," Heldo-Bah says, holding a long, smoldering shard of the fallen South Gate before him as a barrier. "This is no time to be running off. You've heard what Linnet Niksar said: there is to be a new order in this kingdom, one that will sweep away the past and be of enormous importance to the safety of the Bane tribe—especially now that the Broken army's commander knows, if only roughly, where Okot is! So long as this is the case, and great as my respect for your companion— or rather, now, your *companions*—may be, you are not going anywhere, just yet."

"It is not a moment for wisdom and justice to desert this city and this kingdom, Lord Caliphestros," Veloc says, attempting greater conciliation than his fellow forager, but achieving even less effect. Caliphestros remains upon Stasi's back, his face a stone mask that betrays no emotion save determination: an immovable determination to get out of the city that once was so welcoming to him, but which ultimately came close to costing him his life and, says the expression in his eyes, has not in fact changed so much that it may not try to do so again, should he stay.

Keera urges silence on her brother and their friend, then humbly implores, "My lord—" But very quickly, she catches her mistake. "I am sorry—you do not wish that title. Caliphestros—can you not see how much your influence will be needed in the actual building of this new style of kingdom that the proclamation Linnet Niksar has read will bring? Can you not undertake to contribute to it, for our sakes, if not for the people of Broken's?"

But Caliphestros refuses to speak, even to Visimar, who stands nearby; and Arnem can see that some sort of intervention is required. As he moves his wife and son closer to each other, stepping out from between them as all soldiers present come to rigid attention and salute, he catches sight of Niksar, sitting astride his pure white mount, holding an unrolled piece of parchment as if its announcement was meant to resolve this and all problems, and betraying in his face complete surprise that it has not done so. Rather than approaching the participants in the confrontation at the gate directly, Arnem moves to his aide, his voice deliberately calm and inquisitive.

"Niksar," he says.

"Yantek!" comes the reply; and the rank suddenly sounds stranger than it ever has, to Arnem's ears.

"What have you been about, Linnet?" Arnem asks. "It was my understanding that you were attending to errands in the Fourth and then the First Districts."

"As I did, Yantek," Niksar explains quickly. "Well, that is, in the First.

Your charge that I visit the Fourth District was delayed by the appearance of these—" Niksar indicates the bodies of Baster-kin's men that litter the ground about them.

"And my children are safe?" Arnem says, wishing to be certain.

"Entirely safe, Yantek," Niksar replies quickly. "They await outside the walls with a *fauste* of our men and Radelfer, as you directed. But I have carried out the second of my charges, and upon doing so thought it perhaps best to wait, and bring the children in only when we had resolved this matter of—Lord Caliphestros and his panthers."

For the first time, Caliphestros turns his head, but only slightly, in Niksar's direction, as if the remark was no more than what he had expected. "And so now they are dangerous animals to you, Niksar?" he asks, his voice bitter. "When for many days you have traveled with Stasi, and seen that she means no harm to anyone that does not threaten her?"

"But my lord—" Niksar begins to reply.

"*I am not anyone's 'lord,'*" Caliphestros says, not loudly, but with a rage that is unmistakable. "If I have not made that much clear during this campaign, then I have lost far more of the art of communication with my fellow men than I had thought the case."

"Well—" But the moment is beyond Niksar's negotiating skills, and he turns again to Arnem. "You see, Yantek, I went, as we had discussed—"

"As *you two* had discussed," Caliphestros interrupts, his tone the same. "Apparently. I knew nothing of any such plan, nor did any member of the Bane tribe."

"It is a minor point, Lord—" Arnem catches himself. "Your pardon—Caliphestros. Our purpose was only to discover the true intentions of the Layzin and the God-King, and to make our future plans accordingly. Was I in the wrong?"

"Since your 'purpose' evidently included revealing my presence in the city," Caliphestros answers, "then I would say yes, you were in the wrong, by not consulting your allies."

"Perhaps," Arnem says. "But do you seriously suppose that Baster-kin, having observed our actions outside the walls, had not already made your presence, and that of the Bane, known within the High Temple, and thus to the royal family? And do you doubt that I only wished to explain that your presence was not to be feared?" These questions seem to mitigate Caliphestros's fury, for an instant, and Arnem pursues the opening:

"And, since Niksar evidently brings good news—well, what *is* the news you bring, Niksar?"

"Read for yourself, Yantek," Niksar replies, handing the document down to his commander and himself saluting.

"I really do wish you could stop calling me that," Arnem murmurs. "However, I suppose it is inevitable . . ."

"According to the God-King," Niksar says, "it is more than inevitable: it is a heightened necessity, for you are a man of new standing—and power."

As Arnem quickly reads the proclamation, he can see just how and why its actual wording—founded so basically in the Kafran faith and system of rule—would have inflamed the passions of the participants in the current disagreement when Niksar first read the thing. Such being the case, and not wishing to make matters worse, he simply and quickly summarizes its points: "It declares that Rendulic Baster-kin—the *late* Rendulic Baster-kin, I might add, Caliphestros—"

"That was his doing, and not ours," Caliphestros angrily declares, his fears reignited rather than calmed. "My companions and I sought only to escape this damnèd city, that has done each of us such injustice." He glances at the panthers: Stasi's daughter paces in growing and dangerous confusion, and is clearly prepared to commit more violence of the variety that was inflicted on Baster-kin and his Guardsmen but moments ago, if such becomes necessary. She is only prevented from doing so by her mother: Stasi seems able to communicate to her offspring that these men—particularly the Bane before them, but the soldiers, as well—are not to be feared or attacked: not yet, at any rate.

"It is true, Sentek Arnem," Keera declares, using the title that the commander of the Broken army seems, for the moment, to prefer, as a method of appealing to him. Veloc and Heldo-Bah nod in agreement. "We arrived just as the two parties met," the tracker continues. "Caliphestros, Stasi, and her child were attempting only to leave the city, when Baster-kin goaded the Guardsmen with him—who, we now discover, had murdered the priests dispatched by your own God-King to arrest the Merchant Lord—into another, similarly treacherous attack: a decision that they would have been wise not to have taken, if escape was their goal."

"Although," Heldo-Bah says, "had they continued to try to run, and made for the East Gate, they would have encountered us, and met with the same fate—if delivered through slightly different means . . ."

"You would have done murder within the city walls, Heldo-Bah?" Arnem asks.

And for the first time, the three Bane look at Arnem with expressions in their faces that somewhat resemble Caliphestros's own. "Murder— *Yantek*?" Heldo-Bah replies, deliberately provoking Arnem. "Were those not your orders—to hunt down and bring to justice every member of Baster-kin's Guard that could be found?"

"I make no complaint about the Guardsmen," Arnem answers. "But I gave no orders as to what was to be done with Baster-kin himself."

"The *chief* of the Guard was not to be considered a *member* of it?" Veloc replies, somewhat astonished. "One who had already ordered the killing of an escort of priests who acted under the direct instruction of *your* God-King?"

"There is troubling inconsistency in that, Yantek, you must confess," Keera adds gravely. "And, as I have told you, it was *they* who, in accordance with the Merchant Lord's orders, attempted to bring about the completion of the sentence—the *unjust* sentence, as I have heard you yourself say—that was passed upon Caliphestros, so many years ago. The panthers acted in self-defense, and defense of their benefactor—and by urging them all to stay here, we sought only to make that great man's wisdom available to you, as you assume your new powers." Keera's expression changes from surprise to suspicion. "But perhaps we have misunderstood the matter . . ."

"Yes," Caliphestros says to the three Bane, nodding. "Now you begin to see it . . ."

"What 'new powers' do they speak of, Sixt?" Isadora says, moving with Dagobert to her husband's side.

But affairs at hand command Arnem's attention: "Allow me to say that, on the contrary, it is *you*, Caliphestros, who do *not* begin to see," the yantek calls to the sage. "If this proclamation is true—and it bears the royal seal—then you *shall* be a lord and an advisor again."

"*I?*" Caliphestros laughs. "To whom? To a king whom I knew to be perverse from boyhood, and whom I watched become still more treacherous than ever Baster-kin was as he grew? Or perhaps to his sister, who will wish my throat cut at the earliest opportunity, to rid herself of certain—*inconvenient* memories? Or is it to the Grand Layzin that you will recommend me, when he himself pronounced me a sorcerer, a heretic, and a criminal deserving of torture and death?"

"No, Lord Caliphestros," Arnem replies. "You shall become an advisor to *me*." The commander glances about at the collected crowd of soldiers, Bane, and residents of the Fifth District. "You have all heard the words that Niksar has proclaimed?" To their general assent, he turns to his wife and son, and summarizes the principal points it contains: "The Merchants' Council is to be abolished, and the Merchants' Hall destroyed. Rendulic Baster-kin is declared an enemy of the kingdom, to be arrested and suffer whatever punishment the God-King desires. The Yantek of the Army of Broken—"

"You, Father," Dagobert says.

"It would seem so," Arnem replies, not without some reluctance. "The Yantek of the Broken Army will become the chief secular official and power in the kingdom."

"Father!" Dagobert declares, his recent battle seeming somehow and wholly vindicated.

"The 'secret children' of Rendulic Baster-kin—" And to the confusion of most of his assembled audience at this statement, Arnem raises a hand. "I know of this reference, so be calm, all of you. It is enough to say that they are alive, and that their 'cursèd nature' is declared an innocent inheritance, passed down by the traitor Baster-kin. They are decreed mere unfortunates, to be placed under the healing care of Lady Arnem." He glances for a moment at his wife. "The *Kastelgerd* Baster-kin shall, for the time their healing takes, be returned to the supervision of its seneschal, Radelfer. Other members of the Baster-kin family may serve the God-King in their offices in other parts of the kingdom, unless and until they reveal similarly treasonous intentions as the former chief of their clan. Finally, one *khotor* of the Broken army, rather than the now-finished Merchant Lord's Guard, shall see to peace within the walls of the city, in cooperation with the household guard that Radelfer has informally assembled in the *Kastelgerd* Baster-kin." Rolling the parchment and handing it back to Niksar, Arnem continues, "And you, wife, are absolved of all wrongdoing. As is Visimar. The Fifth District is to be rebuilt, not destroyed. That siege, along with the attempt upon the life of the God-King blamed upon the Bane, were parts of Baster-kin's pernicious plan to gain near-absolute power, and did not originate with his superiors or with those in Davon Wood. There are more but lesser details, all in the same spirit. And I remind you, Caliphestros, it bears the God-King's seal."

Shaking his head in disbelief, Caliphestros finally answers, "Sentek—Yantek, whatever rank you now accept: have you seen the proclamation that was posted throughout the city before our entry? It also bears the royal seal."

Seeing that Arnem has not, Niksar takes a sheet of parchment—this one coated with some kind of glue or lacquer—from a nearby soldier. "One of the scouts cut this from a wall in the Third District, Yantek—they have been posted throughout the city."

Arnem quickly reads the thing, then passes it to his wife. "And what of it? It simply states the same information, in briefer form."

"Sixt . . . ," Isadora says, her voice suddenly worried.

"Your wife sees the truth now as clearly as she did when she studied with the wisest woman in Broken," Caliphestros declares, somewhat mollified. "My lady," he goes on, putting a hand to his chest and bowing as much as he can from his place astride Stasi's neck and shoulders. "Though I did not myself know you, then, I knew your mistress—a fact she doubtless withheld from you. She even suggested that you become one of my acolytes—an offer I refused, for your own safety. It required no great insight to see that you were destined for an important place, and should not risk your life in my service. The fate of Visimar—though he is, thankfully, with us today—and the even worse ends met by the others who followed me will attest to the wisdom of that decision."

"My lord," Isadora answers, with no little surprise and gratitude. "Praise from you is honor indeed—my mistress ever said so." She turns to her husband. "And for this reason, Sixt, I must, as your wife, echo his concerns. This proclamation, issued before the conflict was decided, favors neither you *nor* Baster-kin. It is, indeed, so worded as to have made the citizenry believe that whichever side emerged triumphant, the God-King and the Grand Layzin had divined and approved the outcome."

Reviewing the pronouncement, Arnem tilts his head in confusion. "That is one interpretation, surely. But it is the most cynical, to say nothing of the most sinister . . ."

"*Cynical?*" Heldo-Bah declares. "*Sinister?* Yantek Arnem, we, too have seen this decree, and know that your wife speaks only good sense, by the bloody, piss-stained face of—"

"Heldo-Bah!" Keera is forced to order. "Do not worsen matters with your foul blasphemies—of *any* kind."

"Blasphemies or no, Yantek Arnem," Caliphestros says, "you reveal with the smallest statement that you give credence to all this royal . . . maneuvering."

"A hard word, Caliphestros," Arnem declares. "I may have doubts. But if this latest proclamation gives me the power to do the things I must, then this city and kingdom can be reformed. With your help, and that of Visimar, we shall find the source of the first pestilence—"

"From what I understand, your wife already understands the essential problem, and needs no advice from me," Caliphestros replies. "The same can be said of the second ailment and Visimar's diagnosis. Between the two of them, and backed by the authority that you yourself have been given, they can devise a pair of solutions. If permanent solutions truly do exist . . ."

"But we have *need* of your wisdom, my lord," Arnem pleads. "I do not offend Visimar, I believe, when I say that yours is a mind without equal."

"You offend me not in the least," Visimar rushes to say.

"And you make a flattering plea, Arnem," Heldo-Bah declares, throwing aside the piece of charred oak he had used to block the panthers' path. "Save for one thing: with your wife and Visimar both here, you do not need my legless lord, as he says. While the Bane will require their own wise man somewhere in the Wood. And, although I am sure that this is not the main reason that Caliphestros wishes to go back, any arguments against his return—especially arguments made by *you*, who, of all people, has suddenly become the precious creature of that God-King who starves the poor and shits gold—are self-serving demands against which the two panthers, in particular, will prove deaf. So I would suggest that if you continue to fight their departure, you do so at your peril. *Yantek.*"

From where they stand and sit atop rubble, Veloc and Keera join their suddenly eloquent friend, and the three proceed to stand by the side of Stasi, her rider, and her daughter; and it is quite as clear from their expressions as it was from Heldo-Bah's words that their opinions on where Caliphestros truly belongs have quickly changed.

"That we may fully understand one another—you continue to believe in the righteousness and honesty of the God-King and the Layzin, Yantek?" Veloc queries. "Because of two pieces of parchment that bear the 'royal and holy seal'?"

"Do not presume to speak for me, Veloc," Arnem warns. "My beliefs and reservations are well known. But I have the authority. It shall not be reversed—for I command the only power in Broken that *could* enforce such a reversal."

"Ah," Caliphestros noises. "So we come to it at last: *power*. Your power will put all things right. Tell me, Yantek: did it never occur to you that it was power that destroyed Rendulic Baster-kin—who was, I have told you, not doing evil, as he saw it, but obediently enforcing the will of the God-King?"

Arnem nods. "'The last good man in Broken,' you said."

"As indeed he was—by your kingdom's standards. Your wife knew him as a youth. Was he the same soul then, lady, that power would later make him?"

"In his essence," Isadora answers, now wishing to defend her husband. "Later, when he had the ability, and was not troubled by pain—"

"Yes—when he had *power*. He planned the death of his wife—who died during our march—and thought to have rid himself of a belovèd daughter, while keeping an unfortunate and disowned son virtually enslaved. Power allowed him to do all this, yet he thought himself doing only right—for his God-King and the realm. Even when he both courted and threatened you, Lady Isadora, and attempted to arrange the death of your husband and his men, he believed that he did so for the good of Broken, with the power given to him by the *true* evil that inhabits this place. Well . . ." Glad in his heart to see that the three foragers have moved to the South Gate and have apparently decided to accompany him as he departs the city, Caliphestros finally says, "Believe it all, if you will, and if you must, Sixt Arnem. Do your very best, for remember"—and suddenly Caliphestros turns a look on Arnem that cuts the yantek to his very soul—"*you* are the last good man in Broken, now, and therefore the most dangerous. You will do all manner of evil in the name of good—and your first test will come immediately. For I swear to you, if you wish me to stay, you must kill me, as well as my Bane friends—who will, I suspect, advise Ashkatar and his men to take a similar view. We who belong in the Wood will return to it—and you interfere at your peril, less to your life than to your soul."

"But, master," Visimar says, as Caliphestros at last moves toward the gate. "You will not even *advise* us from afar?"

"Visimar, my old friend," comes a more congenial reply. "You have learned to survive in this city—now you shall even thrive. But, once again, beware. The day will come when *each* of you will come to understand, in his or her own way, that Baster-kin was not the sole, or in many cases even the primary, source of Broken's perfidy. You know such in your heart even now, Lady Arnem. But I will promise you this—" Caliphestros leans over to stroke Stasi's neck, urging patience on the increasingly anxious panther. "If the day ever comes when you do discover and realize what that true evil is, and wish to confront it—then, if I still live, I shall return to assist you. But for now, I must bid you all farewell . . ."

The old man at last allows the panthers to move toward the gate, the resigned Arnem indicating to his own men that no last obstacle is to be put to either the rider, his mount, the second panther, or the three foragers; and, as Caliphestros finally passes through the South Gate, he laughs once: a complex sort of laughter, of a type Keera has come to know well. "Fear not, Visimar," the departing scholar calls. "We shall be in contact by the usual means." He gives his old friend a final, earnest glance. "For it would indeed grieve me not to know how you *do* fare . . ."

"But—where shall we find you, master?" Visimar calls.

"You shall not," Caliphestros answers, passing out of the gate. "Only three humans know of my—of *our*—lair. And I believe—" He casts a glance at the three foragers. "I believe I may rely on them never to reveal that location."

"The golden god may descend to Earth, and I shall carve him a new anus with the sword you gave me, old man," Heldo-Bah says with a grin, his disposition utterly changed, "before I will ever reveal any such thing."

"The Moon's truth," Veloc adds. "I may compose the saga of our journey—but I shall never reveal just where we found you."

"Trust in it," Keera assures the rider gently. "Those two shall never reveal the location, nor shall I. But may we—may I—not visit you, from time to time?"

"*You* are always welcome, Keera," Caliphestros replies. "As for your brother and the other?" Suddenly smiling gently, the old man seems to soften at last. "I suppose they may come, if they wish. But in the name of whatever *is* holy, make Heldo-Bah bathe. As to now—you must be away, to advise Ashkatar of all that has taken place. I will make directly for the Wood with my companions." He glances down at Stasi and her daughter, deeply contented. "Yes—we shall make for home . . ."

And at that, the two panthers and the man who still, somehow, has the strength to stay astride the greater of the two, immediately begin to run at full pace, the foragers struggling to keep up. But it is not long before they have all vanished, into the last stands of trees on the high slopes of Broken and then amid the strange mist that continues to encircle the mountain.

Watching the group disappear from sight, Arnem, his wife, and son say not a word as they walk to the ruins of the gate. Only Niksar breaks the silence:

"Yantek! Shall I detail a *fauste* of horsemen to pursue?"

"And what would your purpose be, Linnet?" Visimar asks, his eyes growing thinner, hoping for a last glimpse of his master. "You, your men, all of us, owe that little troop our lives, it would seem. Would you try to bring Caliphestros back, and break his will? This kingdom attempted that, once, and failed."

"Failed rather badly," Isadora murmurs, reaching inside her husband's armor to ensure that the medallion she put there upon his departure remains in place.

"Yes—rather badly, indeed," Arnem agrees, looking at her briefly.

"Yet having aided you thus far, Father," says Dagobert, "they will simply—disappear?"

"I have never been given cause to doubt Lord Caliphestros," Arnem answers. "Nor do I think that he has given me any such, now—he says that if and when a day comes that we discover a deeper evil at work in this city than has yet been discovered, we may contact him through Lord Visimar, who will now, I hope, take the position of high honor I offered to his master."

Visimar bows, if only briefly. "I shall be honored, Yantek." And with that his eyes turn to look down the mountain again, still hopeful for a last sight of the great philosopher he has been so proud to call friend.

"And so," Arnem concludes, "he may be back, one day—but I shall try with all my being to ensure that there will be no cause. As for the Bane, our relations with them shall not only return to what they were prior to this crisis, but shall improve, now that at least two exceptions—the Baster-kin children—to the kingdom's policy of exiling the imperfect have been made. And I intend to make those exceptions precedents. For, I confess, I ever found such rituals unnatural . . ." At that, the new supreme secular voice in the kingdom of Broken turns again to his wife and son. "Well, then? Shall we see how the rest of the children fare? I must inform Radelfer of his good fortune, as well."

Pleased, for now, to have the moment of possible internal strife at last ended, Isadora and Dagobert gladly voice their agreement; yet it cannot be said that Lady Arnem is yet easy in her soul . . .

Visimar, for his part, scarcely seems to hear these remarks, so fixed are his eyes on the distance. Finally, however, he abandons the search; unfortunately, as it happens, for had he but waited a short while longer, he would doubtless have been most gratified to make out—emerging from the forests at the base of the mountain—the forms of two Davon panthers racing back toward their home within the Wood, with an agèd and truncated human attempting with all his strength to keep to the shoulders of the larger and more brilliantly white of the two . . .

ACKNOWLEDGMENTS

The opening chapters and outline of the book that would become *The Legend of Broken* were first put on paper in 1984. The story's central elements have evolved, of course, but not so much as one might be tempted to think: it was a truly "perennial project," because the themes at its core were never resolved, either within me or in "the kingdom" itself. In those first days, I was living in the back room of the apartment that my grandmother, Marion G. Carr, owned on Washington Square, and working, first for and then with, my friend and mentor, James Chace. My grandmother died in 1986; James we lost more recently, in 2004. One made it practically possible to begin this story by offering, as she always did, a roof and a retreat. From the other I learned more about the rules of the writer's life than I can say. Of course, this was not the kind of writing that James ever thought more than a diversion; but if I kept at it, he thought, I "might be able to earn a nice little stipend, one day," while I was pursuing my serious work in diplomatic and military history. As for my indomitable grandmother, she greeted such projects as this with the flat statement, "Well, dear, I don't know what you think you're doing." I miss them both terribly, especially on the occasion of the finished book's publication.

The project physically tormented me, on and off, for many years: when I was working on it, I could not be prevailed upon to take care of anything: my health, my residences, or several girlfriends. I apologize to the latter, and only hope that, if they read this, it may help them understand what was driving me. Then, last year, with the finish line more or less in sight, I had one of my periodic brushes with death, which was brought on in no small part by the overexertions that always consumed me when I was writing *Broken*. That I survived and recovered was due in no small part to the patient exertions of my family, particularly my mother, Cessa, and her husband, Bob Cote, my brother Simon, and my niece Gabriela, the last of whom made all the Jell-O as well as doing whatever else was asked. I thank them, and I also thank Dr. Marcus Martinez, and, at Southwest Vermont Medical Center, Dr. Eugene Grobowski, Dr. Ronald Mensh, and the extraordinarily kind group of nurses who saw me through.

When a writer takes on the life of a "gentleman farmer," living alone with a cat at the foot of a mountain called Misery, he becomes very aware of the daily contacts that make his life work; he also becomes aware of the high price that his neighbors place on privacy. However, I have to risk it and thank Pat Haywood, Arnie Kellar, and the various reliable workers who don't wish to be named. I must also thank Dennis and Joan Masterson, and, of course, their daughter Catherine, who for long periods during this effort was the only human bright spot in many otherwise rough days. And speaking of bright spots, if not human, I have to once again thank my late, beloved Suki for bringing Stasi into the real world, and the present wild child Masha for bringing me Stasi's cub.

I don't even know how to thank the cast of thousands at Thorpe's for their truly life- and sanity-preserving help, so I'll just say that Jim Monahan and Dennis Whitney and all the troops there are models of what the healthcare industry should be but rarely is. They are all valued friends, even if they never thought this book would get done.

My brother Ethan has done an extraordinary job of helping me work out the legalities that will keep the immensity that is Misery Mountain and the estate surrounding it secure as a wilderness sanctuary; I thank him, as well as his wife, Sarah, for supporting the endeavor, and for allowing Marion to hang out with her crazy uncle. From ice hockey to RC planes, she's a real education.

To say that the publication of this book has been a complex affair would be a grotesque understatement; for in its initial incarnation, *Broken* was quite the beast in need of taming. For her astoundingly capable first swipe at editing it into a tame animal, I have to thank my niece Lydia. The recent publication of her own first book is a further and vivid demonstration of her dedication and talent (of course, she *has* had the advantage, which she's shared, of her patient and kind husband, Michael Corey).

At Random House, I have to thank Jennifer Hershey and Gina Centrello for faith and indulgence above and beyond the call of, well, anything. And most of all, I have to thank Dana Isaacson for more than I can adequately say: tireless and expert editing skill, along with real friendship and, beyond that, the ability to learn how to handle the unforgivable and byzantine ill humors that difficulties piled upon difficulties could throw me into.

My agent at WME, Suzanne Gluck, learned that trick during our days at Friends Seminary, long ago; but she had to use every ploy on this one, and I thank her once again, along with the ever kind and patient Eve Attermann and Becca Kaplan.

Barry Haldeman has been a good friend, and shepherded the legal side of the project even when there wasn't a dime to pay him with. My agent and old friend in Los Angeles, Debbie Deuble, always makes time to help and endure my rants, and even more to cheer me up; I hope she and her husband, Tim Hill, know that I'm eternally grateful.

And, concerning matters Out There, mention should be made of the encouragement and feedback offered during this undertaking by my old friend Tim Haldeman. The fact that he ultimately felt he must end so vital a friendship is both impossible and easy for me to understand: most men have at least one Alandra in their lives—Tim was unlucky enough to father his. This is not an indictment, but rather a simple statement that the events and characters chronicled in these pages, while drawn from various sources, are nothing if not real; fantasy doesn't enter the discussion.

My nephews, Sam and Ben, have done their always-yeoman service with only the occasional grumble and usually great and good humor; they've been on the front line for a lot, and I thank them once again. Patty Clayton took the pictures on short notice, which did nothing to hamper her skill and judgment. My cousin William has shared not only the travails of the book but the far more brutal extremes of being a New York Giants fan; anyone who's been through such torment knows the extra demands on work, and on sanity, that it brings.

Dana Kintsler visited when she could and tried to pump blood back into my veins; and Scott Marcus, from distances far and not so far away, has been a solid rock of friendship. Together, we three endured the far too early and awful death of one of our original quartet of noise, Matthew Kasha, and I thank them deeply for being there. I'm sure they'd join me in telling Matt, wherever he is, to pick up the damned bass and practice, so he'll be ready when we get there.

NOTES

x † Bernd Lutz, "Medieval Literature," in *A History of German Literature,* Clare Kro-
jzl, translator (London: Routledge, 1993), p. 6.

Part One

3 † **seat of unholy forces and unnatural rites** Gibbon did not live quite long enough
to see his characterization of the mountain *Brocken* echoed by another great
genius of the age, Goethe, who used the site in just the manner Gibbon
describes—as a setting for unholy rituals—in his most famous work, *Faust.* The
first of the play's immortal *Walpurgisnacht* scenes, during which Faust meets
unnatural creatures as well as characters from Greek mythology, takes place
atop the supposedly cursed mountain. Because of the play's great success and
continuing influence, it both perpetuated and heightened the mountain's notorious reputation. —C.C.

4 † **the** *Bane* Gibbon writes, "When we encounter the word 'bane,' here, we must
understand it not as it is currently defined in English—that is, as a 'spoiling
person or other agent'—but rather in that sense in which it was originally intended throughout the Germanic languages: *bani* in Old Norse, *bana* in Old
English, *bano* in Old High German (pronounced 'bahn-uh,' and eventually
spelled *bane*), which, in turn, translate as, 'slayer,' 'murderer,' and simply
'death.' Only in this way can we see how deep was the impression that this diminutive race made on the citizens of Broken." [An IMPORTANT NOTE, here:
The reason for the shift in vowel sound, and later spelling, that Gibbon cites in
the third of these examples is the famous "vowel shift" of Old High German, by
way of which vowels in almost all unstressed syllables were reconciled (or reduced, the vowel shift sometimes being called the "vowel reduction") to a uniform short "e," which then became the most common vowel sound in Middle
High German and finally in modern German. Along with the famous "conso-
nant shift" in the same language, which is more arcane and of less concern, for
our purposes, the vowel shift was responsible for transforming, from the sixth
to the eleventh centuries, a language that was more phonetically akin to ancient German—as well as to the cousins of that earlier tongue, Old English
(Anglo-Saxon), Old Dutch, Old Norse, etc.—into one that was its own distinct
branch of the Germanic family. That transformation would, in turn, eventually lead to modern German. —C.C.]

5 † **still deem the destruction just** Gibbon writes, "Here is the first of the puzzling
temporal inconsistencies that seem either the careless phrasing of an undisci-

plined mind, or something far more mysterious: and any critical reader of the Manuscript who is possessed of even rudimentary insight will recognize and know full well that the narrator's mind, while afflicted with many peculiarities, was far from undisciplined. Yet he speaks, in this statement, of destruction that is *to come* to his city and kingdom, and then of the destruction that 'evidently' *has come* to pass, leaving us to wonder how, if he is writing before that destruction, he can know not only that it will happen, but what form it will take, down to the smallest details. On this, I shall elaborate in later notes."

6 † **wars to the south** Gibbon writes, "Just what the narrator means by the 'wars to the south' is made unclear by his continued temporal ambiguity: He speaks of Broken in both the present and past tenses, suggesting that he may have been a visionary priest or some such; or that he was a later historian, assuming a guise for dramatic effect (which is my own belief). At any rate, for all of the period he discusses, the Western [Roman] Empire was, of course, in varying but constant states of distress, disarray, and, finally, dissolution, making employment as an auxiliary uncertain and irregular. It seems that his only secure posting there must have arisen out of his loyalty to the famed general Aetius, who, after defeating Attila and his Hunnish horde at Troyes in A.D. 451, was murdered by the jealous emperor Valentinian. It seems also that Oxmontrot, after participating in the vengeful murder of Valentinian, journeyed east to serve under the Byzantine standard, finding employ in the wars between the Eastern Empire and its various enemies, most notably the Persians, but also Oxmontrot's own Germanic 'relations.' After some fifteen years of such service, the founder of Broken returned home to oversee the building of his new kingdom."

6 ‡ **my voyage . . . across the Seksent Straits** Gibbon writes, "Here we may be more certain that the narrator is referring to a journey to either Celtic Britain, Celtic Scotland, or Ireland, the only places in Europe across any 'Straits' (certainly the Dover Straits, the narrowest point in our own English Channel and the most common point at which to cross from France to the British Isles, then as now) where he would have found monks capable of thus tutoring him." One need only add that the term "Seksent Straits" takes its name from the Broken name for "Saxons," who were considered the equivalent of peasants in that kingdom, despite the fact that, operating from their main base in the Calais region (the south side of the Dover Straits), the Saxons had already proved a formidable people, launching raids across the Dover Straits and into Britain, as well as in other directions; but they were still not, apparently, considered more than vagabond trash within the borders of Broken. Gibbon's translator did not put the word "Seksent" in italics, here, perhaps because it was the proper name of a place. —C.C.

6 †† **Davon Wood** The name betrays a Germanic origin, though it cannot of course be taken literally, in the modern German sense: Besides the fact that we know Broken to have had its own dialect (mainly a mix of Old High German, Gothic, and Middle High German, although at times, as we will see, this can be a gross oversimplification), one finds it unlikely that the place was called *"Thereof Forest,"* "thereof" being the standard contemporary meaning of *davon*. But there is a secondary connotation to the modern word that is much more inter-

esting, especially as it seems to have fallen out of use—and would have been more likely, therefore, to have derived from one of the ancient Germanic languages, and thus to have formed a part of the Broken dialect's vocabulary. That connotation is "therefrom," suggesting that *davon* was used to denote a "source" of things, including and perhaps especially evil and dangerous things. When coupled with the use of the word "bane" (see definitions in the note to p. 4), this seems all the more likely.

Judging by its location relative to Broken (assuming that "Broken" and *Brocken* are indeed the same peak, which seems, as Gibbon says, almost irrefutable), it appears that Davon Wood was simply a different name for the vast Thuringian Forest (as Gibbon concludes in a later note). Its hundreds of square miles of thick, rugged woodland, covering mountains and valleys alike, as well as its sudden and frequent drops into cascading waterways, match the narrator's description of Davon Wood precisely—or rather, it would have matched it precisely, during the period under discussion (from the fifth to eighth centuries), when the forest was still primeval, and large tracts had not been cleared for lumber and firewood, and afterward reforested with secondary growth that, while still impressive, does not have the overwhelming dimensions of those portions of the ancient forest that have survived. If we accept the proposition that the Thuringian Forest and "Davon Wood" are one and the same, then we can further conjecture that the mountains which the people of Broken knew as "the Tombs" were the same range that today is known as the *Erz*, or "Ore," Mountains. Situated on the border of Germany and the Czech Republic, the Erz contained (as the name makes clear) a wealth of mineral deposits and forbidding, icy passes that conform closely to the narrator's description of the Tombs. —C.C.

7 † **marauders** This word, used repeatedly throughout the text, may of course be a generic term for all nomadic tribes; but the emphasis on their appearing from the east, "out of the morning sun," along with repeated later references to "eastern marauders" who attacked with the sun at their backs in order to blind and confuse their enemies, seems to indicate that it is a term applied primarily to the Huns, who did indeed prefer such avenues of attack—and who, despite their reputation as fearless and undefeatable warriors, may well have elected to bypass a kingdom as relatively small and capable of defending itself as was Broken. —C.C.

7 ‡ **with this limitation as with so many** It's as well to establish early on that this sense of nostalgia on the narrator's part for the "limitations" of the past fits with the nature of many Barbarian Age Germanic states. The word "barbarian" is often associated, in the popular consciousness, with a warlike, nomadic lifestyle, as well as with undefinable borders and anarchic governments; but the truth (or rather, what little truth we know) is that many if not most of the small, vanished kingdoms of central-northern and northeastern Europe occupied discrete, relatively well-ordered regions. This is particularly true of those kingdoms that, like Broken, retained heavy Gothic influences, although the Goths had long since moved on—if, indeed, they had ever actually "invaded," or were in turn invaded, which is one of those time-honored yet ultimately

unproved theories of population migration that has of late been seriously questioned.

The standard notion of what has come to be known as (to use the phrase employed in one of the early twentieth century's key works on the subject, written by the important if somewhat outdated British historian J.B. Bury) "the barbarian invasion of Europe" may represent less firmly grounded scholarship than it does the culmination of centuries of historical conjecture and pseudo-hagiography among academics across Europe, and even, eventually, in the United States, as well. But the central flaw in this notion of wave upon wave of non-agricultural, raiding tribes—pressed by the need to gain food for their people and forage for their ever-expanding herds of horses and ponies, as well as by a desire for wealth that they could not or did not wish to earn through settled hard work in trading towns and ports—has become suspect, in recent years: in fact, the "barbarian hordes" theory may be a piece of *propaganda* that is far, far older than is that modern term for the deliberate deluding of whole populations. Indeed, it may be an unusually effective bit of fiction that dates back to imperial Rome itself, and especially to the western portion of that empire, which needed an explanation for why their proud legions were regularly repulsed and sometimes overwhelmed by the tribes north of the Danube and east of the Rhine.

Any emperor, much less a commander of a legion, who could allow himself to be fought to a standstill, to say nothing of defeated, by such barbarians would have had a great deal of explaining to do, both to the Roman aristocracy and to the larger group whose acronym the Roman legions bore into battle: "SPQR," *Senatus Populusque Romanus,* "the Senate and the people of Rome." Yet such defeats *did* occur, from time to time, especially at the hands of the Germanic tribes. In fact, the number of defeats only rose as Rome's life as a republic became a distant memory and its transformation into an empire was consolidated. It became necessary, therefore, to concoct a more elaborate rationalization than the simple combat superiority of the Germanic tribes; and the theory of wave after wave of "barbarian invaders" may have been cut to fit this need. Such men (and women, too, for Norse and Germanic females often fought alongside the tribes' male warriors) could be—indeed, *had* to be—portrayed as the worst of all possible dangers, if the indomitable reputation of the Roman legions was to be maintained on other frontiers. And so those tribes were widely declared to be not only every bit as wily as the leaders of those empires and kingdoms that lay beyond even Persia, but as treacherous as the Egyptians or the Carthaginians, and as savage as the crazed Picts in the northernmost reaches of Britannia—with the added attributes, of course, of being uncanny horsemen and expert seamen. Small wonder, then, that Caesar himself eventually declared that he would not campaign in or try to conquer Germania: To face "the Germans" became akin to engaging a semi-supernatural force, and the generally disastrous encounters that occasionally did take place, if they ended in temporary Roman successes, were characterized by punitive measures against German warriors and civilians alike that were unusually horrifying, even for such ruthless troops as the imperial Roman legions.

This inflation of an enemy in order to explain defeat or disaster is hardly an unprecedented or a unique tactic in world military history; indeed, it is all too common when governments need to rationalize not only failure but the enormous expenditures of blood and treasure that usually accompany such failures, as well as the cost of constantly manning a hostile frontier that ensues. But the specific point, here, is that Broken's not having fit into the larger story of the "barbarian invasions" of Europe may have been a fact less rooted in Broken's never having existed than in the very real possibility—most strongly put forward, in recent years, by Michael Kulikowski, in his seminal account of "Rome's Gothic Wars"—that the warriors the Romans faced when they crossed into Germania were fearsome precisely because they did *not* represent violent hordes from the exotic East, but rather because they were the longstanding inhabitants of those lands, as brave as the Romans and more determined to defend their homelands than the legions were to conquer them. The logical conclusion of all these considerations—that there was a limit to Roman military and imperial power—was a notion that the great empire simply could not see propagated; and so any reference to the kingdom of Broken, whether during Western Rome's pagan imperial centuries, or during its early Christian era, was excised, explaining why we find no direct reference to it in the ancient annals of Roman history. —C.C.

7 †† **they are not *too* small** Before dismissing as poetic license the idea that many if not most of the Bane tribe were adult humans of exceptionally small stature (without, apparently and importantly, being characterized in the main by dwarfism), we should remember everything that modern science has learned about genetic inheritance and adaptive breeding, in humans as well as in other animals. The Bane, therefore, were almost certainly the product of interbreeding among people with certain distinct characteristics, exceptionally short stature evidently being first among them.

However . . . there is a possible and intriguing second explanation, not only for the existence of the Bane, but for the common appearance of diminutive peoples in many such stories and legends from the Barbarian Age, as well as from more ancient eras—stories and legends which have, of course, influenced many modern works of fiction based in those periods, as well as in well-known works of fantasy. This possible explanation has only become available through several contemporary discoveries in archaeological anthropology and zoology; and I must stress that the theory is, obviously, highly speculative (some will say fanciful) in nature; but it nonetheless deserves mention:

In recent years, a group of scientists have found what they claim is a new species in the genus *Homo, Homo floresiensis,* who seem to have been, in effect, "miniature people," meaning that they grew to a height of no more than four feet or so, but were not characterized by dwarfism. To date, the fossilized bones of this "species" have been found only on the small Indonesian island for which they are named, Flores; and the claim that they represent an entirely new variation on our own genus has been challenged by scientific skeptics, who believe that these people were nothing more than members of *Homo sapiens* who were afflicted with microencephaly, a disorder in which the brain does not grow beyond a limited size, and the rest of the body follows suit proportionally. But what is particularly intriguing is the assertion that such "miniature humans" (nicknamed by their discoverers "hobbits," for obvious if anatomically incorrect reasons) may also have been present in the Harz Mountains, a notion based on human migration patterns as well as the fact that fossils of "miniature dinosaurs"—close relatives of the brachiosaurs, but *one-fiftieth* the size of those familiar and enormous plant eaters—were discovered in the Harz range in 1998.

Could "miniature people" have existed in the same Harz Mountains as did these "miniature dinosaurs," separated by the same interval that separates *Homo sapiens* from the larger dinosaurs? Again, such is no more than a suggestion that the narrator's claims about the Bane are plausible, and an intriguing alternative to the more likely (but less innovative and, admittedly, less entertaining) explanation of genetic adaptation; although, at the same time, there is nothing to say that the two explanations are mutually exclusive. —C.C.

8 † **Kafra** Gibbon writes, "Their god Kafra is, as I have said, an interesting variation on such deities as Elagabalus [sometimes written *Heliogabalus,* in part to distinguish him from the Roman emperor Elagabalus] and Astarte, whose cults of worshippers became quite large and did indeed interpret physical perfection and material wealth as signs of divine favor. But in the case of Kafra, the evolution of certain of the more sensual and degenerate elements of those cults receives a decidedly Germanic treatment, with their elevation to a pragmatic and highly organized system of theocracy." Kafra also demonstrates the generalized shift in the barbarian West away from religions that assigned a prominent place to a female figure (often a goddess of fertility), and toward both pagan and monotheist religions in which supreme authority was invested in a male figure. Certain superficial similarities between Kafra and Jesus are noteworthy (the facial features, the serene smile that is so often mentioned, and which purportedly reflects a benevolent nature), although Gibbon himself, ever anxious not to alienate Burke before the latter had even looked at the Manuscript, makes little mention of them. —C.C.

8 ‡ **the sacred Moon** One fact concerning the identity of the Manuscript's author, a fact that had apparently escaped Gibbon's attention, is illuminating: In every instance, the narrator pays such respect to the word "moon" that the translator felt it appropriate to use the uppercase "M" throughout. The Broken dialect apparently had the equivalent of an upper case (although we, today, do not know what the written form of the language looked like), and it is possible that the narrator used it simply to show respect for the deity of the Bane, as modern publications use the upper case for the Christian "God" or the Muslim "Allah"; but it is not out of the question to hold that the usage means much more— means, in fact, that the narrator himself was likely a moon worshipper, a notion that presents intriguing possibilities as to his identity. —C.C.

8 †† **the rocky Cat's Paw** Returning to the geography of the kingdom of Broken, we can infer that the somewhat smaller mountains north of the Tombs, unnamed in the Manuscript, are the Harz range, the highest point of which, as Gibbon says, is the mountain that has long been known as *Brocken*. This would make

the river that the citizens of Broken called "the Meloderna" the modern Salle, the sources of which are in those same Harz Mountains. The middle and lower valley of the Salle was long surrounded by rich farmlands, although today (and we should perhaps be careful about drawing any superstitious inferences from this fact) much of the river is badly polluted, with the usual accompanying effects of industrial waste on the surrounding farmlands.

The sole remaining geographical mystery is the modern identity of the river referred to in the Manuscript as "the Cat's Paw": While there are several possible candidates between *Brocken* and the Thuringian Forest, it seems impossible to state with absolute certainty which of them the narrator is actually describing. —C.C.

10 † **called the Groba** On the surface, the connotation here would seem plain enough: *Groba* is a Gothic term for "cave" as in a dwelling or den, and this council meets in just such a place, while its healers work in similar chambers, above. But when we come across such words (to say nothing of even more exotic personal and place-names), we are also reminded of Gibbon's statement that the language of the people of Broken, though basically a German dialect, had Eastern influences, the reasons for which we cannot be certain of, beyond noting the deep influence of Gothic, which apparently seemed "exotic" indeed—at least to Gibbon. And yet, the Groba system, structurally, is not exotic, at all; not for a Germanic tribe. Indeed, it more closely resembles the usual Germanic system of government—which most often featured elected officials, executives, and in many if not most instances, even elected kings—than does the government of Broken. The Groba also reflects, therefore, the type of traditional indigenous government that ruled the communities of the region between the Cat's Paw and the Meloderna rivers before they were consolidated into Oxmontrot's kingdom. —C.C.

10 ‡ *"Ficksel!"* It is interesting to note that Gibbon did not choose to comment on this particular word: Since there are vulgarities in modern German that closely resemble *ficksel* in both sound and meaning, one presumes that there must have been in Gibbon's day, as well, and that the omission was made out of tact—a most peculiar tact, given both other accounts of various perverse behaviors that Gibbon seems not to have had any qualms about describing, and the general trend, in European literature of the late eighteenth century, toward the bawdiness and ribaldry that would provide much of the impetus behind the turn toward more reserved, even prudish, writing in the Victorian era. —C.C.

10 †† **Veloc** Not for the first time, Gibbon speaks here of "the great frustration of not being given lingual tools sufficient to the task of picking apart the enormously colorful names of many of the characters in the Manuscript." His inability was most often caused by the limited advances of scholarship in his day, but they were also, on occasion, the result of what Gibbon called "the almost unbalanced insistence of the man who translated the document and purveyed it to me [an interesting turn of phrase, since, especially in this context, it implies selling scandalous information of some sort] that he would not share his translational techniques, or part with the Broken Codex, for which I would gladly have paid as dearly as I did for the Manuscript itself." But this rather peevish

portion of his note is designed, one suspects, to make him look all the smarter for having come up with what he believed were solid explanations for the three foragers' names: "It is essential to the drama to know all we can of these names," he says truthfully, "as they are characters so very key to the story. That of their leader, *Keera,* requires so little effort as to scarcely want mentioning; we still find the name in use (more often in the forms of *Kira* or *Kyra*) in the Scandinavian and Low Countries, as well as in Russia; and these nations took it, of course, from Greece, by way of Rome. The sole point of interest lies in the fact that it did not originate with the Greeks, but rather their longtime antagonists, the Persians; for it is but the feminine version of *Cyrus,* a name made most famous by Cyrus the Great, ruler of that people in the sixth century B.C. and the first to expand their state to truly imperial dimensions. The meaning of this storied name has been variously described as 'of the sun' and 'farsighted': it seems, in this case, that the second of these interpretations was emphasized. And it is possible that Keera's parents waited until she had begun to display her character and her several sensory gifts, before giving her a permanent name: various tribal cultures are known to practice such a style of naming (including, most importantly, several northern barbarian tribes), and even in our own nations of Europe, a name is not considered permanent until the child has been baptized, which most often occurs during infancy, but can occur later, a practice more common when names were thought to hold formative power over the individual offspring: a practice that Keera's parents evidently embraced. These notions, of a northern influence on the name, and a delayed selection of the same, is supported by the styling of Keera's brother, *Veloc,* although the thrust of this appellation is somewhat less apparent. Its first syllable seems to be a Broken approximation of *valr,* a term in Old Norse for 'the dead'; whereas the second syllable is clearly (taken in context with the first syllable) the Broken styling of the old Norse demi-god, *Loki* (also *Loci, Loge*), either half or blood brother to Odin, as well as master of mischief, shape-shifter, and sometimes noble friend to Man. It would seem that Veloc's parents named him when they had already divined his dual nature, and either aimed to ward off the increasing influence of Loki on their son, or were paying homage to Loki in the hope that he would employ his benevolent side by assisting their troubling boy."

But it is in trying to interpret the name *Heldo-Bah* that we observe Gibbon at his most imaginative, and even whimsical: "It is my contention," he wrote, "that we [of the British Isles] may claim this remarkable little fellow as one of our own: not only because of the filed teeth, a practice not unknown among such primitive tribes as the Picts, but because he only reached Broken as a child-slave, and thus could have come from almost anywhere, including Britain. The first component of his name is clearly a Germanic interpretation of our English *Hero* (in modern German *Held,* or *Helden,* in the plural), a name that also comes to us from the Greeks, by way of Rome; and the dismissive-sounding *bah,* along with exclamations very much like it, were then already in use among Britons, Saxons, and Frisians alike—making it reasonable to assume that the boy was taken from Britain by seafaring plunderers from the North (quite probably Frisians, with whom the people of Broken apparently both fought and traded), and that these warriors took his given name of Hero and made of it a term of derision. And when the boy became a man, he likely kept the name, either because he had never learnt its meaning, or out of no more complex a cause than spite. The first of these explanations is the more likely; but the second displays a taste for irony among the Bane that we shall encounter again." Gibbon is repeating a popular legend about the Picts filing their teeth (an idea picked up on by Robert E. Howard in his "Conan" stories); he could not have known that, if anyone filed Heldo-Bah's teeth, it was likely those same northern captors, for Vikings, it has recently been discovered, often "beautified" their teeth in this manner. —C.C.

11 † **Daurawah** Gibbon writes, "The town of Daurawah, which served as a port for Broken traders, as well as for those foreign commercial vessels that brought goods to the kingdom, was certainly located on the Saale, the river referred to in the Manuscript as 'the Meloderna'; and should one find it difficult to believe that so obvious a group of Bane as these three foragers could have entered such a town freely, one must remember the general air in and condition of Daurawah, at this time, which is clearly elaborated in a later chapter."

11 ‡ **"Hafften Falls"** See note for p. 81 concerning waterfalls in the Cat's Paw.

12 † **oozing** As mentioned in the Introductory Note, the text contains many elements and words that have a vernacular quality that might make them sound relatively modern, to our ears, but that are quite appropriate to and consistent with the era—and "oozing" is an excellent example, being derived from a Dark Ages, Middle English term for "juicing." Conversely, words with similar meanings that might seem more formal and therefore "older"—in this case, say, "seeping"—were only coming into use at just the time that the translator was at work on the Broken Manuscript in the late eighteenth century. This fits a pattern that will soon become well established, of many onomatopoeic words that sound familiar and contemporary to our modern ears actually having deeper roots than many other, *seemingly* more antique words; all of which reminds us that Old High German, one of the parent languages of the Broken dialect, was perhaps the first European tongue to inspire significant written works in the vernacular; whereas the notion that barbarian and early Middle Age tales are more naturally or authentically expressed in stuffy, florid language really originates with such late medieval "courtly" writers as Thomas Malory, and especially with such revisionist Victorian interpreters as Sir Walter Scott and Alfred, Lord Tennyson. The number of modern authors who have followed in Scott's and Tennyson's footsteps is too high to list here, although notable exceptions—Robert E. Howard, for instance—do exist. Of course, there are also modern writers who have gone in the opposite direction, and who have characters speaking not only in the vernacular of either the actual medieval or fantasy-medieval eras, but speaking in utterly and anachronistically modern vulgarities; but they are not the concern of this study. —C.C.

16 † **"the *mang-bana*"** Gibbon writes, "The names of the various rituals of exile, mutilation, and execution cited in the text show the entirely cosmopolitan nature of life and language in Broken. Like some of the Bane curses, the phrase

mang-bana contains elements of words that have both survived into modern German (we may translate this phrase, very roughly, as 'the exile of the imperfect') yet also display a distinctly Gothic influence—or so, at least, we may suppose, based on our limited understanding of that language, which shows us that these words contain elements quite common, not only to Gothic names, but to Gothic terms, as well. The remainder of the Broken dialect's peculiar vocabulary was apparently made up of words imprinted with Eastern and far more obscure origins, many of which we shall doubtless never be able to trace or identify—considering the fact that entire dialects, and even languages, that were used in Barbarian Age Europe have disappeared entirely."

16 ‡ **"three weeks"** Although there was some variation in the number of months in the calendars of the people of Broken and the Bane, they would all seem to be broken down, as indeed were almost all calendric systems, into seven days. —C.C.

17 † **"Tayo"** The name of Keera's husband is one of several intriguing examples of Bane names which have their roots firmly in more than one of the languages that first influenced the Broken dialect. In this case, the languages are Old High German and Gothic, and the meaning is almost certainly the same as our modern *Theodor* or *Theodore*, that is, "gift" or "gift of god"—or goddess, as in this case the reference was almost certainly to the Bane's Moon deity. —C.C.

18 † **"Sentek"** The founding king of Broken must indeed have served as a Roman auxiliary warrior, as Gibbon postulates, because the system of military organization he devised so closely resembles the basics of the late Roman imperial order (with numbers of men in each unit adjusted drastically downward, obviously, given the much smaller size of the kingdom of Broken): The rank of *sentek* is roughly equivalent to the Roman *legatus,* or legion commander, while *yantek* corresponds to *praetor* (although, having no true provinces, and with the Merchants' Council serving the function of consuls, the rank becomes simply "supreme commander" in Broken); a *linnet,* meanwhile, seems no different than a tribune, while a *pallin* is a simple legionary. A *khotor* is, fairly obviously, the equivalent of a legion, though taking its name from the smaller Roman unit of a cohort, and made up, in Broken, of ten *fausten* (sing. *fauste,* or "fist," neither term to be confused with modern German's *faust* or *fauste,* the singular and plural words for "fist." Why the Broken dialect sometimes retained the somewhat longer versions of words may be no more cryptic than the fact that Old English did the same with words we have shortened: the very name "Broken," for example, was rendered, in Old English, "Brokynne," as we shall see). There also appears to have been a rank slightly beneath the linnet: *lenzinnet,* "first lance," a rank that anticipated the future, equating to a grade that would exist among certain formations of modern cavalry. But more importantly, here, the rank is grounded firmly in Roman tradition, being a less formal version of that empire's *pilus prior,* "first spear" (or, in the case of *lenzinnet,* "first lance"). The final proof of this theory of a Roman model for the Broken military is the apparently interchangeable nature, in the text (or so the translator apparently thought), of the words *khotor* and "legion." —C.C.

18 ‡ **Sixt Arnem** This is a wholly German name, the components of which have

been passed down intact into modern times, further supporting Gibbon's contention of the tale's cultural and historical plausibility. The spelling is very often changed to *Arnim*, although it is unclear whether this is a mistake or a mere result of translation and dialect adjustment/confusion (in Old High German, *Arnim* would certainly have become *Arnem*, in keeping with the shift by which all vowels in unstressed syllables became the short "e"); and, although the family's original associations were, not surprisingly, military, by the mid-nineteenth century we find what are by now the *von* Arnems and *von* Arnims (*von* denoting "of" or "from," and used to indicate an honorific aristocratic connection to a family home or a location of some great achievement, in the same sense that the British aristocracy uses "of") branching out into the humanities. The reason for this broadening of interests among the Prussian military caste (and most wise officers in smaller German states followed the Prussian example) is that, during the second half of the nineteenth century, it came under the increasing philosophical as well as doctrinal influence of Helmuth von Moltke, creator of the modern general staff system, military right arm of Chancellor Otto von Bismarck, architect of the wars that would fulfill Bismarck's dream of uniting the German empire, and, finally, a firm believer that officers, especially junior officers, should train themselves as he had: nearly as much in the humanities as in purely military studies. (Women shared in the German liberal humanist movement, and the von Arnems and von Arnims were no exception: by the early twentieth century we find the wife of one of them, an Englishwoman, becoming an established enough writer that one of her books, *The Enchanted April*, was sufficiently well received to become the basis of two film adaptations, one in the 1930s and another, nominated for several Oscars, in 1992.)

There were generals of consequence who bore the name von Arnim (still often spelled *Arnem*) in the Franco-Prussian, First World, and Second World Wars; the youngest of them played an important role in Rommel's Afrika Corps, while the eldest even bore the Christian name Sixt. However, the meaning of the name itself is obscure, as there appear to be no provinces, towns, mountains, or battles of consequence (the usual determining factors for the *von* honor) in modern Germany that bear the name, whatever spelling one uses—and this raises the interesting question of whether the *von* was intended, in this case, not to imply the usual geographical connection, but instead as a link to a distant ancestor, Sixt Arnem. —C.C.

19 † **unadorned steel plate helmet** Remarkable as it may seem, little to nothing is known definitively about what "Dark Age warriors" employed for helmets and armor; and, while we know a little more about their weapons, it is only a little, forcing us to rely on the descriptions of these items in texts such as the Broken Manuscript—which, thankfully, is (as we shall see), unusually rich in its descriptions of these items, the crafting of which forms a very central part of the tale. We can divine, for instance, that this particular reference is to the basic helmet design of the early Middle Ages, which was developed among the Germanic tribes, called the *Spangenhelm*, *spangen* referring to the clasps of the metal framework of the helmet, to which varying numbers of steel plates were either

welded or riveted. It became the basis for the similar Norman helmets (also unadorned, for the most part), as well as for the helmets of many other non-Germanic tribes, during this period, although just how many we cannot, of course, say; but we can add that the number of plates often depended, not only on the shape of the helmet's dome, but on how many metal "flaps" (movable parts that were tied during battle, and swung free at other times, alternately giving protection and allowing access to the neck, ears, cheeks, nose, etc.) were incorporated into the particular design. —C.C.

20 † *khotor* See note for p. 18 on the military organization of the Broken army, above. —C.C.

20 ‡ **Torganian** Gibbon writes, "Surely this word 'Torganian' is little more than a dialectal cousin of *Thuringian,* being as the only modern forest which closely resembles 'Davon Wood' in scale, impassability, and proximity to Broken (or *Brocken*) is that which today gives the fabled region of Thuringia its name: a wilderness which, in the period under consideration, was likely far more vast than is the already enormous woodland that we encounter in the area today. 'Torganian' also suggests an interesting etymology in Middle (and likely Old High) German, some melding of the concepts of 'gateway' and 'pass' or 'passageway': geographic features that would have been much prized, in such a landscape. The Thuringian people are thought to have been displaced by Frankish tribes in the sixth century, but whether they or anyone else ever inhabited the deepest Thuringian Forest is unclear. We do know that, at the height of Broken's power, the dislocation of the Thuringians by the Franks had occurred south of the Erz Mountains ('the Tombs'), from whence the 'Torganian raiders' seem to have originated. Thus, even if the raiders herein described as attacking Broken by way of passes through the Tombs were Franks, it is logical and perhaps even probable that so isolated a society as Broken's would have been unaware of the shift in populations, and would have assumed that the new invaders were simply the latest generation of their ancient enemy. Whatever the case, we can only marvel at how stalwart this Arnem must indeed have been, if he could rally his men to fend off such renownedly ruthless and capable warriors as the Thuringians and the Franks for an entire winter amid high mountain snows!"

20 †† **Herwald Korsar** A particularly interesting name, *korsar* still being a German word for "corsair" or "pirate," but *Herwald* being an archaic name, its meaning apparently lost to time along with its use. Following the common system for determining the origin of such appellations, especially in the early and high Middle Ages, we are forced to conclude that Herwald Korsar came from a family of river- or seafaring adventurers—but whether they acted on behalf of the kingdom of Broken, or were among the enemies who agreed to join the kingdom at the time of its unification under Oxmontrot, is a question that must remain, for the moment, unanswered. —C.C.

21 † **Korsar's dead wife, Amalberta** Gibbon writes, "The appearance of the name *Amalberta* is significant in helping us determine the various influences of surrounding societies on that of Broken. *Amal,* which appears with respectable frequency in early Germanic writings, is believed by some scholars to connote

a representative of the eastern [Ostro-] Gothic royal family known as the *Amelungen;* whereas *berta,* of course, is simply another variation on the group of modern names centered on *Bertha* that imply 'radiance,' or 'golden.' Together, these components raise the rather interesting possibility that this wife of the supreme commander of the army of Broken—a woman who is acknowledged to be 'foreign-born'—may in fact have been a Gothic princess of some importance."

21 ‡ **"some dog-bitten lunatic"** This last word, when used by the soldiers and citizens of Broken, naturally has an especially pejorative connotation, its root almost certainly having been, in the Broken dialect as in English, *luna,* or "moon," both based on the Latin *lunaticus,* or "moonstruck," reflecting the ancient notion—which Kafrans would have highlighted, given the Bane tribe's (as well as their own ancient) worship of that heavenly body—that the moon's powers included the ability to cause mental illness. —C.C.

23 † **Home to the God-King** Gibbon writes, "One cannot help but pay special attention to this idea of the 'God-Kings' of Broken, particularly given the location of the kingdom and the historical era during which it achieved its zenith of power: Germanic tribes of the Barbarian Age were well known for electing their leaders, whether they called them 'kings' or 'barons.' Such leaders, obviously, were not yet what we know as 'divine right' kings, nor was their power hereditary. Once again, then, the people of Broken anticipated European institutions and styles of rank by generations, if not centuries—no small accomplishment!"

23 ‡ **Oxmontrot** Of the many interesting silences that punctuate Gibbon's comments on the Manuscript, none is more eloquent than his apparent refusal or inability to even attempt to determine the origin of this name. The most obvious and literal explanation, if we make allowances for the influence of Gothic and Old High German on the Broken dialect—which, as we have already seen and will see many more times, often reverted to what Gibbon called "phonetic approximations"—is that *Oxmontrot* meant simply "man as strong as three oxen," or perhaps "man as fast as three oxen," although this last seems less likely, as oxen have never been renowned for their speed, but rather for their plodding pace and power. But if we allow other possible meanings of the name's components to enter the question, we find that the first two syllables in *Oxmontrot* may originate with either the Gothic *Audawakrs* and its German counterpart, *Odovocar,* both of which mean "wealthy and vigilant"; or with the Old German equivalent of Old English's *Oswald,* "the rule of God"; or, finally, with *Oskar,* the still-used German equivalent of *Oscar,* translated either as "deer lover" or "godly spear." The determining factor would seem to be what meaning we ascribe to the third syllable. It may be descriptive, based in early German phrasings and spellings of *rostrot,* or "russet, auburn." One immediately thinks of the crusader and Holy Roman Emperor Friedrich I, also called Friedrich Barbarossa, or "Redbeard," although the likelihood of any inspirational connection vanishes when we consider that Friedrich did not rule until the twelfth century; still, Adolf Hitler thought enough of Friedrich's zealous attempts to rid the world of the "racially inferior" Muslims to code-name his invasion of Russia "Operation Barbarossa"—and when one considers Oxmontrot's

policies in Broken, one cannot help but wonder if Friedrich's name was not meant to recall, in some way, the founding king of Broken, and whether there is, therefore, a link between all three names. Or, the final syllable may relate to the more literal *trott,* a jogging pace. Lastly, *trot* may simply reach back to the early development of not only German, but to the Germanic languages of Saxon and Old English, as well, and translate as the number and quantity "three." Why this should be significant, however, is obscure: much like the ruler himself. —C.C.

23 †† *Lumun-jan* Gibbon writes, "We can be in no doubt that the 'vast empire' to which the narrator refers was Rome, despite the fact that the name *Lumun-jan* does not seem to appear in most Germanic dialects." Gibbon could not have known, of course, that he was looking in the wrong place; if we turn to the Gothic vocabulary, we find that *lumun* is a root common to various terms for "light," or in this case "lightning," while *jan* is a suffix incorporated into many words which imply "protection"—especially "shield." The tribes who eventually made up the kingdom of Broken before (perhaps long before) the fifth century included Goths as well as smaller groups, and all must have had some contact with Roman military detachments before Broken's establishment: despite Caesar's vehement warning that Rome should never try to conquer the region north of the Danube and east of the Rhine, some ambitious emperors and generals did dispatch scouting and punitive parties into those areas, usually with mixed or disastrous results. At least some of the tribes of those areas evidently came to associate Rome itself with one of the most effective and time-tested Roman instruments of war, the *scutum,* or large rectangular infantry shield, which was usually embossed with some representation of lightning bolts. Hence *Lumun-jan,* apparently a Gothic-based Broken term for "lightning-shield," and *Lumun-jani,* or "people of the lightning shield." Thus deriving a name for a people from a weapon that they commonly use is not unique in world history, or even in the history of the areas making up and surrounding Broken: perhaps the most famous example is the Saxons, who are believed to have been named after a comparatively small, if still fearsome, weapon, their characteristic *seax,* or single-edged combat knife. —C.C.

23 § **had been labeled "Mad"** It should not strike us as strange that the people of such a kingdom would refer to their founding monarch as "mad," nor is the case by any means unique, in history or in legend—and it was certainly not inspired, as we will see some of the kingdom's officials try to state, by his apparently heretical religion alone. "Madness" was often equated with vision or genius of any kind, particularly in less intellectually developed societies, which Broken evidently was when Oxmontrot began his reign; and the fact that the term would later be used, at least by many, in a pejorative way does not change this fact. Nor does the frequent use of the phrase "Mad King" in countless popular works of legend, fiction, and history from later periods: whether the very real, as in the case of Mad King Ludwig of Bavaria, or in fiction, as in Edgar Rice Burroughs's *The Mad King.* Indeed, there were apparently many in Broken, Sentek Arnem among them, who looked back on this supposedly "mad" king with

great admiration—something they would certainly not have done, had they considered him simply insane. —C.C.

24 † **Thedric** This is another distinctly Gothic name, suggesting that Oxmontrot married a woman of those tribes. —C.C.

25 † **the remarkable Isadora** Isadora is one of those rare Gothic names to have survived intact into the modern age. It is also a useful tool for helping us understand why the influence on Arnem's wife of certain persons considered "exotic" would have been so frowned upon in Broken: like Amalberta Korsar, Isadora Arnem appears to have come from good Gothic stock, although in her case, the blood had definitely thinned, and the family had fallen on hard times, even before the deaths of her parents. But the notion that more northerly influences would have been viewed, in Broken, with the kind of suspicion usually reserved for persons from sunnier, more southeasterly lands is a noteworthy variation on the very old story of European distrust, prejudice, and arrogance. —C.C.

26 † **Reyne Niksar** Reyne appears to be either an archaic or a Broken dialectal spelling for *Reini,* the shortened version of *Reinhold,* or "counselor [to the ruler]." *Niksar,* however, is more obscure: it seems, at first, a variation on *Nikolas,* and therefore yet another obvious confirmation that the influence of classical antiquity on the society of Broken was pronounced, *Nikolas* being a Germanization of the Greek *Nicholas,* or "victory of the people." But there may be an alternate meaning, as *sar* may have been the Broken dialectal version of *saller,* which means, literally, "one who dwells by a sallow," sallow being a type of small willow native to Germany. —C.C.

26 ‡ *khotor* and *fausten* See note for p. 18, for Broken's military organization; in brief, here, *fausten* were, perhaps obviously, detachments of some fifty men, ten of which made up a *khotor.* —C.C.

29 † **"At attention"** Although this phrase did not come into common use, among armies, until the fourteenth century, there were and are generally analogous phrases contained in nearly every language, ancient and modern, all of which are descendants, not surprisingly, of the Roman command, which Oxmontrot would have known and respected; but, because the Broken dialect remains lost to time, the Broken Codex having disappeared with the translator, we will likely never know what the specific term was. —C.C.

30 † **the Merchants' Council** The close identification of the patron god of Broken, Kafra, with the city's merchant class and leaders reinforces Gibbon's earlier point about the way in which the kingdom's rulers and citizens gave a "decidedly Germanic treatment" to what was originally, in all likelihood, a mere cult of hedonism and materialism, turning it into "a pragmatic and highly organized system of theocracy"—a theocracy whose most visible and powerful underpinning was a determined merchant oligarchy, rather than the kind of warrior-based aristocracy that could be found in most barbarian states and tribes of the time. —C.C.

31 † **"let alone a sacred bull"** Gibbon writes, "The close association of lunar worship with male cattle—or, indeed, horned animals of almost any kind—was common to societies as ancient as early Mesopotamia, and likely existed in the vicinity of Broken long before the city came into being. Animal horns were

identified with the 'horns' of the crescent moon, and from this comes the mystical association with virility and sensuality that was, evidently, a part of Old Broken's lunar worship, and which survived among the Bane long past the arrival of Kafra. Indeed, in many parts of the Far East even today, high prices are paid for the horns of exotic animals, which are ground to powder and form the ingredients of traditional virility tonics; only one of the many paradoxes afflicting such Oriental peoples as the Chinese, who are capable at once of great works, great learning, and yet absurd, even vicious and exterminating superstitions." It remains only to be said that this traffic in the horns and other parts of endangered animal species, illegally, brutally, and immorally harvested, has only grown with time; and that various peoples of the world—but especially, as Gibbon states, those of the Orient—will pay unheard-of amounts of money for such "virility tonics," the efficacy of which has been found to be absurd again and again by modern scientists. —C.C.

34 † **"Blast it"** Etymologically speaking, the persistent use of various oaths based on the word "blast" is interesting—and again, adds plausibility to the Manuscript— as it is one of the few words to originate in Old High German that has survived intact, but into *English* (by way of Old English), rather than into modern German: thus it becomes, in a sense, one of the "ghost words" of a dead language. This may seem implausible, if one assumes that the expression is somehow associated, as it usually is today, with explosives; but in fact, "blast" is another example of a phrase that might seem an anachronism, on first look, but which dates back to the early Middle Ages, where "blasts" of wind or man-made air (as in horn-blowing) occurred long before Europeans had divined the secret of how to blow each other up with gunpowder. —C.C.

35 † **"your accursed city was built"** Gibbon writes, "We ought not think that the Bane are speaking, here, in any but literal terms. As our great British explorers— most recently the late and much lamented Captain James Cook—have discovered, the exile of tribal members who have proved unable to contribute to the advancement of a given society, onto some neighboring island, or into some wilderness or other in a remote location, is a practice found the world over—as are societies formed by those same exiles. The fact that, in this case, the exiles appear to have taken on a distinctive physical feature—reduced height—ought not surprise us, either: we have only to look to advances in, say, the breeding of livestock within England itself to understand the physical ramifications, positive as well as negative, of the careful selection of mating partners. If the citizens of Broken deliberately bred their progeny to grow tall, strong, and handsome, it only stands to reason that those exiled from the city would produce a significantly smaller—and less attractive—race." Thus did one of the great historians of his own or any era instinctively anticipate a major scientific principle. —C.C.

40 † **"our unfortunate new recruit"** Gibbon's claims about the cultural mimicry of the people of Broken continue to be borne out in small ways: use of the word "recruit," rather than simply "warrior" (or some one of the many similar terms used by barbarian tribes in Europe at the time), further calls to mind a society in which military service had been highly systematized and regimented along

Roman, rather than early feudal, lines—a theory confirmed by the fact that such service was not, evidently, compulsory, even for the lower classes. —C.C.

40 ‡ *"Hak"* It is impossible, of course, to determine if the original translator of the Manuscript has left this exclamation intact, or if he has approximated some similar sound from the original dialect of Broken; but its close resemblance to the still-common German *Ach* is noteworthy. —C.C.

40 †† **built for the healthy** If the policy of "culling" weak members of those tribes that eventually made up the kingdom of Broken seems to contemporary sensibilities so drastic as to be mythical, we should remember that, even in Gibbon's time (as he makes clear in an earlier note) there was awareness of societies great and small that had employed—that still employed—similar policies; although he fails to mention how often his own Britain did the same, to rid itself of those citizens who lacked financial sense or scruples—debtors and thieves—as well as other petty criminals, all of whom were sent to America, Australia, and other distant colonies.

Nor should we be smug about Gibbon's deliberate blindness on this score: such practices have no more vanished from the twenty-first century world than they had from the eighteenth. Various tribes that are "indigenous" (a word that almost daily loses meaning, in a world increasingly marked by transient populations) to South America and Africa allow parents to have only the number of children that the tribe generally can support, killing off surplus numbers. The ancient Roman practice of weeding out physically deformed children by exposing them at birth to the tender mercies of mountainside wildernesses, meanwhile, is currently echoed both in the Chinese practice of selling or simply drowning unwanted female children—a "traditional custom" that occurs with regrettable frequency—as well as in the license that so many Muslim societies give to individual men and entire families to disfigure, murder, and anathematize women who are perceived as having disgraced themselves and their families, often by "allowing" themselves to be raped. —C.C.

40 § **the Celestial Way** The appearance of the word "celestial" in the name of Broken's main thoroughfare—assuming, again, that it is a literal translation, and not a whimsical choice of the translator—underlines the diversity of cultural influences on the city's society as far back as its founding, "celestial" being a word that is far more commonly found in descriptions of Eastern palaces and potentates than in those of Western. —C.C.

43 † **"The *Denep-stahla*"** Gibbon writes, "These more serious rituals of mutilation contain one common element: the use of *stahla* after the hyphen, which may indicate that they are derived from the sacred instruments used to inflict the punishments, *stahl* being a modern German word for 'steel,' particularly as pertaining to 'blades.' The origins of the first parts of the phrases, on the other hand, are matters for sheer speculation: They seem to have been adaptations of terms peculiar to the original cult of Kafra, and to have therefore been brought into Broken with that god and that faith. We do not know where, precisely, this religion originated, as I have said; but the physical manifestations of these strange words are made fully, indeed hideously, clear by the narrator's descriptions of the rituals, and suggest an Eastern, even an Oriental, morality." [*Note:*

Gibbon is being, as was sometimes his tendency, openly prejudicial, here—it was, after all, the *Western* Romans who perpetuated such ancient and "progressive" punishments as crucifixion and being mauled to death in arenas by wild animals. —C.C.]

45 † **narrowed to sharp points** Here we find more evidence to support the contention that Broken's first king, Oxmontrot, served as a foreign auxiliary in the Roman army: the style of military fortification and housing in Broken's Fourth District is almost identical to those outposts and forts that Roman armies of occupation constructed, particularly in central and northern Europe, where tall, stout pine and fir logs were to be had in abundance. —C.C.

47 † **the emblem of his rank and office** Again, the emulation of the Roman military by the soldiers of Broken is striking, even down to such small details as the baton of rank and authority that was carried by senior Roman officers as well as the leaders of several other outstanding armies, most if not all of them imperial. In more modern times, it was bestowed on German field marshals during the Nazi era: indeed, as Gibbon occasionally notes, it almost seems that the society of Broken may have been something of a "missing link"—culturally, governmentally, and militarily—between Rome and those states of the modern West (especially but not solely Germany) that have had imperial pretensions and ambitions. —C.C.

47 ‡ **beyond the Meloderna** If we accept Gibbon's contention that "Meloderna" was the name used in Broken for the modern Saale River, then the "river valley beyond the Meloderna" where this battle, presumably against the Huns, took place may have been the Mulde, although it seems far more likely that it was the Elbe. The latter represents the more significant barrier, in military terms (it was along the Elbe, of course, that American and Russian forces met to complete their fatal division of Germany during the Second World War), and is only some seventy-five to a hundred miles from the mountain *Brocken*—certainly within just a few days' riding and even marching range of an army as organized and powerful as was Broken's. —C.C.

49 † **detachment** Here is an example of the translator, while not necessarily taking a greater liberty, at least using a much more modern word (which had come into use among military forces only at the end of the seventeenth century) to stand in for whatever the original Broken phrase was. The most common modern German word for a military detachment, *verband* (pl. *verbände*) might suggest to some that the translator would have done better service had he translated whatever the Broken dialectal word was into English as "band"; but that is a far more vague term, militarily, than "detachment"; and, as we have already noted, we cannot rely on modern German, when speculating on the Broken dialect, to be anything save a partial descendant of what remains a lost language. —C.C.

51 † *Kastelgerde* This is the plural (as we shall soon see) of *Kastelgerd*, a word that Gibbon chooses to ignore, almost certainly because, again, experts of his day did not have the tools to interpret it; nor, indeed, can we say with any certainty that experts of our own time do. But, because of the great advances made during the last century in understanding both Old High German and Gothic, we

can at least make a much more educated guess than could Gibbon: *Kastel* (a noun here, using the upper case, as most German nouns did then, and all do, today) is almost certainly a slight variation on the common German *Kastell,* a secondary and less frequently used term for "castle" (the more common being *Schloss*), while *gerd* is almost certainly a Broken variation on the Gothic *gards,* incorporating the vowel shift borrowed from Old High German, meaning "houses" as in important clan households. The purpose of the entire term is evidently to convey that these structures are "castles" as in palaces and family seats, not necessarily fortresses, although they seem to have had more of that utilitarian purpose early in the kingdom's history. —C.C.

53 † **service as a *skutaar*** Gibbon writes, "The appearance of the word *skutaar* is another example of the bridge that Broken's society formed between imperial Rome and Europe in the Barbarian Age: the word itself is doubtless derived from the Latin *scutarius,* or 'shield-bearer,' which is also the source of our own words 'esquire' and 'squire,' as well as several similar terms we find in other European tongues—the French *esquier,* for example."

57 † **the panther enters** The legendary "European panther" is far more than a myth. In fact, there are two likely candidates for the "panthers" referred to in the Manuscript, both of which originated in the Pleistocene era and were, until recently, thought to have become extinct anywhere from eight thousand to two thousand years ago. The first example, commonly known as the "European jaguar," is of interest because of its known preference for forests (although this preference has been challenged by recent research) and its solitary habits— as well as the fact that fossil evidence indicates that the last of its kind lived in Italy and Germany as little as two thousand years ago, and possibly far more recently. In fact, there have been unproved but insistent claims of sightings of the European jaguar up to, and even in, the present era. The second candidate, the "European (or Eurasian) cave lion," is the great cat depicted in Europe's famous Ice Age cave paintings, as well as ivory carvings and clay sculptures. Clearly, it played a vital role in the religions of those peoples, and one can easily understand why: It originated earlier than the European jaguar, and was a more massive animal. Males could reach a length of twelve feet and a weight of six to seven hundred pounds (females were about two thirds the size of males). They had the physical appearance to match the description of "Davon panthers" in the Manuscript: golden fur, short leonine manes, and tiger banding of varying hues. They could easily bring down the largest hoofed animals, including and especially horses, and therefore represented a significant problem for cavalry operating within Europe's most ancient and thickest virgin forests, of which the Thuringian certainly was one, and in parts remains so.

Perhaps the most intriguing clue regarding both of these animals is their classification: like modern lions and tigers, and unlike the smaller wild cats that existed in Europe, they belong to the *Panthera* genus (the European jaguar is the *Panthera gombaszoegensis,* the cave lion the *Panthera leo spelaea*), making the Manuscript's consistent reference to them as "panthers" not at all far-fetched. —C.C.

57 ‡ **the neck and shoulders** Two additional facts about the narrator's description of

the "panther" are significant: he has apparently never seen a true "mane," the male European cave lion having possessed only a short, wispy approximation of the version found on their African cousins (less, even, than the infamous cave lions of Tsavo, Kenya), and he consistently refers to the animal as "he" rather than "it." This and other clues reveal that, if he was not a Moon worshipper himself, the narrator is for some reason very familiar with the customs of that faith, which included, as we have heard Keera say, deep reverence for the souls of animals, especially the Davon panthers. —C.C.

58 † **red velvet** Here is an indication of how advanced Broken's textile production, or its trade with other kingdoms to its south in Europe, or both, must have become: velvet had only just reached that continent from the Islamic empire at the time that the Broken Manuscript was most likely written (the late eighth to early ninth centuries) and was considered an enormously rare and valuable fabric, worn only by the elites of the countries it made its way into. —C.C.

66 † **the cavernous Temple** Gibbon writes, "This description of the High Temple of Broken is revealing, and further confirms the notion that the city and state were something of a stewpot of cultural and aesthetic influences: while termed a 'temple,' the building has the evident design and attributes of a European— and Christian—church or cathedral. We know that, in the Eastern Roman Empire during this same period, rulers beginning with Constantine were devising ways to adapt the Christian faith to the pagan rituals of the various populations contained within the empire's borders, and vice versa. Is it possible that the royal family of Broken was involved in some similar enterprise, or, even more intriguingly, in a precisely opposite undertaking, that is, in adapting Christian architecture and rites to their own faith of Kafra? Certainly, we cannot exclude the possibility—particularly as we know (and I myself have seen) that the 'Broken Codex' used by the Manuscript's translator consisted of portions of the Bible written in the Broken dialect. It has been heretofore assumed that this was for missionary Christian purposes; but what if the intention was to alter the biblical text, and make it serve the purposes of the priests and priestesses of Broken?"

67 † **a distant region of Davon Wood by the Bane** Gibbon writes, "The narrator's consistent references to the quarrying and mining activities of the Bane will not surprise anyone acquainted with the Harz mountain range, as they are rich not only in fine quality stone, but in silver, iron, lead, copper, and zinc; and although the exploitation of these deposits is generally thought to have begun on a systematic scale only in the tenth century, it is by no means overly imaginative to think that a people living in the mountain and forest wildernesses around *Brocken* during an earlier age should have developed the means to create a primitive series of mines and quarries, all evidence of which would have been overtaken by Nature in the centuries following Broken's downfall." What Gibbon could *not* have known was that, during the early Industrial Revolution (within, ironically, mere decades of the great scholar's death), the mines of the Harz Mountains would rapidly be worked to complete exhaustion. —C.C.

68 † **glittering, durable mortar** This was likely either stucco or concrete—both of which were evidently used by Broken builders—mixed with reflective flecks of

the many kinds of granite and quartz that were mined from both the Harz and the Tombs (that is, the Harz and the Erz mountains) by the Bane. —C.C.

69 † **every society that surrounds Broken** As Gibbon writes, "The importance of this seemingly obscure detail of Broken craftsmanship cannot be overstated: the ability to maintain the production of glass windows throughout much of the Barbarian Age, when its secrets were thought to have been lost to all of Europe, was aesthetically, religiously, and governmentally significant." Modern archaeologists and industrial historians agree that, while many barbarian tribes and nations maintained the skill of manufacturing glass beads and receptacles of various kinds, their ability to fabricate far more complicated window glass, whether clear, opaque, or colored, largely disappeared from Europe in the Dark Ages, confirming the enormous role that the ability to produce such glass played in how the society of Broken "saw" both itself and the world around it. Cf., for instance, Macfarlane and Martin, *Glass: A World History.* —C.C.

70 † **known across the Seksent Straits as "ermine"** "For the first time," says Gibbon, "we are given the impression that the narrator's journey to our own region may have brought him into contact with persons more majestic than mere scholarly monks."

71 † **Grand Layzin** Gibbon writes, "Again, we are forced to suspect a mere phonetic approximation in this word *Layzin;* for the sound is identical to the German *lesen,* 'to read,' but seems almost certainly to imply, in this more ancient form, a gerundial noun, 'reader,' for this appears to have been the Grand Layzin's responsibility, as well as the source of his power: to read and give practical meaning to the thoughts and pronouncements of the God-King, as well as, presumably, to those of Broken's god, Kafra. This ability—to translate divine intent into pragmatic action—was the source of authority for many similar pagan holy men (or what German scholars have taken to calling *schamanes* [shamans]), although few seem to have had the executive authority of Broken's Layzin."

72 † **brocade mantle** Here we get an idea of just how many intrepid foreign traders and raiders ventured to Broken's ports and borders to sell their goods, and vice versa: brocade originally appeared in Persia during the Sassanid Dynasty (ca. A.D. 225–650), and was evidently quite common in Broken by the time that the Manuscript was written (presumably the eighth century). It is possible that the techniques involved in producing brocade had been mastered by Broken textile craftsmen by this point, or that the city's merchants were still bringing it up from the river Meloderna. Whatever the case, the fact that it is viewed by the narrator as an item worthy of remark only in reference to an important state figure is important. —C.C.

77 † **his raiding sword** The names given to weapons, among both the soldiers of Broken and the Bane, seem to have been determined either by the names of the peoples they borrowed their design from, or, more simply, by the names and/ or activities by which those foreign peoples were themselves known. Ergo, "short-sword" refers to the Roman *gladius,* a weapon that the Romans adapted from a Spanish blade, but which was often referred to among even Romans by the more descriptive and informal term—simply "short sword"—that the sol-

diers of Broken used. "Raiding sword," meanwhile, seems to link the weapon to a people—in this case, to the early sea- and river-faring raiders that the modern world would come to know as Norsemen and Vikings. The straight blade of the "raiding sword," along with its length (longer than the late-imperial Roman *spatha*, a weapon that was a compromise between traditional Roman and barbarian weapons), matches the simple yet devastatingly effective design that the Scandinavian tribes and nations employed for nearly the whole of their history. —C.C.

78 † *"Visimar"* Another solidly Gothic name, although the man's assumed name, as we shall see, was not, suggesting that at some time, perhaps in the distant past, the Gothic- and Old High German–speaking peoples who inhabited the area that would become the kingdom of Broken lived in some unidentified (and now unidentifiable) state of animosity. —C.C.

80 † *profilic* and *freilic* Gibbon writes, "These words offer us some insight into the development of the Broken dialect in its later period. As at other points in the Manuscript, we find, here, words that are more Germanic than Gothic, and more like modern German than Old High or Middle High German; yet the suffix 'ic' may well be a holdover from Gothic, if we accept that the two terms refer, respectively, to flanking wings of cavalry (*profilic*) and the free-roaming (*freilic*). The former were units literally on the flanks, or 'profiles,' of the army, the latter those 'free' to reinforce weaknesses in lines of battle, as well as exploit openings in the enemy's lines. Why the translator should not have been able to divine as much, I cannot say, save that his knowledge of things military seems to have suffered from severe limitations, as is often the case with deeply cultured men." This analysis—and the questions regarding the translator's apparent limitations—have endured, and time has affirmed Gibbon's interpretation of the words; although it ought to be said that Gibbon's notes reveal that he was another "deeply cultured" man who suffered (periodically, at least) from intellectual weaknesses concerning "things military"—especially as far as the military histories and cultures of the barbarian tribes in comparison to the Romans went. —C.C.

81 † **Moon worshipper symbols** We can reasonably assume that these symbols were more sophisticated variations on those found on the "Sky Disc of Nebra" (see note for p. 82, below), probably incorporating runic interpretations, and making up what little written language certain members of the Bane tribe employed. —C.C.

81 ‡ **the *Ayerzess-werten*** Gibbon wrote of this term, "Both the names assigned by the Bane to particularly dangerous waterfalls in the Cat's Paw River—*Hafften* Falls and the *Ayerzess-werten*—are as yet, for reasons which I have explained elsewhere, undecipherable to scholars of this region and period: an irritating fact, as they seem to have imparted some definite sense of Bane irony." The statement is almost certainly an honest expression of true ignorance, since experts only began to gain anything like a detailed knowledge of Gothic toward the very end of Gibbon's life, while any systematic understanding of Old High German was out of the question, given how few documents were available to serve the purpose that the Broken Codex served for that kingdom's dialect. The

discoveries of modern scholars, however, in addition to consultation with them, reveal first that the word *Hafften* is likely an early forerunner of the modern German verb *anhaften,* "to cling to"—which could be taken simply as a literal indication of what travelers were forced to do when they met with mishap while trying to cross the first of the named waterfalls. But examination of the second name, *Ayerzess-werten,* shows that Gibbon's suspicions about Bane irony were well founded: both terms were, almost certainly, intended (in accordance with the narrator's description) as a sort of black humor. *Ayerzess-werten* derives from a known Gothic phrase, *airzeis-wairthan,* which translates as the fairly pedestrian term "fall into error." The double entendre created by the Bane when they applied the phrase to a sudden and steep gorge leading down to a deadly series of rocks and waterfalls is evident, and further demonstrates that the Bane were very much more than a tribe of uneducated and deformed criminal exiles. As for the change in spelling, it can be attributed to the influence of Old High German and the now familiar "vowel shift." —C.C.

82 † **gneiss formations** Gneiss is igneous rock of a quality inferior to granite, as well as a name for the second most common type of stone found in the Harz Mountains, granite itself being predominant. The name *gneiss* seems to date back to the first Saxon settlers; and while most of these tribes had, by the sixth century, moved out of the area that would soon become the kingdom of Broken, some members stayed behind, perhaps explaining why *seksent* was the Broken word for "peasant" (as earlier noted). —C.C.

82 ‡ **the position of the Moon and stars** It may seem strange that, up to this point in the story, the Bane appear to have a better mastery of time and navigation as measured and charted by the heavens than do the citizens of Broken—but we must remember that the earliest known European instrument used to determine the timing of the solstices specifically, and to measure the movements of celestial bodies generally, was the "Sky Disc of Nebra," created no less than 3,600 years ago—in these same Harz Mountains. Indeed, one of the points of triangulation used in the famous Sky Disc was the mountain of *Brocken* itself. It would appear that there was a long-established tradition of such primitive scientific study among the people of the area; and it likely survived more intact among those tribes that maintained traditional belief systems (i.e., the Bane) than among those that pretended and aspired to greater scholarship (the subjects of Broken). See the explanation of Buhmann, Pietsch, Lepcsik, and Jede, "Interpreting the Bronze Age Sky Disc of Nebra using 3D GIS." —C.C.

83 † and *passim* **gutting blade** Again, one cannot help but wonder, especially given the aforementioned general use of the *seax* among the Saxons, who took their name from the weapon, if these knives that the narrator persistently refers to as "gutting blades" did not in fact have a far broader and greater purpose, by design or by accident, than the name might suggest: if they were not, that is, like the *seax,* as close to a sword as a utilitarian knife. The Bane evidently relied on gutting blades so greatly in situations involving close combat that one is led to the strong suspicion that the "gutting" in question must have included not only dead animals, but living humans, too, and perhaps even more so—indeed, to so great an extent that the narrator does not even consider it worthy of expla-

nation. A wound to the gut of a man, then as now, was the next best thing to an actual kill, given that serious abdominal wounds are paralyzingly painful and usually fatal; and the death, being slow and agonizing, renders the unfortunate victim unfit for continued action. —C.C.

85 † **The hysterical woman** Gibbon writes, "The phrase employed here, in the original Broken dialectal version of the Manuscript, apparently translated, literally, to 'moonsick,' which the translator of the work immediately associated with 'hysteria.' The two concepts do, indeed, have much in common, 'hysteria' being a feminine illness which arises out of the womb, and is generally supposed to be governed by the lunar cycle: hence, 'moonsickness' becomes 'hysteria.'" We should not fault the great scholar for what may appear to us a ludicrous interpretation: in 1790, many if not most violent mental disorders in women were still considered forms of hysteria, which was indeed thought to arise from the womb (the ancient Greeks, of course, first came up with the idea, *hystero-* being the Greek root for "utero" and "uterine"), and to be governed, therefore, by the phases of the moon. What *does* seem odd is Gibbon's failure to connect "moonsickness" to "lunacy," both being illnesses attributed, obviously, to the moon (see note for p. 21). —C.C.

87 † **to form a *skehsel*** Gibbon writes, "Again, there remain, alas, several words and phrases, the precise meanings of which the purveyor of the Manuscript could not, or would not, determine; and, even more irritatingly, he persistently refused to say *why* he could not. I have left these words and phrases in quotations [changed to italics here], and have tried to extrapolate meanings as best I can from context." *Skehsel* was apparently not one of the words he could so extrapolate, and, as in the case of the names of the waterfalls, it appears in its original form because the scholarship of Gibbon's time simply had not caught up to the Broken Manuscript. We can now speculate with reasonable certainty, however, that the word is some sort of an Old High German variation on the Gothic *skohsl*, the term for an "evil spirit" of neutral gender. Why the Bane should have feared such spirits above others (and they mention several) is unknown, but we can also speculate, based on the very high priority the Bane placed on the natural ordering of the world, their reputation as a highly sexed people among the citizens of Broken, as well as the frequency with which "gelding" is mentioned as among the worst of fates, that it is precisely the gender neutrality of the demon that so disturbed them. The Bane evidently believed, as did many Barbarian Age peoples, that humans could, as a course of last resort, mate with most spirits and other mythical creatures, as a means of appeasing them; the *skehsel* do not seem to have offered that option, and, as has always been (and still is) the case in traditional societies that are followers of certain pagan religions, both polytheistic and monotheistic, the failure to produce offspring, any kind of offspring, implied personal annihilation. This may well have been true for the Bane, as well. —C.C.

89 † **"bested by Welferek"** Gibbon writes, "This man *Welferek* must, indeed, have held a position of importance among the Outrager 'knights,' for his name cannot but be a Broken-Germanic variation of the name we encounter in Old English as Wulfric, the 'lord (or king) of wolves.' Given the activities of the

Outragers, such a title implies high honor and authority, as well as loyalty to the Priestess of the Moon strong enough to earn him the right to carry out the most sacred punishments—as he does in this case." Since Gibbon's time, the word "wolf" (or "wolves"), used in this connotation, has been identified as having the secondary, metaphorical meaning of "hunter(s)"; and it is almost certainly true that the knight *Welferek* was the Priestess of the Moon's chief "hunter," as in executioner—or even assassin. —C.C.

97 † **"can only be the *Halap-stahla*"** Gibbon writes, "Again, the peculiar formulation of the names of the rites of punishment and execution in Broken frustrate almost every attempt we can make to determine their origins. Whether the *Halap* in *Halap-stahla* has any basis in some early Germanic variation of *halbe,* itself a variation, in certain German dialects, of *halb,* or 'half,' or if it is derived from the Gothic *halba,* which shares the same meaning, or from some other term entirely undiscovered, we cannot answer with certainty—although it seems at least possible, given the 'halving' nature of the mutilation."

99 † **warriors will meet once more** Gibbon writes, "In stating that many if not most of the tribes of the region surrounding Broken shared the faith that fallen warriors went on, in the afterlife, to a great hall where perpetual carousing and other indulgences were on offer, Arnem (and the tale's narrator) spoke more truly—and presciently—than they likely knew, for it was not merely, or even especially, in Germany that this belief had taken root, by this time, and would become elaborated in centuries to come: Most schoolboys of our day are familiar with *Valhalla,* the Norse version of this myth; but, in truth, the idea pervaded many northern European 'barbarian' faiths, and not a few Eastern tribes, as well. On the other hand, there were also warrior cultures of the time that had little or no faith in an afterlife (for one example, consult the *Beowulf* Manuscript acquired several decades ago from Sir Robert Cotton during the founding of the British Museum), and which therefore placed all the more emphasis on a man's achievements in this life, thinking that such was the only way to keep one's name and spirit alive after death."

103 † **the feet of which** During this period, it was common for European working classes to wear cloth pants that extended all the way down to encase even the toes, much like modern-day children's pajamas with "feet," to which these older garments have often been compared. Such covering obviated the need for "foot stockings," or socks, but were often more vulnerable to wear and tear. —C.C.

104 † **"the Lord God of the *Lumun-jani*"** Gibbon writes, "This is the first ambiguous reference to Christianity in the text. By the seventh or eighth century, nearly all the barbarian tribes, with the exceptions of a few small clans in discrete domains [including, evidently, Broken], had adopted what was by then the long-established state religion of Rome; and, as at least a few of the Bane must have come into contact with missionaries of that faith and other representatives of Rome—probably during their trading sessions in the Broken town of Daurawah—we can reasonably conclude that both Broken's subjects and the Bane knew the general story of Jesus Christ, including the crucifixion, which is the subject of the Bane forager's allusion, here." Stated more graphically than

Gibbon was apparently willing to do, we can assume that Heldo-Bah is declaring that Welferek's being pinned to a tree with knives in a vaguely outstretched position resembles the most infamous ritual punishment inflicted on so many slaves and criminals by the Roman Empire. This underscores the point of how fluid the religious situation during the Barbarian Age was: as Gibbon says, Heldo-Bah would have been most likely to come across a crucifix in the Broken trading center of Daurawah, which the narrator has already spoken of his having visited. The fact that Gibbon let this remark go with only an explanatory comment was almost certainly a fruitless effort to keep Burke from reacting to the story in precisely the manner that he ultimately did. —C.C.

113 † **patterns of profound complexity** Again, we tend, today, to take the many uses that glass serves for granted; but if we remember that most of the tribes and kingdoms surrounding Broken had either lost the ability to create window glass, or, as in the case of nomadic tribes like the Huns, had never had any need for it, we can begin to get an idea of how little the narrator is exaggerating, here: light, in its various forms, was more than simply a source of illumination, during the period of Broken's existence, and could, when cleverly manipulated, inspire faith in one's deity and confidence in the wisdom of one's leaders. Oxmontrot would indeed have seen this process at work (in a number of ways) if he had been a mercenary in the employ of both the western and the eastern parts of the Roman Empire; and it is small wonder that he would have placed such emphasis on preserving and advancing the art of glassmaking in the kingdom that he founded. —C.C.

113 ‡ **a marble initiation font** Gibbon writes, "The use of the words 'marble initiation font' may be taken by Christians less informed than yourself [that is, than Edmund Burke] as 'proof' that the Kafran religion was nothing more than a polluted form of their own faith; and, of course, certain similarities do exist. But, they are minor; and the more important aspect of the Kafrans' use of 'fonts' and 'altars' is its reinforcement of the fact that, among the barbarian tribes of Europe during the Dark Ages, religion was in a state of near-constant turmoil and adaptation, a condition that saw Christians borrowing rites, holy days, and customs from pagans—and, more to the point (although far less popularly recognized), pagans doing the same with regard to Christianity. Thus, we can no more cite the existence of an 'initiation font' within the High Temple of Kafra as evidence of Christian influence than we can say that the original baptismal practices of early Christians were adapted from the 'blood-baptisms' of more than a few barbarian tribes, at least some of which took place in just such fonts and receptacles, which were often located in temples." Gibbon, although attempting again to be tactful, cannot entirely suppress his own passionate feelings on the subject. Still, given his personal agnosticism and Edmund Burke's repeated and public defenses of the Christian faith (even, in his *Reflections on the Revolution in France,* of *Catholic* Christianity), the above statement is an admirable if unsuccessful attempt at restraint. —C.C.

113 †† **A small, circular piece of brass** It should surprise no one to learn that the metalworkers of Broken, as well as those of the Bane, were capable of producing such alloys as brass, bronze, and steel (although the Bane were, of course, la-

boring with far less advanced equipment than was available in Broken, and therefore were unable, up to the time of these events, to achieve the kind of alloys that were available to their enemies). The mountains of the area, as has been noted several times, are rich in all the ores necessary to produce these important materials, or rather, they were, at the time: again, the originally plentiful deposits were exhausted relatively early in the Industrial Age. —C.C.

120 † "Atta Pass" Gibbon would have been unable to do more than guess at the full meaning of this name, which is perhaps why it goes unnoted by him. Now, however, we can reliably translate *atta* as one of many Gothic terms for "father," this one in the sense of "forefather"—but it may also have been intended, in the case of such an important and deadly physical location as this mountain pass, to carry a religious interpretation; and, while any reference to a masculine deity may at first make us think of Kafra, the state of religious flux that dominated Europe (even, to some extent, in and around Broken) at the time poses intriguing alternative interpretations, and suggestions of the Christian "Father" who is more familiar to us today—and whose faith was spreading throughout the Germanic tribes. —C.C.

120 ‡ "dwarfish exiles" Obviously, given the repeated explanations of the Bane's height as having not been, in the main, a result of dwarfism, references on the part of anyone in Broken—especially Lord Baster-kin—to "misshapen dwarves" must be taken as a slur. They also offer consistent reinforcement of the fact that the Bane were not *de facto* dwarves, at least in the main: had they been, "dwarf-*ish*" would hardly have been such a common insult used in reference to them. We return, then, to the notion of "miniature" human beings, as well as the more likely question of genetic adaptation. —C.C.

121 † "the Varisians . . . with their longboats" Gibbon writes, "Once again, we must consider the words *Frankesh* and *Varisian* to be, like *Torganian*, mere phonetic approximations: the first for 'Franks,' or more precisely, the 'Frankish,' tribes who, as I have said, may already have driven the *Torganians* ('Thuringians') from the region south of Broken. Varisian, meanwhile, is clearly another such approximation, this one for 'Frisian,' a northern tribe notorious for their sea and river raiding."

122 † "our enemies" It is important to understand that this discussion of torture, while it may seem anachronistic, is anything but, if one understands the history of warfare in any sort of detail. The torture of enemy combatants and noncombatants, and the question of whether any useful information gleaned by such methods outweighs the risk to the soldiers and people of the torturing side, is hardly unique to our own era: it is, in fact, at least as old as the Roman Empire, where it was debated in much the same fashion as it is today. The arguments have resurfaced regularly throughout Western history ever since; and we should therefore not be surprised to find it cropping up in these pages. Indeed, Gibbon himself is so familiar with it, apparently, that he does not even deem it worthy of mention. —C.C.

128 † the *Lenthess-steyn* Gibbon writes: "I must repeat, would that we had sufficient knowledge of the Broken dialect to comprehend the meaning of every phrase, particularly some of the most obscure yet revealing. One such is this place

where the healers among the Bane, who appear to have been skilled in the use of herbs and the extracts of forest plants, did their noble and comforting work, and also, apparently, achieved advances in the knowledge of anatomy that religious superstition prevented in more 'advanced' societies and tribes—Galen himself [the father of Roman and, many believe, Western medicine] would have envied their freedom, in this regard!" Gibbon's frustration over the lack of a precise translation perhaps prevented him from reasoning out the strange but appropriate meaning of the title of these caves. The phrase *Lenthess-steyn* can be pieced together from Gothic, Old High German, and Middle German (the usual mixture of the Broken dialect in its later phases): it seems to translate as "the Soft Stones," implying caves in which the aged, the ill, or the wounded either recovered or had their journey to the Lunar afterlife eased, or "softened." —C.C.

129 † **effective in battle** Before proceeding with any detailed discussion of the armor, helmets, and swords employed by the Bane and the army of Broken, one scholarly fact (best argued by Ewart Oakeshott in his *Dark Age Warrior*) must be reiterated, particularly regarding this region of northern Europe during the period under consideration: *there are no definitive sources on the subject of just what "Dark Age warriors" employed for armor and helmets (and precious little concerning their manufacture and use of swords), and we must therefore judge largely by what we read in individual accounts—of which the Broken Manuscript is one of the most elaborate.* Hence, we can infer, in this instance, that the presence of scale armor among the Bane is further evidence that Oxmontrot likely fought for the Roman armies of the eastern empire, as well as the western, since such "scale mail" was preferred by the formidable Byzantine (or Eastern Roman) armies. However, while the armorers of Broken appear to have been able to reproduce effective examples of this alternative to chain mail (an alternative that offered greater protection but limited range of motion), the Bane were apparently less able to do so. They likely had some quality examples (captured or stolen from Broken soldiers), but, as the narrator says, their craftsmen simply could not yet work in such detail, largely because of the quality of their iron—which, although about to improve, limited them to merely a few such suits, probably used more often for show than for combat.—C.C.

129 ‡ **the iron itself** Again, the Bane were not, at this point, able to produce steel of a high enough grade to make the manufacture of truly quality blades and helmets possible, although they would soon gain the capacity to do so. This subject will be discussed in greater detail later in the story itself, but it does not spoil that story—and, more important, it is necessary—to note here that their swords were either of low-carbon steel, or steel laminated onto simple iron cores, as was common in barbarian Europe. Their helmets, meanwhile, were based very generally on those of the Broken army, which appear to have been within the family of Germanic adaptations of Roman helmets (and known collectively, as has already been discussed, as the *Spangenhelm* design) which included roughly conical or rounded helmets onto which were riveted or welded segments to cover the nose, cheeks, and sometimes the lower neck. The hinges in such designs were almost universally leather, save in the case of the highest-

ranking soldiers, who could afford metal hinges. Without the latter two features, the Bane would have been left with something closer to the Norman
helmet, a simple one-piece, conical design with a fixed nose guard as an organic
extension, not a component: a sound enough protection, if the steel was of sufficient grade, which the Bane's was not—a condition that was, again, about to
be altered. —C.C.

131 † "Ashkatar" Here is a name that appears to have vanished completely, along
with the society that gave it birth; and the best estimates of those experts consulted is that *Ashkatar* was an approximation, in the Broken dialect, of some
altered or corrupted form of *Augustus,* the imperial name of Octavian Caesar,
the famed architect of the Roman Empire during the bridging of the B.C. and
A.D. eras. If so, this would indicate that Ashkatar's ancestors had once been
people of importance, perhaps quite close to Oxmontrot, for it would have been
the Mad King and his fellow mercenaries who would have heard the story of
Augustus during their years of campaigning for Rome. —C.C.

142 † twelve-year-old Dalin The collection goes seemingly unnoticed by Gibbon,
in all likelihood because they only offered him more frustration. Even today,
one remains obscure: *Dalin,* which may or may not be some dialectal interpretation of the Gothic term for "share," and may have been given to the boy at his
mother's urging precisely because of the child's remarkable physical (and, apparently, behavioral) resemblance to his father, even at birth. We can be more
sure, however, that the remaining names reflect either a general trend toward
modern Germanic names in the kingdom of Broken, or a conscious effort by
Sixt to emphasize his own heritage over Isadora's apparently Gothic background (the Gothic tribes were, of course, "Germanic" in the broad barbarian
and early medieval sense of the word, whereas "modern Germanic names" refers to those appellations belonging quite distinctly to the languages and dialects that would one day meld to form modern German): *Anje* is a variation of
Anna, Dagobert a fairly common medieval combination of the terms for "good"
and "gleaming" (and the name of one of the great Merovingian Frankish kings,
just before the period during which the Manuscript's tale is almost certainly
set, and possibly, therefore, borrowed by the worldly Arnem from those same
Franks), while *Gelie* is a derivative of *Angelika.* The remaining name, *Golo,*
seems to be some kind of variation on or nickname for "Gottfried." It is still in
use—as, indeed, are many of these names, in some form or another—but *Dalin*
remains a riddle without a definite solution. —C.C.

143 † two large, crow-like birds of Isadora's clasp, Gibbon writes, "Without doubt,
we are faced, here, with a representation of Odin, patriarch (or 'All-father') of
the Norse gods, who traded one of his eyes for wisdom, and was attended by
two ravens, one representing Thought, the other Memory. What is of particular interest is the fact that, while we now think of this mythology as quaint, it
was quite vibrant, during the period that Broken existed, and was such a threat
to the Kafran faith (as it was to monotheism generally) that those who worshipped the Norse gods were declared to be, not wayward primitives, but
doomed heretics, in Broken—just as they were by the early Christian church."
Once again, Gibbon reveals his fascination with other-than-Christian faiths,

although worship of the Norse gods can hardly have been considered a "cult" or "mystery" religion—whereas (ironically) the Kafran faith does indeed fit the mold of either a cult or one of what are known as the "mystery faiths". —C.C.

144 † **"Nuen"** The name of the Arnem children's nurse and, later, governess is ignored by Gibbon, scholarly works on Eastern history and culture being relatively few, in his time, and many if not most of those relying on the work of ancient historians. Presuming *Nuen* to be an ancestor of the modern *Nuan*—which, in Chinese, is intended to connote warmth and geniality—may seem a logical conclusion, save that the connection between the Huns (almost certainly the people from whom this woman emerged) and the Chinese has long since been effectively dismissed; and even the Huns' relation to the *Xiongnu* (or, in the older form, the *Hsiung-nu*), a tribe of nomads that occupied northern and northeastern Asia (an area that included much of Manchuria, Mongolia, and the Chinese province of Xinjiang) and may have given rise to some of the similarly restless peoples that sprang out of those regions, is a relationship that, while once considered likely, has recently come to be deeply questioned and in some cases dismissed. Thus the Chinese background of the name is unlikely, but we have few theories to take its place; and so we are forced, like Gibbon, to simply accept the name—although with greater, if therefore more frustrating, awareness of just why we must. —C.C.

146 † *breck* Further evidence, if any is needed, that Isadora's ancestors were indeed Goths who interbred, over time, with other, "newer" Germanic tribes: the word that we know as "brook" winds its way back through most of the related languages of the region—German, Dutch, Middle English, and Old English—until its earliest ancestor is found in the Gothic *brukjan*. The diminishment of the Gothic influence, added to the Old High German vowel shift and the few peculiarities of the Broken dialect that we can speak of with confidence, more than explain the specific form encountered here. —C.C.

148 † **Gisa** The name of Isadora's guardian and teacher, the woman who raised her following the robbery and murder of her parents, is another tantalizing clue to the pattern of religious and social evolution in both Broken and northern Germany generally: although identified as an Old High German name, *Gisa's* precise meaning has been lost. We can, however, fairly safely assume both that it was a shortened form of the Germanic *Gisela*, which connotes both "hostage" and "tribute," and that it was therefore probably not her original name. Thus, given her activities, was this woman of Nordic extraction perhaps sold into servitude in Broken after being taken as a slave by some unknown armed force or band? And, if she was indeed a "hostage," was she a person of some importance in her northern homeland? Many such hostages during this era (as today, in parts of the developing world) were never redeemed—a fact that would explain both her bitterness and her indoctrination of Isadora into what was, in Broken, considered a heretical cult, but which was already an established religion in the region, and perhaps a major one; certainly, it was one that would undergo an enormous revival when it was reasserted by the Nordic tribes, many of which blended it with various interpretations and narrative chapters of Christianity. —C.C.

158 † **his saddle's iron stirrups** A detail that goes unnoticed by Gibbon reveals itself, in the modern era of military history (and military technological history, especially), as being of enormous importance: Broken's mounted troops were using metal stirrups. The ancient Romans had no such advantage, accounting for why their cavalry units were not the most feared parts of their armies: it was the bracing offered by metal stirrups that created the stability necessary for men on charging horses to drive spear and lance points into massed infantry, as well as the control needed for mounted archers to fire without gripping the horse's reins. (There were Asian steppe and American Indian tribes whose warriors could perform this action by way of using their thighs alone to control their mounts, but such were highly exceptional troops, at this time, and relatively rare.) Without the stability and control made possible by iron and steel stirrups, horsemen were relatively easily knocked to the ground; whereas, possessed of this seemingly simple advantage, they were very hard to dislodge from their mounts. Two questions concerning Broken's cavalry, however, remain: If they were indeed using stirrups, why were their mounted units not larger, more heavily armed, or trained in the performance of massed shock tactics that the innovation allowed? Furthermore, from whom did they borrow the all-important advance in mounted technology, which would literally change the face and fate of Europe? Whatever the case, by failing, on the one hand, to increase the size of units that had been given drastically increased shock power, and, on the other, to arm them with the full range of weapons that heavy cavalry mounted with metal stirrups could employ, and by electing instead to maintain their imitation of the old Roman model despite possessing a tremendous advantage, the Broken army committed an error of enormous magnitude. —C.C.

165 † **elected officials** It is worth underscoring the point that the Bane's process of electing various governmental officials, including their chief, was in keeping with the "barbarian"—or at least the Germanic—norm of the Dark Ages. Indeed, Western democracy owes as much (or more) to the codes of these societies than it does to those of ancient Greece and Rome. The Bane's granting of an at least occasionally preemptive right of fiat to the High Priestess of the Moon does reveal, however, as the narrator suggests, a paradoxical, simultaneous, and deep tie between the exiles' government and that of the city out of which they had been cast. —C.C.

167 † **raft of parchment documents** Although both the people of Broken and the Bane could make parchment from the organs and hides of calves, goats, and sheep, "the Tall" were considered the more advanced of the two peoples, in this context, mainly because they preserved the technique of manufacturing parchment scrolls: long sheets of parchment wound around two rods, or batons, with "pages" being "turned" by unwinding one rod and winding the other. The Bane, for their part, relied on loosely bound sheets of parchment, the irony being that, today, the image of the scroll has become emblematic of the archaic: indeed, it is virtually synonymous with ancient and early medieval cultures, while the bound sheets of parchment that the Bane employed were of course the earliest forms of modern books, and were symbols, therefore, of progress.

171 † **four-year-old Effi** The names of Keera's children, like those of Sixt Arnem's, offer important clues as to the cultural drift of each society, Bane and Broken. *Effi* is a form of the modern German *Elfriede, Baza* is an Old High German variation of the Slavic *Boris,* while *Herwin* is related to the modern *Erwin,* which is itself a variation of *Hermann,* still a common enough name in contemporary Germany, despite its original meaning: "friend of the army." In short, the Bane, for all their imagined "inferiority," may have been more closely linked to the modern German people than were the subjects of Broken. —C.C.

180 † *ackars* Ackar is believed to be the Old High German word for "acre," and the amount of land it represented was reasonably close to that which we continue to assign to the term today. Some premodern definitions of an "acre" can vary a little, since the word literally refers to the amount of ground an ox can plough in a day, and certain unscrupulous, land-hungry authorities used teams of two oxen to get an increased measurement. Then, too, not all ground is equally easy to plough; but despite these and other considerations, the differences between the several legitimate versions tend to be small, and come out somewhere near the modern number of 43,560 square feet. —C.C.

181 † **"Alandra"** Another Broken dialectal rendering, this time of the modern German *Alexandra,* which is derived from the older *Alessandra.* Like its male counterpart, *Alexander,* the name means "protector"—a fact that, in the case of this particular woman, will prove accurate in one sense, but far more ironic, and even sinister, in another. —C.C.

182 † *sukkar* The Arabic term for sugar, Arab traders having introduced granulated sugar made from Indian cane into the West only in the early eighth century: very shortly before the events recounted in the Broken Manuscript took place. Gibbon may have let this usage go without comment simply because he found its meaning obvious. —C.C.

186 † **phrenetic** There are cases in which an archaic spelling for a word that we might think anachronistic goes a long way toward demonstrating how very old some seemingly "modern" concepts are, and I have therefore left them in their original form; "phrenetic" is one such example. —C.C.

187 † **surmount their backs** The color and general appearance of these creatures, together with their living in northern Germany, mark them as almost certainly being Great Crested Newts (*Triturus cristatus*), whose range once included almost all of Europe, and who have been reduced in number in modern times only by the loss of their habitat due to human development, to the point that they are now a threatened species. Newts are not, as Isadora seems to indicate, precisely the same animals as salamanders: but both do make up the two classes of the family *Salimandridae,* and it is therefore likely that no distinction was drawn between them in the ancient world, or during the Dark Ages. In addition, while the differing feeding, mating, breathing, and breeding habits and techniques of the seventy-odd members of this family are impossible to completely detail here, both newts and especially salamanders did, indeed, possess certain very important mystical and spiritual properties, in certain religions and folklores of those eras: they were fire spirits, or "elementals," just as undines (or, variously, *ondines*) were water spirits, gnomes Earth spirits, and

sylphs spirits of the air. Elementals were thought to be actually composed of their basic element, and the human who could control such a creature could, at least temporarily, control that element. —C.C.

190 † "Emalrec" Though it passes unmentioned by Gibbon, this name contains a mild irony: if we account for the vowel shift of Old High German, it becomes the fairly common *Amalrec,* a variation of *Emmerich,* both of which connote "powerful worker"—hardly accurate, in this case, and perhaps an intentional comment upon the state of affairs in the Fifth District, and in Broken's society generally. *Berthe,* meanwhile, is obviously an archaic form of *Bertha,* drawn from the root *beraht,* meaning "bright" or "famous": also an irony. —C.C.

190 ‡ **such rough material** Gibbon continues to pay little attention to the questions of how, and to what extent (a considerable one), judgments concerning wealth and station were drawn from elementary statements about clothing, particularly among women, in Broken as elsewhere in "barbarian" Europe. Nevertheless, it is noteworthy that we find still more proof, here, that a woman's clothing and therefore station in life were signaled by, in descending order, material(s) used, the quality of needlework, and color (expensive dyes obviously being available only to people of means). "Fashion," as we understand the word today, scarcely existed, even in one of the most advanced societies of the time. In the case of the unfortunate Berthe, for example, the flat statement that she wears "a simple piece of sackcloth . . . poorly stitched" (sackcloth being a material that, since the time of the ancient Hebrews, had been used by penitents and mourners, who wished to deliberately torment themselves) seems intended to fix her station, in our minds. And indeed it can, if we are aware that sackcloth was no more than the burlap-like substance used, as the name indicates, for making sacks to hold grains, cotton, root vegetables, and similar items; it cannot, in short, have been a comfortable garment, even if "well stitched," especially not for a woman who was pregnant, and even less for one who had no "smock," which, again, during this period referred to a simple robe, usually cotton, that women wore as an undergarment, *if* they could afford it. —C.C.

191 † "plague" If this seems a leap to a conclusion on Isadora's part, we should remember that the bubonic plague was constantly on the minds of people throughout Europe, Asia, and especially northern Africa (where most outbreaks began) during this period. Its principal symptoms were widely known, enough so that someone like Berthe could realize that if her husband's sores had not developed into *buboes,* the near-black sores that gave the Death its name, the disease was likely not *the* plague. On the other hand, many other people were not capable of such discrimination, leaving open the possibility that Berthe's ability was only a product of her association with Isadora, a gifted healer. —C.C.

191 ‡ "rose fever" Variations on this term can be found in more than a few ancient and medieval manuscripts, as can the many other names given to what was almost certainly *typhoid fever;* but it is important to note that "rose fever" could denote several other mortal fevers and sicknesses that shared crucial symptoms. The most common of these was *typhus,* and the general inability to tell

the difference between the two during ancient and medieval times—evident in the similarity of and relationship between their names—was a problem especially pertinent to and within the Broken Manuscript, as shall be seen. Even Gibbon, given the extent of medical knowledge in his eighteenth century, was in no position to make such distinctions (indeed, it was only in the nineteenth century that typhoid fever and typhus were definitely identified as two different illnesses); and at the time during which the events in the Manuscript were taking place, the lines between pestilences were far more blurred, so that the term "rose fever" likely included several other candidates, as well. Today, we can be more discriminating, and try to accurately distinguish between what were certainly (as we shall soon see) two illnesses that struck at the kingdom of Broken and the lands around it at the same time, but that were collectively labeled "plague" by the stricken peoples; and the most important differentiating factor, in terms of understanding the events that the rest of the Manuscript chronicles, lies in the methods of transmission of these illnesses: direct physical contact with the afflicted, breathing of the same air or drinking of the same water, and finally (as we shall soon see) eating the same diet, a practice that brings into the picture yet another widespread disease with certain similar (actually, more horrific, but, ironically, less virulent) symptoms, a further confusion that would make the situation even harder to analyze. *Note:* To say more of this last method of transmission at this juncture would be to spoil the suspense that the narrator is working hard to construct, at this as at other points: it is enough that we note, here, that two diseases were actually at work in Broken, and that none of them was actually "the plague" or "the Death," phrases generally reserved for the Black Death, or bubonic plague.

Finally, it also should be noted that this phenomenon of two diseases being identified as one was not at all unusual, during this historical era; in fact, it is in many ways typical, especially of how little medicine had been allowed to advance by the various monotheistic faiths (for which dissection of the bodies of those killed by the afflictions was a sin), in the four or five hundred years since Galen. —C.C.

192 † **"Bohemer" and "Jerej"** Both Slavic, and probably Slovak (given the geography), names, of which Gibbon comments, "We know the Slavs to have followed earlier invader tribes into central Europe by the beginning of the sixth century, and we must concern ourselves here with one of the principal groupings of this race, the Bulgars, whom we know to have undergone, by the late seventh century, a fractious division into two or more 'empires' of 'great khans'—neither of which 'empire,' we should note, was as powerful or even as large as Broken. One of the chief factions thus produced moved east to the familiar ground of the Volga, while the other pushed on to establish itself upon the lower Danube; and from this forcefully acquired territory, the second group immediately commenced raiding the settlements, not only of the Byzantine [or Eastern Roman] Empire to the south, but of other barbarian tribes in other directions. It therefore seems entirely credible that, by the moment of Broken's crisis two centuries later, superfluous, criminal, or merely adventurous members of this empire—which had by then become firmly entrenched—might have struck

out on their own, to find their fortunes in such famously wealthy kingdoms as Broken. Or, they may have been prisoners of war—or perhaps they even entered Broken, like Heldo-Bah, under the rather sinisterly ingenious policy of indentured servitude that allowed flesh-dealers to cheat Broken's laws concerning slavery." The two names, like the two servants, have rather contradictory natures, each being Broken dialectal versions of Slovak names, in the first case for "god of peace," the second, "worker of the earth." —C.C.

192 ‡ *bulger* Gibbon writes, "While we have no specific justification for believing as much, it seems plain, given the information gleaned thus far, that this adjective is connected to a name: 'Bulgar,' which remains the shortened form of 'Bulgarian.' But there is a matter of interest here that makes the word, perhaps, more than just another Broken adaptation of another people's name: when the narrator refers to the *Frankesh* ('Frankish') or to the *Varisian* ('Frisian') tribes, the first letter of each name appears in the upper case, as a measure of respect, one not accorded to such tribes as the *seksents* (Saxons), a name which, as we have seen, the subjects of Broken likely equated with 'peasants.' Apparently their attitude toward *bulgers* was similar; indeed, it is possible that this little piece of the Broken dialect contributed to one of the modern German terms for 'vulgar,' *vulgär*, as much as did the commonly-cited Latin *vulgaris*." [It should be noted, here, that Gibbon is indulging his sometimes wild taste for speculation. —C.C.]

193 † **"red poppy lip paint"** Ignored, perhaps not surprisingly, by Gibbon, are these examples of ancient and medieval cosmetics from opposite ends of the safety spectrum: rose water (produced when rose oil is created through the steam distilling of rose petals) was used then much as it is today, for harmlessly scenting and softening the skin, while galena is the naturally occurring form of lead sulfide, with all the toxic implications that the term carries. Fortunately, Isadora is using it, as did many, as eye makeup alone, which would limit the area of application, diminishing absorption through the skin and making accidental interaction with the eye the only real danger. "Lip paint," in which flower or berry juice was used for tinting, usually had a beeswax base, making the only possible toxic reaction in this case the effect of the poppies themselves: not a concern, as the plants had to have flowered to produce petals for tinting, whereas opium is derived from first scoring the immature seedpods of the plant, then harvesting the thin latex that oozes from the cuts, and finally processing it. —C.C.

194 † **surcoat** Both Old Saxon and Old Low German had terms that contributed to the word "coat"; and so, while "surcoat" itself is derived from the French and is also a term that came into use in a later period, there was almost certainly an analogous concept in the Broken dialect. The more interesting question here is not one of etymology, but of the object itself, since surcoats bearing heraldic figures are not even thought to have been in use in Europe until well after the eighth century. Yet, because the crest that appears on the surcoat in question—the rampant bear of Broken—involves the emblem of a kingdom, instead of a family or an individual knight, it is consistent with the development of European heraldry, which was still using such crests as most ancient peoples (par-

ticularly the Romans) did: to connote national, imperial, or individual military unit identity, rather than family or personal distinction. —C.C.

194 ‡ **best marauder sword** The debate over which Eastern "marauding" tribes— that is, those who raided into Europe, such as the Huns, Avars, and Mongols— as well as which Muslim armies (or, more precisely, which parts of which Muslims armies) carried the kind of curved blade that Dagobert is said to be girded with, here, is one that has persisted for well over a hundred years. Some authorities claim that there is a widespread misperception—largely created by fiction and Hollywood—that such "exotic" or "Oriental" peoples as the Muslims and the Huns used curved, single-edged sabers and scimitars, in keeping with their non-Roman, non-Western appearance. But in fact, while there is strong reason to think that raiding peoples may have adopted such a weapon during the period under discussion for their cavalry units (curved blades being easier to withdraw from an enemy's body at high speed), those marauder and Muslim soldiers who made up their infantry arms almost always copied the enormously successful double-edged, straight weapons of the Sassanid Persian Empire. As is so often the case, in such debates, one can scarcely do better than to go back to the remarkable archaeological work done by the famed traveler, adventurer, and "Orientalist," Sir Richard F. Burton, contained in his *The Book of the Sword*, originally published in 1884, but wisely kept in print by Dover in an only slightly edited and abridged edition of 1987. —C.C.

196 † **skulls . . . piled as high as mountains** Gibbon writes, "This mention of the infamous piling of enemy skulls, usually associated with later leaders such as Genghis Khan and Tamburlaine, is of use in dispelling those same legends: it demonstrates that the notion of enormous piles of skulls is a far older bogey for children than has previously been imagined, thus weakening the idea that it was ever anything other than a useful nursery tool." In fact, the exact truth may never be known about such infamous and dramatic tales concerning the warriors of the East and their kings, caliphs, emirs, and emperors; but since, in this same passage of the Manuscript, we find mention of another legendary practice for which there is actually a good amount of reliable evidence—the cooking of meat between the legs of Eastern riders and their horses' backs—we cannot agree with Gibbon's skepticism too quickly, simply to obey the imperatives of political correctness or a more basic revulsion at the very idea. Certainly, for instance, the great Turkic Emir Timur (or "Timur the Lame," often contracted, variously, to *Tamerlane* or *Tamburlaine*, A.D. 1336–1405) had his own spies disseminate rumors of "mountains" built of tens of thousands of skulls among populations he hoped to conquer, as a way to weaken resistance and sow panic, a trick practiced more than two centuries earlier by Genghis Khan; and in both cases, we have reliable accounts to prove that these men at least sometimes made good on their threats—as they must have done, in order to be sure that the threats themselves carried weight. "Mountains" is doubtless an exaggeration; but a pile of human skulls numbering in the tens of thousands must surely have *seemed* a mountain, to horrified onlookers. —C.C.

198 † *Allsveter* and 198 ‡ *Wodenez* Two of the most common terms used to describe the deity whom Gibbon has already and correctly (but not adequately) termed

"the patriarch of the Norse gods," Odin (also known, as in Richard Wagner's operatic cycle, *Der Ring des Nibelungen*, as Wotan). He had even more obscure names among the Germanic tribes, since their adherence to this faith (again, contrary to much popular and even some scholarly opinion) predated the arrival of the Norse invaders, perhaps and importantly explaining the German people's consistent fascination with the myths. For the purposes of these examples, however, *Allsveter* is almost certainly the Broken dialectal term meaning "All-father," or "Father of all," a concept that, we should note, is not, in any of its variations, synonymous with "all-powerful" or "supreme being," as in the Christian sense of God: Wotan, like all the other great polytheistic patriarchs, had challengers, mistresses, and weaknesses; could suffer defeats; endured not only self-doubt, but regrets; and enjoyed the distinction of having been the only pagan patriarch to endure facial disfigurement, when he traded one of his eyes for Wisdom. —C.C.

198 †† **"the runes"** Evidently, Gisa taught Isadora not only the practices of a skilled healer, but other talents, as well, talents that, under the old, traditional faith of Broken, would have gone hand in hand with healing: those of a seeress, a woman (and such divining figures were almost universally women, among the Germanic tribes) who could cast runes—anything from collections of bones and sticks to chosen stones carved with runic symbols—and gain, not specific details of the future, but an idea of general trends, most importantly for her tribe. —C.C.

199 † **the family's modest litter** Gibbon writes, "Although this was doubtless another of Oxmontrot's attempts to ape Roman customs, it also served, as so many of his policies did, a secondary and pragmatic purpose: Romans rode litters borne by slaves, as opposed to horses, as both a mark of status and as a method of limiting the amount of horse dung and urine that cluttered their already narrow, foul streets. The imperative for the second of these purposes in a city of stone, built upon the summit of a lone mountain some three and a half thousand feet in elevation, would have been even greater."

202 † **Selke and Egenrich** Although evidently inscrutable in Gibbon's day, the names of Keera and Veloc's parents can now be traced more certainly: *Selke*—like *Elke*, in Frisian, from which the name was derived—is apparently a Broken "pet name" for the Germanic *Adelheid* (or *Sedelheid*, in the Broken dialect), the usual meaning of which is "kind and noble." But in the Broken version, "noble *because* kind" would be closer, and the fact that *Selke* appears to have been a name used only by the Bane reminds us that compassion was a quality found in greater abundance among the exiles in Davon Wood than in Broken. Besides being a virtue, for the Bane, compassion was also good sense—it kept the tribe open to new outcasts, who thus increased their numbers, brought new blood into the breeding pool, and increased the Bane's strength and good fortune accordingly. *Egenrich*, meanwhile, is the Broken version of the very common German name *Heinrich*, by way of the Old High German version, *Haganrich*, all three of which mean roughly the same thing, "strong ruler." Thus, the couple together stand for "compassion and strength": not only the highest of Bane virtues, but an apt description, to judge by their

actions, of the role they played in the lives of their two natural children and their one adopted (if wayward) son. —C.C.

INTERLUDE

205 † **the title Interlude: A Forest Idyll** It is unclear whether Gibbon detected any note of either irony or outright sarcasm in the title of this section of the Manuscript: whatever the case, while the subject matter broadly resembles what we would expect to find in a typical "idyllic" pause between more narrative episodes, and while the central relationship between the two characters introduced in these pages would certainly seem to justify such a label, each of the histories of those characters is so marred by tragedy and violence, the examples of which are so carefully, indeed graphically phrased (and with so little concern for the elements of poetics or aesthetics), that it seems probable that the narrator, rather than attempting a true idyll, is attempting an earnest—indeed, a grim—broadside against some of the most fatuous popular misconceptions and literary foibles of his time. —C.C.

207 † **the forces of revolutionary destruction** Gibbon refers to the growing Romantic movement, and particularly to that school most obviously represented by the philosopher Jean-Jacques Rousseau (1712–1778), whose theories centered on the Natural World, the "Social Contract," and what is perhaps unjustly dismissed as the theory of the "Noble Savage." Rousseau's views on social and societal relationships among humans were indeed twisted and prostituted to the cause of excessive, unchecked violence during the French Revolution, as well as other unsavory episodes during that period and others to come. The most sensible of Romantics recognized the limitations of the philosophy, to say nothing of its dangers, during the French Reign of Terror; but many held on to the ideas tenaciously, rationalizing brutal behavior among human societies that any animal species would certainly have disdained. —C.C.

209 † *neura* Gibbon writes, "This is, of course, a term taken from Greek antiquity, one originally employed by [the fourth century B.C.] physician Praxagoras of Cos to describe what he thought were a special set of arteries that transmitted the 'vital force,' or 'divine fire' which all progressive Greek medical minds called *pneuma,* an invisible substance in the air that is inhaled and traveled from the lungs to the heart, vitalizing the blood that was to be sent to the various appendages and organs of the body, making function and animation possible. However, Praxagoras's student, Herophilus of Alexandria [335–280 B.C.], building on his teacher's work yet pushing well beyond it, realized that the *neura* were in fact not arteries, but instead represented an entirely separate method of transmitting the *pneuma.* In the modern age, of course, when we have learned through the work of the chemists Lavoisier and Priestley that it is *oxygen* that in fact fulfills the role assigned to the *pneuma,* such opinions may seem quaint; but we ought not underestimate their importance as steps along the way to the

truth." One need only add that we ought, too, to recognize that the work of the ancient Greeks is remembered in the name eventually and correctly given to that other "special set of arteries," the *nervous system,* or *nerves,* the adjectival root for which is, of course, *neural,* and whose basic units of signaling all sensations are *neurons,* using electrochemical transmission. —C.C.

209 ‡ **the** *thirl* A term used by various northern tribes—including, apparently, the old man's unnamed steppe horse people, who were likely from the Ukraine or some other pseudo-European area—in the same sense that we use the word "thrill" today. Indeed, there is an obvious etymological connection between the two, and a behavioral one, as well: the old man's tribe, like many modern people, actively sought such experiences. —C.C.

210 † **the endless steppes** The background of this character (prior to his becoming a traveling scholar, apparently well known throughout what we today call the Middle East, Europe, North Africa, and even parts of India for his expertise in fields ranging from medicine to warfare) remains obscure, although certain logical conclusions may be reached that are important to the tale, as it contributes to a more comprehensive understanding of the old man's character and behavior. We can safely rule out any chance that he came from one of those known horse peoples who dominated the critical southern and central regions of the Pontic-Caspian steppe well before and then through the early Dark Ages: the Scythians, Sarmatians, and Goths during the Roman era, as well as the Huns and Alans from the fourth to the eleventh centuries A.D. None of these were noted trading tribes; farther north, however, there were peoples who not only better matched the old man's physical description, but whose history at this time accounts for his ancestors having become apparently changed from horsemen to successful tradesmen, with ships and caravans that visited the Mediterranean basin and northern Europe, as well as the Middle and Far East, in the latter case using what was already being called, in the old man's time, the "Silk Path" (later the Silk Road), the only known land route to China. Now referred to as "proto-Balts" (possibly of Finnish origin), in their earliest incarnation these tribes were Indo-European peoples who had, by the eighth century, been pushed into concentrated communities, first inland, to protect themselves from coastal raiders, but, when they grew strong enough, on the Baltic Coast itself. The exact nature and range of goods available in these important ports and towns—known as "emporiums"—is not known, but it was certainly extensive: soon after the establishment of the Islamic empire during the same era, for example, Islamic silver was being traded in Baltic ports, marking their inhabitants as distinctly different from the Slavic tribes that were coming to dominate lands to their south.

Among the most noteworthy Baltic peoples were (and in many cases remain) Lithuanians and Latvians to the east, as well as Pomeranians and Prussians to the west. These last two regions are of special interest in determining why the old man may have found Broken such a congenial home: Saxony (the German region in which *Brocken* was and is located) was close by, and may also have been "close," in ethnic and environmental characteristics, as well as general feel, to those places where the old man's family and tribe had been forced

to go when they were pushed away from the great steppe, and became tradesmen rather than a horse people. —C.C.

210 ‡ **still understood and respected** Here is the first solid reference on the part of
the narrator to the notion that scholarship and learning have been disappearing
in the "known" world, suggesting that he is writing toward or after the end of
Broken's history (ca. the early eighth century), rather than toward the beginning (sometime in the fifth century): while the fifth was certainly not a century
renowned for scientific advances, it would still have been too soon for a scholar
to declare the onset of a long "dark age," whereas by the early eighth century,
that pattern was clear and unarguable, and had not yet been reversed by the
establishment of the great Islamic centers of secular learning in Spain and Iraq.
—C.C.

210 †† **Wearmouth** The fact that Gibbon feels no need to identify these characters
both demonstrates the high level of even a "basic" education among the "educated classes" of his day, and is a special tribute to the historical awareness of
Edmund Burke: Herophilus is explained in the note to p. 209, above, while
Galen (A.D. 129–216) was the most important figure in medicine between
the legendary Hippocrates (ca. 460–ca. 370 B.C.) and the advent of the Enlightenment in the late seventeenth and early eighteenth centuries. True, Galen
based his work on the humoral system: the idea that the body had four primary
organs of importance—heart, liver, spleen, and brain, the last considered
directly tied to the lungs—that produced four basic fluids (blood, yellow bile,
black bile, and phlegm), the harmonious balancing of which was the definition
of good health. But he also made leaps and strides concerning anatomy
and other areas of practical medicine so significant that he became the only
doctor by whom more than one Roman emperor would consent to be treated.
In addition, by telling us that Galen wrote his famous work on dreams "nearly
five hundred years before the old man's time," the narrator would seem to be
making an unusually definite statement that the old man we are now meeting
lived during the early eighth century (although he may have been born in
the last years of the seventh), which fits with all other actual chronologies
in the Manuscript.

Bede, in the meantime, often called "the Venerable Bede," was a monk who
was indeed born in the important monastery of St. Peter at Wearmouth, in the
present British county of Durham, in A.D. 673. However, although often identified (as he is by the Broken Manuscript's narrator) with that institution, he completed his adult works—most importantly his *History of the English Church and
People* (A.D. 731)—in nearby Jarrow, at the newer monastery of St. Paul, which
one expert (Leo Sherley-Price) identifies as a "joint-foundation" with St. Peter's.
The library apparently shared by the two monasteries was one of if not the
most extensive in Britain, and Bede played an important part in translating and
critiquing great authors of the past, particularly those of Greece and Rome, and
he had a mastery of subjects ranging from music to medicine. He was at the
height of his powers when he would have received the visit from the Manuscript's old man, who had been roaming the Far East, North Africa, and Europe; it is possible, in fact, that the old man crossed the "Seksent Straits"—again,

almost certainly the English Channel at its narrowest point, between Calais and Dover—with the specific purpose of seeking out both Bede and the library at Wearmouth-Jarrow. —C.C.

211 † **Galen the Greek** Apparently unnoticed by Gibbon (or perhaps, again, deliberately ignored, so as not to call attention to an apparent inconsistency in the Manuscript) is the use of "Greek" here, rather than what we will soon discover was the Broken dialectal term for that nationality, *Kreikisch*. This sort of shift occurs too repeatedly, throughout the "Idyll," to be mere accident—it seems, instead, to clearly indicate a desire on the part of the narrator to display the far more learned, cosmopolitan background and personality of the old man. —C.C.

211 ‡ **from their dreams** It is both amazing and frustrating to note how very close such early scientific minds as Galen's and the old man's came to unlocking the secrets of dreams, and thus stealing Sigmund Freud's (as well as Carl Jung's) thunder, at least a thousand years before those pioneers of psychiatry, psychology, and dream interpretation completed their work on the subject: had those earlier authorities only been able to realize that dreams are particularly revealing *symptoms* of mental and physical disorders, rather than analogous *identifiers* of disease, one is tempted to wonder how much earlier the development of Western psychology would have commenced, and thus how very different the course of Western history would have been. —C.C.

212 † *Roma* Again, the use of the proper Latin name for the eponymous capital of the Roman Empire raises questions about when exactly the narrator chose to use particular forms of words, and in what languages, to achieve desired effects: that effect once more being, here, to underline the great learning of the old man. —C.C.

212 ‡ **the Cilician Dioscorides** The narrator refers to the eminent first-century pharmacologist, Pedanius Dioscorides, author of the five-volume *On Materia Medica.* Thought to have lived between about A.D. 40 and 90, Dioscorides traveled throughout the world known to Western scholars, gathering samples of botanical, mineral, as well as what we would today call animal-based homeopathic remedies, although it is as a medical botanist that he was chiefly known and would be remembered. To provide practical tests of the various cures he either discovered or compiled, he sometimes campaigned with (and may actually have served in) the Roman army. His monumental work, published in about A.D. 77, was definitive enough to remain what Vivian Nutton, in his *Ancient Medicine,* calls "the bible of medical botany," one that was still in use "well into the seventeenth century"; and, as we shall see, Dioscorides' life certainly served as an example for the old man, just as Galen's did; but the old man was able to include, in his own (unfortunately lost) pharmacopoeia, plants gathered in both Afghanistan and India that Dioscorides had heard tales about, but never encountered. —C.C.

212 †† **museum** Gibbon writes, "The 'museum' at Alexandria was, in fact, a building that reflected the early and literal meaning of the word, which is to say, a structure dedicated to the Muses, or to artistic and scholarly endeavor. It would be flattering to think that our own 'museums' have retained this character;

plainly, it is not always or even usually so." Yet this note does not seem aimed at Edmund Burke, who likely knew the classical meaning of "museum" as well as Gibbon did; and it's therefore hard to shake the feeling that Gibbon was at least considering publishing the Manuscript, before he received Burke's reply. —C.C.

213 † **the *patella*** Gibbon writes (with the possible end, as stated in the next note, of distracting Burke's attention from the horrors immediately following), "Here is proof, validated by the off-hand nature in which it is mentioned, that both the narrator and the priests of Kafra knew far more of human anatomy than we today associate with those ages we call 'dark': the *patella* is the Latin classification of the 'knee-cap,' a fact that the narrator of the Manuscript—whose expertise does not seem to have extended into medical realms—nonetheless seems to have taken as commonly understood."

213 ‡ ***Roma . . . gangraena . . . crurifragium*** As extraordinary as the horrifying detail (both historical and anatomical) provided here may be, Gibbon's silence on the subject is almost as shocking. He likely maintained it because of how close the narrator comes to describing the Passion of Jesus Christ: Gibbon probably felt (and if so, correctly) that Burke would have already been inclined to view this brief description as near-blasphemous, without any further elaboration on his own (Gibbon's) part.

Textually, we again encounter the use of Latin, apparently employed, here as elsewhere, not only to further convince us of the old man's knowledge and erudition, but out of disdain: the narrator's own contempt for the sadism of Roman punishment rituals is obvious and palpable, and is echoed in the translator's sudden use of what we now suspect to have been the bitter and perhaps pejorative title for Rome, *Lumun-jan. Gangraena*, meanwhile, is again the Latin (and therefore, in Barbarian Age and medieval Europe, the official medical) term for gangrene, clearly meant to display the old man's great medical knowledge; while *crurifragium* refers to a little-known detail of many Roman crucifixion rituals. Victims of this already nightmarish torture often lived—like Jesus—for a day or even two on the cross, in almost unimaginable agony: as the text here says, almost every joint, especially in the upper body, was either torn or horrifically strained. The only "relief" that the unfortunate prisoner could even try to get was offered by the block of wood placed beneath his feet, which he could use to hoist himself up by his feet and legs. But after enough time, and as much out of tedium and the need to return to more important duty as out of any sense of mercy, the Roman guards supervising the ritual would use a mallet to break the victim's shins: which, as anyone who has ever broken or known someone who has broken these bones knows, is a particularly painful fracture to endure. The victim would either die instantly of the shock of this final outrage, or, being as he was unable to further support himself, quickly suffocate, the position of his arms having already badly constricted his breathing.

Again, any suggestion that such Romans had anything to learn about torture from "the East," as Gibbon elsewhere implies, is quite clearly revealed, here as always, to be fatuous. What the narrator calls the "fiendishness" of the Kafran religion—so clearly embodied in the at least partial ligature and cauterization of both the flesh and the arteries and veins (mainly those descending from the femoral, the *popliteal* and *tibial*) of the severed legs, which was, as the text says, intended to avoid their victims' bleeding out too quickly—cannot realistically be contested. This point alone would have been enough to justify the stridency of Burke's reaction in his letter to Gibbon. —C.C.

215 † **derived from . . . opium and . . . *Cannabis indica*** We never learn the old man's precise methods for such derivation, although we know in modern times that such strengthened alkaline drugs (as opposed to their chemical imitators) are their most potent and least dangerous forms. Opium, of course, leads most immediately to heroin and morphine, the latter almost certainly what is meant in the Manuscript when "opium" is referred to, as its uses are always medicinal rather than recreational; as to *Cannabis,* prior to the twentieth century, *Cannabis sativa,* our own marijuana or hemp plant, was not only used in the production of rope (the fibers of its stalk being particularly strong), but was commonly available from druggists and pharmacies (no prescription required). This was true going back to the ancient world: the ostensible use of the drug was as a sedative and narcotic painkiller but, then as now, there were many people who used (and abused) it recreationally. The subspecies *indica,* which came from, among other places, the mountains of what are now Afghanistan, Pakistan, and India, was preferred in the West precisely because of its hardy nature, which allowed it to survive in the climates and mountains of northern Europe (and North America) as easily as it did in warmer climes; but *indica* was also considered by doctors and folk healers as superior to other subspecies of *Cannabis* for medicinal reasons, because it supposedly produced greater pain and anxiety relief with fewer of the "druggy" side effects. For this reason, it was often reduced to its resin form (what we know as *hashish,* the Arabic word for the resin), which doctors in the West would eventually market—as they did morphine, cocaine, and other narcotics—as a commonplace medication that could be eaten or drunk as a tincture, thus avoiding the telltale signs and physical dangers of smoking or injection. Whether the claims that *indica* was less stupefying than, say, the other *sativa* subspecies has, however, long been in doubt; and some drug researchers have argued for the formalization of *indica* as its own species of *Cannabis.*

It is also worth noting that, from ancient times to the late nineteenth century, such unregulated drug use did not produce greater numbers of addicts and "fiends"; whereas the illegalization of such substances (like the prohibition of alcohol) created an entire "subspecies" of violent criminals. The society of Broken was an excellent example of this: *Cannabis* was one of the only crops the Bane could grow in the harsh wilds of Davon Wood, and was one of their most prized trading crops (cultivated land within Broken itself being used exclusively for subsistence agriculture); yet the Bane themselves showed no signs of having been a race of marijuana abusers. —C.C.

216 † **the *dauthu-bleith*** Gibbon writes, with the same frustration we have seen elsewhere, "Here, once again, the influence of Gothic upon the dialect of Broken is hinted at, for this term almost certainly arises from that language: although we do not yet have the capacity to translate it literally, the spellings and word com-

binations are far more indicative of Gothic than they are of Old High German." Developments since Gibbon's time have allowed linguists to corroborate Gibbon's speculation, and to more precisely translate this phrase as akin to a Gothic "coup de grâce." It had originally been translated simply as "condemned [or sentenced] to death," but *bleith* is one of several Gothic terms for "mercy"; and, as the original meaning of *coup de grâce* is a "merciful" as much as a "finishing" blow, it seems that the most recent translation relates the true intent more clearly. —C.C.

221 † **his new, insulted form** The word "insulted" is used in one of its archaic forms, here, to mean "assaulted," "injured," or "demeaned"; Gibbon makes no note of it, as it was still generally used in this sense during his own time (as opposed to being specifically used in the verbal or medical sense, as is the case today). —C.C.

222 † **prevent festering and control fever** Here we get a good idea of the old man's pharmacological skills: despite the above average medical knowledge that Gibbon had gleaned through coping with chronic physical problems of his own, the extent of the old man's understanding of the medicinal power of plants remained a mystery to the later scholar, as it would have to most people (even most doctors) in the eighteenth century. Hops represent an excellent case in point, particularly the wild hops that the old man would have found growing in the mountains that became his refuge: long before they were first cultivated as an ingredient in beer in the eleventh century, hops were recognized as having very real "anti-festering," or antibiotic and antibacterial, powers, as well as narcotic effects (although this particular label was almost certainly unavailable to Barbarian Age healers). Similarly, honey was used (as it continues to be used, by some homeopathic and tribal healers) as an agent against sickness and infection, although many of the people who made or make such use of it did and do not realize that the human body metabolizes honey as hydrogen peroxide. Citric acid taken from fruit, meanwhile, can kill bacteria in both wounds and on food, as well as in the digestive tract (which is the original reason that lemon was used as a condiment on raw oysters). The extract of certain willow barks (as is more popularly known) provides a naturally occurring form of aspirin, and it was and is sought as an analgesic. The roots and flowers the old man initially used are not mentioned specifically, but we can imagine that they must have included wild species of such families as nightshade, or the *Solanum* genus—which, in uneducated or evil hands, had long been sought as the poison "deadly" nightshade, or belladonna, but which were also used (more carefully) as hypnotic anesthetics. In short, given the old man's situation at this key point in his recovery, he could scarcely have assembled a better set of ingredients to use as both poultices and infusions, and there is no contesting that his knowledge was extensive, indeed. —C.C.

222 ‡ **so guttural were its sounds** Given the conjectures already made about the old man's possible origins, we're faced with several candidates for this language of "guttural" sounds: certainly, it could have been a proto-Baltic tongue, but it could just as easily have been one of the early German dialects, including Broken's own. —C.C.

223 † *laboratorium* Gibbon writes, "You may be tempted, my friend, here as else-where, to think that this use of a later form of a Latin term (this for 'place of work') is a contrivance of the Manuscript's translator—yet he assured me that the term appeared in just this form in the original text. As to why, or even how, the narrator of the tale should have been aware of that later form, hints again at his temporal inconsistencies; and, things standing as they do in the narrative, we can but note it, and press on." Unfortunately, we can offer no deeper insight today: unless the narrator was the first to use this original version of "labora-tory," or the old man himself was, we are hard-pressed to say how it made its way into the document. —C.C.

228 † **Bactria, and from India beyond** Bactria was the fabled and very independently minded province, or satrapy, of the Persian Empire in southwest Asia. Most Bactrian territory comprised lands that today form much of Afghanistan and northern Pakistan. Conquered but never really pacified by Alexander the Great, these ruggedly fertile hills, mountains, and valleys continue, in our own time, to produce some of the most potent opioids, as well as other narcotics, in the world—and have also continued to be a thorny problem for would-be West-ern conquerors or liberators, as American soldiers have recently spent over a decade discovering. —C.C.

228 ‡ **wild Davon sheep** The phrase is evidently taken at face value by both the trans-lator of the Manuscript and Gibbon, despite the fact that for "wild" sheep to have existed in the lands between the Erz and Harz mountains, they would al-most certainly had to have been domestic sheep that had become feral; and, while such a development is certainly possible—there were several places in Europe where flocks of sheep were known to have undergone just such reversion—it would have represented a new phenomenon for Barbarian Age or medieval Germany. In addition, the fact that the old man is said to have "har-vested" the wool suggests that these sheep were either of a variety that simply shed their fleece during warm spring and summer months (certainly, he could not have captured and shorn them) or that his companion hunted them and brought them back to the cave for meat. The latter seems by far the most likely explanation, since, while "shedding" of fleece is not unheard of, especially among feral sheep, it is not a common occurrence, and would likely not have yielded the quality or quantity of wool that the old man required. —C.C.

228 †† *metallourgos* The Greek root of "metallurgy," and seemingly left untranslated, again, to give us some idea of the breadth and depth of the old man's knowl-edge: if he wrote Greek, we can logically assume that he spoke it, at least enough to conduct technical conversations with the most advanced scientific minds of his age. —C.C.

229 † **alchemical sorcerer** The fiction that alchemy was purely or even primarily a science devoted to vain attempts to turn lead into gold persists into our own day, and certainly dominated in the periods leading up to Gibbon's: perhaps the greatest scientific mind of his own or any age, Sir Isaac Newton, was deeply fascinated by alchemy, but had to work hard to keep his experiments a secret, one that would keep him from the often-gilded gallows reserved for those con-victed of the supposedly black art.

The truth is that alchemy and metallurgy were, in ancient times, almost indistinguishable: after all, when a man could turn rocks into such precious metals as iron, and then iron into that supreme (along with gold) utilitarian metal—steel—the transformation did seem otherworldly, indicative not only of the possibility of changing one metal into another, but of attaining some superior mystical and perhaps spiritual state. Certainly, what the old man was doing and experiencing in Davon Wood during the period described in this section of the Broken Manuscript more than fits under these scientific and spiritualistic rubrics. —C.C.

229 ‡ **his most precious books** First, it's important to remember, here, that the word "book," in the pre-Gutenberg Dark Ages, was a very transitional term: it not only included early, bound stacks of parchment (often called *folios*), but also more informally fastened collections of parchment, such as the old man was producing during his time in Davon Wood; and finally, it also referred, very often, to "books" in the sense that the Romans knew them, *volumen* (obviously, the precursor of the modern "volumes"), which were the rolled parchment scrolls of which mention has already been made.

As to the specific books mentioned in this list, most speak for themselves; although perhaps the most interesting feature of the collection is the inclusion of the *Strategikon,* a Byzantine military manual concerning, in the main, cavalry tactics (heavy cavalry being the mainstay of the Byzantine army) but also dealing with other important issues, such as discipline in an army and how best to achieve it (as well as what punishments to mete out for infractions), and what would today be called "military anthropological" studies of the peoples that made up the main enemies of the Eastern Roman Empire (although the emperor Maurice, the compiler and main author of the work, ambitiously spoke of the Roman Empire as unified under his rule). The *Strategikon,* like the work of China's Sun Tzu, is a work of a startlingly enduring nature, with impressive implications for modern military organization and conduct, both on the battlefield and off; but Maurice has enjoyed none of Sun Tzu's modern vogue, a new edition of the *Strategikon* having only recently appeared, after a long absence from bookstores in the West. This new enthusiasm likely has to do with the important comments Maurice and the other writers who contributed passages to the work made concerning styles of warfare between large states and non-state enemies, what we would today call counterterrorism and counterinsurgency. Certainly, by applying the precepts included in the book to the intellectual wasteland that was Western European military doctrine and practice during his own lifetime, the old man could indeed have presented himself in any court as a near "sorcerer" of war—a fact that would have brought him renown and wealth, while placing his services in high demand, thus explaining why he was so consistently welcomed in courts throughout the region, and was also allowed, during his sojourns in such places, to pursue medical experiments—notably dissection—that, while once common in cities such as Alexandria, had become ghoulish anathema to Christian and Muslim nobilities and leaders.

As to the remainder of the authors cited, only one statement by the narrator may seem questionable, because of its seeming political incorrectness: the claim that Procopius and Evagrius had determined that most if not all outbreaks of the bubonic plague—*Yersinia pestis* and its related disorders—originated in "Ethiopia." Historical research, however, has proved the theory that the disease most often known simply as "the Death" originated in that region: the rats who carried the fleas that were and remain the initial spreaders of the contagion (which has never entirely disappeared, a vaccine against it never having been developed) apparently boarded Nile trading ships, and reproduced wildly, as did their fleas, in the granaries of Egypt, whence they took ship for all the major ports of Europe. Further genetic research on the subject remains to be done (see the authoritative volume edited by Lester K. Little, *The Plague and the End of Antiquity*), but it seems altogether likely that, whether politically correct or not, the Justinian Plague of the old man's era (the outbreak having occurred sporadically during the sixth, seventh, and eighth centuries, taking its name from the Byzantine emperor Justinian, who was struck down by it, but survived) did indeed follow this geographical contagion pattern. —C.C.

231 † **pains** Gibbon validates this account of the old man's experiments with soldiers, as well as his self-diagnosis, by remarking that "such pains are a thing which almost anyone who has known a soldier, sailor, or ordinary citizen who has lost a limb to war, mishap, or disease can confirm, and in which many scholars who were also medical professionals or simply possessed medically inclined minds took an interest. [René] Descartes [1596–1650] himself took welcome time away from his syllogistic aphorisms to investigate the subject, although praise for its initial identification rightly belongs to an earlier Frenchman, the surgeon and anatomist Ambroise Paré [1510–1590], royal physician to no less than four French kings, who described patients who had undergone amputation feeling continued pain, not at the site of the severing, but *in the missing limb itself.* He noted, as well (further agreeing with our as-yet anonymous friend in the Manuscript), that this pain could be heightened with the onset of certain atmospheric conditions—what we have come to know as rapid changes in barometric pressure—as well as by the aggravation of the general state of agitation in which the patient lived: the root of this last assertion being that drugs which had sedative but no analgesic effects proved to be of use in reducing the distress. Many other, lesser lights have studied the phenomenon, but we are no closer to understanding it than was the former court physician of Broken." Today, the psychogenic distress experienced by amputees—which was given its popular name of "phantom pain" by the American physician and surgeon Silas W. Mitchell, who, working in the 1860s, was provided with no end of subjects for study by the American Civil War—is better understood; but the entire subspecialty of neurology that deals with such problems as severed nerves, neural entrapment in scar tissue, etc., remains one of the most challenging fields in medicine, as the persistent distress caused by the cutting of nerves (which can be a result of surgical malpractice or even surgical routine, as much as or more than by amputation or accident) endures as a principal cause of chronic pain syndromes. —C.C.

231 ‡ **than logic might lead one to suspect** Counterintuitive as it may seem, doctors

have discovered that gentle massaging of the parts of the body affected by an amputation does indeed afford many patients some mitigation of pain; and, as we will see, the particular way in which the old man's companion "massaged" the stumps of his legs was quite unique, and generally successful. —C.C.

234 † *"Stasi"* A shortened version of *Anastasiya*. The full and pointed meaning of that longer name is explained in the text, as well as in the following note; but there is an additional and fascinating coincidence (or is it mere coincidence?) concerning this particular nickname in connection with the modern uses of the mountain *Brocken* that causes one to wonder if the narrator did indeed possess genuine gifts of foresight and prophecy:

As has already been noted several times, *Brocken* was, prior to the twentieth century, popularly considered the most sinister mountain in Germany and perhaps all Europe, the meeting ground not only for human witches and warlocks, but for the supernatural demons and other unholy creatures with whom those humans cavorted, as well. It is perhaps fitting, then, that after the assumption of national power by Adolf Hitler in 1933, the mountain found particular use to the propaganda machine of his Nazi party—as the site of the world's first long-range television broadcasting tower. It was *Brocken's* tower that broadcast the 1936 Summer Olympic Games to a very large (by the standards of that day) area of northern Germany: the first time the Olympics had appeared on television anywhere. A weather station and hotel had also been constructed; but Josef Goebbels, Hitler's propaganda minister, preferred radio to television as a tool for indoctrinating the German people (and when one considers the physical peculiarities, not only of Goebbels, but of nearly all the Nazi leaders, one can understand why); all activity on *Brocken*, along with broadcasting from the television tower, was therefore suspended during World War II. The mountain was bombed by the Western allies at the very end of the European war (April 1945). Although the hotel and the weather station were destroyed, the television tower miraculously survived; and when American troops occupied the mountain, they rebuilt the weather station and used the television tower for their own propaganda purposes. But when *Brocken* fell into the Soviet zone of occupation in 1947, the Americans disabled both the tower and the station before relinquishing control of the mountain.

During the early decades of the Cold War, *Brocken* comprised a "security zone" for the Communist government of East Germany: it was the site of an enormously ambitious fortification project, one that recalled the achievements of the "Mad King" Oxmontrot some thirteen hundred years earlier. Both *Brocken's* continued suitability as a site for a television tower and, even more importantly, the mountain's larger strategic significance were recognized: in the hands of the Western powers, *Brocken* could have proved a strong threat to the advance of East German and Soviet troops into West Germany along the route that eventually leads through the Fulda Gap to the southwest, the most obvious path of entry for such an invasion. The East Germans and their Soviet "protectors" therefore declared *Brocken* a top secret security zone in 1961. Large numbers of troops began using the area just as the army of Broken had once done, as a location in which to train for what seemed an inevitable war. The summit of the mountain was once again turned into a fortress, this time for the use of the East German and Soviet militaries; and construction soon mushroomed into one of the most ambitious Cold War building projects ever undertaken:

The military installation was enclosed by a massive concrete wall, built of 2,318 sections, each of which weighed two and a half tons, and the whole of which was of a scale almost equal to the natural stone walls of Broken. Within the new walls, the mountaintop became the site of a major Communist listening post, from which were monitored any and all broadcasts in West Germany, private and public, military and civilian—an operation that was controlled by the Soviet KGB and the East German *Ministerium für Staatsicherheit* (the "Ministry for State Security"), or secret police, whose popular name was the *Stasi*.

German reunification occurred before the long-expected invasion of Western Europe through the Fulda Gap by the forces of Eastern communism, and the massive concrete walls atop *Brocken* were dismantled along with the more famous wall in Berlin; the television tower now broadcasts one of the television stations run by the democratic government of the unified Germany. Tourism has come to the mountain, its former secret status having made it a haven for rare species of flora and fauna, and it was included in the Harz National Park in 1990; but memories of the Stasi remain burned into the memory of the people of East Germany—hardly what the old man had in mind when he named his savior and companion. —C.C.

234 ‡ *Anastasiya* Gibbon provides no explanation of this name, and little need be added to that in the text, except to say that the name was and remains ubiquitous among Baltic, Nordic, and Slavic peoples, in many slightly varied versions, and that it long ago entered English as *Anastasia*. Other than that, the narrator's interpretation of its meaning is quite accurate; although we may pause in wonder at how many times it has been the name of females destined for remarkable feats of survival, in fact, legend, or both. The most obvious of these cases, of course, is the Grand Duchess Anastasia of Russia, famous in legend as the sole child of that country's last tsar and tsarina, Nicholas II and Alexandra, to have (purportedly) survived the family's savage massacre in Yekaterinburg, in the Ural district, in 1917: even if this "survival" is wholly apocryphal, it only underscores the resurrectionary associations of the name. —C.C.

236 † companion It is worth noting, here, the true meaning of the word "companion" in the Manuscript (and indeed the English language), especially as it relates to the old man and his great cat. Because of one of the many misapprehensions popularized by Dan Brown's engaging yet nonetheless terribly misleading *The Da Vinci Code*—this one claiming that the word "companion," from before the time of Christ to well after it, could imply "wife" (as Brown claims was the true meaning of Biblical and Gnostic gospel references to Mary Magdalene as Jesus's "companion")—one might be tempted to assume that some sort of bestiality was occurring inside the great panther's cave. According to the Oxford English Dictionary, however, and a list of experts too long to list here, such a connotation only applied *retrospectively*: in other words, a man's or woman's "companion" (say, in the phrase "companion in life") *could*

indeed be their legal spouse—but only if they were established as being in such a relationship. It did not mean, in other words, that companion was *always an alternate word* for "legal spouse," if the couple in question had not already been legally joined. This point needs to be stressed because Stasi is so often referred to as "the old man's companion," and because her very intimate—but, of course, platonic—relationship with the old man was used by the rulers of Broken (and even, at first, the Bane) as further evidence that he was actually a sorcerer. —C.C.

237 † **traces of those markings** Although he could not have known it, the narrator is describing both the metallurgical formula and the color associated with the gold amalgam that would gain great popularity, in the 1920s and thereafter, as "white gold." —C.C.

237 ‡ **the long, dipping spine** Gibbon, again, dismisses the panther's dimensions, since fossil evidence that such massive creatures existed so comparatively recently in Europe was either unknown or seriously misunderstood during his era. Regardless of whether this particular specimen was a representative of what is today known as the European jaguar or the European cave lion (the latter being somewhat older and larger), we cannot help but be struck once more by her amazing—and yet, for her species, apparently unremarkable— size: with a nine-foot body (*excluding* the tail, meaning nine feet from nose to rump) that stood roughly half that at its spine, this is an animal more than capable of all the remarkable feats attributed to her in the Manuscript. The "white" fur was not, if we are to judge by the color of both the eyes and the dark "eyeliner" around them, an indication that she was either an albino or a separate species or, indeed, truly white; rather, it is a color that still appears, occasionally, in lions and other great cats around the world, which is very nearly white. (The faint, light markings also confirm the presence of pigmentation.) We also can see, with the revelation that the "warrior queen" was in fact a great cat, why the old man's medicines and poultices would have been so helpful to her: his treatments appear to have been grounded in opiates, willow bark (the "natural aspirin"), and naturally occurring antiseptics, none of which are or would have been toxic to cats, as so many other, seemingly milder, drugs are. Acetaminophen, for example (most popularly known by its major brand name, Tylenol), is generally considered an extremely benign drug, among humans— but it is fatal to cats, even in very small doses.

237 †† **against his nose and face** It will not need stating or restating, to those who live with and/or work with cats, large and small, that this delicate touch is their most intimate indication of affection, and of the granting of their trust—rarely gained (particularly in areas like northern Europe, the nations of which, especially France, have a long history of believing cats the familiars of witches and creatures of Satan). —C.C.

238 † **the Northeastern Sea** Gibbon writes, "Having reliably determined that the 'Seksent Straits' to which the narrator refers is our own Channel, we may infer that this 'Northeastern Sea' is that which lies in the direction indicated, relative to the position of the mountain *Brocken*—in other words, the Baltic Sea. Yet, even if this is so, we can draw few conclusions from the fact, little as yet being

known of the tribes who inhabited the Baltic coast during this period." We are, as already noted, at no such disadvantage today, however, and this interpretation only reinforces the notion that the old man came from the trading peoples who had been pushed to the Baltic coast by larger and more warlike tribes, such as the Huns. —C.C.

240 † **should stir disbelief** Gibbon writes, "While we may indeed, as the narrator suspects, scoff at the further idea of a crippled and bleeding old man being taken in and cared for by so carnivorous a beast as a panther, anecdotal Natural History is too full of tales of humans thus cared for by various animal species (for what reasons, we may never know) to permit our immediate dismissal of this part of the tale." Indeed, the fact that the panther had very recently lost her cubs in the most traumatic manner possible actually reinforces the Manuscript's account, according to the results of recent experiments on animal brains ranging from our relatives, the apes, down to the tiny wasp and bee: it has been discovered that the brains of every species of animal life contain that core region—the amygdala—that both feels and preserves emotional trauma. Thus, as Gibbon suspected, we have no good reason to reject the narrator's account at face value; rather, we have sound cause to accept it. A recent and excellent illustration of this is the case of the "lion man" of modern Africa, George Adamson (foster parent, along with his wife, Joy, of Elsa the lioness, in *Born Free*), who lived among and was protected by lions until his tragic death at the hands of poachers. Indeed, the story of Caliphestros and Stasi has many elements that closely resemble the tale of Adamson and his lions, too many for us to be able to dismiss the former as mythological. —C.C.

Part Two

245 † **legitimate legislature** Gibbon refers to the French Revolution's second phase, during which the National Assembly that had sworn the famous "Tennis Court Oath" became, in response to the persistent refusal of the royal, aristocratic, and clerical sectors of the ruling class to evolve with anything like real alacrity, the National Constituent Assembly, which issued the famous "Declaration of the Rights of Man," and revealed as its noble purpose the official abolition of feudalism and the formulation of a French constitution. Unfortunately, the makeup of this Assembly also saw the emergence of wily leftist members who sought to prostitute the Revolution to their own ends—chief among them such characters as Honoré Mirabeau, a particular target of Gibbon's ire in other letters, and the chief "manipulator" of whom he speaks here, as well as far more radical revolutionaries (Gibbon's "basest scoundrels"), the most extreme of whom, of course, was the man whose name would all too soon become synonymous with the "Reign of Terror," Maximilien Robespierre. —C.C.

I: Water

248 † **cuirass** Another encounter with a word that, while it has a modern story (*cuirass* being a fifteenth-century French term), also puts us back in the largely unknowable realm of the armor employed by Dark Age warriors. We are left to wonder just what concept it was that the translator felt comfortable denoting with the immediately recognizable "cuirass": it might have been anything from the Greco-Roman bronze pieces that covered the front and back of the torso (although we have no other indication that either Broken soldiers or the Bane still employed bronze weapons in the field), to the steel and leather cuirasses of the Chinese and then the Persians. Again, we must rely on the text, and on the original translation, to supply details. —C.C.

249 † *quadrates* Gibbon writes that this formation is "easily identified, by those with even a basic knowledge of Latin, as growing out of that language's *quadratum,* or 'square'; and we can safely assume that these 'squares,' whether composed of the smaller *fausten* ('fists,' *fauste* being the singular, 'fist') or the larger *khotors,* were rooted, not in imitation of the closely ordered, distinctive checkerboard pattern of the Roman *quincunx,* but out of the imperatives of the traditional, even ancient, German military doctrine of expecting attack from all sides. Apparently, Oxmontrot at this moment saw, for the first and perhaps only time, something in the Roman military model that he (rightly) did not believe suited his Germanic legions, and that he believed he could improve upon; and in organizing Broken's marching and defensive order-of-battle formations, he altered the Roman pattern to a prototype of what would come to be identified as both a modern German and an Anglo-Saxon way of war—for in modern times, it would remain both a characteristically Prussian/German, and then British, trademark: the famed square."

250 † **the chaos of conflict** The effect of madmen on troops in the field is a recurring tradition in various traditional cultures, and so the Talons would have been far from alone in their belief that somehow a madman or madwoman could divine present and future order in what was (and very often remains, to the average soldier) the incomprehensible context, purpose, and results of battle. The first Muslims, the Vikings, and certain American Indian tribes were only a few examples of early peoples who sought the counsel of such characters at such moments (ascribing to it varying levels of importance); and it cannot be denied that the results were often remarkably productive. —C.C.

250 ‡ *seksents* As explained earlier, this appears to have been the Broken dialectal word for "peasant," an interesting fact, in that it has a clear phonetic (and likely etymological) relationship to "Saxons," a tribe who may well have first entered Broken, not as fierce, proud conquerors, but as peasants, in many if not most cases "indentured" peasants, who thus occupied the lowest rung on the ladder of Broken's fairly unique social hierarchy. —C.C.

255 † *thatch*-roofed . . . **forges and smiths** Gibbon writes, "We have become so accustomed, in our own age, to tales of thatched roofs put to the torch, or set alight by some ordinary household mishap, that we forget that there ever was an era when thatch was viewed as *progress*. But, at the time of the events de-

scribed in this narrative [the late seventh and early eighth centuries], thatch was only beginning to appear in northern Europe, and was an expensive technique that was also far more advanced, pleasant, and efficient than were the mud, sod, and mere tree-limb roofs that set the dubious standard for most of the era's dwellings." As for the "forges and smiths," while, as always, it is impossible to say with anything like certainty, the description of the bustling town called "Esleben" in the Manuscript, along with its approximate position on the map, create at least the possibility that it might have been some early forerunner of the town of Hettstedt, which became famous for just such a variety of commercial activities, from the agricultural to the proto-industrial. —C.C.

256 † **"Akillus!"** Gibbon writes, "Here is further proof of how great the influence of classical Greek and Roman culture was on Broken, having made its way in, again, through the experience of the 'Mad King' Oxmontrot and his comrades, who served in the Roman legions as foreign auxiliary troops (which, by the later imperial period, comprised the bulk of the 'Roman' army). Although the epithet 'Greek' or, in the Broken dialect, *Kreikisch* was, as seen elsewhere, employed as a thinly veiled insult, there nonetheless appears to have been ample knowledge of and respect for ancient Greece's heroes. We may infer this, not only from the fact that various counterparts to such names (in this case, 'Achilles') made their way into both Gothic and the various ancient and modern Germanic dialects, but by the already-demonstrated and crucial fact that the Roman—and, thereby, at least *some* of the Greek—military systems were studied and emulated in Broken, and even improved upon." Today, there remain Germanic and Nordic counterparts to the name *Achilles* in various countries, although they are used infrequently, in keeping with the very *un*-martial societal values and national narratives that such societies have at least tried to project in the "postmodern" age. —C.C.

256 ‡ **"lad"** Gibbon writes, "My translator did inform me that the Broken grammatical form for 'children' was remarkably close to the modern German *kinder;* however, while it has always been something of a tradition for German commanders to refer to their men as such, the same effect is not achieved in English, 'children' sounding far more condescending than any military officer would wish to. He therefore chose 'lad' or 'lads' when he encountered the word, which seems fitting."

256 †† *Lenzinnet* Gibbon notes, "A typically German compounding of the rank of 'linnet' with what, it would seem, was the Broken dialectal term for the modern German *Lanze,* or 'lance.' Hence, the term has a distinctly *Romani,* or Latin, influence, analogous to the 'first spear' [or, *pilus prior*] rank of the Roman infantry, but transplanted to the cavalry, where it anticipated the later European terms 'first lance' and 'lancer.'"

256 § **ball-headed spurs** An interesting detail that may reveal something of the people of Broken's earliest history and attitude toward animal life during their pagan era. Spurs had been in use at least since the Roman Empire, yet the Romans almost exclusively used a "prick" or "spike" spur, a simple, straight piece of iron tapered to a sharp point, and meant to inspire their mounts to obedience and speed, like most spurs, through pain. The ball-headed (or, in the parlance

of modern dressage, the "Waterford") spur, however, has persisted among various riding cultures as something of a counterargument to the belief that horses will respond only to discomfort, for the small, spherical piece of metal used causes little pain and no bloodletting, and has sometimes been called an instrument of cooperation rather than of absolute command. One can find advocates even today of both types of spurs—a fact that indicates that the ball-headed model is at least as effective as the elaborate forms of pricking and cutting spurs that have been developed since the Romans, particularly in the American West, Latin America—and, of course, nowhere more so than in that homeland of animal extermination and abuse, Texas. —C.C.

257 † **cavalry sword** By the time of the fall of the Western Roman Empire, the various styles or "models" of the classic *gladius,* the Roman short sword (which had been "borrowed" from Rome's Spanish Celtic enemies), the shape and image of which are closely identified in the popular consciousness with the Roman legions to this day, had been largely replaced by a somewhat longer blade of lesser width (or, in some cases, simply greater tapering), the *spatha,* which fell somewhere between the *gladius* and the various, classically medieval blades, most notably those Viking models referred to in the Broken Manuscript as "raiding" swords; especially popular among horsemen, this is likely the version of the "Broken short-sword" that Arnem and his mounted troops carried. —C.C.

259 † **The scouts shrug** There truly are moments in the Manuscript when any reader will find his or her own credulity at the choice of words strained past belief; and the use of the word "shrug" is certainly among them. However, research reveals that "the raising and contracting of the shoulders to express uncertainty or indifference" (in the nearly identical language of several prominent dictionaries) has been going on since at least the fourteenth century, when Middle English gave us the *shrugge.* Why note such examples? Because they continue to demonstrate, first, the surprisingly direct and "modern" sound of so many texts from the early Middle (or Dark, *or* Barbarian) Ages, and, second, the extent to which the florid language that we so often associate with those epochs was the invention of later authors who were anxious to propagate a mythic chivalric code that had supposedly existed since ancient times, and had been passed down directly to modern European nobility. —C.C.

263 † **"an easy gallop"** A moment of validation for the Manuscript, and for its translator: some may wonder why Niksar does not order the men to ride at a canter, which is actually defined as an easy gallop; but the word did not come into use until the mid- to late eighteenth century. —C.C.

272 † **"'fire wounds'"** Gibbon writes, "The modern German term for 'gangrene,' *Wundbrand,* must have closely, if not precisely, matched the Broken dialectal term, *Wundbrend,* meaning, as it does, 'wound of fire' or 'fire wound.' This burning sensation, which nearly always originates in the extremities, is one of the first, but hardly the most horrifying, of the symptoms of gangrene. And, as Visimar himself notes, his initial term for the illness, *Ignis Sacer* ['Holy Fire'], was indeed the popular Latin term for the terrible malady that, into our own age, features *gangraena* [gangrene] as one of its principal (and fatal) properties, but is not 'true' or 'pure' gangrene. The Holy Fire, I am told, is still imperfectly

understood; but we can say with confidence that it was the same malady that eventually took on the rather more colorful title of 'St. Anthony's Fire' (St. Anthony, as you know, being the patron of the victims of pestilence)." St. Anthony [ca. A.D. 251–356] was an Egyptian Coptic Christian, and the patron of an extraordinarily large range of diseases, infectious and otherwise, having spent much of his life working among their victims. Prominent among these illnesses was the "disease" which Visimar here describes, which was indeed and actually not gangrene proper, but a form of poisoning, ergot poisoning (or "ergotism"), which *results* in gangrene, but is not identical with the form of gangrene that Arnem associates with battlefield wounds; the first is caused by alkaloid agents, and is accompanied, as well, by other, often outlandish symptoms (hallucinations, convulsions, loss of feeling, rotting flesh, and miscarriages, the last so often that ergot was often deliberately employed as an abortifacient), while the latter is the "simpler" result of festering wounds. Not a few experts think that many mass outbreaks of delusional madness throughout history and the world have been the result of the first malady, ergotism: the deranged behavior surrounding the seventeenth-century Salem, Massachusetts, witch trials are a celebrated, but by no means the only or strongest, candidate (for an even more widespread, calamitous, and recent possible outbreak, see John G. Fuller's classic in the field, *The Day of St. Anthony's Fire*, which describes the near-self-destruction of a small French town in 1951—possibly due to ergot, possibly to mercury poisoning). Ergotism was also destructive and globally widespread enough to be one of the few such diseases to receive particular mention in the medical texts of nearly all ancient and medieval societies—Eastern, Middle Eastern, and Western.

An important point that must be reemphasized: Both the narrator and Visimar have by now suggested that two diseases are at work, in the kingdom of Broken; yet we will see that they were often lumped together—by average people ignorant of even the limited medical facts available to them at the time, as well as by Kafran healers and physicians little better informed—under the heading *"a plague"* or *"a pestilence."* This was not an uncommon occurrence; indeed, it is not unheard of, in our own time. The desire of doctors to explain a constellation of symptoms by finding one malady that covers them all has long been entrenched in medical minds; and is often as responsible as blatant ignorance for incorrect treatments. —C.C.

274 † *Wildfehngen* Gibbon writes, "Although many, if not all, military commanders of high rank engage in some similar practice, German commanders especially have ever employed idiosyncratic terms of affection, when speaking of and to their rank-and-file soldiers: terms which, when translated literally, simply lose much of their weight and meaning. These range from the relatively simple *meine Jungen* and *meine Kinder* ['my boys,' 'my children'] to the host of more esoteric names of which this *Wildfehng* (or the plural, *Wildfehngen*) seems to be an ancestor (for we find a very similar word still in modern German, in the form of *Wildfang*, which may imply anything from a madcap male 'wild child' to a female 'tom-boy,' that is, a particularly boyish and boisterous young girl). English commanders, like all others, share such terms of affection for many of

their troops, but it is really in the ancient warrior culture of Germany that we find the practice at its most elaborate, profound, and sometimes paradoxical: for however 'wild' such troops may have been or may be, they were, have been, and are expected to obey strict codes of honorable conduct, the breaking of which can bring punishments that make even the justly notorious extremes to which our own British naval officers often go when dealing with disciplinary infractions seem rather mild in comparison."

276 † **Gerolf Gledgesa** The name is the sort of mix that we can now identify as fairly common: *Gerolf* is clearly Germanic (implying a combination of the often-used roots "wolf" and "spear"), while names or terms close to *Gledgesa* are found only in Anglo-Saxon, suggesting the possibility of this character's having come from Saxon Britain. The surname connotes "fiery terror," and the justification for it becomes clear, as his personal history is recounted; but its ultimate irony will only grow apparent later. —C.C.

276 ‡ **Ernakh** Significantly, Gibbon makes only a few references to the Huns—doubtless among the principal peoples identified by the rulers and soldiers of Broken as "eastern marauders"—in his six-volume *Decline and Fall of the Roman Empire;* and, in this particular case, he evidently did not know (or did not think it worth noting) that *Ernakh* was originally the name of the third son of that greatest of all Huns, Attila. Whether the nurse/housemaid Nuen had this fact in mind when she named her own offspring, or whether *Ernakh* was merely a traditional and perhaps common Hunnish name, we do not know. —C.C.

278 † *"Donner Niksar"* Gibbon writes, "We will discover soon enough just what this noble yet unfortunate young son of Broken's achievements were; what should concern us, for the moment, is the form that the spelling of his Christian name takes. One finds, in the few bits of Germanic documentation that survive in their various dialects as well as in the many Norse sagas, nearly every spelling possible of every aspect of the name and life of *Thor,* son of Odin, god of thunder, and paragon of youthful Germanic-Norse virtues, who spent nearly all his time aiding other gods, demi-gods, and humans with his great strength, command of thunder, and magic hammer, *Mjolnir.* The important element, however, for our purposes, is that his name in Old High German appears to have been spelt *Donar,* which would have been pronounced 'Donner'—the same form we find here in *Donner Niksar.* The variations of the names are all of little importance, of course, as they are mere variations on the dialectal terms for 'thunder,' although it is interesting to note that the modern German word for that phenomenon, *donner,* has hewed so closely to at least one ancient version: Broken's. Thus, there is the strong suggestion not only that the myths of the supposedly 'Norse' gods were likely those of the entire Northern European region, but that they may well have *originated* with those Germanic tribes who inhabited the area we today consider Germany, calling at least some of the aspects of the Norse domination of civilization in that region into question." Without realizing it, of course, Gibbon is anticipating the notion advanced most forcefully in our own time by Michael Kulikowski, and discussed at length earlier in these notes: that the myths of the Gothic migrations and the

Norse invasion and cultural domination of northern Germany may have been largely just that: myths. —C.C.

286 † **"the *Krebkellen*"** Gibbon writes, "The practice itself is explained in the text; we pause only to reassert the fact that Oxmontrot, its creator, considered not even the most fundamental Roman tactics to be above improvement. The practice of the *Krebkellen,* which we may confidently translate as 'crab colony,' certainly takes its inspiration from the Roman *testudo,* or 'tortoise,' the tactic, which had long proved successful, of having Roman soldiers form a sort of shell by interlocking their great convex shields, or *scuta,* to their fore, back, sides, as well as over their heads. But again, this tactic, while ingenious, could also be clumsy, designed as it was to mirror the essentially steady, deliberate movement permitted by the formation of the *quincunx*—that is, a primarily frontward-and-rearward motion—to say nothing of the continued relegation of the role of cavalry as essentially support troops for those infantry formations. The contrast with Broken's *Krebkellen,* on the other hand, can indeed be likened to the difference between a tortoise and a crab—or, to complete the terminological explanation, a 'colony of crabs,' in which such creatures are known to live and defend themselves. While both species use their external shells for protection, as both infantries used their shields for interlocking protection, the Broken troops sacrificed some strength of defense for speed, maneuverability, and, hence, offensive potential, the last especially embodied in the cavalry units, which acted as the faster-moving 'legs and claws.'"

287 † **"worthy of our claws"** Gibbon lets this part of the discussion go without remark, perhaps because it's unclear whether Akillus is talking about the "claws" of the *Krebkellen,* or is referring to the pride that every man in the Talons took in the raptor's claws that adorned his cloak. It makes very little difference to the ensuing action. —C.C.

287 ‡ **"this aptly named fellow"** Taankret An obvious source for what would become the famous chivalric name of *Tancred,* the word itself is combined of elements implying "thinking" or "thought" and "counsel"—and is, indeed, suited to its man, as so many names in the Manuscript seem to be. —C.C.

289 † **Fleckmester** Gibbon writes, "Here is a name that, given all the guidelines we have established for the Broken dialect, is not at all difficult to understand: 'fleck' is an ancestor of the modern German *pfeilmacher,* counterpart of our own 'fletcher,' or arrow-maker, while *mester* is plainly some Old German variation of *meister,* or 'master.'"

290 † **longbow** As is perhaps apparent, this use of the word "longbow" simply implies a greater length than the bows used by the Bane—it is not, apparently, an anticipation of the later English invention that would famously carry the day at battles such as Agincourt. —C.C.

290 ‡ **"Nerthus"** Gibbon ignores the name, perhaps because scholarship in Germanic and Norse mythology had not yet reached the point that the Germanic goddess of fertility could be identified precisely; this would be a very strange omission, however, for it is one of the goddesses that Tacitus actually names, using this same spelling, in his *Germania* (pub. ca. A.D. 98), placing her firmly in the original pantheon of ancient Germanic, rather than Norse, deities, and supporting

the theory that a very great deal of what we still think of as "Norse" culture and mythology was actually taken from Germanic traditions. Indeed, one senses that Gibbon is reluctant to give so much credit to the Germanic tribes (perhaps because of their repeated thrashings of the "indomitable" Roman legions), but, being even more hesitant to go up against a scholar of Tacitus's standing, he simply passes the name over, as he does so many uncomfortable subjects.

The sole question that remains, then, is just what extraordinary creature we are discussing; and from the behavior, the extraordinary size and strength, and the markings, we can definitely say that we are dealing with the Eurasian Eagle Owl (*Bubo bubo*), a bird of immense size and power, as great or greater than its formidable cousin, the Great Grey Owl of North America (*Strix nebulosa*). The differences are mainly of appearance, the Grey Owl having an ovular or circular face and no "ear tufts," the feathery "horns" that actually are no more than cosmetic, having nothing to do with hearing. The Eurasian owl is more like the North American Great Horned Owl (*Bubo virginianus*) in appearance, but the size of the Eurasian Eagle Owl is much greater. Needless to say, these creatures caused enormous fear among humans, in part because of the fact that, like all owls, their weight was and is amazingly light in comparison to their power: it is always remarkable to come upon a recently deceased owl of any type and feel its extraordinary lightness, in this regard—a lack of weight designed to assist their silence and agility in flight and the hunt. And the Eurasian owl could take not only such normal prey as rabbits and other small mammals, but deer fawns: it was therefore believed, quite logically and rightly, that they might do the same to important domestic livestock such as lambs, kid goats, and even newborn calves and foals (always a real danger), to say nothing of human infants and toddlers. —C.C.

296 † *skutem* shields Gibbon writes, "Having so closely aped so many of the most crucial Roman military customs, it is not altogether surprising that we here find the soldiers of Broken almost directly transposing the Latin word for shield, *scutum,* into their own tongue." It is also true, however, that by the time Oxmontrot served as a foreign Roman auxiliary, the classic Roman *scutum* had changed in size and shape, becoming more ovular and slightly smaller; so it is possible we do not, in fact, know precisely what Broken shields resembled, just as we do not know the precise details of so much of their culture. —C.C.

298 † dance his deadly round At this point in the general history of northern Europe, as well as many other parts of the continent, "dance," as a form of recreation, still consisted almost solely of "dances in the round," that is, the joining of hands and then unchoreographed movement to one direction, then the other, etc., rather than of the courtly steps and masques with which we associate the later and higher Middle Ages. The only other forms of dance commonly referred to were quite sinister, in both origin and meaning: there were the "dances" that were associated with severe illness, generally nervous—such as St. Vitus's Dance, a name given to various forms of chorea—and there was (as is mentioned here) the "Dance of Death," or *"Danse Macabre,"* which involved that entity leading the wicked or the sickly to a generally unhappy end in the hereafter, either through trickery or sheer power. The Dance of Death could

often involve witchcraft, which was blamed for many disorders, especially after the rise of the monotheistic faiths: again, medicine was poorly served by the predominance of those faiths, except in the cases of those who took their piety with a grain of salt, and refused to let it interfere with reason. Even these last were largely preservative movements; that is, they kept existent knowledge that had been gleaned centuries ago from vanishing, rather than advancing or building on it: progress that would not begin again, after brought to a virtual standstill in the fourth and fifth centuries, until the fifteenth or sixteenth centuries—a full thousand years or more that could obviously have been used to great advantage. —C.C.

299 † **the Great River . . .** *Hel* The name of the river over which one crossed, in Germanic/Norse mythology, to get to the underworld, was never so important as the route one took to reach its complementary and unique paradise, *Asgard*, home of the gods and fallen warriors, or of the figure who guarded that loftier route. The famous "rainbow bridge" connected *Asgard* to *Midgard* (our Earth), and was guarded by a figure variously known as *Heimdall* (usually in the Norse) or *Geldzehn* (literally, "gold teeth") in Germanic tongues, who made sure that those who died less-than-glorious deaths in battle on *Midgard* were consigned to the realm of *Hel*. This last was one of the evil children of *Loki*, the most mysterious and shifting of the gods and demigods in this tradition, but basically half-brother to Thor, the god of thunder, and himself the god of mischief. *Hel* had been banished by *Wotan* (*Odin*, *Wodenez*, the *Allsveter* referred to earlier) to rule the closest thing to a traditional netherworld that appears in the Germanic-Norse pagan faith. The name of that netherworld and of its ruler became one, over time, giving us "Hell," a place that was said to lie across various rivers (depending on the version of the tales one reads), but which, in each case, seemed to fill roughly the role of the river Styx in Greek mythology, although the reasons why one would be consigned to this dark world in the Northern pagan system were based almost purely, not on the nature of one's life, but of one's death, that is, whether one was a warrior (which often included, it should be remembered, women) and died fighting. *Hel,* therefore, claimed not simply "evil" souls, but the spirits of people who had died of anything from disease to mere accident: an arguably unjust system that reveals much about Germanic and Scandinavian values. —C.C.

301 † **"***ballistae***"** Gibbon writes, "Here is a either a particularly clear demonstration of the influence of Rome upon Broken, by way of Oxmontrot and his subordinates, or one of the greatest linguistic mysteries of the entire Manuscript. At first suspecting a third answer to the question—simple laziness on the part of the translator—I pressed him particularly hard upon the matter. Had he found a description of something that, in his mind, closely matched the mainstay of Roman offensive war machines, I asked, and simply borrowed the name? [*Ballistae* were, in effect, close to catapults—which the Broken army also, apparently, possessed—save with greater power: if a catapult resembled a giant slingshot, *ballistae* could be seen as enormous crossbow, in an era, of course, before crossbows existed. —C.C.] But he was adamant that he had found the word intact, and used it for that very reason. It is therefore possible

that many, if not most, Broken troops used the term without knowing anything of its origins, or of the significance of those origins, in terms of cultural transmission."

301 ‡ **"artillery"** The word may surprise some, in this context, but the fact that Gibbon does not even think it worth mentioning shows that, even in his time, "artillery" was still understood to encompass any weapon that hurled what men could not over great distances: for the purposes of the Manuscript, primarily *ballistae* (sing. *ballista*) and catapults. The arrival of gunpowder simply added a new dimension to this phenomenon; but the term had been in use since ancient times, and indeed, purely kinetic artillery—especially the high Medieval *trebuchet*—could hurl heavier shot faster and harder than almost any of its gunpowder-based competitors of the time, though admittedly, the engines themselves were far larger and more difficult to maneuver. —C.C.

303 † **a sheet of white silk** The white flag was already the well-established signal of surrender, as it had been since the early *anno Domini* period. —C.C.

305 † **"exchanged for molten metal"** Gibbon writes, "In the ancient and early medieval periods, it was not unusual for patients who suffered the kinds of disease under discussion, here, to suffer from the delusion that their blood had become some kind of 'molten metal,' absurd though the notion may seem to us."

309 † **plainsong** Obviously, in this case, the word is being used in its most basic sense—that is, to describe a simple, unembellished melody, often heard in the countryside—and not to connote the more formalized and elaborate version developed by the Catholic Church; a distinction understood well enough during Gibbon's time that he felt no need to explain it. —C.C.

309 ‡ **"Weda"** The name of Gerolf Gledgesa's daughter is of obscure origin, having only a surviving male counterpart, one that is associated with "wood," although in what sense it is difficult to say. It may have been only a matter of pronunciation, for in German dialects of almost any age, it would have been—indeed, today would still be—pronounced "*Vay*-da," an unusually pleasant-sounding (if, again, difficult to define) name for girls and women. —C.C.

311 † **"she feels no pain"** This is, indeed, a common feature of the last stages of the gangrene that results from ergot poisoning, and one of its most pathetic symptoms, since both humans and animals who lack whole limbs attempt to behave as if they still possess them. —C.C.

II: Fire

314 † **thud** This is another of the words that are often mistakenly considered "modern" and onomatopoeic, but which in fact are medieval in origin; and it is the imagined need, on the part of many writers and translators, to come up with terms more genuinely "old" with an "e" (*ye olde*) that accounts for much of the stuffiness of modern renderings and/or imitations of what were already, by the eighth century, an athletic set of northern European languages. Indeed, in this case, "thud" is not even thought worthy of comment by Gibbon, familiar as he

likely was with Middle English's *thudden* and Old English's *thyddan,* the parent terms of "thud." —C.C.

321 † **"if he yet lives"** There is something strangely sad about the fact that Bede (who, as was noted earlier, Caliphestros knew, from having spent time in Bede's home, the Monastery of St. Paul near Wearmouth) had almost certainly died by the time that the events described in the Manuscript were taking place. From the many historical, cultural, religious, and scientific references mentioned, it is possible to place those events at circa A.D. 745; whereas "the Venerable Bede," a man of faith who nevertheless did honest and solid work in the cause of scholarly history (and, it should be said, legend, as well), died some ten years earlier, in 735. Caliphestros evidently had great respect and affection for Bede; and his never learning of his friend's death seems not only melancholy on its own merits, but a stark underscoring of just how isolated the "sorcerer" had been during his ten years in Davon Wood. —C.C.

328 † **"a special beer"** The beverage that we today think of as "beer" could in fact only have started to be made in Europe at this time, because the turn of the seventh and eighth centuries saw the first domestic cultivation of hops, although most sources say this was for medicinal purposes, and that hops were not used in beer until the eleventh century. Thus, Broken appears to have been ahead of the European world around it yet again; for, while other forms of beer had existed since ancient times, it is the use of such hops (which originally grew wild in the mountains) that gives "modern" beer the capacity—as Keera asserts—to drive people "mad," through their pseudo-narcotic effect. —C.C.

328 ‡ **"woad"** and † 329 **"meadow bells"** Woad (*Isatis tintoria*) is a plant that did indeed produce a popular blue dye (and as a result, is often confused with indigo). But it has recently been learned that, taken as a medicine, woad may contain twenty to thirty times the amount of *glucobrassicin* (a powerful cancer-preventing agent) than is found in broccoli, the modern vegetable most commonly cited in connection with preventing and fighting cancer. And scoring or bruising the leaves of woad can heighten its powers along these lines many times over (much as scoring opium poppy seedpods intensifies the amount and power of opium produced); thus, Keera's claim that woad is effective against growths, "especially inside the body," almost certainly refers to some power to inhibit or shrink tumors. What she calls "meadow bells," meanwhile (by which informal name modern Germans still know *Pulsatilla nigricans*), was another herbal wonder drug, used for a long list of purposes and problems, ranging, as Keera says, from menstrual pain to the invigoration of the uterus during pregnancy to, most commonly and importantly, counteracting the causes of what were then simply dismissed as life-threatening "fevers." It could and can also be used (according to which source one consults) to treat everything from hemorrhoids to tooth- and backaches. Was it a kind of Barbarian Age snake oil? It seems unlikely, since it is still used in various traditional medicines today, with effect; although the complete list of problems it is said to affect is implausible. —C.C.

334 † **"tiny men like vegetables"** Heldo-Bah speaks of the ancient alchemical "arts," as they were known by both their practitioners and their detractors: for even

the most enlightened of its practitioners did not treat alchemy as a *pure* science. Like so many areas of learning during the Dark and Middle Ages (and not unlike certain fields of science today), alchemy became more famous—or infamous—for the most nonsensical of its practices than it did for its very real, but less dramatic, contributions to science, medicine, and philosophy (and through philosophy, as Carl Jung later explained, to a kind of proto-psychiatry and psychology). Heldo-Bah names two of these extreme activities, the attempt to turn base metals into gold (the most famous, of course, of alchemical efforts), as well as the peculiar desire of some practitioners to create a miniature human called a "homunculus," basically by nurturing sperm (in which, it was thought, *all* of the elements that eventually became a human being resided) in some place other than a woman's womb. Many but not all alchemists saw the womb as nothing more than a nutrient-rich, protected sack, one that could be imitated, preferably in the Earth, thereby removing what post-tribal medieval thinkers often called the "pernicious influence of the feminine" from the life produced.

What is worth noting about alchemy, for the purposes of understanding the importance of the Broken Manuscript, is that many alchemical undertakings became very valid advances in fields ranging from metallurgy to chemistry to common household applications such as cosmetics, dyes, glasswork, and ceramics. But its most important achievements were those centering on military chemistry: alchemists would eventually discover gunpowder, as well as that most mysterious and elusive weapon of all military history, Greek fire (about which the Broken Manuscript will soon have a great deal to say); and the effort to refine base metals—the pursuit behind the famous "lead into gold" legend—led to the creation of ever-stronger and more sophisticated forms of steel out of "base" iron ore and carbon. —C.C.

334 ‡ **"quietly stream away"** Caliphestros seems to be intentionally playing on the unnatural fear of and prejudice against most cats, great and small, that has haunted European and Asian history since Roman times. And the especially irrational reaction to big cats (whether tigers in India, lions in Africa, or even leopards in South America) malevolently turning into "man-eaters" displays this ignorance and fear at its clearest and worst: after all, wolves and other dogs have been hunting men down since the dawn of time without being invested with the particularly and peculiarly evil intentions that are given so readily to "man-eating" cats. The result, however, is that great cats have been hunted to the point of, or into, extinction everywhere in the world, yet at the same time have become the object of fascination and ownership for such people as wish to prove that they can either master or (seemingly more benignly, but in fact just as destructively) "tame" these wildest of wild animals: today, for instance, there are more tigers owned by private individuals in the United States (and usually kept in abominably cruel circumstances) than in all the jungles of the world.

Anyone interested in exploring an organization and center that does invaluable good in the cause of offering such animals rescue and homes, while simultaneously educating Americans and anyone else concerned with (or merely inquisitive about) this problem should contact Big Cat Rescue in Tampa, Florida; their website can be found at www.bigcatrescue.org. —C.C.

339 † **Davon dog-owl** Keera's initial skepticism is justified: nearly all large, "hooting" owls are capable of making "dog-like" sounds (John James Audubon called the American Barred Owl "the barking owl"), whereas very few can do what it is claimed the bird mentioned here has and will, making the European cousin of the barred owl an unlikely suspect. In all probability, the mysterious bird in question is the Eurasian Eagle Owl, and probably the same "Nerthus" we have already encountered, explaining why Caliphestros would be evasive on the subject, at this point: his trust of the foragers is not yet complete. —C.C.

342 † *Heldenspele* Gibbon writes, "Here we encounter a phrase, the meaning of which can only be half-interpreted with any certainty. Clearly, we have the word that has survived to the modern German, *Helden,* or 'hero'; but as to *spele,* we can but posit educated guesses. Does it have some Gothic or other Barbarian root? Or should we take it as an early form of the German *Spiel,* or 'a play,' or *spielen,* 'to play'? All we can say with certainty is that Veloc intended to compose some sort of heroic, spoken tale." Once again, Gibbon has been stymied by the limited scholarship regarding Gothic of his day: if he'd had the advantages we now do, he would certainly have identified *spele* as the Broken dialect's synthesis of *Spiel* and *spill,* the latter the Gothic term for 'tale,' especially in the sense of 'heroic tale,' or *thundspill.* —C.C.

344 † **"the ash tree of the Frankesh thunder god"** Perhaps the most enduring legend to emerge from St. Boniface's time among the Germanic nations was his famous cutting down of a tree supposedly favored by Thor, the Nordic-Germanic god of thunder, after calling for Thor to stop him by striking him dead, if the god truly could. After Boniface dealt the tree a few blows, this legend goes, a great wind rose up and uprooted it, blowing the thing over, at which the local tribesmen converted to Christianity and built a chapel on the spot where the tree had stood.

But Heldo-Bah, repeating a mistake that many before him had made, and would continue to do in ages to come, confuses the type of tree, in his telling: it was Thor's Oak that supposedly fell to Boniface's divine wind, whereas Heldo-Bah is doubtless substituting the Ash of Life in Norse-Germanic mythology, *Yggdrasill,* the roots and branches of which supposedly encompassed all of the nine worlds in that religion's mythological system. —C.C.

344 ‡ **"'Vat of Turds'"** As Gibbon points out, "Yet again, we encounter evidence of just how much of a link the Broken dialect must have been between various older, even ancient, Germanic dialects and modern German—for the homonym discussed here remains very similar today, the German *Bohnen* meaning fecal 'droppings' (and also 'beans'), while *Fass,* although the letters themselves appear as parts of many other words, on its own does indeed connote a 'vat.' Yet this ribald connotation has not survived in any other of the many accounts and legends concerning the life of St. Boniface [A.D. 672–754] and his long career of converting the Germanic peoples to Christianity, possibly because, after being renamed 'Boniface' by Pope Gregory II in A.D. 719, the man in question often

continued to travel under the name 'Winfred'—although apparently not in Broken."

345 † **"what became of him, if he did"** St. Boniface did, indeed, enjoy great success in converting the Germanic tribes to Christianity, and he attempted to carry that success over to the raiding tribes of more northerly regions; however, his luck ran out during the latter endeavor. Although still alive, in all probability, when the events in the Broken Manuscript took place, he was eventually killed by pagan raiders, in A.D. 754, and if we accept Gibbon's contention that *Varisian* was the Broken dialectal term for "Frisian," then Heldo-Bah's skepticism here is justified, as it was Frisians who did the missionary in. —C.C.

347 † **"the river *Nilus*"** Again, Caliphestros uses the Latin term for a place or thing (in this case, the Nile river), and both the narrator and Gibbon's translator leave it in that form, forcing us to wonder why; but, as the reference in that tongue seems important (and the meaning is fairly obvious), I, too, have left it alone. —C.C.

348 † **"the rats that infest those same grain ships"** Caliphestros once more mentions a notion that is tantalizingly close to being the truth: the Black Death did indeed travel the grain routes from the upper Nile to the ports of Egypt, and from there to Europe—carried by the rats who bore the fleas that were responsible for spreading the infection. He saw the connection as metaphorical; yet if he'd had the time and the instruments, it is more than likely so perceptive a scientist would have found that the connection was actually causative. —C.C.

352 † **"bedding her own brother"** Gibbon writes, "No one familiar with Norse and Germanic mythology will be surprised by this remark, for the tales of their gods, like those of nearly all pantheons in the known world, contain important instances of the incestuous coupling (knowingly and otherwise) of brother and sister. And in those Northern tales, specifically, is contained one of the most famous among such myths, that of the hero who, in Germany, was known as *Siegmund,* and his sister, *Sieglinde.*" Unfortunately, Gibbon lived just over half a century before the appearance of perhaps the most famous reinterpretation and retelling of this myth: that contained in Richard Wagner's *Die Walküre,* second of the four installments in his monumental *Der Ring des Nibelungen* cycle. The opening installment of the work, *Das Rheingold,* would be sprung upon an unsuspecting public in 1869; and, when completed, the Ring cycle would quickly become one of the most successful works of operatic literature, albeit an endlessly controversial one. —C.C.

352 ‡ **"*Alandra*"** here and *passim* Gibbon writes, "The reference here would seem to be to the siege of Troy, *Alandra* being, apparently, the Broken variation on the name Helen. Whether it would have been possible that the rulers and people of Broken would have had knowledge of the Trojan War, based on a translation into their own dialect of (in all probability) a Latin text of Homer's *Iliad,* is far more difficult to prove, names often traveling where their context does not. Certainly, it is possible that Caliphestros himself created such a translation, although this Alandra was already a child of some seven or eight years by the time he arrived in Broken, leaving out the possibility that he had suggested the name in the first place. In addition, one can easily anticipate the difficulties that

would have accompanied propagating such stirring foreign legends in as closed and self-admiring a society as Broken's, thus making it far more probable that Caliphestros did not translate the work, and that the name made its way into the kingdom with some earlier emissary—quite probably, that greatest admirer of Hellenic and Roman culture upon the stone mountain, Oxmontrot himself."

352 †† *"Kreikisch . . . Graeci"* The first open statement, ignored, at this point, by Gibbon, of the Broken dialect's term (often derogatory) for "Greek" is accompanied by the second word, the Latin term for the same people. Caliphestros himself explains the reasons for the different uses—perhaps the reason Gibbon ignores them. —C.C.

353 † **can actually *taste* scents** This is an extraordinary statement for Caliphestros to make, and it seems obvious that it was rooted in his anatomical, which is to say his dissecting, work earlier in his life: certainly, no one among either the Bane or the Tall could have been aware, based on their levels of scientific advancement and their terror of the Davon panthers, of such a relatively arcane aspect of the feline sensory system, which is found throughout the feline tree, from housecats to their great relatives. The reference is also further evidence of how frustratingly close scientists came, during the eras before and during the rise of Christianity and Islam, to a truly modern understanding of anatomy and medicine, even veterinary medicine: for cats do, indeed, have unique sensory organs inside their mouths, but they do not "taste" scent with them. Rather, they *smell* with their mouths, adding considerably to their ability to detect scent, often from amazing distances. —C.C.

353 ‡ **roseberry** Almost certainly a precursor of "raspberry." The thickness and slightly thorny aspect of the bushes suggest as much, while raspberries are indeed a branch of the wild rose family. —C.C.

355 † **"Plum brandy . . . Slivevetz"** Gibbon takes this claim at its face value, either because he is unconcerned with the history of particular forms of alcohol or because he has no reason to dispute the claim. In more recent times, however, it's been postulated that brandy (or "brandy wine"), the distilled form of wine, was not invented until after the turn of the first millennium, despite references to it in various Dark Age histories and heroic tales (which, as has already been discussed, were often the same thing). This discrepancy may be accounted for by the possibility that brandy was being made long before its recipe was written down and formalized by the monks and other vintners of the French province of Cognac; or it may be one of many proofs that minor as well as major inventions were little noted until they appeared in one of the "great" European states, among which the kingdoms of the Balkan region—the original home of plum brandy—were certainly not ranked, at this time as during our own era. Interestingly, however, Heldo-Bah gives a name for the drink, *slivevetz,* that, once we account for the vowel shift of Old High German, is very close to one of the many Balkan variations on the name of the libation, *slivovitz,* derived from *sliva,* the Slavic word for "plum"; and anyone who has encountered that drink today (particularly in the immensely potent forms that its not-for-export variations take) can attest to the continued and

rather shattering power of what has formally become the national drink of Serbia. —C.C.

355 ‡ *"napthes"* More on this subject will follow; for now, it is safe to say that *napthes* was an archaic German (perhaps Broken) dialectal term for *naphtha*, which, particularly in its early days, could take the form of anything from mineral spirits to low-grade gasoline; and that Caliphestros's future statements about it may well contribute to unraveling one of the great riddles, not only of Broken's history, but of military history, more generally. —C.C.

364 † *" 'Ther is moore broke in Brokynne, thanne ever was knouen so.' "* Gibbon's lack of any explanation for the appearance of what is the solitary sentence written in Middle English in the entire Manuscript may be a demonstration of the level of scholarship during his era; we simply don't know. Fortunately, the meaning of the phrase is quite clear. —C.C.

368 † "evil vapor or bad air" Gibbon did not bother refuting or moderating such references, of which there are several in the Manuscript, because he couldn't—the science of infectious disease in his time did not yet allow him to. —C.C.

III: Stone

381 † **Radelfer** One can't say with any real certainty (and, perhaps because of that, Gibbon makes no attempt at all), but this name appears to arrive from another ancient popular Germanic name denoting at once "counselor" and "wolf"—an entirely appropriate connotation, given the role this Radelfer played in the Baster-kin family, and especially in the life of Rendulic Baster-kin. Indeed, it is entirely possible that he changed his name, or that it was changed for him, when he was chosen from the ranks of the Talons to watch over the scion of the Merchant Lord's family. —C.C.

384 † **megrem** The youthful Rendulic's condition can be readily identified as "migraine": *megrem* is evidently some sort of precursor to Middle English's *megrim*, the word used to identify what had been, since ancient times, a well-known and extensively described condition. Gibbon's failure to take note of this passage may have grown out of his considering its explanation obvious, although it seems more likely that his silence was caused by his aversion to discussing chronic ailments—a habit that grew out of his self-consciousness concerning his own incurable condition, *hydrocele testis,* a swelling of one testicle that, in an age when the fashion was tight-fitting trousers, was not only painful and serious but the source of enormous embarrassment for him. —C.C.

384 ‡ **a healthy manhood** Before anyone thinks all this some kind of witchcraft or fanciful explanation, we should note, as Gibbon was in no position to do, that for hundreds of years, traditional healers had been successfully treating the terrible symptoms of migraine with a combination of strong opiates, willow barks, and "nutleaf," a translation, in this case, of the German *Mutterkraut,* the term for the flowering, daisy-like plant we call "feverfew": *Tanacetum parthe-*

nium, or, variously, *Chrysanthemum parthenium,* an anti-inflammatory still in wide use by homeopaths, and of interest to Western doctors for its possible efficacy in inhibiting cancer cell growth. —C.C.

385 † **"Healer Raban"** This is apparently an ancient Germanic name denoting "raven"—not the most propitious association for a healer, but not an uncommon sort of appellation, either: it was often popular to give healers of the time, who were seen primarily as ghoulish tormentors whose successful remedies were dependent on unseen forces far beyond their own control or ken, names and macabre accoutrements that matched their miserable systems of knowledge and rates of success. Healers whose work actually could approach systemization and higher rates of success, at the same time, were treated with even more distrust; for their every advance inevitably called into question some central tenet of one of the new monotheistic faiths (as the cases of Gisa, Isadora, and most of all Caliphestros demonstrate). —C.C.

387 † **"Klauqvest"** As was often the case with some of the more arcane or titillating, yet academically inexplicable, aspects of the Manuscript, Gibbon touched on this name only obliquely: he seems to have been convinced that further explorations into the Gothic tongue would one day show that *Klauqvest* was a name given by the man's parents to reflect their reaction, not only to the disease from which he suffered all his life, which seems to have been leprosy—and, probably, something even more devastating, for he clearly lacks the immunity to superficial pain that marked so many lepers—but also an apparent deformity of the hands, almost certainly in evidence since birth and not at all uncommon within the annals of medicine. The fusion of the skin and muscle, and sometimes even the bone, of the fingers, so that the hands resemble the claws of crustaceans—a disease known as *ectrodactylism*—was documented long before discovery of this Manuscript, and before Grady Franklin Stiles (1937–1992) became the popular freak show performer "Lobster Boy." And, since *klau* can be easily identified, in many German dialects, as meaning "claw," we can be sure of the meaning of the first syllable, while the second, *qvist,* is easily conjectured— or so, apparently, said Gibbon's translator: "To those who have labored to understand Gothic," Gibbon wrote, "it is the root of a term denoting 'destruction,' the inserted 'v' being a misread 'u,' which would nearly always have been paired, as it still is paired, with 'q' in Germanic-Anglo-Saxon languages, giving us a name implying some sort of 'destruction' or 'death' by 'claw'—ultimately an ironic, to say nothing of cruel, name to have given this unfortunate fellow." —C.C.

391 † **bearing a towel** The latter is yet another word that may strike the modern audience as being anachronistic and contemporary, but which, it is worth noting, not only is in fact quite old, but has roots in the two languages that Gibbon and his translator of the Manuscript were both convinced made up the principal influences on the Broken dialect: Old High German (the antecedent word being *dwahilla*) and Gothic (*thwahl*). —C.C.

394 † **"Loreleh"** This is a variation on the ancient Germanic name *Lorelei,* the alteration in its final syllable accounted for by the vowel shift of Old High German. It connotes a "luring rock," and is the Germanic variation of the Sirens' Song,

referring to a beautiful female spirit or spirits who sang from a rocky point in the Rhine, luring ships and sailors to wreckage and death. —C.C.

395 † **is clubfooted** Most will be familiar with this condition, which is now quite correctable through surgery, but was once the incurable source of enormous humiliation, even for the great and admired, from the Roman emperor Claudius to Lord Byron. The Latin name for the condition—*talipes equinovarus*—is still the medically technical term, for it means "horse foot," or "foot (and ankle) like a horse," as it causes the ankle to be drawn upward like a horse's foot, while the rest of the foot is bent inward, sometimes in an unsightly enough manner that it could be cause for severe mockery and even persecution in ancient and medieval societies. —C.C.

397 † **Chen-lun** As stated earlier, we can do little more than speculate as to any Hunnish names across which we run, explaining why Gibbon ignores the name. But if we do engage briefly in such speculation, we find that *Chen-lun* suggests some sort of Chinese influence, turning us back to the ancient theory of the relationship between the Huns and their supposed ancestors, the Xiongnu (against whom, primarily, the Chinese built their Great Wall). If we were forced to translate it into a modern Chinese dialect, for example, we would find a general meaning along the lines of "morning flower" (or "bright orchid," more particularly); whereas, if required to translate the name into one of the principal modern Western descendants of Hunnish (or Hunnic)—for instance, Hungarian—we draw an almost complete blank. And, since "Morning Flower" and "Bright Orchid" are both suitable names for a princess drawn or descended from an important family, it seems safe to go with such a translation, for the purposes of understanding not only this particular mystery of the Manuscript, but also for the question of why Chen-lun seems to have features that are neither particularly Hunnish nor Chinese. In fact, we may well glean more from certain details of the "handmaiden's" appearance, as explained in the text, than we do from her mistress's name. —C.C.

398 † **properly brewed wild hops** There is much speculation that hops, having pseudo-narcotic properties, as explained earlier, were used first for medicinal purposes, and only later for beer; this would doubtless have given their original purpose a "proper" connotation, and aided in the understanding of the behavior of young people who imbibed great quantities of beer made with hops. —C.C.

398 ‡ **Ju** The name of Chen-lun's "handmaiden" (actually, one gets the feeling, her bodyguard) is another that appears—not surprisingly, by now—without note from Gibbon, and faces the same translational problems as that of Nuen and Chen-lun. Indeed we can learn more about this woman from the weapon she carries than from the name itself; for the only definite result we can find for the name *Ju* is a Chinese girl's name connoting "chrysanthemum": not a particularly apt term for this woman. On the other hand, it is true that combat knives of the type carried horizontally, as here, were specific to the "Black" or Western Huns who invaded northern Europe (in contrast to the Hephthalite or Eastern Huns, who relied more often on a single sword as they moved into areas to the south, regions we know as Turkey, Iran, and Hungary, among others). The

appearance and names of both Chen-lun and Ju, therefore, are perhaps less important than this lone dagger —C.C.

398 †† **Lady Baster-kin's shadow** Here, Gibbon writes, "In more than one ancient culture, we find reference to the closest of servants, especially a woman's, referred to as a 'shadow,' a term that evidently included some sort of protective role, and could be either a man or woman, though most often, of course, the latter." This may or may not have something to do with our own familiar modern term—usually, now, a verb—to "shadow" someone, which originally was used in a protective, as well as a detective, sense. —C.C.

400 † **Adelwülf** Gibbon writes, "It is perhaps surprising, given how much they were feared—particularly in those northern European regions where the scarcity of food in winter has always made them a particular threat—that wolves have always figured prominently in the mythologies and nomenclatures of tribal-based nationalities. *Adelwülf*, for example, is plainly the Broken dialectic form of a name, common to all such areas, which translates as 'noble wolf.'" What Gibbon could not have known was a stigma would eventually be attached to the modern form of this name, due, obviously, to a quite modern man who was enormously preoccupied with likening the troops and sailors of his fatherland to wolves, in the most sinister sense: *Adolf* Hitler. —C.C.

400 ‡ *alps* Here is an ancient Germanic variation on a supernatural character that appears in almost every culture's mythology since the beginnings of civilization, and that, in the West, is usually known by some variation on the Latin term *incubus*. The word *alp* itself is thought to be a German variation of "elf," and indeed, the first legends concerning the *alps* told of creatures carrying out such mischief as was usually attributed, in Anglo-Saxon-Celtic mythology, to various kinds of elves, although very powerful and sinister kinds of elves. The emphasis here on a sexual component, on lying with human women and producing half-breed offspring, is where the *alp* myth swings back to the incubus model: one of the most famous half-human, half-spirit creatures in Western mythology, for instance, was and remains Merlin, the Arthurian sorcerer, who was said to have been fathered by an *incubus*. As for the *alp* and *incubus* myths themselves, their origins are obscure; but they are generally said to have been concocted to provide explanations for everything from "mystery" pregnancies (often the results of illicit sex, incest, or rape) to sleep apnea and night terrors.

A female form of the *alp*, the *mareh* (or *mara*, or *mare*, in other dialects), also existed; it is considered by some one root part of the word "nightmare." —C.C.

407 † *"marehs"* See note for p. 400, above. —C.C.

408 † *"the 'Great Imitator'"* Caliphestros is employing terminology and classifications of illness that were well in advance of their use in the rest of Europe, likely due to his extensive travels: syphilis was indeed called "the Great Imitator" in many parts of the world, and for the reasons he cites. The great dangers associated with pursuing scientific investigation during his era in Europe would cost other scientific visionaries harsh treatment at the hands of the Catholic Church: small wonder so many advanced thinkers in these fields would either seclude themselves in monasteries and remote cities such as Broken, or would pursue the hermetic life in the wilderness. —C.C.

409 † "the *mang-bana*" See note for p. 16, above. —C.C.

412 † river *Rhein* The correct and ancient (as well as modern) Germanic spelling
of "the Rhine," the most famous river, along with the Danube, in Germany, not
least because they made up the two borders, eastern and northern, across
which Julius Caesar advised Rome never to try to send military forces: the
great conqueror considered the land and the peoples too primitive to be worth
any such ventures. (And, indeed, nearly all Roman emperors who disobeyed
Caesar's warning paid dearly, starting with the very first of them, Julius's
nephew and adopted son, Octavian, called Augustus when he took power.)
This spelling of *Rhein* would have been so well known to scholars in the late
eighteenth century that Gibbon thinks it unworthy of comment, for various
dialects of German, and certainly the modern form, were languages almost as
important as Latin for those who studied the history of ancient Europe. —C.C.

425 † "*heigenkeit*" Gibbon writes, "Here we again come upon a particularly striking
example, not only of the linguistic inventiveness and adaptability of the Broken
dialect, but of its rapid development and refinement from generation to generation, as well as of the attention paid by the rulers and responsible subjects of the
unique kingdom to some of what were then the most advanced scientific and
social concepts, especially in northern Europe. The closeness of the first portion of the word to our own 'hygiene,' which is based, as *heigenkeit* almost certainly was, on the name of the Greek, and later Roman, goddess of health,
cleanliness, and sanitation, *Hygieia* [or, variously, *Hygeia*], demonstrates that
Oxmontrot was deeply impressed by the attention Roman city planners paid to
such matters, and was determined that his mountaintop city would embody
the most advanced techniques and practices that he witnessed in the 'empire of
the *Lumun-jani*.' But there is an additional detail, in the development of Hygieia's myth, that may supply the clue to why 'the Mad King's' reaction to what she
stood for seems to have gone beyond the responsibility of a ruler, and to have
been almost personal: in the later eras of her worship, Hygieia also became
the Roman goddess of the Moon. It is not beyond question, in other words,
that Roman principles of public and private hygiene were interpreted by
Oxmontrot (a Moon worshipper by birth and choice) as not simply a wise but a
sacred policy, in Roman paganism, certainly, but more importantly (as Roman
paganism was dying, by the time he became an auxiliary in their armies), in his
own Moon faith. One of the many tragedies that resulted from the eventual
domination of Broken by the cult of Kafra, is that this intimate connection between public hygiene and religion was lost, with, as we shall see, cataclysmic
results."

426 † *obsese* Gibbon writes, "Of this term the only immediately recognizable variation is, of course, *obsessio*, being an actual Latin term for a 'siege.' The adaptation of that term, however, to the meaning implied here—that is, the connection
to a person who suffers from what the latest psychological writings of our own
day would describe as (in words that reflect a Greek as well as a Latin etymology) an *hysterical mania*—is fascinating, and surely something we do not expect
to find in a *barbarian* Germanic kingdom. And yet this is hardly the sole point
at which we find discussions of either the primary (that is, the empirical) or the

secondary (the theoretical) implications of such ideas, which have received a title for the collected activities they have inspired—*psychology*—some eight or nine hundred years *after* the period under consideration in this tale of Broken." Gibbon does not indulge his frequent penchant for overstatement, here: like the earlier reference to Galen's attempt to discover the medical meaning of dreams, this citation suggests a complexity of thought in Broken's intellectual community—particularly before the death of the God-King Izairn—that was unique, and, obviously, far ahead of its time. —C.C.

430 † *"Plumpskeles"* Gibbon writes, "This is, according to my translator, a man of broad experience, simply a more colorful word for 'latrines.'" We can only suppose that Gibbon knew the effect that the apparently literal translation of the word would have on the somewhat staid Burke: for *Plumpskeles* is another transitional word between Old High and modern German, the latter possessing *Plumpsklos*, or, quite literally, "shitholes," as in holes cut for toilets, which for some reason were/are apparently referred to in pairs; hence the plural used by Isadora, as we have seen four latrine holes in the yard behind Berthe's house. —C.C.

431 † **"Kriksex"** Gibbon writes, "Here is a name that must have been utterly idiosyncratic, even within the Broken dialect. Although it exhibits pieces and aspects of elements common to both various forms of German as well as Gothic, we can make no sense of it, given the present scholarship—a fact which I note only because it seems, somehow, fitting." As, indeed, it does, given the character's nature and role; and modern scholarship hasn't helped us very much more, if at all more, than did that of Gibbon's era. —C.C.

447 † **"Gerfrehd"** The name of this sentek of the regular army evidently was judged unworthy of Gibbon's time to explain, perhaps because it is one of those compound Germanic names that often seem oxymoronic: it is almost certainly the Broken dialectal version of *Gerfried*, often translated as "spear of peace." But it becomes more comprehensible when we consider that its original meaning is probably more general, a "guardian of peace." (And given our general ignorance of the Broken dialect, we may never know what this version means, precisely—but if it were "guardian of peace," it would be a uniquely suitable name for a man whose role seems ultimately to have become the patrolling of what would prove the key section of the city walls.) —C.C.

Part Three

473 † **M. Rousseau** Burke speaks of one of the most famous philosophers of the time, Jean-Jacques Rousseau, for whom he had little but contempt. Burke thought Rousseau's theories on Romanticism and introspection to be nothing more than vanity and self-promotion, and his theories on society to be dangerously destabilizing. But Burke's vindictiveness toward Rousseau, whom he never met, was extreme and admittedly *ad hominem*, much of the time, although, to

be fair, Rousseau drew sharp attacks from far more liberal corners than Burke's: the fledgling feminist movement, for instance, led by such pioneers as Mary Wollstonecraft, could not forgive Rousseau's relegation of women to a completely domestic role in his description of the ideal society. —C.C.

473 ‡ **the time at which he composed the thing** Burke did not necessarily believe that the confusion over the time at which the narrator composed his tale, which Gibbon considered a literary device of some kind, was necessarily anything of the like: he was bothered by the fact that, while it *might* have been an important personage looking back, it might also have been one looking forward, not, as Gibbon says, with prophetic pretensions, but with the *gift* of prophecy—and he makes it clear that his candidate for who this latter person would most likely have been was Oxmontrot, whom Burke would have found (unlike, say, the soldiers of Broken) genuinely mad. All this accounts not only for Gibbon's aforementioned "temporal ambiguity," but for the sense of responsibility that the narrator feels early on: for the future rulers of the state were his descendants, and the city's important ministers, such as Lord Baster-kin, their choices. —C.C.

474 † **Competing Religions, . . . strict and sometimes Cruel Fathers, and . . . perverse hedonism** Burke strikes with intent, here, for these were three of the most tender subjects in Gibbon's life, the first and second having to do with his conversion from Anglicanism to Catholicism and back again, the last due to his father's threat to disinherit him. But formal, popular religion in general held no interest for him, and his attraction to "perverse hedonism" was caused in part by this fact, and in part by the solitary life inflicted on him by his *hydrocele testis,* or badly enlarged testicle, which became so embarrassing that he endured three cruelly ineffective surgeries to try to correct it, eventually being killed by the last surgeon's infecting him with peritonitis: it is not difficult to see, in all of this (just as Burke says) the origins of Gibbon's reasons for being so compulsively attracted to the "legend" of Broken. —C.C.

483 † **squirrels, and tree kittens** The word "squirrel" descends from the Greek and Roman through an identifiable sequence of Romance languages, as well as through early Germanic and Norse terms, and was likely used as a familiar and convenient term by the Manuscript's translator, the modern German term being *Eichkätzche,* or "tree kitten" (really "oak kitten," so named because of the well-known proclivity of squirrels for acorns). The remaining question becomes why did the translator use the phrase "squirrels *and* tree kittens" [my emphasis]? Was there a distinction that the Bane drew, perhaps between two different species of squirrel? Or did another creature exist at the time, one that has since disappeared, a loss far more tragic than that of a dead word? Such are the types of questions raised by the disappearance of words and languages: questions that can, unfortunately, never be answered. —C.C.

484 † **tufts of feathers** It is one of the enduring mysteries of zoology that we still do not know why some species of owl have this feature. It seems definite that it is a defensive ruse of some kind, as the tufts become heightened and more pronounced at moments of challenge and danger; but whether they are intended to make the owl appear more "mammalian" to other predators, or whether they

are intended as camouflage, designed to allow the owl to blend into tree trunks and limbs more effectively, is an ongoing debate. —C.C.

508 † *Muspelheim* A seemingly offhand phrase that in fact references an important element of Ancient German and Norse mythology. In the Dark Ages and before, many ores, such as iron, were often taken from sites where they could be easily harvested, such as bogs, marshes, and moss fields, and then worked in the kind of deep hill (or *pfell*) that served in many parts of the world as primitive smithies. So deep an impression did this practice make on the Germanic and Scandinavian tribes that it became enshrined in their mutual mythologies, and in one of the earliest Old High German epics, *"Muspilli"* (a title that may or may not be etymologically related, but is certainly thematically connected, to the fiery pagan realm of *Muspelheim,* or *Muspell*); and, even though the poem attempts to Christianize many elements of the legend—perhaps becoming another of the nexus points between Christianity and the pagan world of the Germanic-Norse gods—a vivid portrait is painted of this cataclysmic inferno, which in pagan lore was the first of the nine worlds that existed under the world ash *Yggdrasill.* Out of the sparks of *Muspell* the stars were formed, and out of it, too, at the time of the Armageddon-like *Ragnarok,* the three sons of *Muspell* would ride, their way led by the fiery giant, *Surt,* who (according to which source one consults) is accompanied by a wolf who will swallow the sun. The Sons of *Muspell* shatter the great rainbow bridge to *Asgard* and make all earthly creatures and creations fragile or doom them altogether. The Bane, believing in the old faith, apparently also gave credence to some version of this tale; and their fear at what Caliphestros was creating seemed to clash with their excitement at the power they knew his work would give them, creating a state of general tension that was rooted in their childhoods. This anxious state of affairs apparently motivated Keera to find out all she could about the old man's motivations, and could not have been helped by the constant presence of Stasi near the openings of the various mines: was she, rather than a wolf, the giant animal that would swallow the sun? —C.C.

508 ‡ **near-miraculous grade of steel** What is given here is a very shortened account of the transformation of coal into coke, a fuel which, upon incineration, produces greatly increased temperatures in furnaces. Caliphestros would have learned his criteria for determining which coal would best suit for "coking," once again, during his travels to the East on the Silk Path, as the process was used by the Chinese at least as early as the ninth century: but it may well have been another technological innovation that, while somewhat automatically credited to the Chinese empire, actually came out of domains in and near India even earlier. Certainly, Caliphestros's knowledge of it would suggest so. —C.C.

508 †† **the most fiery of the Nine Homeworlds** Another reference to *Muspelheim,* the most and by some accounts the only fiery underworld beneath the world ash tree, *Yggdrasill,* and the place from which the cataclysmic fires that both began the universe and would initiate its end, or *Ragnarok,* were generally expected to originate. —C.C.

509 † **other elements might be** The Bane smiths were not (entirely) exercising their imaginations, as trace amounts of other ores and elements did indeed make

their way into the steel, affecting both the strength and the color of each batch. These could have included ingredients as varied as nickel, zinc, hematite, and, later, vanadium (another argument for the later composition of the Manuscript, as vanadium was used, informally, at the end of the periods under discussion, although only formally recognized in the West much later). When heated and worked, these ingredients could produce remarkable bands of color ranging from grey to red to brown to yellow, appearances that increased the reputation of the metal as some sort of "super" or "unnatural" steel. —C.C.

510 † **the realms of the East** This statement cannot help but bring to mind that supreme example of laminated, layered steel: Japanese samurai swords. Such swords were also, because of their combination of strength and sharpness, considered to have otherworldly powers: Westerners who encountered them said that they were nothing short of miraculous. It was said that there was one sword made that contained four million laminations (folding and refolding): and these are not thick blades. Whether or not this is true, the fact is that these swords could inflict devastating damage on all Western weapons, even rifle and small gun barrels. —C.C.

516 † **"the dance of mating"** This is not poetic excess: among many species of bear, apparently including the Broken brown, the motions and noises that the male makes on encountering the female's deliberately distributed scent is known as a "dance." Keera's reference to the area covered by that female scent as being too limited is also correct, as such females will spread their scent in as wide a range as possible to attract a mate. The only real question, soon to be hinted at, if not answered, is why this second fact should have been the case. —C.C.

527 † **primeval** In this case, we find an anachronistic term that helps us confirm the time of the *translation* of the Manuscript, rather than contradict it: contrary, once again, to common belief, "primeval" was a late-Enlightenment–early-Romantic notion, not a medieval one—a supposed rediscovery of how ancient forests were viewed in the Dark and early Middle Ages that had little to do with facts, and was only popularized because of the rise of industrialized society and man's ability to control and indeed destroy such places, and therefore feel safe from their threats. Like the tired notion of the "noble savage," whose nobility was attained only when he had been for the most part subdued, the primeval forest did not account for the absolute terror with which most people at the time of such legends as that of Broken viewed the wilderness: as, to repeat the earlier discussion of Davon Wood (note for p. 6), a source of terror and death, not Romance and a reconnection to an earlier and more fundamental way of life that would prove somehow cleansing to the spirit. —C.C.

532 † **"knucklebones"** Tacitus wrote of the German tribes' passion for gaming—particularly, again, knucklebones (usually made of ordinary sheep and goat knuckles) and dice, during games of which young men would routinely bet their own freedom, if bereft of funds, and submit dutifully to enslavement if the result went against them. Indeed, said Tacitus, in *The Germania* and elsewhere, "What is marvelous [is that] playing at dice is one of their most serious employments, and even sober, they are gamesters." As to losing their freedom, "Such is their perseverance in an evil course: they themselves call it honor."

Thus, gambling of all kinds was indeed a powerful part of the culture of the people of Broken, and of most of the tribes around them. —C.C.

536 † **Linnet Crupp** A name of which Gibbon would not have taken any note, but which, today, stands out for its similarity to that of the Krupp "dynasty," Germany's greatest steel and armaments manufacturers, who first came to prominence in the late eighteenth and early nineteenth centuries, and who were in fact based in the city of Essen, which was and is indeed "an ancient city to the west of" Broken. Was this Crupp a self-imposed exile from that clan, and has the spelling merely been changed by the Broken dialect, or were the two unrelated? The fact that both were concerned with the artillery of their respective periods is intriguing, but not conclusive, as the Krupp fortune relied on iron as much as armaments production. —C.C.

536 ‡ **onset of a rain** The connection between chronic pain syndromes (such as those suffered by people who have sustained wounds or broken bones) and the approach of rain has long since been established as more than an old wives' tale, or a collection of purely anecdotal experiences. The precise mechanism of the relationship is not yet understood in its details, but is believed to lie in the fact that drops in barometric pressure affect the balance of cerebrospinal fluid, changes which in turn immediately reach any abnormalities in the peripheral nervous system. Again, this was an area in which Galen the Greek and those who followed him could have done much good, had they not been driven into hiding, and their reliance on autopsies forbidden, by the major monotheistic faiths. —C.C.

537 † **Bal-deric** Gibbon writes, "An intriguing name, another of those that must have come down from one of two directions, yet we cannot say which direction is the more likely: it could be a variation on the Norse *Balder*, the name of Odin's most handsome and virtuous son, whose death, in that same set of myths, brings about the onset of *Ragnarok;* but it may also be the Broken version of the Germanic *Derek*, itself a variation of the Ostrogothic *Theodoric*." The addition of an extra syllable in both cases remains unexplained; but the combination of the two may be a further signal of the Broken dialect's serving as a melting pot of regional languages. —C.C.

538 † **steel wheels and wires** Anecdotal accounts of prosthetic limbs have endured since ancient times, although it is not until the late-medieval–early-modern period that scientists began collecting actual examples—perhaps because, before then, they were not considered religiously acceptable and were, like most other scientific advances, destroyed; or, the earlier accounts may in fact be mythological. Certainly, this would not be the only area, as we have seen, in which individual scientists and inventors from Broken anticipated what most would consider a future development. —C.C.

540 † **Weltherr** Gibbon writes, "There is at least no great mystery associated with this name: *Weltherr* must have been the Broken cognate of the ancient Germanic *Waldhar*, which has come down to us in the fairly common form of *Walther* (or our own Walter), whose constituent parts translate roughly to 'master of the army': evidently, this fellow's parents had something more ambitious in mind when they named him than the composition of military maps, despite the

verity, proved century after century, that the army possessed of the better maps—both of locations and topography—enjoys a distinct advantage."

568 † 3:{xi:} For this final chapter of the Manuscript, we find yet another of the, for Gibbon as for, perhaps, many modern readers, maddeningly inconsistent styles of organization. Gibbon's passion for uniform organization is well known: but it does willfully ignore the varied styles of most legends, sagas, eddas, etc., of the period, which often do not represent anything more than the manner in which these tales were told and retold (often by different authors, although not, it seems, in this case) down through the ages; and while the Broken Manuscript may be confusing, in this sense, it is entirely historically consistent. —C.C.

570 † that same misty halo . . . until the end of time Gibbon notes that, in his day, "this is indeed the case, much of the time, on the mountain called *Brocken*, although whether the 'ring' first formed during this march that saw an alliance between the Talons and the Bane is impossible, of course, to say." We could as easily make the same remark today; however, in more contemporary times (even during Gibbon's, although he does not mention it) this mist would add to the sinister reputation of the mountain, rather than connoting some divine blessing, as the narrator seems to imply. —C.C.

571 † allied This is another of those words that might sound anachronistic to many ears, because of its heavy association with the Second World War; but in fact, it comes to us from early medieval times, from Middle English, and its component parts stretch back farther than that. And certainly, the notion of allies and "allied forces" was known to the most ancient world, one of the first and most famous such having been the thousand Greek ships that sailed on fabled Troy. —C.C.

581 † "ponies" Gibbon writes, "Once again, I had no luck in persuading my translator to tell me what the original word for 'ponies' or 'pony' was, in the Manuscript, which is something of a pity, as it might have helped to clarify the origins of this subspecies of the horse, a 'subspecies' that may have a longer history than the 'species' itself, at least in northern Europe: for there are those who believe that ponies were animals bred and then abandoned by several migrating tribes that originated in Asia and were, like their ponies, smaller in stature than their conquerors, the Europeans and the contemptible Byzantines, with their enormous armored warhorses." Gibbon's disdain for the Byzantine Empire has already been noted; and although the actual word "pony" was just over a century old, in his day, the species or subspecies had many other, much older names in other parts of Europe. —C.C.

583 † "the *Kreikisch* called the fire *automatos*" Gibbon writes, "The translator used, no doubt for the benefit of his contemporary readers, the most recent form of the Greek word for 'automatic,' while remaining with the Broken dialect's term for Greek itself, *Kreikisch*, since we have seen it before. There is no point to explaining too early what the term 'automatic fire' implies, as the text will do as much; but as to the question of whether or not it was a myth, it is sufficient to say that chemists have attempted to re-create this most mysterious subcategory of 'Greek fire' without success, although various other formulas for Greek fire have been tested with far happier results; and, as Caliphestros's represented a

particularly volatile form of the substance, we must continue to wonder, until some chemist can prove or disprove the notion, whether or not this part of the story is indeed legend, or mere myth." While it would be unfair, yet, to say why Gibbon's assessment is wrong, we should at least note that it is, and state that what "the sorcerer" Caliphestros was brewing was a weapon familiar in both its component parts and its assembled whole to modern armies, especially the American; and that the fact that it had disappeared from the world for almost a thousand years, in Caliphestros's time, and would do so, following Broken's history, for another twelve hundred ought not shock us: if there is one lesson to be learned from the Manuscript and all the details of the history of Broken, it is that the trend of civilization, as we are learning once again in our own time, is not always upward or forward. —C.C.

606 † *"Kafra's infernal piss"* Here is an entry about which Gibbon could have known little, even anecdotally, and even less scientifically; yet he, not atypically, chose to comment upon it because nearly every report of the scientific composition of the "fire *automatos*," or automatic fire, had and has come down to us through Byzantine sources, and therefore would have roused the great scholar's preju-diced ire to no small extent. Thus, when he says that "this aspect of the tale of the invasion of Broken must be viewed with jaundiced eyes, to say the very least, as the types of 'authorities' upon which it is based spring from a society well-versed in both exaggeration and mendacity," it is far less a statement of true fact than of those same personal prejudices. It was the Byzantines, after all, who would devise new forms of Greek fire so devastating that their use influ-enced battles of immense importance: see, for example, J. R. Partington's excel-lent *A History of Greek Fire and Gunpowder.*

Within such authoritative texts, as well as within the Broken Manuscript, we find not only effective refutation of Gibbon's willful ignorance, but tantaliz-ing evidence as to what it was that the mysterious "missing ingredient" that separated automatic fire from more common forms of Greek fire might have been. And in this context, the account in the Broken tale is not only not to be viewed "with jaundiced eyes," but is in fact to be taken quite seriously. For not only do all the other elements involved in the substance's creation—everything from naphtha to asphalt—match the description that the narrator gives of the stench given off by Caliphestros's creation, as well as of its consistency, but the manner in which it was said that those elements must be transported—in brass containers—conforms to reality as well. But it is several other aspects above all—the description, violence, and action of the flame produced—that give us an additional and, perhaps, key revelation: for the fire *automatos* used at Broken is described as burning primarily "white," not the usual range of fiery colors, at the time, and as doing so *into,* not atop, its target. This is extraordinarily remi-niscent of what we today know as "white phosphorus," a controversial twentieth-century weapon (particularly, again, regarding its use by the United States in Third World countries), the antecedent of which, carbon disulfide, was known to have been used on more than one historical occasion: in an Irish nationalist attempt to destroy the Houses of Parliament, among others. Fire created using such elements can indeed be ignited by water, and made to burn

fiercer the more one throws water upon it; and European chemists at work before science's great suppression at the hands of the Catholic Church would have
been very capable of mastering the creation of such a substance. Did they? The
Broken Manuscript certainly suggests as much; and it is therefore, again, typical that we are suspended, in this key aspect, between what we read, what Gibbon originally thought of it, and what modern military history and science tell
us might have been possible, if viewed without prejudice. —C.C.

632 † *"sarbein"* Neither Gibbon nor his translator could make sense of the origins of
this Broken dialectal term; however, the great scholar was wise enough to
draw a correct (although perhaps obvious) conclusion from its use: "Neither
the translator of the document nor I could make sense of this term, save that,
placed in context, it seems apparent that it refers to 'greaves,' those armored
leggings worn for centuries by warriors in both the East and the West, from the
age of bronze to that of iron and steel; although how the Broken dialect should
have formed such a unique term for them remains a mystery." And, again, we
confront that fact that, in Gibbon's day, very little scholarly work had been done
into either Gothic, or the various manners in which Gothic and German could
and did become hybridized: *bein* being even the early German term for "leg,"
and *sarwa* the Gothic plural for "armor." Thus, we can now fairly confidently
solve another problem that frustrated Gibbon, who knew both the question
and the answer, but not how the two were connected. —C.C.

632 ‡ the basic rules of Broken infantry training Here, Gibbon is not at all confused,
and one gets the feeling that this fact gives him some relief: "The exchange
outlining how Arnem and his son will meet attackers who lack formal military
training not only gives us some idea of why the Broken Army was so feared, but
once again of how much to heart the kingdom's founder, Oxmontrot, had
taken the better elements of Roman military tactics. Any late Roman commander would have been pleased and proud to have men willing to form up in
such seemingly close and perilous, but ultimately fearsome and victorious, formations; it was, indeed, the inability of too many Roman commanders to convince (or even try to persuade) their men to muster the courage to carry on the
close-order tactics of the early empire—tactics that had allowed Rome to establish her dominance over so much of the Western world—that was a contribut-
ing factor to the downfall of the great empire." Nothing needs to be added to
this explanation, save another reminder of how Oxmontrot, unlike so many
"barbarian" tribal leaders in northern Europe, did not view the way the Romans fought as alien and even inhuman, but sorted through those tactics to
pick out the pieces that would best serve his new kingdom: an impressive accomplishment, to say the least. —C.C.

ABOUT THE AUTHOR

CALEB CARR is the critically acclaimed author of *The Alienist, The Angel of Darkness, The Lessons of Terror, Killing Time, The Devil Soldier,* and *The Italian Secretary.* He has taught military history at Bard College, and worked extensively in film, television, and the theater. His military and political writings have appeared in numerous magazines and periodicals, among them *The Washington Post, The New York Times,* and *The Wall Street Journal.* He lives in upstate New York.

ABOUT THE TYPE

This book was set in Monotype Dante, a typeface designed by Giovanni Mardersteig (1892–1977). Conceived as a private type for the Officina Bodoni in Verona, Italy, Dante was originally cut only for hand composition by Charles Malin, the famous Parisian punch cutter, between 1946 and 1952. Its first use was in an edition of Boccaccio's *Trattatello in laude di Dante* that appeared in 1954. The Monotype Corporation's version of Dante followed in 1957. Though modeled on the Aldine type used for Pietro Cardinal Bembo's treatise *De Aetna* in 1495, Dante is a thoroughly modern interpretation of that venerable face.